WHERE THE MOON HAS BEEN

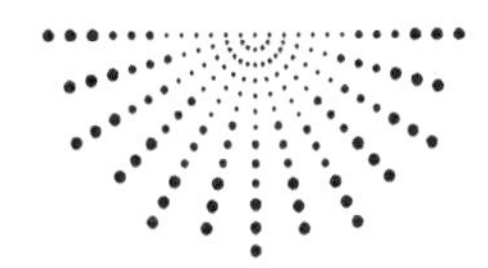

JUDITH LEPORE

For my son Orion, always remembered, always loved.

CONTENTS

PROLOGUE

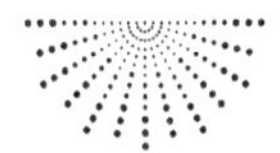

*T*his, the seventeen hundredth turning of the Age of Sorcerers, was destined to be the last, according to the ancient, crumbling scrolls of Anniste lore few bothered to study any longer.

The Night of the Dead came to the North on a balmy spring evening. Had anyone glanced upward, they would have seen a wraith drifting slowly over the rooftops, almost pearly in her luminescence. She stopped, hovering for a moment above a miserable hut and its adjacent hulking forge on the outskirts of the village of Stern.

The wraith made a soft, keening sound, like an animal mother makes when she has lost her young. Then the silvery glow floated away, far to the South. Many miles, she floated over the stark Taboran Mountains that separated North Miraven from the South. She stopped beside a small but well-kept cottage on the outskirts of the City of Meed.

No lights burned in the cottage, but inside, the inhabitants rustled a little—uneasy, without knowing why. A tall young woman rose and went to the window. She halted at a terrified gesture made by her elderly companion.

From the wraith now came a different sound, no longer a mother's lament but a strong, commanding voice that lifted to the very heavens.

"I am Neela, Guardian of the Anniste healers. And they shall not be hunted down like prey, not while the power of the Goddess Anna still holds sway." The voice echoed through the still, fragrant air, past the heavy burgeoning scent of southern flowers and ripening olives.

The wraith spoke again in a tone of unmistakable summons, although she uttered one word only: "Reika!" The old woman sank to her knees, hands covering her face. As the younger turned to face her, the elder stifled a moan. Then all fell silent once more.

CHAPTER 1

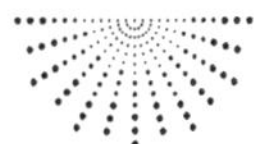

BOOK 1: THE BERRIES OF SUMMER

When Tekoah had first learned her letters, or perhaps even before that, she began to shape poetry, small spare verses. Pictures, smooth as shiny corn kernels, slipped through her mind, capturing moments—joyous or painful—that she feared to lose. Sketches; rough becoming smooth; blurred, becoming sharp and clear. In a strange way, her poetry became her friend as the years of her childhood passed; a companion that kept her from despair.

And yet she could not shape her deepest wound into words, because she must then acknowledge its existence. She could not shape it, weave it, think it, or remember it. In this blind pain, her poetry companion deserted her.

She felt no wounds at all as she walked home from the village of Stern at the end of a late-summer market day. The sun warmed her back. Shouldering her way through the crowded square, she used her large basket like a shield in front of her—a wise precaution, for the livestock were unpredictable, and the lads playing stick-stones in the streets even more so.

Tekoah was revising a poem as she walked. She ran the lines through her mind over and over, not yet satisfied.

. . .

THE LILACS WEEPING drops of dew
   Could sparkle yet in sunlight
   But violets, dry-eyed, wept alone
   Their petals scattered underfoot.

WHAT EYES? Tekoah brandished her basket at a belligerent-looking ram that stood in her path. *Flowers have no eyes. Hmm. Violets, silent, wept alone; silent violets wept alone.*

She sidestepped a black sow bolting, wild-eyed, for liberty, and she barely noticed when its owner plunged through the crowd after his charge. She frowned at the boisterous shouts of laughter that arose at the farmer's plight.

Only three miles of sunlit freedom stood between Stern and the blacksmith's forge that was her home. Three miles in which to mould word-wings for herself, and take the brief, dizzying flights that somehow made her more resigned to her life when she landed.

So, she brushed aside the distractions: laughter, shrieks, and barnyard smells; the sweaty reek of the northern country folk of Stern. She ignored all these assaults to the senses. Her mouth was set with determination. She had wound her plaits of gold-brown hair around her head like a helmet, and though her blue eyes gazed outward, their attention was fixed within.

But as Tekoah walked, a creeping dread descended upon her, which drove even the obstinate violets from her mind. At first, she thought it was connected to a sound, but panic and confusion gripped her, for she had never heard—or not heard—anything like it.

Silence. Utter and complete. In the centre of the village, at the height of a market day. And with it came a terrible stillness in the surrounding air, as if time had stopped in the space between one heartbeat and the next. Tekoah's basket dropped at her feet from fingers gone numb with shock.

Everyone in the square had frozen in place.

Not only the owner of the sow, still crouched to leap on his fugitive, but the pig herself had become still; so had the muttering, cackling women in the stalls. And pigeons, ducks, and geese; mercurial, inquisitive goats; doomed calves separated from their dams who never seemed to cease their mournful calls: all were quiet, hushed. Waiting.

And the children—those stick-stone urchins who never ceased moving—had halted where they stood. Apart or in clusters, statues, all of them; bright eyes stared straight ahead in their dirt-smudged faces, and not a single blink came from their sooty lashes.

A wind had been blowing a moment earlier, rattling the thatched roofs of the cottages and shops, swishing through the narrow alleys, tugging at Tekoah's skirt. Even that had ceased. Stillness was an ominous cloud that had moved across the sun, on a late summer market day in the village of Stern.

How could silence be heard? How could stillness move?

Terror coursed through her, a nameless shadow struggling to take shape; a darker version of poetry, her lifelong friend.

And, like a flash, even before she turned to look over her shoulder and found that she could not do so—could not move so much as a muscle in her little finger—Tekoah knew who it was. Who it must be.

In that dawning, which was like a sudden explosion of sparks from a hearth fire, she saw him.

The sorcerer Braith.

Her face had been frozen in profile, so she could see but a distorted fragment of his hair, his face, his cloak. Scarlet and black engulfed her mind. The surge of her blood roared in her ears. It could not quite drown the awful silence.

Tekoah would be seventeen turnings of age in an annaspan.

Enough turnings in which to grieve like a weeping violet for vanished mothers, for brothers who had left to join the Queen's army without saying goodbye, for a life in which she had never felt truly alive. Yet this was her first glimpse of Braith, although he had spent his youth in her village.

She had heard much of him, of course, in whispers over the wavering light of tallow candles, and in her father's nighttime ravings. Braith was the youngest sorcerer of Miraven. Three sorcerers now lived, although this in itself was an aberration; only two had ever been spawned in a generation.

This difference alone was enough to make people mutter and shake their heads with foreboding. A third seemed a dire omen, indeed.

Everyone, even children, knew that no good ever came from any sorcerer, despite what they liked people to think. Not that anyone would dare speak those words to one of those shape-shifting tricksters. It was just something that was known, like black clouds bringing thunderstorms.

Braith was only thirty turnings of age, and his youth added to the elements of fear and wonder surrounding him. Sorcerers rarely came into their power until they were already well past middle age—did that mean he would become more powerful than the others? Speculations had spread like wildfire.

It was a wellspring of both pride and discomfort for the villagers that Braith had been spawned in the village of Stern. The pride was because of the sudden fame in which Stern now basked, almost rivalling that of the royal city of Rhantor.

After the last turning, when knowledge of the new sorcerer had spread, folk had travelled to Stern from all over the country in droves, just to see the birthplace of the only sorcerer born in their lifetimes. They stood in throngs before Chalvern the apothecary's shop, because, as a boy, Braith had been his apprentice—at least until the day that venerable old man had marched onto his tiny balcony and tipped the contents of his chamber pot upon them.

The discomfort stemmed from the persistent rumour that the village priest and treasurer had driven Braith from Stern fifteen years ago, repelled by his strange and secretive ways. And, woe betide them, ignorant of the power lying dormant within him.

Had they known, they would never have dared to shun Braith. The abstract and capricious approval of the Sun God Rhan was no shield against the genuine menace of a slighted sorcerer.

High Priest Grindhor, paunchy and jovial, denied this rumour, as did the cadaverous-looking Melnich, who was the Village Treasurer. They insisted that they had known—sensed, somehow—Braith's latent power. When he had left Stern, they protested, it had been with their benediction. Skeptics, meaning almost everyone in Stern, laughed their scorn and disbelief.

No one would say a word against Braith now. No one save Veld the blacksmith, Tekoah's father. But everyone ignored Veld, he being a drunkard of ill-repute who had taken to ranting fits and hallucinations, and was judged by most villagers as mad as a skunk-bitten dog.

Tekoah had been a toddler fifteen years ago, and oblivious to these events. But Veld was her father; she believed everything he said. It was part of the fabric of her being.

There was an old saying among the women of the Anniste: *embrace one possibility, and all others vanish in a cloud of uncertainty.* That was how it was with Veld and Tekoah. He represented a possibility, and it became the stable sun around which her heart and soul revolved. And so, she believed that Braith had cursed her father and was endeavouring to destroy him.

This possibility was not so hard to believe, after all. Tekoah saw her father was unhappy, and knew that her mother Neela had disappeared, leaving a gaping hole in the heart of the family.

All this misery had to lead back to the relentless cat-and-mouse game Braith played with Veld's mind. A sorcerer's malevolent amusement—the slow destruction of Veld.

Not to believe it, even for a moment, was to contemplate the yawning ravine in her mind where nothing made any sense at all.

In Tekoah's bitter quarrels with Weslan, her elder brother, it made no difference when he pointed out how Veld's sense of reason and logic had deteriorated in direct proportion to the amount of corn lightning he drank. Tekoah retorted that this was further proof of the sorcerer's vindictive subtlety—making it look as if it was Veld's own doing, so no one would pity him.

"Can you not see his delusion? If you ever left this cursed place for longer than an hour, and talked to people in the actual world, you could not fail to see! What motive could Braith have for persecuting Father? Why would a sorcerer deign to notice a drunken peasant, even if they were born in the same place? He left long ago, and as far as I know, they never crossed paths when he dwelt here. Ask Chalvern! I am certain he will tell you the same."

Exasperated, Weslan would rail until Tekoah put her hands over her ears and defied him silently. With their blue eyes blazing and faces flushed, they looked so alike it was startling. But their quarrels could not separate them for long.

They needed each other.

Until Weslan left. Suddenly, without saying goodbye.

She had heard from him just once afterward—a travelling peddler had brought a message that her brother had joined a band of mercenary soldiers. In his letter, he pledged to make his fortune and return for Tekoah and their twin brothers. And Mother, of course.

"Don't hold your breath." Neela's voice was curt as she dropped the smudged scroll into the fire—quickly, for Veld's footsteps hammered toward them from outside. She had said nothing more, and her words over the ensuing weeks had grown fewer and fewer, drying up like a thirsty well in a drought.

And then Mother had left as well. Without saying goodbye.

Even now, trying to remember that time never failed to give Tekoah a terrible headache. All part of the sorcerer's curse, her father reminded her, looking bleary-eyed and defeated. Turning everyone against him—except for his beloved daughter.

And so, this past turning, Tekoah had nurtured her hatred of Braith like a small but steady flame. She had never seen him, but in the glow cast by the smouldering fire of her rage she held the image of a sinister, hook-nosed man, looking older than his thirty turnings.

What would his Source be? A bat, perhaps—high, narrow shoulders, hunched up toward his ears. Jet-black hair combed straight back, a startling widow's peak, his high forehead gleaming and oily like the raiding devils that swooped across the border from Berlot. Yellow teeth; skinny, no doubt; spindly legs. Malevolent, deep-set eyes gleaming in a rodent's face.

She had seen this image each time she heard her father's high, terrified screaming in the night.

And now, on a midsummer's day, as sudden as the storms that raged down from the Taboran Mountains, there he was. And although the spell had caught her facing sideways to Braith, still Tekoah strained to see more of him, to determine if her imaginings had been accurate.

For there was nothing else to do, caught in this enchanted web of immobility. Stare, then die.

He was by the ancient stone well at the centre of the village square, seated on a huge black horse. A Taboran stallion, Tekoah thought, looking at the steed with the trained eye of a Northerner.

Braith wore black and crimson, his bearing no less fastidious than one of the foppish and disdainful nobles she saw when they stopped to replace a shoe at the forge. But Braith did not look like one of them. He was bareheaded, and his longish dark hair rippled in the hot wind.

Tekoah's eyes watered in the bright sunlight as she focused on his hands. *Are those crimson leather gloves? It is so hot. How can he bear it?*

Braith sat on his restless mount with practised ease, adjusting to its movements until they almost seemed to be one creature—wild, restless, and very dangerous. He looked like a demigod from the legends the village women worked into tapestries on cold winter afternoons.

All this Tekoah observed in a series of sidelong glimpses from the corner of her right eye. When she tried to blink, she found she could not, and mysterious figures from the temple tapestries danced before her face: transparent, insubstantial, like the wraiths said to walk abroad on the Night of the Dead. Her mind, she realized, had begun to wander along the grey borders of delirium, and she had to force it back to reality.

But the unexpected sight of Grindhor, High Priest of Rhan, was no vision borne of delirium. He was leaving the temple, pigeon blood still spattered on his robe. Beside him sauntered Melnich the Treasurer, the priest's long thin shadow. They strode straight toward the market square, laughing. Then they walked into the silence.

Grindhor gaped at the frozen tableau, and then his eyes went immediately toward the well, as if drawn by some secret shame. A spasm of horror crossed his face. He dropped to his knees right there in the square, his white robe billowing about him, its crisp folds settling incongruously into the refuse of market day. His heavy jowls were quivering.

The silence was so complete that Tekoah heard that quiver. She almost felt like laughing. Grindhor, so majestic, such a self-professed lightning rod for the wrath of Rhan, kneeling in the muck. It was not possible.

Melnich kneeled also, his face ashen and his turkey-wattle

throat bobbing convulsively. The elders remained in this attitude of supplication for what seemed like an eternity but must only have been a few seconds.

Tekoah had never gazed long at either man before. Now each line and valley on their faces was etched into her brain forever. In her peripheral vision, she looked again at Braith, and thought he smiled.

"My lord Braith," began Grindhor, his voice cracking after the first word into a trembling squeak. He sounded like a feeble mouse in a trap. Beside him, Melnich sucked his knuckles like a babe and sobbed.

Before the priest could continue, Braith raised a hand—it looked like a nonchalant wave—and Grindhor was no longer there. He simply was not.

Mouth dry, Tekoah stared at the small pile of greyish dust where he had been. Melnich uttered a choked scream and stumbled to his feet as if to flee. Then he, too, was transformed into dust, forever gone beyond pleading.

The wind returned, a sudden gust that blew away the little piles of dust. It stirred her hair, and Tekoah almost wept with joy, for it was the touch of life. She tried to move, and still could not. But the wind was in her hair. She was alive.

And then Braith rose in his saddle and scanned the square full of frozen villagers with death in his eyes.

So, it was not to last, then, this reprieve. The wind did not mean life, after all; it would merely scatter her ashes as it had done the two men's. Despairing thoughts assailed her: *will Braith's revenge encompass everyone? Of course, he probably killed Father first. Oh Rhan, what will happen to the twins? Even if they are left alive, what will they do without me?*

A desperate cry came into her mind: *Mother! Where are you? Where did you go?*

At the height of her terror, just when it seemed to be choking her, a sudden calm descended. Tekoah felt as though she was floating slightly above her body, and her fear dissolved. She strained her sidelong gaze at the sorcerer, wanting to see the face of her death, knowing she was no more than a leaf, a feather, hurled into the vast whirlpool of his vengeance. He had nursed his hatred longer than she.

Is this what life is, then? she wondered bitterly. *Who can hate the most? Not so hard to let go, after all.*

With a sudden shock that made her scalp prickle, she realized that Braith's eyes were settled upon her. At the same time, she discovered that she could now turn her head. She tried to raise her hand to her face, but still could not stir anything below her neck. And so, raising her eyes, she gazed upon Braith's face for the first time.

He looked astonishingly different from the hunched, oily image of her fantasies. She found herself staring into green-gold eyes set beneath thick black brows. They were hypnotic, those eyes; unblinking, like a bird of prey. His cheekbones were high, his skin was the smooth porcelain of a child, but his red mouth betrayed an arrogance at odds with his youthful face.

I did not think he would be so young. Tekoah's heart pounded as though it would burst through her skin at any moment.

Braith leaned forward in his saddle. Tekoah was flooded with such terror that she would have fallen if she was able to move her limbs. A light breeze moved over her, and she staggered, almost fell. Then, gasping, she righted herself. She could now move her body. She was free.

Tekoah turned in small semi-circles left and right, taking in the motionless villagers. In their stillness, they all seemed noble and beautiful, as never before.

And doomed. So utterly doomed—like the insects in clear amber on the shelves in Chalvern's shop—that it brought tears to her eyes.

She stared at these living statues. It dawned upon her that

only the two of them existed in this moment, alone, in this world of Braith's making. She and he.

A searing intensity was directed toward her, like a white-hot beam of light, and she knew Braith was looking at her. This drew her gaze back to him in helpless fascination. And then he smiled, red lips curving upward, white teeth flashing.

At that moment, he entered her mind the way another man might have opened an unlocked door. The shock of the violation was almost unbearable. Tekoah clapped her hands over her ears. Felt him, probing.

"Do not weep, little violet." Five words, spoken in a whisper.

He slipped from the stallion and whispered in its ear. The gleaming black horse shivered and snorted and trotted off, picking his way between the breathing statues. Once clear of the market square, it gathered its haunches and galloped off into the growing dusk.

Tekoah watched in silence, captive—by choice now—and captivated. All this took place in just a few seconds. She turned back toward the sorcerer, only to find that he had disappeared as well, as if he had never been there—gone. And Tekoah was left standing in numb shock, mouth dry as ashes, heart pounding a fateful drumbeat, basket fallen and fruit spilled at her feet.

The village of Stern returned to life. Pigs squealed, old men muttered, women shook their heads as if waking from a dream. They knew not from what they had been spared, or why. And neither did she.

CHAPTER 2

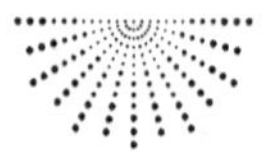

Chalvern the apothecary was forced to play the statue at a most trying moment, when laboriously pouring a few drops of belladonna into a beaker. He was striving to make a tonic of just the right strength for an infant with chest inflammation. A tricky thing.

For the hundredth time, he wished for the healing powers of the Anniste clan. He was accustomed to prescribing, not healing. But a young mother had burst into his shop this morning, half-frantic with worry about her baby, and the fool of a priest hadn't done her much good, had he?

Ah well, they all came to him now. Even the priests. He had hardly caught a moment's rest since they had strictly forbidden the Anniste from practicing their healing arts early that spring. His small, dark shop with the loft perched above it was the most frequented place in the village; not counting the Pitaya Pit tavern, which contained healing powers of its own.

Chalvern had up until recently been content in his gloomy, musky-smelling shop, lined with rough wooden shelves; filled with packets of powder, bottles, bunches of herbs tied together and hanging to dry in neat rows from the rafters. And then the Anniste ban had turned his entire world topsy-turvy.

Neela had disappeared abruptly soon afterward, and then her daughter Tekoah became ill with a fever that almost killed her.

Something was wrong in the timing of all that. Something didn't make sense.

Chalvern finished measuring the tincture and sealed the small bottle with care. He shook his head and muttered aloud, a new habit that annoyed no one more than himself.

Nothing quite makes sense anymore, was what he muttered. Although some nonsense was rather amusing. Take Grindhor, for instance—who hated Chalvern, hated anyone who wielded any power separate from the priesthood—even he had reluctantly swallowed his pride an annaspan ago when he had discovered the alarming growth on his...

The apothecary allowed himself a mischievous, slightly vindictive grin. Then his head moved sharply toward his balcony above the square, as the wind rose to an unnatural shriek, followed by ominous silence. He paused, holding the bottle of belladonna tincture; cocked his head to one side for a moment, a strange foreboding like the buzz of an insect in his ear. He stared down at the bottle in his hand, which was beginning to tremble.

And then felt his body stiffen as if turned to stone.

Although Chalvern could not move, his brain raced wildly. If he was alive, and not felled at last by those pains in his chest which had assailed him more and more often of late, then this must be—enchantment! Something he had never experienced firsthand in his sixty-something turnings on Miraven.

Another thought swiftly followed: *He is here, it must be he. Braith has returned at last!* And, absurdly, joy was the first thing he felt.

Chalvern had no other sensations until the grateful tingling in his body, when a short time later he found he could move again. He barely had time to straighten before Braith was suddenly in the room. His tall, lean frame made the cramped little shop even smaller.

"Hello, Master," Braith said, his voice much deeper than it had been when Chalvern had last seen him.

Chalvern's cramped fist opened, and the bottle of belladonna tincture dropped to the floor. Clay shards shattered in a spectacular display of sound and chaos.

Braith chuckled, and the sound was disconcerting. At fifteen, his voice had often cracked, becoming high and thin, an affliction common among boys-becoming-men, but one that tormented Braith particularly, fuelling his adolescent self-loathing. Now he sounded very assured.

Chalvern had seen a sorcerer once—the story was not pleasant—but had never heard one speak until now. And there was so much conjecture and exaggeration, that one could seldom tell the truth from falsehood. But little could he have imagined that this sorcerer would be a boy he had known and loved.

"Braith," he replied, his voice quavering a little. And then, because he could not keep himself from doing so any longer, he stepped forward and gripped the other one's shoulders tightly, then embraced him. "My son," he murmured huskily, stepping back once more and looking searchingly into Braith's eyes. "How is it with you?"

Braith smiled, the brief glow in his eyes kindling a warmth in his features. "Better than it was the last time we met, Master. And I see you are well, for your dome has gained a most amazing gleam—a beacon, it could be, for ships lost in a storm."

Chalvern tried to look outraged, and then chuckled ruefully, passing a hand over his bald pate. He shot a shrewd glance at Braith and contented himself with saying, "But not all ships come seeking refuge. Some bring the storm with them."

Braith gazed back at him, wordless, refusing to answer the

unspoken question that hovered like a dark moth between them: *And will you misuse your powers as other sorcerers do—have always done?*

The boy had always been stubborn, sometimes cloaking himself in bleak, impenetrable silence that could go on for hours —or even days—when he had first come to Chalvern at the age of twelve. By the time Chalvern crossed paths with the lad, Braith's parents had long been dead, and he lived with his aunt, an ancient Anniste woman who dwelt on a small plot of land a few miles east of Stern. Farala sent her nephew on frequent excursions into the Taboran Woods at Stern's End, seeking the herb pothang, highly prized for the soothing effect of its long, waxy leaves when placed on inflamed joints. Farala suffered greatly from this affliction, and so it was perhaps inevitable that Chalvern encountered in the wood one day a skinny lad with dark hair and wary eyes.

The memory of these first days with Braith came to Chalvern so vividly that he had to grip the table to steady himself. He let himself slip into that time long past, when Braith had been vulnerable and innocent.

Seeing he had startled the boy, Chalvern waved his own herb basket cheerily. "Hail, fellow wanderer!" Braith gave him a tentative smile.

The two struck up a casual conversation, and over the next few months they met in the wood by chance several times. Chalvern was drawn to the lad who balanced, awkward as a nocturnal creature in sunlight, between boy and man. Chalvern's own sons had married and gone, and there was also a more recent ache in his heart that had not yet subsided. When scouring the forest with Braith for lavender or pothang, both of them becoming disproportionately exuberant at a rare find of trell root, the sorrow left him.

Word came that Farala had died. The next day, Chalvern watched from his balcony as a winding procession of brown-robed women moved like a slow caterpillar down the street toward the high way.

The Anniste went to collect Farala's body. They would lift the shrunken form, swath it tenderly in a white linen sack, and convey the sack to the foot of one of the towering crohm trees in the woods; there to bury it deeply, so that the sacred tree could absorb the spirit of the Anniste healer into its roots.

The tree would then become stronger, more powerful—a passive immortality granted to Farala, in exchange for her life of selfless dedication to the needs of others.

So the Anniste believed, at any rate. Chalvern had never been sure of anything he could not confirm with his own five senses. He abhorred speculation, distortion, imagination running rampant—all fevers of the brain which drove away logic and reason, as sheep are driven in a frenzy of fear when pursued by hungry mountain cats.

Although the Anniste had to him always appeared calm, unflappable. He could not deny it: he deeply admired them.

And there was no need for the priest to make such a fuss about these religious rites. If the Anniste wanted to bury their own, let them do it. To hear Grindhor carry on, one would think they had desecrated a statue of Rhan.

Watching that line of women, Chalvern felt a great sense of peace wash over him. Just seeing the Anniste was enough to make a man believe the world would be all right, in much the same way as a fretful child is soothed by the taste of warm milk and the low murmuring of a lullaby.

But peace is short-lived when love stirs the soul. Chalvern swallowed tears in his throat on the day of Farala's burial. Although he had known she would not be there, he looked with hopeless yearning for a glimpse of Neela's form—slim and supple, uncoarsened by childbearing, though her delicate face reflected the ravages of marriage to Veld the blacksmith.

Veld the drunkard, the tyrant, the madman, and many epithets not yet invented.

Bitterly, Chalvern wondered how much Veld had been paid by the priest for convincing his wife to abdicate the Guardianship of the Anniste. And how long it had taken Veld to drink the money.

Neela, he lamented, gazing at the mourning procession, his longing a silent, ever-present shadow.

Turning with a heavy heart to go back into his chamber, the thought suddenly struck him with the force of a smashing beaker. Old Farala was dead! What of the boy—Braith! Where will he go? I must be getting old, he groaned to himself, slapping his forehead with his palm. Every thought is one-half beat of the drum behind.

The next day, Chalvern went to seek out Farala's little hut, walking the three miles slowly but at a steady pace, hailing acquaintances as he went. He had accepted a cold cup of buttermilk at the farmhouse of Hanta the hen-keeper—and well-known gossip—and asked her for directions.

"Anna's tides!" she clucked, sounding much like one of her prized chickens. "You should not be walking this far at your age! More than sixty turnings, are you not? Not that I'm saying you look it. But Farala is beyond anyone's help now, Master, even yours. And you've no wish to run into that sulky nephew of hers, who snarls and snaps like a wild umbray if you go near the place."

Chalvern thanked Hanta gravely for her help and went on his way, chuckling to himself a little at the thought of Braith chasing away that plump busybody. And, when he entered the open doorway at old Farala's hut, he was gratified that Braith did not seem displeased to see him. The boy was as suspicious and taciturn as ever, though, as he squatted over the tiny hearth, making himself corn pancakes and flipping them with his fingers.

When Chalvern asked how he was doing, he muttered something about mother hens, looking up briefly to glower. "Don't they know I can take care of myself?"

Chalvern hid his smile at the wounded vanity of youth.

"I know you can take care of yourself," he replied, striving to sound nonchalant. "But why not come back with me? I am looking for an apprentice, you know. My eyes are becoming as cloudy as mud puddles. And my legs are beginning to tremble when I return from the woods. I enjoy the walk, but I would enjoy it more if I did it less.

"You would like the village," he continued, suppressing his enthusiasm, for Braith's stare was cool and appraising. "There are many young-

sters your age. I know, because I have taught them all. I am the scourge of Stern, the dreaded schoolmaster."

This brought—finally—a smile to the boy's lips, and he retorted, "I cannot imagine you as a scourge." He then turned back to the smoking pancake with deft fingers, his black brows knitting.

Chalvern waited, and finally Braith said, "I do not make friends easily. My father was a peddler, and we moved around so often... And, besides that, I enjoy being by myself. I am used to it."

"There are lots of pretty girls," Chalvern said conversationally, delighted at the flush this provoked. "May I have a pancake? I'm famished after the walk," he added.

Braith looked instantly remorseful, sitting him down on the only chair—a wooden stool—and handing him pancake after pancake.

The boy is not such a snapping umbray, Chalvern thought.

"What do you say?" he ventured, after a companionable silence punctuated by contented munching. "Come back with me today. We can discuss the details on the way."

Braith sat, his jaw working. After a moment, he replied, almost angrily. "Thank you for your kind offer. I cannot believe that your eyes become cloudy or your legs tremble, however. You are stronger and more agile than most men half your age, so I must conclude that you are doing this out of kindness. I thank you for this. But I am accustomed to fending for myself, as I explained. Why, I took care of Aunt Farala, more than she ever did of me. I only need to find a trade, that is all."

He looked defiant, but a little frightened, too. Chalvern saw it in the hunch of his thin shoulders.

"Ah, the perfect solution," he replied smoothly. "You shall continue in your life of solitary bliss—only agree to collect my herbs for me and add a few years to my miserable life."

He made his voice brisk and businesslike, carefully avoiding any hint of kindness in his tone.

"I shall pay you, of course, in coins or kind, for the valuable service, and extra if you will assist me with my sorting and labelling. As for the other idea, well, one day I will find a dedicated apprentice, someone who *will carry on my work when I am gone. Rhan knows it will not be my sons… But, come, what do you say?"*

A spark of eagerness leaped into Braith's eyes, and Chalvern knew he had hit on the right thing. They agreed on wages, and he left feeling a glow of satisfaction that he had given something to the boy who seemed so reluctant to accept anything from anyone.

But his gift had been double-edged and steeped in the bitter irony of all gifts from the fickle hands of the gods.

Emerging from his reverie, Chalvern found he was still gripping the table. He looked at Braith, standing stark as black iron, finding it hard to believe he was capable of being injured. Yet hurt he had been, and now he was irrevocably transformed. Perhaps it was a death, of sorts. A death of innocence.

The boy had gone. Now it was the invulnerable sorcerer Braith who gazed back at him so enigmatically. Nonplussed, Chalvern bustled about, filling the kettle for tea.

The past was the past, and some things did not bear speaking of. But they were with you all the same, like shadows, waiting to swallow you whole. He set the kettle down, hands shaking, back to Braith, and the memories gripped him again.

Everything had gone well in the beginning. Young Braith proved to be a reliable worker. But then, two annaspans after they had struck their agreement, Braith failed to appear on the appointed evening with Chalvern's supply of herbs. Annoyed at this display of unreliability from the lad, Chalvern at last went upstairs to bed, where he tossed and turned for some time on his pallet.

As often happened when his head first hit the pillow, an image of Neela arose before him, her hair dishevelled in a glorious bright cloud swirling around her, her blue-green eyes gleaming at him, whether in passion or desperation he did not know. She had given birth—a girl, he had heard. Chalvern fought a wild urge to go to her, to ask to see the baby. It took many tortured, writhing minutes to resist this urge, and to banish Neela's image from his mind.

But sleep still eluded him. His irritation with Braith refused to evapo-

rate; it whined and circled around his head like a biting gnat, and he remained wakeful. Therefore, when quick, urgent raps came on his door, he stumbled to his feet with alacrity, almost dropping the tallow candle he snatched up from his bedside table.

It was Beula, Neela's elder sister, a scurrying, damp-eyed widow. Her twitching face and bowed frame always seemed comical beside Neela's luminous form, but Chalvern was above such thoughts now. Beula looked most worried.

"You must rouse yourself, Chalvern," she said, "there is trouble."

Chalvern's mouth became dry. Not Neela, please. Let it not be her. An iron band tightened in his chest. Beula knew him well enough to read his thoughts, for she whipped her head sharply from side to side. Not Neela, then.

"It is a young lad, someone has hurt him. He was lying by the roadside, near the forge. One of Neela's boys found him and came to tell me."

"Who is it?" Chalvern asked, the iron band easing a little. "Do you know him?"

"Old Farala's nephew, Braith. Who knows what he was doing? He is a loner, that one. Anyway, you know Neela refuses to heal any longer, although the forge was close by and she could easily have tended to him."

Beula's voice trembled a little in outrage. "So, we had to bring him here. We must help him, poor boy. He has lost some blood."

The iron band tightened again, so that it was difficult to breathe. Chalvern's eyes clouded over until he could see nothing but a grey mist. He must clear the clouds. He must not faint.

Braith had not been late, not intentionally.

Oh Rhan, this is my fault, Chalvern thought, sickened. A drunken soldier or Southerner had robbed or beaten the poor lad. He had acted so proud and independent, but he was just a boy.

"What happened?" he had asked, keeping his voice calm.

Beula dropped her eyes, shaking her head, and he saw tears drip down her weathered cheeks, shimmering in the candlelight. This, more than anything, shook him, for Beula was not by nature a weeper. She had never done so in his presence, in fact, although at Neela's wedding she had looked as if she would.

Chalvern stared at her.

"Someone wicked"—she whispered, shaking her head as if to dispel a dark cloud—"someone truly evil."

Chalvern felt a dawning of comprehension and, with it, a lurch in his stomach.

The sound of heavy footsteps in the darkness behind her had interrupted them. "Ah, here is Raol," Beula said, wiping her eyes. The tranquillity of the Anniste healing trance had descended upon her, infusing her humble bearing with an indefinable radiance.

The priests cannot not quench that light, Chalvern thought, calmer despite himself.

"And here is your charge." Beula's voice lingered on the last word.

Chalvern reached through the open doorway and took Braith's limp form from Neela's deaf-mute son, Raol. The boy's impassive features shifted, as if wrestling with some shadow within.

Chalvern looked down at the crumpled body in his arms. The boy was pale, so pale.

Chalvern turned from the doorway, hearing it close behind him. Time slowed to the beat of the boy's heart against his own chest in the endless crossing of the room to his tiny hearth. Chalvern staggered a little from the load of the muscular twelve-year-old, yet, as he looked into the white, still face, he felt it not at all.

The kettle hissed and seethed, hot drops flying from the stove. Chalvern jumped back to avoid the spatter.

All that had been long ago, of course. Fourteen turnings, almost. Since then, Braith had come into a power so vast, it made ordinary men quake just to think of it. *Some bring the storm.*

Braith's eyes continued to follow him with that unblinking gaze. Chalvern smiled ruefully and removed the kettle from the stove. There would evidently be no tea drinking.

He turned to ascend the narrow stairs that led to his sleeping chamber and—rare luxury—the small wooden balcony that overlooked the square. Braith followed him. Chalvern opened the shuttered doors and stepped out onto the balcony.

The sun was low in the sky, and long shadows were everywhere. He blinked as his eyes adjusted to the light, for it was very dark in his shop.

Chalvern inhaled the late summer air, finding a measure of calmness in the familiar scents—lilac and honeysuckle blended with the more pungent odours of animals and their offal, the inevitable aftermath of a market day. He watched as the last of the stragglers dawdled toward home, and he thought an aura of unease lingered in their furtive glances, and in the sudden distant howl of an umbray. But, otherwise, everything looked as it should be.

Braith stood beside him. Studying his sun-bronzed face, Chalvern realized, with a twinge of paternal pride, that he had become—not handsome, his face was too sharp, but—interesting-looking, and confident in himself. The thin, tormented shadow-boy had gone.

As he studied the sorcerer, questions boiled up within him like herbs in a cauldron. What had transpired since the night he'd left for good? Whence had he fled—driven by sticks and stones and jeers?

Braith's high, tormented voice pleading, *Why are you doing this? I have done nothing to you!* Then, becoming ferocious, *You will be sorry you did this to me one day.*

Or so Chalvern had heard, later, from Beula. He had not been there, otherwise they would never have dared. Although small in stature, he was as doughty as a badger when crossed. Did Braith know he had been unaware of those village bullies? Or did Braith think he had lurked in cowardly complicity behind his shuttered doors?

Another question: when had Braith found his Source—tapped into that animal power that transformed mortal men into sorcerers? What was his Source?

Knowing Braith, he might never find the answers to those questions.

But there was one urgent question now. With an abrupt, jerky gesture toward the villagers below, Chalvern asked, "Why did you spare them? Did you not swear vengeance?"

Watching from beneath lowered lids, Chalvern saw an almost imperceptible shudder pass through the sorcerer. He kept still, not wanting to shatter what might, perhaps, be a moment of rare confidence.

A long silence followed, and Chalvern watched an abandoned lamb bleating forlornly as it wandered alone in the square. Then Braith spoke, in a voice so low and quiet that Chalvern had to strain to hear him.

"It was what I had dreamed of from the moment I found my Source. Annihilation, so complete that I would blot out even the memory of this place. Except you, of course, Master." He looked up, his expression almost timid, and tears sprang hotly to Chalvern's eyes. He forced himself to look away.

When Braith spoke again, his voice was bemused. "But I have harmed no one, except for the priest and his toady, and they are worth so little that nothing will have changed." He paused, and then glanced at Chalvern, smiling. "I am glad to see you, Master," he said.

Chalvern was trembling, and so he took hold of himself. But his mind was reeling. Braith was speaking calmly of murdering Grindhor and Melnich, and in the next breath sounding sentimental. *This is what they become,* he reminded himself. *When they meld with their Source, they lose their compassion, their humanity. And we remain at their mercy because of their vast power, which they wield with as little judgement as children with firebrands.*

Chalvern thought of the only other time he had seen a sorcerer; he could not tell whether it was fear that made his ribs ache, or only that nagging pain in his chest which sometimes spread to other parts of his body.

He shuddered, and could not bring himself to ask how Braith had killed the two unfortunate men. He had never liked them, but that was utterly beside the point.

"Why did you not kill everyone else?" he demanded, making his voice that of the schoolmaster, the father, the judge.

Braith spoke again, his voice taut as a bowstring. "I saw her. And I could not destroy Stern while she walks upon this ground."

Chalvern's head shot up in astonishment. This, least of all, was what he had expected.

"She is the bud of a flower that has not yet bloomed, but already surpasses any of the full-blown flowers that grow. She was spinning poetry as she walked through all the filth and stupidity that is at the heart of this village."

Braith flung a gloved hand out toward the square in a savage gesture. "She was creating beauty in her mind as artlessly as a silkworm streams silk." He stopped, grimacing, as if it had pained him to say this much. "I must see her again," he added, fixing Chalvern with a gaze of frightening intensity. "You know who she is."

Anna cradle my soul, Chalvern groaned to himself, *he means Tekoah.*

Sorcerers did not form attachments for ordinary folk—it was unheard of. What a horrid mess. Braith was still staring at him, and he gazed back, speechless. This kind of pain only the Gods could heal, though they seemed to enjoy inflicting it more.

"Yes," Chalvern said heavily, "I know her."

CHAPTER 3

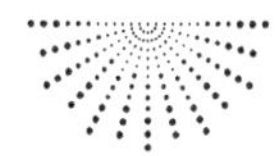

*T*ekoah walked home in the growing dusk like a sleepwalker. Moving with jerky steps, often stumbling. Now and again, she paused, striving to withstand the shudders which swept through her. After a time, she stopped, as dizziness swirled around her in brightly coloured rings.

She leaned for comfort against the trunk of a massive crohm tree. This towering monarch had stood for ages before she'd trodden this earth, and would be here well after she became one of the piles of dust which she had witnessed disappearing into the wind. Tekoah trembled again at the memory and clasped the trunk as if a storm buffeted her. The sobs came at last.

When her weeping ceased, Tekoah's dream-like state vanished, leaving her weak and nauseated. *I cannot go on,* she thought. She could not bear to see what Braith might have done to her home, her family. Then another memory struck her: Braith, entering her mind, touching hidden places.

The memory of that strength pushing dark fingers into her was like the threat of madness. It would drive her mad. She pressed her face hard against the tree.

Coarse bark chafed against her forehead, and the sensation

revived her a little. It was solid, not vague and threatening. The old stories said the gods had planted crohm trees at the dawn of time, and the trees possessed some ancient power from that time.

She looked up at the gnarled branches. In the twilight, their black shadows spread in inky waves above her, crisscrossing each other, their intertwining leaves creating endless patterns against the sky. The branches were arms, and the leaves were hands holding wisdom in their fingertips. Tekoah imagined the tree limbs enfolding her, and her breathing deepened. She yearned to be one with this ancient being, to stay here forever; her legs becoming roots, twisting down into the cool, dark earth —her arms flung out in a benediction to the world and all its creatures.

Into the cool respite of this image came another notion. *The sorcerer Braith—he means me no harm.*

For a moment, Tekoah accepted it as a simple truth. Then, vivid as the spilled fruit at her feet in the square, came a picture of home. Did Braith go there? Was it now a smoking ruin and her family small piles of dust?

Tekoah felt dizzy again; but not knowing was worse, and her legs would not become roots however long she stood in this spot. Stumbling into the road once more, she turned her face toward home, and whatever desolation awaited her.

It was dusk by the time she reached the yard. The place stood empty—eerily so, for it was the dinner hour and on most days Veld and the twins would now be out at the well, pumping water to wash the soot from their blackened faces and hands, removing their soiled aprons and stretching their cramped muscles.

And on most days, she would be in the small, thatched hut, assembling their evening meal, or performing the hundred other household tasks left to her alone, now that her mother was no longer there.

But this day was not like most days. As she peered into the twilit gloom, she saw that her home was still there, a small wisp of smoke rising from the forge. But it was silent. The only audible sound was the mournful call of a dusk-bird from the nearby woods. The light was fading from the sky, and Tekoah's knees buckled beneath her.

There was the solid thud of footsteps, and Fanco came around the corner of the hut, pushing a heavy barrow filled with coal for the morrow. His chestnut brown hair, rough and thick as a bird's nest, hung over his forehead and into his eyes, and Tekoah marvelled that he did not trip and fall. Chalvern had once said that the twins, deaf-mute though they were, seemed guided by some inner voice. It seemed so, for Fanco strode confidently over the rough turf leading from the house to the forge, despite the deepening darkness.

Tekoah thought he looked, in his too-small breeches and tunic, like a hulking mountain scantily forested. Fanco stopped; cocking his head to one side, he listened. Then he straightened and turned, looking behind him to where Tekoah stood.

He had never seemed so dear to her as in that moment. She half-ran toward him, legs unsteady, until she could clasp his enormous arm, the words flooding from her although she knew he could not hear, could not understand.

"Fanco, he spared you! I thought you would all be gone. I am so happy—I have never been so happy since Mother left!"

"Is that you, daughter?" Veld came out into the twilight, squinting as he untied his leather apron. When he saw Tekoah, his voice took on a whining, resentful note.

As Tekoah gazed at her father, a strange fascination took hold of her. It was as if she had never seen him before. She could not tear her eyes away.

It was often said that Veld had once been handsome. His greying hair still had strands of the rich chestnut brown the twins had inherited from him. He was above average height, but walked with a blacksmith's stoop. His eyes were a piercing blue, shot through with the reddened veins common to madmen and drunkards. His skin was as pale as the underside of a mushroom growing in the darkest woods, except for the purple-black pouches beneath the ravaged eyes. With a prominent brow and thin but well-formed mouth—all the features together some-what supported the blacksmith's arrogant boast of descending from a noble lineage.

When Veld's thin lips parted with a snarl—or a smile, as he was now attempting for his daughter—his few remaining teeth seemed long and white and somehow feral, compared with the other blackened stumps. His whole bearing, in fact, resembled that of an umbray waiting to seize a piece of carrion from some larger, nobler beast and slink off with it into the night.

"Girl," Veld was saying now, licking his lips as if in thirst. She knew he wanted a drink. "This half-wit brother of yours would stand like a dolt, thinking about Rhan-knows-what, while I am waiting to bank the fire and get myself in to dinner. Likely to starve, I am. Is it ready, then?"

Tekoah stared at her father in dismay, barely able to hear his words. *He does not know about the sorcerer,* she thought. But how could that be? It made no sense. Perhaps a new enchantment had occurred that she could not see.

"Fanco saw me coming, so he was waiting for me, Father," she answered. Inside she repeated to herself in disbelief, *He does not know, truly, he does not know!*

"Are you all right, Father?" she asked.

Veld, who had been removing his leather apron, stopped, and stared back at her, his face flushing with annoyance. "All right? I am half-starved, with one of your idiot brothers counting ponies at your aunt's all day and the other one only here as a plague on my days."

"And you just come in, girl," he went on, his voice rising.

"Where were you, rolling with some tinker in a barn somewhere?" His face had mottled with spots of red.

Tekoah backed away. "Of course not, Father. There was a disturbance in the village. Did you not hear of it?" Keeping herself out of striking distance, she observed his face a reaction. He must have felt some twinge of Braith's presence.

After all, Veld claimed that Braith the sorcerer dwelt inside his mind at will. He had done so for over a turning, shortly before the priest had announced Braith had become a sorcerer.

"BEFORE!" Veld would shout wildly. "Not after, but *before*! So, if I am mad, or lying, as that scum of a priest says—who was once my friend but now won't spit at me in the street—then how do you explain the fact I knew he was a sorcerer before anyone else in Miraven knew? Explain *that*, filth!" he would shout, standing in the doorway, shaking his fist in a frenzy.

According to Veld, the malevolent sorcerer had projected images of dread demons and beasts, monsters so terrifying as to drive most men mad. These phantoms appeared night after night with relentless ferocity, so that he could sleep no longer than an hour or two at most. This much at least was true. Several times a night, Tekoah heard her father awaken with a wrenching cry which echoed throughout the hut.

The nighttime visions began to appear in the daytime as well; the sorcerer delighted in deceiving Veld, so that he would see a terrible apparition where instead there stood a member of his beloved family. At these times, his beloved family fled for their lives.

The sorcerer Braith had driven away Veld's wife Neela and eldest son Weslan. Braith had brought illness and blight upon his life. And Braith might return one day, Veld would intone, to wreak some final and terrible revenge.

Rhan grant I am dead before then. He would moan and shake his head, while Tekoah stroked his arm soothingly.

But Tekoah saw now that her father was not dead, although Braith had come and gone, leaving dust and darkness. Strange, that.

She was thinking of Chalvern as she watched her father's face, although she could not have said why, having seldom seen him since her illness at the start of summer. Tekoah preferred not to dwell on that time, for such thoughts were very sad. Her mother had abandoned them and Tekoah had collapsed soon afterward — from the weight of the grief, Father had told her.

Chalvern had downplayed his own part in her healing, but without the apothecary, she might have died. He had nursed her through her fever, and those terrible dreams. It was the dreams Tekoah was thinking of now, and Chalvern's face hovering over hers as she recovered, like a pale light to guide her home. A song had come to her that night just as she had fallen over the edge of sleep, the singing voice high as a reed flute:

Only a hole where the moon has been

Oh Mother, where have you gone?

Tekoah shook her head to dispel the memory, for Father was shouting questions at her, arms windmilling, and she must think of a reply. For a moment, Tekoah could not hear his words; it was as if a hive of bees was buzzing in her head. Then Fanco's firm hand settled on her shoulder, and the buzzing stopped.

"I asked you, what are you speaking of, slattern?" Veld yelled. "What disturbance? I am likely to starve, I want my beans and bread, and you stand here like a string puppet, spouting nonsense, with your eyes popping out of your silly head!"

"I—why—I don't know, Father," she answered, struggling to appear calm. All at once, she knew that she did not want to tell him what she had just witnessed in the square. "All I know is that people were shouting, and shoving me so, and an enormous pig escaped from the market and ran right into me, spilling my basket," she finished, making her voice sound plaintive, but nothing more.

Veld smiled unpleasantly. "What a shame. What a pity. But perhaps you might remember not to stand gawking and simpering in the market while your family starves. You were probably looking for a lover. Well, the first pitaya merchant with a fat purse who comes along can have you, and then all you will have to remember is to warm his bed!"

"*Father*," she protested, feeling herself blush as she always did when he spoke like this. It had been more and more often of late.

"Come now!" he shouted. "Beans and bread. And stir up the fire, it is chilly in the evenings now." He turned to rinse his head at the well, scowling at Fanco, who stood holding a wet rag to his head.

Father must have struck him a quick blow. As she thought this, she saw her brother's eyes resting upon her as she walked to the hut and wondered what he was thinking.

Tekoah made haste to stir up the hearth fire and then hurried to the stove. The day's events were like a dream—she must put them behind her. But of course, she could not, and as she heated the meagre evening meal, she felt an unfamiliar flash of contempt for her father.

Stirring the stew with agitated vigour, she tried to quell this disloyalty. But the feeling came again, stronger than before.

Veld the blacksmith is nothing to Braith the sorcerer—less than a fly! she thought fiercely. And as she stared into the fire, the memory of Braith's voice and face came to her. She shuddered, but whether in fear or elation she could not tell.

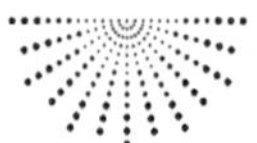

CHAPTER 4

*S*omething *utterly solitary,* Chalvern was thinking, watching Braith's green-gold eyes as they gleamed in the dark. Night had fallen, and they had gone inside so that Chalvern could sit in comfort on his cot. He heated tea for them, but Braith refused all offers of food and drink, so he sipped his own and watched the black-clad sorcerer who had been his apprentice and tried to guess his Source.

"Never mind trying to guess my Source," Braith said, with a faint smile. "Tell me more about Tekoah. I know she is the daughter of the blacksmith Veld, and that she is young, too young for me. But who is to say, Master? Youth and age, they are tricky things, are they not?"

CHALVERN WONDERED how much Braith had guessed as a boy about his feelings for Neela, who had been twenty turnings younger than himself. Or perhaps the sorcerer was bespeaking his mind. He had heard tales of this. But Braith would not dare such disrespect. Even now.

"I was not aware that sorcerers could care for mere mortals, or anyone at all," he snapped.

Braith sat in a wooden chair in the corner, beyond the glow from the single bedside lamp, so Chalvern could not gauge his expression. He paused a long time before answering.

"Neither was I. For all I know, it has never happened before. But then never has a third sorcerer been spawned in a single age. Dare I theorize I may be unique? And you are hedging, Master." Braith touched his crimson-gloved fingertips together, forming a triangle.

Chalvern found his eyes drawn to it as he struggled to find the right words—although no words were right for this. "Braith," he began, "Tekoah knows of you already, of course, and—"

"—she hates me." Braith finished for him, leaning forward intently in his chair.

"DO NOT BESPEAK MY MIND!" Chalvern barked, unnerved.

Braith held up his hand in a commiserating gesture. "I did not, Master—nor would I, please be assured. But I did *hers*, I confess, just for a moment. I could not resist knowing what thoughts lay beyond those great blue eyes. I heard a poem. When she realized I was there, I felt the heat of her rage, smouldering beneath her fear. Do they all hate me so?"

Chalvern shook his head. "No, they do not. Most villagers feel a rather misplaced sense of pride that this was your birthplace. We can brag we have one in the North now, so the Southerners and Berlotans cannot pretend to any superiority because of 'their' sorcerer." He smiled. "Of course, when a crop is blighted, or milk comes sour from a cow, it is because a sorcerer. Or at least it was until the drought in the South. Now everything seems to be the fault of the Anniste. People always need someone to blame for their troubles."

"But she truly hates me," Braith mused. "Why? I must find that out, for I will not violate her mind in that way again. It is not a simple thing at any rate, for it ages me. Tell me!"

Chalvern's eyes were drawn again into that crimson triangle; his answer seemed to come from him almost against his will.

"She believes you cursed her father and caused his madness, which revealed itself last turning, though there are many that would argue the seeds were sown long before. Veld claims you plot to destroy him, like a cat with a mouse.

"Veld's eldest son Weslan left in early spring—he ran off with some soldiers. He has ended up in Rhantor, of all places, at the court of the Queen. Neela, Veld's wife, disappeared shortly after Weslan left. Veld claims she deserted him, but that it was all part of your diabolical plot to take away his family."

Chalvern's voice faltered. This talk fell too close to striking open the wound in his heart. Had he said all this of his own free will?

"But?" Braith persisted.

"But what?" Chalvern knew he sounded querulous, but he was becoming tired of this. "You have been told all you need to know. And no good will come of this, I feel compelled to tell you. You may have significant power, but there is no enchantment that can change hate to love!"

"What do you think happened to her mother?" Braith asked this as if Chalvern had not spoken at all.

Chalvern stared at him, bristling, for a few seconds. Then the heaviness of fatigue settled on his shoulders. Bearing down upon him, oppressive as a wet and moldering blanket, was the weight of all the years, the punctured hopes, the plans which had crumbled like dried herbs, drifted away to nothing.

He said in a leaden voice, "I have a suspicion about something—impossible to prove and likely unfounded—that in a drunken rage Veld beat his wife once too many times, and drove her away at the start of this summer. Or perhaps it is worse. I nursed Tekoah through a fever after her mother's disappearance, and in her ravings were some terrible visions. There may be memories that are too painful to recall, so she forgot."

Chalvern paused, fighting back tears; the wound had re-opened and bled. "I am not so fortunate."

He could not say another word, but sat with his head bowed, hearing nothing but his own laboured breathing. He had spoken of these suspicions to no one. No one.

After a moment, he felt Braith's hand on his shoulder. "Neela." It was not a question. "You speak of Neela, and now I remember her a little, from before. She was someone you cared for. Where were Neela's other sons at the time this happened? She had twins, did she not, or did they die?"

The questions were put gently, but Braith's hand remained heavy on Chalvern's shoulder until he replied. "Weslan had left by that time. The twins, who are deaf-mute if you remember, were away on that day, breeding ponies over at their Aunt Beula's farm."

Braith stood up and paced the room, taking it in two or three strides, making it seem smaller than ever. "And you, Master. If you worried about Veld's violence, why did you never give that voice at the Village Council?"

Chalvern looked up, fists clenched. But, seeing an answering spark in Braith's own eyes, his outrage evaporated.

"I told you, this notion of mine stems from nothing more than the delirious ravings of a girl's fever. Veld had beaten Neela many times. Perhaps she finally had enough. When she was coherent again, Tekoah insisted that her mother had left in the night. I could never accuse Veld without proof—it is common knowledge I despise him. And I had to consider above all else this one thing: if we ever dredge up anything about her mother, it may well destroy the girl."

A fire gathered in Chalvern's chest, and his voice rose. "But I tell you this: more than anything, I wish Tekoah gone from this place—and the poisonous beast that is her father. She is fragile. Perhaps her brother Weslan will send for her and settle her in Rhantor. She might be able to start her life anew."

Looking up at Braith's face, Chalvern saw his folly at once, but said defiantly, "She is like a daughter to me. Do you think I would see her hurt again?"

"I would not hurt her." Braith said this in a soft voice, but his face was frightening to behold.

"How do you know?" Chalvern countered.

Braith rose. His black cloak rippled as a wind whistled through the small chamber. Chalvern drew a sharp inward breath, bracing himself.

"Braith," he said, his voice harsh with desperation. "Think! What will you do, swoop down and just take her? If so, you have made true every falsehood Veld has ever told her. You will lose any hope you have of gaining her trust."

"*Think*," Chalvern repeated, as Braith turned, slapping his hands against his thighs.

The wind subsided. The sorcerer stood weighing Chalvern's words, head cocked to one side, a small tic working near his jaw. After a long moment, he nodded, slowly. Then he covered his face with his hands.

Chalvern watched him. His knees trembled, and he sank down to his cot, gripping the rough woolen blanket with grateful fingers. Where would this end?

Perhaps the Anniste could counsel him on this dreadful matter. They knew more of sorcerers than he did. *I must talk to Beula,* he thought, with a rising sense of urgency. She was Tekoah's aunt and, being Anniste, would do her utmost to help. It would be difficult to find Beula, of course, because she was in hiding now. But this was more dangerous.

Galvanized by the need for action, Chalvern rose from his cot and went to trim the lamp. He resisted the urge to embrace Braith, who remained standing, shoulders rigid. Casting about for words of comfort, he said over his shoulder, "I said that I thought of Tekoah as a daughter. Well, I speak to you as if you were my son, and in this my feelings are unchanged, though you be a sorcerer."

Chalvern meant this, but the words sounded hollow and inadequate. He put the lamp down, wincing as a few drops of hot oil slopped over his wrist. Braith did not move or make any sign. Chalvern kept his voice steady as he continued.

"If you wish her well, then do not disrupt her life or frighten her further. Hers is not an easy lot to be sure, but many have hard lives and end up well. What do you offer her in exchange? Can you make her happy? Or do you wish to? Have you given it any thought?"

Another long Braith silence followed, in which Chalvern had ample time to study the flickering shadows cast by the lamp dance on the cracked wooden floor, and wonder if he had pushed the boundaries too far. But when he looked up, Braith was standing in the circle of lamplight and smiling his rare, quirky smile.

"You have given me no words which are not of wisdom, Master, as usual. I thank you. I will take up no more of your time. Perhaps I may come again, and we will reminisce of happier memories?" He turned to go.

Chalvern nodded, uneasy still. "Where are you off to?" he asked before he could stop himself.

A raised eyebrow answered him as Braith paused on his way to the stairs. "I have not yet paid my respects to the young Queen Darielle. I think now is the time for a visit to Rhantor. Many thanks again, Master."

"Why bother using the door?" Chalvern called, feeling peevish at Braith's remote tone. "Why not just vanish as suddenly as you appeared, and frighten me half to death, as befits a sorcerer?"

"What?" Braith grinned, teeth white in his face, "Are you

trying to age me before my time?" And down he went, taking the stairs two at a time, just as he used to. *Just as he used to.*

CHALVERN HEARD the clatter of hooves in the square. Going to stand on his balcony, he watched as a beautiful black stallion galloped out of the dusk. He saw Braith leap and ride away, his form somewhat shadowed, for the moon had not yet risen. He could have been mistaken for one of the Rhantoran nobles that sometimes rode through Stern, elegant and haughty.

Chalvern closed the shutters and stood in the wavering light. He was very tired. But it was not a fall-asleep-immediately tired, so he moved his stiff legs down the stairs, one at a time, and unearthed a precious bottle of pitaya brandy from a dusty shelf.

It was rare as gold, usually reserved for amputations or women deep in childbearing labour. Chalvern drank the brandy now in tiny fiery sips until he felt the molten honey ascend from his stomach to his head. Only then did he climb into his cot.

He lay there watching the velvety shadows, while the room circled gently around him. Just before he fell asleep, the thought came to him.

A hawk, of course. That was Braith's Source—a hawk.

CHAPTER 5

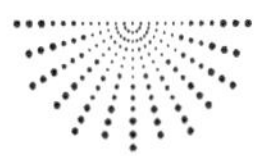

$\mathcal{W}$eslan lay back in the thick, soft grass of the pitaya orchard. The sun's warmth was like honey on his face and shoulders.

This was the life he had always sought. There was so much to which he was eagerly looking forward.

Just now, things were a little dull, however. Heyg's company of mercenary soldiers had spent the past few days patrolling the pitaya orchards by the Berlotan border in a seemingly endless circuit. Weslan did not know which was more suspenseful: the lack of any interesting action, which he had been anticipating since he had joined this band a few annaspans ago, or that Rhantor—and the beautiful Queen Darielle—were less than an afternoon's ride away. But he was not complaining. He had never dared to imagine he would have the chance to see Darielle.

Weslan had glimpsed the queen only once, but that vision had been so sublime that the barest chance of seeing her again had fuelled his impulsive decision to leave Stern. Of course, his father had provided the most powerful motivation of all.

Weslan's initial excitement at leaving Stern had been dampened by the monotony of pitaya orchard patrolling. However, Heyg, their fiery, red-haired captain—whom the soldiers liked and respected almost equally—had refused to leave for Rhantor even one hour sooner than scheduled.

It was summer's end, harvest-time, and the grim, tough, exhausted pitaya farmers could not fend off the raiding Berlotans all by themselves.

"Any devout Berlotan would give his life for a basket of pitayas," Heyg had reminded his men, as they rode along the line of the Taboran Mountains, toward the vivid green lushness of the pitaya groves.

Weslan thought of this now. "Why do they not just grow their own?" he wondered aloud, as he stared up at the sky. After all, the soldiers had been patrolling for two days, and seen nothing more threatening than leaf-worms. "Why not sell the Berlotans some pitaya pits to plant, and then all this stupid fighting will stop?"

If the fighting stopped, we could ride to Rhantor and see the queen! he thought but did not say. He had already been in enough brawls over her name throughout this summer, and Heyg's patience was growing thin.

Weslan's query was greeted with rude guffaws.

"Wash the country cobwebs from your eyes and ears, my lad." Nolvern grinned from beside him on the grass. "That is the whole point! If the bastards could grow 'em, don't you think they would? They cannot, though, for their soil is too sandy. So why don't they use dates for their ruddy rituals? Or figs, or pomegranates? Who knows, lad? It's a shame thinkin' on all the good men wasted all these years over pitayas..."

"Our men, that is. Who gives a rat's tooth about theirs?" Tulok broke in coarsely, showing his own blackened stumps.

Weslan looked at him with disdain. Tulok was a fisherman from Yant, a tiny seaside village close to the larger and more imposing fishing village of Liandon. Along with his mate Brieze, he had joined Heyg's company a few days earlier, claiming that they sought revenge against the Berlotans who had stolen their fishing boat. Nolvern had whispered knowingly to Weslan that it was more likely that they were fleeing from bad debts.

Whatever the reason, Weslan was glad of their presence, because he was no longer the "recruit" and sole target of taunts and laughter from the more seasoned men.

"Always remember, lads"—Captain Heyg was standing nearby, and he leaned his elbow against a tree trunk as he spoke—"pitayas mean more to them than to us, and that makes them dangerous enemies. We use pitayas for naught more than making wine…"

There was a chorus of protest.

"Of course," Heyg amended, grinning. "Pitaya wine is the most fabulous drink in the world—smooth as silk going down, and no head pain the day after. But for the poor buggers in Berlot, this fruit is serious business. They cannot bury their dead without anointing them with pitaya juice to preserve the flesh. It is their sacred custom."

"And a bleeding barbaric custom it is, too"—Nolvern shuddered—"pickling them like ruddy cabbages. What a waste of pitayas."

"Well, we must work hard to provide them with more cabbages to pickle!" Tulok said this with a swagger, provoking a barrage of insults.

The leisurely midday interlude stretched on into the heat of the summer afternoon, and Weslan thought he could guess why—Heyg had judged that day safer than most. Across the border, the Berlotans were celebrating the name day of their monarch, the Jinta. Their foes were probably too drunk to even contemplate a raid.

Weslan leaned back in the grass once more, folding his arms behind his head, forgetting his irritation with Tulok. The honey-warm sun softened his mood. He grinned tolerantly as the clownish fishermen climbed into the branches of two adjoining pitaya trees, holding between them a large fishing net, and shouting down boastfully to their fellows.

"Look! The perfect trap if we get raided. It is a brilliant plan —flawless!" Ignoring the jeers that greeted their every move, they spread the net, crouching into position and miming the move with which they would drop the net onto the heads of unsuspecting intruders.

Weslan squinted up with amusement. Tulok and Brieze were continually bragging, although they still could not carry their swords straight. They were fools without a doubt, but in that moment Weslan was suffused with a euphoria that encompassed all his fellow creatures. That night, they would ride into Rhantor, the royal city of the North; and, if he was lucky, he would see Queen Darielle.

At times like these, he was certain Rhan had destined him to be someone great, someone who mattered in the grand scheme of history. Otherwise, why would things have unfolded in such a way? Unconnected events, stitching themselves together into a pattern, like those patched quilts sewed by the village women.

Yes, every scene was a small quilt piece, meaningless when looked at by itself: a mercenary captain's shoeless horse; drunken snores from his father as he lay unconscious in a corner of the forge; Heyg's fierce and impatient face, alarming the first time he had seen it. Then, as Weslan had done some quick and competent work over the forge, the sudden flare of camaraderie.

All building up to that miraculous flash of light in a dark world, as Heyg had turned on his roan gelding and had said, "Why don't you come with us then, lad, if you have always wanted to be a soldier? You've a quick eye, you are strong, and no slouch." Winking his bright, hard eye beneath bushy red brows, he'd added, "We are due in Rhantor at summer's end. The queen dotes on fair lads like you, they say. But come or stay—do not stand gaping. We have leagues to go before dark."

Gasping at the audacity of what he was about to do, shaking away the knife-wrench of guilt at leaving his family, Weslan had stammered, "Yes. Yes, I will come. Give me just a moment to gather a few things."

Weslan had bolted to the hut, which stood empty, for the rest of them were at Aunt Beula's pony farm that day. He'd hastened to pack, telling himself that he would return some day soon, grand and rich, and take his family far away from Stern, and from Veld.

It had only been one summer, although it seemed much longer. But the dream was just as clear. Sometimes Weslan became frantic when he thought of his mother and sister held in Veld's clutches, like fragile nuggets of precious metal trapped in tongs. But how could he have hoped to help them except by leaving?

He listened to the drowsy hum of bees, letting visions of glory dance on his closed eyelids: Weslan, Captain of the Queen's Guard, splendidly cloaked, striding into the hut and withering his father with a look of careless contempt, before dispatching him with a scornful kick that sent him sprawling. Tekoah's girlish cry of astonishment, his mother's eyes wide with admiration and gratitude.

Shouts shattered the stillness of the afternoon from over the hill, and then an unmistakable, bloodcurdling battle cry. Weslan's eyes flew open. Berlotans. Rhan! A fight—he must fight, and he was barely awake. Fear hurtled him to his feet.

Heyg was barking orders interspersed with oaths, moving quicker than Weslan had ever seen him. But the raiders were already upon them, riding bareback, daggers between their gleaming teeth. Maces or swords in hand, they galloped faster than should be possible, considering they stayed astride by the grip of their knees alone.

It seemed painfully slow, the time it took for Heyg's company to galvanize into action. It was like moving against the current of a great river. Yet in reality it must have taken only a few seconds before they were all standing, then running toward their horses, tethered a few feet away.

But it was already too late, Weslan thought as he ran—heart pounding in his chest, throat and eyes burning in the late summer heat.

Too late. His ears buzzed with a sound like the hum of the bees, magnified a thousand times—but louder still were those chilling Berlotan war screams of triumph. Of death.

Nolvern streaked past him, yelling, "Three of them to every one of us—look to your bow!"

The words dispersed the buzzing, and Weslan leaped into his saddle, fingers trembling as he strung his bow, glancing up desperately every few seconds.

He could never take aim. He was shaking too hard. No one had said it would be like this. Why had not someone told him?

But all at once, to Weslan's astonishment, the Berlotans came to a confused halt between the two pitaya trees where Heyg's soldiers had sprawled a few moments earlier. Weslan spurred his horse into the confused, howling mass of man and horseflesh.

With a surge of hilarity, he saw that the first of the Berlotans was trapped in the fishermen's net, which dangled from the tree limb—exactly as predicted—by Tulok and Brieze from Yant.

Weslan heard Heyg's bellow of laughter, and his own mirth rose in a hysterical bubble from his throat.

But there was no more time for laughter. Once the other raiders realized what was happening, they wheeled to avoid the confusion and continued their charge.

It cannot be that I am to die, Weslan thought incredulously, *without dressing in that splendid cloak, without ever going home again, without saying goodbye to Mother.*

After that, everything became a blur. Some disciplined part of him, trained by Heyg over the past season, seemed to know what to do; and he followed that part, numbly. He bloodied his sword between the ribs of a soldier who hurled himself to attack —knife arcing—from his dying horse. Weslan stared at his dripping sword blade with disbelief, thinking it was the first time he had stained it with another man's lifeblood. He never would have dreamed that his first battle would be part savagery and part buffoonery, where laughter and fear fought to remain uppermost in his heart.

What amazed him the most was how well he fought through the fear and panic, doggedly slashing at any Berlotan face or horse that came within range. His father's derisive face reared up before him each time he struck, so that after a time it became a game—how many Velds he could kill. And it became apparent there were never enough.

Weslan suffered a deep slash on his sword arm. He barely remembered receiving it, for he was riveted watching Tulok fall from the pitaya tree, felled by a hurled mace to the temple, and landed like a fish in his own net.

Before he could react, a lanky Berlotan was standing astride the fallen man. He bent, and his dagger thrust into Tulok's heart shook Weslan as nothing else had thus far.

Weslan's first battle-wound came at that moment. A blow to his arm like liquid fire tore him from his reverie. Screaming with pain, he dropped his sword.

The Berlotan who stood before him grinned and raised his dagger again. Weslan jerked his leg forward in a reflexive attempt to kick the other man, but his brain was swimming with pain, and he only succeeded in tripping and falling to the grass.

Soft, sweet grass. He saw the raider standing over him, wearing the green and gold colours of Berlot. Green and gold. The colours of a summer day. He closed his eyes.

There was a shriek, and he opened them again. The Berlotan was sinking to the ground, and Captain Heyg stood above Weslan, his sword drawn, looking down at him with an expression that was almost affectionate.

I *must be delirious*, he thought. Heyg never looked this kindly upon anything but a roasted pigeon or a jug of ale.

"Rhan is with us today, lad," his commander proclaimed, jerking his head to the west. "The bastards are leaving!"

Weslan sat up, wincing, and glimpsed the raiders riding swiftly back over the hill, sweat and dirt-streaked, and not a single pitaya in their saddlebags. Although many of them would not leave, for their bodies were strewn all over the orchard, surrounded by the pitaya trees for which they had died, and within an arm's reach of the sacred burial fruit in which they would have been embalmed—if there was anyone to carry them home.

It was over. Weslan was still alive, not one of those grotesquely sprawled corpses lying so incongruously in the sunshine. He wanted to weep with the joy of it.

As if reading his thoughts, Heyg said wryly, "It looks as if you will get to see your precious queen after all. Let us get that arm bound up first though, before you bleed to death."

Fourteen of their number died in the space of a quarter of an hour. Nineteen more were injured, two seriously. Heyg told them this later, as they rode toward Rhantor, although how he could keep track of who fell and when, Weslan could not fathom. Heyg said, in a voice hoarse with emotion, that it was thanks to the surprise offering of the two clumsy fishermen from Yant—neither of whom survived the skirmish—that they had defeated the Berlotans.

. . .

T HEY RODE FOR HOURS, and then it was night, had been night forever. The colours of green and gold, the drowsy hum of bees. They had all been a dream, Weslan thought. And he began to hear his father's voice, laughing at him, just below the sound of hoofbeats.

"Almost there," Captain Heyg said to him, drawing his horse alongside and glancing at him.

Weslan smiled. He knew his captain was worried about him, although he would never admit it.

By the time they rode into the palace courtyard, Weslan was swaying and dizzy in his saddle, dirty and bloody, knowing but not caring that he did not at all resemble the nobleman of his indolent fantasy. He was barely aware of his surroundings, and he held himself upright in his saddle only by the strength of Heyg's voice.

So when Heyg called a halt, Weslan did so automatically, but then slumped forward, letting his eyelids remain closed. The sensation was wonderful. *We must be at a well. Get a drink soon. Cool, cool water. Pretty girl with a dipper, maybe.*

Weslan's arm was throbbing beneath the makeshift bandage Nolvern had helped him fashion from his under tunic. His mouth and face were caked with dust, and there was a painful crust of dried blood and salt when he moved his lips in thirst.

But at least he had not been left to die by the side of the road as had Brieze—eyes haunted, punctured rib poking through his chest.

Heyg had said gruffly, "There is nothing we can do for him and, if we stay, we are in danger. Who knows how many more Berlotans there are between here and Rhantor? I do not wish to find out—not in the dark."

But Heyg had decided that there was one more thing he could do for Brieze, after all. He had stayed behind a moment while the rest had ridden on, eyes turned grimly ahead.

Yes, Weslan was grateful to be alive, but he was thirsty, so thirsty. And although he had looked forward to his first view of the royal city, he had only disjointed impressions of passing through it at all: smoke rising from countless chimneys; narrow, twisting streets, like the mazes he used to run through in his nightmares as a child; many voices hammering together until they became one discordant clamour, and throngs of people everywhere, the air thick and steaming with the stifling press of bodies.

If he had not been mounted and caught up in a trance from the shock of the battle and loss of blood, Weslan might have been terrified. But he felt safe, remote, almost as if he was floating on a soft pillow of thistledown, like the ones the peddlers in Stern sold on market day.

Once, as a very small child, he had let go of his mother's hand and stolen over to one of those great cream-coloured mounds lying heaped carelessly behind the stall. He had sunk down upon the cushion, then curled up like a stray kitten and drifted off to sleep, amid the noise of his mother arguing with the egg-woman, and the clang of copper pans from the stall beside him.

He felt the same dreamy detachment now, in the courtyard where the company had come to a halt. For he had become aware that he was not at a well, and instead of the girl with the dipper, a stableboy was at his side, smiling, trying to take his reins. There was a pillar beside him, made of some sort of beautiful marble, purplish-grey, like that famed palace of the queen's. Weslan realized with a shock that he was in Rhantor, at the palace.

But he could not quite grasp it, somehow. He stared dazedly down at the stableboy, and then up again, at a sudden tumult of voices.

More Berlotans?

But no, they were women's voices, high and sweet, chattering like warblers. An alien sound, after so long in the company of men. Weslan tried to see them, but his vision blurred, and he saw only indistinct forms, wavering in the torchlight.

It grew silent. Weslan forced his eyes open by a great act of will, and beheld a woman walking into the courtyard, unaccompanied. All made way for her. As his vision cleared, he glimpsed the stables to his left, made of good, solid wood—cedar, probably. And the looming edifice beyond the courtyard was, of course, the palace.

The woman came closer. She was richly clad in a long robe of indigo linen, and she carried a huge bunch of long-stemmed yellow flowers— lilies, perhaps; Weslan had seen none like them. Swaying in his saddle despite his best efforts to remain still, Weslan realized he was looking at Darielle, the queen.

Yes, it is she! Weslan became giddy with joy. For there was the narrow gold circlet on her forehead, and, beneath, wide brown doe-eyes glowed in her delicate heart-shaped face.

Weslan had carried the memory of that face with him for five turnings. Darielle had been travelling through the North in preparation for her coronation. He had been fifteen, watching in awe from inside the forge, as her honour guard had halted to replace a lost horseshoe.

Darielle had sat on her pony, waiting patiently, but peering curiously into the gloom of the forge, like a child. She had not noticed his eyes gazing hungrily at her from within the dark room, burning like bits of coal.

She is a child, Weslan thought now, staring at the tiny face. Then she moved again, toward them, shoulders and hips swaying slightly as if to the rhythm of a cintar. And he thought, *No, she is a woman.* And found that he was shaking so badly he could not hold his reins. So he finally relinquished them to the hovering stable boy. And then it was worse, for his hands had nothing to do.

Heyg cleared his throat, frowning, and Weslan saw that all

the soldiers had dismounted and were bowing. He lifted his leg from his stirrup with an effort and slid off his mount. He put his palm to his forehead and genuflected with the others, and then leaned back against his gelding's lathered flank, so he would not fall.

And all the time his heart leaped gladly in his chest like a silvery trout in a sunlit lake, and his blood sang, "It is her…"

Queen Darielle moved among the men, smiling. Her ladies had joined her, and they smiled, too, somewhat indulgently. She began to hand out flowers. This was obviously a ritual.

Weslan saw Heyg move forward, hand on his heart, and protest at his queen debasing herself before such unworthiness. But the words were surely formalities, for Darielle pelted him playfully on the head with a flower and continued to mingle with the soldiers, speaking to them all, missing no one.

Heyg smiled courteously as he stood beside his men, but his jaw was tense. Weslan wondered vaguely at that. They had made it to safety, had they not?

Then he saw a tall, stately woman move from the crowd of attendant ladies, and approach Heyg, her eyebrows raised questioningly. They spoke together in low voices.

Heyg evidently knew her, for Weslan heard him say "Lady Saura" several times. He could not hear much else except a few snatched phrases, something about "men wounded" and "need rest before flowers."

Then Weslan stopped listening altogether, for the queen had come to stand directly in front of him.

A single flower was left in her hand, and this seemed fitting, somehow—the last one for him. But just as she held it out, his horse shied and stamped, letting out a nervous, high-pitched whinny. Startled, Darielle dropped the flower.

Weslan stared at it as it lay, trampled in the mud, feeling an unutterable sense of grief and loss. The queen shrugged, smiling at him helplessly, and then her smile faded.

She reached up and touched his arm, drawing her fingertips away bloody. He heard her as if from a great distance saying, "Poor fellow, standing here all this time, bleeding to death probably. Quick!" She clapped her hands. "Saura. Have him tended to at once—and anyone else who needs it. I have been selfish and stupid."

Two strong arms were instantly on either side of Weslan, holding him up. He heard Heyg murmuring respectfully to Queen Darielle, describing the battle and the gruelling ride that had followed. But Weslan cared nothing about Heyg or anyone else.

For he was watching, through the mist that rose up before his eyes, as the queen reached up, her wide sleeves falling away, revealing slender white arms. She plunged her hands into the cloudy dark masses of her hair. And then, smiling triumphantly, she brought forth a single yellow blossom.

Darielle held the blossom out to him, and her eyes seemed to send out whispers and songs and dreams. Weslan leaned forward, taking it from her hands, wanting to tell her he would die a thousand deaths for her. But he could say nothing. He knew the eyes of all in the courtyard were on them. Then, with a great surge of relief, for he could not bear such happiness a moment longer, he fainted dead away.

CHAPTER 6

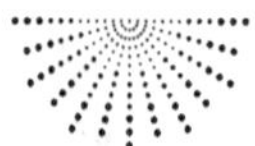

eslan took his loaf of bread and strode over to the table in the eating hall where Nolvern had saved his usual spot. He stumbled and almost fell, so hard was he trying to avoid meeting Heyg's eye.

His commander would have heard about the small skirmish at the Fallen Maiden the previous night. And Heyg did not tolerate skirmishes, outside of proper battles, that was.

Weslan was desperate to explain to Heyg that it had been the queen's honour at stake. Men, tavern scum, all of them, had been wagering about how many lovers Darielle had taken since her coronation in Rhantor five turnings ago. The numbers being bandied about were so large that Weslan had felt compelled to teach the rogues a thing or two about sums.

He had not even been drinking, he would tell Heyg. And he *hadn't*, either. Drinking was something he seldom did. Rhan forbid he should turn out like his father.

Heyg was more like Weslan's idea of a father, come to that. If only he did not breathe down a fellow's neck quite so much.

"How's the eye, lad?" Nolvern murmured with a sidelong wink. "Can you do this?" He winked again.

"For Rhan's sake, shut up," Weslan hissed. "Can you not see Heyg is looking straight at us?"

"How would you know? You haven't raised your face from your muddy boots since you came in looking like an umbray with its tail between its legs."

"I'll give you muddy boots!" Weslan kicked Nolvern under the table. He was about to do it again when Heyg rapped his tin mug with his wooden spoon, signalling an intention to speak.

Everyone became silent. "Morning, lads," Heyg said. Something about the way he said it made Weslan look up. His commander stood at the front, one foot up on a wooden stool, surveying the men as they sat eating their breakfast loaves.

He looked pale, as though he had slept little. His eyes were bloodshot, and his mouth was a grim line. He regarded his silent company for a moment before he spoke again.

"Summer is ending," he said, "and you all know that the queen has invited this company to stay on in Rhantor, naming us as the official Queen's Guard—owing to a few exploits we pulled off this past turning."

A few of the more seasoned men cleared their throats. Weslan fingered the bandage on his arm. It was almost ready to come off, but his wound still ached at night.

"I wager you all think you will toast your arses by the hearth in the hunting hall. And you deserve it, I won't begrudge you that. We've earned our place here—even you, young firebrand." Here, Heyg fixed his fierce gaze upon Weslan, who almost choked on his bread.

"But I am afraid there has been a bit of a complication, lads. No, it is not what you are thinking—not a Berlotan invasion. Not yet, anyway, though with King Darian on the throne in the South paving their way as nice as you please, it won't be long before he and the Jinta carve up the North between the two of them."

A volley of oaths followed this remark, and Heyg waited for

the voices to die down. *This is why Heyg is such a superb commander,* Weslan thought. *He knows when to let the men yell and when to shut them up.*

Once all was quiet, their Captain spoke. "We are expecting an important guest. The sorcerer Braith has announced his intention to pay his respects to the queen."

Weslan gripped his mug so hard his fingertips burned. *Braith! Coming here?* It was impossible. Braith had been part of the fabric of his childhood, along with the giant mountain cats that waited to snatch children who stayed out after dark. But unlike the cats, Braith had never seemed more than a hallucination in Veld's drink-maddened brain.

Sorcerers did not belong in the actual world, and certainly not anywhere near the queen. Looking around, Weslan saw the others had turned chalk-white to a man. For a long moment, no one said anything at all.

Then, "Why now? Why us?" Nolvern groaned for all of them.

Heyg took a moment to gulp tea from his mug, then grimaced. "Rhan's balls, that tastes like—you don't want to know, lads. Just eat your bread and avoid the tea this morning. The cook had too much to drink last night." There were a few weak chuckles.

Weslan's mind drifted to a dream he'd had the night before, about Tekoah and his mother. His mother had been calling to him from the doorway of the hut, over and over, but every time he'd tried to go to her, he'd ended up outside, sitting beside the grassberry patch, feeling alone. At the end of the dream, Tekoah had walked past without noticing him at all, carrying a shovel and weeping softly to herself.

When Weslan had awakened, he'd found that he was weeping as well. Luckily no one had seen him, or he would have never heard the end of it.

But Heyg had stopped clowning around and was speaking seriously now, so Weslan made himself listen.

"I feel compelled to tell you, in case there are any of you addled enough not to know it already, that there is not a bleeding thing we can do to guard the queen or anyone else from a sorcerer, any more than we could guard her from a hurricane or the plague. So do not suppose that I have called this meeting with some idiotic scheme in mind to get rid of him.

"He will come when he pleases, do what he pleases, and leave when he pleases, and I only hope that his motives are friendly. Treat him with the utmost respect should you encounter him and avoid such encounters when you can. That is all my advice about that."

Heyg sighed and ran a hand through his wiry mop of hair, making it stand up like that of a comic minstrel. He gazed into space, seemingly oblivious to his men, until Nolvern raised his hand.

"Begging your pardon, Commander," he said, "but do we know why Braith is coming here?"

"It is Lord Braith, to you," Heyg said testily. "Well, you sure as Rhan do not."

Everyone laughed, and the tension in the room seemed to ease a little.

"That is what we are trying to puzzle out," Heyg continued. "But it may not be an altogether bad thing. The leader of the Kalesh has given me some interesting information about the sorcerer Zant's doings in the South, and it seems from some overheard conversations that there is no love lost between Braith and Zant."

"Are they not all in league together?" Weslan burst out with the question before he could stop himself. He came to regret it just as fast when Heyg turned to him with a baleful glare.

"How is the eye, lad?" Heyg asked him conversationally.

Not again. Weslan sighed.

There were loud guffaws.

"Fine," he muttered.

"Try a slab of raw venison on it," Heyg said in a sympathetic voice, which hardened to steel in his next words. "And stay indoors after dusk for an annaspan. That is a command, soldier! During that time, you will think about what it means to be a member of the queen's own guard, the Kalesh. They are composed of noblemen, and you are more than fortunate to have the chance to rub shoulders with any of them. If Dirken hears of this, you are in disgrace at best, or expelled from the Kalesh—which is worse, but not *the* worst. The worst would include a public flogging. Understood?"

"Yes." Weslan looked down miserably.

He kept forgetting that they were part of the Kalesh now, because of the Queen's Guard posting. Heyg's company had been elevated to the ranks of the far loftier men led by the lord of Mirrand, or Dirken, or whatever he was called—it seemed to change from day to day. The leader of the Kalesh—that was the only title that mattered to any of the soldiers.

It was important, Captain Heyg kept emphasizing, to cultivate manners, gallantry, and courtesy, or else they would look like louts beside the noble-born soldiers.

The principal reason the Kalesh had recruited them was because Heyg knew the North like the palm of his hand, better than any man in the country besides Dirken. And with a full-scale Berlotan invasion becoming more likely every minute, it made sense to have men like Captain Heyg around.

Weslan reminded himself that it was an honour and an incredible stroke of fortune to be present in such a moment in history. The North had not had a proper army for years, and Dirken was trying to assemble one in readiness for the invasion. It was exciting—the stuff of Weslan's dreams.

Only nothing was happening yet. And the queen had not spared him a glance since the day that she had handed him the flower. Things had gotten to be boring, even after a day of spear-throwing and target practice, and the other endless gruelling drills which Captain Heyg and Dirken seemed to delight in thinking up for them.

Yes, things got to be boring, and so Weslan occasionally lost his temper. Must Heyg humiliate him in front of everyone?

"Getting back to your question," Heyg said in a neutral voice, "I am not a scholar of history, but as far as I know sorcerers are not always in league. Sometimes they scheme together, and sometimes they hate the sight of each other. Morogh and Zant see eye to eye, from what I hear, but Braith is another story. He is a third sorcerer, and they are suspicious of him, perhaps? Bit of an upstart, they think? Who knows? We are not privy to the inner workings of their dastardly minds.

"But if Zant is at the palace in Meed, plotting with King Darian to usurp his sister's throne—and that is no big secret, despite all the smooth talk he is spouting about helping to smooth over the relations between North and South Miraven—then would we not be better off with a sorcerer who is on our side?"

"Why would Braith want to be on our side?" someone asked from the back of the hall.

"To spite Zant!" Heyg roared. "Have you not been listening? Of course he does not care a prickly pitaya about us—no sorcerer does! But mayhap we can benefit from his power struggle with Zant. If we are careful not to antagonize him, perhaps we will gain more protection than we had before. If they can use us, why can we not use them?"

Without knowing it, Weslan had reduced the small loaf beneath his twisting fingers to a pile of crumbs on the table in front of him. *She might be in danger from Braith.* His queen, his love. And because Braith was a sorcerer, there would be nothing Weslan could do about it.

He could not save her in the heroic fashion he had envisioned when tossing on his cot during the hot summer nights; creating endless scenarios in which, transfixed by his courage and devotion, she would fall in love with him.

Heyg had taken a bite of bread and was chewing slowly, knowing he had everyone's attention. He swallowed, brushed the crumbs from his red beard and, leaning forward, he struck the wooden table with a sudden force that made the eating hall quake.

"This does not mean that there is nothing we can do to protect our queen"—he shouted—"and make a name for ourselves from here to the deep green Sea of Mira!

"Rhan's Fiery Breath, you should see your faces," he added, grinning. Stepping back a couple of paces, he folded his brawny arms and surveyed them with satisfaction.

Weslan wondered if he had left the forge of his father only to end up with another madman. Still, he waited with impatience to hear what Captain Heyg would say next, as he knew did every other man.

"I speak, my lads, of the hornet's nest in the South. How long do you think Darian will wait for his sister to give up her throne? The old king has been dead these five turnings, and the period of mourning is done. Darian cannot control his own country, but still he hates his sister because their father gave Darielle the most fertile part of the land to rule, when *he* had expected to have it all. He had counted on the pitayas and the ponies, in fact, to provide for his extravagant living. He was always a greedy man, for the South had its own riches.

"But now in the South there is the drought. And there is also Zant, who is acting as the brain for that scurvy runt who calls himself a king. Zant is behind this slander—this talk that Anniste witchery started the drought. It is all an excuse to take over the North, a holy war to purge the witches in Rhan's name. All they want are the pitayas and the ponies. So, King Darian has been turning a blind eye, and a deaf ear, to the Berlotan soldiers coming across the border and lining up in the Taboran passes."

"Traitor!" bellowed Liant, a hairy, black-eyed giant of a fellow who had been born in the South. "Old King Garan must be tossing in his grave."

"He will, now that you have woken him up." Heyg scowled, but his eyes twinkled. He was fond of Liant. "Of course Darian is a traitor and is intent on selling Miraven to Berlot. He cares nothing for his own people, but feasts on candied pitayas while starving peasants scrape the bark off trees to feed their children. But that is not the worst of what he is."

Heyg's voice had dropped to a hoarse whisper, and the room was so quiet that Weslan could hear himself blink.

"There has never been less family feeling between brother and sister that I have ever seen. He cares nothing for her. *Nothing.*"

For a startled, guilty moment Weslan thought Heyg was speaking of him, he and Tekoah. And then he realized it must have been his dream, making him feel guilty.

He drew circles in his breadcrumbs; full moons, then crescent moons. Darielle's brother cared nothing for her. But who in Rhan's name could see her and not care for her? Who would not want to lay his very life down for her?

Heyg continued, "I have it on good authority that King Darian is sending an assassin after his sister, and soon. We must not let this happen, not only because we worship our queen and have sworn to protect her, but because, once she has fallen, Darian has the excuse he needs to seize the throne. If he does, we are at the mercy of Berlot.

"It is your duty to expect and forestall even the slightest chance that someone can gain access to the queen, let alone harm her. When you leave here this morning, know this and remember it: the queen's life, and thus the very fate of the North, depends on your vigilance."

Heyg's company sat, their half-chewed bread sodden in their open mouths, eyes riveted on their commander. He nodded, then began giving quiet, succinct orders.

Although Weslan tried to concentrate on Heyg's instructions, he barely heard the next words. He had forgotten even Braith. All he could think of was Darielle, felled by an assassin's arrow, sinking like a doe in the woods. He wanted to rush out of the room, that very instant. Go to her, never leave her side; take the arrow for her, shield her with his body. Feel her trembling beneath him, soothe her fears.

He shook his head, fighting to dispel the distracting visions. *Listen,* he told himself. *Listen to Heyg.*

"Double the watch in the south tower," Heyg was saying. "Any rider is to be reported, stopped, searched and questioned— regardless of rank. Except Lord Braith, of course," he amended hastily. "He is not to be interfered with, except to be bowed at, from whatever direction he comes—be it north, south, east or west, or down from the sky on a bleeding eagle."

"Sir..." Nolvern interrupted, sounding more uncertain than Weslan had ever heard him. "How shall we tell if it is Braith? I mean, how can you tell it's a sorcerer? I have never seen one."

Heyg made a curt gesture with his hand. "You will know him. Without question."

"You have seen him, then?"

"Not him. Morogh. When I was a young man, and he was still far older than Braith or Zant."

He paused, looking down at his large, calloused hands. "But although he was old, and I young and strong, I was afraid." He looked back up, scanning their faces, gauging their reaction to his words.

Weslan had never seen Heyg act frightened. He could not even imagine it. Most of the men were looking embarrassed; and some were downright shocked, as if their Captain had suddenly dropped his breeches or started weeping.

Heyg smiled, but his eyes were hollow. "I am not speaking of bodily fear—that survival instinct in all of us that tells us when our lives are in danger and galvanizes us into action. No, that kind of fear is our comrade. Soldiers go to sleep with it every night and wake up with it every morning. When I say I was afraid, I am describing something else. All he had to do was look at me, and it made me feel like a small animal caught in a trap. He could do with me as he liked, when he liked."

Heyg gulped down the rest of his tea, making a sour face. "Luckily, he chose to ignore me. I was too insignificant for his notice, and that is how I would have preferred to stay, had Rhan seen fit to grant me that wish."

Weslan listened, shifting in his seat. Heyg's words brought back unwelcome memories of Veld's screams in the darkened hut.

"No, you will have no doubt when you are in the presence of a sorcerer," Heyg repeated, shooting Nolvern a sharp look from under his grizzled red brows. "But back to business. As I said, the Queen's Guard for Darielle is doubled, starting today. I want Nolvern, Malak, Baerd and Weslan. Report to me directly after this meal. The rest of you have your patrolling orders."

Everyone began talking at once, but Weslan's brain was reeling. *My chance,* he thought. *Finally, my chance to be near her.*

All his life had been a waiting for this, he could see that now. Nothing more, nothing less.

He had been like an insect that lies in one of those soft, grey sacs, never seeing sunlight, but one day breaking from the sac in a burst of glory; iridescent wings glinting with every colour of the rainbow. Soaring with noble pride over its fellow creatures— the other poor, blind, crawling things below. Going forth to meet his destiny.

Rhan's warm light poured over Weslan, imbuing him with an ecstasy such as he had never known before. All the misery, the fear, the aching in his bones from beatings; the burns from the forge, the smell of his father's vomit and his mother's hastily muffled sobs in the night—they were but a test. He had passed that trial. Now here was another one, and if he was strong enough, he would reap the sweet reward.

But beneath the swift triumphant surge of his blood, there came a slow, deep drumbeat, intoning, *Let me not fail.*

CHAPTER 7

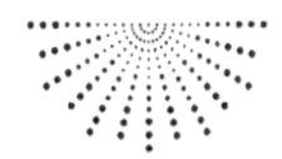

*A*nd so it was that when the sorcerer Braith came two days later to the court of Queen Darielle at Rhantor in the North of Miraven, that Weslan was not even thinking about him.

Nor was he on patrol outside, riding the grounds, marching along the palace ramparts, or tensely scanning the horizon from one of its white towers.

He was in the stiflingly small antechamber outside the queen's suite of rooms, playing at dice; chafed and restless and bored.

Pride warred with resentment. Weslan had been euphoric when Heyg had appointed him to this sacred task, the assignment of which carried the added advantage of placing him close to the object of his desire.

However, now it was nearly midnight, the end of a long day of trailing after the queen and her ladies from room to room in the palace. Weslan's body fairly screamed for exercise. He was not accustomed to being inside so much and was sorely missing the freshness of the fall breeze on his face. Worse, his nerves had become increasingly frayed from the suspense of being in such proximity to his beloved; and his pride was suffering torments, for she had not taken any special notice of him at all.

Her ladies, however, had lost no time in engaging the guards in pleasant bantering flirtations, and this eased the monotony somewhat. Until they were all called away to assist in the queen's bedtime rituals.

Weslan tried to keep in mind his vision of transforming into a splendid other-worldly creature, but it was difficult. He kept yawning, and the air in the anteroom was stale with the breath and the sweat of four restless young men.

Do we really need four? Weslan wondered grumpily.

Heyg was perhaps overreacting somewhat. The sorcerer Braith had not even arrived at court yet, in spite of all the dire warnings, and there was certainly no evidence of deadly assassins. An excess of available women, perhaps, but was that a situation that heralded a call to arms?

"Your roll," Nolvern prompted him testily, giving him a shove.

Weslan shoved him back, harder than he'd intended, and then curbed himself.

His captain had put him on notice the previous day: "Any more fighting and you're out, and not only out of the palace. Out of the Kalesh. And then you can fight for your *dinner.*"

Weslan listlessly picked up the dice, shaking them in Nolvern's face to provoke him. At that moment, the door to the queen's chamber opened and Lady Saura, Councillar to the Queen, appeared, closing the door carefully behind her. Weslan looked up at her, a chill washing over him as her grey eyes swept the room.

"Where is the messenger?" she asked imperiously.

A young boy peeked timidly from around the corner, and she strode past the guards to meet him, ignoring the stammered apologies and scattering of dice.

Word had it that Lady Saura exerted a great deal of influence over the young queen. There was an air of quiet authority about her, although she kept herself very inconspicuous. Perhaps it was her very unobtrusiveness that was so perturbing. She walked like an Anniste.

Weslan winced guiltily at the thought. He wondered how Tekoah was faring now, and his mother.

Thinking of Neela, his surge of helpless love for her mingled, as always, with a kind of scorn. Once he had seen his father for the man he was—or was not—it had been his mother for whom he had lost respect. He did not know why; it made no sense, and it certainly was not fair to his mother. At least he was spared confusion in his feelings for Darielle. There was only heartache, pure and simple.

Lady Saura came back into the room abruptly. There were beads of sweat on her forehead below her wimple. Heyg came in immediately behind her. Weslan and the others were back on their feet in an instant. Saura did not even glance at the soldiers. She slipped into the queen's chamber and shut the door behind her.

Heyg remained behind, looking at them and smiling tightly. "He is here, lads," he said.

THE QUEEN of North Miraven stood in front of the roaring fire in the hunting hall to receive her distinguished guest, the sorcerer Braith. There was a startling lack of formality in this greatly anticipated meeting, but evidently it was at Braith's request.

Weslan had overheard Heyg telling Lady Saura that Braith desired a very brief reception, as he was travel-stained after his journey, and unwilling to besmirch the finer rooms at this hour.

Saura—who, it was rumoured, had established a more than passing friendliness with the sorcerer Zant—had enquired drily why a sorcerer would endure travelling in a manner that could impose such discomfiture to his person—to strike a pose of rustic charm, perhaps? It was apparently the latest fashion for courtiers to look like country bumpkins, was it not? One only had to look at all the Northern nobles at court — joining the Kalesh and dashing around in ridiculous homespun tunics.

Still, it seemed rather ridiculous, Saura had observed, because everyone knew that Braith could transport himself from one place to the next the instant he wished.

Heyg had refused to take the bait, although Weslan could see his captain's eyes narrow with anger at her remarks about the Kalesh. Darielle had asked in a sweet voice, laced with iron, that everyone keep their minds fixed in the exact moment in which they found themselves.

At the queen's direction, she was accompanied to meet Braith by Heyg and the Lady Saura. Weslan and Nolvern were stationed at the entrance, their only function being to open the doors of the hunting hall and stand, eyes forward, bodies rigid, as they tried to quell their fear.

But taking precedence over any of them was the unexpected appearance of Dirken, Rhantor's Court Minstrel and unofficial Advisor to the Queen, who had by strange happenstance returned the very evening before. He walked beside Darielle now as they entered the hall, his hand lightly cupping her elbow.

Not so strange, Weslan thought, seething—if you were privy to the fact that Dirken's role at court went far beyond that of a musician and entertainer. For he was the leader of the Kalesh.

Weslan did not like Dirken, for several reasons: because he was handsome in an elegant, lithe way that Weslan knew he himself was not. And it was obvious that Dirken commanded the respect of nobles and soldiers alike—even Heyg—through his vast and intricate knowledge of not only his own countryside, but of the South and Berlot. He also seemed to know a lot about military strategy and just about everything else on Rhan's green world.

But, most of all, Weslan disliked Dirken because the man could make Darielle laugh as no one else could, peal after kittenish peal. All the while she clapped her small hands together in delight at his wicked imitations of her brother, a Berlotan diplomat, or a drunken shepherd.

Yes, for Darielle's laughter alone, Weslan would gladly strangle Dirken. But, in that moment, he was glad of the man's presence. He could not imagine himself acting so unruffled.

The sorcerer entered the room, walking with a silent, measured tread past Weslan and Nolvern as they stood on either side of the door. He slapped his crimson-gloved hands together as he approached the hearth.

Weslan started at the noise. Beside him, he could smell Nolvern's acrid sweat—or was it his own? Fear.

They stood back in the shadows as Braith went forward to greet the queen, the two tall and stalwart soldiers obeying their strict orders to make themselves seem invisible. Their only function seemed to be to prevent anyone else from entering, should some fool have failed to hear the news of Braith's arrival by now in this buzzing beehive.

Weslan stared straight ahead of him, but could not resist the occasional glance to his left, where the sorcerer Braith had just executed a perfect obeisance to his queen. Darielle gestured for him to sit and then perched herself on the edge of a divan opposite.

The queen wore a robe of tawny orange and gold, its folds coming together low in her bosom and held in place by a single gleaming Berlotan emerald. The cloth clung to her hips and thighs like butter and then spread out, foaming with lace, past her feet, which were perched on a small, tapestried stool placed in front of her by Lady Saura.

Saura's dress was, as usual, in direct contrast to her

mistress. A modest robe of grey linen fell in a straight line from her neck to her feet, her hands hidden in its wide sleeves. Her wimple, an affectation of hers alone, covered every wisp of hair in its starched white folds. The palace joke—behind her back, of course—was that she had no hair.

But Weslan was grateful for her presence, as well. And Heyg's. Along with Dirken, they radiated a calm which seemed to hold the queen's nerves in check.

Darielle had never looked so beautiful, Weslan thought, or so frightened. He did not despise her for her fear—how could he? Not only was he in love with her, but he was frightened himself.

Beside him, Nolvern stood with sweat visible on his forehead, and Weslan fought to keep his own fingers steady on his spear. Dirken, Saura and Heyg remained stoic and expressionless.

Someday I must learn to do that, Weslan thought.

The sorcerer Braith seemed unaware of the powerful sensations he was provoking by his mere presence. His grave and courtly manners were beyond reproach, although he displayed none of the affectations common to the nobles at court. He seemed more like a country lord, keen-eyed, alert; his lean, intelligent face friendly, but not revealing his thoughts.

They sat sipping wine, conversing politely. There was nothing, really, of which to be frightened.

Yet here I am, Weslan thought, *a grown man, a soldier, sweating like a man with the plague. Why?*

It is his eyes, Weslan decided. They did not resemble the eyes of anyone he had ever seen. They were unnaturally brilliant, glittering in the firelight like hard green stones.

Weslan heard indistinct murmurs from the queen, Braith, and Dirken, with Saura occasionally contributing a crisp monosyllable to the conversation. Now and then the murmur would rise in volume, and Weslan would hear a snatch of what they were saying.

Dirken mentioned Zant's name in a bantering tone. There was a brief, uncomfortable silence, during which the queen examined her embroidered slippers with an intensity that was quite remarkable. Then Braith made a smooth rejoinder, an obvious compliment to the queen, for she smiled and turned a lovely shade of pink.

Then it was over, almost as quickly as it had begun. The queen stood, signalling the end of the interview. Braith stooped over her hand, his black cape obscuring her from view for a moment. Darielle took her leave, Dirken walking beside her. Weslan stared straight in front of him as Saura and Heyg followed. His captain gave him an approving nod as he went by, and he felt the liquid in his knees solidify a little.

Weslan took a deep breath. Braith was coming toward the doorway now, walking with that same noiseless tread. He would go through the door any moment, and they would relax and a go to their beds. Raising his spear in the ceremonious gesture he had not quite mastered, he glanced up at Braith's face, unable to resist.

And saw that Braith's eyes were on him. Staring intently. He dropped his own eyes quickly, and Braith went through the door.

"We are off duty now, remember?" Nolvern whispered to him a moment later. "I think we deserve a jug of ale, don't you?"

Weslan nodded, for once in his life unable to speak.

"It was his *voice*," Nolvern said much later, to an admiring crowd at the Fallen Maiden.

Weslan sat in the background nursing his ale, willing to let Nolvern blow the golden trumpet. Even if it meant Nolvern leaving with the prettiest serving maid later. He had lost his appetite for such things, anyway.

Nolvern had a point about the voice. It was deep, but with a slight rasp, just strange enough to set the hairs on the back of the neck to quivering. But it was the eyes that had struck Weslan. Like something predatory, appraising in a way that was more and less than human. Or maybe it had just been a trick of the firelight.

Eyes or voice, it did not matter. What mattered was that he did not wish to meet Braith face to face ever again.

What mattered was that he drank, long and deep.

CHAPTER 8

*P*erhaps he should not have had that last drink, though.

"Perhaps?" roared Heyg, his face suffused with such bright colour it was difficult to tell where his forehead ended and his hair began.

Weslan winced as the roar echoed in his ears and sent poisoned arrow points of pain winging through his skull. This would not be a day steeped in glory.

"Perhaps, hmm? Soft words for a fighting man." His captain's voice was scorching.

Weslan was silent, looking down at his puffy, discoloured knuckles. After a moment there was a loud sigh, and Heyg's hand landed, large and heavy, on his shoulder.

"How many times have we had this conversation, lad? Too many, that's how many. I have told you and told you—save your fighting for the enemy. You would make a first-rate soldier if you would only get that through your golden locks, boy."

"I know, Captain Heyg," Weslan mumbled. "I apologize."

They were alone in the meal room. Breakfast was over, and they had been given their orders of the day.

Weslan had hoped with an optimism born of desperation that his brawl with Nolvern had not reached Heyg's ears. Nolvern himself had staunchly insisted that his blackened eye, missing tooth and grazed cheek had resulted from a drunken fall down the stairs leading to the barracks. *Good man, Nolvern.*

On the other hand, none of this would have happened had Nolvern not insinuated that vile thing about the queen and Braith. One moment they had been singing raucously together, arms about each other's shoulders, and the next—well, that was ancient history now.

Not ancient enough for Heyg, obviously. Now his voice had become gentle and fatherly, which was truly alarming.

"I *know* you know, lad," he muttered. "We all have a good idea of what we should be doing. It's just having the discipline to do it that makes a Kalesh. Now, listen. I could send you off this minute and, by Rhan's balls, I should. But I am going to give you another chance."

"Thank you," Weslan said fervently. *Praise Rhan!* he thought. *Now I can still be near the queen and guard her from harm.*

Heyg's next words dashed his hopes. "But not in the palace. Not now, when the sorcerer is here, and everything is so touch-and-go. I ordered you to conduct yourself in a civilized manner" —he continued, relentless, while Weslan gazed at him—"but you engaged in a cockfight with Nolvern instead. I am striving to establish our credibility among all these lacy-sleeved noblemen who think they are military wonders. Your farm-boy tussles are over, do you hear?"

He stood up, brushing crumbs from his beard and tunic, and reached for his mail vest. "You will patrol the grounds from this morning on. There are six others, as you know. I want you to keep particular watch for lone men, on foot, who may try to slip through the woods into the gardens. The mazes would be an excellent place for an assassin to hide until nightfall."

I have failed, Weslan thought. *Not even an annaspan in the palace, and already I have disgraced myself. How Father would laugh.* He listened, face burning, as Heyg continued to speak.

"Expect the unexpected," Heyg finished, as he turned to go. "For these are unexpected times."

As Weslan stood up, untouched bread and tea still on the table in front of him, Heyg's hand was on his shoulder again.

"Forget her, lad," he said quietly, understanding and pity in his gruff voice. "She is not for the likes of you."

AT LEAST HE had been alone for the tongue-lashing, Weslan reflected, as he walked out into the bright autumn sunshine. No one else had witnessed his humiliation, and so he could gather the tattered remnants of his pride like a ragged cloak—and ride.

Weslan saddled up his roan mare. As he did so, he whistled a little tune. His spirits were rising a little. He reflected that he had found the palace somewhat confining.

Gripping the flanks of a horse beneath his knees, smelling the damp air, full of the sharp spicy fragrance of evergreens, mingled with the musty scent of decaying leaves and blossoms, all rising beneath the tread of his horse's hooves—this was freedom!

It was colder this morning than it had been yester morn, and he could see his breath. Soon, it would snow in Stern. Weslan glanced northeast at the Taboran Woods and the foothills beyond. He yearned to be in those woods, wending his way through the narrow trails, lost in the dark, friendly gloom that had never frightened him, even as a child.

Weslan heard hoofbeats behind him. It was most likely Nolvern, coming to apologize for the second time that morning. He pretended not to hear.

Nolvern had materialized at dawn outside the barracks, as Weslan had gone to sluice his throbbing head under the well pump. He'd seized Weslan's arm, glancing around to make sure Heyg was out of sight.

"No hard feelings, eh?" he had muttered, lisping a little through his broken tooth. When Weslan had not replied, he had added, "I was only teasing you last night! What has happened to your sense of humour, man?"

Weslan's heart had softened a little, but before he could say anything, Nolvern had shaken his head in exasperation. "You would think she was your personal property, the way you act. Well, she would probably sleep with every lord between here and Meed before she would take a tumble with a lowly soldier like you. And if the rumours are true, she probably has!"

His face must have been something to behold, for Nolvern had retreated quickly after that.

If he comes here thinking to cajole me into a truce, then he is sadly mistaken, Weslan thought. But he heard no voice, only the steady trot of the horse, coming closer.

Remembering in a flash that he was posted on the lookout for intruders, Weslan reined in and wheeled around, sword in hand.

The sorcerer Braith sat on his black stallion, smiling. "I could have cut you down three times before you turned, soldier," he remarked.

Heat flushed Weslan, lashing upward from his chest to his scalp. He stared at Braith, unable to move or speak.

"Forgive me if I startled you," Braith continued. "But I was told that the gardens of Queen Darielle are unrivalled throughout the country—north or south. I wanted to see for myself, but I seem to have taken a wrong turning."

He lifted a hand in a self-deprecating wave. Weslan stared at the sorcerer's gloves. He remembered seeing them the previous night and wondering why Braith had not removed them in the presence of the queen.

Weslan pointed toward the gardens, where Nolvern was

patrolling. *Rhan, is Nolvern in for a surprise!* he thought, somewhat spitefully.

Braith nodded his thanks, but seemed in no hurry to leave. "Is it true?" he asked. "That every gardener of note in the country has flocked here like doves to a rooftop, hearing of the queen's passion for flowers?"

"Yes," Weslan replied, marvelling at the inanity of his first words to a sorcerer. "But the queen herself also has great skill. She tends to her hothouse blooms all throughout the winter, and they say she talks to them as if they were children. And she designed the gardens herself, you know. Except the mazes, of course. A Labyrinth Master helped her there."

Weslan realized they were now riding beside each other. Braith nodded.

"Ah, I shall make a point of exploring the mazes later, on foot. Perhaps I should unwind some thread behind me as a precaution," he joked. "But I have decided that today I do not care to sniff at flowers, with the palace courtiers twitching in fright and pointing at me wherever I go. I long for a brisk ride through the woods."

He pointed toward the foothills, at the dark line of forest which Weslan had been gazing at only a moment earlier. "Do you ever ride there?" he asked.

And so Weslan escorted Braith to the northern gate, which lay at the edge of the foothills. His thoughts were whirling, but he had enough presence of mind to signal Nolvern and Kramer as they rode past the gardens. He was in an awkward position, because Heyg had warned them not to antagonize the sorcerer.

They must have alerted his captain with great haste, for he came riding up to meet them just as they picked their way across the stream at the gates. Weslan strove to keep his relief from showing on his face.

Captain Heyg stood in his stirrups and bowed. "I hope you

are enjoying the morning, Lord Braith," he said in a formal voice.

"It is most excellent," Braith replied, stroking his mount's mane. "And I hope you do not object to my borrowing your accomplished man here for my riding companion. He knows the trails here, and I do not."

Heyg looked at Weslan, and for a moment his forehead furrowed. He refrained from pointing out the obvious, that a sorcerer need not worry about losing his way. Instead, he smiled cordially. "Of course not," he responded. "Weslan does indeed know the trails—as well as any wild pony, I would wager. Report to me upon your return, Weslan."

Heyg signalled the porter. The wide wooden gate swung open, and they rode through.

THEY HAD BEEN RIDING for only an hour when they came upon the foal.

They would never have seen her at all, had she not summoned up the strength to whinny forlornly from the thicket as they rode past. Weslan turned at the sound, and he and Braith exchanged a quizzical glance. Then, in unison, without speaking, they stopped their horses and dismounted.

Weslan drew his sword automatically, although the sound had been far from threatening. When he parted the bushes, he gasped.

A wild pony mare lay on her side, her throat ripped out. Marks that could only have been made by a mountain cat scored her flank. They must have frightened it away with their approach, for other than her neck, it had barely touched her. Beside her, the foal—looking to be only a few hours old—whinnied again, looking up at them with honey-sweet eyes.

They returned to the palace, riding slowly, for Braith carried the foal wrapped in his cloak, and she was an awkward bundle. By tacit agreement, they went straight to the stables and stayed with her the rest of the day, calling for sheep's milk, and warm water, and blankets; but after that, brusquely sending away any stable staff who ventured nearby.

Toward sundown, Captain Heyg came and stood in the stable doorway, accompanied by Lady Saura. He cleared his throat.

"Should you require it, Lord Braith, the Stable Master offers his humble services."

Braith looked up briefly from the mound of hay where he sat, the foal's head on his lap. "Are you saying you are short of men, Captain?"

"Not at all," Heyg answered hastily. "Weslan has my leave to assist you for as long as you wish."

"Good," Braith said. Glancing at Weslan, he smiled, his teeth flashing briefly in his sun-bronzed face. "We are in this together."

Weslan saw the eyes of Heyg and Saura on him—baffled, wary.

They are wondering what Braith sees in me, he thought. His blood surged with pride. *Perhaps he sees something they do not.*

Lady Saura's eyes shifted down to Braith's gloved hands as they stroked the foal's throat, willing her to keep down the sheep's milk they had coaxed into her.

"I had not thought a sorcerer would trouble himself—" she began, then fell silent.

Weslan felt a chill all at once, deep in his back. Braith was looking at Saura, his smile gone, his green-gold eyes as piercing as the sudden gleam of a dagger.

"Do not presume to compare sorcerers, Lady," Braith said softly. "It would be a grave mistake."

"Indeed, I am sure it would. My apologies, Lord Braith," she answered, her voice subdued and taut. She turned and left the stable.

Weslan was very glad in that moment not to be in her place.

Heyg stayed a moment longer, surveying the scene, stroking his red beard thoughtfully. "Since you have scared off Lady Saura, my lord Braith—and, believe me, she needed a good scare —I suppose I must act in her stead, and ask you prettily if you plan on coming to the extravagant banquet they have laid out for you."

Braith smiled again, and Weslan was astonished that he could look so terrifying one moment, and then like a mischievous schoolboy the next.

"I am afraid I must forego the pleasure—until we ensure this little creature survives," he said. "However, a basket of bread and cheese and ale would not be unwelcome, as long as Lady Saura does not bring it."

Heyg gave a great guffaw. "I will see to it myself," he said.

Toward sunrise, the foal fell asleep, but Weslan and Braith did not. They had been talking all night, and Weslan was not in the least tired; rather, he felt revived, as if he had just swum in a river or had a good long gallop across a plain.

In only a few brief hours, they had become friends. This was destiny. And unlike his soldier comrades, with whom he fought and chased tavern girls, Braith wanted him to talk. He listened to everything Weslan said and prompted him for more.

Weslan found the words tumbled from him in a torrent. Thoughts he had not known were inside, memories that had evaporated long ago, more colourful and vivid than when he had first experienced them, or so it seemed, from the glow of interest in Braith's eyes.

During that long night of the foal, as Weslan would come to think of it later, he talked much about the village of his birth, and Braith nodded. He, too, had lived in Stern.

"Master Chalvern," Braith mused now, sounding affectionate. "What a character! He taught me everything I could wish to know about herbs, and much I did not wish to know. He was like a father to me. My father was a peddler—my mother died before I could barely stand. One day, I became too much of a burden to him, I suppose, so he left me with my aunt, as if I was a piece of goods he had been lugging around for too long, unable to sell."

Braith laughed as he said the words, and there was no trace of self-pity in his voice. But Weslan felt a lump rise in his throat, and a sort of awe, as if Braith had just entrusted him with something precious—his confidence. And he would appear ungracious unless he gave something in return.

And so he described Veld to Braith, and spoke of the hopelessness of his life at the forge; how everyone but he seemed resigned to their fate.

As the night wore on, and the erratic heartbeat of the pony steadied, it became very important to Weslan that Braith understood why he had left Stern, and abandoned his helpless family to his father's cruelty.

Mother and Tekoah deserved so much more than their present lives. And the twins. Weslan felt such pity for them now. Yet he had shoved and cuffed his brothers sometimes, when deep inside himself, he had been angry at Father. How he regretted it now! He confided this also, along with his pledge of how different it would be when he returned.

"There is always a chance to make things right," the sorcerer said in an encouraging tone. "What about your mother?" Braith leaned back, chewing on the end of a piece of straw. "Why did she marry your father?"

Weslan shook his head moodily. "Who knows?"

"What—does she condone the cruelty?"

"No, of course not. It is just that she seems so helpless to stop him. And yet she was so strong until she renounced her Guardianship in the Anniste."

Braith's eyes flared with a sudden light. "She is Anniste?"

Weslan was uncomfortable for the first time. It was not

prudent to talk about the Anniste, now that they were being blamed for the drought in the South. The priests were becoming more vehement on the subject every day. Claiming that Rhan had sent them a divine message about cleansing the land, or something of the sort. Weslan seldom paid attention to such things.

"Mother was Anniste," he said hastily. "But she left the clan a turning ago, for my father's sake. Only she has not been the same since. It was as if she took herself away and left only a shadow. I remember how she was, confident and kind. And, afterward, she just seemed to wait for her life to end, not caring what happened to herself or anyone else. She gave up, and I despise her for it!"

The last words spilled out of his mouth inadvertently, and Weslan was at once gripped with remorse. What a child he had sounded! He glanced at Braith, but could see no trace of disdain on his face.

"Yes, I know just what you mean," he said. "Those who stand by and do nothing, are *they* not guilty as well?"

"Please do not think I have a contempt for my mother, though," Weslan protested. "I did not mean it. I revere her."

"I can tell by the way you speak you love and respect your mother," Braith said. "But you are a man of action, after all."

Braith understood him so well, Weslan thought. And he had known him for so short a time. It was wondrous.

"My mother was once the most beautiful woman in the village," he told Braith, "or so they say."

Braith leaned forward, his face alert. "And that is all of your family, then? Your parents, two unfortunate brothers, and you? Or did you mention a sister, just a moment ago?"

"Yes, there is my sister, Tekoah." Weslan sighed, guilt flooding him again. "And I worry about her most of all."

"Ah."

Outside, the bells of the palace temple tolled.

"Rhan's name!" Weslan laughed. "We have been talking all night. Or, rather, I have. You must be sick of the sound of my voice. Shall we go find some breakfast?"

"Presently," Braith answered. "As for your voice, I am not at all tired of it. You remind me a little of the better minstrels and storytellers I saw as a child. I think you could hold anyone's interest."

Tell that to the queen, Weslan thought, *and perhaps she will find me as fascinating as she finds Dirken.* But he was flattered. The village girls in Stern had enjoyed listening to him as well.

"You were speaking of your sister," Braith reminded him, leaning back against a bale of hay and bunching his cloak beneath his head.

"She is so innocent," Weslan said, "so easily taken advantage of. Father treats her abominably, but she thinks he behaves that way for a reason. She believes—"

He broke off, staring at Braith in horror. He had never meant to broach this topic.

"Go on," Braith said quietly, his eyes very still in his face.

"It is nothing."

"Tell me. Do not be afraid."

Weslan took a shaky breath, then plunged on. "She thinks you cursed Father and made him the way he is. That is what Father tells everyone, but she is the only one stupid enough to believe him."

"You do not believe him?"

"This is only his newest lie," Weslan said scornfully. "None of which I have paid attention to since I was old enough to know what the smell of corn whiskey on his breath meant."

"You are someone who has always known how to think for himself," Braith observed, and Weslan thought he heard admiration in the sorcerer's voice. "Pray do not concern yourself about offending me. Speak whatever is on your mind. I think you will find that I am a good listener, and I have been told occasionally that I rendered some very sound advice."

"Thank you," Weslan said, uncertainly.

"Go on," Braith prompted him. "You worry about your sister, and with good reason, it seems."

"Yes. I want to bring her to Rhantor. She could work in the palace, perhaps. Together we could even convince Mother and the twins to come. They could get a little cottage on the outskirts of the city. But it is taking so long to get settled. And I have saved very little money. I wrote Tekoah a letter as soon as I knew they had stationed me in Rhantor for the winter. I am waiting to hear her reply. I wish I could watch her from here."

Weslan fell silent, staring down at the sleeping foal, watching her chest rise and fall. Exhaustion flooded him. Or perhaps it was just the weight of the responsibility he had shouldered. How could he take care of his family, when he himself was barely a step away from disgrace and poverty? Why had he ever thought he was capable of such an enormous burden?

"Perhaps you can," Braith said quietly.

"What?" Weslan looked up, startled from his reverie.

"Perhaps you can watch her from here." Braith smiled as Weslan furrowed his brow in bafflement. "Through me. I will watch her for you and alert you if she is in distress."

Weslan stared at Braith, uncomprehending. And then he remembered he was in the company of a sorcerer, and his mouth went dry with gratitude and fear.

THE PONY SLEPT QUIETLY, her head in Braith's lap. Sunlight streamed through the stable window and enveloped her in a soft glow. And in that moment, staring with embarrassed intensity at the pure, silky lashes of the foal, Weslan confessed to Braith his lost, hopeless love for Darielle.

Braith listened silently, although out of the corner of his eye Weslan could see the gloved fingers pressing together softly and rhythmically, like the beating of a pulse.

When he finally stopped speaking, his voice was hoarse from fatigue. He was also somewhat mortified. Men did not talk of these things. But Braith did not laugh, or clap a patronizing hand on Weslan's shoulder, as he had dreaded. He caressed the infant pony's mane, staring ahead for what seemed a very long time.

"They say unrequited love carries the deepest pain of all," the sorcerer said at last, his voice kind, but blessedly remote. "Perhaps I can help there, as well."

CHAPTER 9

*W*eslan crouched in the queen's antechamber, trying to stay as still as the carved crohmwood statue behind which he had hidden. A pity it wasn't taller, he thought. Not only were his legs cramped, but this hunched position would make it harder to draw his sword quickly.

And he would need to do this.

The small room looked very different at night, swathed in utter blackness except for the moonlight which filtered through the one round window behind him. Turning, he could see Anna's white curve against the clear autumn sky. Assassins did not favour clear nights. Clouds were much better.

But Braith had said it would be that night.

Weslan heard a small sound, and he jerked upward, hand on his hilt, almost toppling the statue. He righted it, trying to slow his ragged breathing. A tiny brown mouse scittered across the floor. It looked back, and for a moment seemed to smirk.

Rhan's balls! Would that not be just marvellous—to wake up the queen and her ladies, scare them half to death—when he was here to rescue Darielle from a would-be killer! It would fit in perfectly with the way his life was going.

No, Weslan corrected himself. *My luck has changed, because of Braith.*

And it was true. The sorcerer's coming had transformed his life. At Braith's own charmingly worded request, Weslan had been his constant companion since the day they had come upon the foal. He had accompanied Braith to the nightly banquets held in his honour, where Rhantor's nobles scraped and bowed and jostled each other in order to get near the sorcerer, even while their eyes rolled in terror every time he moved within a few feet of them.

"Their curiosity has overcome their fear," Braith had told Weslan in an amused murmur meant only for his ears.

At the sight, Rhantoran nobles craned their necks, dying to know just what the sorcerer was conferring about with his young crony.

The queen's fabulous brown eyes rested on Weslan more often now, and a thoughtful smile played about her rosy lips. Braith had told her that he and Weslan had both grown up in the village of Stern.

He makes it sound as though we have been friends forever, Weslan thought. He half-believed it himself.

Then, walking in the gardens the previous day—the sorcerer stayed outside whenever he could, for he felt confined indoors—Braith had asked him a question.

"To what lengths are you prepared to go to gain the love of your queen?"

"Why, I would do anything, of course!" Weslan had replied, startled. "But how can I gain her love when I can barely gain her notice? She pays the hounds in the hunting hall more attention—at least she tosses them a bone once in a while!"

He fell gloomily silent, thinking of the flower Darielle had given him on the day he had arrived. He still had it, of course; keeping it in a small leather pouch tied onto his belt. But it had long since lost its fragrance and would no doubt crumble into powder next time he touched it.

"If you can stop feeling sorry for yourself, I will suggest a solution to your problem," Braith said. He stopped walking and sat on a bench beside one of the stone fountains dotted throughout the gardens.

"I am not feeling sorry for myself," Weslan protested, offended. "I regret to have given that impression—" He paused, for Braith's face had become very serious.

"What if I were to tell you that tomorrow night someone will enter the palace and attempt to kill the queen?" Braith was gazing at the fountain as he asked the question.

Bewildered, Weslan looked at the fountain also, as if it held the answer. "An assassin?" he stammered. "That is what we have feared—that King Darian will send one. But we could not guess when. How in Rhan's name do you know it is tomorrow?"

Braith looked at him, and Weslan recalled again with a sudden jolt that he was a sorcerer with unfathomable and terrifying power. He refrained from repeating the question.

"Do you wish to be the one to save her?" Braith asked.

"Yes!" Weslan blurted out so quickly that Braith smiled. "Of course I do. I will do anything—I told you."

"Then pay close attention to what I tell you now, unless you wish the queen's regard to be demonstrated only by placing flowers on your grave."

Weslan had listened to the sorcerer's precise instructions, staring at the elegant gestures of the sorcerer's crimson-gloved hands and wondering, not for the first time, which of Rhan's creatures was Braith's Source.

Now he hovered behind the statue, every nerve screaming for release. What if Braith had been wrong? But no, he must have been right—the empty room proved that. Darielle's guards were not there, which meant something was very wrong.

Braith had told him there would be no guards. When Weslan

had asked why, the sorcerer had replied cryptically that not all of the queen's enemies prowled outside the palace.

Someone had gotten rid of the guards. But who? It would have to have been someone with enough authority to be convincing, and with a good pretext. Weslan thought that the excuse would have to be brilliant indeed to convince Dirken. Then he remembered that Dirken had left that night on one of his mysterious errands. *What perfect timing.*

The queen's bedchamber door opened without warning. Weslan held his breath. A woman stepped out, wearing a white nightdress, a cloak wrapped about her shoulders. She stopped to light her candle with a tinder flint, and he saw it was Lady Saura. Her face was grim and set.

Saura left the antechamber without looking in Weslan's direction. He wondered if she was also uneasy about the lack of guards.

Then a terrible thought struck him. *What if Saura thwarts the assassin before I do?* It would force him to slink away like a beaten umbray. Worse yet, what if someone discovered him lurking in the queen's antechamber, with no orders from Heyg and no reasonable explanation?

As he drummed his fingers on his sword hilt, Weslan heard a slight creak and saw that the door to the antechamber was opening, slowly. *It must be the Lady Saura returning.* Then he saw the form of a man slip through the doorway, and a shocked thrill shot through him as the assassin stepped into the room.

He was so stunned that at first, he watched, unmoving, as the man crept stealthily toward Darielle's bedchamber.

But even as he stared, Weslan's soldier eye was evaluating his opponent, probing for weaknesses. The assassin was tall, but no taller than he, although more muscled, and with a shoulder breadth that was rather intimidating. No face was visible, just a black mask with narrow eye holes. He wore no mail, which rendered him more vulnerable and also showed that he was not expecting to meet any resistance.

This last thought dissolved the knot of fear forming in Weslan's stomach. A familiar heat rose within him, hotter and hotter: the righteous flames of Rhan.

The assassin drew a dagger from his belt and reached for the door handle. *Her* door handle. Weslan drew his sword, and with a cry of outrage, leaped out from behind the statue.

The assassin wheeled about quickly, dagger moving upward and then down in a swift, deadly crescent.

Not swift enough, though. Weslan's sword thrust through to his heart before the man could make another move. The dagger grazed Weslan's hip harmlessly and clattered onto the tiled floor.

The faceless killer grunted, eyes in the masked face blinking in surprise. Weslan pulled his sword out and watched the man crumple to the ground in front of him.

Muffled shrieks sounded from within the queen's chamber, and hounds barked from the grounds outside. The heavy, carved door swung open and Darielle stood before him.

Weslan's heart thumped, and there was a rushing sound in his ears. Everything had slowed down. He looked at Darielle's small, white face. She stared outward from the dark doorway with the eyes of a doe facing a pack of snarling hounds.

Looking at her, Weslan realized she had always known this time would come—when her brother would hunt her down. The queen had always appeared so playful and carefree, yet she must have lain down to sleep every night with that spectre and woken every morning with its skull's head still grinning beside her. Perhaps that was why she took so many lovers—to vanquish the spectre, one night at a time.

Weslan faced her, and her gaze fell upon him as he stood astride the moaning figure at his feet. Behind him there was a gathering commotion.

Saura slipped past him like a wraith into the queen's chambers. "I thought I heard a noise," she muttered as she went by.

His captain came in. The Queen's Guard had returned. Heyg's voice was harsh with shock as he asked the sleepy servants short and biting questions. He knew, as did they, that Dirken would be enraged when he heard of this.

Maids were scurrying about, whimpering and gasping as they lit the lamps. Weslan did not move from where he was standing.

Darielle's white nightdress had tiny purple flowers embroidered on the neck and sleeves. A pulse beat in her long, white neck. *She is so lovely,* he thought.

At Weslan's feet, the assassin groaned, and the death-rattle sounded in his throat. Weslan did not spare him a glance.

The heavy, carved door swung open wider, and Lady Saura placed a heavy bed robe over the queen's shoulders, covering the diaphanous nightdress and the tiny flowers. Gently, she tried to propel Darielle away from the doorway. The queen did not budge. Her eyes never looked away from his.

Saura moved away, tucking in a wisp of pale hair that had escaped from her starched white wimple. She brought a lamp back to the doorway, and as she did so she shot Weslan a look of such pure venom that he was momentarily pulled from his trance.

But the moment was brief, and his eyes went back to Darielle. He was drunk with euphoria; his nostrils were filled with her scent, mingling, not unpleasantly, with the smell of blood.

CHAPTER 10

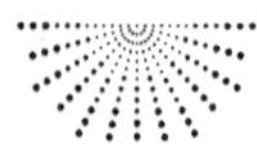

BOOK 2: THE HARVESTS OF AUTUMN

*H*eyg questioned him relentlessly, his manner so severe that Weslan wondered if he had been mistaken for the assassin. But it was all done in whispers outside the queen's chamber, for Darielle had refused to go back to bed unless Weslan was standing outside her door.

He stuck doggedly to the story he and Braith had worked out: he had been patrolling the ramparts—as indeed he had—and had seen Heyg ride off toward the river with the queen's assigned bodyguards, and all but the bare bones of the palace guards. The absence of armed guards had perplexed him. As he stated this, he averted his eyes at Heyg's stricken expression.

"A messenger came with the news that Dirken had returned from the South with urgent information and told us he had called a secret meeting of the Kalesh—every man we could spare," Heyg said.

There was a silence as he and Weslan stared at the floor.

Then, his captain stated the obvious. "We were duped. The first thing Dirken will ask me when he hears of this, is why I believed the message and took the bait like an addled sheep. If he asks me anything at all, that is. More likely he will just hang me from the nearest pitaya tree and use me for target practice."

Weslan doubted it. All the men knew that Heyg and Dirken shared a mutual respect and camaraderie with one another that was puzzling because of the disparity of their ages and stations in life; but not at all surprising when taking into consideration the single-minded ferocity with which both worshipped the North.

"Dirken will not blame you, Captain," Weslan said. "How could he, when you thought you were following his instructions?"

"I blame myself!" Heyg slapped his hand hard on the table. "Now tell me again—you were patrolling the ramparts when you saw a shadow, creeping toward the north gate. And no one was posted at the gate, of course, because the guards were all with me, charging off on a wild-umbray chase like the asses we were. But the gate was locked, was it not? And there were no signs of it being forced. I checked it personally."

"Someone must have let him in," Weslan said staunchly, knowing at least this much was true.

"But who, in Rhan's name? You know what this means. There is a traitor within the palace, we must find out who it is. But go on, go on. You made your way down to the north gate. And?"

"No," Weslan said for the fourth time. "I told you, I came directly here."

"But why?"

Weslan hesitated, seeing in his mind Lady Saura's cold grey eyes; and in that moment Heyg swore softly, striking his open palm with his fist. "Of course, why didn't it occur to me at once? The sorcerer Braith is behind this. He is not on our side after all. Rhan help us now!"

Weslan stared at Heyg with dismay, his fists clenching. "No! You are wrong about Braith."

"You are the one who is wrong about Braith, lad," Heyg said. "Hard as it may be for you to imagine yourself wrong about anything."

"That is not true." Weslan rose from the wooden chair in which Heyg had commanded him to sit while peppering him with questions. The chair leg scraped loudly against the floor.

From within the chambers, a plaintive voice called, "Weslan? Are you there?"

There was no mistaking the queen's soft contralto. Heyg raised his eyebrows ironically.

Face burning, Weslan spoke into the crack of the door. "I am here, my queen. Sleep now."

There was a muffled murmur from within, and then all was quiet once more.

"I tell you it is not Braith who betrayed us," Weslan said. Seeing Heyg's skeptical expression, he blurted out, "It cannot be Braith, for it was he who told me that an assassin would come tonight. Together we planned how to save the queen."

Heyg stared at Weslan as though he had transformed into a wraith. Astonishment warring with rage on his weathered features, he repeated, "Together?" And then, in an acid tone, "Ah, I see. No need to inform the Kalesh. This was a matter only a sorcerer and a wise, seasoned soldier could resolve! My fervent thanks. Dirken's thanks also when he hears of it."

"Oh, Rhan," Weslan had said. "Must you tell Dirken? No one is supposed to know about this—I would have said nothing, except that you got it all wrong about Braith."

"How did Braith know an assassin was coming?" Heyg asked.

"He did not deign to reveal that information. He does not tell me everything, you know."

"I am sure he does not," Heyg said. There was a pause as they glared at each other. Heyg pounded the table with his fist. "Why did he select you to be the hero? Which brings us to the question that minds for many these past few days: why have you become Braith's favoured companion? This 'hail-fellow-villager' stuff wears thin after a while."

"You cannot comprehend how anyone could find me of any interest or worth at all!" Weslan shot back, stung to the quick. He was ashamed of the tears welling in his eyes.

Heyg's steely gaze softened. "You know that is not true, Wes." He clapped a hand on Weslan's shoulder. "You are like a son to me, and that is your misfortune, for of no one does a father expect more than his son."

Weslan averted his face, unwilling to let Heyg see how moved he was. "I do not know what Braith sees in me any more than you do," he mumbled. "But he has been a good friend to me, and I will not have him blamed in this."

"I know you value his friendship," Heyg said. "But it's important for us to know why he did this, lad. We need to think about the North, about the safety of the queen."

"He did it for me," Weslan said abruptly. He might as well tell Heyg and be done with it.

"*What?*"

"A while ago I told him I wanted to impress the queen, and he said he would help me." Weslan stared at his boots, still spattered with blood. He would not have met Heyg's eye right then for all the pitayas in Miraven.

Heyg swore, and then Weslan heard a choking sound. When he looked up, he saw his captain laughing—silently, but with a violence that shook his large frame. When Heyg could finally speak, he said, "Well, you succeeded very well, wouldn't you say, lad?"

WESLAN AWOKE JUST BEFORE DAWN, when the warblers began their first persistent trilling in the palace courtyard. He lay for a moment in quiet disbelief, listening to the soft breathing of the woman beside him. He had conquered her the night before, or perhaps she had conquered him, but it did not matter. It had happened. And all thanks to Braith.

He lay with half-opened lids, hands stroking with a child's wonderment the sumptuous purple coverlet embroidered with a thousand golden flowers. He had scarcely glanced at it the night before. Lifting his head, he propped himself up on his elbow, and at his movement, Darielle sighed and murmured in her sleep.

Perhaps she is dreaming of me, he thought, grinning.

The sunlight was stealing more boldly into the room now, through the gauzy strips of cloth that hung across the window. He had never seen a window like this before he coming to Rhantor. Transparent and crystalline, through it he could glimpse the palace grounds, the winding mazes, arbours and fountains that formed Darielle's fabulous gardens.

Although it was fall, the flowers still bloomed, tended by dozens of gardeners. Many more would flourish throughout the winter, safely ensconced in hothouses.

Darielle's thigh moving against his was a soft, damp hothouse bloom. They had forged, molten, into a single vessel of rare purity during the past few hours.

Heyg would laugh at that. *It is just a joining boy, get your head out of the clouds—before Rhan sizzles it for you!*

Braith might mock his lofty thoughts as well, but then again, he might not. One never knew with Braith.

Any amount of laughter was worth it, though, just to stare down at Darielle's heart-shaped face as she slept. Black curls tumbled about her, and her skin was white—almost as white as her pillow. Her lips were pressed together primly, as if to belie everything they had just done.

Looking at that mouth, a pale, true pink, and at the several livid marks on her white neck, he wanted her. Again. This was astonishing. Drifting off to sleep a short time earlier, he remembered thinking that he would want nothing, ever again. *Utterly sated,* he had thought. *I will die happy, and they can feed my worn-out carcass to her dogs.*

Now, as their limbs entwined sinuously, Weslan put off his demise until the morrow. But he would allow her to slumber a few moments longer. He wanted to savour his moment of triumph. All of those ticking seconds that had led up to this one. More squares in the patchwork quilt.

YES, he had succeeded, Weslan reflected, gazing down at Darielle's sleeping face, which was as pale and luminescent as one of the marble statues in her gardens. Her eyes had shimmered at him with the promise of happiness the day he had first arrived in Rhantor. She had handed him a single blossom from her hair, and a look that he would remember all his life. Fortunately, he had fainted before he could do anything rash.

If he had known how long he would have to wait for another such look, he might have decided not to regain consciousness.

He nuzzled his head against Darielle's breast to reassure himself that she was real, and not some exquisite phantasm. She arched her back and her fingertips stroked his arm, but the gesture was automatic, for she slumbered on. He sat up, thinking he would not sleep again now, although he had snatched only a few minutes during the night. A wave of exuberance washed over him as he recalled how he had come to this bed.

The previous night had been the Night of Masks, the time when men and women came together with an abandon fuelled by the anonymity of their identities behind their hidden faces. Weslan went to the banquet masked as Rhan. He would never have dared on his own, but Braith had suggested it, and Braith had not been wrong yet.

Weslan thought he carried it off rather well, with the golden rays of his mask fanning out and blending into his long golden hair. He was being touted as a hero, and thought he might as well take advantage of it. Next week someone else might supplant him.

Darielle appeared costumed as a radiant Anna—trailing silver and Berlotan lace. Obviously everyone knew it was her, though she wore a mask and avoided her usual chair. No one else would have dared to masquerade as Anna, for two reasons: the civil unrest in the South, where worship of the Goddess was denounced as heresy by the priests; and, of more political importance at court, no lady would risk offending the queen by appearing to place herself higher.

Weslan and Darielle dined at separate tables. Neither ate, but stared with unabashed ardour at each other throughout the banquet. Dirken had composed a poem in honour of Weslan's deed, which he performed with a simple eloquence in his rich baritone, strumming the cintar for effect. Afterward, he sung one of the many well-known northern ballads, a plaintive ballad of unrequited love.

The rest had been inevitable—a slow, dreamy dance toward each other that had ended in Darielle's bedchamber.

Life continued to unfold in such bizarre patterns. Weslan had an image once more of the Anniste women sewing their colourful patchwork quilts—a patch here, a patch there, no square of fabric ever the same, yet all coming together to make a whole.

Feeling drowsy again, he stared at the sumptuous purple window coverings, thinking they looked like crohm leaves after a rain, and closed his eyes.

Braith's face rose before him, lean and strong and kind. *My friend,* Weslan thought, *my brother.* He felt the warmth of Braith's smile like a benediction, lulling him into sleep.

At once, Weslan began to dream, entering a splintered world where his past and present mingled confusedly. A sense of helpless anguish over-whelmed him.

Heyg leaned toward Weslan in one of the many Rhantoran taverns frequented by the Kalesh, tapping the ridged and pinkish scar on his arm.

"Healing nicely, I would say. But you have got a fresh wound in your heart, haven't you, lad? Those don't heal clean like sword cuts. Rhan save you, Wes, you're playing with fire!"

Weslan downed his ale to avoid replying. He stared at the wooden sign outside the tavern, bewildered. It was the Pitaya Pit. But that was in his home village of Stern. It made no sense, because he was in Rhantor.

When he looked up again, Braith was sitting opposite him, fingertips touching to form a crimson peak, head cocked to one side with an alert, waiting expression.

"What am I to do?" he asked Braith, for the ale did nothing to ease the ache within.

Braith said quietly, "I will help you."

And then Weslan was standing upon a hill, carpeted with summer flowers—mountain poppies, orange and yellow and purple—their heads bobbing gaily in the wind, like children nodding to him. The queen galloped by him on her exquisite mountain pony, wearing the soft doeskin breeches that clung to her hips in a way that made him incapable of thought. She turned to wave, and he saw with guilt and dismay that it was Tekoah, a look of gentle reproach upon her face.

Weslan began running after her, stumbling down the steep hill, tearing up great grassy clods of earth with his heavy soldier boots. He had to explain why he had not returned for them. He ran faster, trampling the poppy-children under his feet.

At the bottom of the hill were more flowers, for there were Darielle's gardens—breathtaking, bloom-laden, dense and fragrant as when he had first seen them. He heard the splashing of the fountains, and in the sound was the ripple of Darielle's laughter, cool and mocking.

And then the queen walked by him, on the arm of her latest lover, throwing him a smile like a bone to a dog in the hunting hall.

Weslan's heart, soaring toward her, halted in mid-flight. No, she cared nothing for him. She merely loved all creatures in the capricious way of a child, patting dogs, caressing ponies, handing flowers to poor bleeding soldiers, who were to her as clumsy and grateful as one of the barnyard creatures. Her womanly favours were bestowed on more deserving mortals, like that foppish lord with whom she was walking arm-in-arm.

Unable to stop himself, he followed the couple as they moved into the shadows of the maze, its twisting hedges canopied by artfully entwined ivy and branches.

Sick with rage, Weslan saw the man draw his arm possessively about the queen's slender waist. It must have been Dirken, for he heard laughter. Dirken could always make her laugh.

The man turned, looking directly at Weslan. It was his father.

No! Weslan thought, rage slashing through him. She is mine!

Veld smiled as if reading his son's thoughts. "She is mine," he echoed mockingly, "on the Night of Masks."

His father's voice became a sibilant whisper, and the phrase "Night of Masks" pulsed within Weslan's veins, fuelling his impotent rage.

He awoke, unable to curb the loud cry with which he always burst from these dreams. It promptly provoked an answering shriek from his royal companion and set all the palace hounds to barking at once.

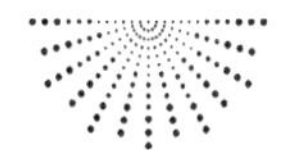

CHAPTER 11

On the Night of Masks, Tekoah would be without a partner again. She had already resigned herself to this, and when she rose from her bed on the morning of the Night, she was determined not to let it bother her. Although, sometimes in the last few weeks since meeting Garth, the Stonemason's son, she had allowed herself to dream that this night would be different.

Garth was gone now, though. Suddenly, and without explanation, like so many people in her life. Was it a curse, perhaps, that surrounded her?

Tekoah's throat thickened, and her eyes misted over as she stood shivering in her nightgown.

But snivelling about it will not help, she told herself sternly. Perhaps she would have time to compose a verse that evening, if her father went to sleep early. She would enjoy some rare and peaceful solitude, staring into the dying embers of the fire, while in one corner of the hut her father snored, and in another the twins lay in an inert, indistinguishable heap.

As for the rest of the day, she would keep herself busy, which was never a difficult thing to do. Tekoah listened to her father curse groggily behind the curtain as he stumbled out of bed. She sighed, tying her apron behind her as she turned toward the stove.

After her father and the twins had finished slurping their cornmeal porridge and headed out to the forge, she painstakingly scrubbed the bowls, spoons and pots in water drawn from the well. A brisk wind was blowing leaves from the trees, stirring the dry summer grass, and she felt the first chill nip on her neck and arms as she pumped the water. It was a breeze that heralded the windstorms that would soon be raging through the mountain passes, bringing snow and ice.

WINTER CAME QUICKLY to the North. There was no coy flirting between the seasons. The cold stalked in with black and yawning jaws and swallowed up the warmth whole, so that the bright mountain poppies had no time to wither, but scattered red and yellow petals instead, caught in a whirling rain by the inexorable wind, like the tears of summer.

Perhaps it was the brisk air that made her restless, for Tekoah impulsively walked to the village, though she had no need to. She did not let herself think about it being the day of the Night. The Night of Masks was not for her, perhaps never would be, now that Garth had left.

Tekoah's fists clenched and unclenched themselves, a habit of her quick-tempered brother. Had Father had anything to do with Garth's sudden disappearance? She could not help but suspect it. Veld had worked with stonemason Kayne, who had recently come to Stern on a commission to supervise the stupendous castle being built for the lord of Mirrand. So Father had had plenty of opportunities to encounter Garth, the stonemason's youngest son and apprentice, who was hale and clever and cheerful, and very interested in becoming acquainted with Tekoah—until Father got wind of what was going on, and forbade her to bring the food baskets up to the castle site anymore.

Tekoah knew it was useless to wonder, for she would never know. There was no point in thinking about it—Garth was gone, that was all. Perhaps he had met someone else and had been reluctant to tell her. Though it did not seem like him to avoid the truth, or to desert his father in the middle of a project.

Stonemason Kayne had at first treated his son's absence as a boyish lark, but now he was asking questions in the village, or so Tekoah had heard from Hanta.

Father had not liked Garth, but then he liked no one who paid undue attention to his daughter. Thinking about it was giving her a headache.

Tekoah covered her hair in a blue kerchief, and threw her cloak about her shoulders, frowning at its shabby, threadbare look.

It was noon when she arrived at the village square, and Stern was buzzing with excitement. It had opened the marketplace to the mask-makers.

Some villagers created their own masks, but there was something thrilling about watching the foreign mask-makers at work in the square, carving wood, painting, or stitching cloth, meticulously plaiting hair that was sometimes real, sometimes made of yarn, to fasten onto the carved faces.

A mask could be as simple as a painted piece of bark or as complex as beaten copper, elaborately engraved. The mask-makers always had sacksful already made, but to lure a customer they would invariably be working on something bizarre or fantastic, their faces themselves masks of concentration and zeal.

Tekoah drifted among the stalls, smiling politely in response to greetings from acquaintances who were passing by, but not lingering long enough to start a conversation. She did not wish anyone to guess that she was longing to be a part of the celebration.

She watched the craftspeople as they worked, silent and intent—shaving a bit of wood here, a bit there, squinting at the effect. The small, precise motions of their hands were soothing, and so she hovered nearby for longer than she had meant to.

A half-formed thought blossomed in her mind: *Father cannot take this from me.*

An old man looked up from his work as she passed, grinning toothlessly. He held up a piece of birch, carved into the face of a bird of prey. The eyes had been painted a hard, brilliant green. Tekoah stared at the mask, uneasy. The old man suddenly jerked it toward her, and she jumped, startled.

As she hurried away, she heard his staccato hoots of laughter behind her. She flushed with annoyance at the old man, at herself. Why had she let him scare her? She wanted to be home.

Tekoah crossed the square with purposeful strides, hoping to escape seeing anyone else she knew. But no—worse luck—there was Norah, detaching herself from a group by the well, coming toward her.

Curse it all! She forced herself to wave and lengthened her steps as if she had no time for chit-chat.

Undeterred and cheerful, Norah bore down on her, her hefty bosom bouncing in her effort to keep up. She shouted so that the whole square must have heard, "Tekoah, if you come to the Pitaya Pit before the moon rises, we will save you a seat!" She added breathlessly, "There is to be a minstrel, if you have not already heard."

"No, I had not." Tekoah looked about for a means of escape.

"Yes, and they say he knows every new ballad sung by Dirken of the queen's court. And is as handsome as Dirken—well, almost." She closed her large bovine eyes, eyelashes fluttering.

Tekoah stifled a smile. Norah had never been to court or

glimpsed Dirken before, but one would not know it from the way she talked. She was annoying and silly, but such a child that it was comical. Nothing at all had ever happened to her; perhaps that was why she was always manufacturing dramas for herself.

"You must come," Norah persisted in a loud voice, holding her by the shoulder to stop her from walking.

Out of the corner of her eye, Tekoah saw some other village youths by the well: Stolk, tall and curly-haired, Brenna and Mirak, all watching with interest.

"We cannot promise you a seat after moonrise, so tell me now you will come."

Norah was enjoying this, Tekoah knew—talking to her, pretending they were close friends. It made Norah seem more interesting to the others. She told them self-importantly that Tekoah confided in her, because only she knew how to draw the poor shy girl out. Tekoah had overheard her saying it once, in a superior voice in Chalvern's shop, not knowing that Tekoah had been upstairs visiting with Chalvern.

It was sometimes amusing that she was an object of mystery —it made her feel *real*, someone who existed outside the endless days and nights at the forge. But at other times she was resentful that they tried to lure her into their childish games. Could these fools not see they had nothing in common with her?

Weslan had dominated them, bullied them into forgetting who he was. He had always acted as if he was destined for great things, and they had believed him. And now look at Weslan: a soldier in Rhantor, someone to respect!

Perhaps that was the secret: convince everyone else that one was who one wanted to be, and then it would happen. But she cared nothing for fame and riches, honour and glory. She longed only for peace and safety—a happy world for those she loved. A quiet place in which to dream and write her verses. Aside from that, Tekoah did not know who she was, except that she was worlds away from these laughing, careless children.

Garth had differed from the other village youths; he'd been wiser somehow. Perhaps it was because he was not from Stern, and he had travelled widely ever since he was small with his father, the Master Mason Kayne. He had looked at her with gentle eyes and had understood her need for silence. Although he had done nothing more than hold her hand sometimes as they walked, he had taken away the loneliness for a short time.

"Garth is not here any longer," Norah pointed out slyly, as if reading her thoughts. "A short-lived passion, alas. But that is always the way with summer, pigeon. I myself have suffered from heartache this season—several times, to be honest. But you must not hide yourself away. Life goes on. And I am charged to relay an urgent message: Stolk is pining for you! He says you hold his beating heart in your hands—and he will wait for you to bring it back to him at the Pitaya Pit." She tossed her head theatrically toward the well.

Tekoah folded her arms, her cheeks flaming. "Pray, do not concern yourself about me," she replied. "If I decide to come to the Pitaya Pit, I shall just elbow my way in, or bring Raol and Fanco to be my strongmen." She stared at Norah defiantly, knowing that Father would not let her come, and knowing that Norah knew.

"Stolk is wearing a mountain cat mask," Norah continued coyly, as if she had not heard. "I know this because I saw his father making it, when I went to bring them eggs yesterday."

"You have sharp eyes, but should you not have been counting eggs instead?" Tekoah retorted, glancing at Stolk despite herself. He was staring unabashedly at her, and he caught her eye and smiled. *Oh Anna,* she groaned, *it is another plot. Why do they not let me be?*

"I forbid you to change the subject, sly one!" Norah's black eyes were dancing with mischief, and Tekoah wondered all at once what she hoped to gain by this. "Stolk has begged me to tell you: come! He says he will make you forget that Garth ever existed…"

Enough of this. "Stop!" Tekoah snapped, exasperated.

Norah's eyes narrowed. Her voice dropped to a murmur. "People talk, pigeon, although of course I never listen to them. They say your father got rid of Garth, somehow. Master Mason Kayne has paid people bags of gold to find his son, to no avail. People say that he is so frantic that he may even leave before they complete the castle."

Tekoah did not reply. She dug her fingernails into her palms, bit her tongue, and willed herself to be silent.

"Veld is crazy, dangerous—everyone knows it! You do not wish for Stolk to disappear as well as poor Garth, and so now you refuse to come. You are so kind to others—which is why I have always liked you."

So, this was what they all talked about—clustered in whispering bunches behind her back. Tekoah's face grew hot. She would never come back to the village square, ever. She wished desperately to be gone now, to vanish from view. To do that— what freedom! Weslan had disappeared, as had her mother, Neela, and now Garth. If only she could learn their secret.

Tekoah knew that if she did not leave the square this instant, she would suffocate with humiliation. But she must be dignified in her departure. *Silly children.* Why should she care? She didn't care. Tekoah shook Norah's hand off her shoulder and began walking.

But the other girl was following her, tenacious as one of the leeches in the pond at Stern's End. "Never mind Garth, pigeon. You must think of yourself for a change. Your best chance is to leave here, go somewhere where your lunatic father cannot find you. With your beautiful hair and white skin, you would stand out anywhere, find a husband who is fit for you. Go to Rhantor, perhaps. Your fiery brother has ended up there, I heard? As a guard in the queen's own palace! Now that is someone I miss—the golden-haired darling. Do not be angry with me, dear," she added, looking at Tekoah's face.

Tekoah quickened her step without replying.

"What should I tell Stolk, then?" Norah persisted, a wheedling note creeping into her voice. "He has himself in a fever, poor boy."

"Tell him what you like. Only don't speak to me any more about it." She felt rather than saw Norah's grin. "And if he needs consolation?"

Tekoah said nothing.

"Then you give me your blessing? You know it is bad luck to come between a joining on Mask Night."

"You have my blessing three times over!" Tekoah answered, her voice shaking.

She knew now what Norah's stake was. Hearing the other girl's unmistakable sigh of satisfaction, she felt a surge of envy and anger toward Norah, whose life was simple.

"Goodbye," Norah said gaily, turning away, as if they had just had the most delightful chat. "I will be wearing a spotted pony mask," she called back, from a little way off. "They say the mountain cats go wild for them!"

If Norah had been a man and spoken to Weslan with such condescension, then her brother would have met that simpering smile with a fist to the face. Tekoah fumed at the thought as she hastened away. She allowed herself to imagine, just for a moment, an image of Norah's expression after she had slapped her, hard. Then she shut it out.

Bad enough that anger ruled her father and was in danger of ruling her brother. For all that she adored Weslan, she had seen his bloody knuckles and puffy face more than once when he had returned home from the village. Anger was an evil curse, nurtured in the breasts of sorcerers and spewed across the land like poisonous spores.

Tekoah forced herself to breathe deeply, calming herself the way her mother had taught her when she was tiny.

Breathe in and out, slowly. Focus on an object close by. Forget about Stern and its inhabitants, pretend it is far away, as far as the stars in the sky.

She stared into the dense green of a salmonberry thicket ahead of her on the path where it narrowed before turning north, toward the highway. The berries were large and ripe, glistening orbs of orange-gold. She picked some to feel the coolness of the juice on her tongue.

Breathe in, then out.

At that very moment, a figure darted from the thicket and stood crouched in the path in front of her. Tekoah screamed in real terror and then fell silent. For it was only Aunt Beula, holding her hands up for silence. Tekoah struggled to regain her breath, heart pounding in hard, angry beats.

DARTING nervous glances all around her, Aunt Beula scurried along the path toward Tekoah. She looked like some wary woodland animal. But perhaps that was what she had become, for she had been in hiding since the spring.

"You frightened me, Aunt," Tekoah said, speaking with respect, but unable to keep the reproach from her voice.

"Well, you would not expect me to hail you at Mirveta's Well, would you, child? You know how dangerous it is for us right now!" Beula smiled, her small brown eyes kindling with warmth.

She reached up, her dry, wrinkled hands patting Tekoah's cheeks, a gesture familiar to her since babyhood. Absurdly, Tekoah wanted to cry.

It seemed a long time since she had last seen Aunt Beula.

Beula's son Bhantok managed the pony-breeding farm now that his mother had gone into hiding, but he had told Tekoah that she appeared sometimes at odd hours and took a mug of tea with him before melting back into the shadows. And once, to Tekoah's astonishment, the twins had brought her a message from her aunt, scratched in bark, saying nothing more than that she was well and safe.

Some hid better than others, Tekoah told herself bitterly, thinking of her mother—it would be such a relief to find out she was safe. Though who be sure of that now?

Tekoah herself had seen the sorcerer Braith kill two men in the village an annaspan ago, though no one else seemed to remember it. No one talked about it, at any rate. And now there was a new priest, Zorak, and a new treasurer whose name she could never remember. It was as if Grindhor and Melnich had never existed.

She wondered if Aunt Beula—or anyone else in the Anniste —knew about Braith's coming. Several times, a strong desire to speak to someone about what she had seen had gripped her—to be certain she had not dreamed it. She had almost told Chalvern, once.

Aunt Beula was shaking her shoulder, bringing her back to the present. "You must meet me tonight, child, once Anna has risen. It is an ideal time, being the Night of Masks. Everyone will be occupied, so it is unlikely that you will be followed."

"Meet you where?" Tekoah asked, alarm prickling her in sudden goosebumps on her arms. "And why?"

"In front of the big crohm tree, a league down this road—you know the one. You think of it as your crohm tree." Beula answered. She smiled impishly at Tekoah's incredulous stare.

It was true that after the calamitous day that the sorcerer Braith had appeared in the village square, Tekoah had often returned to that tree, finding a mysterious solace in leaning against the massive trunk. But she had always been alone—of that, she was certain.

"How did you know?" she stammered.

Beula squeezed her arm impatiently. "Never mind, now. Just be there, at moonrise."

"But I do not know if I can manage it. I mean that Father, I could not leave when—"

Beula winked slyly and placed her mouth close to Tekoah's ear as, if there were other prying ears all around them. She whispered, "Surely your mother taught you something of sleeping potions, so if he has not drunk himself to sleep by then you can help him along his way, child." She nudged Tekoah sharply in her ribs.

There was a loud rustling movement in the fir tree beside them. Both women jumped, clutching at each other. But it was only a wren, flapping its wings, before swooshing away, scattering fir needles as it went.

Tekoah began to laugh nervously—a thin, high sound. Beula peered quickly around, and her hand came down on Tekoah's shoulder firmly.

Checking her laughter with an effort, Tekoah replied, "Yes, I will come—at least I will try," she said. "You speak of the crohm tree by the—"

"You know which one," Beula cut in crisply. "Now goodbye, goodbye, I still need to talk with that worthless son of mine before Rhan goes down."

She scurried away, a tiny figure in brown homespun, looking like a mole, or a shrew, or, judging by her speed, a flying squirrel. She disappeared into the thicket, and by the time Tekoah reached it, it was if as if she had never been there at all.

CHAPTER 12

Leaving home that evening proved less tricky than Tekoah had expected. Veld started drinking corn lightning shortly after midday, became belligerent by late afternoon, and fell into a heavy slumber well before sundown, so there was no need to slip any sleeping powders into his mug as Aunt Beula had suggested. She busied herself instead with applying cold compresses to the bruised and puffy faces of the twins. Why they never struck back at their father, Tekoah could not fathom, but she had long ago ceased to let it bother her. Such was simply the order of things.

Before she tiptoed out the door, she threw into the fire the wooden mask that Veld had waved, leering, before he had stumbled to bed.

"It was your mother's, my sweetheart," he had said, a note of braying sentimentality in his voice that nauseated her. "I first met her when she was wearing this—do you know what I am saying? But of course you do, you are old enough to know! Mayhap you should put it on and see if it suits you? It is a dove —soft, compliant, sacrificial dove." He had slurred his last words, swaying, and a sudden shudder had passed over him as he had stumbled toward his cot.

The shudder seemed to move through her now as she watched the mask burn.

But outside, as the brisk night air swept over her, earthy and damp with the smell of fallen leaves, Tekoah was elated. She was going somewhere on the Night of Masks. Not where she should have gone, perhaps, but it was better than nothing. Sometimes she felt so stifled, lying in the hut at night.

Tekoah was prepared this time for the sight of Beula, and she spied the tiny figure crouching by the great trunk well before her aunt straightened and cautiously waved. Anna was full and bright, the colour of clotted cream; and in the moonlight—just for a moment—Beula's face looked like Neela's, and Tekoah started. Something in the cheekbone's glint, the tilt of the chin.

But it was only a trick of light. Beula had never looked like Mother. Neela had all the beauty, it was said, and Beula all the sense. Sense enough to marry well, at any rate. Beula had said this to Neela in Tekoah's hearing years ago, when she was nine or ten. Tekoah had turned away in a panic, busying herself at the stove, hearing the censure in her aunt's voice. Knowing it would lead to another dispute between the two women.

Tekoah wondered if Beula had ever worn a mask, joined with a man in abandon on the Night of Masks. Or had she refrained, as many did, remaining ignorant of the mysteries of joining until she had married Tok? Uncle Tok, large, stolid, gentle—dead now these many years. He would have been horrified to know his wife was now hiding in the woods, desperately trying to elude vengeful priests.

Beula beckoned impatiently as Tekoah hurried up to the tree. "I am here, Aunt!" she announced, her excitement mounting. "But where are we going? Do you not fear that it is too open out here?"

Beula smiled mischievously, almost girlishly, and beckoned

again, around to the side of the trunk which faced the wood. The indigo leaves were waxy and opaque, sliding together in the breeze with a slight whispering sound.

Tekoah had been prepared for the sight of her aunt, but certainly not for the door that now swung open within the massive trunk at a light push from Beula's hand. Nor for the narrow earthen steps that descended into a chamber which, although small, was larger than she would have thought possible. And not—no, never, by sweet Anna's light—for the circle of brown-clad women, sitting quietly among the gnarled roots that twisted through the walls.

They were in her tree. This was why Beula knew she thought of it as her tree. An uncomfortable thrill shot through Tekoah, from the base of her neck to her heels.

Were they women, or were they only roots delving into the ground? Was she just imagining things? Tekoah thought for a moment that she might faint.

She descended, prodded by her aunt's firm hand in the small of her back. In the faint light provided by several tallow candles set in the wooden recesses of the walls, Tekoah turned and looked at Beula accusingly.

Ignoring the look, her aunt led her to the centre of the circle and said in a matter-of-fact voice, "Sit."

And so Tekoah sat on a woven straw mat that was none too comfortable. A crude stone basin, half-filled with water, sat in the centre of the circle, and all the women's eyes were upon it.

"The Basin," Aunt Beula murmured, sinking down next to her, and with another shock, Tekoah comprehended: Mirveta's Basin.

Throughout her childhood, Tekoah had heard of this relic, which was part of the legend of Mirveta, the first of the Anniste healers. For seventeen hundred years they had handed it down from woman to woman. The Basin had been in her mother's care, once, she supposed, but she had never seen it, for Neela had abdicated her Guardianship when Tekoah was much younger.

She stared down to avoid looking at the women in the circle. The Basin was a humble stone bowl, very much at home in this chamber that was so small and full of dull colours—browns and greys, and the musty smell of earth. Looking up, Tekoah saw with surprise that several of the Anniste were darting nervous glances at her. They looked almost as uncomfortable as she felt.

"I only pray, Beula, that we are not making a grave error," one of the women quavered.

She looked dreadfully old, but to Tekoah they all seemed ancient, including Aunt Beula, who now reached out and placed her hand on Tekoah's wrist. Some Anniste were disconcertingly familiar, ghosts from the edge of her memory, gazing at her with patient, half-reproachful eyes from the gloom.

"Do not pray to me, Valeen," her aunt answered testily, "for this was not my idea. I would have kept Tekoah well out of this. But if you are suggesting my niece would betray us, then..."

"Please," a new voice interrupted from outside the circle.

Tekoah turned to look as the speaker came forward. Beula fell silent. The woman drew her hood back from her face, and Tekoah looked at her with astonishment.

She was young and radiant—beautiful—although different from everyone else in this room, because she was as bronzed as a Berlotan, with dark eyes that flashed like lightning in the faint glow of the lantern. Her gaze fell upon Tekoah and she smiled. The smile was to her face as a bird's sudden flight from a tree, soaring and breathtaking.

She spoke again. "I am Reika. Please forgive us. We would not be so apprehensive, were our lives not in constant danger."

"Danger for your lives?" Tekoah asked, unable to take her eyes from Reika's face. "But surely that is an exaggeration!"

"Surely not," Reika returned, still smiling. "Why else do you think we meet within crohm trees? And live in caves? For the comfort?"

The Anniste healers were living in caves? Tekoah had not thought about where they slept. What would they do when winter came? Aunt Beula would not survive the cold, nor would many other Anniste, who eyed her now with such distrust.

Dumbstruck, Tekoah stared down at her lap. When she raised her eyes again, she saw Aunt Beula looking with gentle irony upon her face, as if reading her thoughts.

"And we would not have summoned you here, exposing you to danger as well, had it not been very urgent," Reika continued, her voice strong and musical. "I hope you trust your aunt enough to believe this."

Tekoah nodded. A thought struck her. "You are the Guardian, then?" she asked Reika.

Of course she was. She had to be. Her bearing was so regal and self-assured.

"No," Reika answered, "I am not." She looked at Tekoah as she said this in a way that unnerved her. "But Anna called upon me, on the Night of the Dead, to serve until the Guardian steps in to take my place."

There was a chorus of murmuring among the women. A few voices, louder than the rest, clamoured, "Tell her!"

Beula's voice cut this off sharply. "Not yet, we agreed, not yet!"

Listening to the women, Tekoah's heart beat rapidly. They could not be expecting Neela to come back when she had left the Anniste turnings ago! Her mother would probably never return to her life of drudgery at the forge. Tekoah's head ached dully, as it always did when she thought of her mother.

She wished herself gone from here.

"Please," Reika said again, and the room was silent. She fixed Tekoah with a gaze of great intensity. "I will tell you what you wish to know, which is why you are here." Reika hunkered down by the Basin, dabbling the water with her forefinger.

"The basin you see before you is a relic of incomparable value: Mirveta's Basin. Into it we gaze when the Goddess calls one of us to Journey. You know what a Journey is?"

"Of course she does," Beula muttered beside her.

Reika continued to look at Tekoah, who nodded. Then, as Reika still waited for an answer, she spoke.

"One enters a trance, which the Anniste call a 'Journey,' and in the trance one somehow connects with the Goddess Anna, who then reveals things about events—both past and future."

Beula began to say something, but Reika held up a hand and she fell silent. Tekoah kept her eyes on Reika's face as she continued speaking.

"Mother said the Goddess tells you only what you need to know. And when you come out of your 'Journey,' you are very tired." Tekoah faltered and stopped speaking.

She was uncertain if she had said something which would offend the healers. She could not tell by looking at them. The Anniste women were gazing at her, their eyes watchful and appraising beneath their brown hoods.

But when she looked at Reika, there was nothing but warmth in her smile. "That is part of it, yes. The Goddess tells us things we need to know. But there is more, and it is very important. The Goddess helps us to look inward. We must seek deep within ourselves, and in that way begin our learning. Otherwise, all outward knowledge is useless to us at best, and dangerous at worst. Did your mother Neela not teach you this?"

"No," Tekoah answered, speaking her mind without realizing it. "She only talked to me about this once or twice, when I was quite young. I remember Father heard her speaking to me once, and he became furious. After that, she rarely said anything—about anything."

There was a silence; Aunt Beula's hand crept on top of her

own, patting it. Tekoah looked at the withered skin, the raised blue veins, hardly able to believe that this flesh and blood was hers, as well.

Reika spoke again. "This inward seeing is the centre of the Anniste faith, Tekoah. And it is where we have embittered the priests of Rhan, who call it heresy. 'Rhan's followers shall sanction nothing that Rhan does not show us, clearly. All else is false and comes from the Pit.'" Reika quoted this with an ironic expression on her lovely face.

"And although the Anniste have always shared their Journeys with each other and with others, for many turnings the priests of Rhan have refused to acknowledge their value or listen to anything we have to tell them. Even when the welfare of the people is at stake. Think of the drought in the South—we knew it was coming, and we hastened to warn the priests. The South Raveners could have prepared for the drought, and suffered far less hardship, had they listened to us. Instead..." Reika's eyes closed, and her long brown fingers made the gesture of mourning.

"Instead"—Beula cut in, bitterness in her voice—"the priests waited until the drought struck, and then claimed it was an Anniste curse. And they are using it as an excuse to persecute us more. Where will it end?"

"That is what we intend to find out, with Anna's help," Reika said, "and yours, Tekoah."

"I?" Tekoah responded, startled. She had been lost in a reverie, thinking about how horrible it was that the priests had twisted everything around them into a lie. She reflected that she herself had wondered if the Anniste had caused the drought, although Master Chalvern had said that it was all pigeon droppings.

"Yes, you. For we know now that we are in a graver danger than we had supposed. It is not only the priests who hate and fear us. Behind the priests, there are the sorcerers."

Reika paused, turning to stare down broodingly into the still water of the Basin. Tekoah's shoulders jerked as Braith's face rose in her mind.

"Sorcerers?" she asked, her voice croaking a little. "What have the sorcerers got to do with it?"

"The sorcerers are our greatest enemies of all," Reika said, and for the first time Tekoah thought she heard fear in her voice. Then, so low that no one but Tekoah could hear, she added, "And you have seen for yourself the terrible power they wield, have you not?"

Tekoah stared back at Reika, dumbstruck. How did she know?

"It was revealed to me several days ago in a Journey"—Reika answered in a louder voice that encompassed the entire circle—"that the sorcerer Morogh and the sorcerer Zant have taken counsel together with the priests of Rhan and King Darian of the South. They are in league to destroy us."

A low, apprehensive murmur travelled around the circle.

"Whether the sorcerer Braith is also in league with them, I do not know," Reika continued. "I saw him in my Journey, but he was here in Stern, and you were also present." She looked at Tekoah.

As Reika spoke, an image of Braith came to Tekoah, vivid as lightning in a storm, contemptuously waving his hand, and two small piles of dust that blew away in the wind. "But why?" she asked. "Why should the sorcerers care about the healers, who have never threatened them?"

"The Anniste scrolls prophesy that the Mantling will take place after seventeen hundred turnings," Aunt Beula interrupted, in a grating voice that betrayed her tension. "And that it will end the Age of the Sorcerers. We have all heard the lore of the Mantling—that Anna's face overshadows Rhan's face for a time, and the world becomes dark during daytime. The Anniste interpret this as a sacred Joining of the gods. The priests see it as a desecration—Anna presuming to usurp Rhan's predominant place in the heavens."

"I *know*, aunt," Tekoah answered, impatient. Had Beula forgotten that she was Neela's daughter?

"I am not sure what your mother told you and what she neglected to tell you, once she gave up on things," Aunt Beula said. "And even if you were told, I need to make sure that you remember, because what follows is very important: if there are no Anniste—no connection with the Goddess Anna—then there can be no Mantling."

She stopped, and there was a significant pause. Everyone was looking at Tekoah.

Reika inclined her head in Beula's direction. "Your aunt hits on the very heart of the matter. The Anniste scrolls speak plainly, but no one has ever paid them much attention. Why bother to worry about there being no Anniste, when our healers are needed and loved by all? But now it seems we are not. And some very dark minds have done some very careful thinking about the Anniste. The Goddess has sent us a warning."

"Why am I here?" Tekoah whispered, dry-mouthed. The tree-trunk did not seem so safe, now.

"We need to find out as much as we can about what the sorcerers are up to. Therefore, I must ask you: have you seen the sorcerer Braith?"

Tekoah tried to keep her face impassive, but her jaw trembled. She held her fingertips against it and strove to steady her gaze.

Reika must have seen what she was looking for, for her lilting voice rose with urgency. "Tekoah, it is very important that you tell us anything you can about Braith. We do not know why he came to Stern. It is certain that the other two sorcerers are hatching this vile plot, but whenever one of us sees Braith in a Journey, you are present as well. It is vital for us to solve this puzzle. Knowledge is our best weapon against an enemy whose plot we have only begun to fathom."

Reika fell silent, her gaze sombre, as if she could see something the others could not.

As if in awe of this unseen vision, the women fell silent. There was a palpable thickening of the air, which was already dense with the richness of the earth and the damp minty smell of the crohm tree.

Closing her eyes, Tekoah thought she could feel the heartbeat of the great tree welling up, a thousand times slower than her own. When she looked up, she saw Reika had fixed her dark gaze upon her once again.

"There is also this," Reika told her, voice becoming stern. "In the absence of your mother Neela, the Guardianship of the Anniste is yours, by right, and by duty."

"No!" The cry burst from Tekoah. "I do not want it—or wish to be part of this. I would never betray you"—she stammered, looking at the circle of eyes—"but I cannot. I do not have the wisdom or the strength."

"Child," Reika replied, "do you think we seek to thrust something upon you which you do not desire? But there is no doubt that the sorcerers are determined to annihilate the Anniste, and your mother was the Guardian. How long do you think it will be before you are endangered? If you are not already? You must tell us what you know."

Tekoah thought of Braith, of his quiet whisper in her mind. Why would a sorcerer care about someone as insignificant as she? A shiver travelled from her neck down to her spine.

She looked at the silent circle of women. Rheumy-eyed, tremulous, frail as dried leaves—where was the great strength she had heard of?

A surprising wave of affection for them swept over her, mingling with pity. *They must live in caves and huddle in tree roots like rabbits in a warren, while the fat priests brayed in the temples, spilling the innocent blood of pigeons, and demanding coin from every poor villager.*

So Tekoah told the Anniste everything that had happened in the square with Braith, all except the last bit, when he had spoken inside her mind.

Reika seemed puzzled. "That is all that you remember?" she kept asking until Tekoah wanted to scream. "He does not know that you are the Guardian—he cannot." She pondered, her black brows furrowed, and arms folded as she paced.

"Perhaps he is not in league with the others. It is said that he and Zant dislike each other. It is possible that his mission in Stern was indeed one of simple revenge against his tormentors —if revenge is ever simple. But why did he single you out in that way?"

"Mayhap he likes me," Tekoah answered, seeing with some satisfaction the bafflement in Reika's face.

It was a relief to speak of this at last—to have others know about it. She had dreamed of Braith several times, but these dreams were a secret from everyone. Reika did not need to know.

It seemed to Tekoah that she had been in this cramped chamber for days, and indeed several of the women were standing up now, stretching to ease their muscles, going over to the roots, some of which the women had hollowed out, to breathe great gulps of fresh air filtering down from the surface.

Tekoah drank from a gourd of water being handed around. Beula, who gave it to her, put her arm around Tekoah's waist, in affection, or apology, perhaps. None of this had been Beula's fault, and at least *she* cared—she had not abandoned Stern, like Mother.

I must clear my head, Tekoah thought, *I must talk to someone else about this.* She would pay a visit to Master Chalvern the very next day. He was the wisest, kindest person she knew, and would give her sound advice.

"May I leave now?" she asked, setting the gourd down on the floor. She felt like a child asking permission for some small freedom.

"For your courage and frankness, we are grateful," Reika replied, "yet there is one thing more." She spoke each word emphatically as she moved back into the centre of the circle. At this signal, the other women returned to their places, looking expectant.

Reika continued. "We believe that your life is in danger, if not now, then soon. We fear that the sorcerers Morogh and Zant both are hunting you—and us. And we fear the sorcerer Braith also, although you believe he does not wish you harm." She spoke with no trace of mockery, but Tekoah flushed in vexation.

Reika pointed to Mirveta's Basin. "We ask that you attempt to Journey. If in your heart you are Anniste, then you will Journey. If not, then you need not trouble yourself about accepting or rejecting a Guardianship, for it will no longer be yours."

Tekoah stared at the Basin, and then at Reika, unable to believe that she meant what she had just said. But Reika nodded, beckoning to her.

A dread seized hold of her limbs, transfixing them until they felt as immobile as one of the tree roots that surrounded them. To Journey had always seemed the stuff of legend, not reality. It was all very well to talk about it, but what was it *really*? A trance full of mystical revelations? Or a wild fit of raving, full of babbling, calculated nonsense at best, blasphemous pronouncements at worst?

Regardless, at the moment, the penalty was harsh—a hefty fine or imprisonment—for any meeting which involved Anniste heresy and witchcraft.

But somehow, barely aware that she had done so, Tekoah moved to the centre of the circle. She kneeled and gazed into the Basin, seeing the water murky, but not entirely dark. It was lit up somehow from within. She glanced up uncertainly, looking not for Beula, but for Reika. But just then someone extinguished the candle, and all was dark around her.

Tekoah could hear the women breathing, and their small shifting movements. The sounds frightened her, and she thought: *How do I know they are not witches, as the priests claim?* Then she felt Reika's hand on her shoulder and her fear left her. She looked down again.

The murky water had cleared, and Tekoah saw a crescent moon reflected in the centre. This could not be—it was impossible! She was under the ground, and besides, Anna was full that night. She frowned, leaning closer.

Looking at that strange moon, the familiarity of her life slipped away, like bits of dry, crumbling earth. She was falling forward, into the water, as the Basin became bigger and bigger—as big as a lake—enveloping her in a dark, rushing sensation.

She reached out for something to hold on to, but there was nothing. From far away, a woman's voice—was it Reika?—called, "Let go!" and the words echoed as she fell, clutching at empty air.

After a few more frantic moments, Tekoah obeyed the voice and surrendered. She felt herself caught up in a soft cradling warmth. She was being rocked back and forth. Nothing had ever felt so wonderful. To be held, not floating off into some vast fathomless universe. What more was there?

Tekoah heard a low, soft humming, a tune that she had not heard in years, infinitely sweet and soothing. Opening her eyes, she found she was curled up against her mother, who was walking back and forth in front of the small wood stove, rocking her as she walked. Neela sang an old Anniste lullaby:

Moon Mother brings honey
and almonds to feed you
But now you must sleep
before you can wake

She watched her mother in mute wonder, seeing her calm radiance, wondering when it was that it had faded from her smooth oval face.

Neela stopped singing, looking down at her daughter with a quizzical smile. "Ko darling, you are such an owl tonight," she murmured. "When will you close those great eyes of yours, hmm?" Her mother kissed her nose, then regarded her thoughtfully. "You look so old and wise sometimes, darling. What secrets are locked inside your tiny head?"

Tekoah looked at her mother, flooded by a wave of pure love. She snuggled close against Neela's bosom and, seeing her bare rosy toes poking out from beneath her shawl, she wiggled them experimentally. Neela chuckled and tucked her feet back inside the woolen shawl. She began to pace and hum again, staying close to the warm stove.

Tekoah became drowsy. She had been thinking about something important a moment before, but she could not remember what it was. Her eyelids felt heavy, so she closed them.

Loud footsteps drummed their way into the soft melody. She stiffened reflexively as the door was thrust open.

"Hush, Veld," she heard her mother say reprovingly. "I have just sent her off to sleep. What is it? Why do you look like that?" This was added in a different, apprehensive tone.

Tekoah opened her eyes just slightly, peeking through her eyelashes. Her father was standing in the doorway, panting hard and swaying slightly. His eyes were wild, and bloodshot, and his tunic stained. As if to belie his alarming appearance, he gave his wife a lop-sided, mirthless grin.

"What is it? Good news! They finally chased the apothecary's brat from the village. Stoned him and sent him on his way."

Tekoah felt Neela's breast heave beside her. She nestled closer, wanting to keep burrowing, to burrow right inside.

"Veld—husband—I cannot believe you would be party to this.

Young Braith has committed no crime but wishing to be left alone. To persecute a young boy like this is heinous!" She covered her face.

"I did no persecuting," Veld cut in. "I was merely watching. No one even saw me."

Neela stopped walking and lowered Tekoah into her cradle, settling her onto the soft mattress. From beneath the blanket, she saw her mother go back to stand beside her father, placing her hand on his shoulder.

"Then what is troubling you?" she asked.

"Nothing is troubling me," Veld replied, reaching into his pocket and taking out a flask. He opened it and drank a long draught. Neela stood, watching him. Wiping his mouth, Veld sullenly returned her gaze, saying, "I told you, it is good news! Good news!" he shouted. "Now stop staring at me like an Anniste witch."

"If nothing is troubling you, why are you behaving as if you are frightened?"

In the silence which followed, a sickness rose within Tekoah as she recognized that she knew what was about to happen. She lay rigid in her cradle and watched Veld turn with deceptive slowness and slap his wife fully in the face.

Neela reeled back from the force of the blow. She stumbled and fell, striking her head on a corner of the cradle. Lying stunned, lips moving soundlessly, her face was only a few inches away from her daughter.

"Mother?" Weslan's sleepy, bewildered voice came from the curtained-off chamber where the bed was.

"Be quiet!" Father barked, and there was silence.

Father reached for his flask again and took another drink. Tekoah could see his hands twitching from where he stood by the doorway.

Neela was murmuring to herself. Tekoah tried to catch the words, but even from this close she could not understand. She heard her father walking across the room, and she shut her eyes, squeezing her fingers together under the blanket.

"That brat cursed everyone who had slighted him. And when he did it, he looked straight at me, although I had hidden myself behind some trees. He must have mixed me up with someone else—I never had dealings with him. Not that I care about his curses. Who does he think he is?"

Veld's voice vibrated with fear despite his defiant words. Tekoah risked a quick look at his face and saw terror mingled with rage. She could feel Weslan listening from behind the curtain and willed him not to make a sound.

Her father was bending over her mother, panting. He leaned closer, close enough for Tekoah to smell the corn lightning on his breath. He spoke urgently, "But if the brat is mixing me up with someone else, he might start telling people lies about me. Do you understand? So if you hear any false tales being spread about, then it is your duty, as my loving wife, to defend me. Do you hear?"

Tekoah saw her mother open her eyes, and then close them again, slowly.

Her cradle was rocking back and forth, and it was very dark. She blinked and the swaying sensation stopped.

She was standing in the untilled land by the vegetable garden, behind the forge. A half-moon shone down, illuminating the rows of corn stalks; they stood like sentinels—watchful, silent.

The corn was high, the night was warm, and the sweet smell of grassberries, which she loved, rose to her nostrils. *It must be summer.* Yes, for she was so hot—she felt feverish, and there were rivulets of sweat running down her back, and between her budding breasts. She had been thinking of something only a moment earlier—what was it?

Tekoah heard a dull rhythmic thudding close by and turned

toward the sound. Veld was slapping the bottom of his iron shovel onto a mound of earth, flattening it.

"There," he said heavily. "That's done! By spring it will be all grass and clover."

Tekoah stepped back. There was something familiar about this, it was as if she had been here before. *I need to leave,* she thought. *I cannot think about this any longer.* A muffled cry escaped her, and Father looked over at the sound, startled.

"You will not break down on me now, girl, when you have been so strong?" he asked.

Tekoah could not answer him. She needed to leave. Pleadingly, she looked up at the night sky, to Anna, and on the surface of the moon she beheld the face of a woman, gazing down upon her with boundless compassion and understanding. Then she saw no more.

TEKOAH LAY with her eyes closed and breathed in the musty smell of the crohm tree. Someone was stroking her forehead with cool fingers. Was it Reika? It was, for she murmured a calm response to a question from Aunt Beula a moment later.

"Patience," Reika said. "She was not yet ready for that truth. Who knows our hearts, if not Anna? Patience."

Tekoah sat up, abruptly. She was in the centre of the circle, by the basin. Someone had lit the candles again. A blanket had been placed over her, and a pillow beneath her head. She was back. She looked at Reika, who was kneeling beside her, with those cool, healing hands, and was astonished to see her lovely face streaming with tears. She reached out in wonder to touch Reika's cheek.

She could not remember a time when anyone had ever cried for her.

CHAPTER 13

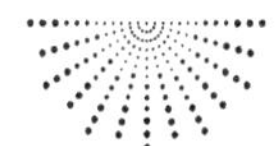

The old wooden door creaked for the tenth time in an hour. Chalvern sighed in exasperation. Why was it that only on the days that he set aside time to transcribe Anniste scrolls, did every villager in Stern suddenly decide they needed a remedy for a bruised toe or puffy eyelids? And naturally, the eyelids outnumbered the toes on the day after the Night of Masks, with all the drunken joining that had ensued. Not to mention other, more delicate complaints. He glanced up, trying to look discouraging without being downright rude.

Tekoah shut the door diffidently behind her and gave him her tremulous smile.

Chalvern straightened, smiling back at her. In her, as always, he saw her mother Neela's face, and his heart contracted with an anguish that radiated outward through his veins. Love. That was what they called it. Another kind of pain.

Neela had looked at him with that same smile, fifteen turnings earlier—the last time he had spoken to her face to face. Their words had been few, terse, and vibrating with intensity.

"I have left the Anniste."

"But why?"

"Veld forbids me. And he is my husband."

Silence.

"My husband! Do you hear?"

"You can remedy that by leaving him."

"You know I cannot, because of the children. Besides, I gave my pledge, and that is not to be taken lightly."

Harshly, "Then why are you here?"

"I do not know." Her voice cracked like a fragile bird's egg dropped from a great height. "After I returned from telling the others—the Anniste —I could not bring myself to go back to the forge. I walked and walked, but I could not stop seeing their eyes, looking at me with such reproach. When I finally looked up, I was here."

He gazed at her stonily, but she did not turn away, and after a moment he seized her arm and pulled her inside, closing the door swiftly behind them.

And Neela looked up at him, tilting her chin, smiling bravely against her fear, challenging him.

Was Tekoah his daughter? It was a question he rarely asked himself, for it thrust deep as any knife. He shook his head to clear it. This was certainly not a seemly moment to pursue the matter, for Tekoah was looking uneasily at him, and then behind her, as if deciding whether to bolt.

"Come in, come in," he said warmly. "I was just now hoping for some charming company."

"Oh, surely not, Master Chalvern"—she smiled nervously— "when you are so busy."

"Never too busy for you." Chalvern kept his voice light and busied himself with rolling up the precious Anniste scrolls and tying them with twine.

He studied Tekoah surreptitiously from beneath his lids. The girl was very pale. It was perturbing, but then everything had been so unpredictable this summer, what with Neela's disappearance, and Braith's reappearance, and the sinister news from the South.

Tekoah tugged at the long, fair braid that hung over her shoulder. She had done so since she was small whenever she was anxious. It gave Chalvern satisfaction to think he knew her habits.

"What can I do for you?" he asked.

"I need some herbs for my father's stomach; it has been very bilious of late."

And no wonder, Chalvern thought, *with all the corn lightning he drinks.*

"Certainly," he said briskly. "It will take me a half an hour to mix you an infusion of the right strength, but that is all the better, for you can sit and tell me all about your doings. We have not spoken since—" He paused, seeing the panic in her eyes.

But she finished the sentence for him, speaking clearly and firmly. "Since I was so ill."

"Yes." Chalvern turned to one of his shelves, selecting a packet of pita-powder and one of turrabalm. "But you are much better now, I see."

"I am." She sounded hesitant. "I thank you for the letter from Weslan, which you so kindly delivered the other day. I was up at the castle grounds, so I did not know you had come."

"Ah yes, I gathered that. Your father spends most of his time there now, I hear, working with the stonemason Kayne. That castle rises higher every day, does it not? But how is Weslan?"

"Very well, he says." Tekoah's face brightened perceptibly. "He is to be stationed in Rhantor for the winter, at the queen's palace. It all sounds very grand."

"And grand is just where Weslan wants to be, is it not?" Chalvern chuckled.

Tekoah laughed along with him, then sobered. "He wants us to join him."

Chalvern kept silent. Tekoah looked down at the tabletop, clasping her hands and squeezing the fingers tightly together. At last, she said, "The twins and me. And Mother, if she can be found."

Chalvern shook out the herbs he had selected into a clay mortar and trickled some honey-mint syrup over it. He began to grind the mixture into a paste, working slowly, although he wanted to pound the stone pestle into the bowl until something shattered.

He kept his voice calm. "So Weslan does not know about your mother's absence?"

"No. We were hoping it would be short-lived, and therefore no need to worry him."

"And will you leave?" Perhaps it was best.

"I do not know." Tekoah watched Chalvern grind away methodically. "There is something else."

"Ah." Chalvern put the pestle down and waited.

"I went to see my Aunt Beula last night."

"But Beula is no longer at the pony farm. She is in hiding with the other Anniste. They are in danger, and best left alone, for your sake and theirs!"

Chalvern's voice was sharper than he'd intended. But he was frightened. The last thing Tekoah needed was to get involved with the Anniste. There had been some very unsettling tales of late about the persecution of the Anniste healers.

"I went to see her in secret," Tekoah repeated, looking worried and defiant at the same time.

Chalvern cursed himself inwardly. The poor girl had enough to be afraid of, without adding him to the list. He gentled the tone of his voice. "I am sorry. Pray continue."

"We met with the other healers who are hiding inside a crohm tree."

"Inside a…what?!"

"They fear that the priests and sorcerers are planning to exterminate them."

Chalvern's hand jerked, and his pestle clattered across the

tabletop. He caught it before it hit the floor, attempting to compose his features. *Could the rumours be true?*

Tekoah was staring at him, her blue eyes immobile in her small white face.

"Go on," he said.

"The Anniste say that I am the rightful Guardian now. That my place is with them. They need me to Journey—to help save them and bring the Mantling."

"The Mantling?"

It startled Chalvern to hear her speak of this. Anniste teachings predicted the coming of the Mantling in this very turning, but few believed it. As for Chalvern, he often made the joke to his pupils that he was a devout believer in everything that had already happened.

"What has the Mantling got to do with it?" he asked in a reasonable voice. He needed to keep Tekoah's trust, because before she left his shop today, he had to convince her not to join the Anniste. At best, it would be the life of a fugitive. At worst —but he preferred not to think of that.

"The sorcerers wish to prevent the Mantling," Tekoah said. "At least two of them do. The new one—Braith—we do not know his motives yet."

Tekoah had said "we" unconsciously, and her voice had taken on the singsong cadence of the Anniste vernacular. Yet when she had mentioned Braith's name, she had faltered.

More things about which to be perturbed, Chalvern thought.

He got up, ignoring the ache in his chest and the sharper pains which shot down his calves as he stood. *Sixty turnings I will soon have seen,* he thought, *yet never did I feel old until Neela disappeared.*

He went over to the stove and poured them both some tea. "Do you wish to join the Anniste?" he asked carefully, handing her the mug.

Tekoah was silent for a time, staring down into her tea as if it held the key to some sacred mystery. When she looked up at him, her eyes were cloudy. "I do not know," she answered slowly. "I was not convinced that I belonged to the healers at all, despite Mother's legacy. But then they asked me to attempt a Journey, and I agreed."

"And what happened?"

"I Journeyed. I truly did," she insisted. "You look as if you do not believe me."

"It is not that! It is simply that the distinction between reality and dreams can be a very tricky one, my dear."

Tekoah looked nettled. "Well, if it had happened to you, you would believe it."

"Very true," Chalvern smiled. "But you have not answered my question."

"In my Journey I became convinced I am one of the Anniste, by birth and in my heart. Yet my choices are still my own. What do you think I should do, Master Chalvern?"

"I think you should go to Rhantor," Chalvern replied promptly. "By any standards, your prospects are infinitely brighter there. You must make up your own mind, of course. But since you honour me by seeking my counsel, I say go home and think about it for a day or two. Do not let the Anniste draw you in by hereditary obligation. You must think of yourself, and you have done little of that in your life."

Tekoah shrugged off his question with a self-deprecating smile. "Thank you, Master Chalvern," she said, standing up. "I will do as you suggest. And I feel a great deal better, somehow. I am able to talk to you as to no one else since Weslan and Mother were here. But I must hurry home now, before Father returns and finds me gone."

Chalvern hastily bottled the herb infusion and Tekoah put it in her woolen sack. As he saw her to the door, she turned and said in a small, wistful voice, "I wish I knew where Mother was."

"As do I," Chalvern muttered. Unable to bear looking at the grief in her eyes, he turned his face away as he closed the door.

Afterward, he swept and swept the shop floor clean, wielding his broom with fierce strokes, long after the sound of Tekoah's footsteps had faded away.

CHAPTER 14

Chalvern watched Priest Zorak's face mottle with fury. He hoped that the anger erupting like hot grease from the priest might prove detrimental to his health—along with his penchant for overeating and his reluctance to move his limbs farther than the temple or the table. He had known such combinations to stop a man's heart cold.

Zorak's plump white fist interrupted Chalvern's pleasant line of thinking by crashing down on the altar where he stood. *So much for sacred relics.*

"You show an appalling lack of respect, Master Chalvern," the priest said in his nasal voice, curling his lip around the word. "How dare you suggest I send you fledgling priests for training? Are you not capable of distinguishing between those chosen by Rhan, a glorious divine calling, and menial apprentices—whose vocation will never rise above gathering herbs, boiling potions, healing paltry mortal ailments, and birthing babes? Women's work."

Chalvern quelled his spark of outrage, refusing to waste the energy. "You strike at my very point, Zorak, when you say women's work," he answered.

He saw the priest's eyes narrow in his pudgy face and knew that his omission of the honorific title "Ray-Zorak" had hit the mark. He was no nearer to making a friend of the new priest than the old. For all his failings, Grindhor at least had not been this short-tempered and long-winded.

Chalvern walked over to the window and gazed out into the temple courtyard. The huge stone dial told him it was nearing midday, almost time for sacrifice. Villagers had gathered in anticipation, their pigeons held in cages or by the feet, their wings flapping as if they knew what was coming and sought to escape.

Like the Anniste? Chalvern thought. Well, that was what he was there to find out, if Zorak did not see through his pretext.

"Women's work…" he repeated, his back still to the priest. "But they now forbid the Anniste women to do that work. I am left to fill that vacuum—I, who know less than the most inexperienced healer." Chalvern turned away from the courtyard. "And yet no one has explained this ban to my satisfaction." He folded his arms.

"The priesthood is not obliged to explain divine instructions from Rhan," Zorak answered in a stiff voice.

"How very convenient," Chalvern said, watching the colour rise again in the priest's face. *There is something about me that irks him to no end,* he thought, amused.

"I need an assistant," he persisted. "There are not enough young men in Stern with time to spare. They are all busy in the fields, or they've joined the Kalesh, or they don't want women's work anymore than the priesthood does."

"Then let the villagers heal themselves."

"Would you have us return to the Dark Ages?" Chalvern asked, his temper flaring despite his best efforts. "Would you have everyone fend for themselves, scrabbling about in the dirt like savages? We are a community, are we not? Yet you have taken one of our foundations away, without warning. Let them fend for themselves. Is that a direct decree from the merciful Rhan onto his people?"

"Of course not!" Zorak snapped, rubbing his chin. "Do not twist my words, Chalvern." But he looked nonplussed.

Chalvern spoke urgently. "Then you must make a choice. The priesthood must move to *protect* the Anniste, so they can practice their healing arts without fear of reprisal. Damn Berlot—and damn the South for their silly superstitions and hatred of Anna. One thing we have always been proud of in the North is our independence of thought. Or am I wrong?"

Zorak's face was stony. He either would not or could not discuss the matter.

"To whom do you answer, Zorak?" Chalvern asked, feeling that he had stepped into a muddy bog, not knowing how deep he would sink.

"What are you saying? I answer to Rhan, of course. And the Patriarch."

"Yes, the doddering Head Patriarch in Rhantor, who is so addled he does not remember the rites. But he is a figurehead only. You answer to someone, I can see that. King Darian, perhaps, who is trying to stir up trouble for his sister the queen here in the North? But why would you do that? This is your home. An Anniste midwife birthed you, and I as well. Why not pay lip service to the new law and ignore it? There must be other priests throughout the North who are doing so."

"You old fool!" Zorak growled, rising to his feet again and leaning both hands on the altar, bunching up the purple cloth with the yellow sun embroidered on it. "It has been too long since you ventured from this village. Too long that you have stayed in your shop, brooding over the past."

The priest shot Chalvern a vindictive, knowing look that made him want to strike that doughy face. What right did he have? He, who fed off the work of others, like all those fat maggots who called themselves priests. He, who knew nothing of love, had never received a woman's caress he had not bought or coerced in the name of Rhan. How dare he?

Zorak was still spouting words, saliva spraying like poisonous foam. *To the Pit with it!* Chalvern thought. Never mind his grand plan to ferret out information about the fate of the Anniste—he could not bear one more moment of Zorak's presence, or he would give the man a thrashing. *Let the priests heal themselves,* he thought. And he hoped Zorak was the very next one who needed healing.

Chalvern turned to go, reaching for his thin summer cloak. But a word caught him, snagged his attention like a sharp stick protruding from the earth.

"—sorcerers," Zorak finished, looking both triumphant and aghast at the same time.

"Sorcerers?" Chalvern echoed, startled. *I have goaded him into saying something he should not have,* he thought. *Now we are getting somewhere!*

"I said you do not know the ascending power of the priesthood. Our instructions now come from the sorcerers Morogh and Zant. You must realize this is a tremendous honour and a great opportunity. For many hundred turnings, the sorcerers have deigned to do little more than accept our offerings and gifts. But now Lord Zant says that we must work together in Rhan's name, to prevent the Mantling." As he spoke, Zorak's face became transfigured. He looked ecstatic.

Chalvern responded with difficulty. His throat was dry with horror. "But the sorcerers have never done this before. Why in the world would you trust them?"

Zorak's cheeks flushed to a purple hue that matched the altar cloth he still clutched. "We will restore proper respect for the priesthood of Rhan to the heretical North!" he thundered. "This, the sorcerers have promised us. As for your outrageous request to reinstate the Anniste, let me tell you something: not one priest throughout the land would dare flout the Anniste ban. To suggest I do so is blasphemy and treason!"

So, it was true. And worse than he could have imagined. "Ah, I see," Chalvern replied. He was about to add, "And so the sorcerers have instructed the priests to annihilate the Anniste clan." But upon reflection, it seemed like a very dangerous thing to say.

"But do you see?" Zorak leaned forward pontifically, as if he was making an invocation at a sacrifice. "And did you hear what I said about blasphemy, old man? Or have you become deaf?"

The first thing I must do is stop antagonizing this priest, Chalvern thought. He made his voice hesitant, fretful. "I am old and weak, and you are also correct, Ray-Zorak, in observing that I have not ventured from Stern in many turnings. And, of course, you know much more of these matters than I. But the fact remains that I need help—I am floundering. And I doubt I will be in this realm for many more turnings, but while I am here, I wish to do what good I can." He shrugged in resignation at the prospect of his imminent demise. "Perhaps you could spare me an initiate? Of your choosing, of course. I would be grateful, and willing to express that gratitude with a generous contribution at Sacrifice. And please forgive an old man his quick temper."

Zorak looked mollified. He gazed through the open window at the crowd milling about in the courtyard. "I have heard your plea, as has Rhan," he replied, his jowls quivering. "I will consider it. Perhaps there is a fledgling or two I could spare. I could use the assignment as punishment, perhaps, for disobedience." He chuckled at the ingeniousness of his insult.

"And now, Master Chalvern"—Zorak spoke in a long-suffering voice, as if it had not been he who had ranted for an hour or more—"I must bring this interview to an end."

Chalvern left the temple, his heart hammering and his head aching; he decided he needed a long walk. Without hesitation, he headed to Stern's End, his favourite thinking spot.

It was cold and windy. A snowstorm would come soon—he could smell it in the air. The vast stands of crohm trees in the Taboran Woods were leafless now, and the beeches, with their close-knit lacy branches, looked like heaps of dark goose-feathers, piled up in cloud pillows against the sky. Sombre green pines held the only remaining colour in the Wood.

Soon, the mountain cats would begin their prowling, edging farther and farther down from the higher mountain ranges as the winter wore on; driven by hunger to seek the prey huddled in the valleys: wild ponies, livestock, unwary villagers.

But there was no snow yet, and Chalvern did not bother to stop by his shop for a thicker cloak. He needed to be moving—to think—for he had to do something. And there was very little time.

He had verified Tekoah's—bizarre—claim that the sorcerers were indeed conspiring against the healers. Therefore, it was quite plausible that they had started the rumour that the Anniste had caused the drought in the South.

Whether the mystical "Journeys" were authentic or hallucinations, the Anniste were in real danger, from both sorcerers and priests.

But why?

The priests had always envied the healers and the regard in which the people held them. They at least had an obvious motive. Sorcerers were different. They had so much power already, and they did not care whether they were popular. Could it be true that they feared the Mantling?

Chalvern himself had never thought of the prophecy as more than a tale of comfort to the Anniste, though he enjoyed reading about it in the scrolls. The Mantling sounded so thrilling and majestic, in a "sweeping-the-slate-clean" way. The thought that one day sorcerers might no longer terrorize ordinary people! But it was all a dream.

Another question followed the first, making him shudder:

where was Braith in all this? He could not bear to think about it, not yet.

Chalvern passed the forge, glancing into the yard to see if Tekoah was about. He saw nothing but the telltale wisp of smoke that showed Veld was sober enough to work that day. At the next bend, he veered sharply off the highway, heading down the well-beaten path to Stern's End.

Who else had been a party to this monstrosity? he wondered. King Darian, most likely. The sorcerer Zant had publicly befriended him, attending his coronation and thereafter remaining at his side as his advisor. People said that Zant had been behind all those speeches about "Rhan's fiery wrath cleansing the land" with which King Darian had been bombarding his subjects, ever since the drought swooped down on the South.

All this was alarming, for sorcerers did not fraternize much with ordinary folk—it was beneath them. Morogh had certainly never deigned to do so.

North Miraveners speculated about Morogh's Source, and his solitary existence in a fabled abode deep in the Taboran hills. Many said it was a lodge built of a curious black stone. Chalvern thought this might be true, for obsidian, the lava stone, was rare and expensive, in keeping with Morogh's arrogance. The sorcerer himself seldom appeared in public, and few could boast of having seen him, although he was over two hundred turnings old.

Chalvern had seen Morogh, though. Once, when he was a child, and he had never forgotten it.

He had been with his parents in Rhantor. They had travelled by mountain pony and cart, a thrilling five-day journey, to attend King Garan's coronation. They had stood among the jostling, colourful crowds outside the palace gates, waiting for a glimpse, not of the ceremony—they were too far away for that—but of the King himself, afterward. He had promised to come out to the palace balcony and wave to the crowd, wearing his crown of the finest Berlotan gold.

Young Chalvern had been among the first to spot him: the bright coronet glinting in the sun, indigo cape billowing in the summer breeze, wheat coloured hair, not curled or otherwise dressed, but simply tied back. The sight of his monarch had filled Chalvern with a glory he had been sure would sustain him all his days, if only he could keep the precious memory intact. But then something else had happened, the memory of which would blot out the first, as a shadow blots out light.

The guards had opened the palace gates without warning, the crowd surging about in helpless confusion.

Soldiers had appeared on the ramparts, their faces flustered. "Make way!" one had shouted, the others echoing it. "Make way for the Lord sorcerer Morogh!"

Morogh had evidently emerged from seclusion for the coronation. Chalvern had been wild with curiosity. As the crowd had parted, he thrust his face forward, trying to catch a glimpse of the sorcerer.

It was meant to be another element of excitement, something else to inscribe onto the tablet of his coronation day recollections. He had looked up to see the sorcerer's white stallion, eyes rolling at the crowd. Morogh held the reins tightly though, so there was no danger of his mount bolting or rearing. The sorcerer had looked neither to the left or the right, but had ridden straight through, his muscular body at odds with the white tufts of hair sticking up over his ears.

Squirming his wiry frame to the front of the crowd, Chalvern had crouched precariously, gazing wide-eyed at the sorcerer, thinking those white tufts of hair looked almost comical. But only for a moment. Then, he had stumbled over a peasant's enormous foot, falling directly in Morogh's path.

He had heard his mother shriek, and several people shouting, "Stop—a child!" and things of that sort.

Morogh had indeed stopped, looking down at the cowering boy who was lying a few yards in front of him, too dazed to roll out of the way. Chalvern had seen the eyes looking down at him, narrowing and widening, cat-like. The tip of his tongue had come out to lick his thick, dark lips.

Then, very deliberately, the sorcerer had ridden over the boy in a flurry of hooves and horrified screams from the crowd.

Chalvern had suffered a broken arm and several shattered ribs, one puncturing his lung; and had almost died of a lung fever. Fortunately, his mother had been Anniste.

Why was he thinking of this now, when he had not thought of it for so many turnings? Because he had learned first-hand more than all the rumours and legends of sorcerers could ever teach him.

They were ruthless and cared no more for people than for flies.

And he had to admit something else, as he held up the tremulous candle to the recesses of his memories: he was frightened. Not only for the Anniste, but for himself. He was becoming involved, something that he had avoided ever since the day that Morogh's steed had crushed him almost to death. His small boy's voice had cautioned him throughout his life—*do not enter the fray or they will hurt you!*

And who was better at hurting than sorcerers? Except for Braith—or so he hoped. The delusional hope of a tired old man, his other self—the young one who danced in circles around him in his mind—mocking him. But he could not permit himself to think about Braith right then. There was too much else to think about.

Morgogh and Zant were devoid of any feelings for their fellow humans. But Zant had not distanced himself from people as Morogh had. *Why?*

Too many questions, and where were the answers? Sunk

deep in murky water, perhaps, as the stones which he was now skipping into the pond at Stern's End?

Chalvern threw the last pebble from his handful and then squatted down a little, watching the loons he had frightened away come back to settle on the water. Their mournful cries reassured each other that the madman had subsided.

Madman. Chalvern's mind leaped to Veld, as it always did at that word, and then back with clutching foreboding to Tekoah. He thought of her as his daughter, although he would have admitted this to no one, not even if they had pulled every aching tooth from his head. It was a small reward, this dream of a daughter, for the woman he had lost. Perhaps she was his daughter.

Neela's daughter, at any rate. And an Anniste Guardian, by blood. Was she in danger—had the sorcerers discovered who she was? *Braith did not know when he first saw Tekoah,* Chalvern thought, *or he would have mentioned it. Does he know now?*

But Braith was so very wrong for the girl, regardless of his feelings for her. It was imperative that she leave, and soon. With a kind person who would take her away from Veld—someone like that Garth lad, who had left Stern without explanation.

A suspicion dawned. Chalvern shook his head. What pitfalls lay ahead for Tekoah? If only Neela were here, she could guide her daughter.

Chalvern could not seem to shake his thoughts of Neela. His past was stalking him like a grey shadow. Strange how some days were such, and others were free of everything but the simple need to be.

His legs became cramped as the late afternoon grew colder, and so he stopped squatting and stood. His head felt no clearer, but he knew one thing. He had to speak to Tekoah and warn her that there was great danger for her in associating with the Anniste.

As Chalvern thought this, although he had made no movement or sound, the cluster of loons that had been bobbing placidly along the water rose in unison, a flurry of gleaming black feathers screeching in alarm. Chalvern wheeled around, knowing instinctively there was someone behind him.

And, of course, it was Braith.

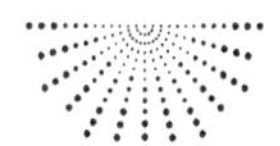

CHAPTER 15

Braith's sudden appearances were getting on Weslan's nerves. Not that he would have dared to even hint as much. Although the two of them had been friends for weeks, he still found the sorcerer daunting at times.

But this time, he gritted his teeth when he looked up to see Braith grinning sardonically at him as he lolled back in the marble bath—a recent addition to the luxurious suite of rooms allotted to him by the queen.

Rhan's Name! Some things are private.

"From the look of bliss on your face, I would judge you had a good night," Braith said.

Weslan sat up with an abrupt movement, covering his crotch with his hands. As he did, he realized how ridiculous he must look, and his face grew hot.

"It was well enough," he answered. He fumbled about for a bath sheet.

Braith stood, reaching beneath him, and threw him one. "Small praise for a noble lady."

An angry retort sprang to Weslan's lips, but he bit it back. *I must allow Braith a bit of teasing,* he thought. "I shall not bore you with the details of my evening," he said, forcing a smile. "How was the Night of Masks for you?"

Braith picked an invisible speck from the sleeve of his black tunic. "Uneventful, compared to yours, I would wager. I produced a display of thunder sparks for the crowd at the waning of the moon. They were duly impressed."

"That is all?" Weslan could not resist a bit of his own bantering. "You must have had your pick of partners afterward!"

Braith did not rise to the bait. "None ignited enough interest to make it worthwhile donning a mask." His voice was brooding.

Weslan observed Braith as he toweled himself off. Did sorcerers ever find anyone who held their interest? It was not a question he dared to ask, although they had spoken of many other sensitive matters with a frankness that Weslan would never have hitherto imagined.

His thoughts meandered. *Why are there no female sorcerers?* he wondered, then answered himself. *Because Rhan has decreed women incapable of handling power or authority.* What a foolish question. Had he learned nothing from the teachings of the priests?

Regarding the concept of romantic passion, he concluded that joining did not hold a fragment of the interest for sorcerers that it did for mortals. The thought brought him back to the glorious present.

"All joking aside"—he stood, wrapping the bath sheet around his waist—"once more I wish to offer my thanks, Braith. Without you, none of this would have happened."

"Do not be so sure." The moodiness had vanished, and Braith smiled at him again, his teeth flashing white in his sun-bronzed face. "Perhaps I only sped things along."

"That is not true! I hope you know I will never forget this. I only wish there was something I could do for you."

Braith went over to the window, a luxury in the palace chambers, and a symbol of the favour in which Queen Darielle held

Weslan. "Be sure that I will not hesitate to let you know," he said over his shoulder. He flung open the white painted shutters and leaned out. "However, it seems I am about to lend you my help once again."

A wind gusted its way into the room, raising goosebumps on Weslan's arms. With it came the unmistakable scent, wild and desolate, of impending winter. He shivered.

As Weslan dressed, Braith asked from the window, "Do you remember that I pledged you two things on the day we found the foal?"

Weslan straightened. "Yes," he said. He remembered everything about that day.

"One was that I would help you, if I could, to win the love of your queen."

"Yes." Hearing the words spoken aloud, he looked away.

"The other thing—"

"The other thing?" Weslan echoed, his heart sinking.

Braith turned around to face him, slapping his gloved hands together. "I promised to watch over your sister and tell you if she was in trouble."

Weslan's mouth had become parched. "Has something happened to Tekoah?"

"Not yet, but it is about to," Braith said. "We must go to Stern at once. Together."

Weslan stared at him. All his visions of endless euphoric moments with his queen, his love—filled with moonlight and flowers, wine and laughter—vanished, flying out the open window where Braith stood, leaving behind only the barren scent of winter.

Sitting on her gilded throne, looking both regal and fragile, Queen Darielle granted Weslan dar Veld a temporary leave from the Queen's Guard, so that he could attend to urgent family matters in the village of Stern.

She spoke in a measured voice, but her doe eyes shone with tears as she held out her hand for his kiss. And when Lady Saura averted her cold, watchful gaze for a moment, Darielle whispered, "Return to me soon."

Riding out of the courtyard at dawn, Weslan turned his head, guided by a tug on his heart.

And there she was. Standing by a turret on the upper balcony of the north wing, leaning against the balustrade. Wearing a thin ivory nightdress and no cloak, though the wind whistled about the battlements, she waved to him from above in an impulsive, girlish gesture.

All his unspoken proclamations of love for her crowded up in his throat, threatening to choke him.

If only there had been more nights together. But there could be no self-pity. Weslan wrapped his fur cloak tighter around his shoulders. He would warm himself with cherished memories as he and Braith traversed the Taboran Mountains where winter crouched, waiting to leap upon the North.

"Never frighten me like that again!" Darielle had commanded, after he had woken up bellowing from that awful dream. "Or next time I shall stuff a pillow down your throat."

Next time. Sweet promises of many nights to come—but there had only been a few more stolen times together. *Will there be more nights?* Weslan wondered. *Or will she forget me as soon as my horse is out of sight?*

"If she loves you, she can do without you for a few days," Braith had told him, in a remote and unyielding tone. But what did Braith know of love, of passion? Like a thirst that could not be slaked, but kept returning tenfold greater each time.

However, turning things around, what did Weslan know of sorcerers?

Braith had instructed Weslan to meet him in front of an inn situated where the city's boundaries ended and the North Taboran highway began. The innkeeper of the Umbray's Bane watched them with narrowed eyes from the front window as he rode up.

Braith sat on his stallion, eyes watchful. "Ready, then?" he asked Weslan, spurring his horse forward in a trot.

A mountain pony frisked behind the sorcerer, the end of the lead rope on her halter looped about Braith's wrist. When her honey-sweet eyes rested on Weslan, she whinnied.

It cannot be! he thought.

And yet it *was* their foal—fully-grown by some strange sorcery. When he glanced at Braith in wonderment, the sorcerer gave an almost imperceptible nod.

She was a real thoroughbred, from the looks of it, delicate and strong, her tawny flanks freckled with small black spots, just as they should have been. She had kept her pleasant disposition and, although small, looked to be a lovely mount for a small rider. But that did not explain her presence.

"What did you do that for?" Weslan sputtered in confusion. "And why is she coming with us?"

"I thought she might make a gift for your sister," Braith said. "Did you not tell me she loves to ride?"

"Yes, she does—she could ride before she could walk—but so does every girl in the North!" Weslan stood up in his stirrups, irritated.

"Also, if she is to return with us," Braith said in a reasonable tone, "she will need a mount."

"Yes, but would not a serviceable mule have been a simpler choice?"

"Perhaps."

Braith's cryptic reply made Weslan feel like a fool, and his ill humour mounted. He thought Braith had presumed in deciding they should present Tekoah with this extravagant gift. Such a gesture toward a young, unmarried girl would in most circumstances be improper.

But he supposed sorcerers had their own rules.

"Why do you bother riding?" he asked Braith, trotting up so that they were abreast on the wide highway. "Why not just wave, or snap your fingers? We could be in Stern in the blink of an eye. We will be fortunate if the snows do not slam us with a vengeance when we cross the Taboran Mountains."

Braith looked at him. "You possess little knowledge of sorcerers."

Weslan sat in his saddle, growing smaller by the moment.

Braith raised his eyebrows quizzically and waited.

"Well, of course not!" Weslan retorted, reaching for the scraps of his dignity. "You are the first one I have ever met, and you so seldom talk about yourself. So how could I?"

Braith's smile was chilly. "Ah, but some make it their business, a pastime of sorts, to study us. We are such fascinating aberrations, after all. Now then, if you had been a scholar, you would know that sorcerers do not wield unlimited powers, waiting to be tapped like water from a waterfall. Use of our power ages us, therefore we must not waste it."

"But you changed the pony and made her full-grown," Weslan protested. "And you have appeared out of nowhere several times."

"The pony was easy," Braith said, "because she *wanted* to grow up, so it took very little power to help her along. As for my sudden appearances: *light travelling,* as we call it, takes little energy when it is for ourselves alone. But to carry another is something else again. One must marshal an external energy, binding it by sheer force of will, so that it does not scatter into oblivion. I could do it, but I would age soon afterward. Whereas a few days of riding is excellent for the health."

There was a long pause. "You are looking rather pale," Braith observed.

"It was that 'scatter into oblivion' part," Weslan muttered. "It makes me rather dizzy to think about it."

They rode on in an uncomfortable silence, the filly trotting obediently behind them, stepping high with her dainty hooves, dark nostrils quivering with delight.

BRAITH BROKE the silence when they stopped around midday to feed and water the horses. "Was Lady Saura present when you said your farewells to the queen?" he asked.

"Yes," Weslan replied. "Why do you ask?"

Braith shrugged and put a nosebag on the pony. There had been something forbidding about him that day. It had daunted Weslan, preventing him from asking too many questions, although he was bursting with them. But now a spark flared within him.

"Listen, Braith," he said hotly, "I have the right to some answers. After all, you dragged me away at a moment's notice. I feel as if I were a child playing blind-man-in-the-barn: I keep bumping into things that I do not know."

Braith's mouth quirked up. In the cold air, the horses' nostrils steamed as they chewed their grain. "What is it you wish to know?" he asked. "I have already told you that your sister is in danger. And you have confided to me your vow to help her escape from your miserable childhood home. You are keeping that promise now."

"That is true," Weslan said. He stared at Braith, trying to keep resentment from his voice. "But I wanted to wait until I was a man of means to set my family up in style. Surely, I had the right to pick my own time, unless something dreadful has happened. If so, am I not permitted to know what it is? From what danger are we rescuing my sister?"

Braith looked back at him, silent.

"It is my father, I imagine," Weslan went on, refusing to back down. "But then where is Mother? She has always protected Tekoah as much as possible. And what has Lady Saura to do with this?"

Braith slipped the nosebag off the pony's nose and took up the lead as he swung onto his stallion's back. "Your mother is no longer living in Stern," he said flatly.

Weslan stared, stunned. Braith continued to speak.

"I heard this from someone reliable —Chalvern the apothecary. As for the Lady Saura, that is a conversation for another hour. Sometimes," he concluded, "it is better to keep the blindfold on. Pray permit me to ponder on this, Weslan, and we will talk more."

Braith would not talk about anything but the weather after that. However, he appeared to be thinking deeply, and his stormy countenance was unsettling. Weslan berated himself for the glib assumption that he was on intimate terms with the sorcerer.

He tried to fathom things out on his own but had little luck. Everything was such a muddle. He ran his formal leave taking of Darielle in the throne room over and over in his mind, but he had no recollection of anything beyond the feverish looks exchanged by lovers. He also scoured his memory for something significant that Saura might have said, but he recalled nothing more than trivialities. *So, you hail from Stern—where all the poor little Anniste healers have flocked? Their last stronghold, poor things. Braith is from Stern also, is he not?*

Inane chatter, though it was at odds with Saura's cold grey gaze. Her eyes were like mountain peaks in winter.

Weslan stared at the three peaks of Tabor as he and Braith rode. *Where is Mother?* he wondered, still reeling. *Did she finally break away?*

But there was no point in trying to decipher this. He had to concentrate on the present.

As if a god had heard his thoughts, the first winter snowflakes landed on his shoulders, feather-soft, melting almost at once. But they had been climbing for the past hour, heading for the mountain pass, and Weslan knew that higher up the snow would not melt so fast.

In less than three days, he would be in Stern. Home. It had never been a haven. Every time he thought about it, he became so anxious that he wanted to turn his horse's head around and ride back toward Rhantor at a full gallop.

An hour later, Braith signalled a halt. The snow was falling thickly now, and it covered the sorcerer's cloak and turned his long black hair white. They turned off the path, and Weslan saw Braith had found a cave.

He had no doubt used his sorcery to do this, which had then aged him by exactly one minute, Weslan thought. A hair or two on his magnificent head might have gone grey. *Must be nice to have things so easy.*

They tethered their horses under the shelter of an immense fir tree, but brought the pony to the mouth of the cave where she could sleep on the fragrant green needles. Of unspoken accord, they treated her as they had when they had found her, as tenderly as a small child. Weslan hoped Braith felt as he did, that the pony was the symbol and seal of their friendship. In that moment, he was not so certain.

Their cold meal of roast venison and bread was not the worst repast, when washed down with flasks of ale. However, Weslan thought of the roaring fireplace in the eating room of the tavern. He shivered. A crackling fire would have been an excellent thing —if only he was not too tired to make one, his fingers and brain numb with the cold.

"Can you not conjure up a fire somehow?" he asked Braith.

Braith chewed for a moment, then replied, "It is dangerous to rely on anything else but hard-won skills unless absolutely necessary. I have told you that using our power ages sorcerers. It is a lesson from the gods: do not take shortcuts unless you must. And by the way, I did not use sorcery to find this cave." He smiled as he said this, but the rebuke stung Weslan.

Outside, a wind began to blow in earnest. The pony whinnied and stood up, circling several times before lying back down in the brush. There were answering whinnies from the other two horses.

"While I am learning lessons," Weslan said pointedly, "perhaps you could tell me why it mattered to you whether Lady Saura was present when I took leave of the queen."

"Lady Saura is in league with the sorcerer Zant." Braith's voice was quiet, but danger prickled like hot needles at Weslan's neck.

Zant. Even the name carried menace. So that was why Braith had insisted Weslan meet him far away from prying eyes, and that he disclose to no one he was travelling with Braith.

"I have heard those rumours," he replied, trying to appear knowing, so that Braith would keep talking to him. "But even if Saura is Zant's accomplice, why would she care that I am going to Stern?"

Braith paused a long moment. He leaned forward, snapping his fingers toward the pony. She opened her eyes and lifted her upper lip delicately to take a bread crust from his hand. "Because Zant is bent on the extermination of the Anniste."

"What? Extermination? You mean death?" Braith nodded without looking at him.

"But why?"

"BECAUSE IF THE ANNISTE DIE, then the sorcerers will not."

"But why should the sorcerers have to die?"

"Have you heard of the Mantling?" Braith asked.

"Of course."

"Do you believe in it?"

Weslan snorted. "No. It is Anniste nonsense. Old women tell stories such as these to pass the time while they make quilts in the winter. No one but the children believe it."

"Zant believes it," Braith said, brushing crumbs off his gloves. "And he also believes, as does Morogh, that by killing the Anniste they can prevent the Mantling."

"But how? I don't understand."

"It is rather complicated," Braith agreed.

"But I still don't know why it matters to us," Weslan said.

"Zant could not enlist my wholehearted support in his endeavour," Braith said. "And with Zant, if you are not with him, you are against him. He will suspect me of going to Stern to aid the healers. We know that most of the Anniste of the North are hiding in the area."

"Oh." Weslan digested this for a moment. He had not understood that sorcerers could be at odds in such a way. It sounded very sinister, especially if one was caught in the middle.

"Oh," he said again, and then winced at how stupid he sounded. "Well, perhaps you could tell him you are helping me and my sister."

"—who is Anniste." Braith's tone chilled Weslan more than the gathering snowstorm.

"Tekoah is not Anniste!" he protested, laughing. He stopped as silence met his words. It was quite dark now, and he could not see Braith's face. There was a sick lurch in his stomach.

"Your mother Neela was the Guardian, was she not?"

"Yes, but she renounced it years ago."

"So that makes your sister next in line as Guardian."

"I am not certain that it does," Weslan answered, holding with an effort a tremor from his voice. "I pay little attention to these women's matters. And even if they had appointed her to this dubious role, Tekoah would not accept the Guardianship. She is much too timid."

"You may know it," Braith said sardonically, "but Zant does not." Shadowed by darkness, he took off his cloak and spread it beneath him, lying back, his arms tucked behind his head. At moments such as these, it was again hard to believe that Braith was a sorcerer. But not when he spoke of such frightening matters. And his deep voice, with its slight rasp, had a strange, primitive quality that was unsettling.

"According to Zant and Morogh," Braith said from the darkness, "the need to exterminate the Anniste is tantamount—superseding anything else—for if the Anniste are extinguished, the Goddess Anna's power is diminished, and this will prevent the Mantling. Thus, sorcerers will continue their rule, undeterred, for another seventeen hundred turnings."

"But Tekoah is not Anniste!" Weslan shouted, his voice echoing in the small cave. Outside, his horse whinnied. "You just told me that the other sorcerers could not enlist your support. Does that mean you oppose them?" He strained forward, bruising his knees on the sharp stones beneath, as he waited for the reply.

"Yes." There was a resounding intensity in Braith's voice.

"Why? Do you not wish to live for hundreds of turnings?"

"No, I do not. It is a hideous thought to contemplate. Besides, sorcerers can be killed, so there is no guarantee of life for anyone in this world. But I do not intend to die this turning, either. And nor do I believe that Zant and Morogh realize the enormity of what they are attempting. One should not tamper with the gods, even if one is a sorcerer."

After a few moments wherein he kneeled in a state of utter panic, his brain racing, Weslan decided he believed Braith's words. If the sorcerer had known about Tekoah being Anniste, he could have killed her long before.

I must place my trust in him, Weslan thought. *What choice do I have?*

At that moment, the full import of Braith's words struck

him. "So, it is from Zant and Morogh whom we must rescue Tekoah, and not my father."

"Yes. But was your father not enough of a danger?" Braith asked, his voice sharp.

Weslan ignored it. He was shuddering with guilt. For the first time, he allowed his thoughts to be entirely about his sister.

Tekoah—hopeful, shy, drifting along in her own world; wanting nothing as fiercely as he did. The little poet, shunning anyone who came too close, with her wide eyes and her way of smiling and nodding, when in fact her mind was far away where no one could capture it. How unfair, if she was to die for a cause she had never embraced.

And I fancied myself a hero, he mocked himself, *striding in to sweep Tekoah away—and Mother.*

A fresh horror seized him.

"What about Mother?" he asked, turning to where Braith lay in the darkness. "Is she in danger?"

Braith's voice came back to him in the gloom, like a sword scraping against bark. "Of your mother, I have no knowledge. You asked me to watch your sister."

It was too dark, both within and without. The blackness threatened to engulf Weslan in its void.

He wanted to stand up and move, but the space was too small to do anything but lie down or crouch. Weslan stared into the whirling vortex of snowflakes outside the cave, and for a moment he thought he glimpsed eternity. It was a game he had played as a child. Stare at anything for long enough and eternity beckoned in ever-widening rings, and one slipped toward it, then pulled oneself back from the brink, just in time.

But this was an eternity of nothing making sense, each event as disconnected as a single snowflake. How had he ever imagined that his life was being woven together like a thing of beauty? It was the opposite—everything was scattering apart. He must have been dreaming—a fool's dream.

Weslan covered his face again. Tekoah. He had neglected her, but at least he could save her now—with Braith's help. And then he would search for Mother, and Braith might protect her as well.

A frightening thought struck him. What if Braith had not befriended him? There would have been nothing he could have done to save his sister against sorcerers. *Nothing.*

Perhaps everything *was* woven together, after all. Weslan burrowed himself in his cloak and slid his aching body down onto the mat of boughs.

"Thank you," he mumbled to Braith. "I thank you." Braith lay beside him in the darkness and did not reply.

CHAPTER 16

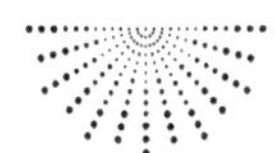

$\mathcal{T}$ekoah could smell snow in the air, although the day was clear. An achingly blue sky provided a brilliant backdrop to the castle, and its bleached stone turrets jutted upward like envious fingers reaching for the colour. A verse formed within her mind.

"What are you gaping at?" Veld barked, making her jump. "Hurry up! Dump off the food and get home with you before Kayne sees you and starts on again about that puling son of his!"

Tekoah hastily set her basket on the ground, where Raol and Fanco circled around it like hungry umbrays. They were at the new castle, the only one for a hundred miles around. It perched on the hilltop above Stern's End, part of the holdings of the lord of Mirrand. It was the first time she had ever seen the castle so close, but like everyone else in Stern, she had watched from a distance for the past two turnings as it rose—slow but steady—from its foundations.

The first stone castle in the North, besides the palace in Rhantor, of course. Another reason for Stern to be proud.

Stonemasonry was something new in these parts, as Master

Chalvern had taught them. In the past, it had been yet another reason for South Raveners to look down their noses at the backward northerners from across the Taboran Mountains.

The Master Stonemason Kayne was therefore a man to command respect with. Born in the North, he had lived in the South for several turnings, learning his trade. "Never wanted to stay there, though," he would often say, spitting on the ground for emphasis. "Southerners cannot hold their pitaya wine, and they cannot ride properly. How do they deserve our respect?"

He had bided his time, he liked to tell anyone who would listen. Waited for a chance to return home. And when old King Garan had died, the opportunity had come like a gift from Rhan. When the King had proclaimed his last wishes: that his son Darian take the throne in the South, and his daughter the throne in the North, Darielle had wasted no time in commissioning a palace in Rhantor. A stone palace, for she would not live in a barbaric castle of wood. In an uncharacteristic state of obstinance, she had refused to leave Meed until it had been completed.

The stonemason Kayne had secured the commission, obliterating his several competitors because he had promised to do it in half a turning. As a northerner, Kayne had known what the others did not: that they could use rocks from the white halestone right in Rhantor. No need to waste time quarrying it from deep within the Taboran Mountains.

Yes, Kayne had told Tekoah more than once, he knew the North. And with the palace at Rhantor, he had made his reputation.

And then, two turnings ago, the mysterious young lord of Mirrand, whom no one had seen since he was a boy, had ordered a stone castle built on his lands just outside of Stern. The subject of lord of Mirrand and his castle vied with the sorcerer Braith as the principal topics of interest that were bandied about in the Pitaya Pit. Villagers ventured out to gaze at the hilltop, wondering aloud when the young lord of Mirrand would come home to his castle, if ever.

Tekoah herself had heard several tales about the lord of Mirrand: he was disfigured, and had been hidden away until his father's death, and he would now return to his impregnable stone fortress and spend the rest of his days in seclusion; he was really the *Lady* of Mirrand, who refused to marry, but wanted to live in peaceful seclusion; he was a Berlotan spy, who would assist the Jinta in a surprise attack, and watch the land pillaged and burned from behind his stone ramparts.

Whoever the lord of Mirrand was, he could be nothing but pleased with Master Kayne's handiwork, Tekoah thought, looking admiringly at the round stone keep, pierced with curious loopholes.

"What are those holes for, Father?" she asked, pointing.

Veld had snatched a loaf of bread from the basket and stood, ripping pieces off and shoving them into his mouth. He ignored her question.

As the only blacksmith close enough to the castle to be there at a moment's notice, Veld had made a good profit from smelting and repairing iron tools, without which the stonemasons could not work. "This castle would never have risen were it not for me," he would often boast to Tekoah after his evening's drinking had commenced.

Raol mimed an arrow flying, and Tekoah nodded at him. Of course—the holes were for arrows. But it was sad to imagine such a lovely place under siege. Instead, she pictured the castle occupied in peacetime, soldiers marching in a dignified parade around the sentry walk, the drawbridge opening to admit throngs of brilliantly dressed nobles, the men riding white Berlotan geldings, the ladies' splendid mountain ponies. And she, Tekoah, standing on the gallery, silken cape billowing in the breeze—

"Oh, Rhan's stinking fire, here he comes again!" Veld exclaimed through his half-chewed bread.

Master Stonemason Kayne was indeed approaching them, his round cheeks apple-red in the stiff wind. He wore a green felt cap jammed down over his ears. Despite the grey hair falling to his shoulders, he looked like a plump, earnest schoolboy.

"Midday mealtime, eh, Veld?" he asked. "Sorry, should have thought to have some extra victuals brought to the workers. But as usual, there was no time for thinking at all this morning."

Veld inclined his head several times, snatching off his cap and then putting it back on again. "Quite all right, Master Stonemason," he answered. "Only, all this fresh air gives a man an appetite. Things are different inside the forge—where the fumes can get inside a man's brain." He laughed as if at some hilarious jest, his shoulders shaking with mirth.

Kayne looked at Veld for a moment, as if unsure how to continue, then went ahead. "Did you hear the news? About the death of the sorcerer Morogh?" he asked.

Morogh's death had been on everyone's tongue that morning.

Tekoah watched her father's face for a reaction. Veld stopped laughing abruptly and nodded at Kayne, grimacing with a knowing expression in the way he did at the mention of sorcerers. Tekoah busied herself with setting out the ale and the seed cakes and then folded the cloth and put it back inside the basket. She hoped Kayne had not noticed her. Now if she could just slip away...

Kayne and Veld had finished speculating on the sordid details of Morogh's death and were talking about a tool which had broken. Tekoah turned away, waving a hand in farewell to the twins.

"Tekoah, lass!" Kayne called.

She looked around. Behind Kayne, her father made a hideous

face at her, so that she had a wild urge to laugh; although nothing was funny about it. Nothing at all.

"Yes, Master Stonemason?" she answered, dropping a curtsy.

"You have not heard from my boy Garth now, have you?"

"No, sir." She looked at the ground.

"Strange," Kayne mused, staring at her. "He talked of nothing but you, day and night. Then he just up and left. No word at all. Frankly, I am worried. At first, I just thought it was a boy's lark, but now I am not so sure. You did not break his heart now, did you? Sent him packing?"

Kayne's voice had become colder, and Tekoah looked to her father for help. But Veld pretended not to hear and was stooping down to examine a chisel. Raol and Fanco were also walking away, back to help with the last of the stone-cutting for the northern wall.

Tekoah wrung her hands together, fretting that she looked guilty, although she had done nothing wrong.

"Did you?" Kayne repeated. "Because if you did, or if there is something you are not telling me, girl—"

She stared up at the wooden squirrel-cage which was turning around, hauling the stones to the top of the wall. Why did she allow herself to be harangued in this way? There must be some dignified response she could make. What would Reika say?

"Kayne, do not tell me you have nothing better to do than badger poor little country girls?" The voice that cut in was unfamiliar. But it was without a doubt the voice of a noble, cultured to sound bored, amused, careless, and masterful all at the same time.

Tekoah looked up in astonishment. Kayne was sinking down to one knee in a bow reserved for the aristocracy. Beside them, a young man sat on a snowy-white palfrey. He was grinning playfully—not at Kayne, but at her.

"My lord, this is a great honour!" Kayne was saying, his voice sounding not at all honoured, but shaken, and a little reproachful. "But if only you had told me you were coming, I could have better prepared for you. A fire in the main hall, a small repast—but I had not expected this honour."

"I like to take people by surprise," the lord of Mirrand answered, still smiling at Tekoah. "One learns so much more, don't you find?"

Tekoah was at a loss on how to behave, but she calmed herself and curtsied. Out of the corner of her eye, she saw Veld gape, a thread of saliva hanging from one corner of his mouth. She wished, disloyally, that this elegant young lord would not discover that Veld was her father.

"So, do you approve of my castle?" the lord of Mirrand asked her, speaking as though they were alone in an intimate alcove of the Pitaya Pit.

HE WAS DRESSED in a green tunic and breeches and wore a rich rust-coloured cloak that picked up the auburn glints in his hair. His eyes were thick-lashed and hazel. He was very handsome—almost beautiful, Tekoah thought. Someone who never got his hands dirty.

"Yes, my lord," she replied. "Although it is the only castle I have ever seen, I am sure it will surpass any other."

"Well then, when I have furnished it fit for a lady's eyes, you must come and see it from the inside." He smiled, showing even white teeth.

Tekoah could see both Kayne and her father looking at her in that appraising way men had. What was the stonemason thinking? *Heartless slut, to break his son's heart and then flirt shamelessly with a great lord?*

She also wondered what her father was thinking, then decided it did not matter. But the three pairs of eyes on her were something she could not bear for one second longer.

"I must go now—please excuse me!" she blurted, turning

away and beginning a swift trot down the hill, lifting her skirts to aid her speed.

"What is your name?" the lord of Mirrand called after her, as if he was any village lad.

"Tekoah," she answered over her shoulder. She stumbled on a pebble, righting herself. She saw the lord smile, but he did not seem to be laughing at her.

"I would remember you anyway," he said, pointing upward. "Your eyes are like two bits of blue sky peeking out when all the rest is covered by clouds."

Tekoah hugged those words to herself that night as she lay in her cot. A compliment. Spoken by a lord. Something a poet or a minstrel might've said.

Norah would laugh if she heard. *Watch out, pigeon,* she would giggle. *All he wants is a joining.* But that was not true. He had been kind. And his eyes were so warm, like melting honey.

She would ask Master Chalvern when she saw him next—he had lived in Stern forever. He had to know something of the mysterious lord of Mirrand.

Mayhap she would dream about him that night.

Tekoah did dream that night, but not about the lord of Mirrand. She lay in bed, twisting and turning for hours on her straw mattress. She propped herself up on an elbow to stare at the banked coals of the fire, and the hulking shapes of the twins curled together on the floor, covered by a rough woollen quilt.

A few days earlier, she had determined to leave the village. Chalvern had advised her to do so, and his advice was sound. Even if there had been no danger for the Anniste, there was nothing for her in Stern. She could not shield the twins from Father—she never had done anything for them other than nurse their wounds and cook their meals.

Only Mother had shielded them, and Mother was not coming back. Tekoah had sensed this with a terrible certainty, ever since her Journey.

As for Father, he was becoming ever more difficult to handle. His fits were wilder, more prolonged, and there was no reasoning with him. It was a wonder he pulled himself together to do any work at all. It was his pride, she supposed. That stubborn streak of unyielding defiance, which Weslan had inherited. Tekoah wished she had more pride.

Then mayhap she would not now be daydreaming about the lord of Mirrand, treasuring his words like a child who holding an unexpected gift.

When is he coming to take possession of his castle? she wondered. If by then she had left Stern, would he notice? Would he care?

She heard her father muttering and moaning behind the curtain. *He will not bother me tonight,* she thought with relief.

She dreaded those nights. Veld would sneak stealthily for someone so intoxicated, but she always heard him. It was after the twins were asleep, of course. Usually she was dozing, or desperately feigning sleep.

Tekoah knew Father missed Mother. At first, it had been her excuse for him. He was just getting her mixed up with Mother, being drunk, being half-asleep. But it was becoming harder, fending him off. He had not stopped with caressing her breasts and belly underneath her nightdress. He had attempted other things.

Tekoah wondered what he would do if she shrieked at him, begged him to stop. He would blame it all on sorcery, of course. But ever since Braith had appeared that day in the village square, and her father had not even known about it, she had doubted the truth of his accusations.

She fell asleep with that thought. And although she had hoped to dream of the lord on the white horse, it was Braith's shadow that beckoned her across the border into that twilit half-world.

Stern slept. Tekoah knew it, even as she slept. Somewhere, a mountain cat cried a cat-cry of hunger and then yowled again at its own echo. The night sky was heavy; she felt its burgeoning heaviness even in slumber. And somehow, she knew the exact moment when—unwatched by all but Anna—the sky gave birth to winter.

In the deepest hour between night and morning, the time of the greatest struggle between Rhan and Anna, she slipped deeper into sleep. And dreamed a dream.

It began with Father. In her dream she lay rigid on her cot. Her father was, taking furtive steps toward her. She felt her stomach twisting in revulsion. She had thought he would not come that night.

Though it was dark, she could see his features clearly, lit up by a kind of inner glow. His eyes were not cloudy or confused as she had always imagined, but clear. Clear and purposeful, holding malice and triumph both.

*HE HAS ALWAYS KNOWN **I am not Mother,** she thought. And she hated him, then.*

But her hate did not overcome her terror. And she realized it was fear that bound her to him, not hatred or love. She closed her eyes, praying for the reprieve that she knew would not come.

She smelled his fetid breath, close to her face. Felt his hands fumbling for her breasts. Then, without warning, he let out a terrible shriek.

Her eyes flew open. Father was kneeling on the ground, covering his face with his hands. Again, he screamed. There was a blinding flash, like that of lightning, only it was inside the hut, and there was no thunder. For a moment, she could see nothing but white light. Then the room took shape again, the glowing coals of the banked fire, the wooden table, the curtain that separated Father's room from the rest of the hut, the stove.

But Father had vanished.

*Tekoah looked toward the hearth, seeking the twins, but they too were gone. **I am alone,** she thought. And just when she should have been feeling relief, desolation swept over her. Alone. Closing her eyes, she lay in a stupor of grief.*

Through her closed lids, she sensed the quality of light and air in the room change. Subtly at first, and then more intensely, almost as though the room was vibrating. Wave after wave of colour and energy swept over her. An irresistible life force, pulling her back from the edge of oblivion.

Then the force became a presence, not so much movement as thought. At first, Tekoah thought her father must have returned, but instantly she knew she was wrong.

Her body told her she was wrong.

A tingling began in all her nerves, and an awareness of her skin, how supple and white it must look in the moonlight. For she was unclothed now, when only a few moments before she had worn her nightdress. Naked, and white as the first real snow that had fallen during the night.

She could see herself from somewhere above, where another part of her floated: her eyes closed, lashes fluttering on her cheeks like trapped butter-flies; thick straight hair falling across slender shoulders, spilling along her back, down to her hips. Lying on her side, knees drawn up to her chest, waiting for birth or death. Was she seeing all this through the eyes of someone else?

Naked and trembling, though not from cold.

Tekoah knew she must open her eyes. But she waited. Her body vibrated like a delicate cintar, its strings quivering with an unbearable need to be played. And the touch came, lightly, on her shoulder. A single note, pulsing long after the trail of his fingers had left.

She opened her eyes. Braith was standing over her. Still as a statue, but for his eyes. They blazed with a hunger the likes of which she had never seen, not from Stolk, or Garth, or that lord on the horse. Not from Veld's twisted soul.

He stood, dark and silent, looking at her, hands still at his sides in their crimson gloves. His desire licked at her like a flame, and she felt her body unfurl itself, as a petal in the heat of the sun.

She looked at him helplessly, unfurled.

He made a slight, ravenous movement with his lips. And then he was upon her.

CHAPTER 17

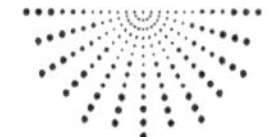

BOOK 3: THE HOWLS OF WINTER

Tekoah might have burned with the shame of her dream all throughout the next day, but for Reika's visit to the forge.

Her public appearance—in daylight—posed a terrifying risk, and Tekoah was so shocked by the sight that her disturbing dream was instantly relegated to the realm of distant memory.

A few moments before, she had been contemplating the prospect of another dull day. The morning had been gloomy and cold, and the afternoon was becoming very grey as clouds drifted down oppressively. Soon it would snow again, only this time it would not stop within a few hours.

Veld was inside the forge, shouting at Raol to clean out the ashes from the furnace. Fanco stood holding a bucket for Tekoah at the well while she pumped water for rinsing the dishes. All at once, he let the bucket tip, and water spilled on the ground.

Tekoah jumped back, annoyed, and then followed his shy, curious gaze to the edge of the rise where the figure of a woman stood.

"Good morning," Reika said in her musical voice. She openly

wore the brown cloak of the Anniste, and as she lowered the hood, she smiled.

Choking back a cry of alarm, Tekoah hurried forward.

"Can you spare me a few moments?"

Tekoah nodded quickly, not trusting herself to speak. She knew she must look like a cowering deer about to dart away. Reika began walking rapidly over the grass, out of the yard. Wiping her hands on her apron, Tekoah followed. She glanced back as they reached the highway, signalling Fanco to keep quiet. He was still holding the bucket, staring after them, and he waved it with a conspiratorial grin.

"Your brother's face speaks eloquently," Reika said.

"That is a good thing," Tekoah answered shortly. "Since with his voice he cannot speak at all. Nor can his twin, my brother Raol."

"I would tell you I am sorry to hear that"—Reika placed a hand on her arm—"except that the Goddess has given them greater gifts in recompense."

Tekoah was uncertain of Reika's meaning, and she could not ask her without seeming foolish. But Reika said no more, and soon they reached the crohm tree.

It appeared spacious in the tree-chamber this time with only the two of them. The minty scent was pleasant instead of overpowering, as it had been on the Night of Masks, and the place was no longer frightening.

"I am sorry to have dragged you off in broad daylight, when your father will demand an explanation," Reika began.

Tekoah shrugged.

"You must know I would never do this if it had not been necessary," Reika said. Her dark eyes dilated in the lamplight. "There is news that you must hear immediately. You know that the sorcerer Morogh is dead?"

"Yes, everyone in the village knows."

"What you do not know is that shortly after his death, an Anniste woman was found murdered, a mile outside Rhantor. Another one was found just before dawn in the Meed River, near Yant, floating downstream. And yet a third was found this morning, in the Taboran foothills, by the place northern folk call the Pony Gate."

Tekoah stared at her dully. "Murdered?" she repeated.

"They were all strangled, then partially devoured"—Reika's voice choked then—"their brains only. And there was something else, strange and horrible. They all bore delicate claw marks on their chests—as if an animal had scored them, but elegantly, in a way no ordinary beast could do. Even the woman found in the river had them."

For several moments there was silence except for the laboured breathing of both women, reminiscent of trapped creatures, waiting in the dark.

Then Tekoah asked, "Do you know who they were? I mean, did you know any of them—their names?"

"Yes."

"Yes, *what?*" she asked, her voice shrill with fear. "You knew some, or you knew them all?"

"I knew them all."

"What were they doing out of hiding? What were you doing?" Tekoah cried wildly, leaning forward and gripping Reika's brown sleeves.

Reika removed her hands and held them in her own. "We are hiding," she said, "but still we must eat."

"And you think the sorcerers are behind this?"

"I know they are. Also, I think Morogh's death signals a graver danger for the Anniste."

"I do not understand," Tekoah said. "I would have thought there would be less danger. Fewer sorcerers, less danger, is that not so?"

"No, we think not." Reika's slender fingers slipped away, and she folded her hands in her lap. "From our Journeys, we gather Morogh restrained Zant somewhat. In their meetings, he was always counselling patience, while Zant pressed him to hurry. Now that he is dead, Zant has free rein. And a great deal of hatred."

She paused, and Tekoah knew Reika was waiting for her to absorb these thoughts.

She tried to pick up the thread, asking with some reluctance, "You saw these things in Journeys?"

She had not allowed herself to think overly much on her own Journey, although she had felt transformed, somehow. It was as though she had been given an invisible thread to hold in her hand, which was there to guide her. Holding onto it, she could walk through the dark mists of the past and the future and would always find her way back.

Reika was looking at Tekoah as if guessing her thoughts. "Yes," she said, "we have seen these things in Journeys, but the visions are glimpses only. Without a Guardian we cannot see clearly, as I have told you."

Although Reika's voice was devoid of reproach, Tekoah felt sick and dizzy. The killings might have been prevented if she had accepted the Guardianship that night.

"We believe this is only the beginning." Reika's voice remained quiet.

How is she so calm? Tekoah wondered. Her own legs trembled, and she gripped her knees with her hands and drew them up against her chest.

Reika spoke again. "We believe that Zant—with or without Braith—will not stop until we are all destroyed." Tekoah stared, uncomprehending. "This means you, as well."

"But I am not Anniste!" she cried.

"You are by legacy. Do you think they will stoop to quibble about whether you have renounced your heritage?"

This was not real. "I cannot believe this," she said. And said it again, like a prayer.

Reika reached forward and took Tekoah's small white hand in her smooth brown one. "You must come when we meet tonight, and Journey once more. At least then we will have a clearer vision of now, and what is to come. I am your friend, am I not? Do you trust me?"

Tekoah nodded.

"Then come."

Tekoah stood. "I have been thinking of leaving Stern, to join my brother in Rhantor and start a new life. Is that so foolish? Is it not possible for me? Could it not be that this violence against the Anniste is a terrible and strange coincidence?"

"The third murdered woman—the one by the Pony Gate," Reika said, speaking slowly, "was your Aunt Beula."

Tekoah stared back at Reika, willing her to take back those words, to say it was not true. But Reika's gaze held pity and sternness both, and the implacable face of a door closing, forever.

TEKOAH'S second Journey was not such a terrifying undertaking. The sensations were familiar—a giddy fear-excitement as she kneeled over the Basin; the indescribable sensation of leaving her skin, like wet soap slipping through fingers. It had frightened her so much before, and this time also she braced herself with clenched fingers. But with the fear came elation. And glancing at the many eyes riveted upon her, there was a small, unfamiliar stirring of power.

Leadership. That was what it felt like. What Weslan craved beyond words.

This time, she let her body relax as she fell, relinquishing the struggle. There was that song again, coming to her like a silvery trail in the darkness:

NEVER SHALL I eat

> *summer berries sweet*
> *or dance in Anna's light*
> *Only a hole*
> *where the moon has been*
> *Mother, where have you gone?*

With no warning, grief engulfed Tekoah. *Anna,* she called, deep within herself. *Where are you? Why do you fill me with sadness?* She listened, thinking this time perhaps the Goddess would speak to her.

Then she had no more time to think.

She stood inside a large, dark chamber. The floor beneath her feet was made of hard, slippery stone. Walls and ceiling of the same stone surrounded her; black shiny stuff, the likes of which she had never seen. The room was unfurnished except for an enormous table in one corner, and a chair beside it. The chair had been overturned with haste or violence, for a leg had broken off.

Tekoah walked toward the table, on which a lamp burned. Several scrolls lay scattered in disarray across the surface. It was so quiet she could hear the oil sputtering in the lamp. Her scalp prickled with unease.

She stumbled over something. Looking down, she saw the large prostrate form of a man, and realized he was dead. His half-opened eyes were yellowish in the lamp's light, and his teeth were bared in a feral snarl. Tekoah cried out, and the sound reverberated back to her from the black stone walls.

Before she could react any further, someone else was in the room.

Was it a sorcerer? It had to be.

Tekoah stood rigid, her breath stopped, heart thumping for several painful seconds before she realized the apparition was unaware of her presence. She gulped in air, her chest heaving. The sorcerer bent over Morogh's corpse, grasping the dead face by the chin.

"Well, old friend..." He sneered—Tekoah thought it must be a "he," though the voice was soft enough to be taken for that of a woman. "You have gone to meet the Worldmaker! How sad for you to lose the power you wielded here in this world and be forced to bow to a greater force." Laughter rippled in the sibilant voice. "But how fortunate that you left me with a last gift—our plan. Now I can move along, unhampered by your commands for patience. A curse on patience—and a pox on your old cat's hide. "

With those words, the figure straightened and kicked the body viciously. "Farewell, Morogh. You will not be mourned, and you will not be missed."

The speaker's hood had fallen away with the force of the kick, and so Tekoah beheld for the first time the sorcerer Zant.

It was a comely face which could have belonged to either sex. Narrow, smooth, high of cheek and forehead, thin of brow and lip. Fair hair, the colour of ash, lay sleekly against Zant's skull. A pale complexion detracted from the beauty of the features, as did the opaque black eyes.

A chill gripped Tekoah, so intense that her teeth began to chatter. This was the predator who hunted the Anniste? What hope did they have?

Zant stopped moving. His narrow head swayed from side to side, black eyes sweeping the room as if searching for something. Had he sensed her presence?

Tekoah held herself still. *Anna, help me!* she prayed. Zant's gaze fell upon her at that moment. She closed her eyes against it.

When she opened them, Zant was bending once more over

Morogh's corpse, chanting strange and terrible words. For a moment, Tekoah thought she saw the corpse move, and the yellowish eyes roll in the shaggy head.

"Let us begin," Zant murmured. Steaming tendrils escaped from the dead sorcerer's mouth, swirling into indistinct shapes, as Zant's fingers moved in sculpting motions.

Tekoah turned away in horror, seeking escape, and then everything—Zant, Morogh's corpse, the black and shiny walls —dissolved.

She was walking, barefoot, on soft, green turf. It must be late afternoon, for Rhan was low in the pale blue sky. She smelled grass, damp warmth rising from black earth, and a spicy scent wafting from flowers which were not familiar, the fragrance making her giddy.

Tekoah stopped, looking up at a looming shape. Before her stood a stone palace. Rhantor? She had never seen the royal palace. But no, it was too warm to be Rhantor.

The south? Yes, she had to be in Meed, at King Darian's palace, for there was the flag of Miraven, flying from the battlements.

It was strange to look upon South Miraven, which was in her own country, yet never saw snowflakes, or heard icy winds whistle through the mountain passes. A place that did not hear the white howls of winter.

An intricately carved wooden balcony was directly in front of her. Massive shutters were flung open at that moment, and a man walked out, closely followed by another figure.

"King Darian!" the one behind him called, and the first man stopped, waiting for the other.

The two began strolling along the balcony, speaking in low tones. Behind them, the sun set in a glorious riot of colour. In the glow, the hues of the lush, unfamiliar foliage that surrounded the palace were breathtaking to behold. Orange petals that were more gold than orange, purple blossoms that were shot through with silver and green streaks, and creamy ivory clumps, so fluffy one wanted to roll in them...

A warm wind ruffled Tekoah's hair. She had heard that the drought was severe, that the rolling red hills of the South held parched mouths to the sky. Garth had told her that even the grapes and olives were withering in the vineyards and orchards.

Yet here the turf was damp and springy beneath her bare toes, and laden fruit trees framed the palace grounds. This king did not believe in suffering along with his people.

Tekoah had flinched involuntarily when the two figures had first appeared. But, just as before, it was apparent that they could not see her, so she stepped closer, matching her footsteps to theirs as she followed alongside the balcony.

Tekoah knew she was looking at King Darian by the beaten-gold crown upon his brow, and because he had just been addressed as such. However, of the two, he looked vastly less royal than his companion.

Darian's eyelids were painted heavily with some purple cosmetic—a southern fashion, perhaps? He moved languidly, and his attitude did not lend itself to the idea of energetic action. His vivid orange vest had the crest of the kingdom embroidered on the back—a red sun, the fires of Rhan pulsing out in every direction. He wore his hair braided back carelessly in the manner of a soldier going to war, as if he was about to jam his head into a helmet and gallop off with a dagger between his teeth. However, this was an obvious affectation, for his elaborate costume, jewel-encrusted coronet, and indolent manner bespoke of a different man entirely.

Tekoah stared in fascination at the notorious monarch of South Miraven, whom she had never seen. She struggled with mirth as Darian posed, legs crossed foppishly in loose blue pantaloons like a Berlotan might wear—she had heard such fashions had been adopted by some young men in Miraven.

Beneath the trousers were slippers stitched from stiff gold cloth, elaborately turned up at the toe.

Tekoah thought they made him look utterly ridiculous, yet Darian paused frequently in his pacing to stare down admiringly at them.

His companion had ceased walking a moment before and leaned out over the balcony, face still, eyes watchful. Looking up, Tekoah recognized with a start the sorcerer Zant.

"Shh!" Zant said abruptly. His head cocked, as if listening, and Tekoah's stomach tightened with apprehension.

"What is it, Zant?" King Darian's asked, his voice high and fretful.

"I thought I heard something, but it is nothing," Zant said.

THE SORCERER TURNED AROUND, arms folded, smiling at Darian. "Now what were you saying, my king?"

"What I do not understand is why it is necessary to ponder every cursed detail of the agreement with Berlot now! Surely all the small things can be worked out later. Promise them the rights to half the pitaya orchards of the North—and the ponies, of course; everything they want. Only let us get on with it. Soon the roads will be impassable and everything I have planned will be for naught."

"Everything *we* have planned," Zant corrected him. Tekoah could see the smile twitching at the corner of the sorcerer's mouth.

"Yes, yes, of course," Darian agreed, waving his hand impatiently. He stopped, staring down at his slippers. "Did I tell you these were a gift from the Jinta?" he asked, wiggling his feet proudly.

"Twice, and I was deeply impressed both times, and am so again. But back to the matter of the agreement. Let me warn you that, golden slippers or no, the Jinta is not a monarch to be trifled with. Broken promises are an excuse for blood. I was born in Berlot, remember, and so my advice has some value, slight though it may be."

"Of course, of course. More than slight, and you know it. I will leave the details of the agreement to you. Once it is drawn up, I will sign it. But then let us take action!"

"You are in a fever to see your sister dethroned, are you not, my liege?"

Listening to the hissing voice, Tekoah wondered uneasily about Zant's Source. Morogh's Source had been a mountain cat. Looking at his corpse, there could be no doubt. She shivered, thinking of Braith.

Zant continued to speak. "Do you truly hate Darielle, or is this merely a family spat?" His voice was mocking.

Darian's face twisted grotesquely. "I would have gladly seen her dead," he said, "if only that fool of an assassin had not bungled it. But your new idea is very good. And if it appeases the Jinta's pride to take as his concubine the Queen of Miraven, it will also satisfy mine to be the sole ruler of this country, as I should have been from the beginning.

"None of this would have happened if she had not curried Father's favour all the time, fawning upon him, so that he preferred her to me!" Darian's voice rose in fury. "You do not know what it was like to grow up with her. Well, now she is going to pay!"

Zant nodded, his taut face lit with an approving smile.

Tekoah watched Darian, revolted. He had become incensed, and spittle flew from his lips. "The time to take charge is now! If I had an army, I would never have accepted help from Berlot. I am not a traitor to my country!"

"Of course not," Zant assured him. "As a wise ruler, you know that this is the only way. Just as it is for the misunderstanding between our two countries—greatly exacerbated by the religious disagreement over the worship of Anna by your witch healing sect. I am honoured that you have entrusted me to rectify that burden."

Darian's face grew troubled.

"Just think," Zant continued, "now we will obtain gold for the royal coffer, and grain enough to pacify your people, who, as we know, are on the verge of revolt."

"Yes, yes," Darian said. He laughed with delight at a sudden thought. "My worthless sister has proven to be of some value after all. I wonder how many bushels, how many coins, we can get for her."

Zant regarded the king, his lips twitching as if in inner amusement.

Tekoah thought of Weslan, stationed at Rhantor, where an assassin had just been intercepted. She hoped her brother was not in danger.

Zant spoke again, smooth and deferential. "You have not forgotten your promise to me, my king: to rename the royal city of the North 'Zantor', and to appoint me to rule there in your name."

King Darian had turned and was standing in front of Tekoah, his back to the sorcerer. At Zant's words, Tekoah saw a spasm of terror cross his face.

He is not such a fool as he pretends, she thought.

"I know better than to cross a sorcerer, Lord Zant," he said. "Ah, look at the moon, how she shines tonight!"

Zant stared at the sky with eyes that were like shiny black stones, reflecting nothing of the silvery light. He held out an open palm to the silver disc, as if to blot the moon from view.

He turned to King Darian, his voice sharp and impatient, saying, "Let us go inside."

Tekoah watched them go, and her own eyes were drawn back to Anna's orb. She was falling again.

∼

SHE WAS INSIDE A LARGE, dark room—not in the South, for the banked coals of a roaring fire glowed against the far wall.

It was a bedchamber, sumptuous by the looks of it, the bed having four wooden posts and the head elaborately carved. On the mattress lay a woman, thrashing about in the throes of a dream. She began to sob. After a moment, she sat up, fumbling about and lighting a lamp.

The woman was older than Tekoah. In the lamp's light, her face looked set and stern. But she was not unlovely. Wisps of golden hair escaped from her nightcap, and she tucked them into place, as someone accustomed to hiding her softness. Was this the queen? Tekoah wondered. No, Darielle was said to be dark-haired.

The air stirred, and then Zant was in the room. Tekoah's echoed the woman's cry of astonishment, but neither turned to acknowledge her presence.

The woman lay back on the pillow, panting. Zant came and stood over her bed, watching her chest rise and fall. After a moment, lithe and quick, he leaned over her, plucking away her nightcap. Long, golden hair fell about her in rippling waves, softening her face, setting her cold grey eyes alight.

"Saura." Zant's whisper was a caress. Smiling, he sat on the edge of the bed. Saura's eyes never once left his face.

"Is it done?" she asked, her voice trembling. He nodded, reaching out to stroke her hair. At his touch, she closed her eyes. "At least Darielle will not die. I never did like the idea of the assassin. But soon she may wish she had died. May Anna forgive me," she murmured, turning her face away.

"Do not speak to me of Anna! The name is like a fruit that has become overripe, and sits, stinking and rotting, waiting to fall. And the fall will come soon."

Saura looked at Zant, her face a struggle between fear and triumph.

He smiled. "Only think, sweeting," he whispered, stroking

her hair. "Of all the freedom, the riches—the power—you will harvest in the days ahead."

"I care nothing for that!" Saura said, holding out her palms. "You must know me well enough by now—I would not be so treacherous for gold. And to whip a few nobles who slighted me is not worth betraying my queen. I did this because it pleases you."

Saura's voice became a supplicating whimper. Clasping Zant's hand, she brought it to her lips. As she kissed it over and over, he stared out at the first feathery snowflakes of winter which fell, his fathomless eyes reflecting nothing.

Tekoah fell toward the dizzying darkness.

SHE OPENED HER EYES. Anna shone full in the night sky, and now it was warm again, a summer night. Tekoah was standing in the field behind the forge. Father was beside her, leaning on his spade. He was drenched with sweat, and something else. Something darker, which also covered her own hands. She kept trying to wipe it off, but it was too sticky. Tekoah fell to her knees, wiping and wiping on the grass, but it was no use. She began to weep.

"Your mother wanted to leave me," her father said sadly from above her. "To take you all away. Promise me you will never leave me."

His fingertips fell upon her shoulder, and she looked up at him. But it was not Veld—it was Braith. He held out a goblet to her, filled with dark red wine.

"Forget," he said, his voice gentle, but in his eyes was the terrifying light of desire. She reached for the goblet and, impulsively, she struck it from his hand, watching it roll away, spilling crimson drops into the earth.

"I cannot forget!" she cried, although what it was that she could not forget, she did not yet remember.

When she looked up, Braith was gone, and it was winter. She was all alone in a snow-covered wood, shivering, shaking with cold. Cold and dark, and no one there.

Then she saw them. The eyes. A cat-creature sprang forward, staring hungrily at her with the yellowish eyes of the dead sorcerer Morogh. It walked on its hind-legs like a man and had claws, long and sharp. It bared its teeth at her with a feral snarl.

She screamed. And was falling, falling, hearing the song again.

"Only a hole where the moon has been,

Mother, where have you gone?"

Tekoah awoke, her head cradled in Reika's lap. Reika had covered her with a blanket. Her eyes looked down questioningly, but she spoke with a soothing voice.

"Your Journey was long—the longest I have ever seen," Reika said. "It has exhausted you. Do not speak now, unless you have the strength."

Tekoah closed her eyes. "You were right," she mumbled, "we are in grave danger." And she fell again, but this time into a deep sleep, sweet and dreamless.

TEKOAH WENT HOME AGAIN EARLY the next morning, determined to stay only long enough to say farewell to the twins, before she went into hiding with the Anniste. There was dread and guilt at leaving her brothers, but it could not be helped. Perhaps they could go live with Bhantok at Aunt Beula's farm.

Veld was not in the forge, and even from the yard she could hear his heavy snores. Tekoah saw the twins sitting on the edge of the well. They leaped to their feet at the sight of her, and to her astonishment, she saw they were burning with excitement.

They signalled with frantic hands, but the sign they made over and over was easy enough to understand, for she had seen it since childhood. A large sweeping circle, with a downward slash through the centre.

Weslan was here.

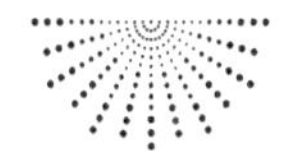

CHAPTER 18

"So." Chalvern said nothing more. The loons were flying high, abandoning Stern's End for a safer resting place.

"So," Braith echoed. "How fare you, Master?"

Chalvern turned and began to walk, stepping gingerly along the spongy ground. He did not yet trust himself to speak. Braith fell into step beside him, his long legs slowing to match Chalvern's pace.

To the west, the massive clouds had broken. Rhan was departing for the day, casting a splendid cloak of colour behind him; the purple, rose, and orange shot through with streaks of gold, seeming to promise a glorious morrow to come.

But Chalvern knew the promise was false. The morning would bring snow and ice. He smelled it in the air. As for glory, that was a fleeting thing. He felt outrage well up within him.

"You did not come here to inquire after my health, Braith, nor to reminisce. Drop the pretence if you please, for I am not so doddering as all that."

Chalvern felt Braith's hand on his shoulder, and the quick hot tears that scalded his eyes made him angrier. He shook off the hand. Braith regarded him, brows knitted with concentration. How many times had he seen that look?

But when the sorcerer spoke, his voice was mild. "I would not be here to seek your counsel if I thought you were doddering, Master."

Chalvern quickened his step. The wind was growing cold now that the light was departing. Plaintive cries came from somewhere above—loons, grieving the loss of daylight.

He looked at Braith, unappeased. "What counsel do you claim to seek? You have no need of my advice, since you do what you please notwithstanding! Do you think I have not heard how you befriended Tekoah's brother, Weslan? The ease with which he has become an object of adoration at the Royal Court of Rhantor strikes me as odd."

Braith shrugged. "Give the boy some credit. He is handsome, brave, and not altogether stupid."

"He is also untutored in the gentler arts, rash, naïve, and hot-tempered. Do not ask me to believe that he has succeeded so brilliantly without your aid."

"I ask you to believe nothing, except that I mean no harm."

"No harm?" Chalvern stopped in his tracks.

They were nearing the highway now, and several oxcarts were rumbling along in front of them, heading back home from their labour at the Castle of Mirrand. The next day, they would bring more stones for the wall, unless it snowed very hard.

"No harm!?" he echoed, his anger rising.

A cart driver turned to stare, and Chalvern realized he must have been shouting. Braith gazed back at him impassively.

"What did you do with Stonemason Kayne's son, Garth?" Chalvern asked. "Turn him into a boulder?" He started walking again, rapidly, though his knees were aching.

"What makes you think I did anything with him?" Braith responded.

Chalvern could hear him slapping his gloved hands together

as he walked. He wanted to grab the boy and shake him. *Only he wasn't a boy, was he?*

"I am not altogether stupid," he replied. "And do not blame Tekoah's father. Veld has the strength only to destroy what is weak. Garth would have thrown that wretch from here to Rhantor, if he had so much as laid a hand on him."

There was a silence. Then Braith said in a low voice, "The lad is making a very fine pig herd on a farm near Liandon. Naturally, he has no memory of his former life. Only I hear he keeps trying to build stone sties. Marvellous creations, but of course everyone thinks he is touched in the head."

There was laughter in Braith's voice, rippling beneath the surface. For a moment, Chalvern felt an urge to laugh himself. At least Garth was not dead. But he checked himself. This was a serious matter, and there were more dangerous things yet in the heart of Braith.

"Well," Chalvern said, sternly. "It is evident you have not forgotten Tekoah, nor ever intended to. May Anna be with her, poor maid. Now tell me plainly, what are you doing here?"

His knees were really paining him now. *Rhan, what a curse to be old.* The brain flitting forward, unfettered as a butterfly on the wind, while the limbs trudged along, protesting every step of way. And he was becoming out of breath as well. If only Braith did not anger him so, he would have more breath to spare.

"Will you take my arm, Master?" Braith was holding out a black-clad sleeve.

Glancing into his face, Chalvern saw only concern. That green-gold gaze was so unsettling, though. Once, his eyes had been a deep shade of brown.

"I do not need your arm, thank you," he snapped. "Just answer my question."

"I am here because Tekoah is in danger. The Anniste are being hunted down and killed in cold blood. It is Zant's doing, and he will not stop until he destroys every woman in that sect."

Fear uncoiled like a serpent in Chalvern's belly. "So, it is the very worst it can be." he answered. "Today I quarrelled with that fat priest; listening to him speak of sorcerers as though they were gods, I became afraid. I was about to go speak to Tekoah again this evening if I had the chance."

"She must be hidden," Braith continued, "and soon."

"But what of your motives?" Chalvern asked. "The Anniste know they are in danger. But Tekoah told me they fear 'sorcerers'—not only one sorcerer."

Braith did not at once answer. Chalvern hobbled along beside him, listening to the silence, imagining a great stone wall, being built between them, higher and more impregnable than those castle walls on the hilltop. Between sorcerers and mortals, there had always been that barrier.

"Morogh—yes, they had reason to fear him. Zant, they have even more reason to fear. But they need not fear me." Braith's voice became hoarse. "She need never fear me."

"Convince her of that."

"Convince *you*, is what you mean," Braith said. "Master, I am here, whether you like it or no. And I mean to see her. Then she may choose for herself whether to trust me."

Chalvern did not answer, and they strode along for some time in silence. Braith started walking faster as they spoke, his agitated gait betraying what his measured voice did not reveal. Pride and anger pushed Chalvern to hasten his own pace.

A few moments later, his breath came in quick, harsh gasps, and his knees were on fire. He stopped abruptly, trying to rally his strength. He would say there was a pebble in his shoe.

But Braith was already at his side—*Rhan curse him*—seizing him by the elbow, taking charge.

"I told you back there to let me help you!" His arm now encircled Chalvern about the waist, taking away almost all the weight from under him so that he floated along ridiculously, toes skimming the ground—like a reluctant child being dragged home by his mother.

Chalvern thanked Anna that it was dark, and no one could witness it. The humiliation would be unbearable. But oh, the relief for his knees, his blessed knees.

Somewhere up on the hill behind them a mountain cat cried, a yowling snarl that stiffened the hairs on Chalvern's neck.

Beside him, Braith spoke. "The mountain cat was Morogh's Source."

"I know," Chalvern answered. "I had the misfortune to meet Morogh once, and the signs were unmistakable. Is Zant's as obvious? A serpent, I thought I heard you say."

"About Zant," Braith said, "there is nothing obvious."

They twisted and turned along the highway, guided by Anna's light. Chalvern had trod this path many, many times as a boy. But now he leaned more and more into Braith's warm, solid form, and after a time he became drowsy. The night air had grown crisp and quiet, waiting for winter.

"Your Source," Chalvern murmured into the darkness, "I think I have guessed it."

Braith said nothing. He had picked Chalvern up now, his hands in their crimson gloves bearing him effortlessly.

They rounded the last bend. Below them the village of Stern lay, lamps burning in cottages and smoke from supper-fires rising from chimneys.

"Almost home, Master," Braith said.

"Stop calling me that," Chalvern answered. A great weariness had taken hold of him. "It has become a joke."

CHAPTER 19

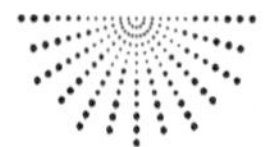

Small rooms, low ceilings, too little light, too little air. How had he ever been able to live in Stern without going mad?

Weslan hunched against the rough wooden table, resisting the urge to pace, to shout, to hurl himself through the door and into the saddle. To ride back to Rhantor, which now seemed more like home than this dreary place ever had.

It was like being a caged animal. Even the garrison at the palace had boasted high, airy ceilings. All one had to do was open the shutters and look out a window to see Darielle's gardens, stretching out luxuriously before one's eyes, like an eternal spring. The gardens were calling to him, beckoning him back across the mountains, whispering that he did not belong in Stern any longer.

But no. It was not the gardens that beckoned him; not the statues with their rich, voluptuous curves, or the fountains that always seemed to murmur delicious secrets to themselves. No, it was a pair of liquid brown eyes, in which laughter swam like lazy fish. Eyes that held no questions. No reproaches.

But it was no good thinking of Darielle. Selfish, in fact. It was Tekoah on whom he must focus. By the holy Mantling, where was she? He had sent word to Tekoah to meet him at midday, and it had been over an hour. He stood up for the tenth time in as many minutes and went to the window.

The goodwife Hanta, with whom he had lodged that night, chuckled from where she stood by the stove stirring the midday soup. She had assured Weslan several times she had given his message to the twins—that very morning—as she rode by with her eggs in a cart for market day. Hanta did not appear to feel confined by her dreary little cottage, but then she had seen nothing with which to compare it, had she?

Had the twins forgotten to tell Tekoah? Had Veld gotten wind of it and locked her up?

Weslan dreaded the meeting in a way he had not even dreaded the knife in the hands of Darielle's would-be assassin. But he wanted it over with. Putting things off was not his style. They only crept back up in the end.

"More tea, Master Weslan? Or should I say 'Lord'?" Hanta had brought a steaming pot to the table, along with a fresh-baked wheat loaf. Her smile was simpering; she seemed not to recollect that she had boxed his ears, not so many turnings past, for boyish pranks he would prefer to forget.

"Weslan will suffice, Hanta." He smiled the smile which always seemed to work well with women but not at all with men. He was careful not to meet her small twinkling eyes, which were brimming with curiosity.

Unspoken questions hovered in the air, thick as flies around pitaya syrup. He could almost hear them buzzing.

Why is there a magnificent spotted pony grazing in the field, without a clear owner? What is the identity of your black-cloaked travelling companion, tall and silent, who left soon after you arrived? What are you doing here in the first place, come to that? And why all the secrecy? A big strapping lad like you, hero and all—are you still afraid of a showdown with your father?

The smile worked, however. Hanta flushed, her plump cheeks quivering with pleasure. She sliced the loaf with unnecessary zeal.

There were three raps on the cottage door, so soft that Weslan first thought he imagined the sound. Then came three more, a little louder, and he leaped up, galvanized. Forgetting his manners, he reached the door before Hanta had the chance to, flinging it open.

Tekoah stood there, panting a little. She smiled, her eyes filling with tears.

More scared than me, he thought with relief.

"String bean!" He swooped down and picked her up. "Light as a feather, string bean."

Tekoah laughed, but surreptitiously dried her eyes against his tunic as they embraced. That was what he had dreaded. Tears. However, she pulled herself together—almost.

"String bean, indeed!" she chided, pulling away from him. "You always called me that, but now I deserve some respect. Mention beans in my presence again and I will bean you—over the head with a wooden spoon. I am sure Hanta will be happy to loan me one."

She glanced over at the goodwife who guffawed, wringing her apron with her hands. Hanta was clearly enjoying the moment and recording it in every detail for later dispatch to the neighbours.

Tekoah held him at arm's length, regarding him with appraising eyes. "Well, you are no string bean! You look as if you were hewed from bronze, brother. Brave soldier, gallant noble—there is no end to the tales. Rhan has shed His light on your path, it is plain to see."

Her voice was playful, but guilt stung him like a wasp. "It has not been all pitayas and posies, sister," he retorted.

"Well said, Tekoah!" Hanta took the moment to rush forward

from where she stood by the stove. "You must be so proud to be the sister of a hero!"

Tekoah nodded, looking a little bewildered.

Hanta beamed. "The greatest hero this generation has known, I'll wager, as he saved the queen by killing her would-be assassin right at the door to her bedchamber." Hanta said these last words with salacious relish and then gazed with satisfaction at Tekoah's astonished face.

"What?" Tekoah cried, her face going very white. "I had not heard this tale. Is it true, Wes?"

"Yes," Weslan muttered, trying to swallow his irritation with Hanta. He had hoped Tekoah did not yet know, so he could tell her himself. He looked over his shoulder at Hanta, who stood, rubbing her floury hands together in anticipation.

"Let us walk," he muttered, taking Tekoah's elbow and steering her toward the door. "There is something I would show you."

They stepped out into the sunshine, leaving Hanta to her speculations.

"No, not that way," he said, as his sister turned toward the road. "Come walk in the fields."

Weslan grinned at Tekoah's puzzled face. *This is my moment.*

Braith had left mid-morning, saying that he wished to visit Chalvern, his beloved former teacher. "I will stay out of your way," he had said, smiling. "And you can spring your wonderful surprise. The reunion is bound to be filled with joyful tears, and the overflow of sentiment will no doubt be unbearable to witness."

He had winked. "Besides, it might be wise not to mention my name just yet. Let your sister become re-accustomed to the sight of you first. Then perhaps we can introduce her to the idea of me—your friend and mentor."

Yes, it was Weslan's moment with his sister, who had long deserved to have some happy dreams come true. The wind was strong, and great white clouds moved across the sky. As they walked along the field behind Hanta's cottage, the light continually changed as the clouds passed over Rhan's face. One moment it was painfully bright; the next it was grey and shimmery, almost as though they were walking in the centre of one of those shellfish Weslan had once eaten in Yant.

He almost said so, knowing Tekoah loved images of that sort. Then he remembered she had never seen a shellfish, had never even seen the sea. Guilt clutched him again.

Tekoah took his arm. "Tell me about the assassin," she commanded, sounding very serious. "Are you really a hero?"

"It was luck, mostly. I will tell you all about it another time." He glanced at her as she strode along beside him. "I hope you will forgive me not coming to the forge," he added awkwardly.

"Of course," Tekoah said at once. She squeezed his arm. "The way things are with you and Father—"

"It is not only that," Weslan said. "I could not bear to go there after I heard about Mother. I would be looking around for her every few minutes, and it would make me very sad. I am determined to find Mother, by the way. I cannot believe she left without saying goodbye."

Tekoah did not reply. She had let go of his arm, and Weslan looked at his sister uneasily. Her face was strange, faraway.

"Yes," she said finally, staring fixedly ahead. "As did you."

He looked down at his boots.

Tekoah began walking again, flinging words over her shoulder as she went. "I have been lonely most of the time since then, living with Father and the twins. There is no one at home to talk to. Not properly. Think of that, Wes. No one."

Weslan heard a tremor in her voice, and he could not bear to look at her. But there was a pause, and when she spoke again, pride threaded stiffly through her words.

"If you wondered why I was late meeting you, it was because

it took me a long time before I could make up my mind to come at all."

"But I am here to help!" Weslan exclaimed, reaching out to touch her shoulder, "I came back, as I planned to all along." It was the truth—almost.

"I do not require your help," she said in a clipped voice.

Weslan remembered how he had pictured their reunion and began to rap himself on the forehead with his knuckle as he walked. *Stupid, stupid, stupid!* he seethed with each rap.

"I can solve my own problems now," Tekoah continued. "I have not had any choice, you see. And as it happens, I am alone no longer. I have friends to help me, to give me counsel. Friends who do not run away."

"I did not run away!"

"You did!"

"I didn't!"

"Did!"

And suddenly they were bristling at each other, eyes blazing, sparks flying, just like the old days.

Weslan laughed first, and then Tekoah also, somewhat reluctantly. Clouds scuttled before the gust, and Rhan shone forth for a brief, golden moment.

Weslan heard a whinny behind them. He seized her shoulders and spun her around. "I told you I had something to show you!"

The pony had heard his raised voice and was cantering toward him across the field. Melted snow from the storm two days ago had made the ground soggy, and wet mud spattered the pony's tawny coat as she came. But she was nonetheless exquisite with a few more spots on her.

Weslan heard Tekoah's quick intake of breath and felt his first measure of satisfaction that day.

"Come here, my darling," he murmured, and the pony sidled

up to him across the fence, rubbing her head against his shoulder and staring up at him like a lovesick girl.

Tekoah gazed, wonder-struck, then spoke breathlessly. "Where did you get her? She is not yours, surely. Are you taking her over to Bhantok's for breeding?"

"No, I am not taking her to the pony farm. Our worthless cousin does not deserve her, and besides, it is not breeding season, is it?" Weslan was enjoying the moment.

Tekoah held her hand out, letting the pony sniff her fingers; they watched the delicate flare of her black nostrils. "Then she is yours? But why? You cannot ride her; she is too small."

He waited. His sister's brow furrowed as she thought.

"I know!" she exclaimed suddenly. "She is your present from the queen for saving her life, and now you are going to sell her for an enormous sum." Tekoah clapped her hands at her own cleverness, then frowned. "But you would get far more for her in the South."

"Are you through guessing?" Weslan asked with a smirk.

She punched his shoulder. "Yes, I am through. Hurry up and tell me."

"Well, you have guessed right about one thing. She is not mine, though I have cherished her since infancy. I found her, in the forest, when I was riding with a friend. Her mother had just given birth to her, but, sadly, had been attacked by a mountain cat, and was dead by the time we stumbled across her."

"Poor little orphan," Tekoah murmured. "Were you very frightened, my angel?"

She closed her eyes, laying her head against the silken cheek of the pony. When she opened them again, Weslan saw that they were filled with tears. *Not again!* He looked up at the sky, willing Rhan to tell him what to do.

He had never been good at this sort of thing. A man could always ride or fight his grief away. For women, it was so much more complicated.

A bird—an eagle or hawk—was circling high above them, a deep black speck against the sky. Weslan envied it its freedom and solitude.

"But you said she did not belong to you," Tekoah prompted him, smiling. She had regained her self-possession but was still puzzled. "If you found her, then she is yours by right, is she not?"

"She is not mine, because I decided from the start that she was yours. And I pledged to myself that I would bring her with me when I came back for you."

Weslan knew that this was not strictly true, but it was close enough, and it sounded very noble. Besides, Braith had asked Weslan not to mention his name, so he could not very well say it was Braith's idea. Either way, it was very gratifying to see Tekoah's face. His sister had always worshipped ponies with a passion almost as great as her obsession with composing her endless verses.

Yes, the transformation that had come over Tekoah was wonderful to behold. Her pale skin—she almost looked as though she had been ill—was now flushed with a rosy glow. Her eyes, still a little red-rimmed, shone like gems through seawater.

Weslan smiled expansively, repeating, "She is yours."

"You do not mean it. You are teasing me!"

But she saw he was serious and, with a shriek, Tekoah threw her arms around his neck. Then, just as quickly, she pushed him away, hitched up her skirt and climbed over the fence. Restless, the pony had turned away and was ambling in the meadow, nibbling in a desultory way at the brown shreds of remaining grass.

"What is her name?" Tekoah called back softly, walking toward the pony with her hand outstretched.

"We did not name her—we left that up to you." He realized his mistake immediately, but it was too late.

Tekoah's head whipped around.

We?" she asked, with a quick frown. "Who is 'we'?"

Weslan fumbled quickly for an answer, but before he could say anything, her frown changed to a sly smile.

"Ah, could the other person have been a 'she'? Perhaps a very *royal* she? Do not think I missed what Hanta was saying—I am not as naïve as all that just because I have not lived in Rhantor. And I am sorry I have been so selfish. I should have told you how proud I am of you. Truly!" She stroked the pony's neck softly.

"What are you going to name her?" he asked, relieved to change the subject.

"I am really allowed to name her? Well, then, it is Flare. That is what I called her in my mind the instant I saw her. Flare." She gazed at the pony, enraptured. "Do you know, Wes, the last time someone gave me a wonderful gift, it was Mother—she gave me that annathyst heart on the chain. Do you remember how I cried when you hid it and said you dropped it into the bottom of the pond? You were a terrible brother!" She pulled a comical face to show she did not mean it.

Weslan's heart contracted at the mention of Neela. It was the only remaining cloud in a sunlit sky. He did not wish to ruin the moment, but it could not be ignored. Where had she gone?

"About Mother—" he said, hesitantly.

"She left. You know that. Therefore, you know as much as I do." Tekoah did not look at him.

"You have not heard anything from her at all? Not a word?" He stared incredulously.

"You know as much as I do, brother." Tekoah's voice quavered. She turned and began walking away.

Weslan followed her, wincing inwardly. "I am sorry, string bean. Forgive me for being insensitive. It is just that things are very confusing. In some ways, it seems as if I left only yesterday. In other ways, it seems as if my whole childhood was only a dream. You will understand what I am saying once you have been away for a while."

"What do you mean?" She had been staring pensively ahead, but turned to look at him at his last words.

"Once you leave. After you get on your beautiful pony, Flare, and ride away with me. She has not been broken, but I should like to see a pony that you cannot ride instantly. We could go tomorrow—before the real snow comes."

"Leave here? Tomorrow?"

Tekoah looked dazed, as if she had never really contemplated it before. But surely, she had not thought to stay in Stern forever. There was nothing for which to remain.

Weslan grew impatient. "Of course!" he said urgently. "Why ever do you suppose I returned? For the scenery? And, string bean, if truth be told, there is someone for whom I am pining deeply at the moment." He smiled broadly at her, provoking an answering grin.

Weslan impulsively grabbed her hands, swinging their arms together. *We have always mirrored each other,* he thought. Only Tekoah's side of the mirror was soft and indistinct, while his was bright and sharp and full of angles.

"What about the twins?"

"They could come with us if they liked. Somehow, though, I always pictured them on Bhantok's farm—if they ever leave the forge, that is."

"I do not think I can leave with you, Wes," Tekoah said slowly. She had that faraway look.

He dropped her hands, watching as she smoothed out her skirts. "Why not? Do you really want to stay with Father?"

"No, of course not. I know I must leave the forge. It is time."

"Then what are you talking about?"

"The Anniste have asked me to join them. As their Guardian. And I have accepted."

Rhan's balls! "You cannot do that, Ko!" Weslan exclaimed,

restraining his voice so that he did not shout. It was exactly what Braith had predicted. "You do not know the danger in that—"

"Yes, I do," Tekoah said, her voice curt.

He stared at her. She had never spoken to him in such a way. "You do?"

"Aunt Beula is dead. They killed her—the priests and sorcerers. We are being hunted down one by one. I know the danger more than you, I daresay, but I will join them, anyway. It is my duty. I will not renounce them as Mother did."

"What Mother did has nothing to do with you!" Weslan shouted.

Startled, Flare threw back her head and cantered off down the field.

Tekoah turned and faced him fully. "And yet I must help them. I am sorry, Wes. But tell me this: if someone had said you should not become a soldier because of the danger, what would you have done?"

Weslan looked at his sister, brow furrowed. Knowing that for this, as for too many other questions, he had no answer.

WHEN TEKOAH LEFT Hanta's place, she was riding Flare, who submitted to her at once, docile as a kitten; turning her head this way and that, following her rider's gentle direction, although she was only halter-trained.

Weslan had protested. "I told you she was yours, but only for riding away from this place."

"You would deny me this pleasure?" She had beamed at him, sitting bareback astride her mount, her skirt tucked carelessly up, a true northerner. Weslan acknowledged to himself that his sister's smile was capable of wreaking havoc among the nobles at Rhantor's court.

Tekoah had grown up. Something bothered him about it—nagging at him like the throb in his healed sword arm—but he could not put his finger on what it was.

She had a mind of her own. Weslan brooded on the ungovernable nature of females, as he watched Hanta clear away the evening meal. His discomfort grew as his mind turned to the inevitable conclusion that Braith would be none too pleased with him.

But at least he had extracted from Tekoah a promise to meet him at the Pitaya Pit tomorrow afternoon, to say farewell. From there, she would depart to meet the Anniste—or so she thought —and he would ride back to Rhantor.

In reality, Weslan would need to kidnap his own sister to save her life. He and Braith had already discussed that possibility. Weslan was uneasy about the plan, but it was preferable to finding Tekoah murdered in some ravine like that poor Anniste woman.

And there been two others at least. Braith had already told him about his Aunt Beula, and, although he had never been as close to Beula as Tekoah and the twins, Weslan shuddered with horror every time he thought of his aunt's small, sweet face.

Mother would want Tekoah safe, Weslan assured himself. But he worried still. Tekoah did not yet know they were travelling with Braith. She would feel betrayed—not only at being taken away against her will—but also because he had not forewarned her about his friendship with the sorcerer.

His sister was angry with him for leaving his family. After tomorrow, she would be much angrier. Worse, she might not trust him any longer.

And what would happen to the twins? The question accosted him out of nowhere, and he realized that he had not wanted to think about them much, because he did not know where they could fit in with his grand plans.

Weslan loved his brothers, but he had never understood them.

They had excluded him. Not that it was their fault, for what choice had they in the matter? They stuck together, speaking a secret language with their fingers, rapid flutters and slashes that Weslan would watch sometimes from the corner of his eye, half-fascinated, half-repelled. Wondering what they could have to talk about.

Would they be happy to know he was a hero? That his name was on everyone's lips? That he had won the love of a queen, and the friendship of a sorcerer?

The twins would make a way for themselves, he thought at last, regardless of whether they chose to come. They would survive, as long as they had each other.

Hanta hastened to refill his ale mug, waving away his thanks with fluttering fingers. Weslan thought that although his brothers might be unaware of his new status, Hanta was not. Her fawning attentions had been flattering at first, but he now wished it was already the next day, and that he was riding home to Rhantor.

For Rhantor was home now, and at least there everyone had stopped questioning him. He sipped his ale, wishing that Hanta would not press him quite so closely for all the details of his encounter with the assassin.

Truth be told, he was sick to death of it.

Truth be fully told, if people knew how the assassin encounter had unfolded, they would cease to think he was a hero.

"But how did you happen to be outside her chamber, right at that moment?" Hanta persisted, her avid face gleaming in the firelight as she swept the floor.

"I was walking in the garden," he answered, reciting the lie which came almost naturally by now. Sometimes he half-believed it himself. "With a—friend," he added enigmatically, for Hanta's benefit.

She snickered behind her hand like a girl. "You are a caution, young man! More than one young lady in this village cried into her pillow after you left, let me tell you. Well, go on, go on. I can't bear the excitement."

"Not much to tell, Hanta," he mumbled, staring into the fire to avoid her avid gaze. "I saw a figure inching its way along the southern wall, moving toward the section that lies below the queen's chamber. At first, I thought that someone was slipping into the palace for a romantic tryst. I did not wish to embarrass anyone, but I had an uneasy feeling. I ducked in by a side door—an entrance for the soldiers. I reached the queen's chamber just before he did."

"And?" Hanta trilled, her goblet hovering halfway to her lips.

"And it was not much of a fight, his dagger against my sword, and I with the added advantage of surprise."

"You are too modest!" Hanta exclaimed.

The wind was crouching and prowling outside the cottage, rattling the window shutters, cold draughts of it blowing through the poorly sealed cracks of the cottage walls. The widow sat and pushed her chair closer to the fire.

"Too modest by far," she insisted, rubbing her hands together to warm them. "I heard you suffered a horrible slash on your sword arm."

"No," Weslan answered, "that was another battle together." *And at least it was my battle*, he thought. He felt a yawn rising in his throat, stifled it, and then decided not to bother. Perhaps she would get the hint.

"But where was your 'friend'?" Hanta asked, ignoring the yawn.

His heart thudded. Did she know about Braith?

"Where was your friend while this was happening?"

"What friend?" He barked the question, then saw by her face that he had sounded harsh.

"I did not mean to pry," she said, in a voice that wobbled. "Only, I wondered what happened to your friend in the garden."

"Oh," Weslan said, relieved. "My friend is *very* discreet."

"Ah."

Hanta looked somewhat ruffled, so he summoned up a smile and a wink. Hanta gave him an answering wink and a complicit nod.

Later, lying on the pallet made up for him by the stove, Weslan thought that the last thing he had said was the truest: his friend was very discreet. Only this mysterious person was not the voluptuous court beauty of Hanta's inflamed imagination.

His friend was the sorcerer Braith.

In a way, Weslan had been like a string puppet in the sorcerer's hands, enacting a play of Braith's making. If he chose to think of it that way.

But he did not choose so. He preferred, instead, to replay in his mind, again and again, the images of his heroic rescue of Darielle: how the assassin had towered above him— had weighed at least a stone more than he. How, in spite of this, Weslan had moved with great power and speed to vanquish the danger to his queen.

Weslan had risked his own life, willingly, for his country and its ruler, who happened also to be the woman he loved.

For that, at least, can I not claim to be a hero? he thought. But somehow, he did not feel like one. Not tonight.

Outside, winter howled its way like a white beast through the Taboran Mountains. Inside, Hanta's snores reverberated through the small cottage. But Weslan was neither here nor there. He closed his eyes and let himself remember every tiny detail of Darielle's face when she saw him standing over the assassin's body, for it was the moment that had made everything worth it.

Hanta began to snore louder, intruding on his thoughts.

Weslan wondered how her husband had borne it. Perhaps it was the lack of a good night's sleep that had killed him.

Weslan spent another hour tossing on the narrow pallet and worrying about the morrow. He tried to calm his mind by reminding himself that Braith had been right about the assassin, and about Darielle. No doubt his judgement could be trusted concerning Tekoah as well.

Tomorrow they would leave for Rhantor, and in three days he would be back at the palace. A wave of longing swept through him to be home in Darielle's arms. *Before another takes your place,* his inner voice jeered. He punched his scanty pillow a few times to banish that thought.

Finally sleepy, an unexpected image of his mother's face rose behind his closed eyelids, and he fought tears. *Perhaps she is somewhere close by, hiding,* he thought, and felt comforted. *She will follow stealthily behind us when we leave. And everything will turn out well.*

He drifted off to sleep, wanting nothing more than for it to be tomorrow.

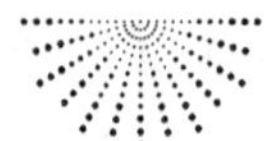

ather had been staring into his half-eaten bowl of cornmeal for what had seemed like hours. In reality, Tekoah knew it was only a few moments. She prepared herself to dodge the flying bowl, or perhaps a flying fist.

But when Veld looked up, his face was tender, and tears filled his rheumy eyes. She wrung her hands together.

"Please, Father. Try to understand."

"Oh, I do, I do." He said this in a quiet, resigned voice, tapping his spoon against his bowl. "You have found a young man. I saw the pony last night, you know. When I went out to make water. It is a fine gift for a betrothed."

"No, Father! I have not found a young man," Tekoah replied.

She wanted to let him think she was leaving to wed some fine young man. But she had promised herself she would speak the truth. It was important, somehow.

"I am leaving to be on my own, Father. It is time."

Her father's face grew mottled. "You are lying! I heard the news from that meddling egg woman. Weslan is here! He has sold you to some Rhantor dandy. You are going with him—do not lie to me! How dare he, that filth!"

He pounded the table with a sudden force that sent the wooden bowl flying. Cornmeal spattered everywhere. Tekoah refused to flinch, because she had promised herself to do three things: not to lie, not to tell the full truth—that was tricky—and not to cower.

Her father grew calm again, as if by a great effort of will. "You must do as you think best, daughter. You have your own life to live." He closed his eyes and held out a hand to her. She took it, sinking down onto the wooden bench beside him.

"Father"—she breathed after a moment, standing up and taking a pace back—"you knew this day must come. But I will return to visit you, as often as I can."

"No!" His voice shook with vehemence, though his eyes remained closed. "I have lost you forever. I can feel it." He sank his head into both his hands.

Tekoah put an arm around his shoulders, feeling helpless. Somewhere in the past turning she had ceased to believe in her father, but it did not mean she had ceased to care for him, or for the twins.

She had already told Raol and Fanco that she was leaving, using their hand signs. At first, she had thought they had not understood her, they had been so unsurprised; and they did not appear worried about being abandoned, as she had feared. But the twins had never been easy to comprehend.

Father felt deserted. It was sad, but she would not change her decision. Tekoah rubbed his back in small, helpless circles.

After a moment, Veld took his hands away from his face, wiping his eyes with the backs, like a small boy. He took a deep breath and smiled at her.

"I am selfish," he said. "It does not matter with whom you leave as long as they can offer you happiness—something which you have never known here."

"Father," she began, but he held up his hand.

"No, no, it is the truth. What house can be happy that has a sorcerer's curse upon it? I will not stand in your way."

She could not believe what she was hearing. But he smiled again. "Let us go have a look at your pony before you depart, shall we?"

It was becoming like one of her lovely, hopeful dreams of Father as he had once been, although perhaps never except in her own imagination. They walked outside together.

Snow was falling, feathery and light. Flare looked up and whinnied, and from the stall next to her in the shed, the donkey Thorn nickered in response. Tekoah removed the blanket she had thrown over the pony's back, shaking it out with a flourish and a proud grin.

"Ah, she's a beauty," Veld breathed, reaching out to stroke her. "Remember the first time you rode, girl? You must have been only three when I hoisted you onto that pony at your Aunt Beula's. And you screamed when we tried to take you off her."

She laughed. "I do not recall that, Father. You are inventing it, I fear."

"It is true, it is true," he protested.

For a moment, they stroked Flare's silky coat in silence. Then her father struck his forehead. "I have it!" he exclaimed. "I will shoe her for you. It will be my last gift to you."

Tekoah felt a lump rising in her throat. "There will not be time, Father. I am to meet Weslan in the village at midday, to say goodbye to him as well."

His face darkened. "Ah, I see! He does not have the courage to come here?"

"That is not fair, Father."

"I know, I know." He waved his hand in the air. "Forgive me, daughter, for feeling bitter. First my wife, then my son and heir, now my only daughter..." His voice broke.

"Father—"

Behind them, there was a sound. She looked up to see the twins standing in the doorway of the shed. They were making the gesture for Beula's farm. They were travelling there today to help Bhantok repair the stables. Tekoah wondered what they were thinking. Their impassive faces revealed nothing.

Tekoah embraced them both, one after the other, while Veld made a grimace of distaste. She watched from the shed door as they walked stolidly down the highway. After a time, she could not see them anymore, for the blur in her eyes.

"Rhan grant that you shed tears for me as you do for them." Father said. He was getting that scratchy, thirsty sound in his voice. "If you walk up to meet Weslan, or catch a ride with a cart," he continued, "I could shoe your pony for you then. It would not take long. You could come back for her this evening. Spend one more night in your family cottage. You have not given me much time to become accustomed to this, you know."

"I cannot stay another night, Father," Tekoah said. "But perhaps I could come back later and then ride her back. It is not a great distance, and she is a swift pony."

"That is my girl." Veld took her face in his hands and planted a kiss on her lips. "Now I go—to stoke up the forge fire good and hot. Let me know when you leave for the village."

Tekoah walked after all, knowing it might be the last time she did so in the open for a long time. Reika had instructed her to be at the crohm tree after dark, so she still had plenty of time to say goodbye to Weslan.

Several drivers hailed Tekoah as she went by, and she waved back. A sense of liberty was sweeping through her, although she was going into hiding.

It was midday, a time of industry, but most people would go to the village to gossip at the market square, or the Pitaya Pit if they were thirsty. There had been so much news in the last annaspan that work had all but ground to a halt. Everywhere, groups of people huddled to discuss Morogh's death, the Anniste murders, and, of course, the latest news about the assassination attempt on the queen.

As Tekoah neared the square, she smiled to think that only a short time ago she had sworn never to return to the village. Her anger seemed childish now. Her excitement continued to rise as she walked, the cold stinging her cheeks. Fear jabbed at her. To leave the home of her childhood was frightening and exhilarating at the same time. *Was this how Weslan felt?*

Weslan would be astonished when she told him of Father's reaction. He had never seen the gentler side of Veld, she thought.

The Pitaya Pit was full. Snow was falling now, covering Tekoah's head-shawl in a frosty mantle. She stood by the door, shaking it off, peering in. It was not a place she frequented. She had been there once only, in fact, with Garth the Stonemason's son. She beseeched Anna for Norah not to be in there.

The door flew open, and two men came out, barrel-chested and brawny —stonecutters from Meed, by the look of their clothes. The castle had drawn many strangers to Stern.

One looked her up and down. "Looks like we picked a bad time to leave, sweetheart," he said. "Next time come earlier, hmm?" He squinted at her through the smoke of his pipe, while his companion leaned on him.

"I will try," Tekoah smiled, ducking past them through the doorway. She shook her head. Rhan only knew what it would be like in here by sundown.

As Tekoah entered the tavern, her cold cheeks flushed in the sudden warmth of the roaring fire of crackling pine logs in the immense stone fireplace.

Even without the flurry of events, the first snow always brought villagers together throughout the North. It was the time to put aside old differences, look to larders, family and friends. The uppermost thought in everyone's mind was to survive winter. Which made a glass of hot spiced wine and a good laugh even more important.

"Get moving, girl, you're blocking the door," snapped a

serving maid, tempering her words with a grin. Tekoah stepped in.

The din was tremendous. At first, she had wondered at Weslan for picking this motley tavern, of all places, to meet, but now she thought he had been clever. Her brother had said he was tired of being pestered by villagers demanding thrilling recounts of his "slaying the assassin". Happily, anything less than a shout would go unheard in this the throng.

Tekoah's fingers throbbed in her woolen mittens as the blood returned to them, so she removed them along with her cloak, which she draped over her arm. She wore an old dress of Neela's, pale green cotton, with a scarlet sash and a dangling bunch of beaded crystal grass berries. Many years earlier, she and Weslan had played with that sash, and she fingered the grass berries as she scanned the room.

I will never find Weslan, Tekoah thought, after being jostled and pinched for several long minutes amid the bustle of din.

At that precise moment, she saw him. He stood in a corner of the room, near the fire—she could just see his face between three farmers who stood in front of her, arguing in animated voices about the drought in the South.

Every time one of them moved to thump the shoulder of another, she lost sight of Weslan. But she could see that he glanced around the room, often. He must be looking for her. Once he turned, speaking to a fellow in a black, hooded cloak. Whoever he was, he was very tall, but he had his back to her, so she could not see his face. There was something oddly familiar about the man, something about the way he stood, the breadth of his shoulders.

Could it be Garth? she wondered, her stomach churning. *Mayhap he went to Rhantor, to seek Weslan and ask for my hand?* He would have known better than to ask her father. No, it was impossible. Garth was tall, but not as lean, unless he had lost weight. And he would have never worn a hooded black cloak of such elegant cloth. She squinted, trying to see through the press of seething flesh.

A hand squeezed her waist. "May I stand you for a mug of ale, my darling?" She turned and saw the broad, ruddy face of an ox-cart driver who lived near her Aunt Beula's farm.

"Thank you, no; I am seeking a friend," she replied, and slipped between the arguing farmers. A good thing, too, for behind her it sounded as if they were coming to blows.

Weslan did not see her until she tapped him the shoulder. To her chagrin, he uttered a loud cry.

The farmers ceased their tussling, looked toward them, and a knot of young people beside them turned to stare.

Stifling a cry of her own, Tekoah hissed, "Weslan, what is it? Are you mad?"

Drops of sweat stood out on her brother's face, and it was drained of colour. He spoke with a visible effort.

"Ah, it is you, Ko. Sorry. But you are wearing mother's dress, and in the firelight, you looked just like her..."

People were still gawking at them. Weslan glanced around, then threw back his head, laughing uproariously. He drew her back toward the corner, near the fire. The gambit worked, and the attention they had attracted evaporated.

"I am sorry," he said again, hugging her. "You are like a block of ice!" he exclaimed.

She shrugged, holding up her sodden cloak. "It has been snowing."

"But where is your pony? You should not have had time to get so wet."

"I did not bring Flare," she replied.

At her words, Weslan frowned. He turned, as if by reflex, to where the hooded figure had stood. No one stood there now.

"You did not bring your pony?" he repeated, looking at her as if she had betrayed him. "What can you mean? You left her at the forge?"

"I will return for her later," she explained. "Father offered to shoe her for me before I depart the forge."

"That sounds very little like the father I remember," Weslan said, taking a swallow of ale.

"It is true, though," Tekoah insisted. "He wanted to do something for me. Do you know, Wes, when I join the Anniste, I shall have to leave Flare at Bhantok's farm for a while. But I am certain that he will take care of her."

Weslan was not listening. He was looking around, as if seeking someone. A serving maid stopped in front of them, carrying hot spiced wine and ale on a tray. Weslan took an ale for himself and handed Tekoah a goblet of steaming wine.

"Where is your companion?" the maid asked Weslan. With her dark eyes and large bosom, she reminded Tekoah of Norah.

Weslan mumbled something into his ale, avoiding Tekoah's eye.

"What did you say?" the serving maid shouted.

"Something called him away," Weslan muttered.

"That is a pity," the maid cooed, glancing sidelong at Tekoah. She held out her hand for payment, then swished away.

Tekoah stared at Weslan until he met her gaze. He resumed their conversation. "I must repeat that I find it hard to believe that Father would do something for you when you are leaving, sister."

"Well, you are wrong. And who was that serving-maid talking about?" she asked. "I thought I saw you with someone."

"You did?" Weslan shrugged.

Tekoah looked at him with exasperation. He might impress silly serving maids, standing there like a lord with his expensive cloak, but she was not one of them. Ever since they had been children, Weslan had failed to deceive her, for he could never meet her eye when he told an untruth. And he was looking uneasy. Something was afoot.

"Yes, the man who stood with you when I came in."

She turned to face him, stood there until at last he had to meet her eye.

"Yes." He took a great swallow of ale.

"Who is he?"

As she repeated the question, his face seemed to freeze, and she saw that, whatever the next moment brought, he had dreaded it.

"It is the sorcerer Braith."

Someone jostled her from behind, spilling her wine in a great red blotch over her green dress—her mother's dress—but she did not take her eyes away from Weslan's.

Braith? "You are joking," she whispered.

"Tekoah," Weslan said, urgently. "He is my friend. He has helped me more than I can say. Changed my life. And now he wants to help you. Save you from the other sorcerers. They are trying to kill the Anniste, you know."

Tekoah laughed bitterly. "I would say they are succeeding. And yet it is a sorcerer who has come to save me?"

"Yes," Weslan said. "He is not like the others, and you must trust him, as I do. He knows things, Tekoah, things we cannot fathom. That is why you must come with us. Tonight. Before it is too late."

"I know him," Tekoah said, her voice sounding in her ears as if through a rushing torrent of water. "And I do not trust him."

"You know only what you have heard through Father's ravings," Weslan replied. "Braith is not what people think. He is kind—and very powerful as well, of course, that goes without saying—but brimming with compassion and sympathy. And he offers help to Miraven, and to us in particular."

Tekoah looked at her brother as from a great distance away; close by, she saw in her mind's eye the careless wave of Braith's hand and the small piles of grey dust that had blown away in the wind. Close by also was her dream of two nights earlier, of Braith's mouth and hands and burning eyes.

"I know him!" Tekoah said again, in a shriek that came out so small that it was barely audible even to her own ears. She looked into her brother's eyes and saw that he could or would not understand. She turned and fled. Burrowing through the undulating flesh, ignoring the exclamations and oaths left in her wake, heedless of Weslan's desperate voice that rose above the rest.

At last, she was outside, breathing the fresh air in great gasps, as if she had been drowning.

It took her some time to realize that it was very cold and snowing much harder than when she had arrived. At the moment that she stopped running and wrapped her arms about herself, the oxcart driver, Hierd, hailed her from his cart.

"Why, sweetheart, you are daft to be out like that without your cloak. You will have the lung fever before you can draw another breath. Come on, hop up."

She took his proffered hand and stepped into the cart, burrowing into the heavy cloak he placed around her, looking at him with wordless gratitude.

"I live at the forge…" she began.

"I know where you live, sweetheart." He grinned.

She listened to him prattle on all the way back to the forge. Luckily, Hierd did not appear to be overly observant, or perhaps he was just polite. He did not seem to notice that she did not reply to anything he said.

Tekoah stared out into the vortex of whirling snowflakes. The wind blew them into endless circles, becoming smaller and smaller, forming a tunnel of sorts. She stared into the tunnel as if she beheld eternity, the eye of the Worldmaker. It occurred to her out of seemingly nowhere that she could probably Journey without Mirveta's Basin, and she welcomed the thought. To slip away in that moment would be a relief.

But they were at the forge. Hierd had pulled up, was about to turn the cart into the yard, but she hastily jumped down.

"Thank you," Tekoah said, "you saved me from freezing." She turned to go.

"Wait," he called, forlornly. "You did not give me an answer: will you meet me at the well, after the next Temple Day?" His oxen stood hunched in their traces, covered with snow, looking like shaggy white boulders at her as if in reproach.

"Goodbye," she replied, barely hearing what he said. "I must go now." She turned and walked toward the hut. It was becoming dark, and she could see someone had lit the lamp.

Hierd was cursing his oxen into movement again, and Tekoah heard the rumble as the cart moved down the highway. It was almost dark. She would have time to say a quick farewell to Father and saddle up Flare. But she mustn't let him know how upset she was. Or mention Braith's name.

She opened the door. Father was sitting at the table, a bottle of corn lightning in front of him, three-quarters empty.

"Hello, daughter," he said. "Did you bring your brother with you?"

Tekoah shook her head wearily. "Of course not, Father. I told you he would not come."

Her eyes went to the stove. No fire, no soup simmering there. Father had probably not eaten all day. She had better heat him up some dinner.

"Weslan did not visit me," Father said, "and the twins are gone. And you, too, wish to depart." Tekoah ignored him and kneeled to stoke up the stove fire.

"Everyone wants to leave me," Veld continued in a maudlin voice. He took a swig straight from the bottle. A bad sign.

Tekoah picked up the pot and headed to the door to pump some water. She would make a turnip and potato stew, throw in a little pork hock from the day before.

"I will not let you go!" Her father shouted the words, just as she opened the door. She jumped in alarm, turning to look back at him. He waved the bottle at her, grinning. "I have shod your pony, as I promised," he said slyly. And in his eyes lurked the gleam of malicious triumph she had seen in her dream.

Flare. She had almost forgotten about Flare. The pony was the only good thing to come out of the mess. But why had did Father look like that? As if he was baiting her.

Tekoah dropped the cooking pot and headed for the donkey shed. Halfway there, she started to run.

But Flare was not in the shed. Only Thorn, the donkey who stamped and brayed uneasily at her from his stall. She stepped out of the shed, gazing around in confusion. Father could not have left Flare tethered outside in such weather.

Had Father sold her pony? *But he would not be that cruel.* Without quite knowing why, she turned to walk around the shed where the fallow field lay—the one she kept seeing in her Journeys.

Rounding the corner, she stopped where she stood.

Tekoah saw her pony almost immediately, lying still on her side. Already the tawny body was covered in snow; but her head, severed almost completely at the neck, lay in a congealed pool of blood.

Tekoah kneeled beside her, brushing the snow off, not feeling the cold on her bare hands. She laid her hand on her pony's flank. It was still warm.

"Flare," she crooned, inching her way down until she could cradle Flare's head in her lap. While sitting, a dream-like stupor stole over her. Tekoah imagined herself sitting here forever, while gently the snow covered her, covered Flare, covered everything.

When Tekoah heard her father's voice calling, the dreaminess hardened, became a brittle ice which shattered into shards of panic. She slid Flare's head off her lap and stood up. One of her boots hit something hard, and she realized her pony had indeed been shod.

CHAPTER 21

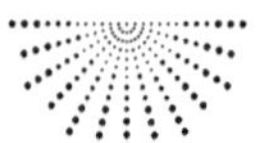

Tekoah looked up. Veld was loping toward her, unsteady, holding out his arms. She rushed past him, dodging the obstructing hand that he flung out. She ran, almost blinded by the snow, toward the highway. Behind her, she heard her father's voice—a high, harsh wail.

"'Twas not me, 'twas Braith. The sorcerer's curse. Trying to turn you against me. Don't leave me!"

Tekoah ran until she could move no longer, and then she stopped, sucking in mouthfuls of snowflakes with every ragged gasp of air.

Somehow, she was down at Stern's End, standing in front of the pond. It was freezing. She had pulled a cloak over her shoulders when she'd gone to find her pony, but it was not enough. She was freezing. But she continued to gaze into the black water. The sun had set, the snow had ceased, the sky had cleared, and the moon had risen, all without her having noticed.

There were great rents in the cloud curtain, and Anna's half-circle reflected in broken fragments, floating on the water.

Tekoah had at first been determined to throw herself in the pond. But now she stared, fascinated. And she realized she was indeed about to Journey, without the Basin. *No one has ever done that,* Reika had told her.

It came as easily as her next breath. She fell toward the dark ripples of the pond, and as she did, she heard the now-familiar song about the hole in the moon, eerie and sad. In a sudden jolt, she recognized the high, reedy voice as her own. Why had she not known it before?

And then she was standing behind the donkey shed again, looking down at Flare's poor battered body in sorrow and horror. But now it was not cold. There was no snow. It was summer, and her feet rustled in the dry grass.

Tekoah heard the thud of a spade striking the earth and lifted her gaze. Her father was standing a few feet away, his back to her. He was digging a deep hole.

She felt hot and feverish. Rivulets of sweat dripped down her face, between her breasts and down her back. A great pulse seemed to emanate from the core of the earth, drumming against her feet, so that she felt unsteady. She wanted to lie down and sleep more than anything she had ever wanted in her life.

Father stopped digging and turned around. His eyes met hers—loving, long suffering, full of silent encouragement.

"It is ready," he told her. Then, "Can you help me lift her, pigeon?"

She bent down and lifted the poor, battered pony—no, her poor battered mother's body—and carried her, holding her back and shoulders. Neela's face was cradled against her bosom.

Her father carried the legs. He was still strong, though weaker from drink than he used to be. He could have carried Neela alone. But he had chosen not.

They slid the body into the trench. Neela lay on her back, her fixed eyes staring up at the moon. Veld threw the first spadeful of earth into her face.

"Mother!" The scream echoed through her soul, ripping it from her, raw and bleeding. And she fell again, still screaming, back through the darkness.

Tekoah stood looking into the pond, but the reflected light of Anna's face was too bright. She lurched away; toward the darkest thing she saw. The Taboran Woods. She ran into the trees and kept running until her legs gave way. She kneeled, chest heaving, on a small grassy knoll, and waited for death to overtake her.

But when she looked up and saw the ring of mountain cats surrounding her, the sudden desire to live surprised her.

She sat still, knowing there was nothing else she could do. The first cat moved forward, out of the shadows of the treeline. And, as the creature moved from the sheltering darkness of the shadows, into the moonlit snow of the knoll, Tekoah saw that she had been wrong: it was not a mountain cat. For it walked on hind-legs, like a man, and its head was of human size. Its paws were hairless, like hands, but the fingernails were claws, sharp and gleaming.

All at once, Tekoah remembered her Journey to the sorcerer's lodge, and seeing Morogh's dead face. This thing looked like Morogh. She realized now what Zant had meant when he had spoken of Morogh, leaving him a legacy—and why he had chanted that incantation over Morogh's body.

As those thoughts flashed by her, the thick black lips of the cat-thing drew back in a snarl. Tekoah backed away, forcing herself not to turn and flee. She wanted two things: a few more seconds of life, and to face the thing that killed her.

Four more cat-creatures came forward, jostling each other. The leader let out a low warning growl, his message as unmistakable and timeless as the wilderness itself: *stay back, this one is mine.*

In a flash, in the second before she saw the cat-creature crouch to leap, Tekoah thought of the Anniste murders, the claw-marks on the women. And there was no longer any doubt in her mind these monsters were Zant's creation for hunting down the Anniste.

Morgs, she thought, the name coming unbidden into her mind. If only she could warn the women, tell them somehow.

The Morg sprang. Tekoah sank to her knees and closed her eyes.

There was a high gurgling sound. After that, a cacophony of snarls, hisses and yowls. Tekoah's eyes flew open. The Morg lay in front of her, writhing in the snow, blood flowing from multiple wounds in its throat and chest. Yet there was no visible assailant. The other Morgs streaked away, their leaping shapes making ghostly shadows on the snow.

Tekoah kneeled on the frozen ground, watching as the Morg died in front of her. When she could bear no more, she put her face in her hands. After a time, the sounds ceased, leaving only a quivering silence.

A shadow fell over her. Then a voice whispered, but the sound shattered the eerie silence like breaking ice.

"So dies any creature who tries to harm you."

Tekoah looked up. Black against white, he stood—Braith.

It is a dream, she thought. But no, it was not. Unless her entire life was nothing but a dream. She tried to smile at the thought but found she could not.

Braith bent over her, scooped her up as though she was only a rabbit or a kitten. She felt a brief, fierce panic. The sorcerer—escape, oh escape! Then, only the warm hardness of his chest, his cloak around her, his breath against her hair. And she let herself go.

CHAPTER 22

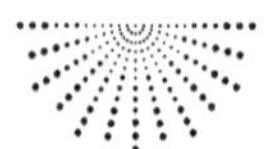

Tekoah sat up abruptly on Chalvern's pallet and uttered a high, wild scream of terror. The sound was chilling. Chalvern, who was sitting on the edge of the cot, thought, *my old heart cannot take much more of this.*

It had been several hours since Braith had carried her in, kicking the door open with a violence that had almost taken it off. The poor girl had dripped blood like a pigeon on Rhan's altar, and Chalvern had feared at first that she was dead. But the blood had not been hers. Whose it was, he had yet to find out.

All Braith had said to his frantic questioning was a terse, "Stern's End. Half-frozen. Badly shocked."

Braith refused to say any more, but stood in a corner of the room, silent and watchful, as the apothecary stripped off Tekoah's bloody clothes, dressed her in an old nightshirt, and put her straight to bed.

Chalvern had been waiting ever since for the girl to rouse herself enough to take a sip of the broth and wine that he had heated in a bowl. But she lay, small and white, reminding him of how it had been the other time he had brought her back from the world of the wraiths.

Now this bloodcurdling scream. Before Chalvern could move or react, Braith was there. Bending over her, enfolding her in his arms. Chalvern stared, struggling with his emotions. He had not thought the sorcerer capable of such tenderness, and the part of him that loved Braith as a son rejoiced. But his fear of sorcerers —their cold eyes, crushing hooves, utter indifference to the pain of others—overwhelmed him.

The boy whom he loved had transformed into another being, and he did not know who Braith was anymore. Perhaps Braith did not know.

So Chalvern watched, his heart torn within him, as the sorcerer sat down on the cot, stroking Tekoah's long, tangled hair, until she closed her eyes again. Her head lolled back against his arm.

It was at that moment that Weslan burst through the door.

Which will collapse first, Chalvern wondered, *my heart, or that old door?*

"I was going to the forge," Weslan explained, panting, "but I thought I would try here, just in case." He halted, gaping in confusion at the scene of his sister, the apothecary and the sorcerer.

The sorcerer, still bent over Tekoah's prostrate form, did not turn around.

"Braith advised me to wait at the Pitaya Pit and hope that my sister might change her mind and come back." Weslan addressed the words to Chalvern. "I waited for over an hour, but all the while I had an uneasy feeling that she would not return."

He spoke faster, casting nervous glances at the pallet. "Is my sister all right? What is all that blood—?" He looked horrified as he caught sight of Tekoah's crimson-drenched garments.

"Ask your father about the blood." Braith lowered Tekoah's head back onto the pillow and turned to face Weslan. Chalvern groaned.

"What happened?" Weslan asked, his voice rising.

"The blood is not hers," Chalvern answered, laying a hand on Weslan's arm. "Come, have some wine."

"I have had nothing to do but drink all afternoon and evening," Weslan's voice shook with impatience. "Tell me what is going on! Did Father try to stop her from leaving?"

"Between your father and Zant's Morgs, you are fortunate to still have a sister," Braith said.

Chalvern shuddered. Morogh's cat-face rose before him, feral, unblinking, just as it had been before his horse's hooves had crushed his ribs.

"What are Morgs?" he asked, finding he could barely move his lips.

"They are what you have already guessed, Master—a new sorcery created by Zant, who does not wish the Anniste to outlive Morogh by too long."

Chalvern nodded toward the bed. "They almost got her, then?"

"Almost." The sorcerer's eyes locked onto his, and Chalvern saw in them an implacable will. But would that be enough to protect Tekoah against every danger? And what if that danger included Braith himself?

"What are you two talking about?" Weslan's voice had become belligerent. He did not like being kept in the dark.

Had the boy guessed of how little importance he was to Braith? Chalvern wondered. Weslan was not the analytical sort. Ah, well, everything would be plain soon enough.

"Weslan?" Tekoah's voice came from the cot in the corner, plaintive, frightened.

Weslan turned and strode to the bed. Chalvern saw Braith raise his hand as though to stop him, and then lower it again.

Weslan sat on the cot beside his sister. "What is it, Ko?" he asked, taking her hand.

Would that you had been here when she had the fever, Chalvern silently accused him. *She cried out for you often enough.*

Tekoah sat up, struggling for words, her eyes cloudy. "I am sorry about the pony, Wes," she said brokenly. "I loved her so."

"It is no matter," Weslan answered, "Flare is yours anyway. Whether or not you decide to come with us. But I still wish you would come."

"If I thought Father would have done that to her, I never would have left her with him, even for a moment," Tekoah continued, as if she had not heard. "It is just that I had forgotten he does things like that."

Chalvern's chest tightened, the same way it had when Raol had come through his door bearing the limp body of the boy-Braith.

"What do you mean?" Weslan spoke the words slowly.

"The blood!" she cried suddenly. "All the blood." She covered her face with her hands. "And the ground was frozen, so Flare could not even be buried as we buried Mother."

The room became still, as if they had all stopped breathing. Beside him, Chalvern sensed Braith waiting, alert.

"*Mother.*" Weslan echoed the word, his voice hopeless. It was not a question.

"I am so sorry, Wes." Tekoah was weeping, choking on her tears. Her long gold-brown hair hung before her face like a mourning veil.

Something died within Chalvern, something precious and irretrievable. *It is true, then.* Deep down, he had known.

Weslan stood up from the bed, his back to Chalvern and Braith. He stood there for several moments, watching his sister. Then he bent down and kissed her forehead.

"It will be all right," he said. "Rest now." He turned and went to the door, stumbling a little. At the threshold he stopped, looking at Braith. "Rhantor can wait another day," he said. "I must pay a visit to the forge."

Braith did not reply.

Bitterness choked Chalvern's throat at the confidence and

authority in Weslan's voice. As if he controlled what was happening.

Into the silence that followed came the muffled sound of hooves in the snow as Weslan galloped away. Chalvern could not look at Braith, for he had seen a gleam in the sorcerer's eyes at Weslan's last words.

There was much sorrow ahead for Weslan. One did not require the heart of a healer to see that. Chalvern covered his face with his hands briefly, then looked back at the sorcerer.

Braith's gaze was inscrutable. Behind them on the cot, Tekoah had ceased weeping and drifted into slumber. The belladonna tincture had taken hold, and her chest rose and fell, her face tranquil.

Let her take her peace when she can, Chalvern thought. He went to the earthen jar to get more oil for the lamp.

"She will be safe with me," Braith said from behind him.

"You can only guess at the truth of that," Chalvern answered.

"I saved her tonight. She would be dead if it were not for me."

"She would not have been out there tonight had it not been for you!"

Braith's eyes flashed with anger at that, but Chalvern cared not. On that bed lay his daughter, whether or not his blood coursed through her veins.

"It was only a matter of time," Braith said. "Between Veld and the Morgs, they would have destroyed her before another turning had passed. And what have you done to protect her, Master?"

That stung. *I, too, have saved her life,* Chalvern wanted to cry.

But it was the truth—he had not done enough. He should have sent her away from her father, by any means he could have mustered. Failing in that, he should have grasped the seriousness of Braith's obsession, and realized he would not let her go so easily.

But now, here we are. And if there was a way to help Tekoah, he could achieve it only by remaining calm.

He answered Braith's inflammatory question with mildness. "We do what we can," he murmured, pouring oil in a steady stream into the lamp, then turning it down a little before sinking into his chair. Weariness shook all his limbs. He wished to be alone, to weep for Neela, but knew he must keep his mind clear.

With a bruised and aching heart, Chalvern also acknowledged that he needed to banish the boy-Braith from his mind and face reality: when dealing with a sorcerer, one had to keep his wits about him.

"I shall take her away from all danger," Braith said to him in a reasonable tone. "And she need not love me in return. I would not force myself upon her, if that is what you fear. You know me better than that."

"*Knew,*" Chalvern said. Braith looked at him. "I knew you," he repeated, "before you became a sorcerer. You are not who you were, having melded with your Source. Even those who know little about sorcerers know what that means: taking on certain attributes of your Source and giving up some of your human traits. Compassion, pity, and understanding are the first traits that disappear."

Braith was frowning at him, so Chalvern hoped he had made his point.

"How can you pledge to protect Tekoah?" he asked. "Do you know yourself that well? Will not your own survival take priority over everything else? I never believed in the Mantling's legend, but what if it is true? If the Mantling threatens to put an end to your kind and you have the means to prevent it, do you imagine you will be so noble as to sacrifice yourself for your love?"

As he spoke, Chalvern began to fear he was in over his head. *What do I know about any of this?* he thought, panicked.

"I would never pretend such a thing." Braith's voice was low and angry. "I have no use for nobility, or sacrifice. I cannot live without her, that is all I know."

Chalvern stared at Braith's tense jaw and averted face. "Is it that bad?" he asked.

"Worse."

"My son," Chalvern murmured. "I am sorry for you. But you must not act with rashness. To swoop off with Tekoah, isolate her from others—she may be safe, but will she be happy?"

"How do you know she will not?" Braith whirled around, his eyes flashing with a dangerous light. He walked over to the foot of the bed and stared down at Tekoah's sleeping form.

"And what about the Anniste?" Chalvern asked. "Zant will hunt them down, one by one. Tekoah is their Guardian by right —without her, they cannot Journey. That is what they told her. Whether that is true or a delusion, it is still their belief—that their Journeys are their only means of defending themselves in this deadly war."

Braith glanced at him, then shrugged. He did not care.

"You would let Zant slaughter them?" Chalvern asked. His voice was shaking with outrage.

"They are nothing to do with me," Braith said. "I refused to take part in any of the recent killings. Nor will I harm the Anniste in the future."

"You can be sure of their undying gratitude," Chalvern said bitterly. "Or should I say, their dying gratitude?"

"They *should* be glad of it," Braith snapped. "There would be many more dead now if I had not refused this undertaking. And I have not earned Zant's gratitude, I can tell you." His voice was brooding, his heavy brows lowered.

He must be very lonely, Chalvern thought, looking at his face.

Shunned by sorcerers and mortals alike. *Where is his home? It could be with me, still, if he wanted.*

"There is another thing, Braith," he ventured. "Have you thought of the danger to Tekoah if Zant finds out she is with you, and who she is? He must want very much to know what you are doing right now. From what you have just described, it sounds to me as if he has drawn battle lines."

"Leave matters you cannot comprehend to me, Master. I beg you." Braith's teeth clenched, and his fists curled at his sides.

A memory came to Chalvern of sitting in the shop when Braith was thirteen or so. He had refused to go into apprenticeship at the temple, and the other boys had evidently been jeering at him for it. Chalvern had heard of the taunts, but the boy had not mentioned one word to him.

Braith had sat at the sorting table, grinding herbs, saying nothing, but his teeth had been clenched so tight it had made Chalvern's jaw ache to look at him.

Then, without warning, the boy had exploded, hurling the mortar and pestle against the wall, crying, "I hate them, I hate them all!"

Braith had no friends to lose, no one whose companionship he would miss. *Except perhaps mine,* Chalvern thought, *but I am probably deluding myself. He did not miss me enough to come back before eleven turnings had passed.*

"I am taking her, Master," Braith said, quietly.

"You are not giving her a choice," Chalvern gestured toward the bed in desperation. "Why do not you wait at least until she wakes up, ask her if she wishes to go with you? Are you afraid of what she will say?"

Braith shook his head slightly, refusing the bait. "There is no time."

"What about Weslan? He thinks you are all going back to Rhantor together, for a fine life. He probably hopes that you will help him find a husband for his sister."

"Weslan must take control of his own destiny now," Braith answered, his voice indifferent, as if Weslan was merely a nodding acquaintance.

Chalvern said acidly, "Oh, and will you excuse me for thinking that when you are done toying with Tekoah, you will abandon her as casually as you do her brother?"

"You overreach yourself, Master!" Braith's voice was like thunder. He raised his arm, and Chalvern automatically covered his head with trembling hands. How elemental was human fear; there was no need for thought.

Braith lowered his arm. Their eyes met. A moment slipped by, an eternity.

"Forgive me," Braith murmured. He bent down and lifted Tekoah from the cot, wrapping the blanket around her as if she was a small child.

"If you take this path"—Chalvern told him, finding his voice with a great effort—"I do not wish to see you again. What we have had together will be severed."

Braith was tucking the blanket under Tekoah's chin. He looked up briefly, his green-gold gaze unfathomable. "That is your choice, Master, not mine."

"You cannot do this!" Chalvern cried.

But Braith was gone, disappearing in a blink of an eye before he had finished speaking the words. And Tekoah with him.

There was a dreadful pounding which reverberated in Chalvern's ears; it was several moments before he realized that he himself was making the sound, smashing his fist repeatedly against the wooden wall of his bedchamber.

He dropped his arm, for he felt no better. In his heart was a great heaviness—a truth which could not be denied: that night, he had lost both a son and a daughter.

CHAPTER 23

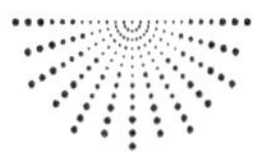

As Weslan rode westward toward the forge, he marvelled, for the true purpose of his return to Stern had now become clear. And, as always, in times such as these, he felt the divine force of Rhan heating the blood in his veins, as though he was a piece of precious metal being purified. Heated into a frenzy of action. He was filled with light, clear-headed, and so charged with energy that it was a little dizzying.

It was the same euphoria that had coursed through him at other crucial times in his life: when the Berlotans had hurled themselves over the hill in the pitaya orchard that day; when he had turned on his mount, scalp prickling, to see his destiny written in the face of an unknown sorcerer; and when he had kept a rendezvous with an assassin in the anteroom of the queen's bedchamber.

It was dawn. Rhan's fingers came stealing over the Taboran Mountains, casting a golden glow over the castle on the hilltop. In the sunlight, snow glittered all around him, as Weslan rode, sick and exalted, into the yard of his childhood home.

No smoke came from the chimney of the hut or the forge itself. He trotted his horse first around to the back, behind the small stable. Dismounting, he led his gelding into the stall next to the donkey.

Knowing where he must go next, he tarried for a moment and stroked his steed's neck, whispering "Good job, Wicker." He spoke a friendly greeting to Thorn, the donkey, and tried to slow his breathing.

Then he stepped back out into the harsh light and walked around to the back of the shed, up to the snow-covered mound that had been Tekoah's pony.

Without quite knowing why he did so, Weslan bent down and brushed the snow away from the creature's face. The pony's eyes stared at the white winter sky. He saw that someone had hacked her neck off the body with a dull axe, and revulsion shuddered through his shoulders. Heyg had instilled in him a respect for clean strokes and sharpened weapons of death.

He stood up, hesitating whether to cover the pony again in some token gesture of burial. The ground was too hard to even attempt a trench. But it would snow more before long, and soon no covering would be necessary. He walked away, and then turned back on an impulse, kneeling to heap great handfuls of white powder over the poor creature's head.

When he stood up, he remembered Tekoah had said that they had buried their mother in the field. He gazed out over the snowy ground. It did not seem possible that Mother was there, alone under all the white glittering diamond points of snow and ice, in the dark. That he had gone on with his life, selfish and unaware.

The smell of wood smoke wafted into the chill morning air. Looking around, Weslan saw grey wisps curling out of the chimney of the hut. Was it Veld who had stoked up the fire, or the twins? But no, Tekoah had told him in the Pitaya Pit that Raol and Fanco had gone to Bhantok's farm. *Good for them.*

Weslan's footsteps crunched in the snow as he strode back

to the hut. He stood waiting for Veld to come out, although whether his father would choose to do so, Weslan did not know.

But Veld emerged a moment later. He must have heard the footsteps, or perhaps the sound of Weslan's horse a few moments earlier. He was smiling as he pulled a stained tunic over his head. Expecting a customer.

Weslan acknowledged, half-admiringly, that his father was a powerful man still. The knotted muscles of his arms and shoulders strained against his sleeves as he drew the laces of his breeches hastily together.

But he was a shrunken image of the man Weslan had carried in his mind over the past turning. Slack, stooped, eyes glazed, face a yellow mask of advanced drunkenness, greying hair thin against his scalp. A dull countenance, seamed with age and self-destruction.

The face of a murderer.

A woodpecker drilled into a nearby fir tree and Weslan heard his gelding whinny from the shed. Veld looked toward the shed and then back at Weslan, recognition dawning like a flint spark in his eyes. They gazed at each other, and a long moment slipped by. For the first time, Weslan was the taller, or perhaps he was only standing on higher ground.

"Ah," Veld breathed, and danced the shuffling, elusive dance of the very frightened.

"You shod a pony last night, Veld," Weslan answered flatly. "Your workmanship is unparalleled."

"My son," Veld answered, backing away, pebbles flying off beneath his frantic feet. "I do not know what you mean. If you are speaking of that poor creature out back, then I must explain. A mountain cat attacked her last night—I heard the screams. It was terrible. I ran out at once and beat the thing off. But, try as I might to revive her—"

Weslan cut him off with a savage gesture. "Is that what happened to my mother as well?"

Veld did not answer. Sweat trickled down Weslan's temples, although the morning was cold.

Did Mother call my name? Did she cry out for me? Weslan wondered. His eyes filled with unbidden tears. At that moment, Veld fled.

He must have known it was a run for his life, for Veld moved quickly for a man in his condition. But Captain Heyg had trained Weslan in combat over the past turning. He felt almost cheated at the ease with which he landed on Veld's back. He flipped his father over, holding him splayed out on the ground.

"Son," Veld whispered. "My eldest son and heir." Flecks of saliva flew from his mouth.

"Heir to what?" Weslan asked, pleased at the evenness of his voice. "Lunacy, terror? Cowardice, lies? Torture, death? Thank you, but no. I must forfeit my inheritance."

Veld shook his head, tears coursing down his cheeks. Weslan's calm dissolved, and he screamed, "Killer! Beast! Demon!" He spat in Veld's face. "Where did you bury my mother?" he asked.

When Veld did not answer, he put his hands around his father's throat and squeezed. After a moment, he stopped.

Veld gasped, "Behind the shed. Where the grass berries grow thickest in the summer."

Weslan nodded, then began squeezing again. He did not stop until all movement in the quivering, thrashing body beneath him had ceased.

EVEN SO, Weslan thought: *This man did not suffer enough. I am sorry, Mother, he did not suffer enough.*

eslan rode back to the village, his hands jerking with involuntary movements upon the reins. Gone were the sword-sharp images, the vivid brightness, the exaltation. There remained only a sick churning in his stomach. Everything seemed dull, muffled. Had it clouded over?

But no, the sky was clear. Whenever he looked up at it, that blue emptiness held a frightening allure. It filled him with a yearning for something that he could not quite name—a cool, unthinking void.

The whitewashed walls of the temple passed him, the chanting of the priests within reverberating in the air. They had not yet finished the Dawn Greeting. He remembered he had once served a brief time as a Son-of-Rhan in that temple—before being expelled for fighting.

Weslan would have made a good priest, Grindhor had intoned to his congregation, for Rhan's fire burned deep within his soul. If only that fire had been channeled toward Rhan's enemies instead of his servants. But Weslan had not wanted to be a priest. There was not enough glory in it.

For a moment, he did not know where he was going, and

then he saw Chalvern's shop, across the square from Mirveta's Well.

Tekoah. He had forgotten about her. Weslan had been moving as if he was half-asleep, when all the time his sister waited here, confused and helpless.

She must be terrified out of her wits, he thought, *stranded with Chalvern and Braith. I did not give her enough time to get used to the idea of Braith as someone who has befriended us.* He hoped Braith had kept his distance, because she needed nothing else to frighten her.

Weslan reassured himself that everything would change soon. They would begin the ride back to Rhantor that very day. Perhaps they should leave at once. *Yes!* What was to stop them?

He reasoned things through: Tekoah no longer had her pony, but she could take turns riding behind the two men. It would not be the most luxurious journey, however Tekoah was accustomed to hardship, and seldom complained. And it would all be worth it once she saw the royal city. Rhantor would dazzle her!

He continued to paint his radiant vision: Darielle and Tekoah would love each other the moment they met—he was certain of that. And no one would ever have to know his sister had belonged to the Anniste. She would be safe. And happy.

Weslan's heart rose, knowing that he would never have to think about any of this again. He could forget all the mangled things lying unburied, half-buried or buried in the snow behind the forge. The memories would be banished forever.

He reined in at Chalvern's shop and sprang from the saddle. In his haste, he almost collided with three old village biddies who were standing in the front, scowling and muttering to each other.

"It is no good," one of them told him. "The Apothecary won't come down. He says he is closed today. And I need penny-royal for my toothache. 'Get it yourself,' he says, 'and leave the money on the table.'" Her cracked mouth quivered in self-pity.

"Get it yourself! How am I supposed to know where it is? He has become a daft old man, has Chalvern."

Another woman nodded. "He needs a real apprentice, not one of the priest's rejects, that is plain as the wart on your face."

The third woman snickered. "Someone willing to hold his chamber pot for him in the morning so he can aim straight."

All three cackled. Weslan brushed past the crones and started up the stairs.

"It is no good," the first one called after him again, as if he had not heard before. "He won't come down."

He entered Chalvern's bedchamber, shutting the door against the flapping and cawing downstairs. The apothecary sat slumped on his cot, staring at nothing. Tekoah and Braith were not there.

"Where are they?" Weslan asked, his voice raw.

Chalvern looked up. His keen brown eyes were filmy, and his face was drawn and grey. Weslan had never thought of the apothecary as old until that moment.

"What did you do at the forge?" Chalvern asked back. He spoke as if he knew what Weslan had done but did not much care.

Weslan's legs shook so violently that he staggered over and sat down in the wooden chair. Outside, he could hear the creaking of carts begin. It was market day.

"You killed your father, did you not?" Chalvern's voice was mild, holding no reproach.

"He deserved more, much more than what I did to him," Weslan answered. To his horror, he started to weep.

Chalvern waited until he had subsided. "Do not think I judge you," he said. In a faraway tone, he added, "I loved your mother, you know."

Weslan looked at him uncomprehendingly. There was too much to think about. "Where is my sister, and Braith?" he asked again.

"Gone." Chalvern said and looked away.

"Gone where? We are leaving for Rhantor today!" Weslan stared at Chalvern's averted face, waiting for a reply. *Stupid old man. Why doesn't he explain anything?*

"Did they go to buy another horse? Supplies? Or did they come looking for me?"

Chalvern still did not answer, but gazed fixedly at the wooden floor. Downstairs, incessant voices buzzed in the shop.

A terror began creeping up from the pit of his belly. For no reason at all, Weslan saw in his mind's eye Tekoah's hand, fragile and white, lost in Braith's crimson glove.

He walked over to where Chalvern sat, grabbed him by the shoulders and shook him. "Where is my sister?" he shouted, using the volume of his voice to hold down the terror.

Chalvern looked up at him, and his eyes were the same as they had been the previous night. Frightened, and something more. Pitying. He did not struggle, although Weslan's grip on his shoulders must have hurt.

"My poor boy," Chalvern whispered, "do you not see that it was she whom he wanted all along? He saw her before he ever saw you. He just needed to get to her. And now he has become her saviour."

Weslan released Chalvern, who slumped forward again, face slack.

"But Braith is my friend!" Weslan told Chalvern, raising his voice, making it ring with authority. "You are mistaken in this. Braith came here to help me. By helping my family, he helps me, you see."

Chalvern did not reply.

It is so dark in here! Weslan thought, panicked. Moving blindly, he threw open the shutters and walked out onto the balcony, willing everything to be as he imagined. Eyes burning, he looked down at the square.

But no matter how hard he looked, they were not there, and so he turned and left.

SHORTLY AFTER HE had passed the forge once more, heading out at a flat gallop along the highway, Weslan heard the voices. A man's and a woman's, arguing with each other. He glanced about him out of habit, although he knew that there was no one around within sight or earshot.

They were arguing, low and fierce. At the beginning, he could not distinguish most of their words, and now and then their dialogue would fade away to the faintest of whispers, infuriating him. Weslan sang a drinking song to drown them out, but could not bear the sound of his own hoarse, frightened voice. He took charge of the situation.

"I am not mad," he shouted, drawing his startled horse to a halt. "My father—he was mad! But I am not. Go away."

There was a moment's silence; but then, as he broke into a canter, the voices came back, relentless, their mocking laughter drumming beneath the hoofbeats. He ignored it, riding on until a company of soldiers bearing the Kalesh emblem on their tunics came toward him from the opposite direction. When Weslan did not stop after being hailed—and then surrounded— the men brought him down with a speed and strength which stunned him. He had hardly noticed them.

"Going somewhere in a hurry?" panted the soldier who sat on his chest.

He looks new to the job, thought Weslan, feeling detached. The fellow was strong, but lacked any sophistication. Not someone properly trained in the lethal, elegant manoeuvres of the Kalesh.

"What business is it of yours?" he retorted, although it was hard to breathe with the oaf crushing his lungs.

The man struck him a hard but half-fisted blow across the cheek. "Soon *you* will be nobody's business." He grinned.

"Tarry a moment!" someone exclaimed. The voice sounded familiar to Weslan. "Release him, Parrin—I know him well. He is my cousin Weslan, and closer to the queen than any of you will ever hope to be, so leave off."

Weslan looked up to see his cousin Bhantok. *By the Holy Mantling, it has to be that ass, in this moment,* he thought.

But at least the pressure on his chest was gone, for the soldier leaped off as if he had just discovered he was sitting on a flaming log. "I beg pardon, sir," Parrin said.

He offered a hand to help Weslan stand. Bhantok was smiling, his round face reflecting a ridiculous pride as he pointed at the crest on his sleeve.

"I am aspiring to your heights, cousin," he said. "Just give me time, and I may find my own fair maid to rescue."

Weslan waved at him, unimpressed. "What are you doing, Bhantok? Playacting as you did when we were children?" He brushed himself off.

Parrin handed him Wicker's reins with a sheepish expression.

"Something like that," chuckled Bhantok. "Only this time it wasn't me who got roughed up. That is a turnabout, is it not?"

Weslan mounted his horse, ignoring his cousin's amiable chatter. He did not wish to talk to anyone. The voices were murmuring again. He wanted only to ride fast, away from people.

"Are you not aware that they could imprison you for impersonating one of the Kalesh?" he asked. "This is no joking matter—we attend to serious business."

Bhantok stared at him, his mild grey eyes protruding a little. "Do you mean to tell me you have not heard the news?" he asked.

"What news?" Weslan wheeled his horse around. Wicker

pawed the frozen ground. He was as eager to be off as his master.

"The queen has been abducted by Berlotans—the Jinta's own company. And King Darian has turned a blind eye to the whole thing, that scurvy traitor."

Weslan gazed at Bhantok. He stood in his saddle, legs rigid. Seeing the reaction to his words, Bhantok swelled with self-importance.

"We have verified reports that King Darian has sold out Miraven to the Berlotan scum, and his royal sister is only the first pay-off. The sorcerer Zant engineered the whole thing and has seized city of Rhantor in the king's name. He is changing the name of the city to Zantor. How revolting!"

Weslan did not reply, but Bhantok continued prattling, delighted to be part of the excitement. "War is imminent. The leader of the Kalesh has sent out a proclamation: all able-bodied northerners have been called to join the Kalesh. For the North and for the queen!"

At Bhantok's last words, the surrounding men raised their swords and clashed them together, shouting, "For the North, and for the queen!" with great gusto.

"We must all do our part," Bhantok continued. "Any able-bodied man is now eligible to join the Kalesh, not just nobles and gentry. Whoever proves courageous and loyal in this war will receive many honours—and perhaps even riches—afterward. So here we are. My men and I are doing our part by patrolling the roads, looking for suspicious characters."

"Queen Darielle?" Weslan repeated in disbelief. "They have captured her?"

Bhantok nodded. "Taken as a concubine for the Jinta. But we are going to get her back, of course. With the help of heroes like yourself, cousin. After all, you already saved her once. Everyone is talking about you."

"Are they?" Weslan began to laugh. He could not stop

himself, even when he saw the look of chagrin on Bhantok's face. He gestured at his cousin and the other soldiers, trying wordlessly to explain why it was all so funny. But they did not understand.

This is what it must be like for Raol and Fanco, he thought, *when they speak with their hands to an entire world of uncaring, uncomprehending fools.*

Still laughing, so hard that tears rained down his face, he rode off, straight toward the Taboran Woods.

When he reached the edge of the forest, Weslan dismounted and slapped Wicker's rump, sending the gelding off in the road's direction. *The last of my partings,* he thought. As he walked into the thick wall of trees, he reflected that he would probably would not come out alive. The North in winter, the wilderness, and he alone—it was utmost folly. It would only be a question of time before the cold got him, or the mountain cats.

But then madness was his inheritance, after all. And the thought of living—going on with it all—had become unbearable. At everything he had failed. He had set himself up for glory. Pride had blinded him. Had it not been for his overweening vanity, those whom he loved—his mother, his sister, his queen —might have been spared from heartache and danger. For childish and selfish dreams, he had sold them, one by one.

Blindness. It came from daring to look too long upon the face of Rhan. Well, now he would look no longer. He would bury himself in the heart of winter and wait for death.

CHAPTER 25

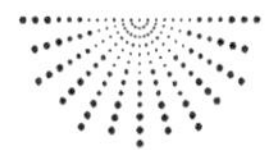

Tekoah glimpsed Chalvern's face, white and frantic, his mouth opened in a cry of protest. He seemed so fragile and insignificant, as he tried to swim to her against the powerful, dark current that was Braith.

Then she saw nothing but blackness. Braith's cloak, she thought at first, for his arms pressed her close against his chest. But when she lifted her head, there was still only blackness. It was like a Journey, and yet not a Journey. The absence of light and sound frightened her more than had all the voices and visions in Mirveta's Basin. With the desperation of someone who was drowning, she struggled for light, for air.

"Hush," Braith said against her ear, and his gloved hand stroked her cheek.

And so, the darkness dissolved. She stood, blinking, swaying against Braith, who held her by the shoulders to keep her from falling. Soft amber light surrounded them, with pockets of shadow, but her eyes stung as if exposed to the harshest sunlight, after that utter dark.

"Where are we?" she asked, her throat dry.

"In the castle on the hill," Braith answered. He smiled at her.

"I do not know why. It was the first image that came to my mind. I was in rather a hurry."

The Castle of Mirrand. Tekoah stared around. *They must expect the lord of Mirrand home soon,* she thought. For it was furnished luxuriously, as if to prepare for someone's arrival, with soft fur rugs on the floor and tapestries on the walls. There were even fresh flowers in an earthen jar, and sweetmeats on silver trays.

"The flowers were my idea," Braith told her, sounding hesitant. Had he read her thoughts, or followed the path of her eyes with relentless scrutiny? Which was worse?

His chest rose and fell against her shoulder, and she could feel his breath on her neck. Even so, she could not make herself turn and look at him. She took an unsteady step away, so that they were no longer touching.

Looking at the flowers, she saw that they were violets, and her cheeks grew warm. "Why have you brought me here?" she asked.

Without answering, Braith turned and walked to a small crohmwood table, with legs carved curiously to resemble the legs of some bird or beast. A silver flagon and two goblets were set upon its shining indigo surface. Braith picked up the flagon and poured wine, dark and red. He held a goblet out to her.

Tekoah stared at him. "Why have you brought me here?" she asked again.

"A haven," he answered. "You looked as if you needed one."

His voice was so kind that unshed tears welled in her eyes. A haven—yes, oh yes, she needed one.

Braith was still holding out the goblet, and now he walked the few steps over to her, putting it in her hand. The fragrance of the wine rose up to her nostrils, like spring earth, summer flowers.

"Drink," he said, his voice soothing, "drink and forget."

She put her lips to the goblet, then hesitated. "There are

wounds I must heal," she told him, not expecting him to under-stand. But he nodded.

"Healing is forgetting," he answered.

I once dreamt of this, Tekoah thought. *Or is this the dream?* She could not be sure.

Forgetting. Reika had told her not to forget, after that first Journey. What was it she had said? Healing began by remem-bering—that was it.

But Reika was not there to guide her, only Braith, holding the goblet to her lips. She drank. It was not until after she had drained the goblet that she looked up into Braith's eyes. In them, she saw not the kindness that had been in his voice, but the same hungry light as in her dream.

He took the goblet and set it down on the table. Tekoah felt his hands hard on her waist. The same hands had decimated men, turning them into small piles of dust; had strangled a nightmare creature without touching it. She should be more terrified.

"You would take me by enchantment, then?" she asked, her voice blurred and far away in her ears.

"There is no power in the world that can conjure love," Braith answered, and his hands moved to her hair, stroking it. "The wine has banished your fear for a little while, that is all. Have you not been frightened enough?"

He steered her by the shoulders, seating her on one of the ornate sofas by the fireplace. The cushions were soft, and she allowed her head to loll back against them. It would be a great mistake to let herself relax, though.

She tried to concentrate. "And should I not fear *you?*" she asked.

"You must not," he replied, "you are all of my world."

Braith stood, and Tekoah watched him take off his crimson gloves, looking at her with the same diffidence as before. His hands were long and brown, with slender tapered fingers. Beautiful hands. Why did he hide them always? Then she saw the gleaming black talons and knew why. Though he kept them clipped short, they still looked deadly. But still she felt no fear.

The sweet wine sang in her veins as Braith bent over her, his lips on her cheek. Black hair brushed her face with a scent like evergreen trees. He kissed her again, on the corner of her mouth. Then he looked into her eyes, his gaze fierce, almost angry. "How you have made me suffer," he whispered. And his mouth caught hers up, not gently at all this time.

And it was as it had been in her dream. She felt the heat along the length of his body as he crushed her to him, and the slow, helpless unfurling of herself to him, to his hot, hard hands and devouring mouth. And in the intensity of their struggle toward and against each other, it seemed that he would devour her.

Then Tekoah understood what Braith had meant when he said that she was all the world to him. For it seemed there was no room at all in the world for anything but their flesh, their struggle.

And at the end, as her body arched itself up toward him, she felt his talons rake her back, but her pleasure dulled the searing pain, as she had known it would.

* * *

Darkness. Whispers. Braith's voice against her ear.

"I must leave you." It was said with an anguished reluctance.

"Why?"

"It is for a short time only. Otherwise, I could not bear it."

"But why?"

"Nothing to disturb your sweet dreams, my love."

"Do you not trust me enough to tell me? Or do you think me a fool?"

"Never that. Do not torment me. I have been summoned by Zant. If I do not go, he will seek me out. I will not compromise your safety. It is all that matters now. There is only us—everything else is a dream. Only I must keep the dream from waking us. Do you understand?"

"No. But kiss me anyway."

A long silence. "That, I understand." Teasingly. "You are an endless thirst. It matters not how much I drink, I can never be slaked."

"But you drink so much."

"I KNOW." A low, despairing sound. Then, "But listen, I have left your wine in the silver flagon. Drink, at evening, as always. Promise me?"

"How long will you be gone?"

"Not long. Promise me?"

"I promise." Sleepily.

"Little Violet." Silence.

"Sleep well."

CHAPTER 26

Time moved slowly, bubbles through still water. Tekoah's surroundings were filmy, softened, the edges dulled and blurred as if seen through gauzy curtains. Toward evening, before it became time to drink the wine, the edges sharpened, regain their clarity. Never for long. After she drank, any thoughts that had taken flight within her mind glided back down to float peacefully on the still water.

Tekoah had counted by scratching her wrists, and therefore she knew the length of her sojourn with Braith had been only three days, but it seemed much longer than that. Her memories of anything else were so far away that it took an utmost concentration to remember even the names of her brothers, her mother, anyone. Sometimes she tried to think about that world —the world outside of them. It was never for long.

When Braith left late in the third night, it had also been like a dream. But midway through the next day, Tekoah was uneasy. She meandered through the castle, which she had yet to explore —Braith had consumed her every moment—touching the silken draperies, smelling the flowers, nibbling at fruits and nuts in dainty bowls. It was all so strange.

However, toward evening, Tekoah walked with a firmer tread. The fog in her head dissipated, and sensations became sharper.

Her body was tender. Standing unclothed in front of a gilt mirror, she saw for the first time the bruises and welts on her white skin. Her blue-green eyes glowed feverishly back at her, euphoria struggling with shame. She longed for a bath.

Tekoah drifted into the bath chamber, vaguely remembering that Braith had carried her in there—had it been only the day before?—lowering her into a steaming tub and washing her tenderly.

The water was still in the marble tub. Tekoah trailed her finger in it wistfully, wishing it was hot. Then, without warning, the familiar sensation gripped her, of falling into a Journey. She stared fixedly into the water and let herself go.

Zant stood inside the sorcerer's lodge. She knew it was he, though all was blackness around them. He had not bothered with lights; no one else was there.

Tekoah could hear him murmuring aloud for some moments, as though he argued with himself. Then the black walls vibrated with the great uncoiling of his power as he sent forth the mind-summons to the world's only other living sorcerer.

It was a voice that blotted out all else, making it impossible to think. Tekoah crouched down into a ball, gritting her teeth against the ghastly hissing noise. It was the sound that Braith must have heard when he'd lain beside her the previous night.

She strove to make herself as small as possible, for once again she saw Zant gaze intently around him, as though he somehow sensed her presence. She blinked, and when she opened her eyes, there was a lamp burning on Morogh's table, and there sat Braith, opposite Zant. They stared at each other in silence.

Tekoah leaped to her feet, looking wildly around her. She was desperate to escape this terrible place with its black walls, which no doubt held even blacker secrets! But she was held there, bound by something she could not yet name.

Braith's face was drawn and tired. On his neck she saw a small, red mark, and she wondered with shame if she had caused it. Yet he did not appear weakened. He wore no gloves, and his talons gleamed in the lamplight. A sardonic smile played on his lips and his gaze was steady.

Zant's eyes darted continually around the room and back to Braith. It was he who broke the silence.

"This table bears the marks of our late friend Morogh's celebrated temper," he remarked softly, running a finger over one of many cracks in the wood. "Were he at this meeting, he probably would have struck it with his fist at least once by now. Or bitten someone."

Braith smile became a grin. "A testimony to your forbearance?"

Zant's eyes narrowed to slits in his face. "Perhaps. Morogh died from the overuse of his powers when he created the drought in the South. He believed that I was helping him, but I decided it would be a shame to squander my own powers if I could get him to do my work for me. Morogh thought he was much cleverer than I, but I have proven him wrong."

Braith stifled a yawn, then waved a hand in apology, examining his taloned fingers.

Zant shrugged and laughed softly. "Do not misjudge me, Hawk, or underestimate me. I look before I strike. That is true. But when I do strike, it is with a speed and force that you might be hard-pressed to match."

"Indisputably," Braith agreed, still sounding bored.

Is he feigning nonchalance? Tekoah wondered. Zant's words had struck a chill into her heart.

"But let us go back to the topic of the judicious use of one's powers," Braith continued, his fingertips drumming the table lightly. "Perhaps you can explain to me why you have wasted your precious power, not to mention mine, by summoning me here. Surely it is not for comradeship, or to hold a belated wake for Morogh."

Zant leaned forward with a poisonous, thin-lipped smile. "Now that you mention it, I have expended more energy than I had anticipated or desired, which is vastly annoying. You were difficult to reach. You seemed very occupied." Zant's words hung in the air for a moment.

Then Braith murmured, still drumming, "I value my privacy."

"Just so, just so," Zant replied smoothly, "we are two of a kind in that regard, are we not? Well, you know I would not summon you were it not urgent." He paused, and his skin tightened across his narrow forehead. "When last we met, you seemed to lack the dedication of Morogh and myself, in preserving our kind. Though it is a matter of extreme urgency to ensure the obliteration of the Anniste witch sect, you seemed reluctant to dirty those gloves of yours in attaining that goal, which would be our salvation."

Braith was silent. Zant's voice rose a notch higher. "To prevent the Mantling was the primary goal of Morogh and I for many turnings. I had hoped that once you tasted the power of your Source, you would join our cause. But now Morogh is dead, and I find that I am alone in my pursuit of survival."

He paused, and Tekoah saw a curious thing; his head began to sway softly from side to side, as a snake did when it was about to strike. She looked at Braith in terror. He remained calm, although he never took his eyes off Zant for a moment.

"I have also discovered that not only do you not share my

goal, you actively seek to hinder it!" Zant's voice was full of venom. He leaned forward so far in his chair that his pale, contorted features were almost touching Braith's face.

Braith stood, and with an indifference that shadowed contempt, turned his back on the other. "Of what do you speak, Serpent? And please make haste, for I have other plans for this evening."

"I speak," Zant murmured, "of your interference in my plan for the assassination of Queen Darielle. And do not deny it, for I know that all would have gone smoothly were it not for you. No mortal would have been able to thwart me. You knew what it meant to me to have her dead. The North would have fallen into a state of confusion, and the execution of our other plans would have been accomplished with ease and elegance."

"And why would I bother to deny it?" Braith asked. In the lamplight, his teeth flashed.

"Ah. Then may I ask this: why you are determined to defy me?" Zant mastered his voice with an effort. His black eyes seemed like gleaming bits of the shiny black walls that encircled them.

"Balance of power," Braith answered. "Do not expect me to follow in your lead. Only a fool would place all his trust in the hands of another. You will forgive me for saying I do not find you entirely trustworthy?"

Zant gazed at him for a moment, as if at a loss for words. When he spoke again, his voice became smooth, conciliatory. "But the Mantling…is something we must stop at all costs, my friend. We can quibble about other things later. We will have plenty of time for that. What do you care if a few human lives are sacrificed to achieve our ends?" He stopped short, and then an incredulous smile stretched his skin.

"Unless," he said slowly, "you do care for a few human lives, some more than others. The lore said you would be different from the rest. It just did not say how." His eyes narrowed again, appraisingly, as if he was seeing Braith for the first time.

There was a growing pressure in Tekoah's chest until it became pain. It was not until a moment later that she realized she had stopped breathing.

Braith's face was impassive, betraying nothing. "I did not mean to give the impression that I am an advocate for mankind," he replied. "Some irritate and affront me, and those I do not hesitate to destroy, the way one swats a buzzing fly. Some amuse me for a short time; mostly, they bore me. I thought it was the same for all of us?"

Tekoah began breathing again, in quick, ragged gasps. But she could see that Zant was not quite convinced. "And it did not matter to you that the lovely Queen Darielle, whose court you honour with your presence, was about to be murdered in cold blood?" he asked.

"And does it matter so much to you," Braith parried, "that the noble King Darian achieves all that his petty heart desires? Of course not. They are pawns, that is all. You have yours, I have mine." His voice was suddenly like thunder as he added, "But I say to you, Zant, do not expect me to embrace your obsession with the Mantling as a blind, obedient child, simply because I am new to my power. I will do what I will do. You do what you must do."

"It is not enough!" Zant answered, and his fist smote the table in the same place he had pointed to earlier. "You are interfering with me, and you will not tell me why. I warn you now, for the first and last time, do not hinder me or you will be sorry you were ever spawned."

"And I warn you," Braith replied, his eyes green and unwinking in the lamplight, "to stay out of my way."

The sorcerers glared at each other in silence in that dark cavernous hall, until Tekoah thought she would go mad with terror, waiting for them to kill each other.

Finally, Zant spoke again, his voice reasonable once more. "Let us not waste our power fighting each other, or we will both end up like Morogh."

Braith did not answer him.

"Enough, then," Zant said crisply. "I will not summon you again unless it is a matter of great urgency."

But before he turned away, Tekoah saw that his eyes rested briefly upon the livid mark Braith bore on his neck.

And she thought—was she imagining it?—that the Serpent's pale face gleamed with triumph.

Tekoah opened her eyes again and found herself staring into the grey marble tub. As always after a Journey, her strength was drained. This time, though, she was curiously exultant. Anna had not deserted her. The Goddess must think she was still of some value, though she had joined with a sorcerer, an enemy of the Anniste.

But Braith was not their enemy. She had just witnessed that. More than anything he could have said to her, this proved it. He had not betrayed her, although by protecting her he had made a very dangerous enemy. He had risked his life for her.

Or had he? Could it be that he wanted more power for himself, and that was why he refused to align himself with Zant? Perhaps he had his own secret plan for the destruction of the Anniste—and she was part of it.

Oh, Anna, why did these visions only show a portion, never the whole?

Her inner voice chided her: *You know he would not destroy you— you are his life. You could sooner destroy him.*

Tekoah felt this to be the truth. But she almost preferred to think of it the other way. To think of him as a danger to her. That would make it a little easier to—

To what? *To leave.*

She began to tremble. Going from the bath chamber into the bedchamber where they had spent almost every moment of the past three days, she threw open the painted wooden shutters of the window. She had not looked outside since she had been brought there.

It was dark. The air was cold and clear. Stars were already pinned against the sky like ice crystals in a vast cavern. Anna's crescent hung among them, a frozen talon. Tekoah breathed the air, deeply, in and out, but she could not stop trembling. A drink of wine, that was what she needed.

That was it, of course. By sunset each night, she had drained a goblet of the wine in the silver flagon. And any stirrings of uneasiness had dissolved. Was that what she would have felt all along, had she refused to drink? She looked down at her quaking limbs. Where was Weslan, she wondered suddenly? Were not Braith and her brother supposed to be together?

Yes, the dark, thick wine was what she needed. To forget. Braith would return soon, and all would be well. She would be once again have a warm soothing blanket in which to wrap her wounded soul. She headed for the staircase. The flagon was in the main hall, by the fireplace.

They usually went down together. But this time, Tekoah was alone, and a part of her did not wish to drink. However, she propelled herself forward, thinking of Braith's voice, his eyes like shining green flames against his bronzed skin.

All at once, unthinkably, there was a sound. It was the front door of the main hall opening to her right. Heavy footsteps followed. Tekoah froze. It could not be Braith, whose tread was almost eerily silent.

There were voices.

"What the devil—the housekeeper must have been in and lit the fire. It's as warm as Rhan in here!"

That voice sounded familiar, Tekoah thought. Who was it?

"Or else someone not so welcoming is expecting you. Tread carefully, my lord, these are deadly times." The other voice was gruff, wary, and Tekoah heard the scraping of swords as they were removed from scabbards.

I must hide, she thought desperately, looking around. *But where?* She stood frozen, three steps from the bottom of the staircase.

"Would that it were Darian himself, that lamentable waste of skin," murmured the first voice. "So that I could separate his heart from his blackened soul and call this a day well spent."

Of course, she thought suddenly, and the blood surged in waves to her cheeks. It was the lord of Mirrand, whom she had seen that day on the white horse. It made sense, after all. The castle was his new home.

What should she do? She stepped gingerly down the last two stairs and peered cautiously around. The two men, dressed in travel-stained clothes and mail vests, stood with their backs to her in the doorway of the main hall, looking at the blazing fire in the hearth.

If she could reach the door, it was only a few feet away. She rushed forward, just making it to the door. Struggling frantically —she had not known it was so heavy—flinging it open, at last. And then she was grabbed roughly by the shoulders, spun around. The lord's companion, a peppery red-headed fellow, let go of her shoulders and, as she tried to flee, seized her hair, which flowed loosely down her back. The point of his sword touched her throat.

"And what be you doing in the castle of an absentee lord, miss? Answer quickly or my sword will make up its own answer."

Tekoah looked back at him, unable to speak.

"Wait, Heyg, I know this girl." The lord of Mirrand stepped forward, pushing the sword down, away from her neck. "Let go of her hair, for pity's sake, Heyg. You will pull it all out, and it's gorgeous."

Heyg released her. Tekoah stood panting, feeling the cold air from the open doorway behind her. Freedom. What she had wanted all along. Only now it was too late.

"You are the blacksmith's daughter, are you not?" The lord spoke gently, stooping down to catch her reply.

"Yes," she whispered. "I am sorry I am in your castle, I have not taken anything. Please, let me go!"

"But why are you here to begin with, sweetheart?" Dirken spoke teasingly, as if she had done nothing more than play a childish prank.

"I—I was seeking my brother, and I lost my way. I became cold and confused, and I heard mountain cats scream nearby, and when I saw this place, I ran in here for shelter. I lit a fire—I was going to leave when I warmed up, but I must have fallen asleep."

The lies rose to her lips like bubbles, thin and easily burst. The lord of Mirrand was nodding as if he believed every word she said, but she saw his eyes on her thin nightshirt, the one Chalvern had lent her. Her stomach sickened.

Of course he does not believe me, she thought. Ashamed, Tekoah hugged her arms across her chest. The lord of Mirrand smiled indulgently at the gesture.

But the other one, Heyg, was not about to let her off so easily. "And who is your brother?" he barked, adding sarcastically, "And why would you be seeking him in the snow, in the middle of the night, in a man's nightshirt?"

Both men looked struck by something as Heyg said this. Putting his finger to his lips, Heyg ascended the stairs. Tekoah stood beside the lord of Mirrand, listening to his footsteps as he walked around, searching the rooms.

"My lord," she murmured urgently, "there is no one here but me, I swear it."

"Call me Dirken," he smiled.

She could not smile back, but stood awkwardly, her arms still wound about herself. Praying that Braith would not come back. She did not want to see what he might do if he saw how the young lord looked at her.

Dirken took off his russet red fur-lined cloak and put it around her shoulders. "There, now you are dressed for company," he joked.

Just then, Heyg came back down the stairs, his grizzled brows still furrowed.

"No one there," he told Dirken in a clipped voice. Turning again to Tekoah he said sternly, "Now, who did you say your brother was? If you are indeed telling the truth, he should be able to confirm your story."

"Yes, I will tell you—only, first I must say that I do not know where he is." Seeing the suspicion deepen in Heyg's eyes, she added hastily, "Weslan is his name. Veld the blacksmith is our father. Everyone in Stern knows us!"

Dirken raised his eyebrows at this. Heyg exploded into astonished oaths. "Weslan! You are Weslan's sister? He was in my company, before the queen befriended him. And he rides with Dirken's men, with the—"

Dirken held up a hand, a light gesture, but Heyg's voice instantly trailed off.

"It is an honour to be formally introduced to you, my lady," Dirken told her, taking her hand and kissing the palm. "I have met your brother and might have been a better friend to him had I known his sister was the loveliest creature in the world. Now forgive me, I know you told me your name before, but I have forgotten it."

"Tekoah," she said, taking her hand away. Her panic was rising. She must get away before Braith returned. Yet there was this man, play-acting as if they were all at court.

"Please, I must go," she entreated, looking into Dirken's hazel eyes. "Truly."

"Of course," he answered, "but can you tell me where your brother is? We are anxious to speak to him as well."

"I assure you, I do not know," she said. "He was to meet me in Stern a few days ago. We became separated, and I have no idea where he is." Tekoah knew she sounded vague, and she strove to speak more coherently. "If I see my brother, I will tell him you are here, I promise."

"Dirken," Heyg growled, a low warning sound.

"Be kind enough not to tell *anyone* you saw me here," Dirken said courteously. "We shall catch up with Weslan in our own time."

Tekoah nodded.

"The events of the last few days have shaken us all," Dirken continued.

He said some other things, but Tekoah did not hear a word. Her heart pounded and her ears buzzed. She waited patiently for him to finish.

"May I go, please?" she asked timidly.

Heyg looked dubious, but Dirken smiled, saying, "Of course."

Before anyone could speak further, she hurried through the doorway.

Behind her, Tekoah heard Dirken's voice calling, asking her a question, but she did not hear him for the wind in her ears. She waved in farewell and broke into a frenzied run. It was only after she was at the bottom of the hill that her feet began to ache with cold, for she wore only thin slippers.

And it was not until she reached the road that she realized that she still wore Dirken's cloak.

❧

Standing directly in front of her, as if she had been waiting patiently for an eternity, was Reika, wearing a black shawl instead of the brown hood of the Anniste. Her smile was joyous; but beneath her eyes were dark rings.

"I have been seeking you, sister," she said, holding out her hand. "With all my heart. And yet the Goddess withheld you from me until now. I feared that I had lost my faith, so futile was my search. I reached the end of my strength, the limit of my hope—yet now, here you are! Sometimes Her will is hard to fathom."

Reika took Tekoah's hand, and, in silence, they walked away from the castle.

After what seemed an endless time, Tekoah saw they were at her Aunt Beula's farm. She was too cold and tired to ask why. *Perhaps Weslan is here,* she thought numbly. Then they were walking through the weathered door of her childhood haven, and she stood in the large open kitchen where she had played as a child.

Beaten copper pots hung from pegs along the wall, shimmering softly in the lamplight. A fire crackled briskly in the hearth. And, though it was late evening and well past mealtime, there came from the soup cauldron a tantalizing smell of lamb and barley stew.

It was all completely familiar, and at the same time utterly strange.

Several things happened at once.

Tekoah's cousin, the fidgeting, loquacious Bhantok, sprung from his chair by the stove as he saw her, uttering a sharp exclamation of surprise. Raol and Fanco leaped forward from two low stools by the fire and embraced her, jostling with silent ferocity for proximity.

Reika let go of her hand and slumped to the floor in a half-faint, her face exhausted and triumphant at the same timeAnd overhead, uttered by some solitary bird in the darkening sky, came a cry of such loss and rage, that it froze the hearts of all who heard.

CHAPTER 27

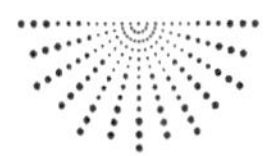

*B*linking like a mole in the bright sunlight, Chalvern thought that if he had stayed inside his shop much longer, he would have been blinded by this glorious vision of Rhan dancing on the snow.

He drank in the frosty air in grateful gulps. The market square, the shops, Mirveta's Well, were all covered by a puffy white quilt of snow, and from the eaves hung jagged icicles, sparkling rainbow prisms captured within each one.

Beauty when one least expects it, Chalvern thought, his throat tightening with emotion. *The gods always throw us just enough morsels to whet our hunger for life, then later they let us starve.*

There was a tentative touch on his shoulder, and he started. He had forgotten Fanco was there. The lad had appeared at his door, refusing to go away until Chalvern emerged. He had his sister's eyes.

The mute boy—although the hulking giant could not be called a boy, could he?—looked at him, half in apology, half in reproach.

"Yes, yes, I am coming," Chalvern told him, using his hands to echo his words.

Fanco took his arm, a thoughtful gesture for someone who had known less kindness than a donkey or an ox. The ground was slippery, and Rhan so dazzling in his eyes. Chalvern let himself lean on Fanco's arm and, supported so, the walk became very pleasant.

After they had turned out of the village onto the highway, Chalvern asked, without turning his head, "Where are we going?"

He knew by the boy's face that there was secrecy involved. It might have something to do with the Anniste, though likely it would be Fanco revealing Veld's murdered body at the forge. If so, Chalvern would have a hard time feigning astonishment, and he would not even try to *pretend* sorrow.

Fanco continued walking as if he had not heard, which of course he hadn't.

I left my brains in the belladonna bottle today, Chalvern thought. Squeezing Fanco's arm to get his attention, he raised his eyebrows in mild interrogation and shrugged his question: *Why did you drag me out of mourning, back into a world I no longer care anything about?* But his look could not convey that thought.

Fanco dropped Chalvern's arm. Placing both hands on his head, with his fingers splayed out, he touched his thumbs together underneath his chin like a kerchief. His eyes darted around while a nervous grin played across his mouth. His impersonation of Beula was so uncannily accurate that Chalvern felt laughter and tears fighting for space within his throat.

"Ah, the farm. I suppose Bhantok is all the family you have left, now," he mused.

Fanco smiled politely at the changing, meaningless shapes Chalvern's mouth made, and his eyes became distant.

It was not far to Beula's pony breeding farm, a mile at most. But it was slow going in the snow, and Fanco carried him through the deepest parts.

Do I look like a sack of corn? Chalvern fumed, irritated at the way he was swung up in the air with no warning. *Or perhaps I appear so fragile that I will die if I walk a mile.* No doubt it was the latter. The last two turnings had aged him.

Fanco set him down on the doorstep and swung the heavy door open. There was Beula's homey kitchen, strewn with the bright rag rugs she had made, walls hung with the gleaming copper pots and kettles for which she had loved to haggle with peddlers.

At the stove stood a woman, her back to him, stirring something in a pot. It smelled tantalizing, and Chalvern realized it must have been days since he had last eaten. Four days at least, for that was when Braith had disappeared with Tekoah. He had not left his bedchamber once, except to take a dipperful from the water bucket when his thirst grew too great.

Beside her, Raol stirred like a great restless beast. Chalvern saw he gazed at the dark-haired woman with something akin to worship. Before he could ponder this, she turned, holding out her hands.

"Welcome, Master Chalvern. You are here in time for dinner, and you look as though you could use a hot meal."

Chalvern had never seen the woman before, and yet she seemed familiar. She was quite young, and exquisite in a dark, exotic way. Her warm smile seemed to illuminate the room, but that did not mean she was trustworthy.

"Where is Bhantok, master of this house?" he asked.

"I am Reika," the woman replied, unperturbed. "Bhantok is out patrolling. There is great unrest, as you know—or perhaps you do not," she finished, seeing his bafflement. "Berlot has captured the queen," Reika told him, while he stared at her lovely olive-tinted face. "Three days ago, by the Jinta's men. So far as anyone knows she is alive, at the palace of the Jinta in Hacinta-Car. King Darian has announced his alliance with Berlot, and many are interpreting it has a signal of his intention to annex the North."

Reika turned back to the stove, ladling stew into wooden bowls. One she handed to Fanco and the other to Raol, who sat down and began to gobble it up with their fingers. Chuckling, Reika handed them spoons. She brought the remaining bowls to the table and seated herself on the wooden bench, motioning for Chalvern to sit.

He did so. Then he put his head in his hands. This news was too much to absorb all at once.

"The word today is that Rhantor has fallen," Reika went on, speaking through small mouthfuls of stew. "King Darian himself was at the palace to watch it razed. He had the gardens destroyed first. They say if you are on any of the roads within a mile of two of the palace, you can smell the flowers burning like incense." She fell silent, staring straight ahead.

Acknowledging how famished he was, Chalvern had started to eat. He stopped at her words, his wooden spoon halfway to his mouth. Reika seemed not to notice and, after a moment, she sighed.

"How Darielle's brother must hate her!" she murmured.

"To give her to the Jinta?" Chalvern asked.

Reika's dark eyes flashed. "Yet perhaps she will be safer in Berlot than she is here. At least in Berlot they establish the rules. Women know where they stand. They do not worship Anna, only Rhan. Here there is a pretence of freedom. It sounds all very well, but when you get close, the pretence dissolves— the thing you *thought* was there isn't there at all."

She gazed at him, adding "Like a Shifting, you know."

Chalvern thought it was apt, her comparison to the magically created mirages of legend, those shimmering doors to other worlds. Or were they only pathways to death? No one could say, for no one who had stepped into a Shifting had ever re-emerged. To his regret and relief, Chalvern had never seen one, but then it was not necessary to see an illusion to grasp the meaning of emptiness.

"I know," he repeated, laying his hand on top of Reika's and patting it.

Then he slid his hand up her arm, pulling the sleeve away before she could stop him. She gasped and pulled away. But too late, for he had seen the scars.

"I know who you are," he told her.

Reika said nothing, only sat with her head bowed, face averted. Fanco had stopped eating and was looking at them with a worried frown. Chalvern threw him a reassuring glance, but he continued to watch them, his gaze protective.

"Do they cause you pain, still?" Chalvern asked Reika, looking at her with respect. He felt very humble.

After a moment, Reika looked up. Her face was wet. "There is no pain that does not bring me joy," she answered, and though she was weeping, her voice did not falter. "For it was the pain that brought me to Anna."

They sat for some time in silence. "And will you ever go back?" he asked.

"Never," she answered. "This much the Goddess has told me, and I am grateful." She smiled, and the glow in her eyes made a silver curtain of the tears on her face.

Chalvern thought that her radiance rivalled that of Rhan on the snow. But it was a gentler vision of glory: the matchless light of Anna shining through a woman's eyes.

"Of course I am not Anniste by birth," Reika told him. "Anna called me, chose me for my past pain and future longing. I am here because of the healers' great need for a leader in this time of danger. But I am not to *be* the Guardian, only to guide her until she can make her own way."

Chalvern opened his mouth to speak, but Reika held up her hand. "She lies in the room yonder." Her head inclined toward Beula's bedchamber. "If any priest or sorcerer knew she was here, her life would be over, and with it any hope the Anniste have to survive this darkest of all times."

Chalvern's heart was beating erratically. He dared not let himself think, but took Reika's hand, trustingly. She stood, and they entered Beula's chamber.

"She has raved or wept most of the night," Reika whispered. "And now she has begun to heal, and with healing comes a strength which is being woven into her soul. Soon, she will discover that strength, and it may be our salvation."

She opened the door.

Tekoah lay propped up on several pillows, face pale, lips cracked and dry, but her blue-green eyes were calmer than Chalvern had ever seen them. She held out a hand to him, and his heart flew to it, perching on her outstretched fingers like a captive bird that had just been released.

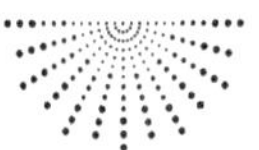

CHAPTER 28

Now that there was a renewed purpose to his life, Chalvern felt years younger. His hands no longer trembled as he measured out precise heaps of pungent-smelling powders and placed them on the tiny copper scales. He could even muster a smile as he listened to the gossipy old women who tottered into his shop, speaking of the fall of the North as if it was only a neighbourhood spat.

"The new palace is being built out of black stone; no one knows from where they quarry the stones, for it is all done at night. They dump every morning new mountains of rock in piles, where Darielle's gardens used to be. The word is that Zant unearths the stones himself by incantation, from the bowels of the earth, and that the stones are the same as the stuff as the sorcerer's lodge."

The women gasped with wonder and cackled with excitement. Icy fingers touched Chalvern's spine, but he said nothing.

"The city is being renamed Zantor, in honour of the sorcerer Zant. He will live in the palace whenever it pleases him. A new era of plenty is being promised, now that Berlot is no longer our enemy. Gold is already pouring over the border like water."

Chalvern listened to all the babble, trying to glean the truth from the falsehood. He possessed an instinct for ferreting this out, which he knew he inherited from his no-nonsense mother. One of the greatest gifts she had given him were words she had said when he'd been no taller than a stalk of wheat:

You must learn to think for yourself, Chalvern. Never heed gossip and never decide the facts are what you wish them to be. Always seek the truth, and welcome Truth as your friend, whether the friendship be bitter or sweet.

That Zant still dangled King Darian like a string puppet was easy to believe. Together they had opened the door for Berlot to rape the North, and to destroy any vestige of the Goddess Anna and the threat of the Mantling. What better ally than Berlot, if that was the purpose? Berlotans believed the very name of Anna to be blasphemy when spoken with Rhan's name—Anna was a woman, and therefore only a servant, unworthy of washing Rhan's feet.

Such was the country into which Reika had been born. And she was even more misfortunate, for she was the firstborn child to the Jinta, elder sister to the Jinta who ruled there now. If she had not had the audacity to be first born, she would not be now bearing the thick scars which covered her from neck to ankle.

Chalvern shuddered. He knew the story; everyone had heard it twenty-four turnings past—how the Jinta's new girl child had suffered immersion in scalding water as was the custom for royal infants in Berlot, if they were female and firstborn. Purification, they called it, for the royal line was contaminated. Barbaric, *he* called it.

If the babe recovered from the ceremony, she would be permitted to live out the rest of her natural life in seclusion, in the women's quarters of the palace. Only how could any child survive such purification?

Five turnings later, the rumour had swept Miraven that the royal girl-child had disappeared from the women's quarters. Too young to survive on her own, they thought her to have died. No one in Berlot cared, of course. But throughout North Miraven, people whispered that an Anniste woman had been working in the palace nursery, and that she had smuggled the child across the border to Miraven, thus saving her life.

Reika, the royal princess of Berlot. Even though Chalvern saw her almost daily now, still he couldn't believe that the Jinta's daughter dwelt in a farmhouse a stone's throw from him, protecting the life of his own daughter.

Daughter. He no longer tried to stop calling Tekoah that in his mind. She was too precious to him, and life was too short. The past few annaspans had been the happiest he could remember since he had dared to dream that he could win Neela's love.

Chalvern visited Bhantok's place whenever he could, ostensibly to help with the running of the farm. It was common knowledge that Bhantok had volunteered to patrol with the queen's men, and so there was nothing suspicious about the apothecary's efforts to help the poor dim-witted twins, who were bereft of family and left to tend to both the forge and the pony farm.

What no one knew was that the farm was now a refuge for any remaining Anniste who could reach it before being torn apart by Darian's soldiers or by Morgs.

However, the Morgs were relentless hunters, and Chalvern knew he must be vigilant. Hanta had become curious of late, and that was also worrisome. If word of the Anniste's whereabouts ever reached Darian's soldiers—he closed his eyes against the thought.

Darian had promised fifty gold pieces for each Anniste captured. That bastard.

Struggling against the dark throng of sorcerer-led brutes that had risen against them, the women depended on Chalvern, and a few others, for their survival. Yes, life had become very busy. *But I can manage,* he thought, energy coursing through him.

He had hired a couple of apprentices, recalcitrant acolytes from the priesthood sent by that tallow-pot priest Zorak. One sulky boy tended Chalvern's indoor winter herbs, and the other dullard weighed, measured, and waited on customers. They were not capable of much else, besides trading unsavoury jokes, after which they jerked their heads in his direction with furtive hilarity because they thought he was deaf. *No matter*.

Chalvern was in his shop when he needed to be and continued to visit ill villagers who required his attention. The rest of his time he spent at Bhantok's, with Tekoah.

It was the middle of the week, his quietest day in the shop, and he was relieved and happy to arrive at the farm. He knocked on the door, rapping three times, then two, then four, as they had agreed. When no one answered, he grew alarmed. Had there been a raid? But if so, he would have heard something.

Perhaps Braith has returned! This fear was a frequent visitor in Chalvern's thoughts.

But just as he lifted a frantic fist to hammer on the door, it creaked open, and there Tekoah stood. Her face was tear-stained and her eyes dull as she motioned for him to enter.

"What is it?" he asked, closing the door behind him before taking her arm.

"It is Reika," she murmured, and beneath the listlessness he heard desperation in her voice. "She has gone."

"Gone? Whatever do you mean?" Tekoah was silent. "Why would she leave?" he continued, trying to keep his voice even. "Is it not much too dangerous to go anywhere at the moment?"

"Of course," Tekoah answered, going to the stove and pouring him a mug of tea. She always did so when he first arrived, and that she remembered even in her distress touched him.

"Reika Journeyed, two nights ago," Tekoah continued, handing him the mug and going to the window. She took hold of the shutters as if to open them, and then dropped her hands again, in resignation.

"It is hard for me," she confided wistfully, "not being able to look outside. Despite the danger to Reika, I envy her, a little."

"Reika Journeyed?" Chalvern prodded her, blowing on his fragrant tea to cool it. *What has that brave girl done now?*

"Yes," Tekoah repeated. "Reika was told in her Journey that she must leave—that there is someone wandering the Taboran Woods who needs a healer without delay, and that the Goddess had chosen her."

"In the woods near Stern?" Chalvern asked. "But there is no one that ill. I would have known! There is no need for that child to risk her own life!"

Tekoah shrugged. "She did not yet know where she was being sent, when she left. Or to whom."

"She did not even know where she was going?" Chalvern exclaimed, incredulous. "But that is madness!"

"Anna will guide her," Tekoah answered, a hint of reproach in her voice. They had argued several times about his lack of faith in the Goddess's ability to protect her followers.

"Let us just assume She is taking a nap at the moment," Chalvern would quip, "and She has been taking too many as far as I'm concerned."

In that moment, he struggled to subdue his anger at the terrible risk Reika was taking. What if soldiers captured her— and tortured her into revealing the whereabouts of the others?

He could not resist saying, "If you are so certain Anna will guide Reika, then why are your pretty eyes all swollen up with crying?"

Tekoah faltered, turning back to the window. "Because she has left me in charge. She told me I was ready to take my place as Guardian of the Anniste. But she is wrong." Tears choked her voice, and her fingertips reached out blindly to touch the closed shutters.

Chalvern was silent, searching for words to comfort her, the right words spoken by a wise father. None came. Only a rat gnawed at his entrails: *Obviously she is not ready—she is nothing but a child!*

Footsteps sounded behind them and Chalvern turned to see one of the Anniste—Valeen—enter the room, her eyes anxious until she spied Tekoah's form by the window.

"Tekoah!" Valeen called.

Her tone was deferential, which seemed odd to Chalvern, coming from a grey-haired widow who was near his own age. Irritated, Chalvern raised his hand to wave her away. Embarrassment at being found in tears should not add to the list of Tekoah's troubles.

But before he could move, Tekoah had turned, and her transformation astounded Chalvern. All traces of tears were gone, her eyes glowed, and on her face was a serene smile.

"Yes, Valeen?"

"Marta is about to Journey and asks for your presence."

"I will come at once." Throwing him a look of apology, Tekoah hurried from the room. "Stay and eat supper with me," she said over her shoulder. "If you have time? I should not be long. We can talk more then."

Chalvern sat swirling the tea leaves in the bottom of his mug. Perhaps if he just thought hard enough, he could persuade her to depart this place. But he had seen her expression, had seen it before on Neela's face. Implacable, and even more so because it was bound by gentleness.

He sighed, staring down at his tea. No answers floated upward through the murky liquid.

Perhaps Reika is right, he thought, pride and fear embracing reluctantly within him. *Perhaps Tekoah is ready. But for what?*

CHAPTER 29

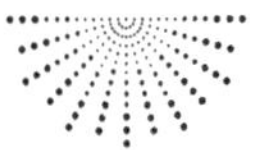

lthough Tekoah had told him she would not be long, Chalvern spent the rest of the late winter afternoon drinking lukewarm tea and waiting for her. Several times he got up to leave; he was only in the way—an old man for which no one had any use. But he nipped the thoughts at their onset, reminding himself that self-pity was not something to which he ever thought he would stoop. After that, he stirred up the stove fire and sat down to wait some more.

Fanco had left on some mysterious errand a few hours earlier, so there was not even his friendly face at which to nod. The lad seemed to look more intelligent every time Chalvern saw him, as did his brother. Chalvern supposed it might have had something to do with the fact that their faces were clean, and their unruly hair neatly combed and tied back with leather thongs. It was because of Reika's gentle prompting, no doubt.

But the twins had changed beyond their groomed hair. Veld's death had somehow freed them, allowing their inchoate spirits to solidify into something forceful. Though of course they still did not speak, and folks continued to regard them as idiots.

The twins had buried their father without a tremor or a tear. He had heard it from Reika.

How do you know that? He had demanded, shocked.

I was with them, Reika had answered, turning her calm gaze upon him.

It had been during Chalvern's second visit to the farm. He had still been reluctant to speak of Veld's death to Tekoah. She had seemed so fragile, easily broken.

Do not hesitate, Reika had reassured him. *Talk to her.*

So Chalvern had mentioned it in a faltering, roundabout way, by asking Tekoah if she had heard from Weslan. She had wept softly. But after a moment, she had calmed herself and, leaning close, she had told him in a whisper that she had seen her brother kill her father in a Journey.

I weep, she had said, *because I do not know why Anna does not show Weslan to me. Wherever he is, he needs a healer.*

Tekoah was so like her mother, Chalvern had thought. Neela always ignored her own troubles, as if they were no more significant than a wisp of cloud seen from the corner of her eye, but allowed the sorrows of others to engulf her like a storm.

But Tekoah was too young for such burdens. Had Neela ever been that young? She'd been Reika's age when Chalvern had first seen her, and he a crusty widower of almost fifty turnings.

Better not to think of that time. It brought nothing but pain.

Chalvern stood up again and went to open the shutters. It had to be dark by that point. All the women were down in the cellar, so he risked a quick look outside.

There was a sound behind him, and he turned. Tekoah had come into the kitchen. He closed the shutter.

She looked white and tired. Smiling at him, she turned to the stove, rubbing her hands together to warm them. "I cannot wait until winter is over," she said. "It is so cold down there."

"You need not stay, my dear," Chalvern answered.

She chuckled as if he had spoken in jest. "I am hungry—famished," she said, reaching into a basket for a heel of bread. "All the others are sleeping now, but I thought you would be here still. Thank you for staying."

Chalvern shrugged.

"There is something I must confess," Tekoah continued, smiling as she cradled the heel of bread in her hands. "I think of you as my father, much of the time. I have done so ever since I had the fever, and you nursed me." She looked away, biting into the crust.

Chalvern had never been so thankful to all the deities, real or imagined, as he was at that moment, for Tekoah was not looking at him, and he had a moment to master his emotions.

"You should have been born a woman, for you would be a wonderful healer," Tekoah added, turning to look at him, her playful tone at odds with her drawn face.

"That has always been my deepest desire, for as long as I can remember," Chalvern told her, not believing he had said it aloud to another person.

"To be a woman?" she asked, laughing.

"To be a healer!" He mock-glowered. "And if I *were*, I would tell you now to finish your bread and find a warm place to sleep. It looks as if that woman's Journey took you to Rhantor and back in a blizzard."

"You mean Zantor," she said, the smile leaving her face.

"You look fatigued," he persisted. "I am concerned. You have spent an entire winter in hiding, never leaving this house."

"It is safer in this house than out there," Tekoah countered, and then added, "or at least it was."

"What do you mean?" Chalvern asked, for her blue eyes had taken on a wild, cloudy look, and she hugged herself as though gripped by icy fingers.

"Marta's Journey," Tekoah told him, lowering her voice,

although they were alone. "She saw soldiers, searching the farm. A raid is coming. And soon."

IT TOOK ALL of Tekoah's persuasive powers—and they were considerable—to convince Chalvern to leave that night. He was more help to the Anniste in his shop, she reminded him. Besides, had he not told her he did not believe in the prophetic truth of Journeys?

She entreated Chalvern to go and return in a few days to assure himself of the Anniste's safety. When he hesitated, she posed the question: What would they do for medicine if it were not for him? Bhantok and the twins could provide most of the food, but none of the herbs they required. They needed him.

Still, he protested. Resorting to petulance, Tekoah had cried that she would not sleep a wink until he left. So Chalvern had left, grumbling. By the time he'd gone to bed that night, he had convinced himself he was the victim of his overactive imagination, caused no doubt by too much fraternization with those brown-shrouded hens.

But he refused to wait. He would go to Bhantok's the next afternoon to make sure all was well. He would bring Tekoah a little gift—a warm shawl, perhaps.

But the shop was busy the next morning, and kept on throughout the day, and so he did not go after all.

Come back in a few days, Tekoah had told him. Very well. That way, he would not appear too anxious.

Chalvern spent a brisk afternoon selling herbs, and it was not until after sundown that he heard the thundering hooves of a company of soldiers riding through Stern. *It must be Bhantok and his company of Kalesh, swooping in for supplies.* Or—a fresh worry— King Darian's tax collectors, scavenging across the land to pay for that snake-pit of a palace in Zantor.

It was not until the next morning that Chalvern learned it was not a band of Kalesh riders, nor a tax-collecting party, but Darian's elite band of soldiers-assassins, seeking the Anniste. And that, among other places, they had stopped at Bhantok's farm.

CHAPTER 30

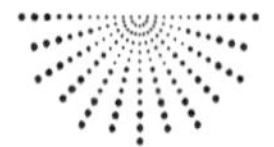

Weslan walked into the Taboran Woods in the frozen heart of winter to wait for death. But death eluded him. What came instead were muffling layers of greyness, like a wet cloud. And the voices.

When it was too cold, or he was too tired to light a fire, he ate his meat raw. At first, it bothered him. But he grew accustomed to it, cutting the red frozen hunks into small strips, which he chewed as he walked. He never stopped moving, except to build a fire or to sleep. His slumber, he could barely distinguish from his waking time. The forest was not kind, nor was it cruel—the forest was an implacable, impartial judge.

Weslan found that his lucid moments came at crucial times of great danger or need. The stifling layers would disappear, as a bubble burst from without; his immediate surroundings gaining a brilliant clarity. Suppressed sensations would belabour him: *I hurt, I bleed, I hunger, I am afraid.*

This clamour to survive always galvanized Weslan into action. He leaped onto the rough trunk of a leafless crohm and shimmied up with agility to avoid the springing mountain cat— readying his bow and stringing his arrow as he went. Or he sent a different sort of arrow to fell the rabbit he was stalking. Arrows of life. Arrows of death.

Breathing quickly, flushed with exhilaration. Staying alive, from moment to moment. Thinking, *At this, at least, I have not failed.* But then the grey clouds would descend again.

The voices came and went, making it difficult to think in a straight course. Sometimes their words filled his head, and Weslan's thoughts zig-zagged, like the myriad of criss-crossing tracks of the hardy animals that had also survived winter in the Taboran Woods.

When Weslan first answered the voices, he shook for hours afterward. But more and more, he could not resist joining in the incessant squabbles that took place within him. Desperate to drive them away, he sometimes shouted, or struck himself repeated blows on the head and shoulders. He startled the few remaining birds from their perches on the stark black branches above him, and sending his smoky breath upward in spirals, like prayers toward the sky.

Once, during a brief thaw, he leaned over a pool in a still, quiet glade he visited on fair days, along with the deer. Weslan saw his own face and did not recognize it: sharp, arrow-lean, canny, and shaggy-haired as an umbray. His eyes glowed with a distant flame, as if he lived in another world. It did not seem to him as if he dwelt anywhere at all. But if he did, it was not in the frozen woods of white on black; it was with the voices.

After a time, Weslan ceased to fear them, and they became almost welcome. He listened for the courteous murmur of the man, and the woman's voice, light and mocking. His loneliness was such that their presence might have been comforting, if only they were not forever quarrelling.

The squabbles were always about Weslan, but whenever he tried to express an opinion, they discounted whatever it was he had to say. As though he was only a distant acquaintance, denied the right to pass judgement upon himself.

One day, Weslan stood in the sunshine, the first of Rhan's warmth he had felt in many weeks lulling him into a somnolent daze as he stared at a frozen waterfall. It was fascinating to look at a seemingly unstoppable force, held in check; stilled in mid-rush. As he gazed, the jagged tips of ice dripped water—small droplets at first, which soon became a steady rivulet.

He stood at the base of a mountain whose name he could no longer remember and let the warmth caress his back. Soon, all around him, he heard the continuous, delightful gurgle of snow and ice melting.

Winter was over. Spring had come to Miraven, and he was still alive.

The waterfall curved in a great arc; a thousand rainbow prisms trapped inside its frozen heart. It was the most beautiful thing Weslan had ever seen, and soon it would vanish. His chest ached at the thought.

"See," the woman murmured, "how weak he is. Tears fill his eyes, like a babe."

"He is not weak," the man said, "except from hunger. Remember, he has not eaten these past four days. Lack of food does strange things to a man's temperament."

"It must indeed, if it can make him weep over a chunk of ice."

"I am not weeping!" Weslan shouted.

At the sound of his voice, a hare leaped, startled, from behind a boulder. Spotting him, it became motionless, staring wide-eyed.

The woman laughed. She had been baiting him of late, even more than usual. Weslan had disciplined himself to not answer, but now he could not help it. She called his very manhood into question.

"Put a roasted rabbit and four hours of uninterrupted slumber into him and he will be born anew," said the man, in a placating tone.

Weslan squatted down, never taking his eyes off the hare. Stone or arrow, which would it be? He felt the roughness of a rock beneath his hand. It was just the right size.

"Yes, and squalling like a newborn as well," the woman quipped.

Weslan gritted his teeth in anger, but said nothing, thinking, *I must eat today.* He knew that, if nothing else. He held the rock, curled within his forefinger and second finger, steadied by his thumb. Drawing his arm back, he took aim.

"Perhaps he did not weep enough as a child," the man ventured. "Unshed tears do not evaporate, you know. They remain deep within the cisterns of the heart."

"How poetic!" the woman commented, acidly.

Weslan's hand trembled, and his eyes misted with fatigue. Was the hare gone? He blinked. No, it was still there.

They are not supposed to speak when I hunt, he thought desperately. *They are breaking a rule!*

"Many are the unshed tears for his sister," the man said in a doleful tone, though there was a secret triumph glinting in his voice. "For he failed to protect her—first from her father, and then from the sorcerer Braith, in whose clutches he left her."

The woman's voice was soft, musing. "Yes. How fares she now, I wonder?"

Weslan's arm jerked spasmodically at those last words, sending the rock awry. With a certain insolence in its tail, the white hare bounded away, its coat soon disappearing against the snow. White on white, the ghost of hunger.

Weslan sat on his haunches, staring at the dripping waterfall, and let the full, weak sickness of starvation descend upon him. It pulsated through his weakened muscles, swirled dizzily in his head, and curled like a bitter worm around his belly.

"You broke the rules," he said flatly into the green, vibrant air of spring.

As if issuing a final taunt, no answer came.

ON THE SEVENTH day of emptiness, after countless stalkings, aims, and misses, Weslan found a cave to crawl into. It was roomy, with a high rock ceiling—the best he had ever found, although he did not need the room. He only needed enough space to lie on his side, on a bed of soft leaves, his deerskin cloak wrapped around him. There were worse endings.

It was pleasant, not moving any more. Not stalking or being stalked, or running to keep his blood from freezing, and running faster to blot out the knowledge there was no longer any reason to stay alive.

When he closed his eyes, he saw a yellow flower, and smelled its exquisite fragrance, as his queen handed it to him gently. Her warm brown eyes locked with his, and in them he saw awe and adoration. A sweet vision to carry him away.

THE VOICES WERE with him all the time now, and he listened to them patiently, as a drowsy child listen to his parents bicker by the fireside.

"I told you it would come to this," the man said, accusing.

"Come to this?" she answered, scornfully. "This is what he intended from the beginning, you fool."

"If that was true, he would have fallen on his sword before he ever entered these cursed woods."

"Ah," the woman said, "that would have been too easy. He wanted to punish himself."

"No!" the man protested. "He had hope. Hope that something would happen, to save him. He loves life, that much is obvious."

"For someone who embraces life, he has caused little but death and misery."

The woman's voice stung, and Weslan tried to shake his head in denial, but found he could only make a slight movement.

"See?" the woman continued mercilessly. "And his own death quickly approaches. Why, by tomorrow's sunset, I will wager you—"

"Be quiet!" the man cut in, voice throbbing with fear. "We are no longer alone."

Hearing his words, Weslan struggled with all the strength left in him, and turned his head. He saw a female figure standing at the mouth of the cave.

This cannot be, he thought.

Weslan closed his eyes and then opened them again. The figure was inside the cave now, crouching over him. She wore the brown hooded robe of the Anniste healers. She was beautiful.

"Hello," she whispered, as if sensing that anything louder would overwhelm him. "I am Reika."

CHAPTER 31

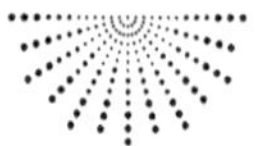

Tekoah kneeled, for the cellar ceiling was so low that she could not stand upright. Beside her was Mirveta's Basin, and before her, fifty-four Anniste women sat with their knees drawn up to their brown-robed chests, looking like so many dusty lumps of earth.

She made the sign of Anna, a sweeping crescent with her arm, and hoped the women would not notice that her fingers were unsteady.

The eyes of the Anniste women flared in the lamp-light, tiny flames of dying hope that wavered as if even the slightest breeze would extinguish them. Tekoah smiled at them, knowing that she must look as if she meant it. No one smiled back. She cleared her throat.

"We are frightened," she said into the silence. "Marta's Journey warned us of impending danger. We must act if we wish to save ourselves."

"Act how?" a voice piped up from somewhere in the centre. "All we can do is cower here like mice, waiting to die."

"We must run," another woman answered, her voice sharp and bitter. "Better to die like women under the open sky than

288

down in this hole. Let the people hear our cries! Perhaps they will not sleep so soundly for a night or two, knowing we are an unjust target. We, who have dedicated our lives to others."

The rest of the women began speaking in a discordant jumble, some weeping and others shouting.

"Listen!" Tekoah called.

No one heard. Why did she not have Reika's voice, vibrant with authority? If only Reika would appear and make everything all right. But it did not happen. Tekoah clenched her hands. *I do not need Reika. I will do this!*

Stooping over, she waded into the midst of the women, shouting, "Stop!"

The voices quieted instantly.

"Sit, and listen," she told them, "if you want to live."

The brown robes rustled as the Anniste resumed their seats. All eyes fixed upon her, waiting for her to explain those last five words. At least she had their attention.

"After Marta's Journey, I was exhausted, but could not sleep," she told them, speaking so low that they had to stop rustling to hear her. "I slipped from the house."

There was a simultaneous gasp at her audacity.

Tekoah continued, gesturing outward to encompass them, "Like you, I asked myself what choice we had but to wait and die. Reika has gone. So many of us have perished already. Even Bhantok is not here to give us counsel. I walked and walked, almost not caring if a Morg scented me."

At the sound of the word, there was an uneasy ripple of movement.

"But then I saw the answer, as I know Anna meant for me to see." Tekoah hoped she sounded confident, and that she was not wrong about what the Goddess had shown her. "But we must have courage, and we must not falter, for if one of us falters, we are all doomed."

She waited a few seconds for that to sink in, trying to meet the eyes of as many of the women as possible.

And then she told them her plan.

TEKOAH STOOD in the farmhouse kitchen, kneading bread dough. It was the perfect thing to do when one could not stop one's hands from trembling. She had put it in the bread pan and then taken it back out three times when the huge wooden door burst open.

But it was not one of King Darian's soldiers, as Tekoah had expected. It was her cousin Bhantok, wearing the mail vest and helmet that had hitherto caused her to turn away, lest she giggle at the sight of "Bhantok, the soldier."

Her cousin's plump cheeks were crimson, a sign of agitation since childhood. He was not a child any longer though, as she had observed these last few annaspans. If anyone had asked her even a turning ago, she would have said that she did not think Bhantok had it in him to do anything more adventurous than halter-train a pony, and only because he had been doing that since infancy. Over time, though, he had developed an air of authority. Despite the quivering cheeks, he spoke in a clipped voice, devoid of the adolescent stutter which Weslan used to mimic with wicked accuracy.

Bhantok rushed to Beula's cedar chest in the corner, stripping off his armour and thrusting it inside. When he turned to face her, he looked like a farmer once again, except that his face was serious.

"You must remove the women from the cellar immediately, cousin," he warned. "I have it on reliable authority that the farm is about to be raided by Darian's men."

"I know," Tekoah answered quietly from the kitchen table, hands in the dough.

"We have not much time," he continued, his brow furrowing. "The best thing is for the women to scatter, make a run for the woods. Hopefully it will only be a few hours. The men of Kalesh are very near, and their leader is the nearest of all, disguised among the enemy soldiers, in fact. Wait—" he said suddenly, staring at her with his round eyes. "Did you say you *knew?*"

"Yes," she replied. At any other time, she would have snickered at the look on his face, but right then she could not even manage a smile.

"But how?" Bhantok looked around the kitchen as if the answer lay hidden somewhere near, awaiting discovery.

"Marta saw it in a Journey."

"Oh." Bhantok looked awed. "And where are the women? In the woods?"

"No."

"Where are they?"

"It is better if I do not tell you. That way, if the soldiers ask you, you do not know."

Bhantok's eyes widened with alarm, and he strode to the table, grabbing a handful of bread dough and pointing it at her. "If they are still in the cellar, or on the farm somewhere, they will be discovered! Do you think the soldiers are fools? What in the name of the Mantling are you thinking, Ko?"

"Calm yourself, cousin—" Tekoah answered, retrieving the dough.

He glared at her. Right then, a loud pounding came on the door.

And this time there *were* soldiers, a half-dozen of them, crowding all at once into the kitchen.

As one of them began barking out a search proclamation, Bhantok muttered in her ear, "The one in green, he is with us. Trust him." Then, with no warning at all, her cousin gave her a nasty shove, sending her sprawling onto the floor.

"Must you bring your lovers home with you from the tavern?" he bellowed. "Like a sniffing pack of umbrays following you around, and different ones every time." He wheeled around to face the soldiers, pointing to the door. "Get out, you drunken mongrels. Back to the Pitaya Pit with you, and better luck next time."

One of the soldiers, a burly, balding fellow, let out a guffaw. Another, a sallow southerner who looked to be part Berlotan, silenced him with a look.

"That is all very well," he told Bhantok with a sneer, "but we care not about your domestic squabbles, swineherd. We are here to search this place for witches. Your mother was a witch, and we suspect you of being a sympathizer. So stay out of our way if you know what is good for you. And if we find you to be hiding any Anniste, swineherd, you will wish you had come clean with me now!"

He gestured to the other soldiers, and they scattered at once throughout the house, except for one tall soldier with a green sash who stayed with him.

"*Pony breeder,*" Bhantok replied.

"What?" the Southerner asked, startled.

"I am a pony breeder, not a swineherd."

"My mistake," the Southerner replied, grinning to show blackened stumps.

He stepped forward and struck Bhantok a hard blow in the stomach. Bhantok exhaled with a small hiss and sank to his knees beside Tekoah.

The Southerner turned away, toward the door. He beckoned to the soldier in green. "Come on," he said, "let us search the grounds."

Tekoah glanced up from where she had been staring numbly at Bhantok's hunched-over form and briefly met the eyes of the soldier in green. His eyebrows had been blackened, and he wore a moustache, but there was no doubt: it was the lord of

Mirrand.

Swallowing her shock, she dropped her eyes, and at that moment he spoke. "I do not trust that girl, sir," he growled, his voice sounding very different from the gentle one she remembered in the castle. "Let us bring her with us."

"Good idea," the southern captain replied. "We can save her later for a little relaxation—give the swineherd something to whine about."

Tekoah swallowed as the disguised lord strode over to her. He grabbed her wrist and dragged her off, sparing not a glance for Bhantok, who still kneeled, gasping for air. But as they stumbled through the doorway he bent swiftly, his mouth to her ear, whispering, "Where are they?"

"The hay-barn," she whispered back, so faintly that she thought he could not hear.

But he nodded, staring straight ahead once more. His finely wrought features were such a mask of brutal indifference that Tekoah thought she must have imagined the whispered words.

Striding across the snow-covered grounds, Tekoah blinked. The day was overcast, but she was no longer accustomed to the natural light of day. It was this that Chalvern wanted for her, the freedom to walk in spicy pine-scented air, snow crunching beneath her feet, the wind stroking her hair away from her forehead, the hesitant, far-off sounds of finches as they found roosting spots for the night. All the sensations accumulated one by one, blending into a glorious harmony.

They stopped at the pony stable. Her aunt and uncle had erected the building with the pride and care of dedicated northern pony breeders. Aunt Beula had not neglected it after Uncle Tok's death, but ensured it was maintained and white-washed twice every turning. Sturdy and spacious, housing the finest ponies in the region, the stable had not only been a symbol of Beula's livelihood and passion for ponies, but also a frequent shelter and playground for Tekoah and her brothers in their childhood.

Villagers had often joked that the guests Beula liked, she allowed to stay in her best bedchamber, but those whom she loved dwelt in her stable.

They wintered there only a few ponies, ones that had not sold before the first snows hit. There was also a magnificent white stallion, stamping and snorting in his stall. He had been brought in the autumn, and would lure mares down from the mountains in the spring.

"Shall I look, or shall you, Kirt?" the lord of Mirrand asked his companion.

"I will look," the other answered. "You go on ahead to the hay-barn. I will meet you there in a minute."

Tekoah found herself pulled along almost at a run; her wrist smarted from the grip of the lord's fingers. He did not speak until they were standing in front of the large, weathered barn, in which they kept bales of hay and sacks of oats as livestock fodder for the winter.

"I assume it is this barn you were speaking of," the lord of Mirrand murmured, staring straight ahead of him. His hand on her wrist had loosened, and she felt the blood return, tingling, to her hand.

She nodded. "Yes, my lord."

"You must call me Dirken," he said, turning his warm hazel eyes upon her. "But the soldiers will find them, I am very much afraid. We had better tell them to run for it now."

The door to the hay barn was ajar, and as they went forward, Dirken pushed it with his foot. It swung open wide, creaking. Within the barn, loosely tied bales of hay stood in stacks all around them. The sun broke through the cloud cover as they stood there, sending fingers of bright light between the rafters. In the fingers of light, dust motes floated, making the air shimmer.

The lord of Mirrand looked all around the barn, and then back at her, his charcoaled brow furrowed in puzzlement. "But where?" he began, then halted abruptly.

Behind them, heavy footsteps sounded.

Please Anna, oh please, do not let anyone lose their heads, Tekoah prayed. *Give them courage.*

Dirken's hand grasped hers and squeezed it reassuringly, then quickly let go, as he turned to face her, hand on his sword hilt. A moment later, the Southerner Kirt cursed as he tripped over a sack of oats lying just beyond the door.

"Any luck?" Dirken asked.

Kirt shook his head. "A beauty of a stallion in the barn, though. He'll fetch a good price in Zantor. What about here?"

Dirken shrugged. "Nothing so far. That farmer looks like too much of a coward to risk harbouring fleas, let alone witches. I say we make a quick sweep of the woods and then head to the Pitaya Pit. What say you?"

Kirt shifted his gaze over to Tekoah. "First, perhaps, we should have a little sport."

She bit her cheek to keep herself from crying out, not wanting him to have the satisfaction of seeing her fear. Involuntarily, she glanced at Dirken, but he leered at her.

"Please, no —" she babbled. "I am a virtuous woman!"

Kirt threw his head back in a guffaw. "That is not what I heard moments ago from your poor husband, my darling," he chuckled.

"Are you forgetting what happened in Berlot?" Dirken cut in, sounding aggrieved. "I saved your life, you said—I knew how to speak the language just when you were about to get your throat cut over a silly little misunderstanding. You owe me a favour, sir."

Kirt glared at him for a moment and then began laughing again. "So, this is the favour? You want her all to yourself? Well, I've got off easy, and no mistake! You could have had the first go, you know. Tell you what, lad, you stay here and disarrange the hay, and I'll lead the sweep. If we don't find any crones crouching in the crohms, then we will reconvene at the Pitaya Pit after sunset. But be sure not to scatter too much hay, or the swineherd will think we have all had a good time, and it will pierce his poor faithful heart to the quick."

Chortling, Kirt pulled out his sword and plunged it into the nearest bale of hay for emphasis. There was a muffled sound, and at that moment Tekoah threw herself on top of the bale, shrieking again and again, as if falling into a fit of hysterics.

Dirken strode over to the bale, pulling out Kirt's sword and then dropping it on the ground behind the bale. Tekoah saw him wipe the blade off with his boot before handing it to Kirt.

"Sorry, sir," he grinned. "It looks as if she might need some taming."

Tekoah allowed her shrieks to subside. Kirt put his sword back in his scabbard, looking at her with contempt. Dirken had gripped her arm now and was squeezing her wrist again—a warning.

"But is she worth it?" Kirt asked, spitting on the ground. He looked around the barn once more. "Do not be too long," he ordered. Then he turned and strode from the barn, tripping over the same sack of oats and cursing again.

Tekoah stood upright until Kirt's footsteps had died away, and then she pulled her arm away from Dirken and hurled herself forward. She saw the blood from Kirt's sword staining the hay a bright scarlet. Biting her lip—the other women must not know, or they would begin to weep, and then all was lost— she crouched beside the bale, ripping the strings with her fingers, tearing at the straw, her breath coming in ragged gasps.

It was Marta. Her seamed, kind face stared up at the light-laden rafters, transfixed as if in astonishment. The sword had pierced her through the throat; that was why there had only been one cry.

Tekoah stroked Marta's worn cheek and tried to close the eyelids, but they would not shut, despite her dogged efforts. Finally, she felt Dirken's hands on her shoulders, lifting her up from where she kneeled. She had forgotten he was there.

He turned her to face him. His eyes were a brown-flecked hazel, holding more warmth in them than any eyes she had ever seen. Tekoah felt as if she stood before a glowing hearth fire. She tried to speak, to tell him it was Marta who had warned them—to ask him why this had happened to her. *It was so unfair. Why?*

But Dirken put a finger to his lips, and with the other hand he gestured around the barn, to the other bales of hay. In each one, an Anniste woman lay, breathing shallowly through a piece of straw. Waiting for this it to be over.

Dirken's arm circled her waist, holding her up so straight that her spine became rigid, and her knees cease to tremble.

Thus supported, Tekoah spoke into the dusty air. "It is well. Not much longer now," she told the silent bales.

There was not a single sound in response, a good sign. Dirken had been right—they must not panic, not until the soldiers had left.

Tekoah did not watch while Dirken moved Marta's body from the hay-barn. She sat on the floor gazing at the dust motes float in their endless, dreamy dance around each other. Some time later—she did not know how long—Dirken returned. He squatted down beside her. She stared at his black boots, wondering how he kept them so polished.

"Darian's scum have left," Dirken told her in a low voice. "And now I must go meet them. But wait another hour, until twilight comes, before you bring the women out, all right?"

Tekoah found it hard to concentrate on what he was saying. Much easier to just stare at the dancing motes. But he waited and, after a moment, she nodded.

"Was the hay your idea?" he asked her. She nodded again.

"Brilliant!" he whispered, showing his even white teeth in a sudden flash.

Tekoah closed her eyes, thinking of Marta.

"It was *brilliant*," Dirken repeated, as if reading her thoughts. "Do you think they would have gone undetected in the woods? Little brown rabbits in the snow, waiting to be picked off? Never."

All at once, he bent toward her, touching her cheek lightly with his forefinger. He held his finger up to the light, and she saw a tear she had not known was there, glistening now in the sunlight, transformed into a tiny rainbow prism. Then he touched the finger to his lips, and his gaze became unfathomable.

"The next time I see you," he murmured, "it will be for longer than five minutes." He stood up and turned to go. Reaching the doorway, he caught her eye, and pantomimed Kirt's clumsy encounter with the sack of oats so cleverly that she could not help but smile. Then he was gone.

Tekoah sat waiting on the floor, looking at the rays of light disappear one by one. Then she stood, and told the women they could come out.

The fifty-three remaining members of the Anniste emerged from the bales, bits of hay sticking to them everywhere, so that they looked like little hedgehogs as they padded back to the house. It was dark now, and quite cold; but in the chill blue air, Tekoah caught the scent of spring—faint, indefinable, almost unbearably sweet.

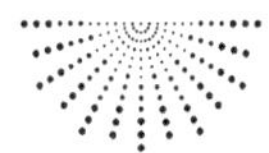

CHAPTER 32

That night, Tekoah dreamed of the sorcerer Braith for the first time in two annaspans, although the dream did not begin with Braith. It began in the hay-barn, and it was the face of the lord of Mirrand who looked at her, his warm hazel eyes saying more than the words that came from his lips.

"You must call me Dirken," he told her, laying her down gently on a mound of straw.

The name seemed important, somehow. It was as if he had given her the piece of a puzzle which she was expected to solve. Surely, he was not the same Dirken as the devil-may-care minstrel over whom all the girls swooned. She had never laid eyes on the minstrel, so she could not say.

She saw he was about to kiss her. His breath was on her cheek, and she closed her eyes.

When his lips touched hers, they were not full and soft as she had imagined them to be, but thin, with the edge of teeth behind. A dusky scent of red wine was on his breath. When she opened her eyes, she realized it was Braith who had kissed her.

They were lying on the sumptuous white sofa in the Castle of Mirrand. All around her, hidden inside pieces of large and magnificent furniture, she heard the women of the Anniste, whimpering with terror.

She rose to reassure them, but Braith held her down. She struggled against him, beating her hands against his chest in fury, clawing at his face. But still he held her, and his eyes were pleading, mournful.

He whispered, "Will you not stay with me until the Mantling? I will be gone, then."

"I must save them," she panted, as the sounds grew more desperate.

The dark weight of Braith pressed down upon her. He would not let her go. But then his hoarse whisper was in her ear, "I will save them."

When Tekoah awoke, her body was hot and restless, just as it had been during her sojourn with Braith at the castle. She hugged her knees to her chest, rocking back and forth in the dark cellar; faster and faster, until at last, her fingernails dug into her arms and her teeth ground together. But it was no good, for she could not rock away the shame.

THE EVENING AFTER THE RAID, Chalvern reappeared at the farm.

"Poor old fellow looks like he's all done in," Bhantok told Tekoah when he came to fetch her up from the cellar. "He must have heard about your ordeal, and it looks like he took it worse than anyone. Almost anyone," he amended, averting his eyes, and she knew he was thinking of Marta.

"It was your ordeal also, Bhantok," Tekoah told him. "And we want you to know we are grateful. Reika will be so proud."

Bhantok blushed to the roots of his thinning brown hair at the mention of Reika's name. "No need to blow my small part out of proportion," he mumbled, but he gave her arm an affectionate pat as she climbed past him.

Bhantok spoke the truth—Chalvern looked as if he had been wrestling with wraiths, his hand shaking as she handed him his tea. After checking her over from head to toe to satisfy himself that she had sustained no injuries, he demanded to hear the story of the raid, and she was not to leave anything out—not a thing, did she hear?

As he listened, there was a spark in Chalvern's deep-set eyes that was at odds with his shaken demeanour. Tekoah surmised he was about to renew his efforts to separate her from the Anniste fugitives and would not let the matter rest so easily this time.

She was not wrong.

"Well, thank the gods young Dirken had some presence of mind," he muttered, after she finished her account. He stared off into space for a moment before adding, "And you performed heroically in the crisis, my dear. But that is beside the point. You must leave, come and live with me. I can hide you safely until all this has blown over. The situation has become very dangerous."

"Dirken?" Tekoah asked, ignoring the rest of Chalvern's words. "That is what he told me to call him! The same name as the minstrel."

"Yes, Dirken. The minstrel, and also the lord of Mirrand. He was pretending to be a southern soldier, but in fact he is the leader of the Kalesh. He prefers to keep a low profile. I know all this because Bhantok told me."

Tekoah recalled the disarming warmth in the hazel eyes of the lord of Mirrand. He seemed incapable of duplicity, yet suddenly she remembered the sullen, stupid expression which had transformed his features when they'd heard Kirt's tread in the barn. And he was also the celebrated *minstrel*?

He must be a very busy man, she thought.

"Dirken is the old lord's son," Chalvern told her. "You were still a baby when the lord Semuel died, but he was a fine man, deeply respected. He had travelled, educated himself, yet he was still proud to be a northerner, and he made us proud as well."

Chalvern held out his empty mug, and Tekoah refilled it, sinking down in silence beside him on the bench. She had heard none of this.

"The Lord Semuel and his wife had only one child, and that was Dirken. And a fair lad he was, too, although his coming caused his father more grief than pride. His wife died in childbirth, and after her death he went into a decline, from which he never recovered."

An inexplicable look of bitterness crossed Chalvern's face. So intense was it, that Tekoah was reaching her hand toward him in alarm when he shook himself and continued.

"When the lord died a few turnings later, they sent Dirken away to live with his wife's family in the South. We, in Stern, never saw him after that, but we heard rumours that when he came into his inheritance, he lived among the Berlotans for several years, and was a great favourite at court. We could not stir up a feeling of pride at that—as you can imagine. I was sad to think that he had become a dandy and a traitor, when his father had been so loyal to Miraven—you must have heard some rumours yourself, my dear? But I did not give him much further thought until recently, when he commanded the castle be built. *Why would he choose to come home, now?* I wondered. *Does he expect a hero's welcome?*"

Outside, an owl hooted, and Tekoah started, covering up her movement by standing and going to fetch a cloth. She wiped the table. But she could not fool Chalvern.

"A little jumpy, and no wonder," he remarked, shooting her a sharp glance from beneath his brows.

"Go on about Dirken," she urged, refusing to take the bait.

Chalvern sighed. "Now Bhantok tells me Dirken has been a spy for the North all along, ever since King Garan died, and that it was Dirken himself who formed the Kalesh. And an excellent spy he makes—he knows Berlot inside out, and has long been privy to closely guarded information, especially as it concerns the court of the Jinta. The North would have fallen much sooner, were it not for Dirken."

He chuckled. "Yes, Dirken: the laughing minstrel, whose tongue trips with honeyed songs at the court of all three kingdoms, and every well-to-do manor within riding distance. No one thinks he can do any harm, so they indulge him wherever he goes. He was at Darielle's court, wooing all the young flowers there, and also at Meed—when he was not in Berlot, sending the Jinta into convulsions with his imitations of King Darian."

"And no one knows he is the lord of Mirrand?" Tekoah asked. She was incredulous. Chalvern knew. Bhantok knew. How could something like that be a secret?

"Some folk know," Chalvern answered. "But for a long while it was not important who he was, as long as he was amusing. But now many more are going to discover his identity—or identities. Because it will be Dirken's highly trained Kalesh fighters who will unite the army in the queen's name, unless I am very much mistaken."

"Oh," Tekoah said, dazed.

Her scalp tingled as she remembered Dirken's flirtatious banter with her outside the castle. What was it he had said about her eyes being like bits of sky? And then an annaspan later, he had discovered her within his castle, and she could not explain her presence. Yet he had been warm and friendly, instead of suspicious. And then there was those sad, sweet moments in the hay-barn.

"There is something else I must tell you about the young lord of Mirrand," Chalvern said.

"What is it?"

Chalvern did not answer for so long that at last Tekoah

glanced at him. She had been gazing into the stove fire, which had died down into brooding embers. Chalvern met her eyes, and on his face was a gentle fatherly smile.

"Dirken told Bhantok something, and Bhantok told me," Chalvern continued, eyes a twinkle. "Do you wish to know what it is?"

The previous night's dream flooded her mind with a vividness that made her hot with shame. She knew Chalvern could see the change in her face, and she was very glad that at least he could not read her mind.

"No," she answered in a whisper, turning away.

"Are you certain?" he asked, and the smile was still in his voice, though she could not see his face.

In a panic, she blurted, "Have you heard anything from the sorcerer Braith?"

"No," Chalvern said, his voice wavering. "I find I must put all thoughts of Braith from my mind for the present." After a moment, he pressed her, "And what about you? Will you not put your thoughts of him behind you? There could be much happiness in store, if you but opened your heart to the possibility."

Tekoah closed her eyes. "You do not know," she whispered fiercely.

"Know what?" Chalvern moved closer to her, and his warm hand stroked her hand. "You can tell me."

"I am afraid."

"Of what?"

"I fear Braith has somehow enchanted me, for I cannot make my thoughts of him go away. And where I should feel revulsion and hatred, I feel—differently."

She had said it. Her shame was out in the open. All that she could not rock away in the dark had spilled out onto the kitchen floor. Chalvern would despise her now. She opened her eyes.

"Ah." Chalvern was looking at her with nothing more than pity and understanding. "My poor child," he murmured, "do not think that it is a terrible thing you did by returning his passion. It is only natural. But the question remains, would you be happy together? And I fear the answer must be no, if he is like other sorcerers. I say this with love and sorrow, for he was once like a son to me. But I would no sooner give you up to him than a lamb to an eagle."

Tekoah shuddered, remembering hot talons on her back. But Chalvern's voice was cool and reasonable, and the weight of her shame dissolved.

"And do not think for a moment," Chalvern continued, "that you cannot love again, and be loved in return."

"But I dreamed last night, and it was terrible—" Tekoah wanted to tell him her dream, to tell him everything.

But he put two fingers against her lips. "You had a nightmare, no doubt. And no wonder, after what you went through? That is precisely why you need to come and stay with me, where I can keep an eye on you. Perhaps that way we will both get some sleep until this thing comes to an end."

"The Mantling approaches," Tekoah answered automatically.

Chalvern waved his hand. "Forgive me for declining to hear of the Mantling," he said testily. "All I know is that a maddened sorcerer is on a killing spree and is using the desperation of a drought-ridden south and the greed of pitaya-hungry Berlot to fuel his power. I refuse to have you in the eye of this storm."

"Is not the eye of the storm always the safest place to be?" Tekoah asked him, sitting up and wiping her eyes. She grinned, glad of the chance to best the schoolmaster.

"Enough of your impertinence, young woman," he replied. "I want you to leave with me, at this very moment! Bhantok agrees, and the opinion of the twins could not be clearer even if they spoke three languages. Bhantok tells me the Kalesh have a plan to move the other Anniste women as soon as possible, but I would have you gone from here tonight."

"I cannot," she told him. "My place is here until the Goddess

Anna tells me otherwise. And besides, there was good news in Valeen's Journey today. The Morgs are dying. They cannot follow the scent in the snow, and they refuse to hunt anything but us, you know. They have good taste, at any rate." She could see the mirthlessness of her jest reflected in Chalvern's sombre eyes.

The apothecary was silent for a moment, looking down. A knot formed in Tekoah's stomach. Why did she have to make such choices? She was not strong—and she did not know half the time if what she was saying about the Mantling was true. It was like stumbling about in a dark forest, tripping over roots and stones, going toward a light one thought to have glimpsed, but which might be only one's imagination.

When Chalvern looked up, there were tears in his dark eyes, and the knot in her stomach tightened into a fist of guilt. She had never seen him weep.

"I loved your mother, you know," he said, and slowly got to his feet. "And yet I could not save her."

Tekoah opened her mouth and closed it again, unable to say anything. Chalvern took his woolen cloak from the peg behind the door and wrapped it around him, hobbling toward the door.

Bhantok materialized, mumbling that he would see Master Chalvern home. Had he been listening to this entire conversation?

Chalvern opened the door, and Tekoah shivered at the chill wind which blew in a sudden gust into the kitchen. She watched as Chalvern and her cousin walked together into the dark night, Chalvern shaking Bhantok's hand from his elbow. Neither man looked back.

WHEN TEKOAH'S next Journey came two days later, she saw nothing but a dark disc hanging in the sky, ringed about by a bright corona which shimmered like white gold. The corona spurted flares in all directions, brilliant hues of red, orange, green and purple. At the sight, Tekoah's spirit strained against her body, as if yearning for flight.

"The Mantling," whispered the voice that she had come to know was Anna's.

Tekoah could not look long upon its glory, nor did she dare to ask the meaning of this sight, so terrible in its beauty.

And then Anna told her she was to make preparations to leave.

"Where?" Tekoah asked, breathless with excitement and trepidation. The Goddess had never spoken to her before, in this clear voice which chimed like a bell. She waited humbly, not expecting to be told where she was going, for Reika had not been told. But she was wrong.

"You are going to Zantor," the Goddess told her.

"But why must I leave the women—if I am their Guardian?"

"There are two reasons," the Goddess told her. "You must warn the leader of the Kalesh that the war is coming sooner than he thinks. Tell him to marshal the army in Stern, wherein lies the greatest stronghold of the Anniste."

"Dirken?" Tekoah asked, bewildered. "But I hardly know him —and I know less than nothing of the war. What if he does not believe me?"

The Goddess continued as if Tekoah had not spoken. "The second reason is because now is the time for the sorcerer Braith to make his choice. He must choose to save the Anniste or let them be killed. If you are with them, he may spare them, because of his love for you. But if you are gone, the choice will not come from his heart, but from his Source. And the Mantling will come—or it will not come—depending on his choice. For he is the Third Sorcerer, the balance between Anna and Rhan."

"I do not understand!" Tekoah cried out, struggling against the sticky cobwebby threads of panic winding around her. "About Braith. Please explain it to me."

But Anna's voice faded away, and Tekoah drifted into a fitful sleep. For a while she dozed, unwilling to wake. However, Anna's words echoed in her ears, and at last she rose from her place between two women, and slowly crept up the cellar stairs.

In the cold dawn, she packed a few belongings and some bread. Thinking ironically that now, at least, she could tell Chalvern she was leaving. But somehow, she doubted that the news would stir any joy in his heart, when he discovered that she was going straight from the fish pond into the cooking pot.

CHAPTER 33

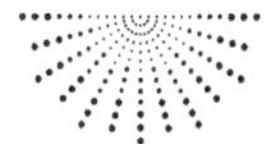

BOOK 4: THE TEARS OF SPRING

For days, Reika was nothing more to Weslan than a lap, warm and soft, in which to nestle. His head cushioned by her thighs, she first gave him only water and broth and bark tea, trickling the liquid into the corners of his mouth. He heard the water boiling over a cooking fire at the mouth of the cave. The fire burned day and night. Howls and grunts, yowls and shrieks, reverberated in the dark hours against the rough stone walls.

"There are many hungry mountain cats out there," he heard Reika muse once, as she rose to stir up the embers in the dead of night. "It is a wonder you survived this long, my friend."

After a time, Weslan found he could sit and, more importantly, that he wanted to. And so he did, legs crossed in front of him like Reika's—was she a Berlotan?—and eating the small flat cakes she made over the fire in a tiny iron pan. Reika also pulled out long strips of dried meat from a pouch at her belt. They would chew them slowly, staring into the awakening forest, softening the tough strands in their mouths until they could swallow them.

She was clever, this Reika, as competent as any soldier

seasoned in Heyg's service. "Spring is here," she told him brightly. "Soon, there will be plentiful fresh food."

Weslan listened to all this when he could, in the brief lulls the voices allowed him.

They would not permit him to speak to Reika, and so he could not tell her that at first, he had thought she was his mother, come to take him away to the Halls of the Worldmaker. And that it had bitterly disappointed him to discover he was wrong.

"Why tell her all that?" chided the woman. "So she can confirm what she already suspects—that you are not in your right mind?"

So Weslan stared at Reika, ashamed and silent, whenever she addressed him. But she remained patient, speaking cheerfully to him, never seeming to notice the intermittent clamour of the voices.

"Would she coddle you so if she knew you had killed your father in cold blood?" the man asked him sternly. "Would she stroke your noble brow, as she does now?"

Weslan ignored him. His head on Reika's lap, eyes closed, he lay listening to the snow geese as they flew overhead. Trapped spirits of the frozen waterfall, freed now to wander the skies, seeking what? Peace?

"How mournful they sound," Reika murmured, her fingers running through his hair like water, like wind.

Weslan wanted to say, *Yes, and I can tell you why they mourn.* But he said nothing.

"I have not yet told you of myself," Reika went on. "You have no doubt guessed by my robe that I am Anniste. But you do not know that Anna sent me to find you. To summon you—for we will need your strength!"

"How disappointed she must be to discover that he is hopeless," the woman said to the man in a snide undertone.

"Hopeless," the man echoed in agreement. And together they chimed the word. It was a game they liked to play.

"You are not hopeless," Reika cut in sharply, and the voices fell silent.

The quiet was so deep that Weslan felt his own heart beating, heard the blood singing in his veins.

"You have not yet made your choice, that is all," Reika said, and her fingers smoothed and smoothed his forehead.

"She could not have heard us, could she?" whispered the woman, sounding chastened.

"No, of course not," the man whispered back. "But—"

"I heard," Reika interrupted flatly, "as I have heard everything you have said. And would that I heard no more from you! But it is not my choice to make."

The voices subsided, but Weslan sensed them waiting in a corner of his mind.

"Before Anna sent me to you," Reika continued, as though nothing had happened, "Your mother Neela visited me. Not living," she added swiftly, for Weslan's shoulders trembled at her words. "Or at least not as you and I know life. She was radiant, clothed in Anna's silver light. And she does not grieve for her time here, or even her death, for this came from choices she had freely made.

"But she does feel sorrow—because others have suffered for her choices, the Anniste especially. And her children." Reika stopped speaking, her fingertips trailing his wet cheeks.

The man and the woman were leaving. As they slipped from Weslan, panic assailed him briefly. However horrible, they had been his only companions for a time.

But with the voices gone, he could hear the snow geese calling clearly, the drip-drip of melting icicles, and Reika's lilting voice, like a lullaby.

"Neela gave me a sacred charge to help the Anniste. But the

Goddess had plans for me as well, because here I am." Reika clasped his hand warmly.

"I am not worth it." Weslan surprised himself with the sound of his voice, creaky as an old wheelbarrow. They were the first words he had spoken to a living being since he had entered the woods.

He sat up, for the softness of Reika's thighs bothered him now. He rubbed the tears from his cheeks, tugged at his tangled beard. Wondering how he must look to her. Not like the beardless, fair-haired boy who had fainted when a queen had smiled at him.

"You judge yourself harshly," Reika said. "Already you have shone with brightness, and your life is still new."

"No!" Weslan cried, the word a burning firebrand in his throat. "You do not understand! I killed my father, and I am infected with his madness. I have carried the seeds within me as long as I can remember, but I could always pluck them out. Then, when I killed Veld, I felt his madness take root within me. And all because of my desire for glory—I have sacrificed everyone I love. My brothers, my mother, whom I left unprotected from my father's brutality, and my sister, whom I led like a bride into a sorcerer's hands."

Weslan stopped, his throat aching with the unaccustomed effort of speech. He dropped his voice to a whisper. "My queen, Darielle, also is gone, and I am lost."

"Not so," Reika answered, her voice strong. She crouched over the fire to stir it up, for the afternoon shadows were becoming long and the air grew cold. "I hear that Queen Darielle is alive—though perhaps not happy—in Berlot. The Jinta has taken a great fancy to her, which should not come as a surprise to anyone." Reika paused, glancing at Weslan in a manner which made him uncomfortable.

"Your mother, as she told me, made her own choices. As for your brothers, Fanco was with me when we found you, although you may not remember. He and Raol both hold you in great regard. I can also assure you of your sister's wellbeing. So, you see, things are not hopeless."

It took a few seconds for her words to sink into Weslan's consciousness. "What?" he croaked. The blood rushed through his skull in a raging torrent, so that her next words echoed strangely.

"Tekoah is alive and well, and not in the clutches of any sorcerer," Reika told him, turning around, and smiling fully into his face. Her black eyes snapped and sparkled in the firelight. "And I will tell you all about it," she added, taking a freshly caught hare from her food pouch. "But first, we must eat."

After that day, the voices sometimes returned, but Weslan heard them less and less, and they seldom addressed him directly, but grumbled in the background, until they were no more distracting than the whine of a mosquito in his ear. Then, one day, they left altogether.

"Will they come back?" he asked Reika—waiting, childlike, for her answer.

"That is not for me to know," she replied, a little tartly. She walked ahead of him and did not turn around.

They were travelling single file along a trail he had not seen before. It seemed to rise steadily, but Reika's pace did not slacken, and Weslan had to run to keep up.

He caught up to her and grabbed her hand. She stopped walking and turned to face him.

"You healed me," he said.

"You healed yourself," she replied.

"But the voices, you made them go away—"

"You exiled those terrible mind-demons," she corrected. "I only reminded you that the choice was yours."

"Whatever you did," Weslan repeated, "you healed me."

"Perhaps, the day you realize it was you who banished your tormentors will be the day they are gone forever," Reika replied.

Reika looked grave and utterly exquisite as she spoke. He wondered how old she was, although instinct told him he was the younger by a few turnings. But her smooth olive face reflected nothing of the ravages of travelling alone in the frozen wilderness, nor of the fear she must live with, being Anniste. Her dark hair was tucked behind her hood, but a few stray tendrils had escaped, giving her a waif-like, dishevelled look.

She is too young to be so wise, Weslan marvelled.

And, before he thought about what he was doing, he had reached out and caught a lock of her hair between his fingers. Reika's cheeks flushed a dusky rose. She turned away, shaking it from his grasp, and walked again even more rapidly than before.

By the time he reached the top of the incline, Weslan was out of breath. His last few weeks of starvation had weakened him. Reika stood very still. Through the stand of bare beeches and elms, just greening with small, hard buds, Weslan saw she was staring down intently. When Weslan approached, she put her finger to her lips and held the other hand, palm out, cautioning him. He lightened his tread, and then almost cried out in astonishment when he stood beside her and looked below.

About fifty men had encamped in a small valley by the side of the River Meed, alongside which he and Reika had been travelling for several days. Weslan saw they wore the colours of the Kalesh: tunics of indigo, embroidered with an emblem of a pony leaping over a silver crescent. They were setting up camp, which made sense, for it was late afternoon, and also dark clouds had gathered.

Weslan had seen no one save Reika for so long that it seemed like a dream to witness so many men milling about. Also disorienting was the volume of their rough voices, jesting and cursing at the rain that had begun to fall.

To his utter astonishment, he caught sight of a large, red-haired man striding about, supervising the organization of the bivouac. It was Heyg.

Weslan had lacked curiosity about his former world once he had discovered Tekoah was well. But in that moment, he clapped his hands around his arms to stop himself from crying out. A dozen questions sprang to his lips at once.

Reika was nodding as if she'd read his thoughts. Taking his arm, she drew him back through the trees—for they were becoming drenched—and back into the shelter of a thicket.

"I see you recognize someone," she observed, smiling.

"Yes, it is Heyg, my old captain." Weslan said, acting nonchalant. But he could not stay still. He began tapping his boot against a tree trunk, and a woodpecker flew off, offended at the competition. "It looks as if he has done well with the Kalesh. At the beginning, he was only being asked for advice once in a while. They are so particular about having only nobility, you know."

"They are no longer very particular," Reika answered.

He stared at her, but she said no more. The tempo of the rain increased, and she squatted down, gesturing for him to do the same.

"He does not look any worse for wear," Weslan added irrelevantly, knowing he must sound foolish. But he could not stop grinning. "I wonder what the company is doing here, holed up in the hills. What mountain is this anyway?" he asked, knitting his brows. Why hadn't he thought to wonder before?

"We are on the eastern side of Mount Naian," Reika answered promptly, "right near the southern border."

"What are they doing?" Weslan repeated.

Reika shrugged, and they squatted for a few moments in silence, listening to the rain patter on the leaves. Weslan found he couldn't stay still long, though, so he crept back, half-crouching, to peer down again. The men had built a shelter from the rain, and a fire was crackling beside it. The torrent had let up a little, and he could see the soldiers passing flasks back and forth. Southern beer, with corn lightning to chase it down. He remembered the taste of it on his tongue.

Still hidden, Weslan watched his captain. Holding a currycomb, Heyg looked upward, scanning the hill above him, then turned to his mount. He removed her bridle, slipped on a halter, and brushed her with gentle strokes, pausing to scratch her behind the ears.

Going back to the thicket, Weslan saw Reika was nowhere to be seen. There was a moment of panic, until she walked out from between some cedars, brown hood framing her face like a halo.

"I have found a cave," she said.

That evening they sat on a nearby log, under a stone outcropping which kept the rain away. They ate a sparse meal— but neither of them was hungry—and then let their cooking fire die down to glowing embers. They entered the cave in silence. Reika had woven tree boughs together as mats; over them, they spread the sleeping roll she had brought with her and the deer-skin Weslan had used as blanket throughout the long winter.

They lay down, side by side, stiffly. Sleeping close together in this way had become uncomfortable for Weslan.

"Are you awake?" Reika asked him, after a few moments.

He grunted.

"Do you know," she continued, "I have thought to myself this past annaspan that on the day you needed to know where you were, you would be ready to return to your world."

"My world?" Weslan replied. He did not like the way she spoke. It sounded too gentle. "Is this not my world?" He propped himself up on his elbow. "Our world? Have you not been happy, these past days, or have I been a fool?"

He sensed her breathing quicken and knew his arrow had found its mark.

But her voice was smooth when she spoke. "You are ready to

return," she said. "You hear the call, and your heart is making its answer even now."

"How do you know that?" he asked, turning in the dark and finding her, warm and soft, beside him. He heard her swift intake of breath, and roughly he pulled her to him in the darkness. She made no resistance.

"How do you know that?" he repeated. "Do you know everything about me? And why do I know nothing about you?"

She did not answer. His mouth found hers, and as he kissed her, he saw in his mind a yellow flower, and seemed to smell the exotic scent of Darielle's perfume. And so he kissed Reika harder, to blot out the sight and the smell.

Perhaps he was kissing her too hard; for he felt her small, white teeth beneath his own and tasted the salt of her blood. But she was still pliant beneath him, and when he lifted his lips from hers, she reached up to run her fingers through his knotted hair.

"I know you love her," she murmured, without censure.

He did not reply, but reached down to her waist to untie the cord of her robe. Her hands were on top of his own, surprisingly strong.

"I am scarred," she whispered.

Weslan froze. Her voice sounded so strange; there was a note in it he had never heard before. Pleading. This was not the Reika he knew.

Weslan untied the cord and let her robe fall open. In the darkness, he could see nothing. But as he ran his awestruck hands over her body, he felt the ridges and weals of her scars go on and on, from her chest to her ankles, front and back.

Who could have done this to her?

She shuddered, and the thought came to him that that no one had ever touched her in such a way before.

He whispered to Reika, trying to soothe her. Her ear felt soft beneath his lips after the brutal puckering of those scars. He did not know what he said, knew only that he must keep saying it, to stop her from trembling. It occurred to him she had very little sensation on those ridges.

So, he brought his hands back up to her face as he covered her body with his own. He stroked her cheeks, lips, ears and eyelids, until she stopped shuddering. He felt her move beneath him.

Much later, lying beside Reika, hearing her soft breathing, Weslan asked himself the question: But who will heal *her*? For he knew he had not. He kissed her while she slept, trying to leave some grateful imprint of himself that she could carry with her, to keep her warm.

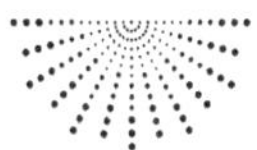

hen Weslan awoke, Reika had gone. He looked around for traces of her, slowly, dazedly at first, then with increasing urgency as he stumbled from the mouth of the cave; but he could find nothing.

No sign she had ever been there, not even a single long, black hair. Though absurd, he searched for exactly that, scrabbling about on the ground. Yet he had wound a curtain of her hair around his neck a few hours earlier, sheltering them both. Without knowing what he was doing, Weslan dug into the half-frozen earth with his fingers.

Voices wafted up from the encampment below him, and Weslan froze, listening. Heyg and his men were breaking up camp. *Where were they headed?*

He rose to his feet, half-crouching. His heartbeat quickened, and its pulse seemed to come from within the earth, the awakened soil, whose musky fragrance he felt clinging to his hands. He walked forward, one step, then two. Then he ran, in long pounding strides, reaching the edge of the plateau in a few seconds. He began the steep walk down, clambering for a foothold on the damp, slippery rocks of the mountainside, trying to stay under cover behind the trees so that he would be within shouting distance before Heyg and his men caught sight of him.

As it was, two arrows twanged past his ear well before Weslan could announce his presence. The Kalesh were not to be fooled with. Crawling the last couple of hundred feet, he zigzagged behind a towering cedar just a few yards beyond the cooking fire.

"Heyg," he shouted, wishing his voice was steadier. "It is me—Weslan!"

There was a moment of silence, in which Weslan could almost feel the tautness of arrows on bows. Then he heard Heyg's gruff exclamation, "Rhan's blazing balls, it *is* him! Show yourself, lad. We thought you were dead."

Weslan stepped out from behind the tree and then stopped. His mouth was dry, suddenly. The thought of all those eyes upon him—too many, too soon. But he must either show himself or they would shoot him as an impostor. He straightened and walked out from behind the sheltering wood, into the camp of the Kalesh.

Later, riding along on one of the pack mules and trying to ignore the sniggers of his fellow-soldiers at the sight, Weslan heard Heyg's voice beside him.

"You tolerate teasing a lot better than you used to, Wes."

Weslan shrugged, hoping it would suffice. His excuse for his absence had been met with a skeptical raising of his captain's eyebrows. And now Heyg had fixed him with a searching stare.

"Running the pony farm with a bunch of clacking hens has made me appreciate the comradeship of men." Weslan grinned, knowing it sounded lame.

Heyg said nothing for a moment, but chewed on his beard, which was shot through with more grey than red. When he at last spoke, he stared ahead as though he was talking to himself.

"You should know, Weslan, that a few days after you went

left Rhantor, I went to Stern—with Dirken. Not to look for you. We had other urgent business. Although I was most astonished to find that no one had heard anything of your intended arrival. Much less the sorcerer Braith."

Someone had trotted up and was riding close to Weslan's other flank. Looking over, Weslan saw with surprise and relief that it was Nolvern, winking at him with delight. He had not recognized his chum in the initial chaos. Upon closer inspection, it looked as if a few more of Nolvern's teeth were missing, and someone had broken his nose. Nothing had changed.

He grinned back, hoping that Nolvern's presence would change the topic. But Heyg coughed in a pointed way, and Nolvern, looking at his captain, reconsidered his riding position. He shrugged at Weslan and rode on ahead.

"As I was saying," Heyg continued, a hint of thunder in his brow and voice, "I was of course concerned about you, lad. I had thought perhaps you despaired when you heard of your queen's capture, or that you might decide to do something foolish on her behalf. But I was not prepared for your complete and utter disappearance."

Weslan started to reply, but Heyg held up his hand. "And, other than a gossipy goodwife and a few villagers in your local tavern, no one seems to have even known that you had been in Stern at all. However, I met your sister under rather strange circumstances, and she seemed even more confused than I. As for your brothers, idiots they are called—though they did not seem so to me—they were unable or unwilling to shed Rhan's light on any of this."

Weslan took a deep breath. He had not been prepared for what it would look like to others. For what he would say. And now he was in a tangled mess. Why had Reika said he was ready?

"Do you know, Wes, what is the worst thing about all this?" Heyg asked, relentless. "It was unpleasant to contemplate that

Braith had done away with you. But the worst of it is that some think you have betrayed your queen."

Weslan reined up his mule so sharply that it stamped its forelegs, braying with alarm. Heyg's horse shied in response, and it took both men several moments to bring their mounts under control.

"What did you say?" Weslan asked through clenched teeth. "*What?*"

"You disappeared at just the right time, you know," Heyg pointed out, looking back at him. "But I did not believe it for a moment. Get over the insult, and get the cramps out of your sword arm, boy. You never know when you might need it."

"Who accused me of this?" Weslan cried. "I wish to know, so that I may deal with the scoundrels!"

"And here I thought you seemed more level-headed than before," Heyg grinned. "Same old hothead for the queen, though, aren't you? Well, that tipped the scales in your favour for me. You would sooner cut your own throat than let a downy hair fall from her head. But you have some explaining to do, my lad, because Dirken does not share my high opinion of—"

Heyg stopped, for there were shouts up ahead, out of sight around a bend in the path. "The bastards must have caught wind of us," he growled, and set off with great dispatch, considering the narrow, wooded path.

Weslan rode right behind him, the anticipation of a fight tightening his muscles and flooding him with a sharp exhilaration. He was in the thick of things again, right where he should be.

They were heading toward a mountain pass southeast of Stern, hoping to cut off a convoy carrying pitayas to the river where dock workers would load them on barges and have them sent to Berlot. Perhaps this time more than the usual small group of soldiers had accompanied the party.

The Berlotans were losing patience with apologies and explanations about pitaya shipments which never arrived. The real reason, of course: the Kalesh derived their greatest pleasure from intercepting such shipments. All was not going the way King Darian might have wished.

It had been a hard winter for the South, Heyg told Weslan, despite all the promises lavished about by Darian and that slippery sorcerer, Zant. Their visions of bounty were long in words, but they were short on bread. Whenever they could, the Kalesh did their utmost to aggravate the situation, at the same time ensuring that any southerner who joined the Kalesh was well-fed, and provisions smuggled to his family.

With no warning, Heyg stopped riding, and Weslan had to turn aside to avoid collision, running his mule into a prickly gorse-bush. Swearing, Weslan looked up to see Nolvern on foot beside his horse, holding the reins and blocking their path. The man's forehead glistened with sweat, and his face was the colour of whey.

"It is a—" Nolvern stuttered, his knees buckling.

"Speak up," Heyg roared at him, standing erect in his saddle. "I cannot hear you. Speak, you fool, or get out of my way so that I can find out for myself!"

Nolvern found his voice. "It is a Shifting. Three men just disappeared into thin air. It is a bleeding Shifting!"

"Out of my way!" Heyg raised his whip, and Nolvern plunged his mount off the path, into the trees.

Heyg is frightened, Weslan thought with disbelief.

Out of the corner of his eye, Weslan saw Nolvern dismount and crouch in the shadows. He had no intention of following them.

First time I have seen Nolvern act the coward, Weslan thought, grimly spurring his mount after Heyg.

They reached the pass within a minute and began the steep, curving descent down into the valley where the North ended and the South began. Weslan could see the great River Mced twisting like a snake below them, its banks swollen with spring rain. The grass was still more brown than green, but it was plain to see that the drought was over for the South.

At the steepest part of the decline, he could observe Heyg's company milling about in noisy confusion, some men on their horses, some dismounted. Weslan heard a soldier's voice rise to a high note of hysteria and an answering trill came, as if in mockery, from a nearby bird.

"What in Rhan's name is going on?" Heyg bellowed, and a soldier broke away from the rest and came running up to them.

"My horse bolted, sir," he said, eyes wide in his boyish face, "and went into the Shifting. That is three men and a horse so far, sir." His voice faltered as he looked over his shoulder.

Heyg frowned and then dismounted, handing his reins to the young soldier. He walked over to where the other soldiers stood.

"Back!" he commanded, and when the men had retreated, Heyg stood staring into the air.

Weslan dismounted and tied his mule to a tree. He edged a little nearer, but could see nothing unusual. Heyg held out a hand, poking his fingers into the air. Still nothing.

"On the *ground*, sir!" someone shouted. "It is like a mirage."

Heyg looked down, and as Weslan followed his gaze, he saw it. A greyish, shimmering ripple that was no longer than a man's height, no wider than a horse's breadth. At first glance, it resembled a flat puddle of water.

Heyg stooped and picked up a stone. "I hate things I do not understand," he muttered, and dropped the stone into the puddle.

There was no sound, no splash, no ripple. The stone was gone, that was all. Behind them, the men had subsided into a silence which was more frantic than the noise.

Heyg spoke in a calm voice, as if reluctant to alarm the soldiers. "I never believed in Shiftings until now, you know. Although the stories say that sorcerers used them for unholy purposes long ago." He was silent for a moment, stroking his beard, stepping back from the shimmer.

"Now at least I know they are real," he continued. "And I fear that there is a sorcerer who has made life unpleasant and precarious for all of us." He turned and locked his eyes upon Weslan's. "I just do not know whether it is one sorcerer, or both."

Heyg fell silent, and Weslan knew his commander was waiting for a reply. When he said nothing, Heyg spoke again, his voice quiet. "I hope that if you knew where Braith is, or what he has planned, that you would tell me, for it could mean life or death for all of us. Think, lad, rack your brains and search your soul. And then tell me: do you know the whereabouts or intentions of the sorcerer Braith?"

Weslan glanced back to the Shifting, which he could barely discern now that they were standing a few feet away.

"No, Captain," he replied, knowing that whatever else he had said, this much at least was true. "I do not."

CHAPTER 35

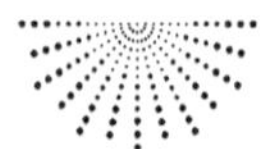

It is truly spring when mud flows through the streets in this way, Chalvern thought morosely, staring at the rain from his open doorway.

A group of boys ran past, soaked to the bone and shouting exultantly. Chalvern envied them the quicksilver flash of their limbs, and he knew why they were so carefree. They were celebrating their release from school: planting time came right after the first rain, so there would be no more lessons until the fall. His duties were also over for two seasons. He was not quite so exultant.

Ah, well, it freed up more of his time. The depressing question immediately following this thought was, *For what, though?*

But Chalvern had always believed that he should pensively ponder on gloomy days, and so he took hold of himself. It was time to close his door against the mud and rain, and make some tea—liquorice, his favourite.

Chalvern often put his mind to good use by transcribing the ancient Anniste scrolls he had in his safekeeping. Until recently, this would have been viewed as an eccentric but harmless pursuit. Now he was breaking a law, so he never embarked upon a session without first locking his door and drawing all shutters fast. Once he had done this, and had his quills all sharpened in a row in front of him, and the copper kettle steaming and hissing on the stove, Chalvern's shoulders relaxed. He smoothed out a scroll, poring over the faded runes before making quick, dark strokes on a fresh scroll with his pen.

He sighed with contentment, thinking, *this is what I do best.*

There was a small sound beside him. Thinking it was a mouse, for they sometimes sought hospitality in his shop, Chalvern ignored it. He heard it again and glanced up, impatient.

Braith stood in front of the shuttered window, hands clasped behind his back, a faint smile playing about his lips.

Chalvern dropped his pen with a muttered oath, knocking over his ink bottle. A black rivulet trickled across the wooden table.

"Did I startle you?" Braith asked. "My apologies, Master. I rapped twice on the shutters to announce myself." He stepped forward. "How dark it is in here! Do you not long for sunlight, and air?"

Chalvern found he could breathe again and snapped, "Have you seen any sunlight today? I have not."

"Yes, indeed I have!" Braith laughed a little and began pacing.

Why does he always do that? Chalvern thought in irritation. It was nerve-wracking.

"I have just descended from the sky near Meed, Master," Braith continued, "where Rhan's light is glorious on the snow peaks of the Taboran Mountains. All blue and silver, dazzling to the eye. Of course, below the peaks are many rain clouds, but they did not concern me in the least."

Chalvern said nothing, watching Braith and trying to conceal his astonishment at the revelation he had just heard. *I was right about his Source being a hawk,* he thought, allowing himself a moment of triumph. Curious that Braith would refer to it directly, though, when he had been so secretive before.

"Yes, I imagine you are right," Chalvern replied in a neutral voice. "Hawks need never bother themselves about clouds."

"Unless they are foolish enough to dip down too low, where they have no business to be." Braith continued to move about. His green-gold eyes had a feverish glitter, and he clenched his jaw.

Where has he been? Chalvern wondered. And, with a lurch in his stomach: *Where is Tekoah now? Has she reached Zantor yet? Does Braith know about it? Why is he here?*

"Why am I here?" Braith asked, voicing his last question out loud. "When our last parting seemed so final. You banished me from your life, as I recall."

"Braith—" Chalvern began, but Braith waved his gloved hand, his voice cutting in before Chalvern could speak further.

"But you won, Master. She left. You were right: love cannot spring from hate, or trust from fear, whatever the enchantment. I have learned that lesson like a schoolboy, and recite it dutifully when I am alone, which I usually am. Do you not wish to gloat, Master?"

Looking at Braith's gaunt face, Chalvern's own tension dissolved, and his heart wrenched with pity. By Anna, how he must have suffered.

Chalvern reached up and clasped the sorcerer's shoulders, whispering, "My son. My son." Braith stood still for a moment, his eyes closed. Then he moved away to pace again.

"Will you not sit?" Chalvern asked. He caught sight of the spilled ink and grabbed a rag, trying to mop it up.

"No," Braith answered. "I cannot stay long. I am here on an urgent matter, and I seek your help."

"My help?" Chalvern echoed, astonished. "What could you need from me?"

Braith stopped in the middle of the room and looked at

Chalvern. "You must tell me where the Anniste are hiding," he said. Chalvern blinked, then blinked again.

"Do not look so apprehensive, Master," Braith continued, "I mean only to help them. They are in great danger."

"What fool doesn't know that?" Chalvern replied testily. "But their peril seems to derive from sorcerers, or am I wrong?"

Braith ignored the remark. "Even if Darian's soldiers cannot discover the Anniste, then the Morgs will," he said. "Have you ever seen a Morg, Master?"

"No, thankfully, I have not," Chalvern replied. "Those monsters are not a common sight for most folk, except the unfortunate Anniste women who have encountered them. Morgs are doubtless terrifying, and I have no desire to verify that theory firsthand. But the word is out: they are dying. Snow does not agree with these abominations."

"Where did you hear that?"

"Is it true?"

"Yes." Braith was gazing at him. Tekoah's name hovered unspoken in the air. "But the Morgs have not all died, Master. And the snows are melting, even in the highest mountain passes."

"Why did they fail to survive in the first place?" Chalvern asked, the scholar in him curious. "It seems rather strange. Even mere mortals have learned to withstand snow."

"Because Morogh expired before he had perfected them," Braith answered. "He died because he aged himself by creating and sustaining the drought in the South. Zant's promise to assist him was a lie—Zant gradually withdrew his own power until Morogh carried the burden alone. By the time Morogh found out what was happening, it was too late."

"How do you know this?" Chalvern asked, electric shivers of horror and fascination coursing through him.

"Zant boasted of it to me, laughing."

"Ah. How wise of you to decide not to trust Zant as an ally."

Chalvern smiled and Braith smiled back, his teeth flashing, the muscles of his lean face relaxing for a moment. *When did we last jest with each other?* Chalvern wondered. He knew, deep within him, that he had failed Braith somehow. Averting his face, he stabbed ferociously at the ink stain on the table.

"But not so wise in matters of the heart, Master?" Braith's voice was quiet, and in its timbre Chalvern heard an echo of the lost, lonely twelve-year-old he had met wandering in the Taboran Woods all those years ago.

Chalvern met Braith's gaze. "I, least of all, can lay claim to that brand of wisdom."

Again, they smiled at one another. Then Braith spoke again. "Will you let me help the Anniste, Master?"

"You mean Tekoah, do you not?"

"Yes," Braith said. "And the others as well."

"What makes you think she would accept your help?"

"Tekoah did not stay long enough for me to demonstrate that she had nothing to fear," Braith said. "I know now that I should never have plied her with the wine to dissolve her apprehension. But now I can prove I mean her no harm. This is my chance to win her trust—and perhaps even her love. Do you not see this, Master?"

"I do not. Please enlighten me." Chalvern drummed his fingers on the table, glaring at the stubborn ink stain.

Braith continued as if he had not heard. "At first, I was angry with Tekoah—she wounded my pride when she rejected me. I fled from all mortal contact and spent the winter as my Source— among the treetops, far from all this. But I could not escape from her. I saw her face among the clouds and heard her voice in the waves when I flew over the sea."

Chalvern listened, mesmerized. Over the turnings, he also had been very lonely, but he could not fathom such desolation.

Braith had stopped speaking. His head was bowed, and his hands clenched and unclenched in their crimson gloves. After a moment, he looked up again, whispering, "I will not let Zant harm her. Not while I live."

I felt that way about her mother, Chalvern thought. *And yet I stood by and did nothing, while a madman destroyed her dreams and then her body.* His heart thudded, and an eternity passed in a few seconds as he decided.

He took a ragged breath. "Tekoah is not with the Anniste any longer," he told Braith.

Braith took a quick step forward, his eyes sparking. "What? Where is she? With Weslan?"

"No one knows where Weslan is!" Chalvern barked. "He is likely dead." He could not help adding, "Did you give that matter any thought throughout your winter?"

Braith looked at him, impassive. "I doubt Weslan has expired, Master. His zest for life is quite admirable, and his survival capabilities are well-honed. I suspect that he, also, needed to lick his wounds."

"What a comforting hypothesis!" Chalvern threw up his arms, extending the fingers as if invoking a spell. "Now if you might just conjure him up, it would quite relieve us. His sister most of all."

"If it would make Tekoah happy, I would do it."

"Is there no one in the world you care for but her?" Chalvern cried, exasperated.

"I care for *you*, Master."

Braith's face was downturned, a tremor in his voice. It caught Chalvern unawares.

"And I for you, my son," he answered, knowing he spoke the truth. "Anna help me."

"If Tekoah is not sheltering with the Anniste, then where is she?" Braith asked. He strode over to the window and threw open the shutter.

"She has gone to Zantor," Chalvern replied, then groaned. *Now why in Rhan's name have I gone and said that?*

Braith whirled around, his eyes flashing.

"You heard me," Chalvern retorted. It was not as if he was dancing a jig about it, either.

"And you let her go?"

"I could not very well stop her. She is not a child." Then, as Braith continued to stare at him with those blazing eyes, he stammered, "I saw her slipping away at dawn—by pure accident. I tried my best to talk her out of it, but she claimed she was obeying the command of the Goddess."

"Does her Goddess wish her well? Or wish her *dead*?" Braith snapped.

"She is in danger wherever she is," Chalvern replied. "Darian's soldiers raided Beula's farm a short time ago, and it was a miracle that the Anniste remained undetected. To be more precise, the miracle was because of Tekoah's brilliant thinking, and a measure of good fortune—not to mention the leader of the Kalesh—who intervened and diverted Darian's soldiers away from the hiding place. Perhaps Anna was watching over her, after all."

"Nevertheless, you should have found a way of preventing her from going to Zantor!" At the mention of Dirken, Braith had frowned possessively. "How could you allow her to venture into that seething snake pit, where all the evil in this world has converged?"

The pains in Chalvern's chest began out of nowhere, piercing him with a sharpness that made it hard to inhale. Clutching his shoulders, he lowered himself into the wooden chair. A blight on sorcerers. What could the gods possibly have to teach mortals through their twisted souls? Oh, why wouldn't the knife-thrusts cease?

Braith's arm was around his neck, and the rim of a mug was pressed at his lips. He sipped the water, grateful.

"Any better?" Braith asked.

"Better," he said. "Thank you."

"I wish to help the Anniste, regardless of where Tekoah is." Braith set the mug down on the table and moved around to squat in front of Chalvern. "Will you tell me their hiding place?"

"How do you intend to help them?" Chalvern asked. He wished with all his heart in that moment that he trusted Braith. But then life would be too simple, and choices too easy to make.

"They must go where no man, nor beast, nor foul combination of the two can find them," Braith replied. "I can take them to such a place. It will age me a great deal, but I can do it."

"They are at Beula's farm, hiding in the cellar," Chalvern murmured, not looking up. *Am I a fool thrice over?* he wondered.

Braith was already at the door.

"Let me come with you," Chalvern stood with an effort. "The Anniste trust me, and I visit them often. They will not welcome you with open arms."

"But are you well enough, Master?"

Chalvern nodded. He stepped toward the threshold. Before he could proceed, Braith's cloak had enveloped him from head to toe. Chalvern struggled, smothered by the folds. There came a strange sensation, like that of plunging from a great height. He cried out, but before his voice had died away, the cloak fell from him and he stood in front of Beula's farmhouse, in the pouring rain.

Chalvern waited for his breath to come back. When it did, he glanced at Braith, hesitating. The women would be very frightened, especially since Tekoah had departed.

Braith spoke again, as if reading his thoughts. "Remember, Master, that Tekoah is also in danger, wherever she is. Greater peril than these women, because she is the Guardian. Zant was particularly interested in finding her. We must act quickly!" He kicked the heavy oaken door open with a crash.

"Quiet—you will scare them to death," Chalvern protested, deeply frightened himself.

"We have no time for niceties," Braith answered shortly. "Where is the cellar?"

"Wait," Chalvern pleaded. "I will fetch them."

He tiptoed through the kitchen. Bhantok was nowhere in sight, thank Anna. The poor man might have ended up getting himself killed trying to defend the Anniste.

He opened the small wooden door and called into the darkness. "Hello, it is only me." He heard a collective intake of breath and several muffled exclamations.

"Chalvern? It is you?"

Their voices were forlorn. He climbed down the steps, willing Braith not to follow.

The women resembled shadows as they stared out at him from the wavering half-light. They clamoured to speak of their ordeal since the raid.

There had been Journeys, they told him—vague, insubstantial images—but every vision had warned them of impending danger. They had been terrified without Tekoah or Reika to guide them. Hearing the door crash open, they had feared it was soldiers or Morgs.

Thank Anna it was only Chalvern. Had he brought some food, perhaps? Something must have prevented Bhantok from bringing supplies, because he had not come for days.

Even in the gloom, Chalvern could see that the women were filthy, dishevelled, and half-starved. "I have something to tell you," he said, "and for the love of Anna, please believe me, for it is your own safety I have at heart."

But when he told them who waited upstairs, and why, the women wept with terror. Some moaned that they were certain it was the sorcerer Braith whom they had seen in their warning Journeys. Others argued it had been the Morgs.

"Why is our Guardian not here to counsel us?" one woman wailed.

Hearing Braith's impatient tread pacing overhead, Chalvern

begged the women to hurry. It took several more minutes to convince them before they began the climb up into the light. At the very last moment, seven women stayed in the cellar, refusing to budge despite his entreaties.

Braith was not in the kitchen. Holding the first woman's hand he could grasp—Valeen's—Chalvern led them outside. Braith stood in front of the house, his back to them.

He turned, and Chalvern saw at once that the sorcerer's appearance had altered in the few minutes since Chalvern had been in the cellar. Braith had aged.

Already? Chalvern stared, vertigo seizing him. He staggered a little, dropping Valeen's hand. But yes, the sorcerer's youthful face had creased with lines, and his dark hair had shot through with silver. *Such is the price of power.*

Braith neither smiled nor frowned as the Anniste came out, blinking and shivering, into the rain. And because of the wet sheets that fell steadily, no one saw at first the grey shimmer that lay on the ground like a large silver puddle.

Braith pointed to the pool, which misted and smoked a little in the wet air. He then beckoned the Anniste forward. "Come. You have not much time."

Gazing upon the first Shifting he had ever seen, it seemed to Chalvern that at any moment everything around him might become equally insubstantial, dissolving into the ripples that lay on the ground before him. He prayed that Braith spoke true about safeguarding the Anniste.

But it was too late to do anything about it. And in the end, all the women who huddled there went in, while Chalvern stood by and watched.

When the last of the Anniste had stepped into the Shifting, Chalvern saw that the rain had stopped; he knew not whether the water coursing down his cheeks had come from the sky. The women had looked so fragile and beseeching. Out of nowhere, he remembered that in three nights was the Night of the Dead, and that it was exactly one turning since Neela had disappeared.

Rhan burst forth from behind a cloud just then, as if mocking his tears. Chalvern caught a movement out of the corner of his eye. He turned his head and saw that Braith had spread his arms out wide, and his cloak fell in downward folds which looked like wings. He was looking up at the sky and, with a lurch, Chalvern realized he was preparing to depart.

"Braith," he whispered, his voice choked with tears.

Braith turned, looking at Chalvern with distant eyes, as though he was already far away. "Yes?"

"Where are you going?"

"To save her, of course."

Chalvern pointed up to the sky, where Rhan burned away the edges of the clouds as a flame burned the thinnest bark. "Do you truly think you can help her? Your power spawned from Rhan. You have been placed on the wrong side in this battle, even if you do not wish it!"

Braith looked at him, his face strange. "What world do you want to dwell in, Master? Did you not once tell me that love will always conquer hatred?"

"Yes," Chalvern said, remembering a spring evening fifteen turnings earlier, when he had bandaged a twelve-year-old's wounds and also soothed his heart. "I suppose I did."

Braith faced the sky again, and Chalvern saw the second mysterious and terrifying thing he had seen that day. He saw the sorcerer Braith raise his arms, and they became wings. And his head became the head of a hawk, with a sharp, curved beak, above which his unblinking green-gold gaze turned briefly to regard Chalvern, eyes unchanged. Then he glimpsed the talons which Braith must have kept hidden underneath his gloves, for all sorcerers changed permanently in one part of their bodies after coming into their Source. Chalvern had read it in Anniste lore and, in that moment, he became certain of its truth.

The Braith-hawk turned away from Chalvern, lifted its wings and launched itself from the ground. It was a magnificent sight as it flew away, crimson-shouldered and robin-red beneath, with heavy dark stripes along its tail and broad, powerful wings. It wheeled above him for a moment and Chalvern heard the hawk's scream: a two-syllable "Kee-ya!" And then it glided away, wings pulled back, tail folded.

He watched as Braith caught an air current and flew higher, the glide becoming a full soar, wings extended, and tail fanned. He turned east, toward Zantor. After a time, he was nothing more than a black speck.

The sunlight was very strong. Chalvern blinked his watery eyes, and when he opened them, the hawk had disappeared.

CHALVERN WAS PACKING up a basket of bread and cheese to smuggle over to the remaining Anniste women that evening when he heard an urgent knocking on his door. Before he could open it, Bhantok burst through, knocking it off its hinges at last.

"Will no one treat my door as a door is meant to be treated?" Chalvern shouted in exasperation. "Why must you all enter as though you are storming a castle with a battering ram?"

When the other man did not answer, he forgot his annoyance and observed him more closely. Bhantok's ruddy cheeks had drained of colour.

Chalvern collected himself. "What is it?" he asked.

"The women. The Anniste. They are…" Bhantok struggled for breath to finish the sentence but failed.

Chalvern put a comforting arm on Bhantok's shoulder, pressing him to sit down in the wooden chair close by. "I know," he said. He cast his eyes about for his sachet of calming herbs. "I was there. Braith has hidden most of the women. I am sure the ones who refused to go must have told you this. They are afraid, as they have every right to be. But we have no choice but to trust Braith—"

"Braith?" Bhantok interrupted in a wild voice. "Braith? I know nothing of Braith. All I know is that there are only seven remaining Anniste in the cellar—"

Chalvern nodded, saying in a patient voice, "Yes, as I told you. Let me explain about the others."

Bhantok stood up from the chair and walked unsteadily over to Chalvern's writing table, leaning against it for support. "And all are dead, with their throats torn out," he finished in a choking whisper, and was sick all over Chalvern's newly transcribed Anniste scrolls.

CHAPTER 36

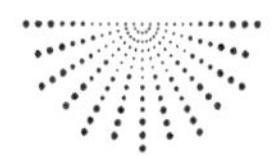

The first thing Tekoah heard when she reached the palace at Zantor was that once again a woman ruled the North of Miraven: King Darian had gone back to Meed, and Zant to Berlot, leaving Lady Saura to act as regent in his stead.

The servants seemed to be divided whether this was a good thing. "Anyone is better than Darian, that damp-eyed, beard-gnawing umbray," a plump scullery maid told her, sniffing. "He looks harmless, but he is as twisted as they come, and cruel. I can judge that better than any fine lady in this court."

Tekoah could but vaguely fathom the meaning of this remark; she thought it must have something to do with the whispered tales she had heard through Bhantok—who had left out a great deal, no doubt—of King Darian's strange pleasures, taught to him by his depraved Berlotan hangers-on, and abetted by the sorcerer Zant.

"You have not had much dealing with Lady Saura, then," said an older woman, in a voice that matched her iron-grey hair.

She was Gerten, the Keeper of the Kitchens, and it was she who would decide whether to take Tekoah on as a servant in the royal palace at Zantor. The scullery maid lowered her head and hurried away to where the platters and trenchers were being washed. Tekoah stood deferentially, eyes down, offering no opinion of her own. However, she breathed more deeply after learning that Zant was not there.

"Lady Saura has eyes and ears in every wall of this palace," Gerten continued, glancing around her reflexively as she spoke. She squinted at Tekoah. "Can you sew?"

Startled, Tekoah nodded.

"And while King Darian has many whims—like a child—at least he forgets one toy easily when another plaything is put into his hand. Not so Lady Saura. She never forgets. No slight, no word once spoken in jest that seemed to mock her, no oversight that she imagined was an insult."

Gerten's voice dropped to a whisper. "Queen Darielle thought of Saura as her best friend and confidante. And where is the lovely young queen now? Caught up in the pincers of that scorpion, the Jinta. And look who rules in her stead. Can you bake bread?" she asked Tekoah abruptly, with a hard stare.

Tekoah nodded once more, smoothing her hands on her worn skirt. Her long gold-brown hair she had plaited behind her and bound up with bone pins. She wore a white cap that she had purchased at a shop nearby. Nothing could disguise the well-used look of her pale blue dress—one of Neela's old ones, patched several times—but she hoped she looked respectable, at least.

"How do you know so much about Lady Saura?" the scullery maid asked over her shoulder, sliding a huge roasting pan into a steaming tub of water. The faint smell of cooked meat and the aroma of baking bread in the ovens caused tears of hunger to stand in Tekoah's eyes.

"Lady Saura is my niece," Gerten answered. "I made the mistake once of telling her what I thought. And look where I am now: in the kitchen with greasy dishes."

An uneasy silence followed her remark.

"Can you serve?" Gerten asked Tekoah. As Tekoah stood hesitating, Gerten shook her head. "I did not think so. We do not need another serving wench with white skin and blue eyes. You would be with child in no time and turned out to fend for yourself in a ditch, for Lady Saura has no tolerance for such goings on. I might as well turn you out now and save her the trouble."

Gerten pointed to the doorway of the kitchen, her sharp, creased face filled with a rage which seemed to encompass everyone and everything within her small domain.

Tekoah walked out of the kitchen. Her face burned with shame, but she determined not to give up. *I will gain entry into the palace under some pretext or other,* she had told Master Chalvern.

"Wait!" Tekoah turned to see the scullery maid coming after her. The girl had glanced at her once or twice while she was being grilled by Gerten, and now she said, "Why do you not approach one of the merchant's houses? They have no prejudices against white skin and blue eyes."

The maid's droll smile reminded Tekoah of Norah. She smiled back. "Thank you. No doubt I will find my way. But perhaps you could tell me where in the palace I might locate Dirken, the minstrel. I must speak to him before I leave."

The girl's smile deepened, even while she threw up her hands in mock-horror. "Oh no, not another poor girl stricken with our Dirken. Watch yourself, my dear—Dirken gobbles up young beauties like candied pitayas."

Tekoah could feel herself flushing, but she spoke coolly. "I fear you are mistaken. I carry a message for Dirken, nothing more."

The scullery maid nodded knowingly. "As many others do. Well, my dear, Dirken went hunting today, but he may have returned. Check the hunting lodge." She pointed down the corridor. "You will see it to your left, as soon as you round the corner."

"Thank you," Tekoah said.

The girl shrugged good-humouredly and sauntered back in the direction of the kitchens. Tekoah walked down the corridor. When she turned the corner, she saw to her left a massive chamber, with its oaken doors thrown open wide.

She had never seen a room so immense. Why, the hearth alone was longer than the whole wall of the Pitaya Pit. Overcome by diffidence, she hesitated for several seconds before she dared to peer deeper inside.

Animal skins adorned the hearth and walls of the room: great mountain cats, with their heads still attached, black lips drawn back from bared, yellow teeth; dog-like umbrays with their scavenging eyes; even two rare white stags. Tekoah had never seen so many animals in one place, either dead or alive.

She stepped forward a few more paces. There was a smaller fireplace in a kind of alcove at the southern corner of the chamber. In it a fire burned, and two men stood facing the hearth. Alarmed, she turned to leave, then froze at a sudden shout.

"Hoy there!"

Tekoah looked back, trying to appear calm. The speaker, a bronzed southerner, lifted his arm imperiously. With a chill, she recognized him as one of the soldiers who had raided Bhantok's farm. He was holding a goblet, and he turned it upside down now, letting a few drops trickle to the stone floor.

"More ale!" he shouted. "Why are they taking so long?"

His companion had not bothered to turn around.

"I do not know. I will send someone—" Tekoah stammered, cursing herself immediately afterward for her stupidity. Why had she not just nodded and then left?

"What do you mean you do not know?" the soldier roared. "Come here, girl!"

The other man had turned around now, and as Tekoah approached, she heard a stifled exclamation. Glancing toward him, she saw it was Dirken. He had camouflaged his surprise in a fit of coughing, but as she opened her mouth to speak, she saw his hazel eyes narrow in a clear warning: *Say nothing.*

"Would a flogging with my riding whip help you remember where to get the wine?" the Southerner asked her, his voice taking on a taunting note that reminded Tekoah of her father.

She shook her head, stepping toward the door.

"Wait a moment," the soldier said, his tone changing. "I know you—you are from Stern. Where a coven of Anniste witches were hiding. I suspected you of being one of them, is that not so?"

"Every blue-eyed northern wench looks the same to you!" Dirken howled with laughter.

"No, it is her," the other man insisted. "And we are under orders to report to Lady Saura if we suspect anyone. Remember?"

"Tell her tomorrow," Dirken said carelessly. "For now, let us drink a toast to the stag you killed today." He turned to Tekoah, who stood frozen in the doorway. He spoke curtly. "Fetch someone else to bring more ale, you stupid girl. You are not fit to serve us. We are weary from a day's hunt—a *brilliant* hunt!" Here he smiled at the Southern soldier. "And we have no patience for a maid who has been kicked in the head one too many times. Go on, I say," Dirken repeated, striding forward and propelling her toward the door.

But in the instant before he pushed her through, he bent and whispered in her ear, "Meet me behind the smaller stable, under willow grove. I will be there as soon as I can."

Tekoah's limbs trembled as she stumbled down the corridor. *Anna, what am I doing here?*

She wished for Weslan to appear—he would tell her the right thing to say, how to behave, so she did not give herself away. Though she wore Neela's blue dress, in her mind she was garbed in the brown, hooded robe of the Anniste, marking her for all to see.

It took some agonizing minutes to find her way out of the castle, and longer still to locate the stables. The palace grounds confused her, and she could not accustom herself to the menacing clusters of soldiers that seemed to be everywhere. She kept seeing Kirt in her mind's eye, with his blackened teeth, slipping his bloody sword back into his scabbard.

Tekoah dodged the stable-boys and grooms who were jesting and singing as they led their charges into stalls for the night. She darted outside and immediately spotted the stand of willows, set apart a little way, densely populated with the green-curtained trees which were just now budding. She could see that this was a perfect choice for a clandestine meeting; the drooping, shadowy branches could hide anyone from view.

By the time the sun had gone down, Tekoah was shivering with cold. She yearned for sleep, thinking she would gladly share a stall with one of the horses, burrowed down under a pile of straw in the corner. It was how she had often found shelter the past six nights.

She must have left her cloak in the kitchen, her brains addled by Gerten's humiliation. Should she go back and get it? she wondered uneasily. She might need to flee that night if Dirken had forgotten all about her. No doubt he had, she thought. He seemed to be a different person here, as well. How many faces did he have? And which was the real one?

As the sky darkened, Anna's face came into view—a full circle that night. But the disc seemed wafer-thin, without substance. Tekoah stared up, hugging her knees to her chest, chin resting on her folded arms. There would be no answers from the Goddess. Why did none come when she needed them the most? She shook her head to dispel her sadness.

Despite the cold, Tekoah grew sleepy, for she had walked many miles that day, fearing soldiers or Morgs would appear beyond every bend in the road. Willing herself to reach the city before dark, fear had given her strength, but it had soon ebbed away. Her head drooped on her folded arms, and she closed her eyes.

There came into her ears that familiar high voice, keening around the dark edges of her mind.

Only a hole where the moon has been
Mother, where have you gone?

Tekoah knew that the reedy, haunting voice was her own, but still she tossed and moaned in response to the singsong words. Wishing to awaken—to get away from herself—but something trapped her in the muffling darkness of sleep. Then a hand was on her shoulder, and she awoke.

It was dark all around, but Dirken's face reflected the moonlight. He wrapped his cloak around her. It was warm against her icy shoulders.

"And here I thought I must go back to Stern to find you," he said, his voice husky in her ear. "Yet *you* have come to *me*."

Shaken, Tekoah sat up, moving so that Dirken's hands were no longer on her shoulders. She smiled to show that she knew he was joking.

"I am sorry I took so long," Dirken said in a different, brisker voice. "I had promised to sing at dinner, and my unexplained absence would not have been prudent, agreed?" Tekoah nodded. "Come now, you cannot stay out here any longer for fear of catching a chill. Let us go to my chamber where we can talk freely."

They entered the palace through an inconspicuous entrance that must be meant for servants or tradespeople. Dirken led her down a maze of dark corridors. He held her hand in a light grip, turning to smile at her now and then. As if all of it was just a game.

Stepping into Dirken's well-appointed but small chamber, Tekoah thought of his castle near Stern, the sumptuous wall hangings and silken pillows. This made her think of Braith, and her recent dream in which Dirken had also appeared. Her cheeks grew warm.

"You were having a nightmare," Dirken said.

She stared at him in dismay. How in Anna's name did he know what she was thinking?

"When I woke you, just now—you were moaning," he explained, ushering her in and bolting the door behind him. "You need not tell me about it unless you wish to. You have suffered enough to warrant a nightmare or two, I would wager." His voice was reassuring, as if he did not expect an answer; Tekoah gave none.

Dirken lit a candle and placed it on a small table beside his cot. He sank down on the pallet with a small sigh, gesturing for Tekoah to come and sit beside him. His eyes danced in the candlelight, and he smiled up at her, looking young and boyish. Perhaps it was because he was clean-shaven again; no longer the uncouth soldier he had been at Beula's farm.

Who was he now? Dirken, the carefree minstrel, of course. Darling of the court, writing verses that made country girls like Norah swoon. Tekoah remembered the words of the scullery maid and remained standing.

"You must trust me," Dirken said, his smile suddenly gone, and his voice sombre as it had been in the hay barn when they'd stood over Marta's body. "For if you are to have a friend in this poisonous place, it is I."

Tekoah stood silent, weighing his words. For a moment, she thought he would rise and come over to her, but he remained where he was.

"I have the honour to lead the Kalesh," he said, quietly. "And I find it diverting and illuminating to assume other identities from time to time. If you were to betray my secret, then I might soon be dead. So, you see, my wary little angel, you hold as much power over me as I do over you! Now pray come seat yourself and let me cover you with a blanket, for I cannot bear to watch you freeze to death. Then please, I beg you, tell me what in Anna's name you are doing here!"

The blanket Dirken held out was woolen, indigo and white striped, like the one Tekoah had dragged around with her as a child. It looked very warm. She walked over to the cot and sat down.

"There, that is better, is it not?" She nodded. All at once she thought of something. She asked him, "When I last saw you, you were seeking my brother Weslan. Have you found him—or heard anything of him?"

Dirken's face lost its softness, became unreadable. "No," he answered. "He was last seen in the company of the sorcerer Braith, and no one has laid eyes on him since the queen was abducted." His words echoed in the silence that followed.

"My brother would have laid his life down for the queen," Tekoah said in a strained voice. "Urgent family business called him home. I can vouch for his integrity—if you will believe me." Her eyes met his defiantly.

"I believe you," Dirken said, after a moment, "for I can spot a liar as most men can feel the bite of a flea. You are very like your brother, you know, only finer by far. As gold compared with brass."

"I do not know where Weslan is now," Tekoah interrupted him, her voice unsteady. "And I fear that some harm has befallen him. But with all that has happened, I have not had time enough even to wonder or grieve for him as he deserves." To her horror, she wept.

"Do not!" Dirken lifted her chin. "You will break my heart, princess. If your brother is alive, I will find him. I give you my promise, and I do not break my oaths, so dry those huge, soulful eyes of yours."

Tekoah wiped her cheeks. "I am sorry," she murmured. "I am tired and easily overwrought."

"And who could blame you? But before you sleep, I must find

out why you are here. Are you seeking your brother? If so, I wish that I had a sister as devoted as you." Dirken grinned at her, so that Tekoah could not help but smile back. But then she remembered the command of the Goddess and knew she must speak "I am Anniste."

"Yes, I am aware of that. I was uncertain before, but I asked Chalvern, and he told me."

Remembering Chalvern's words about that conversation, Tekoah's heart quickened, but she ignored it.

"I am the Guardian," she told him, attempting to sound dignified. "And I have Journeyed." She stopped, expecting Dirken to laugh. But his face was serious, so she repeated Anna's prophecy, reciting it word for word.

She related the rest of her Journey. When she had finished, Dirken stared ahead, his brow furrowed in thought. "That is most interesting," he mused. "Stern was where I planned to marshal the army all along. And yet you say that Berlot will attack sooner than I expected?"

Tekoah nodded. "The Goddess said so. They must not catch you unawares."

"Being caught unawares is something I loathe," Dirken agreed. He grasped her hand and squeezed it, dropping her fingers before she could react.

"Then you trust the prophecy?" Tekoah asked him.

"Yes, no, and perhaps," Dirken said. "But I shall make ready all the same."

"You do not believe me?" Tekoah sat up, indignant, throwing the blanket from her.

"I believe *you* believe it. As for the Goddess—there are many shades of belief." Dirken's mouth quirked a little. "Let us just say I have donned a paler shade at the moment. And speaking of pale, you look exhausted. Here." He tucked a pillow under her head. "Now lie back and slumber, poppet. Without dreams, nightmares, or Journeys of any kind. For the moment, we must assume your Goddess knows what she is doing. Although it seems incredible that she would tell you to come here—when it is the most dangerous thing you could do, short of hurling yourself off a very high cliff. You have heard, no doubt, of the pet that Zant is rumoured to keep in the bowels of this palace?"

Tekoah tried to listen to his words, but she had grown very sleepy with the pillow soft under her head. Dirken's voice seemed farther and farther away.

The last thing she heard him say was, "Never mind, you will be safe with me."

Her eyes closed while he was still speaking. The muffling darkness of sleep no longer seemed threatening. Dirken said no more, and in the next moment Tekoah felt him tucking the blanket around her. Soon there was a deeper blackness behind her eyelids, and she knew that the candle had been blown out.

As she fell asleep, she heard Dirken singing an old northern lullaby, in a wonderful melodious voice that was reminiscent of the wind in the crohm trees of Stern. *This is who he is,* she thought, and then thought nothing more.

When she awoke in the morning, Tekoah's first sensation was that of warmth. Dirken's simple cot seemed as soft as the luxurious bed in his castle, where she had lain with Braith. She sat up quickly, trying to quell the memories of that time. Rubbing her eyes, she looked around for Dirken. He was not there. For a moment, panic fluttered like a trapped insect against her chest. But then the door opened, and he came in, shutting it behind him.

"Did you sleep well?" he asked, smiling.

She nodded, struggling with the diffidence she felt in his presence. It was childish to be so shy. But Dirken seemed not to notice. He looked distracted, despite his warm smile. Walking over to a clothing trunk in the corner, he rummaged through it, whistling to himself.

Bare feet dangling from the bed, she watched him. His curly hair carried a light sheen, as if covered with dew, and his hose and boots were soaked.

"Is it raining?" she asked, puzzled. "The sky was so clear last night, and the sunset red as a berry."

"No, not raining," he replied, still digging. He pulled out a pair of bright yellow hose and a scarlet tunic, shaking them out with clear satisfaction. "Turn around," he ordered her, grinning mischievously. "I will not have you admiring my manly form when we know each other so little."

Tekoah whirled away. "Why are you soaking wet, then?" she asked, her back to him.

There was a brief silence. In a flash of intuition, Tekoah knew she should not have asked that question. Something intangible and dangerous had drifted into the air, made even more so because of Dirken's boyish curls and ready smile. *He will not answer me,* she thought with certainty.

And he did not. Instead, he commanded, "You may contemplate me now—and tell me I am as resplendent as a peacock." She did so and could not help but smile, for he had struck a vainglorious pose that was both convincing and self-mocking.

"I am to sing at a banquet tonight, given by the Lady Saura in honour of spring. And that brings me to our explanation, which is both brilliant and simple. You will masquerade as one of my strellas—from my chequered past, when I sang all throughout this marvellous country. You can sing, can you not?" He paused, looking at her quizzically.

"I cannot sing a note!" she protested, her voice rising with panic. "What a terrible plan! I do not wish to sound ungrateful —but would it not be wiser for me to stay in hiding? Here, or somewhere else, until I can slip away without being noticed? I must hasten back. The Anniste wait for me anxiously."

"I will not consider letting you travel back to Stern alone," Dirken said with crisp finality. "When you have rested a day or two, I will send some of my men with you as an armed escort. Or I will go with you myself—I will be there soon enough, anyway! In the meantime"—and here he made his voice deep and wise, like an elderly scholar or priest—"there is a common fallacy about how to avoid rousing suspicion: hide in the shadows." Dirken strode across the room in a heavy, measured tread, continuing his comic playacting. He paused, hands behind his back. "'If you wish to be caught, then sneak about. If you desire to go unchallenged, hurl yourself into the thick of things, banging a loud gong and shouting at the top of your lungs!'" Dirken raised his arms and let out a yell so loud that Tekoah clapped her hands to her ears, laughing despite herself.

"Are you not worried that someone will come rushing to my rescue?" she asked, wiping tears of laughter from her eyes, and glancing around.

"Not now that you are my beloved strella," he grinned. "But to turn to serious matters, do you really mean to tell me you cannot sing? You look as if you have the voice of a songbird." He bent close, forcing her to meet his eyes.

"I have never tried—my voice is too thin, and it did not suit my family life to sing." She faltered, embarrassed by his scrutiny.

"Ah," Dirken countered, "I knew it! Well, this will be a delightful task for me: giving the songbird her wings. Now, we must practice immediately, for you will accompany me tonight."

"What?" Tekoah shrieked, jumping from the bed as if a wasp had stung her. "Tonight? I cannot. I will die. And then I will faint. And besides, what about Gerten? She turned me away as a scullery maid, and now I turn up claiming an acquaintance with you—"

"Do not worry about Gerten," Dirken replied, his eyebrows coming together. "I have already spoken to her. She owes me a favour, and she will keep her lips shut, and will also answer for the discretion of her staff."

"Well—" Tekoah stammered, casting about in her mind for excuses. "What about that southern soldier you were drinking with yesterday? If he recognizes me, he will wonder why you acted the way you did—pretending you did not know me."

There was an inexplicable silence. From without, Tekoah heard the footsteps and easy banter of servants as they began their morning tasks. It was still early, for the first fingers of light were just stealing through the slats of the shutters. Dirken had left while she was sleeping, before the last of the stars had evaporated from the night sky.

Why does he not reply? Tekoah asked herself.

With dread, she glanced at him, then saw the answer to her question in his fleeting, savage grin. She shuddered as she pieced the story together: Dirken had gone to the river, which was but a stone's throw from the palace grounds and swollen from the melting snows and spring rains. He had returned in sodden clothes and with a secretive face. She turned away from him, hugging herself, arms shaking. *Two* men had been at the river's edge that morning, but only *one* had come back.

Tekoah knew then that she must be very careful in the future not to ask Dirken questions for which she did not wish to know the answers.

CHAPTER 37

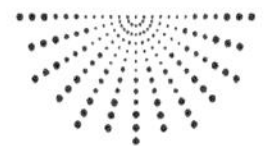

A deluge of rain ended the drought in the South of Miraven the day after Tekoah sang for the first time with Dirken the Minstrel in the banquet hall at Zantor. Such was the torrent that no one could travel the impassable roads for fifteen days. During this half-annaspan, the weather confined Tekoah to the palace—she could not contemplate stepping outside, let alone travelling back to Stern.

It was the happiest time in her life.

She admitted this to herself with a sort of guilty wonder, counting off the days: ten, eleven, twelve. Had it been twelve days? She often shook her head in astonishment, for the time flew by so; it sometimes seemed to be one long day, filled with bright colours, songs, laughter, and so much to eat.

Among a myriad of other discoveries, Tekoah found it shocking and delightful that food could make such a difference to one's mood and sense of well-being. At home there had never been a bounty, but it was not until she went into hiding with the Anniste that she had learned what it was to subsist on so little: stale water, hard bread and onions that Bhantok smuggled to the Anniste women, with occasional strips of dried pork. The women would accept this last luxury with polite hesitation and then gnaw the meat later with silent ferocity.

"It is difficult for everyone right now," Bhantok had apologized when bringing his scanty offerings. "Things will be better in the spring."

And now it was spring, and things were better. But it was because she had landed in the royal palace of Rhantor—Zantor, rather—and was dining like a queen.

Are the Anniste women eating adequately now? Tekoah wondered, eyeing the over-burdened table in the banquet hall. *Half the food in Miraven must be here.* Fluffy breads, dried figs from Berlot, roast boar, and wine the colour of jewels—red, white, sparkling green —savoury pies, dozens of confections that melted on her tongue almost the instant she placed them there.

Looking at the sumptuous dishes, no one would guess there had been a drought in the South, and that the new taxes imposed by Darian were robbing the North of much of its food stores. *It is because the robbers are all here,* Dirken whispered to her, his flinty words belied by that charming, boyish smile.

When she was not enjoying herself, Tekoah sometimes wondered if her last Journey had been a delusion. Anna had certainly not spoken to her since that time. Such worries often assailed her in the middle of a lovely meal, and she would shift uncomfortably in her cushioned chair, eyeing the complacent faces of nobles who couldn't care less who ruled, as long as there was food and drink and music. She wondered if she could ever become one of them. It was a terrible thought.

"What are you thinking of?" Dirken murmured beside her, during one such dark inner moment of reflection, deftly plucking the strings as he tuned his cintar. Tekoah turned her face toward him. He groaned, "No, no—do not look at me in that way, with those great corn-flower blue eyes of yours, or I shall seize you here and now and carry you off to my lair!" He made her laugh, as always.

At first, she had found Dirken's jesting embarrassing. But he had not tried to draw closer to her after the night under the willow grove, and Tekoah bantered with him almost as easily as she used to with Weslan. She could say anything to Dirken; however nonsensical her words seemed, he never mocked her. Soon, she spoke to him of serious things as well, just as she would have with Reika or Chalvern.

Sometimes, right before she fell asleep in her small but comfortable chamber, Tekoah admitted to herself that this minstrel, this secret leader of the Kalesh, this absentee lord of Mirrand, was one reason for her happiness. On such nights she dreamed of him, although sometimes his face and Braith's were once more interchanged.

Tekoah kept so busy during her waking hours, she had very little time to fathom the meanings of her dreams. Dirken was coaching her in the art of becoming a strella.

Her presentation had been uneventful, although Tekoah imagined the Lady Saura face was cold when she'd looked at her. "Your face is familiar, child. I cannot place it at the moment, but no doubt I shall."

One day the rain had stopped for a few hours, and Tekoah and Dirken strolled along an outside balcony, speaking of Zant and his rumoured consort, Lady Saura. Tekoah confessed to Dirken that she was afraid of Saura. "In a different way than most things frighten me," she explained. "I do not know how to describe it. It is as though she has lost her soul. Not in the way of wraiths, who wander for a time because they have a task—but that she has truly lost it."

She did not add that she had seen Saura's face before in a Journey.

Dirken joked at her unease, saying, "Yes, and I wager that when the Lady Regent dies, she will be denied entrance to the feasting hall of the World-maker, or I will choose to dine elsewhere. Send her to rule the Pit of Lost Souls instead—she will be right at home there!"

Tekoah shivered at his last words, and he put a reassuring arm around her before continuing.

"But although Saura holds sway at the moment, it is only by Zant's whim. Who knows how she gained his favour? It doesn't bear thinking of—it turns my stomach. But the point is, I have an advantage, because she knows I am popular and worshipped wherever I go." Here Dirken winked, for it was a joke between them: he was insufferably vain.

"Seriously, though, Saura will not dare to antagonize me," he went on. "She needs all the friends she can get at court, and she has very few, for Queen Darielle was loved by all."

Dirken's animated features became subdued as he spoke of his queen. Tekoah wanted to ask him how well he loved Darielle. However, she bit her tongue rather than sound like a jealous village girl, going to the window instead to watch the rivulets of rainwater sweep down the strange translucent crystal, like tears.

After fifteen days, the rains stopped, and spring sunshine cascaded in bright yellow ribbons through the palace windows. As Tekoah stood in the slivers of light from the emerging sunrise, shivering before the embers of her fire and swiping at her face with a cloth dipped in cold water from the basin, there came a tap on her chamber door.

When she opened it, a servant girl stood there, breathless, announcing that the Lady Regent requested her presence in the royal chambers after breakfast, which would end at the changing of the watch. Casual attire, for the lady wished to walk or ride outdoors. Could she attend?

Tekoah stammered her assent. It was a mere formality, for of course she had no choice. After the girl left, she paced in her small chamber. What could Saura's summons mean? She longed to go to Dirken for advice, but he had stopped by her door a short time before, announcing that since fishing season was over, he was going hunting with a party of Berlotan nobles. Tekoah knew he hoped to glean additional information about the impending war. If the rains had ended, then he wished to gather his army with all haste.

TEKOAH SANK down on her cot, tugging at a loose thread on her nightdress. She sat thus for some time, wondering what she might have done to draw Saura's attention to herself. Perhaps Dirken had been wrong about the shouting and gong-banging business.

The bells chimed, signalling the end of the early watch, and Tekoah started up. She had not even dressed yet, and her hair hung in tangles down her back. Plaiting her hair and changing into a simple rose-coloured linen gown which Dirken had given her took only a few moments. Donning her only pair of shoes, she thought that their shabbiness indeed suited them to outdoor strolls. Ignoring the hammering of her heart, she stepped out of her chamber and shut the door behind her.

When she entered the chambers of the Lady Regent, the first thing Tekoah saw was a glorious, embroidered coverlet thrown across the vast royal bed. She lowered her eyes as she stood in the antechamber, willing herself not to gawk at the thousands of tiny yellow flowers sewn onto the crohm-coloured silk. How long had it taken to do that?

"Pray do not be bashful," Saura's strong, rather deep voice commanded from within. "Come in, I am only fastening my hair. It is an exasperating battle every day, and I have sworn a hundred times to cut it all off. Come in, I tell you—I won't be a moment."

Tekoah stepped into the bedchamber. The Lady Regent was tucking her thick, wheat-coloured hair into an exquisite net of lace and gold. Around this, her maid wound her white wimple, without which no one saw her in public. Saura wore a flowing yellow tunic which looked Berlotan, and doeskin riding breeches.

She nodded at Tekoah. "Shall we ride?" She offered, "I have a lovely mount I can lend you."

"No," Tekoah answered before she had thought. "I would rather not."

"Oh?" Saura raised her thin brows in surprise. "But I can see by your colouring and accent that you are northern-born. Do not pretend that you cannot ride. I was born there as well, and we northern maids could all ride before we could walk. Is that not so?"

"Yes, Lady, but I do not ride now."

"Yet you do not seem injured and are not ill."

"My favourite pony died, and I have not ridden another since." Tekoah snapped the words, then wished she had not.

If she felt a lurch in her breast each time she saw a pony, it was none of Saura's affair. Yet the Lady Regent had a knack, they said, for drawing things out of one in spite of oneself.

I must be more careful, she thought.

"Ah, sentiment. I quite understand, although I am not cursed with a sentimental character myself. But I have heard that such dramatic affectations quite enslave musicians, and other artists. I will forgive you." Her smile told Tekoah that she was very fortunate to be forgiven.

"We will walk," Saura told her servants, her voice imperious. "We wish to be alone."

When they stepped outside into the morning sunshine, Saura drew Tekoah's arm through her own, startling her. "We will walk," the Lady Regent murmured, in quite a different voice than the one she had used with her maids. "And I will console you, for your lover has abandoned you to go hunting today, has he not?"

Tekoah opened her mouth to protest, but Saura burst into a

throaty chuckle. She cut in, "Come now, do not toss your head at me, child! His ardent glances as he sings his love ballads are meant for you, regardless of where he directs them. There, I have made you blush, as I intended. I will say no more about it."

They walked along a winding gravel path leading to the stables, and then out into what had once been the gardens. It was still fairly quiet, except for the chatter of the dairymaids, and clinking of their shiny pails, when they passed the dairy. In the charred fields, workers toiled, planting bright flowers in the wet spring earth.

Saura stopped, looking pensively at them. "I wonder if they will flourish," she said, looking at Tekoah with a disarming, melancholy smile. "I have heard it said that nothing will grow now; that the soil is filled with charcoal from all the burning, and the plants will all choke and die. When the queen was here, the flowers never ceased blooming. You never saw the gardens?" she asked, turning to Tekoah, who had remained silent.

"No, but I heard about them from my brother." Immediately, Tekoah bit her lip.

"Your brother was at Rhantor Court? I must have known him, then. What is his name?" Tekoah hesitated, and before she could think of what to say, Saura snapped her fingers triumphantly. "Ah, Weslan. Weslan. I knew your face looked familiar when I first laid eyes upon you. I can see a striking resemblance, but you lack his flamboyance, for all that you sing with Dirken. Perhaps that is a good thing, hm?"

Tekoah's heart was beating erratically. *Already I have told her two things I should not have,* she thought. *Pray Anna that I do not live to regret it.* She carefully removed her arm from Saura's, smoothing her hair back, shivering slightly as she felt upon her Saura's grey, appraising eyes.

"So how is your impetuous brother?" Saura continued, her voice pleasant, but her eyes dangerous. "I have not seen him at this court at all."

"And I have not seen or heard from him since the first snow-fall of winter," Tekoah said, her voice rising.

"Ah. What was I thinking? Of course, he must belong to the Kalesh, that band of northern hot-bloods who would all rather die than set foot in Zantor's court." Looking at Saura, Tekoah saw a faint flush stealing over her cheeks. Could the Lady Regent be feeling shame?

"No doubt he misses the queen," Saura continued, her even voice betraying no emotion. "He was a great favourite of hers, you know." She looked at Tekoah sharply as she said this. Tekoah shrugged in reply. They watched in silence for a moment as the kneeling gardeners continued to plant bulb after bulb in neat little rows.

"Let us walk down to the river," Saura said, turning away. "That, at least, has not altered."

They stepped gingerly down the steep grassy slope that ended with the narrow, rushing channel of the River Meed as it flowed swiftly eastward. Saura bent down and picked up a stone, flinging it into the frothy, churning water. "In Darielle's court, Weslan was a great favourite of the sorcerer Braith as well," she remarked, raising her voice slightly to be heard over the roar of the water. "Do you know anything of that?"

"No," Tekoah answered, reaching down for her own stone so to avoid looking at Saura. She threw as hard as she could, watching the rock as it hit the water and disappeared without a sound. "I know only that I miss him."

"I miss her, too." Saura's voice was wistful suddenly, and Tekoah looked at the other woman, startled. Saura was gazing far out, to where the channel narrowed even more, watching the endless wild leaping of silver water over grey rocks. Tears stood in her grey eyes, and to Tekoah they seemed like small bits of the river, held imprisoned in her face.

"You speak of Queen Darielle?" she asked softly. Saura made an inarticulate sound, averting her face.

She truly loves the queen, Tekoah thought pityingly. *She is both false and true. The dreadful, unhealed wounds within her—they must never give her rest. She needs a healer.*

Tekoah knew with sudden certainty that she could have been that healer, if the time and place were different. She felt the healing strength of Anna welling up within her, like a joy that must be shared.

And then, without thinking, she spoke from the depths of that strength. "Queen Darielle must care for you a great deal. You are so clever and loyal and strong. The very thought of you must give her strength and solace now, wherever she is."

Saura turned and faced her, her face calm and soothed, as it should be. Tekoah felt a surge of elation. Had she performed her first healing? But a moment later, Saura's tranquillity had dissipated, like a thin mist over the river, and she was looking at Tekoah, hard.

They walked back in silence, but Tekoah felt as though she heard a mocking shriek in every innocent birdcall from every treetop that they passed—a shrill echo of danger. She had given herself away.

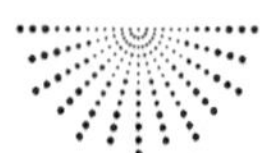

ekoah stayed in her chamber the rest of that day, and most of the next. But Dirken was coming back from the hunt in the late afternoon, and she was to sing with him after the banquet in the evening. So, she forced herself to dress, to practice smiling at herself in the glass—a careless smile, so that Dirken would not guess that something troubled her.

She would have been looking forward with pleasurable anticipation to that night's banquet, if she not been so apprehensive of Saura's scrutiny. Of late, pleasure had outweighed fear whenever she musically accompanied Dirken. Her voice, squeaky and wavering at first, had steadied into a clear soprano blended not unattractively with Dirken's rich tenor.

"Magnificent!" was Dirken's word, but then Dirken was always lavish with his praise of her. Small wonder men loved him and willingly went into great danger at the lift of his hand.

Evening came. Dirken was already seated when she entered the banquet hall, and he made a small grimace of distaste at her, which disappeared instantly when one of the two Berlotans between whom he was sitting turned to speak to him. Tekoah suppressed a grin and turned away, going to one of the lesser tables, where she would eat before she and Dirken performed at the banquet's end. She avoided looking toward the royal dais where Saura sat with a retinue of her favourite nobles, a group which seemed to vary almost daily.

Tekoah ate automatically, without tasting the bread or fruit, imagining that Saura's eyes were upon her. In her mind, she saw the fragile flower bulbs which the gnarled hands of the gardeners pressed into the spring-damp earth. Would they grow?

When Dirken strummed the first notes on the cintar, Tekoah looked up, startled, for in her musings she had not marked the time. She stood, brushing crumbs from her skirt, and hurried to the corner where the musicians and storytellers sat. Dirken smiled at her as she came, and then bent his head down in concentration, cocking it a little to the side, as was his wont.

Tekoah listened to the melody, intrigued. She had supposed that she had listened to all of his new compositions, but it must be a new one—he seemed to pluck melodies from the surrounding air.

Several days earlier, Dirken had been telling her of his verses, how he came to create the ballads which moved his listeners to tears or laughter at his will. The melodies came with ease, he had said with a shrug. It was the words which were difficult; he stumbled across his verses one by one, like tripping over shiny stones on a riverbed.

Shyly, Tekoah had told him of her own verses, how they had bubbled up within her for as long as she could remember. He had demanded to hear some of them, and so—becoming less timid as she'd seen the glint of excitement and approval in his eyes—she had recited some of her best poems, the lighter, whimsical ones. The deeper, brooding verses she kept to herself, for they belonged to her alone.

Dirken smiled at her again as she took her seat, listening to the cintar notes and thinking in a panic. *This is a new song—I cannot accompany him if I do not know the words!* But before she could signal her confusion, Dirken sang.

After a moment, Tekoah covered her face into clasped hands, struggling to contain her chagrin and delight.

He had set to music one of her poems. It was an old one she had composed when she was ten and could finally ride one of the newly broken foals at Beula's pony farm. She was astounded, then touched, for Dirken had remembered every word, and the melody he had chosen made the words seem more beautiful than they had been before. He looked to her as he began the refrain, and she joined her voice with his, blending it behind the rising of his powerful voice, wishing that the moment could stay with her always.

> *Hoofbeats on the hill*
> *echo of my heart*
> *I hear you calling still*
> *Though we be apart…*

Tears stood in Tekoah's eyes. She dashed them away, ashamed to be acting like a child when she should be acting as a proper performer—beyond the sway of simple emotion.

She glimpsed Saura's face and turned away from the knowing smile, not letting herself imagine that Dirken's voice had seemed to impart more meaning to the words than she intended in her ballad of a girl and her horse.

Tekoah was back in her chamber, undressing without hurry, when there was a low rapping at her door.

"Who is it?" she called, a little alarmed. She pulled a shawl around her unlaced bodice. Had Saura betrayed her after all? She had forgotten about the previous day's events in the pleasure of performing with Dirken.

There was no answer, but a second later the door opened and Dirken put his head through, winking. Tekoah put her hand over her mouth to stifle her laughter. Dirken shut the door behind him and produced a bottle from behind his back.

"Pitaya wine!" he announced in a triumphant voice.

Tekoah stared in amazement. She had never tasted pitaya wine. Besides being expensive, it had become a rare commodity in Zantor.

"Where in Miraven did you get it?" she asked. There was outrage at Zantor Court, because the Kalesh had commandeered or destroyed every cartload of pitaya wine destined for the royal city, and for Berlot, since Queen Darielle's abduction.

"My favourite captain, Heyg, had it sent to me tonight." Dirken produced two crystal goblets from somewhere within his person, setting them down on Tekoah's small bedside table. "It is his way of telling me that the roads are passable now. They ambushed another cartload of this precious stuff on its way to Berlot. A very admirable method of communication—is it not, sweetheart?"

He poured each goblet about three-quarters full of the pale amber liquid and handed one to Tekoah. She took a small, tentative sip.

"Why, it tastes just like honey, only better!" she exclaimed.

Dirken made an exaggerated bow. "I have pleased the lady," he said with satisfaction, and seated himself on her cot without further ceremony. He continued to grin at Tekoah.

At last, she said, "You have pleased yourself more, by the looks of it."

"Ah, but that is where you are wrong," he said. His voice had become mysterious. "For Heyg told me something else, which concerns your beloved brother. Weslan stumbled out from the Taboran Woods and rejoined his company ten days ago, near Mount Delnor. He is alive and well, and once again lends his shine to the Kalesh."

Tekoah sprang up with a cry. Dirken deftly caught her goblet before it dropped, saying, "Careful now, that stuff is precious!"

He said nothing more, for she flung herself against him, sobbing and laughing at the same time. It was only after she felt his arms tighten about her waist that she pulled away, shaky and breathless. Dirken handed the goblet back and pulled her down to sit beside him.

"See how good I am for you!" he said. "Now finish your wine."

By the time she had drained her goblet, Tekoah's head was swimming. But she had never thought with such clarity. Dirken was telling her about the ambushes of the Kalesh, and everything made perfect sense to her. The pitaya wine was being stashed away in certain mountain caves by the Kalesh and would be bartering strength for the North when the queen's army proved victorious. He spoke as if their victory was inevitable.

"What about the sorcerer Zant?" she asked him. "He seems determined to bring about our downfall."

Dirken swirled his wine around in his goblet, nodding. "Zant is our biggest worry, for how can we overthrow an enemy who wields unseen weapons? We must hope that he tires of his little game, as sorcerers often do. They never seem to sustain their interest in us for long. Perhaps if the Anniste stay out of his sight, he will forget about them, much in the same way a donkey forgets about the fly once it ceases to buzz in his ear."

Tekoah sat up straight on the bed. Could it be that Dirken did not know of the Mantling? "Zant will not forget about us until we are all dead," she said flatly.

Dirken stared at her face. Whatever he saw there must have alarmed him, for he reached out as if to grasp her shoulder. But then he extended it past her, reaching for the bottle of wine, and refilled her goblet. "Do not say 'us' like that," he told her, his voice taking on a sudden intensity. "He will never touch you while I am alive. Know that."

"Do you know the reason he wants us dead, though?" she persisted.

Dirken shrugged. "I suppose it is because the Anniste

possess certain powers—their healing, their Journeys—and Zant is jealous. Jealous of Anna overshadowing Rhan, if you want to put it that way."

"You are right," Tekoah answered. A shudder passed through her. "You do not realize how right you are."

And she told him of the prophecy, and also how Morogh had caused the drought in the South so that the Anniste would be blamed, and war would begin with Berlot. She described how Zant had created the Morgs by enchantment from Morogh's corpse; and spoke of the Morgs she had seen that night in the Taboran Woods, although she did not elaborate why she had been in the woods.

Of Braith, she did not speak at all.

"Do you believe all that?" Dirken asked her. His voice was calm, though he was paler than before.

"I do believe it," she answered. "I saw it. Though it all sounds quite fantastic talking about it now."

"And where does the sorcerer Braith fit into all this?" Dirken said.

Tekoah felt the need for more wine, and she took a generous gulp. "Besides," she continued, as if Dirken had said nothing, "it does not matter if I believe it or not, does it? All that matters is that Zant believes it. And he has always hated the Anniste— hated all women."

"How do you know that?" Dirken asked, looking at her. Tekoah opened her mouth, then shut it again. "You seem to know rather a lot about sorcerers, come to think of it, sweetheart. Your brother Weslan was friendly with Braith, as I recall. Is that why?" Dirken's voice was nonchalant, but Tekoah knew that whatever else he was, he was no fool. However, she could not think straight at the moment. "Is that why you do not trust Weslan?" she countered.

Dirken looked at her, stroking his chin. "My right-hand captain, Heyg, has nothing but praise for your brother. And we know him to be brave and fearless. In the autumn, his praises were being sung from one end of the North to the other for killing the queen's would-be assassin. On the other hand, Weslan loves the idea of power, but not the work and learning that it takes to achieve the glory he desires. That is not a bad thing, but such people often act on impulse, without regard to the trouble they make for themselves and others around them. I have known many like Weslan, and some become corrupted. Saura is such a one."

"Are you comparing my brother to Lady Saura?" Tekoah asked, folding her arms stiffly, although Dirken's words had described Weslan's character.

"Not at all. But there are some questions to which Weslan must provide the answers. Now, about your knowledge of sorcerers?"

To her dismay, Tekoah slurred her words. "I know about Braith through Chalvern, who is the apothecary in Stern, and the schoolmaster. He once had Braith as his apprentice—long before Braith came into his powers. He still visits Chalvern from time to time, and they have spoken of these things. And of course, the Anniste have learned about them in Journeys."

Dirken nodded. "It is an excellent thing we are leaving tomorrow," he said. "For Zant is due back from Berlot soon. And he likes to make surprise visits as well."

"We leave tomorrow?" Tekoah asked, startled. It made sense, given that the rains had stopped. And she must reunite with the Anniste women, to reassure them, and to exhort them to wait just a little longer for the Mantling. But all at once Tekoah felt a bitter doubt rise beneath the sweet hum of the pitaya wine, and she wondered if the Mantling *was* coming, after all; and if it was, whether it would still be too late for all of them. Perhaps when the Age of Sorcerers ended, the Anniste would end as well.

· · ·

HER EYES MISTED OVER, and her throat tightened. *I am so tired of being afraid,* she thought.

Dirken had not noticed. "Yes, we are leaving tomorrow." he said. He put his goblet down and flexed his arms restlessly. He wore an emerald-green tunic with very short sleeves, and his muscles rippled like small brown waves under his skin.

"But you are going to marshal an army," Tekoah reminded him. "If I go with you, I will just slow you down. I can find my own way back to Stern."

"Do not be ridiculous." Dirken's voice had taken on a clipped, brisk tone that she disliked. He stood up and began walking about, arms now folded. "You will come with me because it is the only safe thing for you to do. Perhaps your Goddess allows for a bit of common sense once in a while?"

Dirken was speaking to her in a rude way. The mistiness in Tekoah's eyes pooled at the corners into tears. She knew she should not be feeling sorry for herself—she had been more than fortunate throughout this time. But it did not seem fair. Just when life had taken on a wonderful rainbow gleam, Anna commanded her to leave. To worry about everything again.

Perhaps she was not destined for happiness. Anna might have decided to punish her for something she had done, only she couldn't remember what it was. *I have strived to be good all my life,* she thought. The tears in her eyes spilled over her cheeks.

Not caring that Dirken had turned to look at her, Tekoah gulped down the rest of her wine. It went down her throat like fire, but she did not choke. That was the beauty of pitaya wine— it was smooth. No wonder men fought over it like umbrays and salted it away in mountain caves.

Maybe I will live in a cave, she thought. *That would solve every-one's problems.* She giggled.

"Why are you laughing, sweetheart?" Dirken asked. He had stopped pacing and stood over her; and now he bent down, very close, his curls almost brushing her face. The clipped note had left his voice; it was low and caressing, the way it had been when he had awoken her under the willows.

"Going to go live in a cave," she told him, lying back on her pillow. "Just me, and tubs of pitaya wine. Everyone else can kill each other until they are all dead."

She closed her eyes, hearing Dirken chuckle above her. Then his fingers were in her hair, loosening it from the bone pins which held it. What a lovely feeling. He stroked it away from her forehead, humming the melody of the song he had sung—her song, his song, their song.

"You will never live in a cave, darling," he murmured. "I am taking you back to my castle. Would you not like to see it again? You were in it once before without permission, remember? Some day, I will make you tell me why, though your pretty blue eyes go all cloudy whenever I ask you. Yes, I will take you back there, and you can stay as long as you like. I will have a guard— five guards—to watch you night and day until this bloodthirsty sorcerer has had his fill. Tell me you will go there with me. Tell me you want to, anyway."

Dirken had the most marvellous voice in the world, and he could change it to sound like anything he wanted, whenever he chose. Right now, it sounded like silk rubbing against a stone; she could see the silk, emerald-green, and the stone, round and white and rough.

For a moment, Tekoah allowed herself to believe that all he said was true. That it would happen, like one of her long-ago dreams as she watched those white towers rise higher and higher on the hill above her hovel. She opened her eyes and nodded at him.

Dirken stopped stroking her hair. His fingertips were at her cheeks, her forehead, under her chin. He was going to kiss her, she thought. She waited, but the kiss did not come. She was a little afraid to open her eyes. What if he had changed into someone else, as he had in her dream?

But when she did open them, it was still Dirken's hazel eyes that gazed back at her, and in their depths, she thought she saw tenderness mingled with his desire. Tenderness. Something she had seldom known.

Does he look at anyone else like that? she wondered, feeling a sudden fierce jealousy. Then, because he had not yet kissed her, she kissed him.

At the moment that their lips touched, his arms were around her, so tightly that she gasped at first in surprise. Another Dirken she had not known existed. But she was glad, glad of this Dirken. He was kissing her, and she was kissing him back, running her fingers through his curls. His hands traced circles along her neck, her shoulders, her arms, pushing aside the shawl.

Dirken paused, lifting his mouth from hers and smiling at her with sudden mischief. "Like honey," he whispered, "only better."

Just then there were shouts from out in the hall, and the sound of feet running. Dirken sat up. "I had better go see what that is all about," he said reluctantly. "Bolt the door and do not allow anyone else to enter. I will knock three times, then two, then three again. All right?"

Tekoah nodded, and then he was out the door. It closed behind him, and it was as if the past few delicious moments had never happened.

Rhan's balls! Tekoah grumbled to herself.

She felt a little better after using an oath she had never dared to even think before. No doubt it was nothing more than a grease fire in the kitchen. Or perhaps the Lady Saura had misplaced her beauty ointments.

She sat up, staring into her half-filled glass of wine.

The liquid seemed to swirl around in her goblet, faster and faster. With no warning at all, she felt herself slip into a Journey.

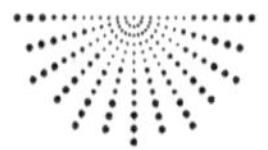

As she fell, Tekoah heard her mother's voice for the first time since the terrible day last spring when she had disappeared forever. The voice was faint, but unmistakable: "Beware, my child!"

"Mother," she cried, "where are you?"

But Neela's voice faded away into the darkness whence it came, and she said no more. Tekoah kept falling.

Finally, there was a solid floor beneath her feet. The darkness was replaced by light, etching itself gradually into the objects which surrounded her.

She was in the sumptuous bedchamber of the Lady Regent, staring at the enormous, canopied bed with its embroidered coverlet. Sitting in it was Saura, upright against the pillows, yellow hair plaited over one shoulder, wearing a high-necked white nightgown. She was staring at the door, her jaw working with small, tight movements.

With a jarring violence, the door was flung open. Huddling in the room's corner where she found herself, Tekoah saw the sorcerer Zant enter.

Zant had aged since she had last seen him within the

obsidian walls of the sorcerer's lodge. His hair, snow-white, was slicked back against his head as before, but it was thin and brittle. His pale face had aged; the lines were few, but etched deep, carving downward from each side of his nose and across his forehead. And though his eyes darted about the room as was their wont, their lids drooped, as if in fatigue. However, the hooded gaze seemed to Tekoah even more frightening. It was as if he could see her now, and she would not know.

Zant turned his face toward Saura, who smiled at him, twisting a corner of the coverlet between her fingers. Tekoah saw in her face the dread and resignation of a small girl about to be punished.

"You are angry with me," she faltered.

The proud voice that could cut like a whiplash across the banquet hall had faded. Tekoah watched her with pity mingled with disgust. The Lady Regent was lonely, Dirken had said, with very few friends. And she had aligned herself with a monster.

"You are a fool." Zant's voice was flat. He walked toward the bed, and although Tekoah could see her terror, Saura remained where she was.

She did not flinch or move, as she replied, "Why do you speak to me so? You know I would do anything for you!"

"Anything but what I asked, and that was for vigilance."

"I have been vigilant."

Zant leaned forward and smashed his fist down on Saura's beside table, toppling a small statuette. It shattered to pieces on the wooden floor. Saura jumped, but her eyes never wavered from Zant's face. His voice dropped to a whisper.

"Everything is going wrong," he hissed. "The Morgs are dying, and we cannot find the witches. I bade you to watch for anyone new at the palace, especially from Stern. Did you do as I instructed?"

Saura had been sitting upright, taut as a bowstring. "Anyone new, I question personally," she answered.

"And?"

"And I have found no one I suspect. They are all simpering milksops!"

Tekoah took a deep, shuddering breath of relief. Was Saura protecting her? It seemed unlikely, and yet—

Zant stood over the bed, his head swaying slightly from side to side. "Ah. Your judgement is beyond criticism, no doubt. But leave that for a moment, my dear, and tell me something else? Did you visit my pet every day that I was gone, as I instructed?"

Saura shuddered. "No, I could not bring myself to go down there. You know that creature frightens me!"

Tekoah thought of what Dirken had said to her as she'd dozed off in his chamber on the night she'd first come to Zantor; and about the yellow eyes she sometimes saw behind her closed eyelids when she lay down to sleep. *Why did Anna not warn me?* she wondered.

She shuddered. All the time she had been there, a Morg had been in the dungeons of the palace.

"Fool!" Zant's hand darted out with a speed that blurred it and slapped Saura full upon the face. Tekoah's own body leaped with shock.

Saura gave a moaning gasp, then cradled her cheek, crying out in a muffled voice, "Why do you punish me, when I only seek to please you?"

"If you had gone below and checked on the Morg as I bid you to do both morning and night, then you would have seen the frenzy come upon it. As it is, it has hurled itself against the bars so long and hard that its face was a bloody pulp when they released it. It will barely be able to complete this task, and everything that we have accomplished may still be for naught. Because the Guardian of the Witches has been here for a half-span!"

"Anna's Tides!" Saura exclaimed, taking her hand from her cheek and looking at Zant in astonishment.

"Do not speak the witch's name in my presence; you cannot imagine how it sickens me." Zant's lips pursed in distaste.

He turned away, and in profile he looked once more female, with a slight swelling at the bust and hip, and a sudden softness to his lips and cheeks. Tekoah shook her head, and when she looked again, the vision had disappeared.

Zant was gazing at Saura again, his black eyes unblinking. "Yes, my pet has been more vigilant than you, my dear," he said bitingly, "and much more valuable."

Saura opened her mouth as if to speak, but he raised a pale hand, silencing her.

"This information would have been useful, for I have spent this last half-span witch-hunting, but I ferreted out only a few of the Anniste in Stern, when I had been confident that I had discovered their lair. They have scuttled away, those dung beetles. And my Morgs are still dying. I fear they are all gone, but for my pet, which you left to languish below."

"The Morgs are still dying?" Saura's startled voice echoed Tekoah's own surprise. "But why?"

"They starved all winter, and starve still, and you ask why? But now at least I know why they could not find most of the Anniste: Braith hid those witches in a Shifting."

As Tekoah heard these words, her knees gave out, and she sank down to slump on the floor. Her heart pounded so hard in her ears she could barely hear the words that came next.

Saura continued to stare at Zant in stupefaction. "Why would Braith do such a thing? It would age him greatly!"

Zant smiled faintly. "He does it for love, my dear."

"For love?"

"Yes. He is in love with the Anniste Guardian, who has graced your banquet hall several times of late."

Saura turned very white. "Tekoah?"

"None other."

"But where did you learn all this?" Saura exclaimed. "Not from Braith, surely?"

"Surely not." The sorcerer put his hands behind his back and tapped his foot on the floor, eyes darting from side to side. "How I discovered this is a very amusing story, and I could tell you, if I cared to, but why bother?"

There was a long silence. Saura stared at Zant, her grey eyes apprehensive but curiously fatalistic. Tekoah watched Saura's face, willing her to scream, to run, to do something besides wait for whatever would befall her.

"So," Zant said at last, "Braith is shielding the Anniste in a Shifting, and you have been shielding the Guardian. Well, I have created some Shiftings of my own, and none of them to shield anyone."

He gave Saura a venomous look. "I will bring this country to heel for protecting those hags. I will make them pay, those northern soldiers who blunder around trying to protect themselves from the beating they deserve. And I will kill every witch!" Zant's gaze moved past Saura's shoulder, toward the corner where Tekoah stood, and his head swayed from side to side.

Tekoah stood still, reminding herself repeatedly that this was a Journey. Zant could not see her, but neither could she run to Dirken, to warn him of the Shiftings.

I must not give way to panic, she told herself.

"And now, I ask you," Zant said, going over to Saura and taking her chin in his pale fingers. "Why did you not suspect who it was? She was under your very nose."

"You are squeezing my jaw too hard," Saura whispered. "Let go! There, that's better. I did not suspect her because she did not hide. I felt uneasy about her at first, but after I questioned her, I satisfied myself that she was not Anniste, and as for being the Guardian, it would have seemed laughable. It still does. She looks too meek to be Guardian of a chicken coop without getting pecked to death. I see now I was wrong."

Lady Saura is not a coward, at least, Tekoah thought, with grudging admiration. Even though beads of sweat had broken out on her forehead, Saura's voice was dignified.

"Yes," Zant replied. "But this is the question: is the Guardian more useful to me alive, or dead?" He sat down on the bed, saying nothing, staring again into the corner where Tekoah crouched, gripping her arms to her sides.

The room was silent for several minutes. Tekoah saw Saura wipe the sweat from her cheeks and smooth her hair. She reached a tentative hand out toward Zant's back, but pulled it back again without touching him. The movement caught his eye, and he turned slowly toward her.

"Dead," he concluded. "For even if I take her with me to bargain with Braith, something could go wrong and one witch might survive. But if I kill *her,* Braith no longer has a reason to let the others live. And it will be easy to convince him of that—for if the Mantling befalls, *he* will perish as well. It is only his ridiculous obsession with the witch girl that prevents him from seeing this."

"I know how he feels," Saura murmured.

"Do you?" Zant asked, his voice mocking.

Tekoah saw anger flare in Saura's eyes. She sat up straight, looking regal once more, as she had been on the dais in the banquet hall, raising a hand imperiously to the nobles who surrounded her.

"Stop treating me like filth!" Her voice vibrated with emotion. "I have sacrificed everything for you."

Zant's forehead lifted, an odd facial movement because he lacked eyebrows. "Sacrificed?" he echoed. "You have gained much, by the looks of it. So much so that you have grown complacent. Have you forgotten that if we do not stamp the witches out, *you* will fall with me? You will lose everything, and your body will be torn apart in the streets, for you are the worst sort of traitor."

Saura held out her hands, imploring, but Zant turned away from her.

"The Mantling approaches," Tekoah heard him mutter. "I can feel its coldness, deep within me."

"You should release your creature upon her now," Saura said. "What are you waiting for?"

"Soon enough!" he replied. "But first, let us talk of you, Saura, and your many attributes: Lady Regent, traitor to a queen, harlot to a sorcerer, and stupid, presumptuous fool! Do you know I would feed you to my Morg, piece by piece, if I thought he could stomach you?"

"What a horrible thing to say! Why are you so cruel?"

"I am angry with you," Zant answered, his face expressionless. "I had supposed you to be superior to your counterpart in the South."

"You compare me to Darian? What an insult!"

Zant grimaced, his seamed skin drawing away from his bones like old parchment. "You mortals are all very boring, and have begun to annoy me dreadfully, my dear. As I told Darian myself, several hours ago."

Whether Saura saw the menace in Zant's voice and face and ignored it, or did not see it at all, Tekoah did not know. But if Saura saw, she gave no sign, putting on a determined smile. "My beloved liege is becoming testy," she crooned. "You are wearing yourself out, making those Shiftings. I beg you to rest, for a time. I am worried."

"Come here," Zant answered her, smiling all at once, and holding out his arms.

"Why?" Saura replied, her voice sulky. But there was a glint of triumph in her eyes.

"So that I can show you how fragile I am."

"All right." Saura moved across the bed to where Zant sat.

Her eyes became cloudy as she kneeled before him. In a graceful, fluid motion, she lifted her nightgown over her head and let it fall to the floor behind her.

"You have never undressed for me," she murmured. "Will you do so now?"

Zant shook his head, holding out his arms. As Saura slipped into his embrace, they tightened about her, then seemed to elongate themselves, enfolding her again.

Tekoah watched from the corner, revulsion rippling through her, thinking, *Anna, why are you showing me this?*

"I knew you could not despise me forever," Saura was saying.

"I hate all women," Zant replied, his narrow face looking impassively over Saura's shoulder. "And you have been a great disappointment to me, Saura."

Saura's eyes were closed, but Tekoah saw with horror that Zant's arms looked even stranger—seeming to join themselves together into one thick arm—and the sleeves were falling away. Then she saw it was the flesh itself that was changing— becoming a flat, dull black, shot through with red and yellow stripes.

"You are holding me too tightly!" Saura gasped.

Tekoah, unable to tear her own eyes away, saw Saura open her eyes and look full into Zant's face. From Saura's throat came a choked scream, for Zant's features were transforming, his undulating face becoming that of a serpent, a long tongue flicking in and out of his mouth.

Beneath Zant's head, his body was nothing but coils now, thick, rippling muscle under dull, leathery skin. The coils had wrapped themselves about Saura's body from her neck to her ankles and were squeezing, methodically.

Again, Saura shrieked, faintly. Looking one more time upon the other woman's face, Tekoah saw she had no breath left. And then Tekoah turned her own face to the wall, closing her eyes, and darkness engulfed her.

TEKOAH HEARD an insistent knocking and realized she was in her chamber, lying on her cot. The vision of the serpent was still so vivid that, in a surge of blind, animal terror, she scrabbled to a corner of the bed and huddled there. The knocking continued, however, and after a moment she remembered it must be Dirken, for the raps came in the pattern upon which they had agreed. She went to the door and opened it with shaking hands.

Dirken's face was grimmer than she had ever seen it. But as he put an arm around her shoulders, he kept his voice light.

"Interesting news, sweetheart." he said.

"I know," she whispered.

Dirken looked down at her, his brow furrowed with puzzlement. "The Lady Saura has just received word that Berlot has closed the River Meed to all trade with Miraven," he told her. "So, you were right. War is even closer than we thought."

"Yes," Tekoah replied, with an intensity that deepened the baffled look on Dirken's face, "I know. Even closer than we thought."

She felt a small measure of gratification that Dirken gazed at her now with deepened respect, the same expression he had worn at Beula's farm after discovering the living bales of hay that surrounded them. Only this time, it was she who was hiding in the bale, scarcely daring to breathe, praying not to be noticed; wondering if her life would end with such suddenness there would be no time even for a last prayer to Anna.

CHAPTER 40

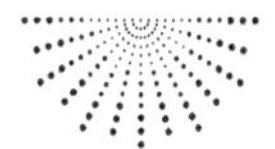

The night was dark as coal, as pitch, dark as nights were only in the Taboran Mountains in the North of Miraven. The blackness carried with it a chill left over from winter, but Weslan did not notice. He was used to it.

He stared into the orange glow of the banked fire, sitting his watch. It was the last hour before the morning, and bats with wingspans longer than a man's arm swooped by occasionally, looking for a final meal before dawn came stealing over the mountain peaks.

Weslan heard the snuffling sounds of small nocturnal animals outside the circle of firelight, and their noises were infinitely more familiar than the restless movements of the men in their sleeping rolls, and the resigned sighs of Captain Heyg, who suffered lately from insomnia.

Weslan waited with some impatience for the sighs to stop, for he planned on leaving when Heyg fell asleep. Not that he blamed his commander for his restlessness. Heyg had a lot to think about: the upcoming meeting of the Kalesh that Dirken had called three days hence in Stern; the Shiftings, which were claiming lives and causing panic throughout the North; the shortages, always, of rations for the soldiers and the endless inpouring of recruits from the South. Wakeful thoughts for Captain Heyg.

But his own thoughts were even less conducive to sleep. *How have I changed?* Weslan wondered. The question surprised him, for he was not usually comfortable with self-examination.

Ah, but that is one of the very things that has changed, is it not? Weslan could almost hear Reika speaking to him—telling him to look within for the answers.

He had been convinced that the burning desire for glory had left him forever. It had not, obviously. Why else would he be planning this mad, impossible, glorious thing?

For love! The reply came swiftly, glibly, and Weslan rejected it, thinking that, if he had learned nothing else, he had learned not to lie to himself.

Of course I love Darielle, he amended hastily. *But that is only part of it. Perhaps the least part of it.*

The "new" Weslan despised self-delusion. He winced at the memory of his often-told, always-embellished tales of vanquishing Queen Darielle's appointed assassin. He cringed when thinking of these self-aggrandizing fables, which he had eventually come to believe himself.

Ruthless with his inner purging, Weslan had admitted to himself that even his fury at Braith's deception was really anger directed at his own failings. For how gladly he had accepted the trappings of glory, without shouldering the work. He had been dazzled by the appearance of gold, when beneath the bright paint lay only dull and shoddy metals, easily pierced by the sword of truth.

Thinking about swords, Weslan took his out of the scabbard, staring at the blade. He had sharpened it earlier that day with great care, coating it lightly with oil. He doubted he would have another chance to do so, for he would probably be forced to leave it behind when he entered Berlot.

His elaborate preparations had not seemed out of place. The rest of the company had also been tending to their weapons, polishing boots and shields, grooming horses, and cleaning in a kind of frenzy. The next day, they were leaving for Stern, a three-day ride—if they did not encounter any Shiftings. It was the beginning of something exciting, although no one knew quite what that was.

News had spread like a brush fire throughout the North: Dirken had called a meeting of the Kalesh, to be held at the Castle of Mirrand just outside Stern, three days hence. They summoned all the Kalesh, even the new southern recruits, and Rhan knew how many of those had joined up by now—hundreds, perhaps.

Yes, Weslan thought, *something exciting is happening! Victory!*

All loyal northerners—men, women, and children—were to appear at the castle on the appointed day. They would admit no one unless they bore the emblem of the Kalesh stitched on their sleeve: a mountain pony leaping over a crescent moon.

Exhilaration overtook the dread which had pervaded the men of Heyg's company since their encounter with the Shifting —a little wild, perhaps—but welcome.

Yes, everyone had been sharpening their swords, nervous but exhilarated, so Weslan had not looked conspicuous at all. But in reality, he was the outsider, for he was not going with them. He did not quite know when the plan had first formed itself within his mind. Perhaps it had been after listening to Heyg speak of Dirken with an awe that Weslan had never heard in his grizzled commander's voice. "He should be king. He would soon put everything to rights!"

"Why him?" Weslan had asked, inexplicably stung. "What makes *him* so special?"

"He has got nobility in his blood, for starters," Heyg had retorted, shooting Weslan a sharp look. "People respect that."

"What do you mean, noble blood? He is only a minstrel."

"Ah, that is where you are wrong, lad! No, do not ask me any more questions. It is not information he wants bandied about. He would rather that everyone believe he is as lowborn as—"

As lowborn as me, Weslan had thought, walking away before Heyg finished speaking. He was tired of it. For the past few days, he had heard nothing from the other men but breathless, worshipful stories of Dirken and his exploits.

Dirken of a thousand disguises, who juggled intrigues as easily as he did Berlotan oranges; slipping over the border and drinking with Berlotans, who considered him an ally. Dirken, singing at Zantor before the Lady Saura and the sorcerer Zant, who indulged him because of his unshakeable popularity at court, regardless of who held the throne. Dirken, leader of the Kalesh, directing with iron reins all the actions of the flourishing underground army. And now—according to Heyg—Dirken, who should be king.

But most significant of all: Dirken, who suspected Weslan of betraying the queen.

Well, I will prove him wrong, he thought angrily.

Heyg's company encamped only twenty miles from the Berlotan border, hugging the southern edge of Mount Delnor. All he had to do was ride south, down to the River Meed, commandeer a small boat from a fisher in Liandon, and slip across the border, somehow.

The "somehow" loomed rather largely—there was the matter of Berlotan patrols—but Weslan determined not to think about it too much for the time being. He did not want to lose his nerve.

Once he was across the Berlotan border, he would travel, by foot or by cart, to the royal city of Hacinta-Car, enter the palace —cleverly disguised, of course—and rescue the queen. After that, there would be no more doubts about his loyalty, from Dirken or anyone else.

Yes, if the bare, bitter truth be told, love was probably the least of it.

How he would escape the palace and dash back across the border, taking with him the queen—who was much more difficult to hide than a sword—he had not yet figured out. But he would find a way. He would be an authentic hero this time, not a puppet dangling on Braith's string.

Weslan grimaced at the puppet image. That was the trouble with all his inner purging—it hurt. He knew he had to summon every ounce of his will and courage, while refusing to be rash and impulsive. Things like this took work and meticulous planning.

He stared into the fire, trying to think of Darielle, to conjure up the yellow flower, the heady fragrance, which had preceded all thoughts of her before... *Before what?* he wondered. *Before I killed my father? Before my winter as a solitary wanderer in the snowy fields of madness?*

Before Reika.

It was Reika's face that Weslan saw now, its strong planes, full red lips, deep eyes, inky lashes and brows, infinite sweetness in her voice and fingertips. *My healer.*

Weslan had been told that Dirken had saved many healers; for that, he was grateful, despite his resentment. *Be safe, Tekoah,* he prayed, his lips moving silently. He did not know whether she was in Stern still, at Beula's farm, or hiding elsewhere. He hoped he would see her again soon, if he was fortunate enough to return alive.

The first grey light was etching itself around the edges of the mountain. It was time to go. Weslan moved to sheathe his sword and then looked up quickly, hearing a small sound. It was Captain Heyg, standing in front of him. He did not look as if he had slept at all, though his wiry red hair was tousled, and he yawned hugely.

"About time to wake me for the watch, was it not, Wes?"

"It looks as if there is no need, Captain," Weslan answered, trying to keep his voice light.

"A shame. I did not mean to rob you of the pleasure of kicking me from my sleep."

Weslan laughed. It was a great joke between Heyg and his soldiers that he could not command their respect. Heyg laughed with him, his low, growling chuckle. But as soon as the laughter died away, his face became very serious. Looking at it in the faint morning light, Weslan saw with sinking certainty that Heyg had guessed his intentions. He sheathed his sword and returned Heyg's look, defiantly.

"Going after her, are you?" Heyg's voice was soft.

Weslan nodded, waiting for the inevitable explosion of wrath, for Heyg's temper was quick when it was roused. But the explosion did not come. Heyg merely turned and looked to the east, toward Berlot.

After a moment, he sighed. "I have been wondering how long it would take you to think up a plan," he said.

"You have?" Weslan asked, startled.

"Of course. I know you as if you were my son. Although you have changed somewhat from the day, I first plucked you from that miserable hovel—and for the better, I think." Behind them, a soldier stirred restlessly in his sleep, and Heyg lowered his voice.

"But has it not occurred to you that the Kalesh would have tried to rescue Queen Darielle long before now, had it been worth the risk? You are not the only one who cares for the queen. Every red-blooded Miravener is smarting from Berlot's slap in the face to the North."

"Then why is it not worth the risk?" Weslan asked. He was impatient to be off.

"It would be an impossibility for a company of soldiers—even a small one—to cross the border unnoticed," Heyg answered, stroking his stubbled chin. "But it might be possible for one man. However, the danger is great, and there are important things for that one man to know in advance to maximize his chances of success. Even then, there are an infinite number of ways it could all go horribly wrong."

"If you say so," Weslan answered curtly. "But I am determined to try."

"Well, then I will tell you everything I can, and if you still want to go, I will not stand in your way. I will even vouch for your whereabouts at the Kalesh meeting in Stern. Fair enough?"

Weslan nodded. At that moment, the first warbler sounded its note—a sweet, bubbling trill. Behind them, he could hear the same soldier mumbling as he emerged from his tent. Heyg put an arm about Weslan's shoulders, drawing him farther away from the campfire.

"First," he said, "getting into Berlot is a bit of a tricky thing."

"I know," Weslan replied, but Heyg cut him off before he could continue.

"Not that it is impossible, for Dirken has our men posted throughout Berlot—from the border to Hacinta-Car—in various guises. There is a ferryman, and a groom at the royal stables. There is even an embalmer, I think. You only have to know who you're looking for, and the right passwords. This will be of some help to you, though I imagine you have already formulated a foolproof strategy."

Heyg's face was grave, but Weslan could see the ironic twinkle behind his blue-grey eyes. He kept silent. Heyg spoke steadily for ten more minutes, reciting names and locations with astonishing precision, as Weslan strove with a whirling head to commit them to memory.

Heyg's voice took on a warning note. "As you must realize, although it may not prove difficult to get into Berlot, coming out with a queen is a different story. If they catch you—"

"They will kill me. I know, and I am prepared for that." Weslan said. His voice was calm, but he fingered his scabbard nervously. He did not mind dying for his queen, but it was common knowledge that the Berlotans were fond of torture.

"That is not what I was going to say," Heyg growled. "Do you think I am about to wring my hands over your miserable life? If you are caught, it will be the excuse Berlot is looking for to invade us! Right now, their hands are tied, because of the treaty with King Darian."

"Where is the problem?" Weslan laughed. "Don't we want to fight them?"

"Use your head, lad. What have we been jawing about these past annaspans? Oh, I forget, you were not here a good part of the time." Heyg cleared his throat. "I could use some tea right now, and it looks like the pot is boiling," he muttered, looking back toward the camp. "To put it simply, we are trying to buy a little time. Dirken wants all the Kalesh together, to assess our numbers, our weapons, and our expertise. He needs time to organize us, and complete a battle strategy, though I suspect he's come up with one already. The point is, we want to strike first. It is our best chance. But we do not want them to suspect anything of the sort, of course. Let them think we are bowing under the yoke of tyranny like obedient oxen."

"So what happens if I rescue the queen and do not get captured?" Weslan asked, trying to keep the edge from his voice. "Won't it amount to the same thing? There will still be an excuse for invasion."

"No, for there will be no proof she did not simply escape on her own, and we will keep her safely hidden until the war is won. The problem with capture is that the Jinta will have the excuse he needs to start the war. You may just lose everything for us."

Weslan stared at the ground, trying to ignore the crushing pressure in his chest. Grass was pushing its way up through the soft, moist earth, along with small clusters of white and purple flowers, whose names he could not recall. Tekoah would have known, as would Reika. And Darielle, of course, his flower queen. The spring rains had drawn the fragile blooms up from the earth, wakening them from dark winter slumber. How brief would be their flowering, but how glorious! Afterward, no one would remember that they had ever been there.

"Second," Heyg said, relentlessly, "there has been talk, some of which you must have heard, that the queen is not as unhappy as we would like to believe. That she does not wish to leave Berlot."

"I cannot believe those words," Weslan said, trembling with anger. How could Heyg stand here and say it? To wear the emblem of the Kalesh and utter such blasphemy!

"I did not say that I believed it," Heyg replied, putting his hand on Weslan's shoulder.

Weslan shook it off and strode away. Heyg followed him.

"Wes, I do not believe it in my heart! How could I fight for her if I did? Or expect my men to fight? Queen Darielle has become the symbol of everything we love about the North. But I must accept the possibility up here." Heyg tapped his forehead. "If there was even the smallest chance at all that she would betray us, then I should not in good conscience send someone in there after her. We have too much to lose. There is our freedom to think of, and that of our children."

Both men were silent for a moment. The birds were all singing now, a chorus of trills and whistles that resounded among the trees. Above them, the sky was getting brighter and brighter. It was going to be one of those rare days in early spring that suddenly behaved like summer; for it was warm already, but the fresh, moist air made it better than any summer day could be. The kind of day when one tossed all plans into the wind and went down to the river to fish.

"You are still going, aren't you?" Heyg asked him.

"Yes," Weslan answered.

Heyg looked toward the east, squinting against Rhan's brilliance. Bits of rosy cloud were still drifting, as if caught in the branches of the evergreens on the mountaintop.

"Remember the Shifting we saw, day before last?" Heyg asked.

"What about it?" Weslan replied, frowning.

"The trouble with Shiftings is that you don't know they are there until you're in them, almost. They always look like something else until it is too late."

Weslan did not answer. He was taking deep breaths, the way Reika had taught him. He wished she was with him.

"Unless you are looking out for them," Heyg added. His last words came as a whisper. "I did not see you leave."

He turned and walked back to his men, and Weslan went to saddle his horse.

WESLAN RODE under the blue bowl of the sky, coming out of the woods just east of the fishing village of Liandon. He had been there once before, soon after joining Heyg's company. Then, as in that moment, he couldn't believe that he was in the South. Liandon seemed as if it should belong to the North, somehow. The people acted more like northerners—slower to speak, but quicker to speak the truth, as the saying went.

From a grassy slope at the bottom of Mount Delnor, Weslan could see the white pebbled huts of the quaint fishing village on his right, and the River Meed twisting like a silver snake ahead of him in the sun. It was along the river he would travel into Berlot.

But first he needed to locate a friendly ferryman, by the name of Hengren. The password would be "the Mantling," Heyg had told him. Hengren would give Weslan the information he needed in order to contact the next link in the chain of Dirken's agents, some of whom had lived in Berlot for several turnings now, doing not much more than waiting for orders from the Kalesh.

Weslan did not ride through the main part of the village. Heyg had warned him it was crawling with Berlotans. He skirted around the riverside and rode the rough path parallel to the village until he found the small, cobbled street of which he had been told. The smell of fish was so strong he gagged, and he wondered how anyone could bear it all the time.

The lane was very narrow. Weslan dismounted and walked his horse to the third hut on the side of the street facing the river. There was no hitching post, so he held his horse's reins while he rapped on the low door.

The crowded huts clung together as if for comfort; from the open window of the one next door, Weslan could see the face of a child watching him, round-eyed. A moment later the door opened, and a tremendous fellow with a beard that spilled halfway down his chest stood regarding Weslan.

"Today is my day of rest," he grunted. "What do you want?"

"To be ferried across the river without delay," Weslan answered, and before the giant could utter the retort that was rising to his lips, he added, "in the name of the Mantling."

At that, the bearded fellow pulled him in and shut the door behind them, scowling ferociously at the waif next door.

"Why they picked you, with your fair skin and blue eyes, is beyond me. Why not just tattoo the Kalesh emblem on your forehead?"

"My name is Weslan," Weslan said coldly. "May I know yours?"

The fisher burst out laughing and clapped Weslan on the shoulder. "Touchy, aren't we, young lord?" he said. "All you noblemen are the same. You feel you have to prove yourselves when it comes to the fight. Well, no matter. I am sure Dirken knows what he's about. My name is Hengren, but I am sure you know that already, or you would not be here. Now, as for our business…"

"That, I cannot tell you, although if all goes as it should you will know before long," Weslan told him. He was feeling slightly mollified at being mistaken for a nobleman. "Are you able to ferry me without delay? I am in a hurry."

"I cannot do it until the morrow, lad," Hengren said. "I've a load of whitefish to carry into Hacinta-Car in the morning. It is always the first of the week that I go with the whitefish. It would look strange if I changed my habits all of a sudden." As Weslan pondered, he added, "If you are in that much of a hurry, you must swim."

The wild fantasy of spiriting Darielle away and getting her back to Stern, just in time to walk into a conference of the Kalesh, disappeared like a burst bubble. Still, Weslan reflected, he was still better off than before he had spoken to Heyg.

All vessels entering Berlot were being thoroughly scrutinized, Heyg had told him. Weslan would have soon been caught on his own. But Hengren had been the jovial ferryman in the border village for thirty turnings, besides supplying the coveted delicate whitefish to the royal palace. He was above suspicion.

But he might have some suspicions of his own, for at the moment his canny face regarded Weslan without expression. "You were not contemplating just walking up to the palace looking like that, were you?" he asked at last.

Weslan's face grew hot with vexation. "I was going to wear a hooded robe, and perhaps a black horsehair wig," he said, and then cursed himself under his breath as Hengren burst into a roar of laughter.

From the chamber behind, a woman's voice said sharply, "Be quiet, the baby is sleeping."

Hengren rolled his eyes at Weslan in a pantomime of terror. Tiptoeing over to the kitchen table with exaggerated movements that were ridiculous on his colossal frame, he motioned for

Weslan to sit on a thatched chair that seemed to be made of straw and rope woven together. He took one himself, drew it up to the table and leaned forward with a confidential air.

"You must darken your skin, and dye your hair," Hengren whispered, nodding with delight at Weslan's look of astonishment. "I know how to do it, don't worry. There's nothing we can do about your eyes, though. You will just have to keep them down as much as possible. And for the love of Rhan, do not glare at anyone the way you're glaring at me right now, young lord," he added, bursting into laughter again and then checking himself as he glanced toward the back of the hut.

Hengren's cosmetic alterations took most of the afternoon and were done in the smelly outhouse behind the hut which was used for cleaning fish.

I will never forget this as long as I live, Weslan thought, cringing as Hengren remorselessly sluiced yet another sopping wet sponge of the foul concoction over his face. It smelled like dung —and probably was. *Someone had better be grateful for this. Hopefully it will be Darielle.*

"And now you can show me your appreciation for my hard labours on my day off," Hengren announced, as they sat in the hut eating bread and cheese with Hengren's unexpectedly pretty wife, Letta.

"How can I do that?" Weslan asked courteously, swallowing a mouthful of wine.

"By helping me clean the last of my whitefish, of course," Hengren grinned, then burst into guffaws at the look of repugnance on Weslan's face. He laughed louder and with more freedom than before, for this time his wife joined in.

THE WIND WAS brisk on the river the next morning. Weslan stood unsteadily on the rocking stern of the small fishing boat, while Hengren shouted cheerful orders to his apprentice. Weslan did not understand one word of what he was saying, so he hoped that Hengren would not take it into his head to shout any orders at him. As it was, it was all he could do to keep from throwing up his breakfast all over the bins of neatly cleaned fish that had been packed in ice and straw and stacked on every available space to be had in the little vessel.

"Hacinta-Car!" Hengren shouted suddenly, pointing at a glittering spot in the distance as they rounded a bend in the river.

Weslan leaned forward, squinting anxiously for a view of the royal city of Berlot, a place he had never thought to see in his lifetime.

It was a dazzling sight. The sun glanced off the gleaming domes of what surely must have been a thousand temples, though the largest one, set on a hilltop, had to be the palace. So many temples in one city! There were not so many in the whole of Miraven.

Weslan knew, as everyone did, that Rhan was worshipped in Berlot with far more fervour than in his own country. But still it was strange, seeing it first-hand, and remembering that the Berlotans believed that pitayas were thought to be Rhan's sacred seed scattered upon the earth. This was what had started all the fighting. Or did it go deeper than that? Was the hatred of Anna a more powerful force than the love of Rhan?

For Reika had told him that in Berlot, Anna was worshipped not at all. Reviled, rather. It was why the Jinta got along so famously with Darian, and with Zant.

Weslan shook his head. Religion usually bored him, unless it had something to do with action. Rhan's fire coursing through his chosen ones, and all that. However, at the moment, religion seemed to be on the brink of killing everyone and ruining everything.

Time you started paying attention, Reika had told him, playfully tapping his cheek.

If Darian had his way, Anna's name would have been stricken from the ancient scrolls or distorted into that of the wicked she-devil who presided over a coven of witches. But thus far Darian had to content himself with blotting the name of his sister from the royal records.

How can a brother hate his sister so much? Weslan wondered. The question made him both sad and angry. He tried to imagine himself hating Tekoah, wishing her dead, and almost burst out laughing with the absurdity of it.

"You look as if you are happy at the sight," Hengren observed, nodding toward the glittering domes. "Judging by your smile, at least."

"I will be even happier when I find myself inside the palace."

"That is an easy matter. Getting out again with your head still attached to your shoulders is another thing altogether. Hail, Brenton!"

They were passing a small sailboat which towed a log boom. The boat's captain waved a cheerful greeting, then tacked wildly as the log boom drifted toward the fishing vessel. After barely avoiding a collision, he grinned at them.

"Last day of trading, I hear," he called.

Hengren shrugged. "They have been chirping that for an annaspan, now. I will keep catching a full load and carting it down until I am turned away."

Brenton nodded his agreement, then was gone around the bend.

Hengren barked "Tack!" to his boy, who nimbly hopped over to the other side of the vessel and, by some magic Weslan could not yet fathom, took the sail with him. The city looked much closer now. They had to be moving faster than it appeared.

The sun was high over the sky, the heat beginning to build like a stoked furnace. Hengren took off his woollen cap and wiped his forehead.

Weslan was also sweating. His dyed hair was tied back with

a leather thong and clung damply to his neck. Perhaps he should have cut it off, as Hengren had suggested. But Darielle loved his hair, so he had been reluctant to cut it. Even so, would she recognize him disguised as he was?

"What did that fellow mean by 'last trading day'?" he asked Hengren, who was still standing beside him.

"Oh, the rumour is always floating around that Berlot is going to attack Miraven, and for the past few days, it has been on everyone's lips. The army has been out, parading around, and the sorcerer Zant paid a visit not too long since, and gave the soldiers the blessing of Rhan, and a promise of victory over the 'land of the witches'". He paused, his sombre eyes belying his casual words.

Weslan stared, incredulous. "Already? Does Dirken know about this?" Heyg had said they needed more time.

"Of course he knows," Hengren answered, as if Weslan had said something stupid. "And I am sure he is doing something about it, just as fast as he can. Am I not correct?" His eyes were hard and searching above his smile.

Weslan realized that Hengren must have assumed that he had been sent by Dirken personally. Only a mission of the greatest danger and delicacy would take its bearer into the women's quarters at the palace of the Jinta.

"I meant," he amended, "I wondered if Dirken knew that today was rumoured to be the last day of trading."

"As I said," Hengren answered, a cool note in his voice, "they have been predicting it for an annaspan now. In any event, we will soon know, will we not? After I unload the fish, I will send you directly to the palace, into the care of someone who knows everything that goes on in this country." Hengren said no more, but Weslan could sense the fisherman watching him covertly from that moment on.

If only Hengren was a woman, Weslan thought ruefully.

Women's suspicions were easy to allay. Men were harder to pacify.

But there was no more time to worry, for they were docking in the strait of Mira. The pier was thronged with people, much like a market day at Stern, and indeed it was like a marketplace, only with fish as its main ware. Great wooden bins full of fish were everywhere, lining the quay; and bright orange shellfish that Weslan had never seen before, and horrible things with tentacles that still squirmed. The stench rolled over them as they docked. He pulled his hood over his face, as much to block the smell as to hide his features.

"Out with you—and be careful where you cast your eyes." Hengren said, his voice terse.

When Weslan glanced at him, Hengren's smile was as affable as ever, and Weslan realized he wore it like a mask. He stepped shakily down to the pier, cursing as he lost his footing, and almost plunged into the water. Someone laughed, but he did not dare look up.

After a moment, Weslan heard Hengren's voice beside him on the dock. "Come, I will walk you to the highway. It leads directly up from here."

They walked along in silence for several minutes. Weslan was careful to avoid gazing around him, but whenever he looked up, he saw soldiers. They seemed to be everywhere, strolling in groups of two or three or ten.

They had reached a wide thoroughfare and Hengren stopped, drawing Weslan to the side of the road, in the shelter of a large tree, with long, flat leaves, the like of which Weslan had never seen before.

Hengren took his arm, speaking in a low voice. "This is where I leave you, young master. I have business to attend to, and I can do no more for you. Now listen, for I will tell you this only once. When you reach the palace, tell the Jinta's steward, who directs all traffic, that you have come to see Faleesh. If he presses for more, tell him you have come from Meed, from the shop of the famous gem-setter Gilboa, about an ebony powder box inlaid with carbuncles for one of the ladies. He will not ask you for papers to prove this. He is far too busy. That is Faleesh's job."

"What shall I do if Faleesh asks me for papers?" Weslan asked.

His apprehension was growing at the thought of being left in this strange city. *The city of the enemy.* The place that had scarred Reika, casually, the way one branded a pony.

He took a deep breath, reminding himself that he was anonymous, safe, as long as he did nothing to draw attention to himself. But there were so many soldiers, with their curved, gleaming swords and pointed boots, wearing the green and gold colours of Berlot. Weslan had a sudden flash of memory: the Berlotan raid in the pitaya orchard; his first fight, the slash that had come out of nowhere on his sword arm, and the Berlotan who had stood over him, grinning, upraised sword glinting in the summer sun.

Hengren was again looking at him as if he had said something ridiculous. "Faleesh is with us, of course," he said irritably. "When you are brought to him, say 'The Mantling approaches' before you say anything else. And now fare you well, and may the Goddess be with you," Hengren finished, looking over his shoulder as he spoke.

Weslan gazed nervously about him as well. Anna's name was not invoked in Berlot unless it was in hatred. He turned back to thank Hengren, but the bearded fisherman had already disappeared.

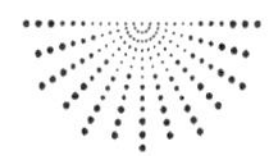

CHAPTER 41

Weslan's journey to the royal palace turned out to be uneventful and not too uncomfortable. He jolted along beside several cheerful, dirty children in the oxcart of a tinker. The tinker and his family spoke nothing but Berlotan, and for the first time Weslan was glad that Heyg had insisted that every man in his company speak that language. The small mob seemed friendly enough after he had jingled some coins about in his hand; and they were going to Hacinta-Car that very morning.

The tinker set him down a stone's throw from the palace gate. As the oxcart jolted off, Weslan had an absurd urge to shout, chase after the cart, and beg to accompany them wherever they were going. The life of a tinker might be enjoyable. Anywhere would be more enjoyable than where he was going.

The enormous palace doors loomed forbiddingly, all dark wood and beaten brass, which dazzled the eyes. As Weslan approached, he saw a long queue of tradesmen and beggars, and realized he must take his place at the end of the line. He had bought some bread, dates, and goat's milk hours earlier, but had not thought to buy anything extra.

Within an hour, Weslan was irritable and impatient; astonished that the merchants resigned themselves to waiting in the scorching sun for so long, chattering away to each other as they stood in their absurd slippers with upturned toes. He tapped his own heavy leather boot restlessly on the dusty ground, wishing for a flagon of foamy ale.

The afternoon wore on, and Weslan surmised that at least one watch had elapsed. His fear dissipated in a pool of misery wherein swam hunger, thirst and fatigue. When he stood before the steward's booth at last, his mouth was so dry he could barely speak.

"What did you say?" the steward snapped back at him. "Speak up, southerner."

Weslan forced himself to stand straight. "I come from the gem-setter in Meed," he said, "about an ebony box for one lady. She was in a great hurry for it."

"Who?" the steward asked.

"Who?" Weslan repeated, dazed.

"Yes, to whom were you directed? Tilaan or Faleesh? They both make purchases for the ladies."

"Faleesh," Weslan answered.

A great relief washed over him as the steward waved him toward the women's quarters. *I have done it!* he thought. His hunger and thirst left him in a wave of exhilaration. He was within the palace grounds in Hacinta-Car. They were beautiful, reminding him, ironically, of the queen's own gardens in Rhantor.

The path he trod was pebbled with shimmering stones of pink, yellow and blue, inlaid within some kind of mortar. All around him were groves of huge, rough-barked trees, with extravagant emerald leaves fanning out. Weslan had seen none like them, and he stared upward, fascinated.

There were marble fountains everywhere, sculpted into a myriad of human and animal shapes. He stopped at one of them, thirst overcoming his desire to reach Darielle before his good fortune evaporated. It was frog-shaped, water spurting from its stone tongue. Avid, he gulped, until he heard a giggle behind him.

"Thirsty, soldier?"

Weslan spun around. A serving girl stood, looking at him with amusement, a basket of fruit balanced against her hip.

"Why do you call me soldier?" he asked, fear making his voice sharper than he would have liked.

The girl laughed, unperturbed. She had skin the colour of the amber southern earth and flashing white teeth. "You drink like a soldier," she answered in a bantering tone.

"What do you mean?" *How in Rhan's name have I given myself away?* he wondered.

"With your hand on your sword hilt-in case anyone sneaks up from behind. I know, for I am almost-betrothed to a soldier," she added.

Perhaps he was not meant for subterfuge. Weslan shook his head and wiped his mouth, considering before he replied. It would be unwise to antagonize this girl, for she might ask why his sword was under his tunic instead of above it, and why he did not wear the uniform of Berlot.

"Lucky soldier," he said, looking her in the eyes and grinning as she blushed. Some kinds of subterfuge he understood very well.

"You are a south Ravener," she said, her voice certain. Weslan nodded, thanking Rhan for Hengren's brilliant disguise. "So am I! Taia is my name. What is yours? And where are you going?"

"Hengren is my name," he answered without thinking. And then, "I am going to the women's quarters."

At the look of bafflement on Taia's face, Weslan added, "I am a soldier when required, but otherwise I am a gem-setter's son from Meed, running errands for my father. "

"Well, there will not be much time for errands after today, I'll wager," Taia said, "when we invade the North three days hence."

Weslan stared at her. His gaze must have burned with an intensity which Taia mistook, for she dropped her eyes, blushing again.

"Come with me, for I am going to the women's quarters—the Jinta's Littlest Flower craves pomegranates today." She turned, broad hips swaying, and continued down the path that wound around the west tower of the palace.

The women's quarters were separated from the rest of the palace, joined only by a narrow, tunnel-like corridor they entered by a small side-door. This ended in a small anteroom, in which there was only one piece of furniture: a large sofa, on which reclined a person of such large proportions that he could barely glimpse the couch for the flesh that overflowed upon it.

Weslan squinted, unaccustomed to the gloom after standing for hours in the sun. It was hard to know whether the reclining personage was a man or a woman, but whoever it was must be important, for Taia was inclining her head and nudging him to do the same.

"And who have you brought with you, Taia, you little slut?" The voice was high, but somehow still sounded more like a man than a woman.

It was a eunuch, Weslan realized in a flash of clarity. He had heard of such creatures. The Berlotans seemed to have no end of ingenious ways in which to subjugate their slaves.

"No one of any consequence, Faleesh," Taia replied. "Only the gem-setter from Meed."

"I saw the gem-setter from Meed not an hour ago," the person called Faleesh said, a silky, dangerous note creeping into his voice.

"The Mantling approaches," Weslan murmured, leaning forward so that Taia could not catch the words, "But I am the new gem-setter!" he exclaimed, "the good one."

"You are audacious," Faleesh answered. "I like that."

The eunuch stretched out a hand and plucked a bunch of grapes from the basket of fruit. His fingers moved with a deceptive quickness in one so corpulent, and Weslan blinked, startled.

Faleesh smiled. "Taia, my pet, you may go in." He waved a plump, be-ringed hand, and Taia stepped forward, casting a glance over her shoulder at Weslan. He risked a small smile.

"Speak fast and get to the point," Faleesh said as soon as they were alone. His voice was urgent. "Tiresome people are always drifting in and out of here. If I dislike what I hear, your life will be forfeit."

"I am Kalesh," Weslan said, folding his arms together, for his hands shook. "I am here for the queen." He said nothing more.

A strange look passed over Faleesh's features, fading away before Weslan could fathom what it was. "You know, of course," he said, "that war is imminent between our two countries."

Weslan nodded. His face had dripped with sweat, although it was much cooler inside than it had been outside. He wished more than anything that he could wipe it off, but he stood still, for Faleesh was looking at him very hard.

"I will not pretend to understand the maze-like turnings of Dirken's brilliant mind," Faleesh said. "You may go in. Darielle's apartment is the first one on your left. Rap three times and her attendant will admit you."

Weslan nodded again and made as if to go past the sofa. Faleesh lifted a hand, almost languidly, and Weslan stopped where he stood.

"Grant me a small favour," Faleesh said, "for I was born in the North. Yes, you may lift your brows in astonishment, but it is true." He was silent for a moment, swallowing convulsively. When he spoke again, his voice trembled with intensity. "When next you make the Kalesh salute, finish by saying 'for the North,' not 'for the queen.' You may understand what I mean before the day is out."

"Certainly," Weslan replied, although he could not fathom the meaning of the eunuch's words. Jealousy, perhaps?

He moved past Faleesh, his eyes searching for the apartment of Queen Darielle.

WESLAN RAPPED three times on the door of the first apartment on his left. The ensuing few seconds were without a doubt the longest he had ever waited for anything in his life.

At last, the door opened and a Berlotan woman stood before him. She was heavily painted and dressed in a brilliant robe of rose and green hues. Notwithstanding, she appeared weathered and sharper than his sword. Her dark eyes regarded him with suspicion.

"I am here with Faleesh's permission," Weslan said, his voice stiffening with apprehension and dislike. "And I bear a message for the Lady Darielle." He shuddered, for he had almost said "queen."

The woman stood gazing at him for so long that Weslan gestured behind him. "Go ask him if you don't believe me, only pray do not waste my time!"

The woman stood back from the doorway only just enough to admit him. Weslan counted her as an enemy to be reckoned with on their way out of the Jinta's palace.

Taia had already been there, for the first thing he saw was the basket of fruit sitting on a low, carved table at the far end of the chamber into which he stepped. It was large and airy, opening onto a large balcony, from which a lilting voice came.

"What is it? More fruit? But I will grow fat, as he well knows."

The laughing voice belonged to Darielle, and it seemed to Weslan that no time at all had passed since he had last seen her. Her courage amid captivity made him ache for her. But then she had laughed at danger before.

The night the assassin had lain dead at her feet, Darielle had looked at Saura, saying, "My Name Day is not for another annaspan, yet my brother sends a gift so soon!" She had smiled, but her lips had been white.

Darielle's companion said nothing, but darted rapidly to the balcony. She was evidently mute, for she gestured with silent, eloquent hands to her mistress, whom Weslan still could not see. He strode forward. Just at that moment, Darielle came into view. She stood in the balcony's doorway, looking quizzically at him.

She does not recognize me, he thought, relieved and pained. Hengren had done his work well. Weslan reached her in three strides and bent low, touching his forehead with his palm, whispering, "My queen."

When he looked up, he saw recognition leaping into her eyes. She leaned against the wooden arch of the doorway, one graceful hand coming up to cover her face. But it took only a second for her to regain her composure. She murmured something to her maid, who made a gesture of protest. *"Leave us,"* Darielle repeated.

Her spine rigid with opposition, the woman turned and left.

Weslan gazed at Darielle, thinking that although her voice had remained unchanged, her face had not. They had lined her eyes with charcoal, giving her a feline aspect that made her look less than innocent.

Perhaps he was only imagining it. But her lips, which were a true, pale pink he had always loved, were stained a bright carmine; and her hair, which she had most often worn braided or flowing, was elaborately twisted and coiled about her head.

She was still exquisite, but Weslan's shoulders sagged, and a mist covered his eyes. He smiled, trying to dispel the sadness.

He told himself this was nothing, only Berlotan cosmetics. She had not changed.

"Why do you look at me like that?" Darielle asked him, sounding petulant. She took a step back.

"I am sorry," Weslan mumbled, feeling awkward. Moments like these were so seldom as he imagined them. He ran his hands through his hair and then dropped them to his sides. Nausea gripped him.

"Am I so different as all that?" Darielle asked, smiling a cool, brief smile. "Your eyes look as if they beheld a Wraith."

"No. It is just that I cannot believe that I am here," he blurted. "It is a stroke of fortune, finding you so fast. Rhan and Anna must both favour us today."

"Do not mention Anna's name," Darielle said, and a frown creased her smooth forehead. "My lord forbids it."

A seed of fear sprouted within Weslan. "Of course," he answered slowly, "One must be careful of what one says, here."

"That brings me to the question which I should have asked you at once, only I felt confused for a moment. What are you doing here, Weslan?"

His pulse quickening with mingled fear and elation, he whispered, "To take you back, of course. To Miraven."

Darielle's eyes widened, and she moved over to a divan, sinking down upon it, taking a melon from the basket and regarding it with fascination, as though she had never seen one before. Weslan moved over to her and sank down on his knees, taking the melon from her hands.

"I heard you pined for the fruit of the North," he whispered.

Darielle's eyes were downcast, and she would not look at him until he put a finger under her chin. Even then, he could not read the expression beneath the painted lids.

"I miss the fruit, from time to time," she said, shrugging. "But not enough to go get it myself."

Before he thought of what he was doing, Weslan had grabbed her by the shoulders, shaking her. "I risked my life to come here," he said, speaking through clenched teeth to stop himself from shouting.

"Stop it," said Darielle, "or I shall scream, and your head will roll in the square below for the Berlotan urchins to kick about in sport."

Weslan stopped. His arms dropped to his sides, and his chest heaved.

"Do not look at me in that insolent fashion!" she commanded haughtily.

She rose from the couch and straightened her disarranged gown, which seemed to be little more than brightly coloured gauzy strips of cloth held together by a jewelled pin the size of a goose egg. She walked across the room and then spun around to face him.

"You risked *your* life!" she snapped. "What about me? Taken from my palace, where I thought I was safe, guarded by the invincible soldiers of the North, the Kalesh!" Her voice lingered on the last word with contempt. "Yet they scooped me up and carried away with greater ease than a sack of pitayas. The moment the Jinta lifted his finger, there was nothing all the pitiful men of the North, or the South, could do. That is power, Weslan."

"And this is what you want?" he asked. "Power?"

"Not power, so much." A dreamy, yearning note crept into her voice. "Though it holds a great deal of enticement, of course. No, it is safety that I desire above all else, and I have not known it since the death of my beloved father. I am the daughter of a king, and I do not deserve to be hunted down like a—"

"Like an Anniste?" Weslan finished, his voice dark.

"The Anniste are doomed, for the sorcerers have decreed it,

and who can hold sway against them?" Darielle said. She waved a dismissive hand. "They are no concern of mine. I do my lord's bidding, and in return I am cared for, adored, protected. Berlot has the strongest monarch. And the strongest sorcerer."

"Do not be so sure you are any safer here," Weslan told her. Reika's face rose before him, as it so often did; his fingertips twitched with the memory of her scars. "Women are not so revered in Berlot as it may seem."

Darielle's lip curled. "You may know a lowborn wench or two who was beaten, but it is different for those with royal blood."

"Do not be so sure," Weslan repeated, bitter laughter rising in his throat. "Your fealty is with Berlot, then?" Although he knew the answer, his throat tightened with the effort it took to utter the words.

"My fealty is with my lord, the Jinta of Berlot." Darielle replied.

Weslan turned, knowing he must go before he struck her. A red rage had descended, blinding him. He struggled to find the door. At last, he saw it; at that moment it opened, and the mute attendant of the queen entered. His face must have looked strange, for the woman started and drew back when she saw him, covering her face as if to ward off a blow. He grinned, baring his teeth just to see her flinch.

Before he sprinted from the room, Weslan turned once more, and saw Darielle's face hovering, sun lighting it from behind on the balcony, glowing like some exotic, poisonous flower. *Why is she so beautiful, even now?*

"I once saved your life—does it mean nothing to you?" he asked from the doorway. She stared back at him, saying nothing. "I loved you," he added, for that was what he really meant.

"Yes," Darielle answered, "both things mean something to me. For that reason, I have not notified my guards that there is anything amiss."

She turned her back on him, returning to the basket on the table. She began to rearrange the glistening pieces of fruit, one by one, and did not look up again.

LEAVING THE PALACE, Weslan knew he should be more frightened—and thinking of what to do next, for he must escape from Berlot with the greatest of speed. Dirken needed to be warned of the impending invasion. Also, Weslan did not altogether believe Darielle's assurance that she had not alerted the guards.

"My fealty is with the Jinta," she had said.

Yet his fury and grief were of such magnitude that he could not think rationally as he had promised himself to do. He kicked rocks viciously as he walked back through the gardens.

Stop it, he told himself. *What would Reika say?*

She would say, "Think, Weslan! There is a time to be guided by your heart, and a time to be guided by your head. Learn to distinguish between those times."

Weslan knew he must flee. He also knew that his guise as a trader was not plausible if war was being declared in three days. The river would be closed off to trade—it might already have happened. He needed another disguise. Weslan could not resist kicking another particularly large rock. At that moment, he happened upon a Berlotan soldier, a palace guard by the looks of it, coming out from behind a large, flowering shrub where he had been relieving himself.

He grinned at Weslan, buttoning his breeches as he approached. He seemed a nice enough fellow, Weslan thought, bending down to pick up the rock. It was a shame to dash the stone against the back of his head, but he did it anyway, lunging forward first to capture the soldier in a headlock. The man grunted with the impact and then slid in silence toward the ground.

Weslan caught him, ignoring the queasy feeling in his stomach, and dragged him back into the shrubbery. Working swiftly, Weslan stripped the soldier of his uniform. There was a leather purse with some money, which Weslan left beside the fellow. He took the sword though; a curved scimitar, shorter than his own, and a small dagger. Weslan felt a pang of regret looking down at the other man. He did not enjoy this sort of thing.

Trying to look purposeful, Weslan strode along the pebbled path until he reached the palace gates. The black wrought iron doors were open, and the steward seemed caught up in some complicated transaction with a plump merchant. He shouted something as Weslan went past, but his voice did not sound threatening, so Weslan waved back and kept going. A minute later, he realized he was shaking, and the hairs along his neck prickled for some time in anticipation of pursuit.

It was still mid-afternoon. Weslan stared about him, somewhat dazed. It seemed as if he had been inside the palace for hours and hours. He was lightheaded, queasy, which made it difficult to think about what to do next.

Reika's face rose before him again, almost as real as if she had been there. As it faded away, he realized he must eat before he did anything else. Passing a market stall, he stopped to purchase some flatbread and fish, drizzled with a tangy sauce. It seemed delicious after the first bite, and before he was finished, he was back at the stall, purchasing another. He chewed slower this time, looking around him, trying to decide what to do next.

He would head back down to the quay. Soldiers would be leaving, going to Liandon; that was the logical base for the invasion; a quick upward thrust through the mountain pass.

Weslan felt panic rise within him. Dirken did not know. That he had not rescued Darielle now seemed almost trivial in comparison with the news he carried. But would the warning do any good? Probably not. Even if he got out by river and was on Miraven soil by sundown, riding his heart out, he could not reach Stern before three more sunsets had passed. By then, the Berlotan army would already be in the South, headquartered in Liandon, making ready their battering ram of men and horses to hurl across the Taboran Mountains.

"Back!" a harsh voice bellowed in the Berlotan tongue.

In the next moment, Weslan was thinking how it was fortunate that he understood Berlotan, for he had only a second to leap out of the way before a procession of horsemen swept forward at a smart clip. Six criers went before them, so there must be important personages to follow. Extremely important, he corrected himself, dropping into the hot dust as everyone around him was doing.

"Jinta!" he heard in a droning murmur that sounded composed of every voice on the crowded street. And then, quieter, a sigh. "Zant!"

Lying like a dung beetle with his hands outstretched and his knees tucked up under him, Weslan still craned his head to one side for a look. It was a sight he did not wish to miss.

And there they came, proud-visaged soldiers surrounding them in front, flanking their sides, and carrying their rear: the Jinta of Berlot, dressed in brilliant peacock blue and gold, gem-studded circlet on his forehead, from which floated a blue and white headdress to protect his royal neck from Rhan's heat. He rode himself, as Weslan had heard, but beside him Zant sat in a litter, muffled to his neck and covered with lap robes as though it were cold.

He caught only a glimpse before they vanished from view, But the image of their faces stayed with Weslan, vividly etched. Both bore some strange connection to him, having changed his destiny.

Haertal, the Jinta, had supplanted him in Darielle's eyes. Weslan ground his teeth. What had *he* to offer her, besides the illusory safety of power? His face, though plump, was thin-lipped and cruel, and his paunch had protruded over the pommel of his saddle.

The sorcerer Zant was the greatest enemy the North had ever seen, if the Anniste were to be believed. The glimpse of Zant had chilled Weslan, though he did not know if it was simply because he knew who Zant was. At the end, he had been frightened of Braith as well. But there was something different about Zant. He was older, thin and pale as a day-old corpse, and seemed cold, utterly passionless.

All around him, the citizens of Hacinta-Car were rising from their obeisance on the ground, stretching and yawning as though it were a new day. But a hideous sense of danger gripped Weslan.

He would never get out of Berlot alive.

"Hello." The voice behind him was familiar. It was Taia, looking very pleased with herself.

"Taia." Weslan smiled back, hand on his dagger, looking around to see if this was a trap.

"I am just going home," she told him. "Where are you off to?"

"Do you not live at the palace?"

"I am a servant, not a slave," she said, looking aggrieved as she pulled up her sleeve to show him her unmarked wrist. "Every evening, I meet my father at market. He is an eel peddler. Then we travel home together."

"Ah." Weslan added, "I am looking for a ride back down to the quay. Are you going my way?"

"Yes, I live down by the water. It will be very crowded right now, with soldiers leaving for Liandon. Isn't it exciting? How I should love to be there for the invasion. I wish I was a man! It will be glorious, a supreme victory for Berlot, and we will all be rich as lords. A parcel of northern land will be given to every loyal soldier, I have heard."

"No doubt." Weslan turned away so she would not see his anger.

"Ah, there is Papa!" Taia exclaimed. "You can ride back with us, of course." She squeezed his arm. "Papa will be honoured."

A surge of unexpected hope shot through Weslan. *I am saved,* he thought.

CHAPTER 42

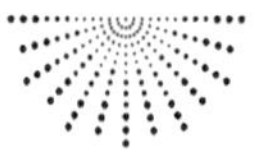

The eel peddler's cart was heaped up with empty, smelly white sacks. Weslan hated the odour of anything from the sea, but a ride was a ride.

"It has been a profitable day!" the peddler gloated, clapping Weslan expansively on the back. He could not conceal his elation that a soldier was travelling with him. He also seemed eager for Weslan and his daughter to become better acquainted. Perhaps he did not approve of her almost betrothed.

"Go sit in the back," he winked. "You are young, you need to talk—enjoy each other's company!" Taia blushed and scowled at him, but he ignored her, repeating, "Go on, settle in—it's more comfortable than this wooden seat that scrapes your rump raw."

"Papa, you are so coarse!" Taia shrieked, hoisting up her skirt and pulling Weslan along with her.

She settled herself on the pile of sacks, moving very close to him and laying her head back to look at the sky. Weslan sat tensely beside her, hoping it was not far to the river. Until that moment, he had focused solely on his sacred task of rescuing the queen. He shook off the galling images that assailed him. They had to be close.

After jolting on for about an hour, the air cooled, and Rhan hung low on the horizon. Purple and golden wisps formed a royal cloak in the darkening sky—night was closing in. How he wanted to be home.

"I can see Anna," Taia said dreamily, nestling her head on his shoulder.

Weslan squinted up into the sky.

"No, there." She pointed. "Look—right near Rhan."

It was as she said. Barely discernible, like a white shadow of a cloud, was Anna. The moon was nearly full.

"Do you think the stories are true?" she asked him.

"What stories?"

"The Mantling, lumpkin. What else? Rhan and Anna joining. Has it ever happened? Will it ever happen? It would be lovely to see it, do you not think? A god and a goddess, coming together for the entire world to witness! Passion such as we mortals can only imagine." Her hand was creeping up his thigh.

"I do not believe the stories," Weslan said, shifting his legs. Reika had believed them, though. "What does your betrothed think?" he asked pointedly, and Taia removed her hand.

"Ah, the river!" the peddler murmured, like a prayer.

Craning his neck to the front of the cart, Weslan glimpsed the silver glitter of the River Meed through a copse of trees. A moment later, the cart rounded a bend in the dusty brown road, obscuring it from view. They were almost at the border.

He peered intently, trying to catch another view of the water. With a sickening jolt in his stomach, he saw a company of horsemen tearing along the road toward them.

Soldiers!

Darielle had betrayed him after all. Weslan's initial terror crystallized into a sort of mad exhilaration, as it always did in moments of genuine danger. He seized Taia by the wrist and, still holding it, dove under the pile of sacks, burying himself from view.

As Taia squealed in dismay, he drew the jewelled dagger from its sheath, held it out so that she could see it, and then let it rest against her ribs, just below her heart.

"I am not here," Weslan whispered. "Not a word to the soldiers!"

Taia nodded, her dark eyes rolling back in her head, and her long teeth biting her lip. She looked like a frightened hare.

"Tell your father," he said through gritted teeth. When she hesitated, he allowed the point of the dagger to prick her with a light touch.

Weslan waited until Taia had made her father understand, which took a precious moment or two. Then he submerged himself beneath the sacks, pulling Taia back so that she was sitting on top of him, with the point of the dagger against her lower back.

He could hear her panting with terror. *Poor girl*, he thought. She had been kind to him, much kinder than anyone else in this stinking country.

But it was not the time for regrets or musings of any sort. The galloping of steeds and shouts of soldiers came steadily nearer.

"Ho, there!" a voice commanded. "Halt!"

Weslan could hear the peddler speaking to his mule. The cart slowed and then stopped. The eel sacks muffled the peddler's tremulous voice even more.

"How may I help you, good sirs?"

Oh Rhan! Weslan thought. He hoped the peddler would not lose his nerve and start babbling. And that Taia's frightened face would not give her away.

"We are looking for someone," the soldier answered. "A northern spy, who has just attempted to abduct the Jinta's Flower."

Taia gasped, and her father exclaimed, "Rhan save us from the night!"

"He will attempt to flee back to his country by the only way north—the river. He has disguised himself as a southern tradesperson."

"Then how will we tell if we meet this villain, may I humbly beg to inquire? For these tradespeople are as numerous as fleas on a donkey!" He said this with forced jocularity, throwing his arms out to show the confusion created by forces beyond one's control.

"Simple enough: his eyes are blue." the soldier snapped back. "As blue as the sky above, and there is no disguising that in these parts. Have you seen him?"

There was a silence that seemed much too long to Weslan. He was just fearing that the peddler or his daughter had pointed him out—that he would have to leap out of the cart and run for it—when he heard Taia's voice say, "No, we have not seen such a pale-eyed devil, and Rhan protect us from one such as he."

"No, indeed we have not," her father chimed in fervently. "But if we do, we will report him at once. The scoundrel. The rogue. How dare he?"

"Do not worry, old man," another voice broke in. "We will soon crush him, and all his countrymen—like the roaches they are." There was laughter.

"Besides," added the first voice, "he hasn't a chance. The army is closing off the river tonight. We were about to do it anyway, so the timing is perfect. He will fall into our hands like a ripe pitaya."

"Soon all the ripe pitayas will fall into our hands," said the second voice, an obvious buffoon.

There was more laughter, in which Weslan could hear the nervous titter of the eel peddler.

"We are off then," barked the officer. "Remember—*blue eyes.*"

"I will remember," the peddler shouted after the flurry of departing hooves.

A moment later, Weslan withdrew the point of the dagger, re-sheathing it, and Taia burst into tears.

~

IT WAS NIGHT. The darkness was kind, for in its protective blanket all eyes were the same colour. Weslan stood in the shadows of the quay, behind a wooden shed that was transformed into a temporary barracks for the soldiers who were patrolling the river. He watched, waiting for his chance.

He had been hiding for hours, and Anna was high in the sky. Looking up at the glowing orb, Weslan resisted the urge to pray. Men did not pray to Anna, only old codgers and boys—and women, of course.

Is Mother up there somewhere with the Goddess, watching over me? he wondered.

His chance came at the changing of the watch. Dawn was approaching, and the guards were at their sleepiest and most befuddled. Weslan saw a soldier exchanging float vests with another in the barracks. The first soldier flopped down at once on one of the straw pallets lined up within a row in the shed. The second soldier went off at a trot toward the pier, fumbling as he tried to tie his vest. It slipped off his shoulders to the ground; running back for it, he encountered Weslan.

A moment later, the vest secured at his waist, Weslan set off for the pier, which was illuminated by wavering torches that looked like giant panicked fireflies milling about in the night. When he got closer, he saw why they moved about so much: Berlotan slaves carried them as they performed their myriad of tasks on the riverfront.

Reaching the pier, Weslan could see the patrol vessel they expected him to board, for two other boats were pulling away, and only one still waited. A figure standing up in the boat waved him over with an impatient hand. Weslan clambered down and felt himself steadied by outstretched arms.

Three other soldiers set themselves to rowing. The fellow who had gestured at him glared, and Weslan realized he must be the captain, and unhappy with the delay. He sat down in the remaining space and picked up the oars, thanking Rhan that he had learned to row in Liandon when he had been here with Heyg's company, although he had never liked it much. He kept his head down, and when one of the other men spoke to him, he grunted in reply.

In the dark, it was impossible to gauge where they were, but listening to the conversation, Weslan learned they would go the farthest of the patrol boats—almost to Liandon. What luck! Where he would part company with the boat, and how far he would have to swim in the black water before he reached land, was another matter.

After an hour, Weslan remembered why he had developed an aversion to rowing. His shoulders ached and his hands were blistering. Soon it seemed he had always been here, pulling the oars with endless monotony, hearing their squeak as they rubbed against the oarlocks, and the slap as they hit the water.

There was nothing to look at but the silver-white of Anna on the black water. The sight was pretty enough, but Weslan wished for a heavy cloak of clouds to descend as camouflage. The men had been speaking of a blue-eyed northern fugitive, and with every remark they made, the moonlight seemed to grow brighter.

At last, the captain shouted, "There! Make for that cove."

The soldiers headed north-east, toward a dark, forested mound nestled within the natural curve of the river. *But where are we?* Weslan's heart thudded from more than the vigorous rowing.

"Only two leagues to Liandon," remarked the man beside him, as if reading his mind. "But it might as well be two hundred now. My sweetheart lives there," he added in explanation.

Weslan nodded, grunting.

"It will not be long, they say, until the river is open again. The Northern heathens will be subdued before the first pitayas ripen. Do you reckon that is true?"

"Of course it is true," growled the captain from behind them, his voice harsh with fatigue.

They were in shallow water now, less than a stone's throw from the muddy beach. The captain threw the mooring rope at Weslan, who stood stunned for a moment. Then, as the captain pointed toward shore, holding up a lantern, he realized he was expected to jump in the water and pull the boat in. This good fortune astonished him. By Rhan, he could not have planned it better himself.

At that moment, there was a sharp exclamation from the man with the sweetheart in Liandon. "By the Sun God's chariot, you are not Berlotan!"

Everyone in the boat turned to stare at Weslan in the lantern's light. "Look at him!" the man shouted, "His eyes are blue! He is the Northern fugitive!"

He leaped to his feet, staggering to regain his balance, and seized Weslan's shoulder. With his free arm, Weslan struck the man a short, furious blow to the face, felling him. He sank to the bottom of the boat, and it rocked violently at the impact.

The other men lunged at Weslan from all directions. He used his elbows and feet to keep them at bay. One he knocked down at once, head striking a tackle box, and another he sent toppling over the edge of the boat.

Then, because there was nothing else to do, he turned and plunged into the river.

❧

Heaving himself gasping onto the shore many minutes later, Weslan could see torch flames reflected on the water, and hear the excited shouting back and forth between the patrol boats as they searched for him.

He discarded his sodden clothing as he ran, his breath rasping in his ears. His bare feet slipped on smooth stones and were bruised and cut on sharp ones. He had kicked his boots off in the water at once, and his sword had gone next. As it was, he had barely made it.

Weslan had braved the river often in its tributaries between Stern and Liandon, ever since he was a boy. And the water was much faster and rougher there than here at its headwaters, with enough merciless currents and rapids to satisfy the violent whims of any demon or sorcerer. But although the water was calm, it was a difficult thing—to be forced to swim suddenly, for one's life, in the dark, weighed down with one's clothes and boots and sword, and arrows coming down, thick as rain.

Fortunately, he was a powerful swimmer. And he had the whiplash of Darielle's rejection to spur him on.

Weslan kept running. He almost sobbed with relief when he saw the lights of Liandon across the channel. It was only half a league to the small wooden bridge he had crossed with Hengren. The bridge was visible in the distance. It was within his reach.

He needed to stop for a moment, though. *Just a moment.* Weslan squatted down, panting, his muscles cramping from the shock and the cold.

Perhaps he could not do it.

Then he thought of Darielle's scornful face, her voice saying, *I do not miss the fruit enough to return for it myself.* And he started running again.

When Weslan reached the bridge, it occurred to him that there might be soldiers waiting for him. But he had no choice. He trotted across, and then westward, threading down through the lane at the back of the fishing huts, until he came to Hengren's. He knocked on the door. When there was no answer, he pounded on it, trying to control the ragged gasps that shook him.

Hengren's voice came from within, rumbling like boulders falling from a mountainside. "Rhan's balls, I'll flay you, whoever you are!"

The door was flung open, and Hengren stood there, wearing a flung-on cape to hide his nakedness. He stared at Weslan owlishly for a second or two and then burst out laughing. "The dye has come off in some spots, but not in others," he chortled. "What, are you back for a touch-up session?"

Weslan gazed back at him with something akin to hatred. "A horse," he choked out, fists clenched.

Hengren clapped him on the back, pulling him inside. "Yes, yes," he replied, his voice soothing, though he still chuckled. "Dry yourself off, and we will get you fixed up at once."

RIDING into Stern soon after dark, three days later, Weslan knew he had reached the end of his store of strength. He'd lived on fear and anger, stale bread and dried fish, which Hengren had packed him in a leather satchel. He had sworn not to eat fish again for the rest of his life. He needed sleep, above all.

Weslan almost rode right past the Castle of Mirrand. He had been falling forward in his saddle, daydreaming, and somehow had become confused—thinking he was going home to get Tekoah and Mother and take them away to Rhantor. But seeing the white towers jutting up out of the corner of his eye, something had jerked him from this dream, reminding him why he was there.

Rhantor is gone. Mother is dead. There is only Tekoah. And Weslan did not even know whether his sister was alive or dead. Should he ride to Beula's farm first, to find out whether she was there?

No. Duty to the Kalesh came first. After he had reported to Dirken, then he could think of himself. He turned his horse and started up the winding stone pathway that led to the castle.

As he neared the gate, Weslan saw with mounting astonishment the crowds gathered on the castle grounds. Soldiers were dressed in the indigo tunics of the Kalesh, all intent on some task: making or repairing armour, performing battle drills, hauling food stores through the gates, and slapping stones and mortar together to make the castle walls higher.

And, indeed, they were much higher than when he had seen them last. Had the mysterious lord of Mirrand allowed Dirken to persuade him to use his castle as a military fortress?

Within the castle were many more soldiers, he saw. The battlements were seething, and the gates were heavily guarded by grim-faced men in full battledress. Two of them crossed spears when he tried to pass.

"I must see Dirken," he said.

"No one is allowed inside unless he wears the colours of the Kalesh!"

"I am one of the Kalesh," he replied.

Then he realized how ridiculous he must sound. He wore a straw-coloured tunic of Hengren's, huge on him, and it flapped about his knees; he probably looked like a child. His skin was still amber in patches, and his feet were bare.

"You look more like a mottled Berlotan, or perhaps Berlotan and umbray mixed together," said the other soldier sardonically.

"Dirken will vouch for me," Weslan told him, too weary to respond to the jibe.

"Dirken is not here."

"What?" Weslan stared, incredulous. "But he was supposed to be here by this morning! I have urgent news for him!"

"So you say."

"Well then, where is Heyg? Second in command of the Kalesh. He must be here! Give him my name—Weslan. He will answer for me."

One of the guards prodded the other with his spear and, looking reluctant, the fellow set off, presumably to fetch Heyg.

The remaining guard regarded him suspiciously, spear point levelled at his chest, as if he preferred to settle the matter differently. And perhaps he would decide to drive the spear home and make up some pretext or another after the fact. Weslan had nothing but a dagger with which to defend himself—and a Berlotan dagger at that. Very incriminating. Sweat trickled down his temples as he held the guard's gaze.

Heyg had better be here.

And—Anna be praised for all eternity—there was Heyg's gruff bellow. "Weslan! At last, lad."

His voice sounded like cintar music to Weslan's ears. He grinned as his captain came striding toward him.

"You have returned, alive!" Heyg shouted, sounding angry. But Weslan saw the tears standing in his eyes, and his own eyes blurred.

"And you have not brought the queen?" Heyg looked saddened but unsurprised. "But you do bring news."

"Yes," Weslan replied slowly, through his dry, cracked lips. He made the salute, one hand to the heart: "For the Kalesh!"

Like an echo in his mind, he heard again the request made to him by Faleesh the eunuch, in the Jinta's palace. Now he understood the bitterness behind it.

"For the North!"

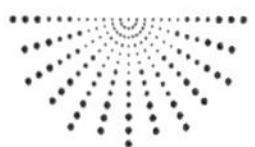

CHAPTER 43

BOOK 5: THE MANTLING

*E*xcerpt from the Anniste Scrolls, The Revelations of Mirveta, founder of the Anniste Healers:

Of all the divine miracles which privileged mortals have observed, the most sacred and full of wonder is the Mantling.

The actual witnessing thereof is so terrible—and so beautiful—as to be beyond our poor capacity for description. Not only has it always been a portent of vast and inconceivable alterations to the hierarchy of our world, but such is the power of the Mantling, that no one who sees it can remain unchanged. Anna has spoken of it to her servants thus: those whose souls are pure will find themselves changed for the better, but those whose souls are something tainted will find only excruciation and death.

There are dissenters, of course, who assert that the Mantling is not a joining of Rhan and Anna at all, but a horror, a desecration, because for a short time Anna's face covers Rhan's, blotting it out, and the world becomes dark as night, though it be midday. Rhan's priests—who do not serve Rhan, but only themselves—claim that the Mantling is Anna's feeble and futile attempt to overpower and destroy the more powerful deity of the Sun God. But these souls are fearful and ignorant. For enlightened souls, the Mantling is the most glorious vision imaginable.

I speak as one who knows, for I, Mirveta, Guardian of the Anniste in the first turning of the Age of Sorcerers, witnessed the Mantling only yesterday. Afterward, as I lay prostrated in ecstasy, Anna herself deigned to speak to me, and told me this:

"This Mantling has heralded the Age of Sorcerers, which will endure for seventeen hundred turnings. Each century will spawn two sorcerers. Their power will be great, as will be their capacity to do harm. The power of the Anniste to heal will also be great. The balance between Rhan and Anna will always exist in the world, in whatever form it takes. This, the Worldmaker has decreed.

And in the seventeenth hundred turning a third Sorcerer will appear. And a Guardian not of Anniste blood shall guard the Anniste for a time, and there will be a drought, and a war. By these signs you shall know that the Mantling is again at hand, and the Age of Sorcerers is at an end, and a new age about to begin."

Might all this be true? Chalvern pored over his scrolls, pondering.

The predictions had been very accurate, especially considering the woman who made them had been dead for almost seventeen hundred turnings. And the phrase "the Mantling" was on everyone's lips these days, though most of the time as a fashionable oath—"by the Holy Mantling"—and all that rot. It was eerie, though.

But then, it was already an eerie day.

It was the day of the Night of the Dead. By sundown, everyone in Stern would be indoors, shutters fastened, doors bolted, fires in their hearth burning low. All to avoid being visited by Wraiths, the spirits of the dead.

I might as well throw my doors open, Chalvern thought. *I know so many dead.*

Veld had murdered Neela one turning past. Her sister Beula had joined her in the Halls of the Worldmaker last autumn, and three days ago seven more Anniste women had died rather than trust a sorcerer to save them. Were they all joyfully reunited somewhere?

Chalvern felt a tug of desire to join them, to find out for himself. It was an urge that had intensified of late.

He was not being morbid. It was simply an acceptance that it would not be long before he himself departed for the Halls of the Worldmaker. He was a tired old man who had seen too many things, that was all.

Chalvern rolled up the Anniste scroll, tying it carefully with a leather string. Outside, he heard the boisterous yelling of the village lads as they spotted yet another company of Kalesh riding into the village.

It had been going on for the past two days; Stern was wild with excitement. Hundreds upon hundreds of soldiers had galloped in, faces dust-streaked, eyes blazing, to the hilltop Castle of Mirrand.

They had chosen Stern for this glorious marshalling of the forces of the North, and the village was exploding with pride. Adding spice to the excitement was the fact that the villagers would at last lay eyes on the absentee lord of Mirrand.

Notwithstanding, provisioning so many soldiers might prove to be a challenge. Chalvern was judging this by the staggeringly brisk trade in his own shop. Shortage of supplies could become an intolerable strain if Miraven lost the impending war with Berlot. But it had been only two days. Stern had reached a fever pitch of enthusiasm, which was most infectious.

Word had it that the next day, the leader of the Kalesh would arrive to call a council of war. Chalvern knew this rumour to be true, for Bhantok—still pale and shaken from his discovery of the dead Anniste women—had confirmed it.

Most villagers did not know that the leader of the Kalesh was also Dirken, the handsome court minstrel idolized by village girls throughout the North. But only Bhantok and Chalvern knew for certain that the lord of Mirrand was both these men. To be precise, all three.

Secrets. He carried too many of them. Perhaps that was the

trouble. *Secrets are told to those who have no life of their own.* He had heard that somewhere, or perhaps he had made it up.

Chalvern fought the waves of self-pity that lapped about him. He was morose because it was the Night of the Dead, that was all.

He had closed his shop early, despite all the footsore, bilious, saddle-chafed men who had come clamouring for remedies. He had sent his lazy apprentice up to the castle, bearing packets of herbal remedies and instructions to send for him if there was anything serious. For the rest of the afternoon, he had pored over the Anniste scrolls. Looking for even more secrets. *No, he* admitted to himself. It was just that it made him feel closer to Neela.

There was a rapping on his door. "Go away," Chalvern barked. "The shop is closed!" The rapping continued. Sighing, he rose from his chair.

Reika stood there, her lovely face shadowed by her hood. Chalvern gave an involuntary cry and pulled her inside, shutting the door behind them, and glancing at the windows to make sure they were all shuttered.

More secrets.

"YOU MEAN to say that Weslan is alive? Praise Anna! This is the first good news I have had in many days." Chalvern knew tears were audible in his voice, and he did not care.

Reika nodded back at him, eyes shining. "Not only alive, but as full of fire as ever, only just a little more tempered. The Goddess led him through a dark time to prepare for an arduous task awaiting him, one which requires both thought and action."

"You know the nature of this task, I presume?" Chalvern asked.

Reika's mystical tone was unnerving, although he reflected that his discomfort was a little ridiculous. After all, he had seen a Shifting three days earlier, and watched a man turn into a hawk and fly away.

"No, I do not," Reika answered, adding, "and I am glad of that!"

They sat for a moment in silence. Chalvern watched Reika's face glow as she spoke of Weslan. He resisted the urge to ask her how long they had been together, alone.

Reika smiled radiantly at him, as if reading his thoughts. Then she stood up, tucking her long, plaited hair behind her as she drew on her brown hood. "I thought I would come to you first, with the news," she said. "And now straight on to Bhantok's place to tell Tekoah about her brother—and see the others. It feels as if it has been forever since I left. How fare the women?"

Chalvern stared back at her, comprehension eluding him for a few seconds. Then he realized she did not know. Why had he stupidly assumed she had learned of Tekoah's departure, of the raid by the soldiers and Marta's bizarre death; of the strange and terrible events of three days past?

Why did her all-knowing Goddess not tell her? Chalvern thought savagely. *Why does she leave it to me?*

"In a way it has been forever," he replied, gesturing for Reika to sit.

She gazed at him intently, her cheeks blanching as she saw his eyes.

"Tekoah is not there," he began, rather hesitantly.

Reika was nodding, as though this did not surprise her. "I felt something," she said. "But I was uncertain what it was. Where has she gone?"

"Zantor," he said.

Fear leaped into her eyes at his words. But a moment later, her face was serene once more. "Anna must have told her to go, or she would not have done this," she said with certainty. "But the other women may be very frightened. Have you seen them?"

"I saw them several times," Chalvern answered. "I went as often as I could. But the shop was busy, and the rains came. I could not go as much as I wished." Why did it sound as if he was trying to make excuses? As though he felt guilty.

"Do not reproach yourself," Reika said in her soft, musical voice. She laid a hand lightly on his arm. "It is my task—and Tekoah's—to guard the Anniste. But their safety is in Anna's hands."

"Then Anna has failed," Chalvern said bluntly, needing to stop this, to wipe the smile from Reika's face, to rob her voice of its music.

For it was all a lie, was it not? Who had guarded Neela? And who would save her daughter? Not him. Not Reika. Not a Goddess who led her followers into dark chambers from which there was no escape.

"What do you mean?" Reika asked him.

"I mean, you should not go to Bhantok's farm. There is no one there now."

"What do you mean?" she cried again. "Where are they?"

"Eight are dead," Chalvern said, softening his voice. Regretting his bluntness now that Reika's face was completely drained of colour.

"Morgs," she whispered; and it was not a question.

He nodded. There was no point in going into every detail.

"And the rest?"

This is going to be the troublesome part, Chalvern thought. For he was responsible. He, alone. "The sorcerer Braith came," he said, holding his hand up so she would not interrupt him. "He warned me about the Morgs and told me that the melting snow brought danger because the monsters could more easily scent the Anniste. He said he could save the women, if I told him where they were."

Chalvern faltered, unable to do more than glance at Reika before dropping his eyes. Her mouth looked like a wound in her face.

"And you told him."

"Braith thought Tekoah was with them. That is why he took such an urgent interest, of course. But he was willing to save them even after I told him she was not there."

"You told him," Reika repeated.

"Yes." Chalvern answered, closing his eyes against the sight of her face. "I took him there. He created a Shifting, and they went in. All but a few."

He opened his eyes to see that Reika had turned away from him and was stumbling blindly, as if seeking the door. Then she stopped. With her back to him, she asked, "And those few?"

"Those few were the ones killed by the Morgs," he told her.

It was silent. Through the closed windows, Chalvern sensed darkness stealing in. The Night of the Dead. He should turn the lamps down, turf over the fire. But he just stood there, watching Reika's back as she wept.

"Why did Anna not show me this?" Reika murmured, as if to herself. "Was she trying to summon me, while I wandered the Taboran Woods with Weslan? Did I shut her out, because I was so happy? Yes, I was too happy to care about what happened to the others. And when the Goddess called me, I did not hear. Perhaps this is all my fault."

"Perhaps," Chalvern said, "the others have their own responsibility."

Reika turned, looking at him with wonder. Chalvern did not know where his words were coming from, but as he said them, he thought they contained a profound truth.

"What are you saying?" Reika asked. "That those poor trapped women should have known it would be their salvation to go with Braith? When even we do not know whether it was the right thing to do?"

"I say that in the end we answer only to ourselves," Chalvern said, still groping for the words as for stones buried deep in the earth. "And our faith."

For a moment longer, Reika gazed at Chalvern, as though he had turned green or sprouted horns. Then she smiled. "Master Chalvern," she said, "you have the soul of a healer."

Chalvern did not want Reika to see how much her words had affected him—that they were, in fact, the words he had been waiting all his life to hear. So he spoke in a gruff tone, "You will stay here tonight. I forbid you to go anywhere else."

Reika nodded compliantly, finally letting him see her exhaustion, the grey sheen of fatigue that hovered over her skin, behind her eyes. She was little more than a child, after all.

Chalvern fed her some bread and goat's cheese and made them a pot of licorice tea. Then, seeing that she was nodding over her second cup, he took it from her slackened hands and led her up the stairs. He put her in his own cot and then went downstairs to wait in his chair until dawn came to end the Night of the Dead.

Just in case Neela plans to visit me, he thought, allowing himself to smile about Neela for the first time since her death.

In the deepest part of the night, he heard Reika's gentle breathing from the cot above. Even healers needed healing sometimes.

REIKA CAME DOWN the stairs soon after dawn. Chalvern was still awake. He found he needed less sleep these days than he used to, though he had become inordinately fond of naps, especially when talking to a priest.

He stirred the porridge as it simmered over the stove. "Hungry?" he asked her, smiling.

"No," she answered. Then, "Yes, I had better eat something. I am leaving for Zantor today."

"You as well? Who will be here to keep an old man company in his dotage?" Chalvern joked, trying to ignore a stab of anxiety. "Better yet, who will tend to the soldiers in yonder castle? They congregate there all the best and brightest young men of the North. No doubt they will need the services of a healer before long."

Reika smiled back, but her face looked taut, strained. "Perhaps not all the brightest," she replied. She took the bowl of oatmeal that Chalvern proffered and sat down at the table, swirling her wooden spoon in the porridge. "I Journeyed last night," she told him. "So, I have no choice."

"Tekoah needs your help?" Chalvern asked. "Is she in trouble? Did you see anything?"

"I saw above all that your words last night were true, Master Chalvern," Reika replied slowly. "Therefore, I would not say that Tekoah needs my help; rather, I would say that Anna has a task for me."

"Ah," Chalvern said, trying to appear wise. If he had the soul of a healer, he should probably have known such things.

Reika smiled. "You look so comical when you scrunch up your face like that, as if you had a toothache."

So much for wisdom. "Will you bring Tekoah back here, do you think?" he asked her. "I cannot seem to do anything properly since she's been gone. I try not to worry, but—"

"That, I cannot tell you," Reika answered, sounding strangely abrupt.

They ate their breakfast in silence. Chalvern glanced at Reika's face; she looked pale, tense. It was probably the thought of all the Anniste women gone—not knowing where they were was the worst of it.

"Braith had said he was going to Zantor," he began.

Reika interrupted him with a terse, "I know." The sound of

her spoon scraping the bottom of her bowl seemed loud in the quiet shop.

What else does she know? Unease crept from the shadows into the room.

He cleared away the dishes, making more clatter than necessary, while Reika sat staring into space. Chalvern had not dared to open them, so it was quite dark except for the stove fire and a lamp on the table. In the gloom, Reika's eyes shone like those of a nocturnal animal. Hiding.

"Must you go?" he ventured.

"Yes."

"But what about the Morgs? Braith said that they can hunt now, because the snow has melted."

"Almost all of them are dead. They fed on the flesh of the Anniste killed by the soldiers throughout the winter. It seems they cannot survive without Anniste flesh for longer than a day or two. So, if Braith has kept the women safe, which Anna has not deigned to relay to me, then they would be free to return now. If you see Braith," she added, bitterness tinging her voice, "you might tell him that."

Chalvern shuddered. "You learned all this about the Morgs in your Journey last night?" She nodded. "So they are all dead?" he repeated.

"They are dead," Reika answered. "All except one."

Before Chalvern could ask what she meant by that, Reika was on her feet. "I must hasten," she said, "before the village folk are about."

"It is a shame you cannot see the Castle of Mirrand, and the Kalesh all gathered," Chalvern said. "We are in for some excitement, it appears."

"I shall be sorry to miss it." Reika said, a hint of her old radiance returning. "Weslan will find his way here, for this is the thing he loves the best. Will you tell him something for me if you see him?"

Reika had gone to the door and now stood hesitating, looking back at him as a child looked when asking for a rare favour. Her dusky skin glowed like amber in the half-light.

Is she even aware of her own beauty? Chalvern wondered. She wore it with such ease, like a rare bird's plumage. He nodded.

"Will you tell Weslan that I loved him? That I gave him my heart, freely?" She was blushing. It had been very difficult for her to say.

He nodded again. Reika lifted her hand in a wave and then slipped through the door. There had been no time to thank her for what she had said about his soul.

Hours after she had left, Chalvern was still trying to find a plausible reason Reika had spoken of her love as if it was a thing long past; as though either she or Weslan—or both—were gone from the world.

CHAPTER 44

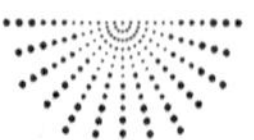

The day became busy, and soon there was no time for thoughts of Reika. Toward dusk, Chalvern wound his way up a steep and dusty path, on his way to see the Castle of Mirrand for the first time. His sullen apprentice lent his arm for support with a grudging air. Chalvern would have slapped it away if he had not so genuinely needed it. The hill was steep.

As he got nearer, Chalvern saw that in the past few days the soldiers had fortified the castle walls, both in girth and height. It had been an imposing sight before, but now it was tremendous, rivalling the castle at Meed. Rhantor he had never seen, and never would, now that it was Zantor.

The Kalesh had accomplished much in the time they had been gathering there. Someone was brilliant, keeping them too busy to get into trouble. Many idle soldiers in one place never boded well for nearby villages.

There was no shortage of men. The Kalesh was no longer an aristocrat's playground. Any able-bodied man or boy—he saw lots of boys—could join, it seemed, provided his wife or mother could stitch on his tunic the emblem of the Kalesh.

They reached the top of the hill. Chalvern could not contain a gasp of admiration, squeezing the arm of his apprentice until the lad drew away, grunting in annoyance.

The castle itself was a beautiful sight. Chalvern had never seen it this close. The rays of the morning sun gleamed behind the white halestone, lighting it up with a beauty that seemed ethereal. Splashes of brilliant colour—blue, red, silvery white and green—dazzled his eyes, and he realized he was looking at windows, made of flat, translucent slabs of some strange material Chalvern had never seen.

The flag of the Kalesh flew from every turret, indigo pennants stitched with white ponies leaping over crescent moons; the new flag of the North. It was at its sight that Chalvern felt his throat constrict with admiration and pride. And also at the soldiers, striding the battlements in their mail shirts, or poised at the towers, arrows slung behind them, bows at the ready; and the captains, distinguishable from their men only by their bright scarlet sashes.

We have an army, Chalvern thought with wonder. *A real army.* That he should have lived to see this!

His apprentice was prodding him. "Come to the gate, old man. You will not get in any other way!"

"Old man!" Chalvern retorted, astounded at the effrontery. The brat must be Zorak's favourite. Well, he would not put up with him any longer. "Get out of here!" he snapped. "Go on!" he shouted, incensed. "Go back and kill some pigeons to fortify your impending manhood. I will make my own way."

Despite his bold words, Chalvern approached the huge wood and iron gates with some trepidation. He had been summoned after breakfast to examine and treat an ill soldier. Water in the lungs. The affliction had pounced upon him without warning, and it was a strange thing, because the season for lung fever had passed.

However, Chalvern had been glad of the excuse to go, although only yesterday he had shunned the prospect of mingling in any crowd as lively as this one. He wanted a distraction to stop him from worrying about Reika, and Tekoah, and *anyone*.

And now he found the energy was contagious, though it was more fear than excitement, with the glowering sentries frowning at him from beside the gates. Chalvern cleared his throat and stated his business.

"But where is the boy we sent to fetch you?" a guard asked.

At that moment, Chalvern felt a hand on his shoulder. The sentries stood aside, swinging the gates open so he could pass. With the hand still heavy on his shoulder, Chalvern walked through.

This must be someone of great importance. Chalvern forced himself to turn around.

It was a twin. Fanco, yes, it was he.

"Anna's tides!" Chalvern exclaimed, astonished and delighted. He clapped Fanco on the arm, for he could not reach any higher. "And what are you doing here?"

Fanco made the gesture of hammer striking anvil. Of course! Raol and Fanco were doing a brisk trade as blacksmiths. He had heard in the village that they ran the forge far better than Veld ever had. So much for being witless.

Fanco made another gesture, a sort of rippling with his fingers, and squinted. Chalvern shook his head, frowning in bafflement. Fanco repeated the pantomime, but Chalvern still could not understand. He shrugged in apology.

"I am here to see a sick soldier," he told Fanco, miming a racking cough.

Fanco nodded, knitting his brows. They had been walking as they spoke, and now Fanco propelled Chalvern toward the eastern face of the castle. They stopped at a side door, and Fanco rapped.

The door was opened at once by a buxom girl in a white cap and apron. She stood grinning and nodding at them. He knew her, Chalvern realized with a start. It was the egg-woman's niece, Norah, as empty-headed a gossip as her aunt and mother had always been. There would be plenty to talk about to her cronies later, and if nothing exciting happened, she would be sure to make something up.

"It is Norah, Master Chalvern." Her tone was brisk. "This way, please. We have no time to lose." She turned and bustled down the narrow corridor.

Fanco seemed anxious also, judging by his heavy hand on Chalvern's back, steering him forward like a small vessel before a great wind.

They followed Norah down the long corridor, which was lit by clear-burning lamps set in wall sconces at regular intervals. No smoky torches for the lord of Mirrand. He was sparing no expense in the castle, thought Chalvern, looking at the exquisite wall hangings. They all had some element in them of the North of Miraven, whether it be mountain ponies, pitaya groves, or the large, purple-black leaves of the crohm tree. The son was as fervent a patriot as his father.

The corridor ended in a large, airy chamber which was meant to be a banquet hall, but had been transformed into an infirmary of sorts. Large fur rugs were rolled up against the walls, and straw pallets lined up in straight rows upon the flagged stone floor.

"Someone expects a fierce battle, with many wounded." Chalvern did not realize he had spoken aloud until Norah answered.

"It was Captain Heyg who ordered this," she said importantly. "He is second in command to the leader himself. He speaks to me all the time," she added, tossing her loosely plaited black hair.

"Oh, he does, does he?" Chalvern asked ironically.

"Yes, he does, for he—but here we are!" They had stopped at

a curtained-off partition. With a dramatic flourish, Norah threw open the heavy curtains.

Weslan lay on a pallet on which several mattresses had been piled; he seemed to be in a heavy slumber, and his breath rasped like a file against a stone. Looking at him, Chalvern felt little surprise, probably because he and Reika had just spoken of Weslan at length, and she had surmised that he might soon be in Stern.

He bent over the sleeping boy. His chest was bare and covered with a fine sheen of sweat. His bright hair lay in dampened curls about his forehead and shoulders.

"Is he not beautiful?" Norah breathed.

Chalvern looked at her in distaste. "Clean, tepid water in a bucket," he said shortly. "Boil some fennel root in apple cider for an hour, then bring it to me still hot. And for Rhan's sake, tie his hair back." Norah sprang into action, and Chalvern felt the weight of Fanco's hand leave his shoulder.

By midday, Weslan was sitting up, sipping his hot apple cider and smirking at Chalvern. "Are you surprised to see me again?" he croaked between sips. "I'll wager you thought I was dead."

"Not at all," Chalvern answered, a little tartly. Weslan's bravado had never impressed him. So unlike his sister, though many said otherwise. "Because, yesterday, I spoke to a close friend of yours, and she not only told me you were alive, but she also predicted that you would end up here."

"Who?" Weslan's voice rose. "Reika? Was it Reika?" His hands jerked on his mug so that cider slopped over his chest and the thin sheet which covered his legs.

"Do not agitate yourself," Chalvern said. "You are ill. Your bath in the River Meed was not taken for the good of your health, if you have not guessed that by now."

"You saw Reika? She is safe, then. I worried that one of those Morg things—is she here, still? I would give anything to see her."

"No, she is not here."

"Oh." Weslan slumped back weakly against the pillows, while Chalvern mopped up spilled cider as best he could.

"She is gone about Anniste business, I suppose," Weslan said after a moment. "She must have been sorely missed. She is so clever, and so strong."

He coughed, a horrible choking sound. Chalvern took the mug hurriedly from his hands.

After a moment, the coughing subsided, and Chalvern said carefully, "Yes, she has gone about Anniste business. In Zantor."

"Zantor? But why? Surely it is the most dangerous place of all."

"Tekoah is also there," Chalvern said gently.

"Oh." Weslan exhaled, and all his strength seemed to leave his body with the expelled air. "I feel so helpless," he whispered.

Chalvern patted his arm, wondering if he had been right to tell Weslan this worrisome news when he was obviously so weak. But who knew how much time any of them had, before they were called to the Halls of the Worldmaker? Weslan had a right to know where his sister was.

There was a rustle at the curtain, and Raol's face appeared, grimy and sweat-streaked. His grey eyes were anxious, but he grinned when he saw Weslan sitting up. Weslan grinned back. Raol's head disappeared.

One twin or the other had materialized at least half a dozen times since Chalvern had been there.

"Why are they not forbidden from just popping in like that— or do they have the run of the castle?" Chalvern asked, amazed.

Weslan coughed again, and it went on and on. When at last he stopped, he sipped at the mug of cider Chalvern handed him.

"It is the strangest thing," he mused, shaking his head. "But the twins can detect Shiftings. The first time was an accident, from what Heyg told me. Raol stopped a company of men who were about to ride down the trail on the far side of the pond.

The one at Stern's End, you know. He was down there, fishing for eels. Well, Heyg said, Raol threw himself right in front of the soldiers; he was lucky they did not stampede him. But he saved them all. The Shifting was right in front of them. And the twins have found three more Shiftings since then—all of them near Stern. Eerie, isn't it?" he added, shuddering.

"Eerie," Chalvern muttered, "but not unfathomable. It makes sense Zant would place them here, since here is where he suspects the Anniste are hiding."

"Whenever anyone wants to go anywhere," Weslan continued, "Raol or Fanco act as scouts—so they have the run of the palace. They have been accorded a status close to that of an army captain—or a sorcerer in Berlot." He chuckled at his own joke.

Pride in his brothers was clear on Weslan's face, probably for the first time in his life, Chalvern thought. Then an appalling thought struck him. "But what about all the men who may still be on their way here?" he asked. "Will they not be in danger of falling into Shiftings? Can we warn them?"

Weslan shrugged. "Whoever wants to be here will get here. Look at the odds I battled against, and I got here! I did not know about the Shiftings—I probably just missed a couple of them." He laughed without humour, then began coughing again.

"It looks to me as if just getting here is not enough," Chalvern pointed out. "The River Meed seems to have posed as much danger to you as any Shifting. I recommend you rest now, so that you can boast later of your great exploits." He pushed Weslan back down onto the pillows.

What did Reika see in this fellow, by the Holy Mantling? Chalvern grudgingly acknowledged Weslan was something for the women to look at, with his golden curls and rippling muscles; but what a vain, simple pup he could be sometimes.

He thought of Neela, and how she had seemed unable to resist Veld, and then caught himself. It was an unfair comparison to make. Weslan had killed Veld, and for reasons far more complex than any that could lurk in the soul of a simpleton or a brute. Chalvern himself had seen the self-loathing and anguish in Weslan's eyes.

The boy was not stupid, nor a replica of his father, but some would never know it. People loved to condemn each other's faults while dissembling about their own, Chalvern thought. Most would never guess that Weslan had depth.

Weslan's eyes had closed now, and his mouth was twitching with the need to sleep. He was past the point of danger, though.

I will go now, Chalvern thought. He reached for his cloak and fastened it about him.

"Reika." Weslan said it without opening his eyes. "Did she say anything about me?"

"Yes," Chalvern answered with a stab of guilt, for he had forgotten his message from Reika. He swallowed; it was hard to say. "She said to tell you that you have her heart, for the first time and forever."

His eyes still closed, Weslan smiled the ecstatic, transported smile of a child.

STRIVING TO STAY INCONSPICUOUS, Chalvern waited on the grounds until he spotted one of the twins. Then, with awkward hand gestures, he requested an escort home. His actual fear was not of losing his footing on the steep path—it was the Shiftings. Seeing those women disappear into oblivion had shaken him more than he wanted to admit.

The thought of death had never disturbed Chalvern much. As for the pain associated with dying—well, many things in life were unpleasant or painful. One gritted one's teeth and got through it. But the contemplation of utter obscurity, nothing-ness; no flesh or bones left to make the waiting earth more fertile. That was another matter. It was even more ghastly than the thought of being embalmed in pitaya juice like the Berlotans.

Fanco smiled at him, as if sensing his fear. But he signalled Chalvern to wait and trotted off. *Of course they cannot spare him for the likes of me,* Chalvern thought. He's gone to ask permission, and now there will be no end of embarrassment.

He waited, shifting from foot to foot, and was just deciding to slip away when Fanco came loping back. Accompanying him was a man with grizzled red and grey-streaked hair and beard and a frowning, preoccupied face. A commander, for he wore the scarlet sash. He came straight up to Chalvern.

"Ah, you are Master Chalvern, of whom I have heard much. I am Heyg." His voice was brusque. "I have meant to look in on Weslan a dozen times today. But there was so much to do. Dirken arrives today, before sundown."

"I had heard he was coming this morning," Chalvern replied, more to make conversation than anything else.

"Yes," Heyg replied, his frown deepening. "Yes, he was. He is late, which is not a usual thing for him. He is a fanatic for punctuality, though he likes to behave as if he hadn't the least idea what time it was." Heyg's face looked unfocused for a moment, and then he gazed at Chalvern. "I heard Wes will be in expert hands with you, so I have not wasted any time worrying about him."

Chalvern nodded. But he was divided in his mind. This was Weslan's commander, the man who had taken him away from the squalor of his upbringing. Yet Weslan had returned and killed his father. What had he learned by becoming a soldier?

However, Captain Heyg cared for Weslan—Chalvern could see it by the tension in his jaw. *Good.* The boy needed a man like Heyg—someone who resembled a proper father.

"Weslan will be on his feet again in a few days," he told Heyg. "But he is unlikely to be strong enough to take part in any fighting, if it lies ahead soon." He gazed back at Heyg, his own unspoken question hovering in the air.

Heyg nodded. "Yes, indeed it does, unless I am mistaken." He turned his face southward, toward the Taboran Mountains, and his grizzled brows plowed furrows into his freckled forehead.

He looks worried, Chalvern thought. *And if he is worried, then so should we all be!* He cleared his throat to get Heyg's attention. "I will take my leave now, if you can spare young Fanco for an hour."

"Yes, yes, by all means. It is the least we can do. And you shall be paid well—I will send someone around with a purse when I have a moment to think."

"Do not trouble yourself about payment," Chalvern answered, as he took a firm grip on Fanco's welcoming arm. "I think of him as family."

FANCO LEFT Chalvern at the door of his shop. There had been no Shiftings lurking along the way, although Chalvern was certain that he saw a telltale shimmer several times. Each time they came closer, however, it turned out to be a bit of shiny rock, or the trickle of a stream. And then Fanco would grin hugely, poking Chalvern's ribs in a jocular fashion.

The boy was probably right to think it comical. Chalvern considered this ruefully. It *was* rather pointless to cultivate the art of cowardice at his age, when there was nothing left to lose.

Fanco waved farewell and walked away, purpose lending a speed and grace to his movements which Chalvern had not previously seen. The sun was low in the sky. It was later than Chalvern had thought. But he was tired, come to think of it, and hungry as well. Tea would be bliss, and some stew, leftover from the previous night's dinner with Reika.

As soon as Chalvern entered his shop, he saw a figure standing in front of the hearth, his back to the door. *Braith!* he thought at once, but almost immediately he realized he was wrong.

For a fire was roaring, although the day was more than mild. This was a thing Braith would never do—he loved the open air and was rarely cold. Also, this person was shorter than Braith, very slender, and a little stooped. The figure turned toward him, and something in the movement of the hips made Chalvern think it was a woman; but again, he thought he must be wrong.

He saw the pale face, narrow as a skull, and the eyes that seemed to be made of some smooth black stone, and at the sight Chalvern grew sick with fear. It was the sorcerer Zant. And suddenly the notion of being swallowed up by a Shifting did not seem so terrible.

CHAPTER 45

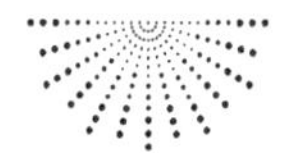

They were walking about on the palace grounds at Zantor, in the hour just after dawn. The spring morning was one of unparalleled beauty: crohm leaves were on display everywhere, their indigo sheen mellowing and diluting the sunshine, scattering it about in green and gold coins among the moist turf. The breeze carried with it promises of tantalizing mysteries not yet revealed; and the warblers sang with a sweetness so piercing they had to know something of the human heart.

Tekoah noticed all this fleetingly, though at another time she would have lost herself in rapture and composed at least three sets of verses in her head. But all she could think of was that it was a good thing she and Dirken were outside, beyond earshot. Otherwise, the ferocity of their quarrel would have been fodder for annaspans of palace gossip.

"Yet Zant is not here," she said, for the third time.

"That is my point!" Dirken struck a nearby laurel bush with his riding whip so hard that she jumped.

He was garbed for travelling. Besides his riding whip, he wore light hose of the forest-green colour which he favoured, and a rust-coloured tunic over a loose white shirt. Hidden under the fashionable clothes was, Tekoah knew, a shirt of light mail. Both sword and small axe were slung from his belt. Back at the stables, his mount waited, loaded with saddlebags for his three-day journey to his castle at Stern.

Dirken was leaving court, as he did every season, ostensibly to travel about and gather inspiration for his melodies and verses. He was to have left hours ago. But Tekoah, after days of vacillating, had told him she would not accompany him, and he was furious.

They argued in urgent whispers in her chamber. At first, Tekoah declined to explain why, beyond telling him she had Journeyed. And then she had made the mistake of trying to bolster her argument by describing her Journey—telling him she must try to stop Saura from being killed. She wished for Dirken to remain, for she was terrified. But there was an army waiting for him, and he could not delay just for her.

Tekoah had made it sound as though the Goddess Anna had told her to stay, although it was she herself who had decided it, as soon as she realized that the events in her Journey had not yet happened. Trying to sound reassuring, she told Dirken she would follow him as soon as she was able and join him in Stern.

At that point, he had become truly angry, for he had ceased speaking altogether. He had fixed her with a wrathful stare, biting the inside of his pale cheeks as though holding back words he should not say. Tekoah, although shaken, had looked at him, resolute. He had left her chamber, then returned an hour later, his manner cheerful but determined, and announced he was taking her for a walk.

Tekoah would have foregone the pleasure, had Dirken given her the choice. She wanted to gather her thoughts and summon up the courage to speak to Lady Saura—though what in Anna's name would she say?

But Dirken had given her no choice. She had pulled on a

cloak and allowed him to take her arm as they walked along the black marble floors and out into the glorious spring day.

Her mind reeled. How had she stayed in this palace for thirteen days, without knowing that a Morg lurked there? How could she have danced, sung, laughed, slumbered? Why had Anna not shown her?

Perhaps Dirken was right. Perhaps she should use her wits, instead of relying on the Goddess. Anna would want her to think for herself, Dirken had pointed out in a deep, reasonable voice. Had she not used them when she saved the Anniste before?

This line of thinking troubled her. Where were the Anniste? Had Braith destroyed them, or was he sheltering them, as Zant surmised?

There were so many questions, and no answers, only a mad whirlpool of fear and indecision whirling about her, made worse somehow by the bright sunshine and the singing birds. Nothing seemed real. Perhaps it wasn't. Perhaps they had all been drawn into a Shifting.

And now, worst of all, she and Dirken were embattled. Soon he would leave, and they might never see one another again in this lifetime. A blackbird trilled from a tree beside them—a sweet, high note; the sudden sound made Tekoah start. Dirken was staring at his hands, clenching and unclenching them. He did not look up.

"I know you think I am being stubborn," Tekoah said, laying her hand on his arm. She wished he knew how deeply she wanted to be back in her chamber with him, kissing his lips with luxurious slowness. "But do you realize you are speaking to me as a commander speaks to his men, laying out strategies and giving me orders? It all makes perfect sense, of course. But I do not have the luxury of blind obedience, as do your soldiers."

"Is that how it seems to you?" Dirken looked astonished.

"And here I thought I was behaving so persuasively. Perhaps I am simply accustomed to getting my own way."

"Perhaps," she answered, smiling.

"And yet I am so frightened for you. And you are acting in blind obedience—to the Goddess. Only your orders make no sense at all." He stopped, taking her hand from his arm and clasping it between both his own. "You are too sweet, too good, to be caught up in all this. I long to protect you, but you will not let me."

It was all unbearable. She wanted to scream, but she could not, for they were too near the stables. Instead, she snatched her hand away.

"You see me as so gentle and innocent," she said, her voice vibrating. "And yet I grew up with violence abounding in my home, choking and poisonous as the black smoke that came from the forge. No, do not shake your head at me in that way, I speak true! My father murdered my mother before my eyes, and my brother Weslan killed my father in revenge last winter." She saw the shock in his eyes and felt a grim satisfaction.

Dirken said nothing for several moments. They were both walking rapidly now, as if trying to escape from each other, but somehow unable.

"And you wish me to trust your brother?" Dirken asked her at last. His voice was heavy with irony.

"Was not justice served? He avenged my mother's murder— and spared me the fate of acting in her stead. But it is clear that you must decide for yourself whether to trust Weslan. After all, you will know if he is lying, will you not? It would feel as if you were being bitten by a flea!"

They had reached the bleached wooden buildings now. Above her, Tekoah felt rather than saw the hawk wheeling above them, and she knew then why she had told Dirken about her father, her brother.

Dirken averted his face. *I have lost him,* Tekoah thought, as the wall of her past rose, bleak and inexorable. But she could not let him continue to see her as someone she was not—naïve, untouched, virginal. She was someone different. She had been with a sorcerer. Yet she could not tell him about Braith, even to save her life.

Dirken spoke without looking at her. "If you hope to shock me into pushing you away, you hope in vain."

Joy flooded unbidden into Tekoah's heart, its force astonishing her. She had not thought there was room for happiness until that moment. Not after that last Journey.

"When I first saw you, you were battling against the fools and bullies who surrounded you, like a blue cornflower which struggles to grow in the dirt." Dirken continued. "And next I saw you in my castle, looking as if you fled from something terrible, yet you did not yield to your fear. You carried your courage before you like a flame. I had the castle searched from top to bottom after you left, that day," he added, "but I found nothing. Nothing," he repeated, as if the word held a secret for him, a door to which he had not yet found the key.

"When I saw you again, you were fighting against great odds to save the lives of the Anniste women. Fighting at least as hard as the Kalesh, and with more nerve than any battle-scarred soldier I ever met. I fell in love with you some time between the second and third time, I think. Though I told myself I did not have time. That has been the story of my life—no time for love."

His voice had a melancholic tinge, but when Tekoah looked at him, he met her eyes, smiling his usual smile.

"And here I am again," he said lightly, "rushing off, no time for love. Only this time, the stakes are very high. Can you see why I am loath to lose you?"

She looked at the ground, holding his hand. "I thought I was only one among many."

"It would have done me good for you to think that, for a while," he answered. "It might have shielded my heart from the arrows that are coming thick and fast." He sighed. "Again, there is no time for that. So I must tell you, it cleaves my heart in two. For the North is my first love, and you are my second, and I would not choose between them. And regardless of whether you return my love, I still would not leave you in this place, for it is cursed. Doomed by the flowers of a lost queen, and by the hopes of a lost land."

Dirken paused, looking up at the pale morning sky. "I would not quarrel with you anymore, sweetheart. Will you come with me?"

Tekoah could hear the grooms cursing and stamping about in the yard. She looked up. The hawk was nowhere in sight. Her heart contracted within her, tight, tighter, so that she could scarcely breathe.

"No," she said. "I cannot." Then, lifting his hand, she kissed the palm.

He took his hand away, touched her cheek briefly. "So be it. Obey your Goddess and rescue Saura—who by all observations does not wish to be rescued. Then, if by some miracle you can escape this place unscathed, come to my castle with all the haste you can muster. Fighting will begin before the next full moon, and it would be wise not to be caught between Stern and Berlot. If—" he added urgently, as she turned away, "if all goes well for the North, and I am alive, I swear upon my mother's ashes I will spend my last breath looking for you."

Tekoah nodded, her legs wobbling unsteadily as she turned and walked away. When she was sure Dirken was not looking after her, she stopped. Concealed behind a tackle shed, she watched him mount his white destrier, back erect, shoulders broad, curly hair glinting in the sun; and wept as he rode away.

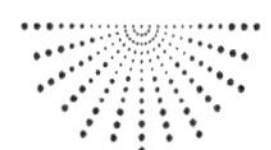

Walking back numbly to her chambers, Tekoah found herself among a group of dairymaids passing by carrying their milk to the dairy for churning. One of them sloshed her bucket against Tekoah as she passed, spilling milk on her skirt. When Tekoah looked up, she gazed into the glowing brown eyes of Reika. She gave a joyful, inarticulate cry, but Reika's forefinger was at her lips.

"I am so sorry, miss," she said, bending down to wipe Tekoah's skirt. The other dairymaids glanced at them, smirking, and kept walking.

"What are you doing here?" Tekoah clasped Reika's hands in her own. Relief flooded her at the sight of those strong, slender fingers. Everything would be all right.

"I came to help you," Reika answered.

"Yes, there is danger—I saw it in a Journey. But I felt I must stay a little longer, in case I can make a difference."

"Did Anna tell you to stay in this Journey?" Reika's face was not stern, but she looked perturbed.

Tekoah rushed on, her words tumbling over each other. "There is so much happening. Everything is so confusing. I should have guessed you would come—that Anna would bring you to me!"

"Yes, I had to come. But you should have left by now!" Reika said, and for a moment her eyes became veiled, and her fingers trembled in Tekoah's hands.

Before Tekoah could question her further, however, Reika whispered, "We must not continue to speak to each other in this way—there may be others watching. Meet me tonight outside the palace. Do you know somewhere it is safe to talk?"

"Yes, the grove of willows beyond the larger stable," Tekoah answered, remembering the night she had waited there for Dirken.

"Very well. Go there as soon as you can get away after sun goes down. Stay there until I come. Do you understand?"

"Of course," she answered, puzzled by the unaccustomed vehemence in Reika's voice. "I am not a child."

"No," Reika said, raising a hand to her cheek, "you are not."

Then she strode off, hurrying along, swinging her milk bucket the way any carefree maid would on an early spring morning.

SITTING in the moonlight under the willows, Tekoah thought not of Reika—or even of Dirken—but of the Lady Saura, who was unaware of her doom. She had gone to the Lady Regent's chamber that day, only to find that Saura had left for the city, to purchase some fine silks. Lord Zant was returning from Berlot at any moment, her maid told Tekoah, and she wanted to look her best.

Tekoah had waited and waited, but Saura had not returned by dinnertime. Perhaps she could seek her out after meeting with Reika. But would Saura believe her? Who was she to Saura but a silly young girl, Dirken's new plaything, easily led?

Tekoah wondered what it was about Zant that had bound Saura to him. Had he pretended to love her in the beginning? Or had the allure of being aligned with a powerful sorcerer drawn Saura into this?

Was that what Braith had sought—for Tekoah to become his creature, manipulated for his purposes and then discarded? Her head ached. She was exhausted, and there was too much to think about. She drifted toward sleep, fought it once or twice, and then succumbed.

Into her troubled slumber came dreams, fragmented and strange: stone tears flying from the Lady Saura's eyes into the River Meed, choking the water so it ceased to flow. Laughing kitchen maids with starched caps, grey shifts, and brown eyes like Reika, who planted flowers, which then grew up, up, up, in brilliant blooms of purple and orange, bursting from twisted stalks that then turned into the coils of serpents.

In the dream, Tekoah was running from a flower which hissed and spat as it writhed along the ground after her. She tripped over the root of a giant crohm tree and fell through a cavernous tunnel inside the trunk. As she fell, she realized her dream had ended, and she was entering a Journey.

TEKOAH WAS STANDING in a luxurious bedchamber, but saw at once that she was not in Zantor. Gold and ivory statuettes and ornaments cluttered the several low tables scattered about the apartment. Tapestries and wall-hangings hung in random order, overlapping each other so that scarcely one was visible in its entirety. The ornaments all had the lavish, overstated air of Berlotan design, so that the room seemed oppressive, as though some sweet, heavy incense burned, making it difficult to breathe. Even as she thought this, Tekoah heard heavy, laboured breathing below her on the floor.

She looked down. King Darian lay writhing on the ground upon a heap of pillows, his ragged breaths interspersed with moans. At first, Tekoah thought he was injured. Looking closer, she saw he was in the throes of ecstasy, and oblivious to anyone around him. He wore a woman's night robe of shimmering pale gold, its diaphanous folds tangled around his limbs.

A maidservant stood by Darian; naked, her skin striped by the marks of a recent flogging. Tears ran down her cheeks, yet there was a slight sneer on her lips as she watched her monarch wriggling about on the floor. It was a revolting sight, Tekoah thought as she looked down at him.

The maidservant drew in her breath; Tekoah saw a shadow fall over Darian's form. Looking up, she saw the sorcerer Zant standing just to her left, so close she could have touched his shoulder without moving. He smiled at Darian.

"That is the way—always follow your darkest desire when in pursuit of your greatest pleasure."

Darian raised himself, flushed and panting, and turned upon the sorcerer a look of undiluted hatred. The silent maidservant crawled from the room, stumbling over Darian's legs as she went.

Cursing, he stood up and threw a quilt around himself; seating himself on the edge of the bed and glaring at Zant like an umbray whose bone someone has wrested away. "I believe you time your visits for the express purpose of humiliating me."

Zant cocked his sleek head. "I, too, must pursue my pleasure."

"Which is making others suffer, no doubt."

"That sounds very righteous, coming from a man who cannot reach the pinnacle of ecstasy without flaying the flesh off servant girls while wearing his exiled sister's apparel."

Darian turned very red, but did not reply.

"I came to obtain your incisive report about the status of

your fighting men, which you promised me days ago," Zant continued in a bantering tone.

"I cannot give you a detailed report at this very moment," Darian answered. "I must summon my military advisers, my commander-in-chief—"

"Do not attempt to deceive me with your drivel the way you deceived the Jinta!" Zant's voice was scathing. "For I know very well that every day more of your so-called troops are deserting you and heading for North, where there is a proper leader, one that men can respect."

"How dare you!" Darian began, but Zant cut him off.

"Now it is more difficult for me to infiltrate the North and wipe out the witch-worship that still prevails. Someone is hiding them well. I have been exceedingly patient, Darian. You have given me no rewards for that patience." He paused, smiling with his pale lips at the king, who sat now wearing a young boy's hangdog expression.

"And I have another problem," Zant said, his voice dropping to a sibilant whisper. "The Jinta is no longer satisfied with the annexation of the north. He wants to rule the whole of Miraven, to assure a prosperous, united land, one country, with one God —Rhan. He claims you are not only an incompetent ruler and a lying cur, but an Anna-worshipping infidel as well. It is in your northern blood, after all."

Darian had turned deadly pale. "You know I have no use for Anna," he stammered, "and you can vouch for my loyalty."

Zant shrugged in boredom, his eyes flickering away from Darian. Darian dropped from the edge of the bed onto the floor, grovelling toward Zant on his knees, the gossamer robe trailing behind him.

"Please," he whimpered.

Zant raised his hand. "I am done with you," he said.

Tekoah's shoulders bunched, rigid. There was a high, thin shriek from Darian which reverberated throughout the room, and then he writhed, much in the same way he had before. Tekoah tried to take her eyes away from him, but found she could not.

"Look away from this sight." It was Reika's voice. And Reika's hand on her shoulder.

Tekoah looked at her in utter bewilderment. *What is Reika doing here?*

"Sometimes it is better not to see. Come."

Reika took her hand, and they floated through the walls of the palace in Meed, out into the air of the spring night. They drifted for so long that for a while everything ceased to matter.

"Am I dreaming?" Tekoah asked, her voice emanating from her body, visible ripples of colour and sound. She felt safe and happy.

"No," Reika replied. "I was Journeying, and have pulled you somehow into my Journey. I suppose Anna must have wanted both of us here, or she would not have sent one just at that moment."

"Yes! I did not know it was possible to Journey together!"

Reika squeezed her hand. "Neither did I. Perhaps we have always been able to do it, only we have not tried before. But why not? It is common knowledge that sorcerers can bespeak people's minds. However, that kind of invasion is repugnant to the Anniste. The teachings tell us to value the privacy of the individual's soul, so I think we avoided the idea of group Journeys. They might prove very useful, though."

"I think this is wonderful," Tekoah answered. "But should we not return now to where I am waiting for you under the willows?"

As she said this, she looked around, wondering where they were, for they seemed to be suspended, in some pearly, luminescent place, far above the world. She could see tiny, dancing motes of rainbow light around them, and in the background, she heard something—like music—only it was lighter, sweeter, than any music she had ever heard.

"Where are we?" she asked in an awestruck whisper.

"I think we are in a place created by my mind and aided by Anna. Can you feel her?"

Tekoah looked at Reika and saw her brown eyes filled with a quiet joy. "I think so," she murmured.

Reika closed her eyes, breathing in and out, slowly. Tekoah watched her, but after a moment she grew uneasy.

"It is lovely here," she ventured, "but hadn't we better be going? There is so much danger surrounding everyone we love. We must help them."

"Indeed, you must go soon," Reika answered without opening her eyes. "And I wish you had left today with Dirken— for your own safety. But we must make our own choices. Chalvern told me that a short time ago. And I will not pretend I am not glad that you are here. Stay with me for a little longer, will you? It is selfish of me, but I need your strength."

She opened her eyes, gazing at Tekoah steadily. All around her, rainbow specks glittered and danced, but Tekoah could not look at them now, held as she was by Reika's eyes.

"You have no need of my strength, you are a thousand times stronger than I. Besides, what did you mean by saying that I must go?" Tekoah faltered. "You mean we must go!"

Reika shook her head.

"Well, why did you say that you were here because of me?"

"I am here because of you," Reika said. "But first let me tell you about Weslan."

"He is alive. I know already—Dirken told me."

"But you do not know where he was before he returned to the Kalesh. When I left Beula's farm to search for the one who needed healing, it was to your brother that Anna directed me."

"What? Where was he? Was he ill?"

"He was wandering the Taboran Woods, in the dead of

winter. He was out of his mind, or others were in it, if you prefer to look at it that way. I helped him to return from his time of wandering."

"Why did Anna not send me?" Tekoah asked, a little jealous. "He is my brother, after all!"

"Perhaps that is why," Reika replied. "And you can rejoice for him, for I healed him of the sickness caused in him when he killed your father. I thought you would want to know this."

"Thank you," Tekoah answered. "But what about the others? The Anniste?"

"They are in a Shifting created by Braith, who hid them there when you and I were both gone. The Morgs would have come for them—they killed those who refused to go." Reika's voice became a whisper.

Tekoah felt Reika's sorrow in the long silence that followed. But she needed to voice the question that choked her own throat.

"Did Braith save them?" she asked. "Or did he betray them? I do not believe he is in league with Zant."

"Neither do I," Reika answered. "Anna has not shown me the others, but I believe Braith did it for their protection. You may soon find the answer."

Tekoah looked down, her face burning. "I have not seen Braith since—"

"I know." Reika's voice was gentle. "And whatever wisdom the gods have given us, it does not seem to extend into matters of the heart, does it?"

For a moment, they said no more.

Tekoah drifted through the downy air, weightless. *I could do this forever,* she thought. Then she remembered something. She looked at Reika, whose eyes were closed, sooty lashes brushing her cheeks.

"Zant! What if he comes to Stern? I cannot bear the thought of it! Zant—near the ones I love."

Reika answered without opening her eyes. "In this moment, we cannot know what will happen to your brothers, or Master Chalvern. I love them as well." A shudder marred the tranquillity of her features for a moment. "But I know where Zant is at this moment."

"Where?"

"Here. In the palace."

"No!" Tekoah had a vivid image of Saura's cold grey eyes filling with sudden tears as she stared at the barren gardens of her former queen. "Can we not save Saura?" she asked, but she knew even as she spoke that the plea was futile.

Reika shook her head. "It is too late. He has finished with her now," she said with certainty. Then, without warning, she let out a low moan. "The Morg," she said, "it hunts!"

All around them, the rainbow slivers of light moved, and Tekoah had the sensation that she was no longer altogether whole, but a loosely bound configuration of dancing rainbow shapes. At any moment, her form could scatter into bright irretrievable fragments. She must try to concentrate, for there was something important she had been thinking about only a moment before.

"The Morg," she said thickly, "It hunts for me. You are keeping me safe."

"Yes." The word came from Reika in a muffled moan.

"Then what is it? What is wrong?" Tekoah asked her. "Are you about to Journey?"

"I am here with you," Reika replied. Her voice grew fierce. "Keep talking to me!"

"I know you are here with me," Tekoah repeated, baffled. Then, following her thoughts, like winding through a dark maze, "Do you mean that part of you is not?" When Reika did not answer, she repeated, "Part of you is not here. Where is it, then?"

Reika was silent for a moment. A spasm crossed her face. "Now it comes," she murmured.

And then, all at once, the awful truth Tekoah had been staving off descended upon her.

And with it the same dread she had when watching the sorcerer Braith lift his hand in that careless, deadly wave toward Grindhor and Melnich in the village square. When walking around the back of the forge in search of her pony. And standing in the moonlit snow as the gleaming yellow Morg-eyes formed a circle around her.

"Reika," she said, and her shriek came out as a whisper. "But you are here! You are safe."

"Yes," Reika answered, opening her lustrous eyes in which the pupils seemed dilated, "my spirit is here, beyond all harm. But my body lies in your chamber, where the Morg will seek you out. And I am afraid. Please—keep talking to me. It is almost upon me, now."

"Why? Why do you do this?" Tekoah could say nothing more through her dry and burning throat.

"Because all the others are in a Shifting. Without you, the Mantling cannot take place." Reika paused, gasping. "If Zant kills you now, he has won."

With a visible effort, she slowed her breathing and took Tekoah's hand.

"This was my destiny from the first. And it is glorious, more than I deserved. I have placed my trust in Anna and have been rewarded. Remember, I am not Anniste by birth, so this is an honour that will carry me like the crest of a silver wave to the Halls of the Worldmaker. Ah…"

Reika's voice rose, and she cried out once, twice, three times.

"I forbid you to sacrifice yourself for me," Tekoah said. Reika did not answer. Tekoah sobbed. "Do you hear me? I reject it! I reject it!"

"It is too late," Reika whispered. Her head lolled back.

Tekoah's grief for her mother fused somehow with sorrow for Reika, and she saw her pain reflected in the pinpoint rainbow lights that danced around her.

Reika shuddered, and then a great calm seemed to descend upon her. "Ah, thank Anna, it is over." She opened her eyes and smiled at Tekoah.

Then, before Tekoah could say anything, Reika's form dissolved into the surrounding brightness; her hand, which Tekoah still held, was the last part of her to slip away.

WHEN TEKOAH CAME to under the willows, she had the wild hope that perhaps this Journey, too, heralded events that had not yet taken place. But from the palace she heard distant shrieks and knew that the servants must have discovered the carnage in her chamber. Morgs were not subtle killers.

She thought of Reika—who had never shown fear even by the flicker of an eyelid—whispering, "I am afraid."

Sitting against a willow trunk, staring at the sky, her eyes were open but unseeing; she wished for tears to come to ease the sandy burning she felt behind her eyes. Remembering her first Journey, how frightening it was; how unwilling she had been to risk memory, to risk pain. And then she had awakened to the sweet comfort of nestling in Reika's lap, while tears had dripped from Reika's eyes like warm rain.

And then Tekoah wept for a long time, holding her hands over her ears so that she would not hear any more sounds from the palace.

When she took her hands from her ears, Tekoah heard a rustle behind her. She stiffened. Was it Reika, still alive somehow, coming to tell her it had all been a dream and not a Journey after all? No. Reika would have said something reassuring by now.

Tekoah could not look. She did not dare. Terror flooded her with an animal urge to burrow into the ground. *Anna, do not let it be a Morg, she prayed. Let the Morg go after someone else, anyone else!* Such guilt overwhelmed her with that thought, that she stood up and looked in the rustling's direction, determined to meet any fate that had come.

Tekoah stood staring, dumbstruck. This, least of all, was what she had expected.

Braith stood just outside the willow grove. In the shimmery spring moonlight, there was no mistaking him for anyone else. He was clad as always in black, so that he seemed to blend in with the night behind him. His crimson gloves were clasped together. He did not speak, did not utter one word; but his entire attitude, from his lean, taut face to his clasped hands, was one of intense supplication.

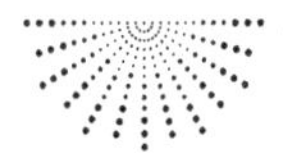

The unceasing, ecstatic blare of trumpets along the ramparts told Weslan that Dirken had finally arrived. And although he was alone in the castle's makeshift infirmary, he sensed the tension break all around him, as at the first crack of thunder in a long-impending storm. His heart thudded painfully in his chest, and he cursed himself for coughing when he finally sat up. It was not how he imagined greeting the leader of the Kalesh.

He smiled wryly at his last thought, thinking that it summed up his life nicely. Perhaps he should rein in his expectations. Reika had said something like that, hadn't she? What was it exactly? If only he could remember. If only he could see her again, then he would ask her.

And then she would take his hand, laughing, saying, "Work it out for yourself, lazy one."

How he missed her.

Weslan heard a mighty cheer go up outside. *Dirken must be riding through the gates now.* Mayhap he was strong enough to get up, go to the window.

He tried to swing his legs over the edge of the cot, but everything began swimming around. What was he thinking of? He was on the wrong side of the castle for a start, so he would not have been able to see anything except a duck pond and a lovely view of Mount Delnor to the west. Ah, what a dismal excuse for a soldier he was at that moment. He slumped back down on the pallet.

He must have fallen asleep without knowing it, for when he opened his eyes, Weslan realized night had fallen. Through his window he could see they had kindled a fire in the great hearth of the banquet room. A candle also flickered on his bedside table.

Weslan stared at the candle drowsily for some time before he thought to wonder why anyone had bothered to light one, when he was sleeping. A slight movement beside him made him turn his head.

Dirken sat in a chair beside the cot, his face wavering in the flickering candlelit shadows. He leaned forward, forearms resting on his knees in the relaxed yet watchful posture of a seasoned soldier.

Weslan sat up, then began coughing. Dirken reached for the water jug which stood on the table, pouring some into a mug and handing it to Weslan.

"I am sorry if I awakened you," he said.

Weslan took a deep gulp of water, and then another, though he did not need one—to give him time.

"That is all right," he muttered.

"I would not have disturbed you at all, for Heyg has told me you are ill," Dirken continued. "But I am to give a speech to the men in the morning, and I must ensure that I know as much as every man here—and more—if I am to keep the small trust I have earned among the people." Dirken's mouth quirked in a wry smile.

"How may I serve you?" Weslan heard his voice, stiff and rusty, as if it belonged to an old man. He cleared his throat.

"I hear you visited Berlot and have returned with news of an impending invasion. We knew about it, of course. But not that it would be this soon. Are you certain of your information?"

Weslan nodded. He found it more difficult to look at Dirken than he had thought it would be.

"Heyg insists it was with his approval that you went." Dirken paused, then added, "That is fortunate for you. Otherwise, your cough might be even worse."

He does not like me any better than I like him, Weslan thought, staring back at Dirken, whom many, many others hoped would one day be king. The nobles at Rhantor had told him half-jokingly that it was acceptable to have enemies, as long as none of them were powerful.

But what about powerful friends? Were they any less dangerous? Braith, for instance.

"Well?" Dirken said, breaking the silence. His chair creaked as he leaned forward.

"I went to rescue the queen," Weslan told him. The words sounded silly as he said them, childish and naïve. Dirken's expression did not change, so Weslan added, "She did not wish to be rescued."

"Apparently not," Dirken said dryly. "Why did you risk so much on such a—if I may express an opinion—foolhardy venture?"

"It did not seem that way to me. We had done a poor job of protecting her, after all our fine words. I thought that any risk was worth restoring her to her throne, and dignity to the North."

"You think we have lost our dignity, then?"

"Perhaps it was my dignity I was thinking of."

Dirken smiled faintly at that, and Weslan wondered why he had spoken such words that revealed his vulnerability to a man he did not know or trust.

Before he had time to think about it further, Dirken began

speaking again, as one commander speaks to another on a field of battle, weighing strategies one against another.

"Well, this is very useful, very important, and so I am glad despite everything that you went. But it raises a dilemma, and the dilemma is this: although I have sworn to be truthful always with my men, I feel that to tell them that their queen has betrayed them, especially now, would impair their spirits. This is a thing we can ill afford; do you not agree?"

Weslan nodded. "Why not just keep silent for a few days?" he ventured.

"Yes, I could do that, but Heyg tells me that rumours of your adventure have multiplied like mosquitoes in a swamp. Is there anything you can tell me, that Darielle did or said, which we might construe in a more positive light?"

Dirken was looking steadily at Weslan, and even in the candlelight Weslan could see the challenge in his eyes. His lips twitched, whether in mirth Weslan could not tell.

He is trying to find out if I am stupid, Weslan thought, *if I am capable of any subtlety at all.*

"The queen was pining for the melons of the North," Weslan said. "She missed them so much, she said, that all other fruit seemed sour to her."

"Ah," Dirken said, smiling in approval. "I have that to work with, at least."

Weslan felt an unwilling surge of gratification at Dirken's smile. He ignored it, saying, "But surely that is not enough to set the men at ease?"

"It must be enough."

Weslan lay back against the pillow; he felt tired all at once.

Dirken spoke again, sounding amused. "You look as if you do not believe me, soldier. And yet when you are out in the court-yard at dawn tomorrow, listening to my call to arms, you will believe me then."

"I?" Weslan echoed, opening his eyes. "But I thought I would be of no use to you, being ill. Chalvern has said—"

"You will come out to the courtyard, cot and all," Dirken answered, "as any true and loyal soldier of the North would wish."

Weslan nodded, feeling miserable. He wanted to explain that he had meant no disrespect, no disloyalty, but what was the point? It seemed inevitable that he and Dirken would always clash.

"Your presence will lend credence to my words," Dirken continued, stroking his smooth-shaven chin.

Weslan wondered how he had found time to scrape his face on his three-day ride to Stern. He fingered his own stubbled chin self-consciously, thinking he must look like a whipped umbray.

"You appear fatigued," Dirken added, as if reading his mind. "And yet I must ask for your indulgence for a moment longer."

At that moment, there came the sound of footsteps in the corridor. Almost at once, the door was flung open, and a messenger came in. He bowed as he came, staggering a little. Weslan could see that he was exhausted—his hair was soaked with sweat, and his clothes were covered with dust.

Dirken stood, pushing the chair on which he had been sitting toward the messenger; tapping the man's shoulder to make him sit. "What message do you bear?" he asked.

For a little while, the man did not speak, and Weslan saw it was because he could not catch his breath. He gasped raggedly, and the sound of it set Weslan to coughing again. Dirken sat, patient.

At last, the messenger looked up, eyes as grey as the dust on his tunic. "King Darian is dead. The sorcerer Zant assassinated him, they say. But the official word is that he killed himself."

Dirken nodded. "Go on. There is more, is there not?"

The man nodded. "Yes. The people are crying for a genuine

leader to take the throne. There is no one in the South, they say, and no one in the North. So let Berlot take the throne—as long as there is someone to ensure they do not starve."

Weslan looked at Dirken to see his reaction; his complexion neither rose nor paled, but his eyes seemed to kindle brighter in the candlelight.

"Anything else?"

"The first line of the Berlotan army is sweeping toward Meed. None are hindering them."

"Thank you," Dirken said. "Be assured that none of this surprises me, except perhaps the untimely death of King Darian, and we shall weep for him another time." He grinned with an unexpected ferocity which startled Weslan. "Go now and find my second in command, Heyg, who will see to it you are fed and found a bed. I shall salute you in the courtyard at dawn."

The man nodded, bowed again, and left the room.

Dirken turned back to Weslan, lifting a finger. "Their stronghold will be Meed, but they are not counting on the Taboran Mountains, where their horses will hinder them."

"Nor are they counting on Shiftings."

"Ah, good point. Shiftings, on which no one had counted. Except perhaps, those who have the exceptionally good fortune of being privy to the councils of sorcerers." Dirken was still standing; he pulled the chair up close to the cot and leaned forward, looking Weslan full in the face. "This brings me to our next topic of discussion. Sorcerers."

Weslan's scalp prickled with unease as Dirken looked at him. He forced himself to look back without flinching.

"When you were at Rhantor court, we well knew that the sorcerer Braith had befriended you. What we did not know was why." Dirken paused, as if waiting for Weslan to respond. When he did not, Dirken continued, "It did not matter so much then, because we did not see Braith as a threat to the queen, or to the North. Quite the contrary. We considered him to be 'our' sorcerer, and even harboured the silly notion that he might champion our cause against Zant, Darian, and the Jinta, who had become very cozy.

"When you left Rhantor—quite suddenly I might add—Braith left with you. Soon afterward, Queen Darielle was abducted and Rhantor fell prey to the childish tantrums of her brother. You disappeared for quite some time. The sorcerer Braith has not resurfaced since."

Dirken let the weight of his words sink like stones into Weslan's breast. Then he asked, "Do you know where Braith is, or what he is doing?"

"I do not," Weslan answered.

"Why did you leave Rhantor?" Dirken was shooting out the questions as if he was interrogating a captured Berlotan.

Weslan clenched his teeth. "I was summoned home on urgent family business."

"Why were you accompanied by a sorcerer on urgent family business?"

Weslan did not reply.

"If you do not answer to my satisfaction, I shall have to assume that you are lying, and it was not family business at all that took you away, but that you had an agreement with Zant to absent yourself from the palace when the queen was abducted."

Weslan felt the colour leaving his face. He sat up, words welling up in his throat, but for a moment he could do nothing more than cough. Dirken picked up the mug of water and handed it to him. His eyes were like stones.

"I was visiting my sister, who is Anniste," Weslan muttered, when he had caught his breath. "I had reason to believe she was in grave danger."

Dirken gazed at him for a moment. When he spoke, his words were slow and measured. "I stood in this castle of mine a few days after the time of which we speak. Your sister was here, alone, disoriented. She fled without giving me a coherent explanation. But the one thing she told me, which I understood perfectly well, was that she could not find you."

Weslan sat silent. What could he say, where could he begin? It was all madness anyway. His forehead throbbed, and the fever gripped him again.

"Your sister did not know whether you were living or dead for many days," Dirken added coldly, "and has been much tormented over it."

"What do you mean? How do you come to speak of Tekoah that way? As if you know her well. When have you seen her?" Weslan's agitation was such that he almost leaped from the bed. A stabbing pain shot through his eye, but still he glared at Dirken.

"I saw her last three days ago in Zantor," Dirken said shortly. "And I tried everything in my power to persuade her to come here with me, for she is in danger, as you pointed out. What I do not understand is why you would abandon her."

"I did not abandon her."

"Then why don't you simply tell me what happened between the day you left Rhantor, and the day you walked out of the woods and rejoined Heyg?"

Weslan looked down, picking at the edges of the bandages Chalvern had wrapped around his hands, which were scraped raw from scrabbling among the riverside stones.

Dirken cleared his throat. "If it helps any, I believe you did not betray your queen. Perhaps you were enticed by Braith under false pretences, and then were reluctant to come forward, knowing you would be suspected."

"What a filthy bunch of rot!" Weslan burst out. Dirken's reasonable tone enraged him. "I am not a coward. If you do not know that by now—"

Dirken held up his hand. "Of course not. No coward would sneak into Berlot alone on the eve of war. Tekoah and Braith both vouch for you, and that is enough for me."

"I must ask you why you feel free to address my sister by her first name?" Weslan said stiffly.

"My question came first."

"Very well." Perhaps he should surprise Dirken, wipe that superior look off his face. "I learned from my sister that my mother had been murdered by my father while I was at Rhantor. I went to even the score."

Dirken's face remained unchanged. "What you say has been verified by Tekoah. I will forget that I ever heard it. Go on. Where did you go afterward? And where was Braith during this time?"

"I went mad and lived like a beast in the Taboran Woods until an Anniste woman named Reika sought me out and healed me." Weslan grinned savagely at Dirken. "And, since you are on such friendly terms with my sister, perhaps she should tell you where Braith was all that time."

And at last, he saw what he had been hoping to see. A reaction. A change of expression in that proud, self-contained face.

Dirken's eyes flashed flint-sparks, and he half-stood before sitting back down on his chair with an effort. "What in Anna's name do you mean by that?"

"I mean, you have guessed half-right," Weslan said bitterly. "I was duped by Braith, but not for the reason you think. He does not give a jot about the queen, or Rhantor, or any of our petty politics. We could all sink into the Pit as far as he is concerned."

"What are you saying?" Dirken asked, his voice deadly quiet.

"Not that it is any of your business," Weslan told him pointedly, "but the sorcerer Braith is in love with my sister. That is the only reason he befriended me. Come to that, it is the reason the Queen Darielle was not killed by an assassin the night that I saved her. Braith told me about it, so I would look like a hero, and get into the queen's bedchamber. I owed him something after that, you see. So, it was not hard to convince me to take him with me to Stern, to rescue my sister. After that, he did not need me anymore. I have not seen him since."

Before Weslan knew what was happening, Dirken had grabbed him by his shirt-front and was shaking him violently. "If you are lying—" he growled.

Weslan did not reply, but let himself go limp and, at last, Dirken stopped. His forehead was covered with a sheen of sweat.

"Why would I lie about something so hideous, and so humiliating?" Weslan whispered and began coughing again.

Dirken gazed at him for a long moment, then handed him his mug of water. "Are you saying she is his mistress?" he asked flatly.

"No. He abducted her against her will. I don't know much else, except what I heard from Reika: that Tekoah had somehow escaped—I think it was outside this castle that Reika found her —and that she had rejoined the Anniste on my Aunt Beula's farm. I had thought she was safe, right up until I saw Chalvern yesterday."

"That is why she was in my castle that day, looking so pale and dazed." Dirken murmured, as if speaking to himself. "And why she would never speak to me of it. By the Holy Mantling, what a monster he is!"

"At least he is not out to murder her, with a pack of fiends from the Pit."

Dirken's eyes flashed those dangerous-looking sparks again. "Are you saying that your sister is *fortunate* to have attracted the attentions of a sorcerer?"

"She seems to have attracted the attention of both sorcerers," Weslan answered. "And others as well." He spoke it as a challenge, as it was meant to be. He was greatly gratified to see that Dirken looked discomfited.

"My intentions toward your sister are nothing but honourable," he began.

"Forgive me," Weslan interrupted, unable to resist, "but my sister did not have the fortune of knowing you at the queen's court in happier times than these. Your reputation was of the blackest when it came to women. In fact, I personally recall a night where several at once—"

"Enough," Dirken snapped, standing up and glaring down at him.

Weslan grinned. After a moment, reluctantly, Dirken grinned back. Then he turned abruptly away, striding toward the door.

"I will see you at dawn in the courtyard, soldier!" he flung over his shoulder.

Wonderful, Weslan thought, turning onto his side and pulling the blanket over him. *That should give me at least a quarter of an hour's sleep.*

CHAPTER 48

*D*irken was true to his word. Raol and Fanco appeared at first light and carried Weslan's cot out into the courtyard. He was slumbering at the time and did not wake until they put him down with a thud among loud guffaws. Blinking, he opened his eyes, scowling up at his smirking brothers and other soldiers who milled around him, each determined to outdo the witticisms of the rest.

They had placed him on a dais of some sort, under a pavilion that must have been erected since he had ridden into the courtyard five days earlier, for he had not seen it until that moment. Perhaps there had been fears it would rain.

It would never do to have the spirits of the army dampened while Dirken made his speech, Weslan thought peevishly.

He was feeling cranky and ill. Why did Dirken insist on having him out there? A punishment of sorts, mayhap, for daring to decide on his own. Dirken would probably have had him executed if he was not so besotted with Tekoah. Fortunately for Weslan, executing the brother of his true love was not the way to advance his courtship.

There was nothing much to look at, except the soldiers

milling expectantly about the courtyard, chewing venison jerky, and squinting at the rising sun. Weslan wished that it had risen just a little later. He closed his eyes.

"We will never win the war if this is how relaxed the army is," said a familiar voice.

He looked up to see Nolvern grinning his gap-toothed grin. Before Weslan could make a suitable retort, a cheer went up from the crowd of soldiers. Nolvern whipped around and then joined in the cheer, unsheathing his sword and waving it exuberantly over his head. The lord of Mirrand had emerged from the castle.

Bareheaded, wearing a mail vest over a white tunic with billowing sleeves, Dirken looked as if he had stepped out of a tapestry.

And he knows it, Weslan thought sullenly, rubbing sleep from his eyes.

Dirken waved as he loped easily along, clapping the shoulders of the soldiers, who parted before him like wheat stalks before a wind. Behind him strode Heyg, with his perpetually furrowed brow, hand on his sword-hilt as if he expected an attack at any moment. They were coming toward the dais.

Oh Rhan, Weslan thought, *I had better sit up straighter.*

There were three wooden steps leading up to the dais. Dirken ignored them and leaped lightly up onto the platform, provoking another cheer. Heyg climbed the stairs, favouring Weslan with a wink before turning to stand formally behind Dirken and to his right.

Dirken held up a hand for silence. He waited until it was so quiet that the only sounds Weslan could hear were the warblers singing in a nearby crohm grove and the shuffling of the sentries' boots on the battlements as they leaned over to watch the proceedings.

Then he lowered his hand and gestured with the other

toward the east—and the sunrise. "A new day!" he shouted, "And with it a new beginning for Miraven!"

There was near pandemonium then, but it died down more quickly than before. Everyone was curious to know what Dirken would say next. Weslan stifled a cough and waited with the rest. He was feeling a twinge of excitement despite himself.

"My father—may Anna cradle his soul—was a close friend to King Garan," Dirken continued, "and they shared a deep desire that came from their noble hearts. That desire is mine also: that the North and the South of Miraven should stand united. Why should we continually strive against each other, merely because the Taboran Mountains cleave us in two? It only weakens and divides us.

"Brothers and sisters born from the same mother and father are separate, but still they form a family, do they not?

"Standing before you today, I see many faces from across the mountains, and to you I say 'Hail brother, come to defend our family, our land, against those who would rape and defile it. Against those who have no reverence for our mother, who is Anna, or her servants, the Anniste!'"

Dirken paused, leaning forward, face stern, waiting for his words to sink in. It was the first time Weslan had heard anyone openly defy the priesthood's injunction against the Anniste. He saw some men shifting uneasily, looking at each other in confusion. Others were nodding at Dirken, nudging each other and stamping their feet.

Weslan thought of Tekoah, Beula, Reika, and wondered how many men had Anniste women in their families who had been murdered. And had stood by, doing nothing.

"There has been enough innocent blood shed," Dirken was saying. "The time to show our strength, our power, is now! By the Holy Mantling, it is now!"

A roar went up from the crowd. Insanely, Weslan stood on his pallet in his nightshirt, clenched fist over his head, shouting

"Now!" with the rest. But his throat was sore and his cough worse, so he could not last long.

As he sat down, he saw Heyg looking at him, openly guffawing. Weslan ducked his head, embarrassed. It was not something he could help, though. Like the man or not, he had to admit that Dirken had a way of putting things.

The soldiers had subsided a little, enough so that a soldier's loud voice could be heard from near the front. "What about the sorcerers?" he asked. "What about the Shiftings? I lost two of my mates in one day to a Shifting, sir, if you don't mind me pointing that out."

"Yah, the stinking Berlotans have the sorcerers on their side!" someone else shouted. "We don't have the chance of a lamb in a pack of umbrays, not with sorcery afoot."

"Good point," Dirken said. "But remember this: the Shiftings will hinder the Berlotan army as much as it does ours. I intend we shall stay put here and make them come to us. In the long run, Zant has worked against himself. Also, there is only one sorcerer that we know for certain is working against us, and that is Zant, the Serpent. Morogh is dead. And Braith has shown himself to be more inclined to aid us than otherwise. This is something that may give us some hope in the days that lie ahead."

There were murmurs of astonishment. Dirken had surprised them with that one.

BUT WESLAN WAS UNEASY. Dirken had not lied, but Weslan knew he was uncertain where Braith's sympathies lay—other than with Tekoah. His mind had been working with far-reaching possibilities in the few hours since they had spoken at Weslan's bedside.

"There is something else I would say," Dirken shouted, "before we prepare for the battle that will come before another sunrise."

He grinned at the men, as intimately as if they were all in a smoky tavern, sharing a joke over a mug of ale.

"In my recent travels, incognito of course"—he paused to smile at the ripple of laughter that swept the courtyard—"I heard it said that Raveners are cowards, because we did not attack Berlot when our queen was abducted."

The crowd vibrated with angry murmurs. Dirken looked pleased at this. "The fools who said this did not take it into consideration that we still had a King—Darian—who, although unworthy of that station, still commanded our fealty because of the respect we had for his father, the late King Garan.

"Even more to the point, we did not have an organized army." He stopped, chuckling. "We had not needed one for many years. Now we do. And we have got one!"

Dirken unsheathed his sword, raising it over his head. Then he pointed it straight at Weslan.

Weslan felt his stomach shrivel and harden into a pitaya pit as hundreds of eyes turned toward him. What on earth was Dirken doing?

"This man," Dirken shouted, "is no coward. He risked a trip to Berlot three nights ago, just before they shut off the river traffic to prepare for this war. Disguised, he made his way into the palace and spoke with the queen for a moment, before being forced to flee for his life."

Everyone was staring at Weslan with undisguised fascination. He sat in his nightshirt, stunned. Dirken was speaking of him as if he was a hero. As he had always dreamed of being, ever since the day he'd run away from the forge.

"Weslan dar Veld," Dirken boomed, "brought back a message from the queen, and it is with this message that I end your call to arms: Queen Darielle yearns for the melons of the North, which cannot be quenched by any other fruit!"

NATURALLY, the men went berserk after that. Weslan reflected on it later that evening, after several hours of restorative slumber, while sipping mutton broth and eating with relish some fresh-baked bread with cheese. Dirken's words—the men's cheers, directed at him—appeared to have acted as a tonic for his health, for he was feeling much improved.

Weslan's uneasiness remained, however, because he had been there, had known what Darielle had said and the way she had said it. But that moment of glory—when everyone had looked at him with admiration and awe—he would never forget it.

He was still baffled with disbelief that Dirken had elevated his status in such a fashion. One part of him suspected that it was probably just a ploy to win Tekoah's gratitude and approval. Still, Dirken needn't have gone that far.

Weslan set his soup bowl down, savouring the moment once again. His mind drifted, thinking about how his family had blossomed. He had not believed his eyes when seeing his twin brothers thriving—so confident and competent. And then there was Tekoah. She had two of the most powerful personages in the land, sparring fiercely for her hand. His little sister. Perhaps his family was destined for great things, now that Veld's curse was lifted. What a marvellous thought.

In the middle of his reverie, Dirken came striding in, dressed for battle, his mail vest augmented by a helmet and thigh-high leather boots.

"We expect the Berlotans will be here within the next few hours," Dirken said in a clipped, brisk tone. "We do not have the luxury of scouts, of course, because of the Shiftings, but based on your information, we think it an accurate guess."

Weslan nodded, wondering why Dirken had taken the time to bother telling him, when he would not even be there to witness the battle, let alone fight. His sword arm twitched in a spasm of longing for action.

"I came to ask you something," Dirken said, and a curious hesitation came into his hazel eyes.

"How may I serve you?" Weslan asked, deferentially. He no longer had any doubt that Dirken would one day be king of Miraven. If they won the war.

"Your sister, Tekoah. I urged her to come here, when and if she can. Will you please look out for her and reassure her if she arrives while I am gone? Tell her I will return as soon as possible?"

"Of course." What else was there to say, except more teasing about Dirken's terrible reputation as a womanizer? And somehow that did not seem appropriate at the moment.

Dirken turned to go.

"Wait," Weslan said. "Thank you. For today. I mean, your speech. What you said about me."

"I spoke only the truth, so there is no need to thank me. It also inspired the men, and so it was very useful. Do not worry," he added, his eyes crinkling up above his visor, so that Weslan knew he was grinning. "This does not mean that we are brothers of the heart!"

Just then there was a great clatter in the corridor. A soldier came running through the open doorway of the banquet hall, slipping and sliding in his boots across the tiles and skidding to an ungraceful halt in front of them. He bowed to Dirken, his face very white.

"It has begun," he said.

Dirken turned and strode from the room. Weslan leaped with the alacrity of a soldier used to sleeping with his sword, and then he fell back onto the cot weakly, gasping and cursing at the same time.

CHAPTER 49

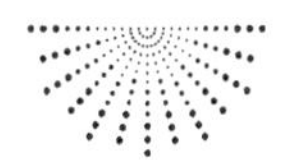

$\mathcal{C}$halvern lay dying on the rough wooden floor of his shop. To pass the time, he recited the names of all the healing herbs he knew, alphabetically. "Anise, annaroot, leaf of aloe, belladonna, bursta-root, bolarberry, crohm-bark, cerise berry gel..." He made his lips keep moving to keep from thinking about how he had failed.

For he had failed in the end, despite all his best intentions. One could never be sure about it until one was at the end, of course. There was always the chance that one could still fix things, make them right. But he was at the end now, and nothing had been made right.

Zant had driven that point home. The sorcerer had stood over him, watching with undisguised amusement as Chalvern had clutched his chest when the familiar pains had begun.

"I shall not bother killing you," Zant had drawled in his sibilant voice. "You have been dying for so many turnings, old one, that there is practically nothing left to kill. And I have enjoyed talking to you, more than to most of your kind. What a funny little man you are! You thought you could make a difference."

Zant had laughed, a high woman's laugh. Chalvern had not

been surprised at this, for he'd thought he'd found out Zant's secret.

Chalvern had held onto the pain for a time, had ridden with it, as he had been taught. Pain was a wild mountain stallion. It bucked and thrashed mercilessly, but he would not let it throw him.

And every so often—as in that very moment—the ride was smoother, and he could look back at his life's experiences with a greater clarity than he ever had before.

Before him rose Neela's face, as smooth and lovely as it had been the first time he had seen it.

She came at his urgent plea. Chalvern had not requested the services of a healer since the death of his wife in childbirth ten turnings before, but he sensed he was not equipped to handle this situation.

Barton, his youngest son, had been bitten by a swamp serpent while fishing for eels down at Stern's End.

It was harvest-time, and his elder son Cedor was out threshing barley. At Chalvern's frantic bidding, the boys who had carried Barton home bolted to the healer's lodge in the village. But Rayena, the Guardian of the Anniste, was busy with a difficult midwifery of twins, so she sent her daughter, Neela.

Alone in his little cottage, Chalvern panicked. Quiet, self-possessed, fiercely independent until that moment, he watched in horror as his son's face grew flushed and hot, and the flesh above his ankle became so swollen that the actual bite disappeared beneath the yellow-streaked flesh.

He waited, ears straining for the sound of footsteps outside his door; suspended in time. He, the revered village School Master—helplessly watching his son die.

Finally, there came a quiet rap on the door and Neela entered.

Chalvern had not looked at her properly since she had been a child, stammering shyly with the other urchins as she learned her letters. So, when she came forward, throwing back her brown hood and moving quickly over to the bed, Chalvern involuntarily caught his breath.

Neela's lustrous chestnut hair was braided down her back, and her eyes like the sky reflected in the sea. Chalvern's heart surged forward like a wave in the tide, foaming helplessly at her feet.

Neela seemed unaware of his reaction. She had saved his son's life, coolly and quietly, practicing the healing arts of the mind and body with a skill that humbled him forever. All his pretensions of knowledge and wisdom had seemed only fleas hopping into a hearth fire compared to her.

Within a few hours, Barton was sitting up, weak but good-humoured, attempting to flirt with Neela as he sipped herb tea. He looked at her in a way that had made Chalvern want to backhand him, forgetting that he had wept over his son's prostrate body only a short time earlier.

Riding his pain, feeling it dull a little, Chalvern could see it all clearly now: he had decided to become an apothecary on that day, after watching Neela the healer at work.

What he had secretly wanted was to be Anniste, but of course that was not possible. Apothecary was the next best thing.

His sons had been ashamed of him; for anything to do with healing was a lowly art—the province of women! Cedor and Barton had gone on to the priesthood and had left for the magnificent temple in the South, in Meed. They seldom bothered to communicate with their father, and so could not know that he was also ashamed of them.

But the Anniste in Stern had been grateful, for Chalvern had shouldered the menial tasks—combing the woods for herbs and barks, flowers and berries; sorting, drying, simmering, clarifying; performing the endless renderings from plant to remedy. He had freed the healers to do what they did, which was to commune with people, gain their confidence, and infuse them with tranquillity even when facing pain and death.

But Chalvern had never believed their power truly came from Anna, for in his heart he did not believe in the gods. Sorcerers, yes; gods, no.

After the departure of his sons, Chalvern had sold his farm and had moved to the shop in the village, closer to the healer's lodge. He had continued to teach the village children, and in return he'd been fed and clothed by the villagers. But he'd known his true reward: a chance to be nearer to the distant, gleaming shore that was Neela.

"Fennel, goldenrod, lavender, lobelia, marigold, nettle…"

Chalvern gasped for air, feeling the knife thrust in his chest. If he could just have a sip of water. But although he tried, he could not make himself rise from the wooden floor.

He swallowed. It would not be long now, and perhaps then he would see Neela again. If only he could truly believe it, he would be glad, so glad. He had waited so long for her—ever since the day he thought she was lost to him forever.

WHEN HE HEARD that Neela was to marry Veld the blacksmith, Chalvern felt his heart shrivel like a handful of herbs in the sun.

Tall, handsome in the way of a hastily groomed mule posing as a thoroughbred, insufferably arrogant, Veld held a great appeal for many of the village girls. But never would Chalvern have thought Neela among them. Not that he had even dared hope she would look at him that way. But for her to marry someone like Veld was an outrage.

Chalvern was not himself that day. He locked himself in his shop, and darkly fingered some packets of powder, a few tiny grains of which he knew would end his life instantly—or Veld's. But he was a thinker, not a man of action. A coward, if it came right down to that. The hoofprints of a sorcerer's mount upon his ribs had molded his destiny as a spectator, not a man of action. He stowed the packets away.

And—worse—in the end, Chalvern attended the wedding, becoming uncharacteristically intoxicated. The next day he endured much laughter from the villagers. They stopped by his shop to remind him he had been carted home in a wheelbarrow by Neela's brother-in-law, Tok, singing mournfully the whole time. Chalvern shrugged, and said he could not remember.

Now it seemed there was nothing to do but remember.

"Plantain, prickly ash, savoury, red sumac berries, valerian root, white willow bark."

"Neela!" The cry was torn from him, hovering in the empty air of his shop, setting the dust motes atremble.

Zant had been right—the worst of it was being alone.

AND THEN ALL at once she was there. Neela. Unlike before, for this was not merely a memory. She was in his mind, salving the wounds, filling the empty places, lighting the dark, cobwebbed corners. Her warm, slightly husky voice was so real that Chalvern lifted his head, craning his neck to see her. Her laughter rippled through him like cool water, and he laid his head back down.

"Will it be all right, then?" he asked her, his voice so weak could barely hear it himself.

"Yes."

"But Zant is going to kill Tekoah. And then she—he—it, will be immortal. There is nothing more terrible than that thought: Zant ruling for another however many hundred turnings —unchallenged."

"No." Neela said it with quiet certainty.

"*No*? Why?"

"Think," Neela coaxed.

"But I am so tired." Chalvern protested. "Why are you making me think right now of all times?". Then it struck him, jolting him into a more wakeful state.

"The Mantling?"

"Very good, my lad," she answered, mimicking his schoolmaster's voice.

"So, it is actually going to happen," Chalvern marvelled. "I wish I could live to see it."

He lay quietly for a few seconds, revelling in the feel of Neela within him. There was no loneliness now. The ache that had lived in his heart for so long had disappeared entirely.

"You should have married me," he chided Neela. "We were meant for each other."

"I know," she answered, adding quietly, "but it is not too late. Soon—"

"You mean I am to join you? Now?"

"Not quite," Neela replied. Her voice was a cool hand stroking his forehead. "First, there is something you must do."

"Do?" Chalvern laughed at the absurdity of it. "But I am dying. I cannot move. What is it you would have me do?"

"There is a healing you must begin, although someone else will finish it. There will be no peace for you, or for me, until you do this."

"A healing? Of what do you speak?"

"That, you must find out yourself. Reach within. Remember that nothing happens without cause. Remember what you spoke of with Zant. About the damage done."

Neela's warm presence faded from his mind. For a moment, Chalvern felt nothing but cold desolation.

But then he thought about what Neela had said. About his conversation with Zant. Yes, it had been strange, that conversation, and more than bizarre that Zant had confided in him. It was almost as if the sorcerer had needed to tell one other living soul, and it had just happened to be he.

This is the tale of my life, Chalvern thought. *Everyone chooses me to tell.*

Now think.

He had entered his shop to see the sorcerer Zant standing in front of his hearth. The door had shut behind him of its own accord, but Chalvern had already grasped the fact that there was no point in running. He had felt terror, of course, but also a great curiosity.

"You stare, pop-eyed," Zant had whispered. "As though you

had never seen a sorcerer before." He had smiled, folding his arms within his wide-sleeved Berlotan tunic. "But we both know you have."

"Indeed," Chalvern had answered carefully. "I had a sorcerer for an apprentice, and now my reputation as a great teacher is undisputed."

He had moved toward the table slowly, feeling Zant's eyes upon him. Whatever happened, he had to sit down. So, he'd reached the chair and sat.

Zant had laughed softly. "You are a wit, Chalvern the apothecary. Master Chalvern, they call you, so I shall as well."

Chalvern had inclined his head silently.

"We will talk a little, you and I," Zant had continued, holding his hands out once more to the fire. "How fares your apprentice now?"

"I fear my apprentice has little time for his old acquaintances," Chalvern had begun, but suddenly there had been a pain in his left temple, so hot and fierce that he had cried out involuntarily.

"Do not lie to me," Zant had hissed without turning from the fire. "Not to *me*."

Chalvern had sat holding his head, staring at the table. Within his mind had arisen the image which still haunted: the trampling hooves of Morogh's steed bearing down inexorably upon him. He had felt another smaller pain in his temple, and a strange probing sensation in his mind.

Zant had continued to speak casually, without looking at him. "Yes, I know all about how you were stamped and stomped by Morogh's horse, who cared not a whit for mortals, and nor did his rider, and nor do I. It is a cautionary tale, carrying a sad lesson, one that folk would do well to learn when dealing with sorcerers."

Chalvern had winced. Zant had smiled a chilly smile before continuing.

"I know you were visited by one called Weslan, just when the first snows came last winter. It is also known to me he was accompanied by the sorcerer Braith. What I wish to know is why."

"They were friends, I suppose."

Again, Chalvern had felt a knife slice through his temple, and then, horribly, he had felt Zant in his mind. It had been a dry, slithering feeling, like something nameless rustling over leaves.

I can take what I want, Zant had whispered from inside his head.

The sensation had faded away, and for a moment Chalvern had seen nothing but darkness, with bright spots before his eyes. When his vision had cleared, Zant had been smiling at him again.

"So, the Hawk *loves,* does he? And what a grand passion it is! Quite touching to contemplate." Zant laughter was an ugly sound. "Astonishingly, the object of his devotion is the Guardian of the Anniste witch sect. I knew there must be a reason why I had failed—that there must be some greater intelligence at work than the simple human mind. Intriguing, is it not?"

Chalvern had gazed back at him in despair. His determination to keep silent, even under torture, had been no good. Zant had just slipped casually into his head and had plucked from him everything he'd wished to know.

What a dreadful violation it was, to invade one's mind.

Zant had looked very fatigued, however. He'd been panting in quick breaths, and his shoulders had heaved.

The plunder of my thoughts has aged him, Chalvern had thought with grim satisfaction. *But is it enough?*

Apparently not, for the sorcerer's pale face had gleamed with triumph as he'd turned back to the fire again. "And Braith's adored love—for whom he would give up power unto another age—is in Zantor, even now," he had murmured. "Lovely.

Although Saura should have detected her. I must punish the Lady Regent for her negligence. And that will be lovely as well."

"What is it you want?" Chalvern had asked. "What do you hope to gain by all the bloodshed? Does it satisfy you to see others suffer?"

"I want immortality, of course, or the closest approximation thereof," Zant had answered. "To prevent the Mantling is a very good beginning."

"But why? You are aged already. What happiness will it bring you to live on like this, with no one who understands you, except other sorcerers—and even then, you all seem to mistrust and dislike one another?"

Zant had turned and had gazed at him intently.

He will kill me now, Chalvern had thought with certainty.

But the sorcerer had sat down on the floor, crossing his legs in the Berlotan fashion. "No one who understands," he had echoed. "And yet you sound almost as if *you* understand, little man. Do you know what it takes to become a sorcerer?"

"No," Chalvern had replied, "but I have always been interested." *And right now, I would rather be interested from a great distance,* he had thought.

"At the moment of bonding with one's Source," Zant had told him, "there must be an alienation from the rest of humankind."

Chalvern had nodded. That much had made sense. Braith had been hideously alienated; driven from the village by a vindictive priest and a pack of bullies with sticks.

"But first"—Zant had held up a finger—"there must be damage."

"Damage?" Chalvern had shrugged, not understanding.

"Yes," Zant had said, his head swaying from side to side. "Damage. Irreparably and irrevocable, inflicted upon one's soul. For example," he had added in a jaunty tone, which made his next words even more horrible, "Morogh inadvertently set his house afire when he was a child, and his family burned to death while he stood outside and watched. He was damaged. I wonder what Braith's damage was. Do you know, Master Chalvern?"

Chalvern had remembered the night that Braith had been carried through his door, while behind him Beula, who never wept, had stood weeping.

"Do you wish to know the nature of my damage?" Zant had continued, marking Chalvern's silence with an ironic quirk of his mouth.

"Very much," Chalvern had answered at once, although he could hardly believe that Zant had made the offer.

"Mine came at birth." Zant had smiled without mirth.

Then he'd leaned forward, looking intently at Chalvern, and his black eyes had seemed to draw light into themselves, so that the room had become darker. Chalvern had shuddered.

"I was born both man and woman," Zant had whispered, "and so of course I could be neither."

"Both?" Chalvern had stammered.

"Both."

Zant had stood, untying his robe for an instant, letting it fall open, so that Chalvern had a shocking glimpse of pale skin stretched across bony flesh; and the rounded, red-tipped breasts of a woman, while below was the body of a man.

Zant had retied his robe. "Ugh, it is cold," he had remarked, turning to the fire. "How can you northern scum live like this?"

"Were you mistreated because of your difference?" Chalvern's brain had reeled with disbelief.

"My deformity, you mean. I would have been, had anyone discovered it. How could things be otherwise, especially in Berlot? I was fortunate, however. When I was old enough that my form could no longer be concealed, my mother took me to the jungle and left me there. She did not kill me, although she had that right. My Source found me just as I was about to become prey to a fanged monkey. Instead, my predator became my victim. And it was sweet."

The image had nauseated Chalvern. Then, in a flash, he'd thought of something, and known that he was correct.

"It is not only about the Mantling, is it?" He'd looked straight at the sorcerer as he'd spoken, unafraid. "The reason you wish to kill the Anniste is that you hate women."

"You are perceptive, Master Chalvern," Zant had replied. He'd smoothed his hair back with a long, slender hand. "Of course I hate women. If it were not for this curse of Anna's mockery that plagues my body, I could have been a man like other men."

"But you could just as easily say that you were cursed by Rhan and meant to be a woman."

Zant had turned, head swaying, mouth tight. With dizzying quickness, the sorcerer had stepped forward and had struck Chalvern across the face with his closed fist, knocking him to the ground.

"In the end, you are a disappointment," Zant had said, standing over him. "Like all your kind. If you truly understood, you would see that I was destined to be a man. Meant for power, strength, and glory."

Zant's voice had risen almost to a shriek. "There shall be no Mantling, no sapping of Rhan's strength by that foul Goddess. Think of that as you lie there, dying your worm's death in the dust!"

Damage.

Chalvern wept, the tears sliding down his temples. He knew what Braith's damage was. Had always known and had purged it from his mind. *Why?* Was it because he had known the culprit, and had been too much of a coward to do anything about it? But no, he had not been certain then. Nothing had been clear as it was now that he was leaving it all behind.

The truth was Chalvern had not wanted to admit that the ugliness had happened. He had wished desperately for everything to turn out right in the end. And so, he had denied its existence. Braith, reticent by nature, had fallen in with the denial. It had been easier in the short run. But in the long run, they had paid such a price.

But what can I do about this now?

Chalvern shook his head, weary. He did not understand Neela's words, for he had no power to begin a healing. All he could do was to lie there quietly, feeling the last of his strength ebb away; and wish, with all his soul, for Braith to come to him.

CHAPTER 50

*B*raith stepped out of the shadows with a movement so swift that Tekoah gasped. Her involuntary sound of fright deepened the furrows on the sorcerer's face.

"Forgive me," he said.

Tekoah said nothing. At the sound of his voice, the aroma of strong red wine filled her nostrils. She shook her head to dispel it.

"I would not have inflicted my presence upon you," Braith continued, "except that Zant will kill you if you do not come with me now."

"How do I know you will not kill me?" Tekoah countered, her hands bunching into fists, seething. *Does he think I am a fool?* "The Anniste vanished," she continued, biting out the words. "And there is only your word that they are safe. Why should I not believe that you are in league with Zant to prevent the Mantling?"

"How can you think that?" Braith answered in a low voice. "After all we were together."

Tekoah had a mortifying urge to put her hands up to Braith's lean cheeks, and stroke away the furrows. She quelled it, squeezing her fingertips together until they stung.

"We have not much time." Braith's voice was urgent. "Please—"

"If I go with you, will you show me that the Anniste are safe?"

"Yes."

"All right."

Braith put out his hand. Tekoah hesitated for a moment. Underneath the crimson gloves were talons, she knew, curved and sharp. Looking into his eyes, the watchful eyes of a bird of prey, she saw a fear in them she had never seen.

Was it fear for her safety? Or that she would refuse to be lured?

Taking a deep breath, she took his hand. Instantly, there was a muffling darkness all around her, familiar. It was as though she was running against a strong wind, trying to take a breath. But the panic did not last for long. The darkness lifted and Braith's arms were steadying her feet upon uneven ground.

Tekoah looked about her. They were standing in the yard in front of Aunt Beula's farmhouse. She shook her head with astonishment. Braith had placed the Taboran Mountains between she and Zant.

Dawn was creeping slowly upward from the horizon, and in the half-light, she could see the yard; the darkened shutters of the house seemed to stare at her in reproach. She had left less than an annaspan before, and yet the place was transformed.

Spring had come. The snow had gone; the white, soft carpet through which she had walked after the raid by Darian's soldiers. Grass was pushing its way up, dotted with cowslips and daisies and tiny, fragrant mirtas, which her mother used to weave in Tekoah's hair, long ago. No, only a turning past. From one spring to the next, how much had changed.

Tekoah glanced toward the door, her mind reaching toward

the cellar. Following her glance, Braith shook his head. And she remembered with a jolt about the Shifting.

"Where—" she began, but he was pointing to the ground in front of them. She looked down and saw a faint silver shimmer, like a large glowing puddle. She shivered. "They are in there?" she asked, incredulous.

Braith nodded, running a hand through his greying hair in a boyish gesture.

"But where is *there?* Is it a place? How can they be alive? Are they altered?" Tekoah could not stop her voice rising.

"They are alive, and I do not believe changed in any way that is harmful or permanent. They are drowsy, and a little confused. It is rather like being half-awake and trying to remember where you are. Lean over, and gaze into the Shifting. Think of one woman and call her. She will answer—you may even see her face."

Tekoah nodded, trying to remain calm, but despite her efforts she trembled. These women had been left in her care, and she had deserted them.

Anna commanded me to go, she reminded herself fiercely. *I was only obeying the Goddess.*

But she needed to be honest with herself: hours, even days, had gone by without her thinking about the others. She had been too busy enjoying herself. Flirting with Dirken, eating candied figs, sitting next to the very priests and nobles who had driven these women into hiding.

And what good had it done—her mad dash to Zantor? She had told Dirken that the war was coming sooner than expected, but nothing had happened to further the cause of the Anniste. He did not believe her about the Mantling, and she had probably increased his suspicions about Weslan.

I have done no good at all. Tekoah clenched her teeth to keep from weeping.

Braith's hand was in her hair, stroking it. "I came to save

you," he murmured. "But you were not here, and so I saved them instead, knowing you would have wished it. I wanted to please you, to make up for everything."

It was true, then, what the Goddess had revealed to her. Braith had made his choice and had saved the Anniste. They would all have been dead if she had stayed in Stern.

Faith in the Journey. The primary tenet of the Anniste teaching kept echoing in her mind, like the peal of a joyful bell.

Braith's hand in her hair felt wonderful, and Tekoah stood still a moment, imagining she was a tree with the wind blowing softly, softly, through her branches.

But she must think before she acted, she reminded herself.

"May I look now?" she asked.

"Yes, whenever you like."

She bent down, hunkering over the Shifting as though it were Mirveta's Basin.

However, the experience did not feel even remotely similar. There was no sensation of being pulled in, or of wanting to fall. Rainbow shapes seemed to swirl beneath the flat, greyish surface, and she was reminded of Reika, her spirit bright among dancing sparks while below her body writhed in anguish.

Please Anna, do not let them be dead, she prayed.

Whom should she summon? For a moment she could not think of a single face, a single name. Then she thought of Valeen, grey-haired, timid, a widow with a soothing voice and feather-soft hands. She had always been so patient with sick children, her comfortable dumpling cheeks crinkling as she laughed away their fears.

Valeen could not laugh away her own fears, though. Of all the women, she had seemed the most frightened when Tekoah had left, clinging on to her hand, biting her lips nervously.

She was struck suddenly by a terrible thought. Reika had told her that seven of the Anniste had refused to go into the Shifting. Tekoah could not bring herself to ask their names, and

Reika had not volunteered the information. What if Valeen had been one of them? She did not think that she could bear it if the first one she called was not there. But she had to try.

She closed her eyes, concentrating, and called softly within her mind, *Valeen.*

For a moment nothing happened, and then, faintly, she heard a reply.

"Tekoah?" There was a slight disturbance on the surface of the Shifting; the swirling translucent lines swirled faster, agitated.

"Valeen! Are you there?" she said urgently.

"Yes," came the reply, a little louder than before. "We are here."

Tekoah heard Braith move behind her, and his quick intake of breath. Perhaps he himself had not been certain.

The surface of the Shifting cleared, and Tekoah saw Valeen's face, a little blurry, like a reflection seen from a smeared cooking pot. She was blinking slowly, like a drowsy owl.

"Are you all right?" Tekoah asked, her voice choking a little.

"Yes."

"You are safe, then."

"Oh, yes." Valeen's frowned a little, as if trying to think. "Yes, we are well. We are warm here, and we sleep a lot. Sometimes it is hard to remember what we were frightened of. Cats, or some such, was it not?"

Tekoah looked quickly over at Braith, who shrugged in reply.

"You needn't be frightened, now," she told Valeen, a little lamely.

"No."

"And you will come home soon, I promise. As soon as it is safe here."

"Yes." Valeen's voice was becoming fainter, and her voice faded away.

"Anna be with you!" Tekoah tried to keep the urgency from her voice.

"And with you." Valeen's replied, her voice wavering, and then she was gone.

Tekoah hovered over the Shifting for a moment longer, trying to compose herself. The Anniste were safe. That was all that mattered. But it was so strange.

She turned to Braith. "Why did Valeen sound so forgetful? It was almost as though she didn't know who she was."

"It is a waiting place," he answered. "There is not enough energy there to 'live' as we know. Shiftings are gateways between one world and the next. Or so we believe." He smiled quizzically at her look of astonishment. "It is a misconception among mortals that we create the Shiftings. We do not create them, we summon them."

"From where?"

Braith did not answer for a moment. Instead, he looked up, scanning the sky. It was lighter now, a pale blue that would deepen into sapphire by mid-morning. What was that song Dirken had sung? *Never skies bluer than the northern skies…*

"Up there," Braith said, his gloved hand making a sweeping gesture toward the sky. "It is said we gather the light from long-dead stars. All I know is that I willed it to come, and it came. And afterward I was fatigued."

It was true, she realized—Braith looked exhausted. His shoulders slumped, and there were faint purplish shadows under his eyes. Tekoah felt a longing to put her arms around his neck. She asked herself for the hundredth time if it had been more than the enchanted wine that drew her to him.

She looked down at her clasped fingers and admitted to herself that she had known the answer to that for a long time. The confession strengthened her somehow, so that when she saw Braith looking at her with his green-gold gaze, Tekoah did not drop her eyes. A long moment passed, and then they smiled at each other.

There were others to think of beside herself, though. "Will you bring the women out again now?" she asked. The question gave her a cold, queer twist in the pit of her stomach. She stared back down at the grey puddle.

"If you so desire," Braith answered. "But I do not think it would be a good thing at the moment. Zant still lives, as does the one remaining Morg. I will obey you, however." He paused. "In this, as in all things."

Tekoah knew Braith wanted her to look at him again, and so she did not. She sat down on the grass in front of the Shifting, regretting it when her skirt become drenched with dew. She stood up again, shaking out the wet cloth, and circled about the Shifting.

"What happens to those who never come out?" she asked. "Those poor soldiers who keep falling into the Shiftings that Zant made."

"They gradually fade away," Braith answered. "Nothing painful, they just become less and less. Unless they enter another world. But I have no knowledge of those."

"How awful!"

"Not as awful as Morgs."

"No. I suppose not." She shivered, and a moment later she felt Braith's cloak around her, his hands lingering on her shoulders for a just a second longer than necessary. "There is no wine in this place," she said, turning her head so he would not see her burning cheeks.

Braith was silent for so long that she looked up at him. "Forgive me for that," he said, "but do not ask me to regret having loved you. It is not a sin. Would you have me cast into the Pit for it?"

"No," she answered. "I ask for forgiveness also," she said in a low voice. "Anna teaches us never to inflict pain upon others if we can help it."

His face turned bitter. "And now I am relegated to 'others,' am I?"

"No, it is just that—" Tekoah stopped. Then, out of nowhere, a wave of anger washed over her. "You never gave me a chance to know whether I loved you!"

Braith looked at her in astonishment, but she rushed on, her voice rising.

"How do you know I would not have loved you without enchantment? I have a mind, a soul, of my own. You did not have to tame me like a captive animal!"

"I did not wish you to be frightened of me."

"You could have given me more time."

"Time," he said. "There was never much of that. And now there is almost none left."

"What do you mean?"

Braith did not reply but looked at the sky again. After a moment he said, "The nobleman at the palace in Zantor, the one I saw you walking the grounds with—"

"Dirken?" Tekoah looked at him. "When did you see me with Dirken?"

Braith put the tips of his gloved hands together. "Outside the palace. I was flying above you, watching you."

The hawk, she thought. How many times had he done this without her knowing it?

"Do you love him?" Braith asked.

Tekoah did not answer.

"I could have killed him, you know," he continued, his voice light. "But I did not, because I swore to never again displease you."

"Wait a moment," she said. "It was you who made Garth disappear!"

Braith said nothing, but she saw a slight smile hovering in his eyes. Her mouth went dry.

"Did you kill him?"

"No."

"What did you do, then?"

"I did not kill him," Braith replied, his voice hardening a little. "But you have not answered my question. Do you love Dirken?"

"What does it matter?" she cried, exasperated. "The world is falling apart, and you sit here talking of love as if we were making daisy chains at Mirveta's Well. What will become of the Anniste? If they cannot come out, they will fade away, you said. I think you had better bring them out, and we must take our chances with Zant."

"Please listen," Braith said. He turned to face her and, before she could stop him, took her hand. "I go now," he said, "to seek Zant. I think I can destroy him. He has spent more energy than I, and he is older. Once he is vanquished, it will be safe for the women to emerge."

"But what if you fail?"

Braith did not answer.

"But do you not believe they have a better chance out here?" she persisted, her voice faltering. "Because if you do not defeat Zant, who will bring them out?"

"If Zant prevails," Braith cut in, "they have no chance at all— wherever they are—and neither do you."

They were silent for a moment. Braith bowed his head, looking at her hand, pale and small, lying in his crimson palm. His greying hair and bent neck made Tekoah's heart wrench within her.

"It is not only the Anniste for whom I fear," she breathed, moving her hand and loosely intertwining their fingers.

They both stared at the sight, entranced.

"I do not want you to die," she whispered. "I have thought

and dreamed of you often these past few annaspans—even when I tried not to."

Then she was in his arms, and Braith was holding her as though he would crush all her bones, and she did not care. As he tilted her head back into the crook of his arm and kissed her, she heard the warblers singing all around them, for it was morning, and why shouldn't they be singing?

But this was not possible. She loved Dirken. Even while she had this guilty, despairing thought, she gave herself up to the heat of Braith's kisses. It seemed only yesterday that they had held each other this way, the spicy smell of evergreens rising from his hair, his teeth sharp and dangerous behind his lips.

Then Braith leaped back as if he had been stung. Tekoah looked at him, astonished. He was holding both sides of his head and had turned very pale.

"Chalvern!" he muttered. "Chalvern just called me. I heard him clearly. He is dying, he said. He wants to see me."

Tekoah put a hand to her mouth. "Not Chalvern—it cannot be!"

"I must go to him," Braith said. "Do you understand?"

"Of course. I will come with you."

"No." Braith steepled his fingertips together, brow furrowed. "Zant may have discovered our connection, and if so, then this could very well be a trick."

"And is it any safer for me to stay?" she argued. "I wish to see Chalvern, especially if he is ill. He has been like a father to me."

"To me as well." Braith ignored her surprised expression, his voice gruff as he continued, "But I will not risk taking you into a trap. If Zant is there, then all the better, for I need not seek him out. If not, I will come back for you as soon as I have seen Chalvern. Perhaps he is not dying."

But even as Braith said it, Tekoah looked at him and saw her own fear reflected in his eyes.

She wondered how in Anna's name Chalvern had summoned Braith in the first place. Bespeaking was a rare gift from the gods, one that she had thought only the Anniste and sorcerers possessed. But the world was becoming stranger every day, so why not? Nothing seemed to make sense anymore.

Braith had taken her hand again. "The safest place for you now," he said, "would be the castle on the hill, I suppose. The bravest and the best of our northern men are all gathered there now, under the command of your would-be suitor."

His crimson glove tightened convulsively on her hand. She nodded.

"Do you know," she murmured, "you may not need to confront Zant, after all. The Mantling is very near—Anna has told us so—and that will change everything."

"Yes, the Mantling," Braith answered, his voice heavy with irony. "The true heart of this holy war, which is being waged by both sorcerers and mortals. And yet if the prophecy is true, if the Mantling comes, my kind will be extinct. That includes *me*, as well as Zant."

He dropped her hand, his lips quirking humorously, but she saw sorrow in the depths of his eyes.

"The Mantling will indeed be an end to all your problems."

CHAPTER 51

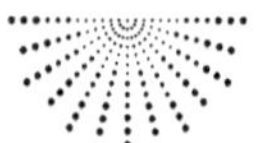

ekoah mulled uneasily over Braith's words as she hurried through the courtyard of the Castle of Mirrand. He thought she wanted to be rid of him. But that was not what she had meant. Why was nothing simple between men and women?

Braith had said nothing more after that. He had transported her by magic to the gates, opening his cloak and setting her down carefully just out of sight of the sentries. As he had released her, she had turned toward the castle. When she'd looked back, he was gone, before she could say farewell.

She had turned her eyes up to the sky instinctively—and there had been the hawk, soaring effortlessly away. He'd looked so invincible up there, and so alone.

All were milling about in confusion in the courtyard. Women bustled along, carrying baskets of food or presiding over long wooden tables, ladling out soup and bread to soldiers, who ate standing up. The soldiers were without exception filthy, exhausted-looking and streaked with sweat or blood or both.

Tekoah's mind still reeled with fevered images of the past few hours: the Shifting, and Valeen's drowsy owl face; Braith's bowed head, his lean, boyish neck contrasting with his greying hair; and persistent, painful flashes of Chalvern, sitting in Beula's kitchen holding a cup of tea between his bony knees and following her every movement with his humorous, deep-set eyes. But gradually she absorbed significance of the surrounding sights. The battle had already begun.

Tekoah sent up a fierce prayer to Anna: *Keep Dirken safe. Please.*

Looking around at the tumult, she felt uncertain, out of place. Dirken had exhorted her to meet him at his castle as soon as she could. But he was not there—he was obviously out leading the soldiers. Should she stay? If not, where could she go?

As she stood hesitating, Tekoah's eyes fell upon a hastily assembled forge, at which a soldier stood lustily working the bellows. Another fellow was hunched over the fire. As he straightened, holding a mended sword between his tongs, she saw it was Fanco.

He grinned at her, delighted. Setting the sword down on the anvil, he bounded over to her like a great shaggy dog, lifting her off the ground and swinging her around while she shrieked with delight.

Fanco pointed proudly to the emblem of the Kalesh, which was stitched on his sleeve. Tekoah nodded, and then he made a small, sweeping crescent with his hand and shrugged questioningly, a wistful look coming into his eyes.

It took Tekoah a moment to realize that he was asking her about Reika. Before she could reply, his face fell; he had seen the truth in her eyes.

She put a hand on his shoulder. He had truly loved Reika. Indeed, who could meet her and not love her?

Zant had not loved Reika. Nor had the Morg.

Tekoah took her hand from her brother's shoulder and made the gesture for Weslan, arms flung out in a dramatic, exuberant gesture. It was an old joke with the twins, and it brought a smile to Fanco's face. He nodded vigorously and, taking her by the arm, he led her toward the castle.

"Is he here?" she asked, confused. "I thought he would be out fighting."

Fanco smiled at her, indulgent. She had often talked to the twins like this after Weslan and Mother had gone. Not expecting a reply, but needing to hear the echo of her own thoughts.

Fanco walked with confidence, as if he knew the castle and grounds. He led her around to the eastern side, rapping three times on a side door. They entered a narrow corridor from which many tapestries hung. Tekoah had seen them before—with Braith—and she averted her eyes, her heart beating erratically.

She was almost certain there was a banquet hall at the end of the corridor. It was so strange to be back there, in the enchanted place in which she had dwelt with Braith, and then encountered Dirken a second time. The castle had been so silent then, echoing with disuse. Now it was a place that was bustling with life, both without and within.

The double doors to the banquet hall burst open, and two women came out, carrying basins and blood-soaked towels. They nodded to Fanco in a friendly fashion, and he stood aside to let them pass, holding Tekoah back with him.

Tekoah thought with amusement that her brother had become downright courtly. They pushed their way through the doors.

Tekoah hesitated as she stepped into the room. Dread gripped her now that she was about to see Weslan. *Why?* Because when she thought of him, Veld came to mind. It was that simple. She had not seen him since he had gone to kill their father—because of her.

Reika had said that she had healed Weslan.

Am I healed, though? she wondered uneasily. Self-probing was never comfortable—but then true growth always took place outside the warm fire circle of comfort, or so went the teachings of the Anniste.

No profound sayings helped now, of course. Or made it easier to put one foot in front of the other. The question was: which did she fear the most—the future, or the past?

A woman carrying an earthenware jug jostled her, muttering in annoyance. Embarrassed and apologetic, Tekoah stepped out of the doorway. As she did so, she saw Weslan.

Her first inclination was to burst out laughing. He wore a soiled apron tied behind him and tucked up into his breeches as though it had hampered his movements. His hair was bound under a sort of kerchief—for the sake of cleanliness, she supposed.

Weslan bent, frowning over one of the many straw pallets that lined the huge room; while the soldier who was lying on it cursed him loudly and colourfully. Altogether, he looked like a large, ungainly, extremely unattractive serving maid.

It was not funny, she knew. All around them rose the moans of wounded soldiers.

Even so, as she crept up behind him, Tekoah could not help but murmur, "How jealous I am of your beauty."

Weslan whirled around. He stared at her with utter blankness for a moment, then said her name slowly; said it again, reaching out to touch her cheek with wonder. "Tekoah?"

She nodded, biting her cheeks to keep back her tears.

"You are safe," he breathed.

No point going into that. She nodded. "And you are as well. I thought you would have been out there with the others, trying to get yourself killed."

Weslan scowled. He seemed to take it as a reproach. "I would have been, had I not caught a chest fever right before the battle started."

"I am so glad," Tekoah said quickly, reaching out to squeeze his arm. Her voice shook a little. "Just think of it, Wes. When was the last time you and I—and Fanco and Raol—were all together?"

They both stood silently, pondering that. A loud moan came from the bed, and Weslan hastily turned back, wringing a cloth that he had been holding in a basin of water.

"Cousin—" the voice moaned.

Bending down, Tekoah saw Bhantok lying on the bed, his apple-red cheeks quivering.

"At last, a true healer. Please, get this madman away from me, or I will perish."

"Turn around," Weslan told him grimly.

"Never!"

"Turn or I will tend to the other side of you and your treble voice will become even higher!"

Bhantok flipped over on the cot like a fish on a riverbank, and Tekoah suppressed a smile.

"Whatever happened to him?" she asked.

Weslan's face wrinkled in disgust. "He sat on one of his own arrows."

There were a few seconds of silence, and then all three burst into laughter.

It was past midday before they could talk any more, for Tekoah donned her own apron after that, and was kept busier than she had been for a long time. The wounded men just kept coming and coming.

"Does that mean we are losing the war?" she asked.

"Yes, we are losing. They have far more men than we do, and so they can afford to lose more. We are killing twice as many from what I hear, but that does not matter, because we are not making a dent on them," Weslan told her. He kicked a floorboard, his face moody.

They were sitting on hard, wooden benches in the same chamber that she and Braith had first been together. Tekoah stared around her from time to time, disoriented. They relayed messages there, and Weslan came whenever he could spare the time to receive news of the battle. He was charged to reassign fresh men whenever necessary. And it was always necessary, he had told her wearily.

The room had once been beautiful, Tekoah recalled, with gleaming tables and soft white sofas. Braith had laid her down on one of those sofas and told her she was all of his world.

Now the chamber was steamy and dank, the tiled halestone floor crisscrossed with muddy boot prints; someone had rolled the rugs back and ripped the opulent cushions from the sofas to use for bedding. Servants and soldiers ran in and out, shouting messages and giving orders. It seemed to Tekoah as though they had violated something sacred, and she wanted to weep.

I must be tired, she thought, pressing her fingertips to her temples.

"Do you believe in the Mantling?" Weslan asked her abruptly.

She stumbled, trying to find the words to reply.

Weslan waited, looking a little sheepish as he added, "Reika always talked about it as if it was a certainty. Listening to her, I almost came to believe it myself. But now—"

"Now?"

"Now," Weslan told her, "I desperately want to believe it, because we are going to need something."

A defeated silence descended upon them. Tekoah remembered with a pang the look on Braith's face when she had mentioned the Mantling. Nothing but good could come of it, though. Reika had said that.

"What are you thinking of?" Weslan asked. "Your face is all scrunched up."

"I am thinking about the Mantling," she told him. "Of course I believe in it. I would not be Anniste if I did not."

"But I mean truly believe in it," he persisted.

"We are not like the priests," Tekoah told him, hearing her voice crackle with anger. "They do nothing but pay lip service to Rhan and, in reality, worship the sorcerers because they have a power that can be seen and felt. The Anniste are not afraid to have faith in things we cannot see."

"And look where it has got you," Weslan remarked ironically.

"You sound like Father," she said bitterly. Without thinking. And could not unsay it.

Weslan looked away, staring into the fire.

"I am sorry," she said, after a moment. "I was angry."

"I deserved it," he said shortly. "An Anniste sought me out and healed me at her own risk. My mother is—was—the dearest person in the world to me, and she was Anniste. Two healers gave me life, and another one to who I am deeply devoted sits beside me right now. I am just frustrated."

Weslan reached out his hand to Tekoah and she took it, hardly daring to believe that he would have forgiven her so quickly.

"You have changed," she said warmly.

Weslan shrugged self-deprecatingly. "Not enough. Reika counselled patience, and patience is just what I lack. I want to be out there, where it matters. Not in here, nursing cranky soldiers, like an—"

"Like an Anniste?" she smiled.

They both chuckled at that, but then she saw the tears standing in his eyes.

"How is Reika?" he asked. "I have been waiting for the chance to ask you. Chalvern told me she was going to Zantor. Did you see her there?"

Before Tekoah could answer, a soldier burst into the room, shouting Weslan's name.

Thank Anna for that, Tekoah breathed fervently, knowing she could not have told him the truth about Reika. Not yet.

"The Berlotans are on the run!" the soldier was bellowing. "They have been routed, do you hear? Many have thrown down their arms, and we are driving them back, down toward the Valley of Delnor. Dirken wants anyone who is resting or eating out there again, now. This may not last long, he says, and it may be our last chance."

Tekoah's blood surged with excitement. She looked quickly toward Weslan. He had leaped to his feet, tearing his kerchief off and looking at the messenger with wild, shining eyes. He clapped his hands on the man's shoulders. "What happened?" he shouted.

Who cares what happened? Tekoah thought, annoyed. *As long as we are winning!* He reminded her of Dirken, needing to analyze everything, even in the heat of the moment.

"The news has just come that the Jinta was killed in Liandon," the man replied, stumbling on the words as if he could scarcely believe them. "And you know how superstitious the Berlotans are. Their leader has been struck down—they think it's a sign from Rhan! They are paralyzed with terror!"

"The Jinta! Killed?" Weslan echoed jubilantly. "By whom? Everyone always said it was impossible to get close to him! Was it the eunuch? Faleesh?"

Tekoah sat with a frozen smile, but she was tense and bewildered. This Weslan—though he was the brother of her heart— was a stranger. He belonged to a world of military intrigue that was far beyond her ken. She guessed that he must be speaking of some spy for the Kalesh.

"No, not a eunuch." The soldier's voice became strained, reflecting none of Weslan's jubilance. As he continued speaking, he lowered his head and began taking small steps back. "No, it was our queen, Darielle."

"What?" Weslan stared at him with such fierce intensity that the man looked frightened, but he plunged doggedly on.

"Yes, the queen—she stabbed the Jinta with his own dagger in the merchant's house where they were quartered, just as he was about to ride out and meet his troops."

Weslan covered his face with his hands, a high keening note escaping through his fingers. Tekoah listened with horror; she had never heard a sound such as this come from her brother's lips.

"The queen turned the dagger on herself immediately afterward," the man continued, doubling over in a macabre mime and then grimacing in remorse. "Sad and terrible news for all of us, but she did the clever thing, our queen. They would have torn her apart like a pack of umbrays."

Weslan lifted his head, cheeks wet, and gazed at the soldier, unblinking.

Tekoah rose, saying, "Thank you. You must be very tired, and hungry. Go to the kitchens now."

"But—" The messenger looked at Weslan uncertainly.

"You did nothing wrong," Tekoah said reassuringly. She propelled him gently through the door and down the hall. "You know where the kitchens are? Good."

When he had disappeared around the corner, she turned back in a rush—Weslan needed her! But she need not have hurried, Tekoah saw, as she looked at her brother standing as still as stone in front of the window.

For it did not matter what she said after that, she might as well not have been there at all.

CHAPTER 52

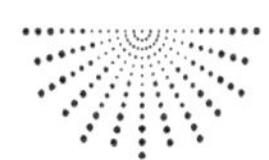

*W*hat did it mean? All of it, any of it? For all her wisdom, Reika could not tell him that. Weslan gazed at the terrible black void in his mind, while around him voices and footsteps faded away into oblivion.

Darielle was dead. Had died by her own hand, in an act of courage that any brave soldier's deed could not match on the battlefield. What bothered him the most was that she had died alone, among enemies.

Knowing that he despised her.

Why had he not connected to Darielle's soul? He should have realized that she had not betrayed her country, but was only playacting, plotting in her disingenuous and charming fashion, waiting for an opportunity to kill the Jinta.

Was it impossible to know someone truly, even if they were one's deepest love?

No, he answered himself. *It is not impossible.* Reika knew his truth. She had seen through all the layers to who he was. She had loved him despite his flawed soul. But he did not deserve Reika.

And he had not deserved Darielle.

If he had just been more persuasive that day or had refused to take no for an answer—knocked her over the head with a vase and carried her off, rolled up in a rug—Darielle might still be alive.

Instead, his overweening pride had foiled his good intentions. The real reason he had left was because Darielle had appeared to reject him. He had felt spurned.

And now Weslan would never know what had been going on inside her beautiful head on that day. He wept, leaning his forehead against the stone wall and scraping it until blood ran down the wall.

This went on for some time, and then, as if waking from a strange dream, Weslan found himself upon his knees. He pledged his soldier's fealty to the queen once more, as he had the first time he saw her. He would keep with him that young boy's first vision of love, and the unforgettable fragrance of yellow flowers, unsullied and untrampled by muddy hooves.

There was one thing only left for him now—to fight, as Darielle had fought.

What was he doing here with the women, moaning and wringing hands? Where was his sword? Weslan fumed; he rose from his knees, gnawed his lower lip for a moment, then spun on his heel and headed for the door.

Tekoah stood in the doorway. She was saying something to him; her voice sounded very far away. He grunted a vague reply. She held out her arms, and he embraced her before bolting from the room and out of the castle.

At the makeshift forge and armoury, Raol was in charge. Smoke rose in thick clouds around him as he wiped his hands on his greasy apron. A dozen soldiers stood about the forge, waiting—stripped of their mail vests and tunics—taking advantage of the chance to feel the warm sun on their backs. Most of them had wounds, bandaged or untended. They all drank thirstily from the dippers of water carried round in sloshing buckets by village maids and lads.

Weslan gestured to his brother, miming a sword slash downward through the air. Raol looked startled and then pointed at him disapprovingly, coughing to make his meaning plain. Weslan gestured again, giving Raol a glare that went far back into their childhood. His brother shrugged, looking resigned. Reaching behind him, he selected a well-wrought sword, freshly cleaned and oiled.

Weslan took it, wondering who it had belonged to, and when its owner had expired. Only hours earlier, perhaps. He stuck it in his belt, feeling a wave of nostalgia for his own sword, mired in the mud somewhere at the bottom of the River Meed.

"Where are you going?"

Startled, Weslan looked toward the voice and saw Tekoah gazing at him reproachfully.

"I must fight, Ko," he muttered.

"And here I thought you worried for my safety," she chided. "Yet we have barely spoken and now you want to rush off."

Weslan took her hand. "Of course I am concerned for you, but you are who we are fighting for—your safety, and that of the Anniste, of everyone in the North. This may be our one chance to win. And you will be protected here, more than anywhere else." He broke off, coughing. He had not moved so much since he had caught the fever.

Tekoah listened to him cough. She nodded, but tears streamed down her cheeks.

"You must understand, string bean," Weslan said, his voice cracking with urgency. "I must do this, or I shall go mad! I did not believe her, you see. I thought our queen had betrayed us, and I spoke harshly to her. My last words." He stopped. Talking about it only made it ghastlier, and the sympathy in his sister's eyes was almost too much to bear.

"I know," Tekoah said, touching his arm. "You loved her from the moment you saw her until the moment she died."

"The problem," Weslan answered grimly, "is that I did not love her enough. And that only makes everything worse. Do you see?"

"Yes," she said slowly, her eyes resting on him. "Yes, I see."

There were loud sounds coming from the courtyard, different from the exuberant war whoops they had heard a few moments ago. Weslan's belly tightened instinctively, overriding his grief. Without thinking, he ran.

He felt Tekoah's hand clinging onto his and wondered suddenly how safe it really was there for her.

Weslan skidded to a stop. The courtyard was a mass of confusion. Soldiers stood arguing with one another; some had come to blows. From the ramparts above, sentries swore and gesticulated to those below. Villagers and servants were running about, the stricken, panicked look of rabbits on their faces, clutching possessions and children close to them.

Why in Rhan's name were they fleeing? The castle was their only refuge.

"What is it?" Weslan demanded, grabbing the elbow of a passing stableboy.

"It is Zant, that's what it is!" the boy yelled back, his face flushed with excitement, or terror, or both.

Weslan felt Tekoah's fingertips flutter like the wings of a trapped bird, and then her hand slipped from his.

"What do you mean, Zant?" he growled, giving the lad's arm a good shake. "Speak plainly."

"The sorcerer Zant has taken the Jinta's place and is leading the bleeding army against us! Their army," the boy added, unnecessarily.

Beside him, Tekoah murmured a prayer, but Weslan could only stare, stupefied.

Obviously impressed with the impact of his words, the lad

continued with a flourish, "The Kalesh are refusing to give ground on the battlefield. But no one believes they can withstand a sorcerer. That is why everyone is stampeding out of here. They want to flee, while they still can."

"Then they are cowards!" Weslan said. His fists clenched involuntarily as he bent over the boy. Hot rage tore aside the heavy curtain of his grief. "Are you a coward?"

"No, sir," the boy answered, dropping his eyes.

"Good." Weslan dropped his arm, and the boy edged away, eyes rolling with fright. "Neither am I," Weslan said loudly to no one in particular. He unsheathed his sword, and called after the lad, "Get me a horse, quickly."

He stood waiting, his temper rising at the sight of all the terrified faces milling around him. They cared not that the Kalesh had risked their lives for them, that the Anniste had been hunted to extinction by Zant and his Morgs all the long winter. No. But at the first sign of danger—they ran!

These craven creatures, was it they for whom he had been fighting?

Tekoah tugged at his arm. "Weslan," she said urgently.

"What is it, Ko?" he muttered, trying to keep the anger from his voice. His fury was not directed at her. "Are you frightened? But I have explained that you will be protected here. Stay in the castle and do not fear."

"I am not frightened," she answered.

Looking at her face, he saw it was true. She has become a lovely woman, he thought. Her gold-streaked hair framed her face like one of those brilliant Berlotan scarves, all coppery in the sun. Her eyes were a wonderful sort of turquoise, a shade darker than his own. Even the pallor of her face held a kind of beauty, like the inside of a pearly seashell. She gave him a tremulous smile.

"I was terrified, a moment ago," she confided, "but then I

remembered, about the Mantling. Everything is going to happen as it was meant to, so we must not worry."

"Do you mean we will win the war?" he asked, bewildered.

She sounded like Reika. Weslan shook his head to dispel the image of Reika's face, the memory of which always filled him with a forlorn longing.

"I cannot say," Tekoah replied. "I know only that everything must turn out the way it should."

The chastened stableboy came running up with a roan gelding, already saddled. Weslan swung himself up.

"Yes, yes, of course," Weslan said. He was not feeling philosophical—he felt more the need to dull the gleam of his sword with Berlotan blood.

"But I must tell you something," Tekoah insisted, taking hold of his horse's bridle to detain him. "About Braith—"

"What is it?" Weslan shifted in his saddle. They had not spoken of Braith since Veld's death.

"Braith," she repeated, her face suffusing in a flush.

"You have seen him again?" he asked her, incredulous.

"Yes."

"I do not wish to hear it," he said sharply. "There is nothing you could say concerning the sorcerer Braith that would interest me."

"I, however, would be very interested."

At the voice, they both spun around, Tekoah faster than Weslan, her shoulders jerking.

A space had been cleared around the speaker, and silence surrounded it in ever-widening circles. Zant stood in the centre of the silence and smiled, as though accepting a tribute. Although the midday sun was strong, he was hugging his arms about himself as if it were bitterly cold. He looked directly into Weslan's eyes.

"You were saying," Zant advanced forward a few steps.

As he did so, Weslan saw, or thought he saw, another

shadow behind the sorcerer's own shadow. He wanted to blink, to clear his vision, but he knew it would be dangerous to take his eyes from Zant's, even for a moment.

"I know nothing of Braith," he said shortly. Good. His voice had not trembled. No matter what happened, he would not stand before this crowd and let anyone hear his fear.

"Oh," Zant said, in a taunting voice, "and who does, then? Your sister, perhaps?"

"Perhaps." Tekoah said this in a calm voice from behind him. She stepped toward Zant, though Weslan tried to hold her back with his arm.

Little fool, he thought. *Shut up, shut up, shut up!*

"I have seen your face many times before, Lord Zant," Tekoah continued, "in Journeys."

"Yes?" Zant was looking at Tekoah with amusement.

And something else. Trepidation?

"You have aged considerably," Tekoah said, her voice like a whiplash.

Weslan swivelled his head, looking at his sister in astonishment. He had never heard her speak in such a manner, not in his entire life. What was she trying to prove?

At that moment, he saw Raol behind Zant, standing in the crowd of cowering villagers, beckoning to him. Had he lost his mind?

But perhaps Raol was suggesting that they make a run for it. That might not be such a bad idea. The horse was right beside him; he could scoop up Tekoah into the saddle and make a dash for their lives. In the confusion, perhaps, they might disappear. It was better than no chance at all. And he owed it to his sister.

For it was Tekoah whom Zant wanted, there was no doubt about it. The sorcerer regarded her now with undisguised hatred. When he spoke, his voice shook with fury.

"Yes, I have aged. I have expended much valuable energy on you, little witch. But I could not help it. And now here we are, and yet you do not even seem frightened, though with a wave of my hand—"

"Indeed," Tekoah interrupted coldly, "it is you who should be frightened, for the Goddess will not forget your deeds, and the day of reckoning is at hand, Zant."

"Be silent!" Zant screamed.

The sound of his voice was a knifepoint pricking up and down Weslan's spine. He saw the shadow again, behind Zant, and knew this time that it was not his eyes playing tricks on him.

The darkness came forward with a measured tread, and Weslan heard the gasps of horror in the crowd echoing his own. There stood a monster—how could it have been hidden in the first place?—half-man, half-cat, the human aspects somehow making the animal aspects more predatory and hideous.

Villagers who had seemed paralyzed moved, screaming "Morg!" and running in blind panic for the gates.

Weslan's mount reared in alarm, the reins jerking in his hand. But the Morg had eyes only for Tekoah.

Weslan, turning in a kind of sick terror to look at his sister, saw that she seemed unable to unlock her gaze from that of the creature. It was as if they were suspended in a kind of gruesome embrace.

Zant reached up his long fingers to stroke the creature's fur, and as he did so, he unchained a leash from around its neck.

At the sight, Weslan was galvanized into action. Without even looking at Tekoah, he seized her arm, pulling her up in front of him as he swung into the saddle. He dug his heels into the horse's flanks with all his might and uttered a guttural war cry.

They leaped upward, the terrified horse's hooves bearing down toward the Morg as it threw itself in their path. They skimmed over the snarling creature, galloping past Zant, and scattering the crowd before them. Again, Weslan shouted at the top of his lungs, as though by sheer force of will they would escape.

And indeed, they were through the gates and down the path. If they could just get far enough...

Two figures had formed a barrier in front of them on the path. Raol and Fanco. What were they doing? Weslan was still galloping headlong, but he reined in his mount as Tekoah shrieked a warning in his ear.

"Are you mad?" he thundered, leaning forward in the saddle, nearly beside himself with rage and terror.

The twins looked terribly frightened. Good. Anyone with a donkey's sense would be.

But there was Fanco, pointing at something just up the road, beyond a log which had fallen across the path.

With a shaking hand, he was pointing to—a Shifting, by Rhan!

We would have ridden right into it! Gasping, Weslan wiped his brow.

"See," Tekoah was saying, "see—I told you!"

What it was she had told him Weslan did not know, but before he could reply, Zant materialized directly in front of them. And Weslan saw it was too late for everything.

Yet he had to try.

As though moving in slow motion, Weslan leaped from his horse, drawing his sword. He did not quite know why, but action seemed required, and he could not think of anything else to do.

Zant's eyes narrowed with contempt. "You would presume to fight me?" he asked.

"Only if you know how to fight for yourself!" Weslan mocked. "But you must rely on monsters to do your killing for you."

Over Zant's shoulder he saw Raol, beckoning again, toward the Shifting. And he understood.

Weslan moved forward a little, jabbing Zant's chest with his sword point. Wanting to laugh at his own audacity. Probably no mortal had ever done that to a sorcerer.

Taken unawares, Zant moved back a few steps. His face contorted with fury, and he lifted his hand. Then, without warning, he tripped over the fallen log and fell into the Shifting.

Weslan stood, stunned with disbelief. He heard a strangled noise come from Raol, the first sound he had ever heard uttered by his brother. Looking at his Raol's face, he saw it was meant to be a cheer, and he grinned back. As if refusing to be outdone, Fanco laughed, a rusty, painful sound.

Then, behind them, the horse whinnied in terror, and Weslan turned around and saw that Tekoah had been thrown from her mount, and that before her crouched the Morg.

Tekoah scrambled to her feet, jumping aside with amazing speed, just as the Morg sprang.

One jump. Into the Shifting.

Weslan screamed, a sustained, despairing sound. The cries of his brothers echoed hoarsely beside him.

Then there was a deathly quiet, as all three of them stood staring down into the shimmering portal. Weslan took a step toward it. But then there was a hand like iron on his arm, as Fanco pulled him back.

Weslan looked into his brother's eyes. Tears welled in them, but he shook his head.

A snarl brought them back to the moment. The Morg still crouched, its narrowed yellow eyes staring with malevolence at the shimmering silver puddle which had cheated it of its prey.

Glad of something to do, Weslan darted forward and thrust his sword straight through the Morg's back. It yowled once, an unearthly shriek, then crumpled and lay still. Weslan withdrew the blade, grimacing in distaste as he wiped yellowish blood on the grass by the side of the path.

Raol and Fanco were gazing with deep intensity at the Shifting.

"Why are you staring?" Weslan shouted. "She is gone, can you not see that?" He began weeping helplessly.

But all at once it had become dim all around them, greyness closing in like a fog. *What is happening?* Weslan wondered. *Am I dying?*

He sat trembling. The descending darkness—like midnight come at midday—Reika had described it to him! And all at once, he knew without a doubt that it was the Mantling.

Raol and Fanco came and kneeled beside him. They moved with a radiant calm that reminded him of Reika.

This was the Mantling.

He had always supposed it to be the light that revealed hidden things. But the darkness had a penetrating quality that somehow stripped away all his pretences, and Weslan saw himself as he was—a child, sweaty-palmed, dry-mouthed, waiting behind a curtained room for his mother to come in and tell him everything was all right.

Nothing had changed, had it?

He felt the solid presence of the twins on the other side of him and realized their silent strength had been there for him all along, had he only known it. The darkness enveloped him like a cradle.

"Mother," he whispered, "I feel you."

TIME PASSED. Weslan did not know how long he had been sitting there in the road, but he had no desire to do anything or go anywhere. His thoughts were far too absorbing. Not thoughts; dreams, perhaps, or thoughts of dreams—only mixed up with the thoughts and dreams of others who had lived before him.

His mother's presence was warm and reassuring in the wordless way it had been when he was very young and needed nothing more than to be held.

Weslan could see nothing, and felt only dimly the hole in the sky, blacker than the surrounding darkness, where the moon had been. And the sun.

Gradually, he regained awareness of his surroundings. The sky was growing lighter. He stretched and looked around him, smiling at the sight of his brothers, who leaned against each other, back-to-back. They appeared to be asleep.

Then, as Weslan kneeled there under the brightening sky, he saw a sight he would never in his life forget.

From the Shifting, brown-robed and with shining eyes, the Anniste women stepped one by one.

CHAPTER 53

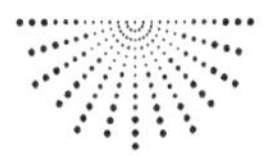

*C*halvern called Braith's name, wordlessly, forcefully, feeling a flood of love so strong it surprised him. Why could he not have loved his own sons in such a way? Cedor and Barton, gone long ago to Meed to join the priesthood. Both underlings, toadies of King Darian, climbing the rungs of power with slippery, bloodstained hands. And yet they despised him.

"Master." Braith's voice was suddenly beside him, filling him with a quiet joy.

"My son," he croaked, astonished at how difficult it was to speak.

"We may talk silently, if you wish," Braith said, taking his hand. "After all, you called me without speaking, and I heard."

"All right," Chalvern said within his mind, and within his mind Braith spoke back to him.

"How long have you been able to do this, Master? This bespeaking gift is not meant for mortals."

"I do not know, because I have never tried. It is of no matter now, though, is it? Ordinary or not, I am dying."

They both fell silent. Chalvern became drowsy; the warmth

of Braith's hand in his was all he had wanted. But there was something else, though, something important. What was it?

He roused himself a little, peering at the sorcerer's face. "Tekoah? Is she all right?"

Braith smiled. "I have just left her."

"I am sorry," Chalvern told him, "to take you away. She cares for you then?"

"I care for her," Braith answered, "and she is allowing me to do so. That is all the happiness I can hope for."

"All anyone can hope for," Chalvern assented, thinking of Neela. Then, in a flash, he remembered their conversation, and the pain washed over him again. "My son," he murmured.

"I am here, Master. Please rest."

"No. There is something I must say."

"Very well." Braith's voice was soothing.

"About when you were a boy. When you first came to me."

He felt Braith's fingers tighten spasmodically for a moment in his hand, but the sorcerer said nothing.

"About Veld."

Braith still did not reply.

"He hurt you," Chalvern persisted against that familiar wall of silence. "And I knew—deep inside my heart—that it was he. And yet I did nothing. I am sorry."

"Peace, Master," Braith's voice said inside his mind.

"I am sorry," Chalvern repeated. "I should have killed him."

"Do not be sorry for who you are," Braith said quietly. "There are others enough who are eager to do bloody deeds."

"But—" It was becoming harder and harder to think. "The lack of action also causes harm sometimes. Doing nothing is a sin, if it begets ten other sins."

"Do not regret who you are," Braith said again, "or who you are not."

"You really did torment Veld, did you not? It was not his drunkard's mind playing tricks on him." Everything was becoming clear to Chalvern now. "You did it to punish him. That part was true."

"Yes. But he did not become evil because I tormented him," Braith replied. Anger crackled for the first time beneath his even tone. "I tormented him because he was evil."

"I know." Chalvern lay pondering. "Did you cause Weslan to kill his father?" he asked. He needed to know.

"No. I cannot conjure hatred or love. But I altered his life's course a little—a slight bend in the road—so that it was easier for him to do it. You may blame me for that, if you wish."

"Who am I to blame anyone?" Chalvern responded, thinking of all the times he had wished Veld dead. Then he asked the most important question. "But you truly love Tekoah, although she is Veld's daughter?"

"Truly." Braith's voice left no doubt.

Chalvern squeezed his hand. "Good. My son?"

"Yes."

"Go to the window and tell me what you see. I want to have a vision in my mind, when I say farewell."

Braith stood, and Chalvern heard him take a few brief steps to the small window. The wooden shutters opened with a satisfying clatter, and Chalvern felt meltingly warm sunlight on his closed lids and sighed with happiness.

"Well," he said into Braith's mind. "Go on, tell me. What do you see?"

There was no reply. Instead, there were Braith's arms beneath him, picking him up as gently as though he was a baby bird, carrying him to the window.

"Can you open your eyes, Master?"

Chalvern's eyelids fluttered and lifted. "Ah…" The butterflies were there.

The wings of summer, as northerners called them. For they came at the end of spring, these brilliant orange, yellow, purple and black creatures, warming their delicate wings in the sunlight with visible delight. Great swarms of them, endlessly coming together and apart, in myriads of shapes that dazzled the eyes.

Chalvern was very tired, but he recalled something he had heard Tekoah say about the butterflies when she was small, standing with her schoolmates, staring up at them in wonder. *They are like music, if only you could see it.*

"Thank you," he said to Braith, and closed his eyes again. Neela nudged him lightly in a corner of his mind. *I am coming,* he told her.

Into his heart there came a rush of gratitude to the World-maker, who had sent the butterflies as a final gift; and who oversaw all these things, tending them like an herb garden; plucking and sorting; patient, relentless.

He opened his eyes one more time, and saw that Braith was looking down at him, his own eyes glittering with tears. The sorcerer did not blink or look away.

"I think I will say farewell now," Chalvern whispered aloud, with a great final effort.

"Farewell, Master."

"Farewell."

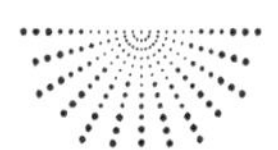

CHAPTER 54

As she fell, Tekoah called Braith's name in her mind, fearing that if he did not hear her and come to her aid, she had little chance to survive.

It was similar to a Journey, except that her surroundings were denser, dreamier. It was more like the place where she had been with Reika at the end.

She was in a chamber of sorts, with walls that seemed less than solid—they vibrated in waves, as though at any moment they would dissolve. Just looking at them made it difficult to concentrate.

Tekoah heard a sound from behind, like someone breathing, only with great difficulty. *What is it?* She looked over her shoulder, craning her neck, but the darkness was impossible to penetrate.

A mist swirled all about the floor, and Tekoah peered down, catching sight of something. There were what seemed to be shapeless brown sacks lying all over the place.

One sack moved and Tekoah realized with a start that it was Valeen.

The Anniste were there. Most of them were sleeping, their

chests rising and falling peacefully. Valeen sat up drowsily, facing Tekoah.

The sound came again from behind her. Valeen's eyes snapped open wide, and she pointed her forefinger, staring past Tekoah with undisguised horror.

Tekoah turned around.

The serpent Zant had wrapped itself around one of the sleeping women and was methodically crushing her.

Tekoah shrieked, calling for Braith without thinking, and hurled herself on the serpent.

The coils froze; then swiftly twisted and writhed, loosening their hold upon the Anniste woman and seizing Tekoah around the chest and throat.

She screamed Braith's name again, just before the leathery noose tightened around her neck.

And before she could blink, Braith was there. He stood wordlessly, his green-gold eyes taking in the scene. Then he lifted his arms.

The folds of his black cloak became wings. His crimson-gloves slipped from his hands, revealing the curved black talons. The hawk rose in the air, up, up, through the mist that seemed to go on forever, above and below them.

The mist enveloped Braith, and for a moment Tekoah could no longer see him. She struggled to free herself—to take just one breath—but a hideous pressure grew behind her eyes, and she saw bright spots of red and yellow and green, and heard a high ringing in her ears.

Zant's coils tightened about her and she knew she was about to die. Then there was a shrill cry from above.

The hawk dove. Braith's powerful, hooked beak ripped through the serpent's leathery skin. Zant twisted and turned in agony, but the talons had dug into him, and they did not lose their grip. Several times, the hawk's beak was so close to

Tekoah's face that she saw the tiny, serrated ridges on its edge. But never once did it touch her.

The serpent's hold loosened and then loosened again. Tekoah took a ragged, gasping breath. At the sound, the hawk's talons slipped for a moment. Swift, the serpent lunged, wrapping a coil around the hawk.

Her arms free, Tekoah wrapped them around the serpent and pulled with all her might. There was a rustling sound, and from all around her, the Anniste women rushed forward, their brown-sleeved arms tugging and pulling the serpent from the hawk, until it could slip loose.

The hawk was unharmed, Tekoah saw with relief. The Anniste women backed away as it rose in the air, beating its great wings. They pulled her with them; she was gasping, and coughing, and half-fainting, as they dragged her off to a corner of the chamber.

Her breaths were coming easier now. Tekoah sat up. One woman supported her from behind, as they all watched the last moments of the battle between Braith and Zant.

It happened so fast they could barely see it. The serpent coiled itself up, keeping its head low. The hawk circled again, gave a hoarse, taunting cry. As if goaded, the serpent rose from the ground, its head undulating.

From Zant came a loud hiss, a sound so full of hate and malice, that Tekoah felt as though she would stop breathing again.

The hawk darted, its beak striking the serpent's face in a rapid series of stabs. There was an unearthly shriek. Braith struck once more, and then the head of the serpent collapsed; smoking black blood dripped from both its eyes. Zant's coils shuddered once and then were still.

The hawk settled on the ground, regarding his dead foe with glittering eyes. His wings pleated themselves into the folds of a black cloak, and then the sorcerer Braith was sitting on the ground, breathing hard. His eyes scanned the chamber until he saw her.

Braith smiled, and Tekoah stood up unsteadily and went into his arms. They sat holding each other, their cheekbones pressed together so tightly it hurt; until behind her, Tekoah heard a throat clearing.

"I think we will go home now," Valeen's voice quavered. "We wish to see the Mantling."

"Yes," Tekoah said, burrowing deeper against Braith's chest. She wept softly. "Thank you. Go."

CHAPTER 55

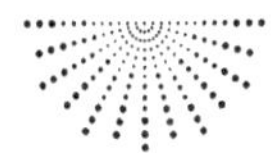

The women slipped out of the Shifting, one by one. After they disappeared, Braith nestled his head into her lap and fell deeply asleep. Tekoah stroked his hair away from his temples. Without warning, she slipped into a Journey. There was no water in which to gaze, and yet the transition was effortless.

The first thing she beheld was the Mantling, and she was glad to see it inside her mind, for she knew that to look directly upon it in reality could have blinded her. She gazed in rapture at the ring of fire with its ruby flares, blazing like gems; light that burned in darkness, fierce, refusing to be quenched. Then the ring faded, leaving only darkness, desolation, a dull grey all around her, the colour of lost hope.

Tekoah understood in a flash the terrible loneliness that filled Braith's mind; heard its dark, mocking echoes, and wondered how he could have borne it all this time.

Such was the price sorcerers paid for power.

Braith's eyelids quivered, but, looking at his face, she knew he was no longer slumbering. He was in a solitary place now, had forgotten she even existed—alone with his pain. But

535

although he was not calling her, she heard him. It was part of the new magic that was blossoming all around, not yet formed, but already gathering the momentum that would propel them all into a new age.

A billowing cloud of darkness appeared before her and slowly took shape. And Tekoah beheld her father's face.

He looked much younger than when she had last seen him in the snow beside her slain pony. The pouches under his eyes were new, and the network of tiny red lines across his cheekbones and nose were faint.

Veld was smiling—a predatory smile—as he stood by the edge of the highway in front of the forge. He stared down the road, toward the woods at Stern's End. It was dusk. Pale clouds, splotched with purple and orange, hung like exotic flowers among the branches of the crohm trees.

Tekoah followed her father's gaze and saw a lone figure walking along the highway, carrying a basket. It was a young boy of eleven or twelve. Dark of hair and eye, thin, walking with a long-legged, nervous gait.

As he came closer, she saw with a shock that it was Braith, and her heart contracted with love and pity, for his countenance was devoid of the pride and confidence that she had always observed in him. He looked diffident and unsure, hunching his shoulders in the self-conscious way of boys who are not children any longer, but not yet men.

The boy-Braith looked down, contemplating his basket, which was packed with herbs and seeds. He smiled, pleased with himself. However, when he lifted his head and saw Veld, his smile faded. He flinched, his eyes casting about despairingly for a means to escape. Tekoah flung her hand up in warning, even while knowing she could not save him from whatever he feared.

Braith dropped his basket and broke into a wild, hopeless gallop.

Teeth bared, Veld gave chase, and soon caught his prey. With a furtive glance about, he dragged the struggling boy into the field behind the forge. Braith's screams became her own, and she felt she would never stop shrieking.

Somewhere deep within, where her very pulse drummed in outrage, she asked Anna, in the small, hurt voice of a child, "Why have you shown me this?"

Then she saw the Mantling again, the glorious ring of fire, and from it came a gentle whisper, "So that you will understand."

The cleansing heat of the Mantling coursed through her veins, its white-hot baptism of pain—healing pain. Healing pain.

And then she was awake. And beside her, Braith had also awakened, and was sobbing like a child on the misty ground. She slipped off her robe and pressed her body against his; compassion in her heart and healing in her hands.

Hours afterward, Tekoah stirred and looked at Braith. She blinked in disbelief. No, it was not a trick of this gloomy, greyish light. Her heart thudded in her chest as she sat up.

The sorcerer's face was wizened, and the flowing black hair that had hung about his shoulders when she first saw him was scant and white, receding from his scalp.

Tekoah turned away for a moment, burying her face in her arm, glad that the aging had not come when they joined. For Braith looked so frail now, that he seemed incapable of even grasping her hand, let alone making love as they had with such silent, desperate intensity. She felt no revulsion, only an overwhelming sorrow for who he had been.

Turning to face him again, Tekoah saw Braith had opened his eyes and fixed his brilliant green-gold gaze upon her. He said something, his voice so low that she could not hear him. She bent over his face, so that her ear was at his lips.

"Little Violet," he whispered.

Hearing the words vividly reminded Tekoah of when she had first seen Braith, sitting on his black stallion, holding up a crimson-gloved hand in judgement over her village; wielding a terrible strength, the embodiment of all her dark, forbidden dreams.

Tekoah cradled the sorcerer's head against her breast and waited for him to say something else. But he only smiled as though he had received a long-awaited gift. His fingers twitched as he tried to lift his hand, but then he shuddered, and was still.

She gazed at Braith's face for a long moment, wishing she could weep; but there was only a dry flaming in her eyes, which she kept upon him, as if by directing all the heat and longing in them toward him, she could somehow bring him back to life.

Has this been a healing? Tekoah asked the Goddess. Her heart told her yes, for Braith had looked truly happy when he died. She had felt it in their joining. But what was the point? Why heal him when he was about to die?

It was not the Mantling which had killed Braith. Tekoah knew that with the inexplicable certainty that sometimes came after a Journey. He had died from using his powers to keep the Anniste in the Shifting—out of harm's way—and in his ending battle with Zant. He had drained himself to the dregs for her, and for the Anniste.

But she was the Guardian. They had appointed her to protect them. It was hideous, unfair, that Braith had sacrificed himself. It made no sense.

Then Tekoah bent her mind again toward the teachings of the Mantling: Anna's face blotting out Rhan's power; bringing the world to its knees. And all at once it made sense: Braith's love for her had driven him to protect the Anniste, to change the way he perceived the healers. In this way, they had swept him out of Rhan's domain and into Anna's. It was the choice the Goddess had spoken of, when directing Tekoah to go to Zantor.

Braith's love for her had made the Mantling possible.

She sat silent, grateful, her head bowed over Braith's face, her long hair enveloping him like a curtain.

SOME WHILE LATER, Tekoah withdrew Braith's gloves from his hands and thrust them into the pocket-fold of her dress. She rose, shaky on her feet, removing her cloak, thinking to cover Braith. But when she looked down again, she saw that Braith the Man had vanished. Braith the Hawk lay on the ground—dark and compact, wings folded tightly together.

So she wrapped the hawk tenderly in her cloak. Then, walking toward the wall that seemed the thinnest and most translucent, Tekoah stepped back through the Shifting.

CHAPTER 56

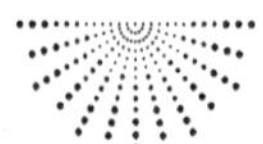

Walking through the wall, Tekoah thought at first that it was nighttime. But then she realized, awestruck, that she was in another kind of darkness—that of the Mantling. However, the sky had brightened, so perhaps it was nearly over. She had no notion of how long she had been gone, but it did not seem at all important.

Around her, all was hushed. Weslan was no longer rushing about, determined to save everyone even at the cost of his life. The Morg lay still, its long white teeth grinning in death. Raol and Fanco stood regarding her without surprise, as if they had been expecting her. Tekoah looked back at them, silent, making no effort to hide her grief.

She began walking. Behind her, she heard the twins' footsteps, keeping a respectful distance.

She strode on and on in the strange twilight, toward Chalvern's shop. Knowing the apothecary was dead. He had to be. His face rose before her, bald, shining pate, ironic smile, and those lively badger's eyes, kind and humorous.

Chalvern, stroking her head with a cool cloth; coaxing warm broth and wine between her lips. Chalvern, striving to protect her from Braith, thundering, "You shall not take her!" Risking the wrath of a sorcerer.

Chalvern, who should have been her father. He had loved her mother, after all. Perhaps he was with Neela now.

He would beam with pride if he knew she no longer needed protecting. That was the gift Anna had been giving her, piece by small piece, throughout her life.

And although Tekoah grieved for Braith, this gift, this strength, coursed through her limbs with a marvellous vigour, bracing her spine in a continuous stream, like a river fed always by the rain.

This was the Mantling.

Tekoah had not felt that strength when she'd first looked into the eyes of the Morg. She had seen everything she had ever feared in those eyes. She had seen her father.

There are wounds that never heal, Reika had once said. *But they need not cripple us.*

Something buoyed her up now, a quiet exhilaration threading through her grief, glinting like a vein of gold through grey rock. It was the joy of being connected with everything around her—the crohm trees, the fallen log, the earth beneath her knees. A sense of rightness.

Above, in the dark sky—she knew without looking—was the ring of fire: Rhan mantled by Anna, so that only the edges of the golden disc showed. A *quenching*, as the priests would describe it.

But Tekoah knew better. She could feel the power of the God and Goddess joining—a power that had not emerged for seventeen hundred turnings. It gave her strength.

The horizon was becoming even lighter by the time she entered the apothecary's shop. Pervasive darkness—irresistible and consuming as the thought of death—was lifting. Soon, there would remain only a memory of this time, a time of terror, but also of transcendent beauty.

Standing in the doorway, Tekoah ran her fingers through her damp, tangled hair. Then, still holding her bundled cloak, she crossed the room and ascended the steep stairs leading to the upper chamber. She saw Chalvern lying on his narrow cot, arms folded across his chest. His eyes had been closed, and in his hands had been placed a fresh crohm leaf. On his face was a faint smile. He did not look at all as she had feared, after Zant's interrogation.

All that befitted him—all that had been proper—Braith had done. Tears filled her eyes.

Tekoah bent down and kissed the top of his bald head, whispering, "Father." Then she turned and went back down the stairs.

She cradled the hawk against her bosom with one hand. With the other, she pulled open Chalvern's door and stepped out into the full sunshine.

CHAPTER 57

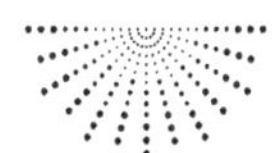

The Mantling had ended; the sky was a summery blue. Butterflies flitted gaily all about Tekoah, as though nothing unusual had happened. Some creatures appeared utterly unaffected by profound events, she mused. Perhaps they lacked souls.

Or brains, she thought, watching with resignation as Norah came bearing down on her.

"Tekoah? Pigeon? It is you, then! How we have missed you!" Norah made a sweeping motion with her arm as if encompassing a welcoming throng which stood behind her.

"But you have had no time to think of us, you intrepid little adventurer! You have been dashing about in Zantor—or Rhantor, as we will call it again, of course, now that we have won the war!"

"Won?" Tekoah echoed.

As she spoke, a company of soldiers came galloping along the road, waving and shouting. Both women skipped to the side, as one horseman swerved wildly.

Tekoah clutched her bundled shawl to her chest. Looking up,

she saw Norah's magpie eyes fixed upon it, and her heart froze; but Norah babbled on, punctuating every sentence with a giggle.

"Yes, we won! The Berlotans ran like stampeding sheep after Zant disappeared. Your strapping hero of a brother pushed that hideous sorcerer into a Shifting—how delightful! Were you there, by chance? I am not sure what happened, because I was not fortunate enough to see it, of course. But I think they must have hightailed it for the border. It was too much for them, following the Jinta's death. And then any remaining Berlotans simply bolted in fright when the Mantling came at last. By the by, I believed in the sacred prophecy all along—not like some others. And now Dirken will be king, of course, which is lovely, because he is so handsome. I have always adored him! And he is our lord, just think of that. Stern has become almost as famous as Rhantor!"

Tekoah tried to concentrate through Norah's unrelenting torrent of words. Where was Weslan? Was he safe?

Stop it, she told herself. *Best not to think, just keep walking!*

But Norah's well-padded body barred her path. Behind her, she could hear the twins shuffling their feet. They had little regard for Norah.

"Ah, poor dear," Norah clucked, gesturing at Tekoah's shawl, her voice somehow sounding motherly and malicious at the same time. "The court is a swamp of iniquity, one hears, even when there isn't a wicked sorcerer in charge. Easy enough for a country girl to go astray."

She thinks this is a newborn infant. Sickened, Tekoah gazed back at Norah so unflinchingly that, after a moment, the other girl dropped her eyes. Tekoah moved past her, nodding a polite farewell.

"I nursed your brother Weslan when he was ill, you know!" Norah called after her in a truculent voice. "Saved his life, mayhap. Days after my own poor Stolk was killed in battle! Do not think badly of me."

"I do not," Tekoah answered, turning to speak over her shoulder, surprised to find she meant it. "But I must go. Goodbye."

"Goodbye," Norah echoed.

Tekoah walked for a minute, then turned around. Norah was still staring after her. She raised her hand in a wave. Tekoah waved back and walked on.

She kept moving, past the hill where Dirken's castle stood, threading her way among the crowd which surged along the highway. They were laughing and shouting and singing victory songs. She wondered again where Dirken was, and Weslan. She acknowledged her longing to see them both and then pushed the burden of attachment from her mind.

In some ways, it was a relief to evade those two—who cared so much for her. She did not wish to explain where she was going next. For she knew with certainty that neither her brother nor Dirken would understand.

The twins moved ahead, helping to clear a space through the crowd as the highway wound back into a wooded path along the edge of the Taboran Woods.

When she reached Stern's End, Tekoah paused for a moment and looked into the dark, rippling water of the pond—so different from the opaque sheet of ice when she had last stood there.

And there—through that clump of evergreens—she could just glimpse the knoll upon which she had stood, facing the ring of Morgs, with no weapon but a deep desire to live, despite everything that had showed her that life had no worth.

Looking at the Morgs and hearing their ravenous snarls, Tekoah had been certain that her desire for life was futile, and that she would die in that very moment. Then Braith had appeared, obliterating the awful creatures with a lethal force that was so controlled and effortless, that it became a kind of beauty.

Tekoah signalled her brothers to remain at the pond. They nodded, watching her as she walked away toward the knoll.

This place had also changed. The clearing was green instead of white with snow, and scattered with summer flowers, peri-winkle and clover. She walked until she reached the centre.

Sitting down, Tekoah let the wind blow through her hair. She listened to the drone of the bees and the trilling of the birds; the busy, friendly sounds ventured closer when she had not moved for some time, and so she stayed as still as she could.

She closed her eyes and envisioned birds flying in the currents of the wind, trying to imagine what it would be like to soar so far above everything that nothing was frightening any more.

For the first time, she noticed how her throat and chest ached from the strangling coils of the serpent Zant. The wonder of her joining with Braith had blotted that horror out. Their lovemaking had been like a violent, beautiful storm that had engulfed them, beyond the simple fact of themselves.

Tekoah bowed her head onto her knees and sat thus for some time. At last, she stood up and buried Braith in the spot where she had sat; digging patiently with a small stick she picked up and leaving him wrapped in her shawl.

It was where he would wish to be—close to home—but with the protective evergreens all around him.

Then she sat down again and waited for Anna to tell her what to do.

Tekoah stayed thus for some time. She did not Journey, as she had thought she might. Perhaps there would be no more Journeys. It was the dawn of another age, after all.

Is Reika watching all this from somewhere and smiling? she wondered. Reika had been right about everything, even about the roles that Weslan and the twins would play at the very end.

What would have happened if Zant had killed her? Could the sorcerer have prevented the Mantling? Did *she* make that much of a difference? The devout Anniste women believed it, as they had believed in Tekoah's mother, and her mother's mother.

It was a humbling thought: to enter the world, and play one's small part, so very crucial for one moment, and then to look back and comprehend that one was but a faint, almost indiscernible thread in the eternal tapestry of people and events; a story that was woven together with such density it was impossible to see where one thread ended and another began.

She would rejoin the Anniste, Tekoah supposed. Except that she did not know where they were. Caring for wounded soldiers at the Castle of Mirrand? That was a likely guess. If so, she belonged there as well. Dirken would be nearby—and Weslan.

What had happened with the battle? Had it ended? Was the North victorious? As the fog of the Shifting cleared from her mind, the need to know gripped Tekoah. But, as she stood, a sound assailed her ears. Very distinct, though it was dim and far away. She had never heard it before, this distant muffled roar, but was certain it must be the sea. And then she saw a vision before her, of great silver-green waves rising higher than the River Meed after a spring rain.

And faintly, on the horizon, Tekoah saw a mound shrouded in mist. The Isle of Mira, she thought at once, with an instinctive shudder. Along with every toddling child in Stern, she had heard the oft-told stories about the Isle of Mira. Her father had once threatened to strap her to a raft and send her there, if she did not cease her bawling.

The Isle was perpetually shrouded in mist, and the few fisherfolk who dared to venture near spoke of strange wailing sounds coming from its shores as they passed. It was whispered to be the waiting place of Wraiths before they met the Worldmaker. And, although Chalvern had said in his no-nonsense schoolmaster's voice that the stories were pig slop, no one Tekoah knew had ever been there, so how could he know?

But now, evidently, this was her purpose. To go to the Isle of

Mira. For it did not matter how many times she opened her eyes and closed them again, it was all she could see.

So, she rose, turning her back on the sinking sun, and walked back to the pond where the twins were waiting for her.

Rhan was sinking again two days later when they reached the fishing village of Liandon. The last of the boats were being hauled onto shore, and the fisherfolk bragged to each other about the weight of their nets.

Tekoah stood on the sand, fingering in her palm a small shell she had picked up and staring out at the Isle of Mira. There was a thud next to her. She looked and saw Raol standing there grinning. In his hand was an oar, and beside him a small white coracle.

She grinned back. *He has done it,* she thought, admiring him.

It took them all night and most of the next day to reach the Isle of Mira. They wended their way down the River Meed to its mouth, where it poured into the Bay of Tarant, with its bracing scent of salt and assertive waves.

Raol had brought cornbread, goat's cheese and water, and also blankets, which she was glad of. For although it was summer, the sea breeze carried with it a chill.

The shoreline was close now, close enough for them to hear a low, mournful wail. This was the sound which had provoked the stories of wraiths.

Tekoah shivered a little under her blanket. She looked over at the twins. Fanco threw her a reassuring smile, and the twins continued to row, stoic and unperturbed.

When they drew near enough to see the shells and polished stones at the island's edge, Raol and Fanco leaped from the boat, holding onto the rope and pulling it up, scraping onto the rocks. Fanco gave Tekoah his hand, and she stepped out, her legs trembling as they touched the ground. Raol steadied her and they walked forward.

The mist was not evident from where they stood, except for where it touched the tips of the three craggy grey rocks which jutted up at the island's centre. However, the wailing had become louder, and Tekoah listened with trepidation as the wind whipped her hair across her face.

Raol touched her shoulder and pointed up at the rocks.

"What? What is it?" she asked, her body twitching with fear, looking for some strange bird or monstrous creature lurking among the stones.

But Raol swept his hand, up and down, until she finally saw what he meant.

The stones were full of holes, small and large; and she saw that birds did indeed perch in many of them, sheltering from the wind, no doubt. But it was not the birds, or wraiths, that were making the sounds. It was the wind, rushing through the holes, ceaselessly, with a high, keening sound in some places, and a deep, sonorous moan in others.

Tekoah stared at Raol and Fanco, rapt. Though deaf, they had solved the mystery of the Isle of Mira. She reached her arms out to them.

The three of them stood, hands linked, while she listened to the strange music. "I will become used to this," she said to herself, at last. "The birds seem to like it, and so will I."

There was a small copse of trees just to the west of the wind-stones, as Tekoah called them in her mind. They walked until they found a sheltered spot to build a lean-to; out of the wind, close enough to the shore that she could watch for boats, and near to a fresh-water spring. Together they worked, lashing together saplings which Raol felled with the small hatchet he had brought. Then they walked again, carrying a small bucket—

they had purchased a few provisions in Liandon—and collecting huckleberries which they had seen earlier. Smiling at each other, eating more than they saved, staining their faces and hands, the way they had done as children.

When it became dark, they crawled into the lean-to, backs nestled close against each other under the blankets, and slept. Once Tekoah woke in blackness, thinking she heard the yowl of a Morg, but it was only the windstones, and she soon fell back to sleep.

In the morning, Fanco kindled a fire and heated water. They gulped down tea with the remaining cornbread and then walked in unison to the coracle at the water's edge. The twins embraced her. After that, Tekoah stood and watched them row away until the small vessel was only a fleck of foam riding on the grey-green waves.

TEKOAH SAW Raol or Fanco once every annaspan throughout the summer and fall. One of them came faithfully, bringing her bread, dried meat, wine and other sustenance that she could not harvest or catch herself.

They never stayed for more than a night. Her brothers seemed to sense that for a time, this place was hers and hers only. And if they noticed the swelling in her belly, they did not show it by a glance or gesture.

By the time the leaves had turned the colour of singed gold and fallen from the sparse stands of beech and elms, Tekoah was moving much more heavily than she should have been by then. She calculated the annaspans on her fingers, puzzled.

Although not an expert on such matters, she had an idea of how long it took for a baby to be born, and it was longer than this.

She walked along the shoreline one day, wrapped in a thick

woolen shawl of Neela's. Summer was over. She heard it in the wind, which was always present, but now wailed through the wind-stones with greater urgency. She glimpsed it in the sea's colour, though she could not have said quite how she saw it—there seemed to be a subtle diminishing of the light, so that the silver-green of the water had shifted to slate-grey.

Tekoah watched the waves hurling themselves upon the surf, squinting her eyes and scanning the horizon for the sight of a boat. One twin should come any day now. It was uncanny, how they always seemed to know where to be. Almost as if they had powers similar to the Anniste.

She was struck suddenly by a thought, followed by the profound certainty that she had hit upon a great truth: this new age had something to do with dissolving the differences between men and women.

Healers and sorcerers had clashed hitherto. But now the stage had changed. A queen—Darielle—had behaved like a king: courageous, unhesitating, changing the course of history. A sorcerer had behaved like a healer, rejecting his power and the tyranny behind it. Saving those who were fragile at the cost of his life.

Closer to home—Chalvern had summoned Braith through bespeaking, a cry of love that brought to bear his latent power, at the very end of his life. No ordinary mortal should have been able to do that.

Reika had reached through her scarred, tormented past, protecting the Anniste, and also rescuing Tekoah's family from Veld's legacy.

And the twins—so different from others, so ignored and belittled—with their strange gifts, they had also claimed a stake in this new world. They belonged to this age.

Whatever it was.

Tekoah felt a dull, insistent cramping in her belly, beginning low and quiet, but spreading upward with an intensity that was impossible to ignore.

All thoughts of the new age and its mysteries fled, as she summoned her strength and will to get from the beach to her shelter. In time.

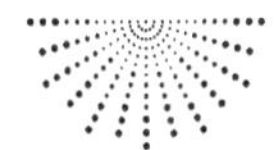

CHAPTER 58

When they first stepped from the Shifting, Weslan was so awestruck that he could say nothing, not one word, to the women of the Anniste. But when they began walking away, slowly but purposefully, he called out to them.

"Do you know where my sister is? Tekoah—did you see her?" It was possible she was still alive, for these women were unharmed, and Zant was nowhere in sight.

One woman looked at him; her eyes were unfocused, as though she had awoken from a long dream. "Yes, I have seen her."

"Where is she, then? Is she still in there?" Weslan pointed at the Shifting.

The woman nodded.

"With Zant?" he asked, horrified at the thought. "Is Zant in there with her?"

"Zant is dead," the woman told him solemnly.

The other women had stopped walking, waiting for her in the path. At her words, a joyful sigh went up from them, like rustling leaves.

"Tekoah is unharmed," the woman added, turning to go. "She is with Braith."

"With Braith? Wait! What do you mean?"

But the Anniste were moving forward again, more briskly, and the one who had spoken to him said, "We must hasten—wounded soldiers are waiting for us."

Weslan stood, watching them go.

She is unharmed, the woman had said. That was a matter of opinion.

He stared down at the Shifting in a hypnotic state of dread and rage. He leaned toward it. Once again, there seemed to be nothing he could do for his sister.

He did not want to think about Braith; it was painful even to say the name in his mind.

The Mantling had diminished a little, darkness fading into grey. Weslan refrained from looking up at the sky, although tempted to do so. When he was a child, he had learned all the lore of the Mantling, including the dire warning: *Do not look upon the sacred sight of Anna and Rhan joining, or you will become blind, in a searing and irrevocable lightning bolt of punishment to the unwary disbeliever.*

Weslan wondered how the North was faring in the battle with Berlot. Within moments, the suspense became almost unbearable, and he was chafing with impatience. *We cannot lose!* he thought. *Almost everyone I love has gone, because of this…*

Beside him, Raol and Fanco were still gazing into the Shifting. Weslan threw up his hands to show them it was no use.

"I am going to the battlefield," he said, pointing south as he spoke. "Where perhaps I can still do something for someone. Are you coming?" He made a beckoning gesture to translate his unheard question.

The twins shook their heads. They seemed these days to have an unshakeable confidence in where they were situated at any given time. Weslan envied them. He clapped each brother on the shoulder in farewell and loped away.

Long before he reached the field at the foot of Mount Delnor, Weslan heard the sounds of fighting: shouting, screaming, swearing, men riding or running for their lives.

It seemed far less dangerous than where he had just been.

Weslan reined in his gelding. He had found the horse, quivering in the woods, a short distance off from the Shifting. Looking around, he was thankful to have a mount.

Hundreds of horses lay dead, Berlotan spear shafts protruding from their flanks. It was an ugly sight to a northern soldier, taught to revere horses. In battle, the steed of an enemy was always captured or left unharmed. Yet the Berlotans had taken a spiteful delight in slaughtering the mounts of their enemies.

And their owners, too, by the looks of it. It appeared to him as though the battle had driven the Northerners almost up to the Castle of Mirrand itself.

Weslan peered around him, puzzled. The fighting had been taking place right there. But now the battlelines were half a league away, though there were still small skirmishes going on close to him. He could see the dust, and men and horses moving, but not much else in the greyish light of the Mantling.

Studying the field, he could see that the Kalesh had—against all odds because of the uneven numbers—driven the Berlotans back half a league in a brief time. Something must have altered the odds in favour of the Kalesh.

At that moment, Weslan's horse shied and whinnied in alarm as two soldiers on foot stumbled toward him.

Their swords were locked; sweat dripped down their faces; in their deadly struggle, they did not even see him. The Berlotan swiped the other man's leg with his foot, tripping him and sending him crashing to the ground. He grinned, raising his curved sword high above his head with both hands.

Without hesitating, Weslan spurred his mount forward and pulled sharply on the reins. His gelding reared up, its sharp front hooves crashing down upon the Berlotan. The Kalesh soldier rolled away, then clambered to his feet, drew his sword and thrust it deep into the Berlotan's belly. He and Weslan exchanged affectionate smiles. It was Nolvern.

"Thanks, lad. I was heading back to the castle to make a report when that bastard came up out of nowhere. Killed my horse, too, may the Berlotan demon rot in the Pit." He spat on the ground. "Where have you been?"

"Fighting sorcerers," Weslan answered.

"Ah, so you've been taking it easy again."

"Yes, taking it easy. How goes it?" Weslan surveyed the field.

Most of the action seemed to take place in the zigzagging line at the foot of the mountain. The slain lay in great numbers, many wearing the colours of the Kalesh. The ground was like a field strewn with crohm leaves, after a mighty windstorm.

"We have lost quite a few, Wes." Nolvern smiled again, a sorrowful smile. "But since the Mantling, things have swung the other way. We are not sure why, my lad. However, Zant has made himself scarce, which I suspect has unsettled the Berlotans somewhat. Where did that snake get off to, I wonder?"

"I can tell you all about Zant. As for the rest of it, let us go find out," Weslan said. He urged his mount into a trot.

They soon had to slow to a walk, with Nolvern striding along beside Weslan as they picked their way, among the dead and dying, to the battleline.

Wending through the bodies was a slow, anguished ordeal. Recognizing many of the soldiers on the ground, Weslan felt his throat thicken; he kept his eyes straight ahead. However, when they reached the front line, they saw an amazing sight.

There were only a few hundred Kalesh at the most, and many of those were on foot. But somehow, they seemed to prevail against the Berlotans, who numbered well over a thousand.

All was confusion in the enemy ranks. Men swore, screamed, fell from their horses like wheat stalks from a swiping scythe. Weslan glimpsed Dirken, riding a white destrier, plunging in and out of the mass of seething flesh; teeth flashing, sword hewing, laughing, by the Holy Mantling!

By the Holy Mantling! Weslan understood what was happening. The Berlotans who had looked up at the sky were going blind. There was nothing in Berlotan teachings that warned about the peril of gazing at the Mantling.

As if to confirm his thoughts, he saw a Berlotan captain—an arrogant-looking fellow who looked enough like the Jinta to be his brother—glance upward, stare curiously at the sky, and then down and up again in horror, passing his hands in front of his eyes. In the next moment, his head was rolling on the ground.

"The Mantling!" Weslan shouted to Nolvern. "It is blinding them. We can win, if we do not lose heart now. We can win!"

Heyg galloped by, leading a grim-faced company of only three men.

"I will tell the Captain," he said to Nolvern, "and you tell Dirken!"

BY MID-AFTERNOON, the Mantling had ended, and the North had won the war. They herded the Berlotan soldiers who had not been killed into a pen to mull over their probable fate. About half of them were now blind. But they would be treated like men, not animals, as Dirken had ordered, before commencing his victory speech in the castle courtyard.

He had added something which soldiers would repeat often in the years to come: *Descending to the level of your foe is to become your own foe.*

Dirken sounds Anniste, almost. Weslan thought this, sitting

in a sulky mood upon one of the wooden benches set up in haste for the comfort of Kalesh soldiers who had come through the fighting unscathed.

Villagers regarded the soldiers with awe, as if they were legendary heroes from the past. The events of that day would be woven into many a tapestry.

The Battle of the Mantling, it was already being called.

Within the infirmary lay the most grievously wounded men. The Anniste women had arrived, by donkey, by cart, and on foot, still looking dazed from their time in the Shifting. But they had begun tending to the injured soldiers, moving with quiet competence among the cots. Despite their efforts, piteous moans and sighs floated out through the open windows, temporarily sobering the celebratory mood of the Northerners.

Any villager who could fight, bribe or flirt their way into the castle grounds had done so on that day to remember. Weslan arose from the bench and stood with the throng, facing Dirken as he spoke from the makeshift platform in the courtyard.

The Mantling was on everyone's lips, and people assured each other, piously claiming that they had always believed in its power.

Except for Dirken.

At least the man was honest. Speaking to the crowd in an earnest voice, Dirken declared that, prior to that day, he had not believed wholeheartedly in the prophecy, but that now he fervently thanked Anna for excusing his stupidity and winning the war for them, anyway.

Everyone clapped at that, whistled, cheered and stamped with wild feet. And then, as Weslan watched with the others, Heyg suddenly leaped up onto the platform.

He held up his arm to Dirken in the Kalesh salute, his face flushing with emotion. "A few of us might have something to say about that," he roared out into the crowd. "A few of us think Anna would not begrudge you getting some of the credit!"

Heyg clasped Dirken's hand in his and raised it in the air. The crowd cheered again, and Weslan had a surge of pride in Dirken. He had looked magnificent out there on the field and was certainly not one of those leaders who hung back and let everyone else do all the work—and then criticized their performance.

Dirken was speaking again. "Talking of credit, let us thank two men for their very astute observations at a crucial time for the army: Nolvern dar Lenk and Weslan dar Veld. May Anna always shine Her light upon you."

Startled, Weslan ducked his head. He realized in that moment that he did not crave attention the way he used to. He would have rather they had not mentioned him at all.

The crowd was yelling and clapping, but it was obvious they did not know what Dirken meant. Looking at the forest of faces and waving arms, mind-numbing fatigue struck Weslan. He wished for nothing more than to crawl into a soft corner and sleep—for days, if possible.

He dozed off in the sunshine, leaning against a post, sliding downward until he was sitting on the ground, then awoke with a start. Someone was shaking his shoulder. It was Dirken, chuckling good-naturedly as he bent down, his sweat-streaked face looming close to Weslan's own.

"Tired, soldier? Or did my speech put you to sleep?"

"Exhausted," Weslan mumbled.

He glanced around. The courtyard still seethed with exuberant villagers, but it was beginning to empty. The excitement was over.

"As am I," Dirken said. "If I do not rest soon, I shall crash like a falling log in front of all these good people who seem to think that I arranged the Mantling."

Weslan smiled. At least Dirken was not so carried away by the crest of his popularity that he himself believed it. And he was not invincible after all, it seemed. At close range, Weslan could see that the other man had innumerable sword nicks and cuts and was swaying a little on his feet.

Dirken squatted down beside him. "But first," he announced, as though he had just remembered it, "I would like to see Tekoah. Where is she?"

Weslan stared at him, bewildered. "Tekoah? She is not here. She—"

"What? A messenger came to the field and told me she had arrived and was in your care."

"My care?" Weslan repeated. He winced at how stupid that sounded, how indifferent.

"Where is she?" Dirken's voice had become deep, reverberating like a war drum.

"Zant came seeking her," Weslan said, raising his own voice to counter the look in Dirken's eyes. "Seeking to slay her," he added, as if there might be confusion on that point.

"We fled, with Zant in hot pursuit. It was all chaos. And then my brothers saw the Shifting. We distracted Zant. I drew my sword and challenged him and then tricked him, so that he fell into the Shifting. I also killed the Morg he had with him."

"You drew your sword on Zant?" Dirken repeated.

All around them, a gathering silence grew, and with it came the heat of inquisitive eyes.

"Yes," he answered.

"That was a shining deed!"

Weslan lifted his chin and pulled back his shoulders. They were the first words of direct praise Dirken had ever spoken to him.

But a moment later, the drum voice was back. "And so, where is your sister? The other Anniste have arrived. Is she resting?"

"No," Weslan replied. The dread was returning. "I do not know where she is."

There was a deep, awful silence, in which Weslan ferociously told himself he would not fear Dirken, not after what he had just been through.

"You do not know?" Dirken echoed. His voice bit deep.

"No. After I pushed Zant in, Tekoah fell into the Shifting as well."

"She fell in?" Dirken's voice dropped to a whisper, and he went white to the lips.

"To be exact, she jumped in—to escape the Morg. It all happened in a matter of seconds. And that was when I killed the Morg with my sword."

Everyone nearby was staring at Weslan with horrified, riveted attention. He ignored all the faces except Dirken's.

"After I stabbed the Morg, I wanted to go in after her, but my brothers held me back. They seem to understand a lot about Shiftings—as you know."

This last sentence sounded as lame as a stray dog begging on the village outskirts. Weslan rubbed his lips, as if to remove the taste of the words. In the quiet that followed, Dirken's face was terrible to behold.

"But I am hopeful that she is unharmed," Weslan said, the words falling flat. "When the Anniste came out a few minutes later, they told me that Zant is dead."

"Dead? How?"

"Braith killed him."

Dirken looked at him a moment without comprehension, and then Weslan saw the flint-sparks in his eyes. He decided he had better stand up, so that they were at eye-level, at least.

"So Tekoah was with Braith when he killed Zant?"

"I suppose so," Weslan said. "I do not know; I was not in there."

"And then what happened?"

"What?" Weslan asked.

"What happened after that?" Dirken said, with exaggerated slowness, as though he was talking to an idiot.

"I do not know. I left."

"You left?"

Weslan looked at Dirken's darkening face. "Tekoah was still in there—there was nothing I could do for her," he muttered.

"You could have stayed. The other women came out. Why would not she?"

"It would not have mattered where she was," Weslan said. "Because she was with Braith."

Dirken struck him then—right out of Rhan's blue sky—as hard as Weslan had ever been struck in his life, knocking him to the ground; amid a collective gasp from the curious onlookers that had surrounded them. He stood rubbing his knuckles, looking down at Weslan lying there on the hard-packed ground.

"I should be sorry I did that," he mused. "But I cannot be. Not yet."

And he turned and walked away.

CHAPTER 59

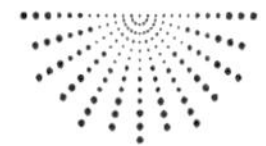

BOOK 6: CHANGING SEASONS

Spring had gone, and summer had come, and summer was almost over. But as he tossed restlessly in his dream, it was winter again, the winter of his wandering.

Not knowing he dreamt, Weslan walked again with Reika through the snow-muffled Taboran forest, moving with a freedom and happiness he had never felt. They stopped, staring into a frozen pool. And as they gazed, the ice began to melt, floating away from the centre so that they could see into the deep black water.

"This is Mirveta's Basin," Reika was explaining to him. "She was the very first Anniste. As with so many of her friends and neighbours, Mirveta's husband and sons had all been killed in the war with the marauders from over the eastern sea. The priests were of no comfort to her, for they claimed it was a holy war, and that she should be glad, proud to give up her family to its cause.

"Weeping with despair, she stooped over this pool, thinking to throw herself in, but as she gazed, she saw a brilliant full moon reflected in the water. And Anna spoke to a mortal for the first time. The Goddess gave Mirveta a reason to live. 'Heal, and be healed,' she said."

Reika was looking at him, the warmth of her eyes reaching out like a kindled fire, and he basked in her love.

"You healed me," he murmured, reaching out for her. Bewildered, he found he held only air.

Engulfed by loss, Weslan stumbled through the woods. All around him the snow was melting, and soon grass and flowers were springing up everywhere. He walked into an open glade; the ground was carpeted with more flowers than he had ever seen.

In the centre of the glade there was a bier, garlanded with roses and lilies. As he walked closer, his footsteps became as heavy as if he wore boots of iron. He had not been strong enough to make the pilgrimage he owed to Darielle. This caused him shame; because, of course, all his countrymen—courtiers and peasants alike—had flocked to the new palace gardens of Rhantor, where their martyred queen's body was laid out in state.

Weslan had dreaded this moment; but it was as if someone was pushing him from behind, and he kept walking until he reached the place where she lay. Almost blinded by his tears, he bent over her. But it was not Darielle who lay in the carved crohmwood box.

It was Reika, her scarred body hidden by the flowing brown robe of the Anniste, the warmth in her lovely eyes taken from him forever.

When Weslan awoke, he was weeping, and he could not halt for some time. The depth of his grief unnerved him. He wrestled with the fear that, although it had only been a dream, Reika was dead.

～

AFTER THAT DAY, Weslan searched less and less for Tekoah. When he went to Chalvern's shop, as the Anniste who gathered there still called it, he questioned the women in a listless, desultory fashion. He admitted to himself, after a wild and fruitless night of drinking at the Pitaya Pit, that he had been also searching for Reika.

Not that he did not care for Tekoah, he thought, feeling extraordinarily clear-headed after retching for several minutes on Hanta's neatly planted rows of radishes. It was just that there was not much point in looking for her. She had gone beyond him—she had gone to Braith.

And if Braith was alive—and no one had seen him since the Mantling—then, wherever he dwelt, there Tekoah would be. Some deep magnetism drew her to the sorcerer, and he could do nothing about it. Although Dirken thought otherwise.

Arrogant bastard, that Dirken, Weslan swore, weaving his way back toward the cottage. *Must be quiet!* he admonished himself. *Do not wake anyone. They have been too kind as it is. Don't be any bother.*

Someone was silhouetted against the back door. Weslan squinted at the shadow. "Is that you, Hanta?" he asked, hearing his voice come out thick.

"No, it is Norah," came the answer. "As always. Let me help you to your bed."

"Not yet," he answered. Restless, he slumped against the doorframe, staring up at the summer sky.

Norah stayed beside him, though he wished she would not. Her insistent presence made him uneasy. When Weslan had agreed to board with Hanta, he had not known that her newly widowed niece would lodge there as well. And the hopes of the two plump women could not have been more transparent than if they had already begun cooking delicacies for the wedding feast.

He did not wish to be unfair. He should leave, and soon. But there did not seem to be anywhere he cared to go. Dirken had grudgingly invited him to Rhantor Court, along with the other leaders of the Kalesh, in the apparently unending rounds of victorious ceremonying. Weslan suspected the invitation was grudging and insincere, but the letter written by the Crown King had been elegant and courteous. Very king-like of Dirken, considering the fact that the man hated him.

Ceremonying, Weslan repeated to himself. *Terrific word, that. I think I made it up.*

"What did you say?" Norah asked, her voice cooing in a way that made his teeth grate.

"Nothing," he blurted. "Why do you not go to bed? It is very late." He hiccupped, undermining his attempt to dignify his demeanour.

"I like it out here. Summer will not last much longer."

"No." He expelled his breath. "Soon it will disappear."

"Weslan," Norah said, and when he did not reply she continued in a timid voice, "You should go to Rhantor. Or something. You are not happy."

Weslan turned his head away from the glittering, star-lit sky and rose to his feet, chagrined. Did it show that much, then?

"Happiness is a luxury, Norah, like pitaya brandy or candied figs. One experiences the pleasure once or twice and remembers it forever. But I was not raised to expect happiness, so pray do not worry about me."

He knew he sounded maudlin, but he was too tired to care. Steadying his hand on her shoulder, he found the doorknob and staggered through the door.

In the night, Weslan heard Norah weeping. He buried his head between his folded arms, covering his ears so he could no longer hear.

THE MORNING after his communion with the radishes, Weslan lay abed, unwilling to get up. He felt a little ill, but there was more to it than that. There was nothing to get up for.

The cottage was silent. Hanta and Norah had no doubt crept out before dawn to gather their eggs and then headed down to the neighbouring farm to thresh barley. That was where he should be as well. Or at the forge, helping his brothers. But he could not bear the sight of the forge—Veld's domain.

Bhantok had offered him a full partnership in the pony farm, but Weslan knew his cousin would try his patience beyond all limits, with his crimson cheeks, his stammer, and his incessant mooning over Reika, whom he had decided was his lost love.

Weslan belonged nowhere, it seemed. After he contemplated the morbid thought for longer than he should have, Weslan decided he had better go help with the barley threshing, before he became insufferable company even for himself. He donned his worn breeches and a loose-sleeved, open-necked shirt. For it would be hot work.

When he stepped outside, it surprised him to feel a hint of chill in the air, and a faint mistiness, just yonder, caught in the tree-branches like bits of jagged cloth. Summer was ending.

The previous summer, he had been patrolling with Heyg's band of mercenaries, never guessing in his most far-flung dreams all the things that would transpire. Yet there he was, back in Stern, lacking even a horse, walking along the highway of a countryside that had lost and regained its freedom within the stroke of a single day.

Why was it that most life-changing events occurred with such breathtaking speed that one was not aware of anything happening until it was all over?

Famished, Weslan stopped by the side of the road to pick some ripe blackberries, and when he looked up, he saw a horseman riding toward him. Even from a distance, he could see by the gait that the steed was a fine one, and there was something in the rider's seat that was familiar.

Weslan straightened and stood still, waiting until they were close enough to see, and then leaped out with a glad exclamation. "Captain Heyg!"

Heyg stopped short, pretending to glower beneath his wiry brows, but breaking into a guffaw an instant later. Weslan grinned back, feeling more alive than he had in annaspans.

His captain dismounted, handing his reins to a nearby soldier, and embraced Weslan with unabashed emotion. Then, taking his arm, he strode forward, facing the harvest fields.

"So glad to find you well. That is obvious. But you can forget about the barley," Heyg said bluntly, pointing at the waving stalks. "Dirken wants to see you."

Weslan winced. It was not Heyg's habitual abruptness that disturbed him. That was as welcome as froth on cold beer after being with Hanta and Norah all summer.

It was the mention of Dirken's name.

"Why in Anna's name would he want to see me?" he answered, keeping his voice light. "Has he not enough to do planning his coronation?"

"You know very well he refuses to contemplate a coronation until your sister is found."

"Still? Then he is a fool."

"So you say," Heyg growled. "Yet for a fool he still saved this country from being pickled in pitaya juice."

"The Mantling saved this country."

"Far be it from me to dispute the interpretations of the holy and the devout," Heyg answered scathingly, "but from a stupid soldier's point of view, our victory was due to the army being in the right place at the right time—thanks to Dirken—and also to the astounding bravery of a dead queen."

Weslan shrugged, a gesture that could be called disloyal,

even treasonous; for Dirken would certainly be the next king—if he stopped moping about long enough to take the throne.

"Why does Dirken wish to see me?" he repeated, as a distraction, for Heyg's head had lowered like that of a bull about to charge.

"That, I cannot say."

"He must be aware that I know his formal invitation was just that: a formality. Is this more of the same? Because I do not wish to waste my time. Harvesting has begun."

"I should think," his captain said, dangerously soft, "that as the next ruler of this country, he can do as he thinks fit."

Heyg had responded in just such a manner to an insolent Berlotan envoy—right before running him through with his sword. Weslan had witnessed the harrowing encounter and thought it best not to attempt a witty retort.

"Go pack your things." Heyg's voice was brisk. "I will ride to the village and bring you back a mount. As I recall, you look your best on a mule."

Relieved that the tender-hearted women were not there to weep and wring their hands, Weslan packed his few belongings and oiled his sword. Strapping it on gave him conflicting sensations of elation and dread. Too much time had gone by—weeks —and the soldier in him seemed diminished and remote.

He sat on the wooden steps of the cottage, munching an apple and some bread, throwing the crumbs to Hanta's hens, until he heard hoofbeats outside.

Heyg had brought a chestnut mare, a little small for him, but at least she was not a mule, as he'd threatened. Weslan swung into the saddle.

"Here we go again," he remarked.

"Hmm?" Heyg grunted. He still looked a little angry.

"Here we go again. This is the second time you have stormed into my village and dragged me away—without letting me give so much as a by-your-leave to my nearest and dearest. Soon I will imagine that I am a valuable piece of goods."

Heyg laughed, a little unwillingly. "Never think that, lad," he cautioned, shaking his head. "Never think that."

THEY RODE HARD for three days, barely stopping to eat and snatch a few hours' sleep. Heyg was vague and taciturn whenever Weslan tried to hypothesize about the purpose of his summons, so he gave up asking. Perhaps Heyg really did not know.

As they approached the royal city, Weslan found his stomach tightening in anxiety, although he tried to tell himself it was only hunger. He was not looking forward to his interview with Dirken. How could he be, when last time they'd met, Dirken had punched him square in the face, knocking him flat in front of a courtyard of people?

He flinched as he remembered the force of Dirken's bare fist on his jaw.

Suppose he said the wrong thing again—would Dirken break his cheekbone this time? And Heyg claimed he was the one who could not master his temper, Weslan fumed. *This country does not know what it is in for.*

Heyg said something.

"What was that?" Weslan replied. He had not been listening.

"Here we are."

And so they were, he saw with surprise—at the very gates of the palace. They had been riding through the city streets of Rhantor for some time, but Weslan had been lost in his apprehensive imaginings, and was only vaguely aware of their surroundings.

"May fortune smile upon you, and all that rot, lad!" Captain

Heyg said sardonically, wheeling his horse around.

"Wait," Weslan called, alarmed. "Where are you going? Are you not attending on Dirken as well? Is this not to be a meeting of the Kalesh?"

"There is no meeting that I plan to attend"—Heyg grinned—"except a very informal one, that I have arranged at the Fallen Maiden tavern. Join us, if you have time on your hands afterward. You know the place. If not, be assured that the Fallen Maiden knows you." Chuckling a little at his own wit, Captain Heyg rode away.

A blind, unreasonable panic assailed Weslan. He did not wish to see Dirken at all. To be forced to see him alone was the worst thing he could think of, worse than having a tooth pulled without a dose of corn liquor first. Perhaps he should catch up with Heyg and let Dirken hunt him down at the Fallen Maiden.

But it was too late. The sentries had recognized his captain, and they swung the iron gates open. So, pulling his features into what he hoped expressed remote dignity, he waved at the soldiers and rode on through.

They led Weslan to a small chamber in which he scarcely had time to wash his face and slap the travel-dust from his clothes, when the same servant returned to announce that his presence was requested. Not in the throne room, as Weslan had assumed, but in the hunting hall.

Well, that is a relief, Weslan thought. *Dirken has not put on too many royal airs just yet.*

Nodding briskly, he followed the man down the corridor, resisting the temptation to bark out that he knew the way.

Knew it well, too. He wondered what the servant would say if he discovered Weslan had graced the royal bedchamber of Queen Darielle, who after her death had achieved the status of a goddess among the common people.

How Darielle would have adored that, Weslan mused, standing in the open doorway of the hunting hall, and blinking his eyes as they adjusted to the dim light. And how unlike Reika she had been in that way, though they had both been born with royal blood in their veins.

"Come in, Weslan."

At the sound of Dirken's voice, Weslan jumped a little, and was immediately furious with himself for doing so.

"Leave us," Dirken said crisply to a dark little Berlotan man who had been crouching beside him over a table covered with a small mountain of clay tablets. "And close the doors," he added, standing and stretching his limbs, muscles rippling restlessly beneath his fine linen tunic.

The little man gathered up an armful of tablets and went scuttling past Weslan, peering at him fearfully, and stumbling in haste.

"Come closer, Weslan, so that we needn't shout at each other," Dirken told him, cupping his hands in an exaggerated movement around his mouth and raising his voice.

Weslan walked across the room, his boots thudding loudly on the flagged stone floor.

"There, that's better. Sit." Dirken gestured to a large, deep chair near the unlit hearth. He threw himself carelessly into another beside it, sighing pleasurably as he did so. He had not given Weslan a chance to bow.

There was a flagon and two goblets on a table between them. Dirken poured them both a generous goblet-full. It was pitaya wine. Sipping luxuriously, Weslan looked sidelong at the other man.

Dirken had changed. It was subtle, though, hard to pin down. He still had the dimpled, boyishly handsome face which had always irritated Weslan. His dress and hair were immaculate, from the silver circlet on his head—he would not wear gold until after the coronation—to his butter-soft leather boots. Something was different, though.

"You have no idea how good it feels to escape from those

eternal numbers," Dirken drawled. "I am a man of action, like you, Wes. This Berlotan treaty is slow torture."

Weslan grunted sympathetically and took another sip of pitaya wine. When had he tasted it last? More to the point, why was Dirken being so pleasant to him?

"Sometimes it appears this short-lived war never happened," Dirken continued. "But the endless haggling that has followed always serves to remind me. Perhaps more monarchs would become diplomats if we forced *them* to deal with the messy aftermath of our glorious scuffles."

"We are getting the best of it, I hope," Weslan ventured.

"Naturally." Dirken grinned. "I may be obtuse with sums and bushels, but not when it comes to pitayas and ponies. When it is all blown out the clay pipe, Berlot will find itself responsible for feeding the South throughout next winter and replenishing the grain stores of the North. We will not even discuss trading pitayas until next spring."

"And they will agree to it?" Weslan asked, incredulous.

He cared little about politics, but everyone knew the Berlotans were rabid about pitayas.

"They haven't any choice. They are still frightened by the Mantling—and it's all chaos and confusion at Hacinta-Car, because their monarch has been assassinated. The new Jinta, a dredged-up cousin of his, has evidently yet to sprout hair upon his body, and is meekly obeying the advice of his councillors. But the Berlotans will soon be back to their usual treachery, sharpening their daggers and hatching their plots. That is why it is vital to get everything underway now." Dirken was quiet for a moment, rubbing his lower lip with his forefinger.

Scrutinizing him, Weslan realized how Dirken had changed: he seemed more thoughtful, now. Before, he had seldom hesitated about any matter, great or small. Not even when there appeared to be no time in which to decide something. He had decided in the blink of an eye, the slap of a palm; coolly, quelling with a look anyone who disagreed with him. And demonstrating his confidence by joking or singing in the next moment, as though he had ceased to give the matter any thought.

Weslan had been jealous of that. But now Dirken had paused for a fraction of a second. Just long enough to make him seem human, like everyone else.

"After the coronation," Dirken said, looking straight at Weslan, "I will need help to ensure that the army stays an army, so that there is never again a chance that we will lose our freedom. I seek to surround myself with men who have been in the Kalesh for longer than a summer." He smiled at Weslan.

Weslan sipped his wine silently, not wanting to reply, for fear of seeming a fool. Surely Dirken was not asking for his help. He had made very plain his opinion as to Weslan's leadership potential.

Why was Dirken acting so friendly? Out of guilt? Or had Heyg intervened on Weslan's behalf? The thought was galling.

Dirken was smiling at him, hazel eyes unblinking, waiting for a response.

"Yes, you will need seasoned men, without a doubt." Weslan added, "And the coronation will be soon, I hope. Your people are becoming anxious, my lord."

"In five days, I hope." Dirken grinned at the look of incredulity on Weslan's face. "I know, I know," he said. "I said not until next turning, unless we found Tekoah."

"I am glad," Weslan said, and found that he meant it. Miraven had been without a king long enough. "I am very glad, my lord. This is the right thing to do. We must put the past behind us."

As he said the words, he thought of Reika, and his dream, and such a bitter sense of loss gripped him that he could say no more. *Ah, how I love to preach about never looking back!* he taunted himself.

Had Dirken's sorrow been as deep as this when he lost

Tekoah? If so, perhaps they had more in common than Weslan had thought. But he saw now that Dirken was looking at him with pure, undiluted joy. It glowed in his eyes and sparked from his fingertips as he leaned forward and clapped Weslan heartily on the shoulder.

"But you have not guessed?" he exclaimed, squeezing Weslan's arm with something astonishing close to affection. He laughed, "I thought you would, in an instant!"

As Weslan continued to stare at him, Dirken stood up, seizing his goblet and hurling it against the hearth, his face exuberant.

He has lost his mind. Weslan ducked a clay shard that ricocheted back toward him. He became quite certain: the war had afflicted Dirken with battle exhaustion, accompanied by euphoric, happy delusions. Quite common among soldiers. It explained everything: the laughter, the camaraderie, the absence of any hostility toward him.

Weslan took a gulp of wine. *I will enjoy it while I can.*

"You still sit mystified." Dirken marvelled. His voice rose to a shout that made the wooden rafters shiver and groan. "It is Tekoah! I have found her!"

CHAPTER 60

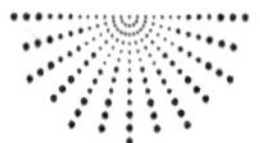

Sometimes it was as though the wind-stones were singing a song for her alone, telling a tale of mourning and loss. The high, keening whistles agitated and then soothed her, so that when she closed her eyes, her body became a wave, rising and falling.

Tekoah sat on the shore, wind whipping her ragged hem around her bare white feet, staring out at the horizon. For days, she had cared about nothing except her own sorrow, but now she found her eyes straining toward the horizon, seeking the image of a small coracle bobbing along on the waves.

However, it was too stormy in the season for that tiny vessel. Would the twins be able to procure another, larger boat? And how would they navigate it? The seas were becoming rough.

No matter, she thought wearily. Her brothers would probably not bother to return, after the way she had dismissed them last time.

SHE HAD BEEN at the crest of her birthing, squatting with her arms braced between two trees: breathing in short, hard gasps.

Looking up through the haze of her pain, Tekoah had seen the twins standing there, awed, and silent. She had been surprised, for they had seldom visited her together since the day they had first brought her there. They had always been in demand at the forge. Yet there they had been.

Why now, for Anna's sake?

Then all at once, the head of the baby had been coming down, crowning, and she had screamed at Raol and Fanco, in a fever pitch of pain and terror and fury, telling them to get out, to leave her alone!

She had been so frightened. She had not known what her child would look like.

There. At last, a boat had appeared on the water, larger than the coracle—probably a fishing vessel, weaving its intrepid way among the jagged waves. Rain fell, and Tekoah turned her face upward, letting the frigid drops mingle with the hot, joyous tears on her cheeks.

The child inside was part of her, and part of Braith, and so until that moment, being alone had not been frightening or painful. Eager, she had waited for the birth, hoping to nourish and sustain them both, and to live out their lives in content on the Isle of Mira.

But even this simple dream was gone.

The boat was much nearer now, but hard to see, for the rain was driving down in sheets, drenching her hair, plastering her tattered dress to her skin.

She would not usually be foolhardy enough to stay sitting there, for it was impossible to stop the shivering once it began, and even more dangerous when it ceased, for one became warm and sleepy. It was easy to die that way. The shivering and drowsiness had happened to her once, but Fanco had arrived, just in time to revive her.

But in that moment, Tekoah did not care about danger. There was no longer the baby to worry about. Her beloved daughter, for whom she had needed to stay alive.

For the little creature had abandoned her, fled from her cupped hands almost immediately after the birth—green-gold eyes wild with confusion and fear, wings unfolding swiftly, heading skyward with an uncanny, haunting cry.

No, Tekoah did not care about such foolish things as living and dying. Everyone did both, and seldom at a time of their own choosing.

But, for the first time in a long while, she wanted to talk to someone. Beyond that, she did not know what she desired. It was as if a blank, colourless wall had reared up straight in front of her, slippery, smooth and insurmountable.

Tekoah stood, legs unsteady. In mockery of her defiance, the shivering had begun. She hoped the twins had brought blankets, for she had hung her bedding on a tree limb to air, and it would now be soaked through.

The boat came in fast, driven by a strong gale behind. A man leaped out, and Tekoah stared, unnerved, wiping the water from her eyes.

He was faster, more agile than the twins. Pulling the small fishing vessel onto the beach, he secured it onto a large drift-wood log. Then he turned and strode swiftly toward her.

And she just had time to register with astonishment that it was *Dirken*, of all people, before he lifted her up and swung her in the air. Then lowered her gently; holding her wet, shivering body against him, murmuring in wonder as though he had just unearthed a rare treasure.

THE STORM STALKED the Isle of Mira for many dark hours, and they spent the night huddled together in the lean-to.

Tekoah's trembling had ceased, in part because Dirken's body seemed to give off a tremendous amount of heat. She clung to him as to a raft in a river, while outside the gale whistled and sighed through the windstones.

"At first I suffered, wondering why you had deserted me," Dirken whispered to her during the night. "But now I know. Why settle for a poor minstrel such as I, when here the gods play for you their most sublime music?"

Tekoah did not trust herself to answer. She clung to Dirken because her body needed warming, and because not a day had passed since their last meeting that she had not thought of him.

Yet she had a strong desire to flee. She had not talked to anyone for days and days—perhaps annaspans. Dirken, with his deep voice and the fiery heat of his aliveness, was terrifying.

She felt his arms tighten about her and she turned her body so that her back was curled against him.

"Do not think I had a joining in mind," he growled in her ear. "You look like a drowned kitten."

"Liar," she muttered, burrowing further under the blanket. She heard his low chuckle, and a measure of peace stole over her as she drifted back to sleep.

But the next morning Tekoah felt the same urge to run from Dirken. His calm assumption that she was going back with him only intensified the urge.

Dirken did not enquire why she had come there, and that made her uneasy. Nor did he mention Braith's name, or anything about her being with child, although it must have been the twins who had told Dirken where to find her.

But several times, Tekoah saw him gazing about, a puzzled look on his face, and a chill swept through her which had nothing to do with the storm. She could not bear the thought of having to talk about Braith or the babe.

"See, you are cold," Dirken said in a quiet voice, as they

stood gazing out to sea, which looked clear and green and tranquil, as it often did after a storm.

It was true that Tekoah trembled. She tried to still herself after he noticed, but her limbs seemed possessed of a nervous energy.

He took off his grey woolen cloak and flung it over her shoulders. "You would not last much longer here, although you do look like one of the savages that used to throw poisoned spears at me in Berlot."

Tekoah smiled, then giggled at the thought of hurling a poisoned spear. Dirken had always known how to make her laugh.

Now, sensing success, he continued to tease her, turning toward her, and twisting a lock of her tangled hair around his finger, saying, "Do you promise you will not throw any spears at me? You are a gruesome sight, you know!"

"I do *not* know," she answered. "I have not seen myself in ages."

"I lied," he said. "You are beautiful."

Looking at his face, Tekoah turned away, smoothing the cloak with nervous fingers.

"You are coming with me," Dirken said, in the stern voice he sometimes used with his soldiers. "Or else I shall stay here with you, and moan and sigh, and sing in a dreadfully off-key voice along with those magnificent stones, until you go utterly mad."

Tekoah laughed, but then halted. "It is just that—"

"Just that what?"

"I do not know who I can be to you, now. Or ever."

She could not look at him as she said the words, so she looked down instead, toeing the ground with her cracked leather boots. In the brief silence which followed, her words seemed to echo.

"Whoever else you are, you will be my queen. This I have pledged, and I have waited long enough."

Looking into his intent face, Tekoah felt a disbelieving wonder. King. She had forgotten about that. He was now the king of Miraven! And she was to be his queen? How Father would have laughed at her, had she ever dared to imagine herself as queen.

She turned and rushed away in a panic, stumbling across the sand. He followed, and they tripped hard against each other, falling in a tumbled heap. Tekoah pulled away from him, sitting apart, shaken and confused.

Dirken refused to listen to her objections, but continued his persuasion—even when she covered her ears—pleading, cajoling, and lecturing by turns. Then the rain began again, and the windstones moaned and wailed, warning against something— desolation, perhaps?

And at last, she agreed.

THEY TOOK with them a few blankets for the journey home and left everything else behind in the little shelter, which for a time she had called home.

As they pushed off, Tekoah looked back, just once. She saw the curved branches of the lean-to, frail-seeming and insignificant against the jutting stone fingers beside it; and wondered if another pilgrim would one day seek refuge from a storm within, or without.

Tekoah soon became drowsy from the rocking and swaying of the boat on the becalmed water. The sun caressed her cheeks as she lay with her head in Dirken's lap.

Tekoah knew she was asleep, and yet, somehow, she could see through her closed lids. She looked up at the vast blue bowl of the sky; unable to stop herself from searching for a speck that was a little larger than a bird.

A speck that would return to her because she willed it to,

with all the strength and yearning left within her. She felt a call rise up from deep inside, as old as time itself. *Come back to me, my child!* And her babe would return, dipping downward, sunlight catching the iridescent feathers of her outspread wings. Smiling, her dark, silky, baby hair flying back from her pure forehead.

Mother! she would cry out, if she could talk—would she ever talk? She'd gaze intently, with her father's green-gold eyes as she hovered, shimmering, in the air. *Mother, l will never leave you again!*

Tekoah's eyes ached from staring at the empty sky, but because they were already shut, she could not close them.

When she awoke, it was with a cry, and her cheeks were wet. Dirken was stroking her hair and singing an old Anniste lullaby. She looked up at him mutely, wondering how many times she had shouted out, and if she had said anything aloud that would give away what had happened.

But Dirken looked down at her with a tender smile, and she closed her eyes again, to blessed darkness this time.

Tekoah woke from her troubled sleep again and again before they reached the shore, crying out for her child. Each time, Dirken was singing softly, and so she drifted back into a fitful slumber.

Then it was Dirken who woke her, shaking her shoulder gently, pointing to shore and the twinkling lights of Liandon.

They were home.

CHAPTER 61

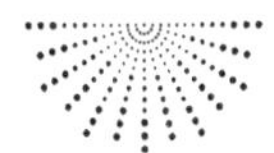

iraven has seen nothing like this since King Garan's coronation!

Tekoah heard the exclamation repeatedly, and each time she smiled, trying to match the excitement that quivered in the eager faces around her.

The coronation at the palace in Rhantor was indeed a splendid affair, made even more thrilling because it had been delayed. That they held it on the day of the Night of Masks was a brilliant, if rather flamboyant notion—for in this way everyone in the country could feel that they were part of the pageantry.

It was also fitting because the coronation included the wedding ceremony of the king and his chosen bride.

Tekoah sat in an ornate chair carved of crohmwood, between her brother Weslan and her husband, the king of Miraven. Hearing him addressed as King Dirken sounded so strange, but this was who he was, among many other things: the beloved minstrel, the spy, the soldier, the far-sighted warrior-king.

Weslan pinched her calf under the table and rolled his eyes. The diplomatic delegation from Berlot was still struggling its word-tangled way through a congratulatory speech, which of course bored Weslan to tears.

Dirken, who had been listening with grave dignity, leaned swiftly behind her and whispered something to Weslan. The two men smiled like mischievous schoolboys.

It was lovely that they got along so well, Tekoah thought. She had never seen them in the same room until that moment, and had feared that they might clash, partly because Dirken had once questioned Weslan's loyalty, but mostly because, although they were both men of action, they were very different. However, her fears had come to naught.

Could it be? she wondered. That her earliest dreams might come true, after all? Everyone she loved, happy and at peace with one another. Smiles and content wherever she turned her gaze? Peaceful dreams, no screams in the night.

There had been no chance to say more than a few words to Weslan. It could wait, she supposed. There was so much to relate, yet it would take few words. He seemed to sense the truth about Reika—she could tell that the moment she'd seen him. His blue-green eyes had lost some of their lustre, and there were lines about his mouth that had not been there a few annaspans ago.

Across the banquet room, Valeen smiled at her. Tekoah smiled back, grateful for the sight of someone who understood.

She wished she could sit with the Anniste at their table, which had been placed in a position of honour, close to the monarchs. She imagined herself, free of the heavy gown, the indigo and white garb of a queen, which glittered with Berlotan rubies and gold-threaded embroidery. In her mind, she saw herself wearing the simple brown homespun robe of the Anniste, and sitting among them, comfortable, unwatched by hundreds of pairs of avid eyes.

But the Anniste did not need her any longer. Although she

was glad to be relieved of the burden, she had times of wistful melancholy.

The Anniste had changed. They no longer Journeyed. Valeen had spoken to her of this when they conversed after the coronation. Tekoah had felt a mingling of longing and regret. But at least she had not been alone in losing the power to Journey.

And, by unanimous agreement, the healers were allowing others, not Anniste by blood, to take up their calling. This included—astoundingly—men.

Not so surprising when one thought about it, Tekoah mused. Chalvern's voice echoed in her mind: *It was always my deepest desire to be a healer…*

Why not men? Perhaps it might make them less eager to kill each other. Some of them, anyway.

With unease, Tekoah observed the artfully concealed hatred on the face of the Berlotan envoy.

It was unnerving, not knowing why the Mantling had somehow heralded the end of sorcerers, or why the structure of the Anniste healing clan had changed. Not understanding where the new power would come from—or where it would take them.

A familiar urge took hold and, unable to stop herself, Tekoah craned her neck and looked upward. But there was no sky at which to gaze, only the polished halestone ceiling. She closed her wet eyes and tried to slow the rapid breaths which came without warning at these times.

Dirken pressed her hand, and she smiled at him, doing her best to look happy, and willing herself not to see the hurt in his eyes.

If she could blot out the memory of one heartbreak, then perhaps she would not become the cause of another.

CHAPTER 62

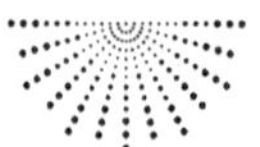

When Weslan heard the news of his nephew's birth, he left his hoe standing upright in the earth and ran shouting at the top of his lungs down the newly furrowed fields.

"It is a boy!" he shouted at Norah as he burst into the kitchen, cold water from the well still dripping from his face and hands. He undressed where he stood. "I will ride to Rhantor today. The planting is almost done."

Norah smiled indulgently from the table where she sat chopping dried apples. "It is about time," she said, glancing significantly toward a corner of the room, where Theena sat playing with a corn-husk doll.

Weslan knew what Norah was thinking as clearly as if she had said it—*and about time we had babes of our own.*

She had already been with child by Stolk when Weslan had moved into Hanta's cottage. Little Theena was now nearly two turnings old. Stolk had been among the first to fall in the battle to protect the North, and his young widow Norah had every right to seek a stable future. Weslan wished he could give her more of what she wanted, or that she wanted less.

He scooped up Theena before he left, pinching her plump cheek. "I will be back in an annaspan," he said to Norah over the child's head.

She nodded. She knew better than to press further.

ENTERING THE QUEEN'S BEDCHAMBER, the first person Weslan saw was the king, sitting on the edge of the bed, where the queen lay propped up on pillows as she nursed the heir to the throne of Miraven.

"He's a proper nuisance, King Dirken is," complained the pretty maidservant who had escorted Weslan. "He will not leave, and he keeps bossing us about, as though he has better ideas than we in these matters. A man!" she sniffed, wrinkling her pert nose in outrage.

Weslan grinned at her. "Nothing but trouble, aren't we?"

She coloured a little, lowering her eyelashes primly. "Indeed, you are," she snapped, but her voice softened a little, and Weslan could not resist winking at her before she turned away.

"Weslan!" Dirken had risen and was striding toward him. "Come see your nephew. He is magnificent. Huge, healthy and an absolute tyrant!"

"Just what this country needs," Weslan laughed, moving toward the bed.

"Shh!" Tekoah hissed, glaring at him.

She gestured with her chin toward the babe who was drifting off to sleep on her breast. He looked distinctly smaller and less menacing than Dirken's description.

The maidservant bustled forward, stretching out her arms to take the child; but this time Tekoah and Dirken both scowled fiercely at her and she retreated, sighing with exasperation.

"We will speak outside," Dirken murmured, taking Weslan's arm. "Rest while you are able, my dear," he said, turning back to the bed with a courtly bow. "I shall not be long."

"There is no hurry," muttered the maid, as she closed the door firmly behind them.

"Let us ride!" Dirken exclaimed exuberantly, as if making an unusually unique and brilliant suggestion. "I have not been out in days. What is the weather like?"

"Wonderful," Weslan answered. "The rains have stopped, and the soil is perfect for planting. There was just enough rainfall this season, not too little or too much. We are almost finished in Stern."

"Splendid, splendid," Dirken replied, nodding sagely, though Weslan could tell he had not listened to a word.

Weslan could not help glancing at the king's face as they rode. Dirken's eyes shone, and his laughter was frequent and unrestrained. He looked happy, finally, and Weslan was relieved, because his sister's future was forever entwined with him.

For three turnings after the coronation, a perpetual gloom had pervaded the palace at Rhantor, although no one knew why. Peace had returned to the land, and the gods seemed to smile benignly upon the Miraven, as if it suddenly suited them to make up for their capricious cruelty in pelting the people with drought, war, and sorcerer-spawned terror.

But in spite of the lightened atmosphere elsewhere in the land, the royal couple had withdrawn into themselves. They seldom held court unless it was necessary, and although King Dirken was fastidious in performing his duties in overseeing the army, judicial matters, and the royal purse, he performed them without enthusiasm. Gone was the charismatic man-of-the-people who had written the stirring *Anthem to the North*.

More than one disgruntled courtier was heard to mutter, "He was once a minstrel, wasn't he? Well, why isn't there ever any singing?"

The people seldom saw the queen outside her suite of chambers. She was glimpsed by the odd tradesperson or gardener, standing out on her balcony, staring up at the sky, oblivious to all else.

Weslan himself had seldom visited Rhantor, and on the few occasions when he had seen Tekoah alone, she had spoken of trivial matters. Once, he remembered, when he had mentioned some antic of little Theena's, her expression had become so pained that he had left hastily on some pretext.

Weslan did not know the details of Tekoah's sojourn on the Isle of Mira, nor had the twins enlightened him in their unique styles of communicating pantomimes or stick drawings in the dirt. So, he knew only that Tekoah was not happy. And when she was unhappy, Dirken was unhappy.

But now the royal couple appeared transformed, radiant. They had produced an heir to the throne, defying the recent despairing speculation among the populace that it would never happen.

When had everything changed? Why had it changed? Perhaps he should not worry about it so much. In the past, Weslan had not been concerned by the "whys" of things. But now he could see that Tekoah was truly happy, no longer living a half-life. He did not know why, and it weighed upon him.

His pensive mood dissolved when Dirken's mount drew up to him, Dirken pointing at a buck standing motionless in a thicket. They had brought their bows, and he threw himself gladly into the hunt, for action was still the greatest salve for any unrest, large or small.

Later that evening there was a banquet, and Dirken sang. The queen appeared briefly, although the babe was only six days old, and she was still fatigued. Dirken sang to her as though they were alone in the room and he had just begun courting her.

Tekoah gazed back at him smiling, cheeks flushed, eyes rapt.

Weslan averted his face in embarrassment. He was thrilled for them, but it was a bit much. He shifted in his over-stuffed chair, thinking he should depart for Stern the next day. Or seek Heyg or Nolvern and have a boisterous reunion at the Fallen Maiden. He made his excuses and left the banquet room early.

They are completely consumed with each other, Weslan told himself, half-enviously, packing up the few clothes he had brought with him. There was no need for him in this place.

But an hour later, he was surprised to hear a knock on his chamber door. When he opened it, the same pretty maidservant he had seen before stood there, delivering a request from the queen to attend her in her chamber.

Tekoah was standing by an open window, wearing a long, rose-pink nightdress, with a light shawl thrown about her shoulders. She turned, holding her hand out to him, smiling.

"Wes. I saw you looking restless at the banquet and thought I had better catch you before you sneaked off."

"You always could read my face."

"And you mine," she laughed.

Her smile faded, and she gazed sombrely out the window for a moment. Into the silence, Weslan felt the past creeping up all around them, as the night shadows crept up the balcony.

"Look," Tekoah said.

When he did so, he saw she was holding something in her open palm, something he had not seen for many years. It was a small gem, an annathyst: the stone of the Anniste. His mother had worn it on a ribbon about her neck, long before, its creamy opalescent shimmer mesmerizing to her young children.

At the sight of the stone, his mother's face rose so strongly before him that Weslan had to close his eyes.

"I wish you to take it," he heard Tekoah say. "Give it to Theena, your daughter."

"She is not my daughter." Weslan could not say the next words aloud: *I want her to be my daughter, but I am afraid.*

"Do not be afraid," Tekoah murmured. "You can be her father, if only you have love enough to conquer the fear. And you know as well as I that fatherhood comes not only because of blood ties."

She paused, and he felt her eyes upon him, though he did not trust himself to look up.

"You are not he," she whispered, taking his hand and pressing the gem with its finely wrought chain into his palm. "You are not Veld," she repeated.

Weslan nodded. He squeezed the annathyst tightly in his hand, so that the edges dug into his skin. It was as if a great weight had rolled away from his chest. His sister was smiling at him with a tenderness and understanding that reminded him of —but he would not think of Reika. Not in that moment, or he would begin weeping.

"Thank you," he said. "Ko, I want you to know that I am happy that things turned out this way. Who would have thought —when we were just squallers with dung between our toes— that you would one day be queen? You were always so shy."

"Yes, I wanted only peace, an end to the violence. A quiet life, and time to compose my verses. And you wanted glory above all things," she finished, sitting down on a stool near the window. "Yet look at where we are now."

"Funny how things—"

"Yes."

They were silent again for a moment. Weslan stared at the tiny purple flowers embroidered on the yellow coverlet of the bed. He had slept on that bed, once, oblivious to the events that had been shaping themselves into threatening clouds at the edges of his horizon.

"I am sorry," he said abruptly.

"For what?"

"For failing to be there when you needed me. I was always so busy thinking of myself as a hero, but when it came down to it, I was not much good to anyone. Dirken was very angry with me for not going after you that day, the day of the

Mantling. But I never knew how you felt about it. Please forgive me."

"But how could you have gone after me?" she exclaimed. "You did not know where I was. Which enemy to fight! Besides —" She broke off, looking out the window.

"What?"

"Besides," she repeated, her voice trembling a little, "I was not there for you either in your greatest time of need. Anna chose someone else to heal you."

Reika's memory hovered between them like an unshed tear. Weslan put his hand on Tekoah's shoulder.

"I think," she said, haltingly, "we were so caught up in our own struggles that we could not be of any real help to each other. We were too close to the same thing, and therefore we only caused one another more pain when we came together. Only now can we begin to talk about the past, without running away in a blind panic."

Weslan nodded. Her words sounded strange, but somehow, they made sense. Or perhaps it was easier to believe this than to remember he had not guarded his own sister as faithfully as Dirken had—or Braith.

Braith. Another name to hang unspoken between them. They could not speak of everything, yet. He thought again of Reika, to whom he could tell whatever was in his heart.

"Do you think it is possible, Ko?" Weslan asked, his voice cracking. "To be in love with two people at once? I mean, truly love them?"

"Oh yes," Tekoah replied without hesitation. She closed her eyes. "I know it is."

Gazing at her face, which seemed pale and weary, Weslan realized that the question must strike her heart as deeply as it struck his.

"You are fatigued," he said, "and I must leave early tomorrow. The planting..."

"You seek escape yet again," she replied, giving him a wry smile.

He opened his mouth to protest and shut it again when he saw her dancing eyes. "Stop teasing your poor, stupid brother," he told her with mock-sternness. He leaned forward and tugged a lock of her hair.

"Word in the market stalls has it you are a strong ruler." He grinned, unable to resist teasing her back. "At least as strong as your husband. You have changed, string bean."

"I have learned to think of myself for a change," she answered, "and it has strengthened me."

"And I have begun to think of others," Weslan said, surprised at his own words, yet knowing he spoke true. "Perhaps it will strengthen me."

"It will," Tekoah answered, with that new certainty in her voice.

"May I ask you something?" Weslan straightened and slipped the annathyst into a leather money pouch he carried about his waist.

"Of course."

"Why are you happy? Now, I mean. You did not look at all so when you were being crowned queen of this country, nor for a long while afterward. What has changed, Ko?"

Tekoah gazed out the window at the star-spangled night. A wind rose, stirring her brown-gold hair about her face. She took her time answering.

"It was something that the twins told me," she said at last, very low. "Something they saw."

"Told you? But they cannot speak!" She did not reply. He became impatient. "Well, what was it?"

Tekoah took a deep breath and stood up, stepping a pace or two away, as though she needed air, or space. Then she turned toward him and placed both hands on his shoulders.

And Weslan was shaken to see in his sister's mild blue eyes a flame, deep and smoldering; and wondered that he had never seen it before. That there was a part of her he could not know.

"Wes," she whispered, low and fierce. A shudder seemed to pass through her, and then the flame in her eyes quieted. "Someday," she murmured, turning back to the window. "Someday I will tell you."

"Well," he muttered, still uneasy. "I am glad for you, and that I have a nephew whom I shall teach to ride and shoot better than any man in the Kalesh. And we will talk more when you come for the summer to the Castle of Mirrand. Yes?"

"Yes."

Weslan stooped to kiss her cheek. "Goodbye then, little mother."

He turned to go, but as he opened the door, she called his name.

"Yes?" he said, turning around.

"Are you happy?"

"Someday," he answered, smiling, "I will tell you."

Weslan closed the door behind him and walked slowly down the darkened hallway to his chamber.

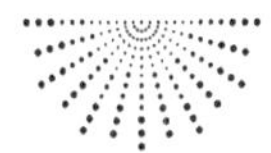

*T*ekoah watched Weslan's proud, unhappy back as he shut the door behind him. *His life is not over yet*, she thought. If only he knew it. But of course it was hard for him to believe, when only emptiness seemed to stretch before him.

She turned back to the window, gazing up once more at the sky. It gave her such peace now, but still she dared not permit herself to do it too often. She did not want things to become as they were before—the endless gazing skyward, day and night, unable to tear her eyes away, ceaselessly searching, even when Dirken's pleading voice made her shiver with pity.

Was her daughter alive? That was the question which had woken her in the night, rustled in her ear like the soft brush of insistent wingtips, until sometimes she had thought that she would descend into screaming insanity.

Until last summer. Tekoah covered her face with her hands and looked away from the sky as she remembered.

Raol hailed her as she walked along the road in Stern, returning to the castle after an hour of berry-picking with her maid. Her brother looked at her with urgent intensity, and so she dismissed her maidservant and followed him back down to the forge where Fanco also waited. She stood for a moment, rigid, looking at the hut where she had been born.

Tekoah had not set foot in the place since she had fled through the snow from her father's drunken, gloating voice. She felt a strong urge to flee, but forced herself to stand still, though she pulled on the fringe of her shawl so hard that the strings of silk broke off in her hands.

But Fanco was tugging at her sleeve. He pointed downward to where Raol squatted in the dust beside the well, drawing on the earth with a stick he had dipped into a bucket of water.

She looked down, watched as the brown, wet lines took shape.

A circle for a head, with long, flowing hair.

An insubstantial body, just a few strokes brushed out; arms stretched out wide, and—arcing above them—wings.

Tekoah found suddenly that she could not breathe. She fell, but Fanco caught her, bracing her from behind. Raol stood, shuffling from foot to foot, smiling expansively as if he had just presented her with a gift. He pointed straight up at the cloudless summer sky, and then his arm encompassed himself and his twin.

"You both saw her," Tekoah said slowly, miming a baby rocking in her arms. Her lips felt parched.

Raol nodded, and Fanco squeezed her shoulders.

"She is alive, then. She is well?"

Again, she mimed, and again Raol nodded.

Almost gasping with the joy of it, Tekoah stammered, "Where? When? I must see her—" She broke off, staring, for Raol was shaking his head emphatically.

"But why not?" Her voice cracked with disappointment. For an awful moment she'd wanted to strike him, strike him down, wipe that knowing, solemn look from his face. How dare he presume he knew her own daughter better than she?

But then Tekoah realized he was right. The knowledge illuminated her from within, like a flash of lightning sent from the deep, unfathomable place from which she used to Journey.

She could not see her child. Not yet. And even this much had been a gift, a miracle.

Still, she wanted to cry that it was not fair, that she had only held her daughter for a moment before the baby-hawk had taken flight. Was that supposed to be enough to last her a lifetime?

The answer came: It must be enough, for now.

Tekoah looked down at the earth-sketch for a moment longer. Then she nodded at Raol to show that she understood, hugged both twins and walked away.

Later that day, Tekoah sat on her balcony, watching the sky. The sun was sinking into the horizon, painting the Taboran peaks the colours of flames and roses.

As she sat, she saw a small movement out of the corner of her eye. She turned to her right. At the crest of the hill, riding toward the castle, was a lone horseman. She saw at once that it was her husband the king, riding from Rhantor to see her, although she had begged him not to bother. It was too far to travel for no important reason, she had told him listlessly when he suggested it.

He had come anyway.

As he approached the castle, Tekoah leaned forward, looking at him intently, playing a game with herself, imagining that Dirken was a stranger whom she had never seen before. She looked at the grip of his hands on the reins, strong but easy; the graceful, boyish way he shook his dark auburn curls. The defensive squaring of his shoulders as he glimpsed her sitting on the balcony.

Behind him, Tekoah watched as Rhan began to sink, a glowing ember in a forge. She asked herself what it would be like to lose Dirken, as she had lost Braith.

She walked slowly back into her chamber, and over to her bed, staring down at it for a moment. Quickly, she reached under her pillow and removed a pair of crimson gloves. Smoothing them in her hands, she walked over to her cedar chest in the corner and thrust them inside, down to the very bottom.

That night, Dirken came in to kiss her cheek before retiring to his own chamber, as he had done every night since bringing her back from the Isle of Mira. This time, upon greeting her husband, Tekoah dismissed the attendant who had been brushing her hair—the girl looking flustered but intrigued as she scurried from the room.

Dirken stood in the shadows of the doorway, watching her quizzically.

She beckoned him forward, forefinger on her lips to signal secrecy. He shut the door behind him.

"Why do you look so mischievous?" A hint of his old teasing crept into his voice. "Tell me, wench, or I shall beat it out of you!"

"Be careful about making promises you cannot keep," she cautioned him, moving over to the bed and reaching into her small bedside cabinet.

"What do you mean?" Dirken followed her, as she had known he would. Straightening, she could see him glancing sidelong at the bed.

"You may find that you are too weak to beat me," Tekoah answered mysteriously.

She produced a flask of pitaya wine, waving it aloft in triumph, along with two goblets. Dirken clapped his hands, whistling softly.

Tekoah took a deep breath, for she was shakier than she had thought she would be. Then she sat on the bed, crossing her legs under her thin night-gown, patting the place beside her. Dirken sat down, a little stiffly. She handed him a goblet.

"Do you remember," she asked him, not quite daring to meet his eyes, as she poured the wine, "a conversation we had in Rhantor once—no, it was Zantor then—that we never finished?"

Dirken did not answer. He took a deep draught of wine, then set the goblet down on the bedside table. She set hers down next to it, and then remained still as he leaned forward, touching her face lightly with his fingertips. Her hair, her cheeks, her lips, like a blind man.

He had not forgotten. For after the first long, hungry kiss, he whispered in her ear, "Like honey—"

❧

Tᴇᴋᴏᴀʜ ᴡᴀs certain that she had conceived her son that night. It was a lovely, sacred thought. She listened to her brother's solitary footsteps echo down the hall. Then, turning to the window, she looked upon the night sky with its dancing stars.

Was Reika was among them? Her mother Neela? And Chalvern—whom she always called Father to herself, now—was he watching her from somewhere, his benevolent smile lighting her path?

Tekoah heard her husband's buoyant stride in the hall, and a sweet mewing sound from the wooden cradle in the nursery. She thought of her beautiful, winged daughter, whom she had not named, and her daughter's father Braith—something he had said, and something Reika had said—that had once seemed to contradict each other.

Healing is remembering, Reika had told her, stroking her tear-stained face after that first, terrifying Journey.

Healing is forgetting, Braith the sorcerer had told her, holding out a goblet of forgetfulness in his crimson-gloved hands.

Tekoah thought to herself that they were both right, after all. Healing was remembering, and then forgetting. Over and over again.

She closed the shutters upon the night sky and turned toward the door, smiling.

THE END

ABOUT THE AUTHOR

If you enjoyed this book, you can sign up here for my monthly newsletter—giving you info on upcoming book releases, plus ongoing musings and snippets from my corner of the fantasy writing-and-reading world. When you sign up, you will receive an exclusive short story—unavailable anywhere else—the back-story of a beloved character from this book: "Reika: Fugitive Princess of Berlot."

https://landing.mailerlite.com/webforms/landing/f3c0b2

ABOUT ME

I am a long-time and avid fiction reader, especially of epic fantasy. I worked in my twenties as a freelance writer, editing and copywriting for radio, television and film, while also raising a family. But during all those years I wanted to write "the book I would want to read" (to paraphrase C.S. Lewis). And then one day, the spark ignited and I was on fire with this story.

I wrote "Where the Moon Has Been" almost twenty years ago, when raising my (then) young children. This was before "Harry Potter" and "Game of Thrones," when fantasy became a 'thing' again. Go figure.

My highly focused intention was to publish this novel, but life interrupted me in several ways, including losing my son in a tragic accident. For a decade I could not think about much beyond basic survival. Then the universe intervened, and told me to get on with it. And so I have.

A born-and-raised Canadian living in Vancouver, B.C., I slip away spend much of my creative time in the interior of this beautiful province, communing with deer and stellar blue jays, and gazing at the ever-changing waters of Lake Okanagan.

This is my first published novel.

A sequel, "Mirror of the Sea" is partially completed.

I would greatly appreciate a review—even just a line or two to let other likeminded readers know about your reading experience. Because, if you have taken the time to read this, then you must know: a *reader's* interest is a *writer's* fuel. Thanks in advance and here's the review link:

http://www.amazon.com/review/createreview/?&=9781777205225

I can also be reached at my website:

www.judithlepore.com.

ACKNOWLEDGEMENTS

I would like to thank my daughter Daria for reading various drafts of this manuscript for years and cheerleading me to the publishing "finish line," during which time she had many other balls to juggle in the air (most recently, becoming a doctor in a global pandemic, planning a wedding in a global pandemic).

I would like to thank my husband Lorenzo for his faith in me, for his unfailing, tireless support, and (equally important) his valuable insight as a genuinely passionate reader of epic fantasy.

Finally I would like to thank my mother, Faye, for teaching me by encouragement and by example to break free of the shackles imposed upon me by others, and pursue my dreams.

*Acknowledgement and gratitude to my brilliant and talented cover designer: Ana Gjorgjijoska.

facebook.com/judithlepore111

instagram.com/judith_lepore_author

9 781777 205256